East Angels

A Novel

by

Constance Fenimore Woolson

Double 9 BOOKS

East Angels
A Novel
by Constance Fenimore Woolson

ISBN: 978-93-71460-43-9

Published by

DOUBLE 9 BOOKS
2/13-B, Ansari Road
Daryaganj, New Delhi – 110002
info@double9books.com
www.double9books.com
Tel. 011-40042856

ABOUT THE AUTHOR

Constance Fenimore Woolson was an American novelist, poet, and short story writer, born on March 5, 1840, in Claremont, New Hampshire. She was a grandniece of James Fenimore Cooper, a renowned American writer. Woolson is best known for her works set in the Great Lakes region, the American South, and among American expatriates in Europe. Her writing often explored the complexities of human emotions, social settings, and the intricacies of life in both familiar and foreign landscapes. Her style combined detailed character studies with vivid descriptions of settings. Woolson's works garnered attention for their realism and insight into the lives of women. Her most famous stories reflect her interest in the social dynamics of these regions, as well as the lives of people navigating change, identity, and relationships. Woolson passed away on January 24, 1894, at the age of 53 in Venice, Italy. She was the daughter of Hannah Cooper Pomeroy, whose influence on her writing is often noted. Woolson's legacy continues through her literary contributions, especially in American fiction.

CONTENTS

CHAPTER I

"I think, more than anything else, I came to be under blue sky."

"Are you fond of sky?" said the young girl who was sitting near the speaker, her eyes on the shimmering water of the lagoon which stretched north and south before the house.

"I can't lay claim to tastes especially celestial, I fear," answered the visitor, "but I confess to a liking for an existence which is not, for six months of the year, a combat. I am mortally tired of our long northern winters, with their eternal processions of snow, ice, and thaw—thaw, ice, and snow; I am tired of our springs—hypocritical sunshine pierced through and through by east winds; and I have at last, I think, succeeded in breaking loose from the belief that there is something virtuous and heroic in encountering these things—encountering them, I mean, merely from habit, and when not called to it by any necessity. But this emancipation has taken time—plenty of it. It is directly at variance with all the principles of the country and creed in which I was brought up."

"You have good health, Mr. Winthrop?" asked Mrs. Thorne, in a tone which was prepared to turn with equal appreciation towards sympathy if he were, and congratulation if he were not, the possessor of the lungs which classify a person, and give him an occupation for life.

"Do I look delicate?"

"On the contrary, you look remarkably well," answered his hostess, sure of her ground here, since even an invalid likes to be congratulated upon an appearance of health: not only is it more agreeable in itself, but it gives him the opportunity to explain (and at some length) that all is illusory merely, a semblance; an adjustment of the balances between resignation and heroism which everybody should admire. "Yes," Mrs. Thorne went on, with a critical air which seemed to say, as she looked at him, that her opinions were founded upon unprejudiced scrutiny, "wonderfully well, indeed—does he not, Garda?"

"Mr. Winthrop looks well; I don't know that it is a wonder," replied Edgarda Thorne, in her soft voice. "He has been everywhere, and seen everything," she added, turning her eyes towards him for a moment—eyes in which he read envy, but envy impersonal, concerning itself more with his travels, his knowledge of many places, his probable adventures, than with himself.

"Mr. Winthrop is accustomed to a largeness of opportunity," remarked Mrs. Thorne; "but it is his natural atmosphere." She paused, coughed slightly, and then added, "He does not come into the ports he enters with banners flying, with rockets and cannon, and a brass band at bow and stern."

"You describe an excursion steamer on the Fourth of July," said Winthrop.

"Precisely. One or two of the persons who have visited Gracias-á-Dios lately have seemed to us not unlike that," answered the lady.

Mrs. Thorne had a delicate little voice, pitched on rather a high key, but so slender in volume that, like the pure small note of a little bird, it did not offend. Her pronunciation was very distinct and accurate—that is, accurate according to the spelling; they knew no other methods in the conscientious country school where she had received her education. Mrs. Thorne pronounced her *t* in "often," her *l* in "almond," her "again" rhymed with "plain."

"Did you mean that you, too, would like to go everywhere and see everything, Miss Thorne?" said Evert Winthrop, addressing the daughter. "I assure you it's dull work."

"Naturally—after one has had it all." She spoke without again turning her eyes towards him.

"We are kept here by circumstances," observed Mrs. Thorne, smoothing the folds of her black gown with her little withered hand. "I do not know whether circumstances will ever release us—I do not know. But we are not unhappy meanwhile. We have the old house, with its many associations; we have our duties and occupations; and if not frequent amusement, we have our home life, our few dear friends, and our affection for each other."

"All of them crowned by this same blue sky which Mr. Winthrop admires so much," added Garda.

"I see that you will always hold me up to ridicule on account of that speech," said Winthrop. "You are simply tired of blue. As a contrast you would welcome, I dare say, the dreariest gray clouds of the New England coast, and our east wind driving in from the sea."

"I should welcome snow," answered Garda, slowly; "all the country covered with snow, lying white and dead—that is what I wish to see. I want to walk on a frozen lake with ice, real ice over deep water, under my feet. I want to breathe freezing air, and know how it feels. I want to see trees without any leaves on them; and a snow-storm when the flakes are very big and soft like feathers; and long icicles hanging from roofs; and then, to hear the wind whistle round the house, and be glad to draw the curtains and bring my chair close to a great roaring fire. Think of that—to be *glad* to come close to a great roaring fire!"

"I have described these things to my daughter," said Mrs. Thorne, explaining these wintry aspirations to their guest in her careful little way. "My home before my marriage was in the northern part of New England, and these pictures from my youth have been Garda's fairy tales."

"Then you are not English?" said Winthrop. He knew perfectly that she was not, but he wished to hear the definite little abstract of family history which, in answer to his question, he thought she would feel herself called upon to bestow. He was not mistaken.

"My husband was English—that is, of English descent," she explained—"and I do not wonder that you should have thought me English also, for I have imbibed the family air so long that I have ended by really becoming one of them. We Thornes are very English; but we are the English of one hundred and fifty years ago. *We* have not moved on, as no doubt the English of to-day have been obliged to move; *we* have remained stationary. Even in dear old England itself, we should to-day, no doubt, Garda and I, be called old-fashioned."

Winthrop found himself so highly entertained by this speech, by her "We Thornes," and her "dear old England," that he looked down lest she should see the change of expression which accompanies a smile, even though the smile be hidden. This little woman had never been in England in her life; unmistakable New Hampshire looked from her eyes, sounded in every tone of her voice, made itself visible in all her movements and attitudes. She was unceasingly anxious; she had never indulged herself in anything, or taken anything lightly since she was born; she had as little body as was possible, and in that body she had to the full the strict American conscience. All this was vividly un-English.

"Yes, I always regret so much the modern ways into which dear England has fallen," she went on. "It would have been beautiful if they could but have retained the old customs, the old ideas, as we have retained them here. But in some things they have done so," she added, with the air of wishing to be fully just. "In the late unhappy contest, you know, they were with us—all their best people—as to our patriarchal system for our servants. They understood us—us of the South—completely."

Winthrop's amusement had now reached its highest point. "Heroic, converted little Yankee school-marm," was his thought. "What a colossal effort her life down here must have been for her, poor thing!"

"Your husband was the first of the American Thornes, then?" he said, with the intention of drawing out more narrative.

"Oh no. The first Edgar Thorne came out from England with Governor Tonyn (the friend of Lord Marchmont, you know), during the British occupation of this province in the last century; he remained here after the retrocession to Spain, because he had married a daughter of one of the old Spanish families of this coast, Beatriz de Duero. As Beatriz was an only child, they lived here with her parents, and the second Edgar Thorne, their son, was born here. He also married a Duero, a cousin named Ines; my husband, the third Edgar, was their child. My husband came north one summer; he came to New England. There he met me. We were married not long afterwards, and I returned with him to his southern home. Edgarda was but two years old when her dear father was taken from us."

"Miss Thorne resembles her Spanish more than her English ancestors, I fancy?" said Winthrop, looking at the handle of his riding-whip for a moment, perhaps to divest the question of too closely personal a character, the young lady herself being beside him. But this little by-play was not needed. Mrs. Thorne had lived a solitary life so long that her daughter, her daughter's ancestors, her daughter's resemblances (the last, indeed, might be called historical), seemed to her quite natural subjects for conversation; if Winthrop had gazed at Garda herself, instead of at the handle of his riding-whip, that would have seemed to her quite natural also.

"Edgarda is the portrait of her Spanish grandmother painted in English colors," she answered, in one of her neatly arranged little phrases.

"An anomaly, therefore," commented Garda, who seemed rather tired of the turn the conversation had taken. "But it can do no harm, Medusa-fashion, because fastened forever upon a Florida wall."

"A Florida wall is not such a bad thing," answered Winthrop. "I am thinking a little of buying one for myself."

"Ah, a residence in Gracias-á-Dios?" said Mrs. Thorne, her small, bright blue eyes meeting his with a sort of screen suddenly drawn down over them—a screen which he interpreted as a quick endeavor on her part to conceal in their depths any consciousness that a certain desirable old Spanish mansion was possibly to be obtained, and for a price which, to a well-filled purse of the north, might seem almost comically small.

"No; I do not care for a house in the town," he answered. "I should prefer something outside—more of a place, if I should buy at all."

"I cannot imagine why any one should wish to buy a place down here now," said Garda. "A house in Gracias-á-Dios, with a rose garden and a few orange-trees, is all very well; you could stay there for two months or so in the winter, and then close it and go north again. But what could you do with a large place? Cotton and sugar are no longer worth raising, now that we have no slaves. And as to one of the large orange groves that people are beginning to talk about, there is no one here who could manage it for you. You would have to see to it yourself, and that you could never do. To begin with, the climate would kill you; and then there are the snakes."

"Being already dead, the snakes would hardly trouble me, I suppose, unless you refer to future torments," said Winthrop, laughing. "Allow me to congratulate you upon your picture of the agricultural resources of the country. They have never before been so clearly presented to me; it is most interesting."

Garda shook her head, repressing a smile. But still she did not look at him.

"In purchasing a place here Mr. Winthrop may not be thinking of agriculture; he may be thinking only of climate," remarked Mrs. Thorne, mildly, to her daughter.

"Climate—that is blue sky, I suppose," said Garda; "I acknowledge that there is an abundance of that here. But I advise Mr. Winthrop to buy but a small piece of ground as his standing-point, and to take his sky out perpendicularly; he can go up to any height, you know, as high as the moon, if he likes. That would be ever so much wiser than to have the same amount spread out horizontally over a quantity of swamp-land which no person in his senses could wish to own."

"But the land about here strikes me as remarkably dry," observed their visitor, amused by the girl's opposition to an idea which he had as yet so faintly outlined. He suspected, however, that she was not combating him so much as she was combating the possibility of a hope in the breast of her little mother. But poor Mrs. Thorne had been very discreet; she had not allowed herself to even look interested.

"It is as dry as the Desert of Sahara," Garda answered, with decision, "and it is as wet as a wet sponge. There is this dry white sand which you see on the pine-barrens—miles upon miles of it. Then, stretching across it here and there come the great belts of bottomless swamp. *That* is Florida."

"Your description is a striking one," said Winthrop, gravely. "You make me feel all the more desirous to own a little of such a remarkable combination of wet and dry."

Garda glanced at him, and this time her smile conquered her. Winthrop was conscious of a pleasure in having made her look at him and smile. For it was not a matter of course that she would do either. His feeling about her had been from the first that she was the most natural young girl he had ever met—that is, in the ranks of the educated. There was a naturalness, of course, in the Indian girls, whom he had seen in the far West, which probably exceeded Garda's; but that sort of naturalness he did not care for.

Garda was natural in her own graceful way, singularly natural; her glance and her smile, while not so ready, nor so promptly hospitable as those of most girls of her age, seemed to him to possess a quality which he had come to consider almost extinct—the quality of frank, undisturbed sincerity.

"I sometimes regret that I described to my daughter so often the aspects of my northern home," said Mrs. Thorne. "It was a pleasure to me at the time (it had been a great change for me, you know), and I did not realize that they were becoming exaggerated to her, these descriptions—more beautiful than the reality. For she has dwelt too much upon them; by contrast she over-estimates them. The South, too, has its beautiful aspects: that we must allow."

Winthrop fancied that he detected a repressed plaintiveness in her tone. "She thinks her daughter cruel to keep on beating down so ruthlessly her poor little hope," was his thought. Then he answered the spoken sentence: "As she has never seen these things for herself, your descriptions must have been vivid."

"No; it is her imagination that is that."

"True—I have myself had an example of her imagination in her remarks upon agriculture."

Garda laughed. "I shall say no more about agriculture, blue sky, or anything else," she declared.

"You leave me, then, to take care of myself?"

"You do not need my assistance, I never waste it."

"I should have pretended to be quite helpless! That's the second mistake I have made this afternoon. If I had only let it be supposed that my health was delicate, Mrs. Thorne would have been much more interested in me."

"Oh no, Mr. Winthrop," said his hostess, earnestly; "you are quite mistaken. Good health is in itself full of the deepest interest, I am sure, and especially at the present day, when it is so singularly rare. I am most glad you possess it—most glad indeed."

"I possess enough of it, at any rate, to go over the place, if you will be so kind," said Winthrop. "You know you promised me that pleasure some day, and why not this afternoon? There is a delightful breeze."

Mrs. Thorne dropped her eyes to the tips of her black cloth slippers, visible beneath the skirt of her gown. These little shoes one could scarcely fail to see, since the skirt, which was neatness itself in its decent black folds, was rather scanty and short. Their age and well-worn thinness, the skilful mending of their worst places, the new home-made bindings, the fresh ribbon bows bravely tied, told a story to the observers of delicate things.

But while Mrs. Thorne surveyed her slippers, her daughter was replying: "It would hardly amuse you to go over the place, Mr. Winthrop; there is really nothing to see but the crane."

"Let us go, then, and see the crane."

"Mamma would be so delighted, you know. But she never walks."

"Not far," corrected Mrs. Thorne. "I am not strong, not able to walk far."

"And I should be delighted, too," continued Garda, "only I am so sleepy. I have fallen into the habit of spending my afternoons in the hammock; that makes me immensely drowsy just at this hour."

"I feel like an interloper," said Winthrop; "say a large mosquito."

"You needn't. It's not well to sleep so much," replied Miss Thorne, calmly.

"Certainly you know how to console. Is that the hammock in which you pass your happy existence?"

"Not existence; only afternoons. You really wish to go?" she added, seeing that he had taken his hat from the chair beside him. "We will send Raquel with you, then, as guide."

"Raquel?"

"Haven't you noticed her? She lets you in when you come. She is an important personage with us, I assure you; her mother, grandmother, and great-grandmother lived on the place here before her."

Winthrop recalled the portly jet-black negress who, in answer to his knock, had opened the lower door.

"Three generations make aristocracy in America," he replied; "I am afraid of so distinguished a guide. If doomed to go without Mrs. Thorne or yourself, why may I not go alone?"

"You would never find the magnolias, you would come into the live-oak avenue at the wrong end, you would look at the ruin from its commonplace side, you would see only the back of the Cherokee roses, the crane would not dance for you, the wild cattle would run at you, and you would inevitably get into the swamp," answered the girl, checking off the items one by one on her pretty fingers.

"I have confessed my fear of Raquel, and now you display before me this terrible list of dangers. Don't you think it would be but common charity to come with me yourself? My conversation is not exciting; you could easily sleep a little, between-times, as we walk."

"I believe you have had your own way all your life," remarked Garda, "or you would never persist as you do. Your humility is nothing but a manner; in reality you expect everything to be done for you by everybody."

"Not by everybody," Winthrop responded.

Mrs. Thorne had coughed as Garda ended her speech. Mrs. Thorne often coughed, and her coughs had a character of their own; they did not appear to be pulmonary. They were delicate little sounds which came forth apologetically, shielded by her hand, never quite completed; they were not coughs so much as suggestions of coughs, and with these suggestions she was in the habit of filling little pauses in the conversation, covering up the awkwardnesses or mistakes of others (there were never any of her own to cover), or acting as hyphen for disjointed remarks when people had forgotten what they were going to say. It was, indeed, a most accomplished cough, all Gracias had been indebted to it. Lately, too, she had begun to use it to veil her own little periods of consultation with herself regarding her daughter; for she seemed by no means certain of the direction which this daughter's thoughts or words might take, and the uncertainty troubled her careful maternal mind. Garda, however, though often out of sight round some unexpected corner, was never far distant; the hurrying elderly comprehension always caught up with her before long; but these periods of uncertainty, combined with cares more material, had ended by impressing upon Mrs. Thorne's face the look of anxiety which was now its most constant expression—an anxiety covered, however, as much as possible, by the mask of minutely careful politeness which fitted closely over it, doing its best to conceal, or, failing in that, to at least mark as private, the personal troubles which lay underneath.

"Mamma's cough means that I am not sufficiently polite," said Garda; "I always know what mamma's cough means." She rose, passed behind her mother's chair, and bending forward over her small head, lightly kissed her forehead. "I will go, mamma," she said, caressingly. "I will be beautifully good, because to-morrow is your birthday; it ought to be a dear little day, about six hours long, to fit you."

"I am fortunate to have asked my favor upon the eve of an anniversary," said Winthrop.

"You are," answered Garda, taking her broad-brimmed hat from the nail behind her. "It's only upon such great occasions that I am really and angelically good—as mamma would like me to be all the time."

"I will send Raquel after you, my daughter, with the umbrellas," said Mrs. Thorne, with a little movement of her lips and throat, as though she had just swallowed something of a pleasant taste, which was, with her, the expression of content.

"Surely it is not going to rain?" said Winthrop, examining the sky.

"They are sun-umbrellas; you may need them," answered his hostess, with a certain increased primness of accentuation, which immediately brought to his mind the idea that the carrier of these articles would represent the duenna whom she considered necessary.

"A Spanish graft, that, on the original New England tree," was his mental comment. "I wonder how many more there are?"

But the descendant of the Spaniards was speaking for herself. "We do not want Raquel, mamma; we can carry the umbrellas ourselves." And she passed into the darkened drawing-room, from which opened the little balcony where they had been sitting.

Winthrop, after taking leave of Mrs. Thorne, followed Garda. But he had the conviction that a duenna of some sort, though it might not be Raquel, would be improvised from that balcony before long, and sent after them.

He had already paid several visits to these ladies, and knew his way through the interior dimness, but the old house still attracted him, and he did not hurry his steps; he looked again at the rooms, which, with their few articles of furniture, had to northern eyes an appearance of cool shaded emptiness, the broad open spaces having been purposely left to give place for the free passage of air. The vaulted ceilings deep in shadow, the archways in place of the northern doors, one room panelled to the top in dark polished wood which glimmered dimly as he passed through—all these he liked to note. Beyond, the stone stairway made a leisurely, broad-stepped descent. The high wainscot on the wall at its side showed pomegranates stiffly carved in low relief, and the balustrade of the same dark wood ended in a clumsy column, with a heavy wreath of the fruit wound round it, the conventional outlines worn into vagueness by the touch of time.

The old house was built of stone, the porous shell-conglomerate of that coast. The thick blocks had been covered with an outer coat of plaster, and painted a shadeless gray-white. The structure extended itself over a large space of ground. Blank, unadorned, covered by a flat roof, without so much as the projection of a cornice to break their monotony, the walls stretched evenly round a parallelogram, and having but two stories of height, looked low in comparison with their length. But the old house in reality was not so large as it appeared to be, these same walls with their lining of rooms enclosing an interior court which was open to the sky; the windows of the inner sides looked down upon a low-curbed well, a clump of bananas, a rose-bush, and an ancient stone seat with a hook above it, where had hung in his cage, until he died of old age, Mrs. Thorne's northern canary, who had accompanied his mistress southward on her wedding journey to Florida.

Viewed from without, the gray-white abode had a peculiarly dumb aspect. On the north side there were no windows; on the south, east, and west the windows of the lower story, few at best, were covered by solid wooden shutters, which, being all kept closed, and having the same hue as the walls, could scarcely be distinguished from them. The windows of the upper story were more numerous, but almost as jealously guarded; for though their shutters were here and there partially open, one could see that in a trice they could all be drawn to and barred within, and that then the old mansion would present an unbroken white wall to all points of the compass. But once allowed to pass the door, solidly set in the stone, without top or side lights, the visitor perceived that these rooms with exterior windows darkened, opened widely upon the sunny court within. Some of them, indeed, did more. The inner walls of the ground-floor had been cut away in four places, leaving rounded open arches with pillars supporting the second story, and, under these arcades, there were chairs and tables and even a sofa visible, articles which presented to Evert Winthrop's eyes, each time he came, a picture of tropical and doorless confidence in the temperature which struck him as delightful. These arcades were not so unprotected as they appeared to be. Still, as the months went by, it could be said with truth that they remained, for five-sixths of the year, thus widely open. Evert Winthrop had spent his childhood and youth in New England, he had visited all parts of the great West, in later years he had travelled extensively in the Old World; but this was his first visit to that lovely southern shore of his own country which has a winter climate more enchanting than any that Europe can offer; to match it, one must seek the Madeira Islands or Algiers. In addition to this climate, Winthrop was beginning to discover that there were other things as well—old Spanish houses like the one through which he was now passing, a flavor of tradition and legend, tradition and legend, too, which had nothing to do with Miles Standish and his companions, or even with that less important personage, Hendrik Hudson. There was—he could not deny it—a certain comparative antiquity about this southern peninsula which had in it more richness of color and a deeper perspective than that possessed by any of the rather blank, near, little backgrounds of American history farther north. This was a surprise to him. Like most New-Englanders, he had unconsciously cherished the belief that all there was of historical importance, of historical picturesqueness even, in the beginnings of the republic, was associated with the Puritans from whom he was on his father's side descended, was appended to their stately hats and ruffs, their wonderful perseverance, their dignified orthography, the solemnities of their speech and demeanor. And if, with liberality, he should stretch the lines a little to include the old Dutch land-holders of Manhattan Island, and the river up which the *Half-moon* had sailed, that had seemed to him all that could possibly be necessary; there was, indeed, nothing else to include. But here was a life, an atmosphere, to whose contemporary and even preceding existence on their own continent neither Puritan nor Patroon had paid heed; and it was becoming evident that he, their descendant, with all the aids of easy communication, and that modern way of looking at the globe which has annihilated distance and made a voyage round it but a small matter—even he, with all this help, had not, respecting this beautiful peninsula of his own country, developed perceptions more keen than those of these self-absorbed ancestors—an appreciation more delicate than their obtuse one. Winthrop's appreciation was good. But it had been turned, as regarded historical and picturesque associations, principally towards the Old World. He now went through a good deal of meditation upon this subject; he was pleased, yet, on the whole, rather ashamed of himself. When Raphael was putting into the backgrounds of his pictures those prim, slenderly foliaged trees which he had seen from Perugino's windows in his youth, the Spaniards were exploring this very Florida shore; yet when he, Evert Winthrop, had discovered the same tall, thin trees (which up to that time he had thought rather an affectation) from the overhanging balcony of the little inn at Assisi—it had seemed to overhang all Umbria—did he not think of Raphael's day as far back in the past, and as completely remote from the possibility of any contemporary history in America as America is remote from the future great cities of the Sahara plains? And when, in Venice, he dwelt with delight upon the hues of Titian and Veronese, was he not sure (though without thinking of it) that in their day the great forests of his own New World untrodden by the white man's foot, had stretched unbroken to the sea? Because no Puritan with grave visage had as yet set sail for Massachusetts Bay, he had not realized that here on this southern shore had been towns and people, governors, soldiers, persecutions, and priests.

"I presume you intend to show me everything in its worst possible aspect," he said, as he joined Garda in the sunny court below. She was waiting for him beside the bananas, which were here not full grown—tall shrubs that looked, with their long-winged leaves standing out stiffly from their stalks, like green quill-pens that a giant might use for his sonnet-writing.

"No; I have withdrawn my guardianship—don't you remember? You must now guard yourself."

"From the great temptations opening before me."

"They may be such to you; they are not to me. I think I have never met any great temptations; I wonder when they will begin?"

They had crossed the court, and passed through a cool, dark, stone-floored hall on the other side; here they went out through a low door, which Raquel opened for them. Winthrop declined the white umbrella which this stately handmaid offered him, and as Garda would not let him carry the one she had taken, he walked on beside her with his hands in the pockets of his short morning-coat, looking about him with enjoyment, as he usually did at East Angels. The façade of the house which looked towards the lagoon was broken by the small balcony, roofed and closely shaded by green blinds, where they had been sitting, and where the hammock was swung. This little green cage, hung up on the side of the house, had no support from below; there was neither pillar nor trellis; not even a vine wandered up to its high balustrade. The most agile Romeo could not have climbed to it. But a Romeo, in any case, could not have approached near enough to attempt such a feat, since a wide space of open ground, without tree or shrub upon it, extended from the house-walls outward to a certain distance on all sides. Winthrop had already noticed these features—the heavy barred shutters of the lower floor, the high-hung little balcony, the jealous open space—he had pronounced them all very Spanish. He now looked about him again—at the dumb old house, the silvery sheen of the lagoon, the feathery tops of the palmettoes on Patricio opposite, the blue sky, and the sunny sea stretching eastward to Africa. "I ask nothing more," he said at last. "*This* is content."

His companion glanced at him. "You do look wonderfully contented," she commented.

"It amuses you? Perhaps it vexes you?"

"Neither. I was only wondering what there could be here to make you so contented."

This little speech pleased the man beside her highly. He said to himself that in the mind of a girl accustomed to the ways of the world, it would have belonged to the list of speeches too obvious in application to be made; while a little country coquette would have said it purposely. But Garda Thorne had spoken both naturally and indifferently, without thinking or caring as to what he might say in reply.

"I was remembering," he answered, "that at home all the rivers are frozen over, not to speak of the water-pipes, and that ice-blocks are grinding against each other in the harbor; is it any wonder, then, that in this charming air I should be content? But there are various degrees even in contentment, and I should reach a higher one still if you would only let me carry that umbrella." For she had opened it, and was holding it as women will, not high enough to admit him under its shade, but at just the angle that kept him effectually at a distance on account of the points which were dangerously on a level, now with his hat, now with his collar, now with some undefended portion of his face. He had always admired the serenity with which women will pass through a crowded street, raking all the passers-by as they go with an umbrella held at just that height, the height that suits themselves; smilingly and with agreeable countenances they advance, without the least conception, apparently, of the wild dodging they force upon all persons taller than themselves, of the wrath and havoc they are leaving behind them.

"No man knows how to hold a sun-umbrella," answered Garda. "To begin with, he never has the least idea where the sun is."

"I have learned that when you say 'To begin with,' there is small hope for us. Might I offer the suggestion, humbly, that there may be other methods of holding umbrellas in existence, besides those prevalent in Gracias."

Garda laughed. Her laugh was charming, Winthrop had already noticed that; it was not a laugh that could be counted upon, it did not come often, or upon call. But when it did ripple forth it was a distinct laugh, merry and sweet, and not the mere magnified smile, or the two or three shrill little shouts in a descending scale, which do duty as laughs from the majority of feminine lips. Its influence extended also to her eyes, which then shot forth two bright beams to accompany it. "I see that it will not do to talk to you as I talk to—to the persons about here," she said.

"Are there many of them—these persons about here?"

"Four," replied Garda, promptly. "There is Reginald Kirby, surgeon. Then there is the Reverend Mr. Moore, rector of St. Philip and St. James. Then we have Adolfo Torres, from the Giron plantation, south of here, and Manuel Ruiz, from Patricio, opposite."

"A tropical list," said Winthrop; "discouragingly tropical."

"But I'm tropical myself," Garda responded.

She was taking him through a narrow path, between what had once been hedges, but were now high tangled walls, overrun with the pointed leaves of the wild smilax. The girl had a light step, but if light, it was not quick; it could have been best described, perhaps, by the term unhurrying, a suggestion of leisure lay in each motion, from the poise of the small head to the way the pretty feet moved over the path or floor. Winthrop disliked a hurried step, he disliked also a tardy one; the step that is light but at the same time leisurely—this seemed to him to mark the temperament that gets the most out of life as a whole, certainly the most of pleasure, often too the most of attainment. Garda Thorne had this step. In her case, probably, there had been more of pleasure than of attainment. She did not indeed strike one as a person who had given much thought to attainment, whether of scholarship or housewifely skill, of needle-work or graceful accomplishments, or even of that balance of conscience, that trained obedience of the mind, which are so much to many of her sisters farther north. But these same sisters farther north would have commented, probably, commented from the long, rocky coast of New England, and from the many intelligent communities of the

Middle States, that no woman need trouble herself about attainment, or anything else, if she were as beautiful as Edgarda Thorne.

For in their hearts women always know that of all the gifts bestowed upon their sex that of beauty has so immeasurably the greatest power that nothing else can for one moment be compared with it, that all other gifts, of whatsoever nature and extent, sink into insignificance and powerlessness beside it. It is, of course, to the interest of domestic men, the good husbands and fathers who are satisfied with home comforts and home productions, and desire nothing so much as peace at the hearth-stone, to deny this fact, to qualify it as much as possible, and reduce its universality. But the denials of these few, contented, low-flying gentlemen are lost in the great tide of world-wide agreement, and no one is deceived by them, save, in occasional instances, their own wives, who in that case have been endowed by nature with much faith (or is it self-complacence?), and powers of observation not much beyond those of the oyster. But on that long New England coast already spoken of, and in those pleasant, pretty towns of the Middle States, observation has been keenly cultivated, and self-complacence held in abeyance by much analysis. All the northern sisters who lived there would probably have answered again, and with one voice, that with simply the most ordinary good qualities in addition, a girl as beautiful as Edgarda Thorne would carry all before her in any case.

Garda was of medium height, but her litheness made her seem tall. This litheness had in it none of the meagre outlines of the little mother, its curves were all moulded with that soft roundness which betrays a southern origin. But the observer was not left to this evidence alone, there was further and indisputable proof in her large, dark, beautiful, wholly Spanish eyes. She had, in truth, been well described by Mrs. Thorne's phrase—"the portrait of her Spanish grandmother, painted in English colors." The tints of her complexion were very different from the soft, unchanging, creamy line which had been one of the beauties of the beautiful Ines de Duero; Garda's complexion had the English lightness and brightness. But it was not merely pink and white; there were browns under its warm fairness—browns which gave the idea that it was acquainted with the open air, the sun, the sea, and enjoyed them all. It never had that blue look of cold which mars at times the beauty of all women who are delicately fair; it never had the fatal shade of yellow that menaces the brunette. It was a complexion made for all times and all lights; pure and clear, it had also a soft warmth of color which was indescribably rich. The lustrous black braids of Ines de Duero had been changed in her grand-daughter to braids equally thick, but in color a bright brown; not the brown that is but golden hair grown darker, nor that other well-known shade, neither light nor dark, which covers the heads of so many Americans that it might almost be called the national color; this brown had always been bright, had never changed; the head of the little Garda of two years old had showed a flossy mass of the same hue. This hair curled slightly through all its length, which gave the braids a rippled appearance. It had, besides, the beauty of growing low and thickly at the temples and over the forehead. The small head it covered was poised upon a throat which was not a mere point of union, an unimportant or lean angle to be covered by a necklace or collar; this throat was round, distinct in outline, its fairness beautiful not only in front, but also behind, under and at the edges of the hair where the comb had lifted the thick, soft mass and swept it up to take its place in the braids above. Garda's features were fine, but they were not of the Greek type, save that the beautiful forehead was low; the mouth was not small, the lips full, delicately curved. When she smiled, these lips had a marked sweetness of expression. They parted over brilliantly white teeth, which, with the colors in her hair and complexion, were the direct gifts of English ancestors, as her dark eyes with their long, curling, dark lashes, the thickness of her brown braids, her rounded figure with its graceful unhurrying gait and high-arched little feet, were inheritances from the Dueros.

But written words are not the artist's colors; they can never paint the portrait which all the world can see. A woman may be described, and by a truthful pen, as possessing large eyes, regular features, and so on through the list, and yet that woman may move through life quite without charm, while another who is chronicled, and with equal truthfulness, as having a profile which is far from showing accordance with artists' rules, may receive through all her days the homage paid to loveliness alone. The bare catalogue of features, tints, and height does not include the subtle spell whose fulness crowns the one, while its lack mars the other, and a narrator, therefore, while allowing himself as detailed a delineation as it pleases him to give, should set down plainly at the end the result, the often mysterious and unexpected whole, which the elements he has described have, in some occult manner, combined to produce. "There was an enchantment in her expression," "There was an irresistible sweetness about her;" these phrases tell more than the most minute record of hue and outline; they place the reader where he would be were the living, breathing presence before him, instead of the mere printed page.

But in the case of Garda Thorne it could have been said that she had not only brilliant beauty, but the loveliness which does not always accompany it. There was sufficient regularity in her face to keep from it the term irregular; but it had also all the changing expressions, all the spirit, all the sweetness, which faces whose features are not by rule often possess. She had undoubtedly a great charm, a charm which no one had as yet analyzed; she was not a girl who turned one's thoughts towards analysis, one was too much occupied in simply admiring her. She was as open as the day, her frankness was wonderful; it would have been said of her by every one that she had an extraordinary simplicity, were it not that the richness of her beauty threw over her a sort of sumptuousness which did not accord with the usual image of pure, rather meagre limpidity called up by the use of that word.

Evert Winthrop, beholding her for the first time in the little Episcopal church of Gracias, had said to himself that she was the most beautiful girl (viewing the matter impersonally) whom he had ever seen. Impersonally, because he would have set down his personal preference as decidedly for something less striking, for eyes of blue rather than black, eyes which should be not so much lustrous as gentle, for smooth hair of pale gold, a forehead and eyebrows like those of a Raphael Madonna. He was sure, also, that he much preferred slenderness; even a certain virginal thinness and awkwardness he could accept, it might be part of the charm. A friend of his, a lady older than himself, upon hearing him express these sentiments not long before, had remarked that they shed a good deal of light backward over his past. When he asked her what she meant, she added that a liking for little wild flowers in a man of the world of his age, and an indifference to tea-roses, did not so much indicate a natural simplicity of taste as something quite apart from that—too long an acquaintance, perhaps, with the heavily perfumed atmosphere of conservatories.

"I don't know what you are trying to make me out," Winthrop had answered, laughing.

"I make you out a very good fellow," replied the lady. "But you are like my husband (who is also a very good fellow); he wonders how I can go to the theatre, plays are so artificial. I suppose they are artificial; but I notice that it required his closest—I may almost say his nightly—attention for something like fifteen years to find it out."

Winthrop happened to think of this little conversation—he knew not why—as he followed his guide through her green-walled path, which had now become so narrow that he could no longer walk by her side. As it came up in his mind he said to himself that here was a tea-rose, growing if not quite in the seclusion of untrodden forests where the wild flowers have their home, then at least in natural freedom, in the pure air and sunshine, under the open sky. There was—there could be—nothing of the conservatory, nothing artificial, in the only life Edgarda Thorne had known, the life of this remote southern village where she had been born and brought up. Her knowledge of the world outside was—must be—confined to the Spanish-tinted legends of the slumberous little community, to the limited traditions of her mother's small experience, and to the perceptions and fancies of her own imagination; these last, however numerous they might be in themselves, however vivid, must leave her much in the condition of a would-be writer of dramas who has never read a play nor seen one acted, but has merely evolved something vaguely resembling one from the dreaming depths of his own consciousness; Garda's idea of the world beyond the barrens must be equally vague and unreal. And then, as he looked at her, sweet-natured and indifferent, walking onward with her indolent step over her own land, under the low blue sky, it came over him suddenly that probably she had not troubled herself to evolve anything, to think much of any world, good or bad, outside of her own personality. And he said to himself that wherever she was would be world enough for most men. In which class, however, he again did not include Evert Winthrop.

The path made a sudden turn, and stopped. It had brought them to the borders of a waste.

"This was one of the sugar fields," said Garda, with her little air of uninterested proprietorship.

Two old roads, raised on embankments, crossed the level, one from north to south, the other from east to west. The verge upon which they stood had once been a road also, though now narrowed and in some places blocked by the bushes which had grown across it. "A little farther on, beyond that point, you will find our ruin," said Garda. "There will not be time to sketch it, I will wait for you here."

"You are deserting me very soon."

"I am not deserting you at all, I intend to take you remorselessly over the entire place. But there are thorns in those bushes, and thorns are dangerous."

"I know it, I am already wounded."

"I mean that the briers might tear my dress," explained Miss Thorne, with dignity.

This stately rejection of so small and, as it were, self-made a pun entertained her companion highly; it showed how unfamiliar she was with the usual commonplaces. Talking with her would be not unlike talking with a princess in a fairy tale—one of those who have always lived mysteriously imprisoned in a tower; such a damsel, regarding her own rank, would be apt to have a standard which might strike the first comer as fantastically high. His entertainment, however, was not visible as, with a demeanor modelled upon the requirements of her dignity, he bent back the thorny bushes of the green cape, and made a passageway for her round its point. When his little roadway was finished, she came over it with her leisurely step, as though (he said to himself) it and the whole world, including his own poor individuality, belonged to her by inherited right, whenever she should choose to claim them. He was well aware that he was saying to himself a good many things about this girl; but was it not natural—coming unexpectedly upon so much beauty, set in so unfamiliar a frame? It was a new portrait, and he was fond of portraits; in picture-galleries he always looked more at the portraits than at anything else.

On the opposite side of the thorny cape the ruin came into view, standing back in a little arena of its own. Two of its high stone walls remained upright, irregularly broken at the top, and over them clambered a vine with slender leaves and long curling sprays that thrust themselves boldly out into the air, covered with bell-shaped, golden blossoms. This was the yellow jessamine, the lovely wild jessamine of Florida.

"You will look at it, please, from the other side," announced Garda; "it looks best from there. There will not be time to sketch it."

"Why do you keep taking it for granted that I sketch? Do I look like an artist?"

"Oh no; I've never seen an artist, but I'm sure you don't look like one. I suppose you sketch simply because I suppose northerners can do everything; I shall be fearfully disappointed if they cannot—when I see them."

"Do you wish to see them?"

"I wish to see hundreds," answered Miss Thorne, with great deliberation, "I wish to see thousands. I wish to see them at balls; I have never seen a ball. I wish to see them driving in parks; I have never seen a park. I wish to see them climbing mountains; I have never seen a mountain—"

"They don't do it in droves, you know," interpolated her companion.

"—I wish to see them in the halls of Congress; I have never seen Congress. I wish to see them at the Springs; I have never seen Springs. I wish to see them wearing diamonds; I have never seen diamonds—"

"The last is a wish easily gratified. In America, as one may say, the diamond's the only wear," remarked Winthrop, taking out a little linen-covered book.

Garda did not question this assertion, which reduced her own neighborhood to so insignificant an exception to a general rule that it need not even be mentioned. To her Florida was Florida. America? That was quite another country.

"You are going to sketch, after all," said the girl. She looked about her for a conveniently shaped fragment among the fallen blocks, and, finding one, seated herself, leaning against a second sun-warmed fragment which she took as her chair's back. "I thought I mentioned that there would not be time," she added, indolently, in her sweet voice.

"It will take but a moment," answered Winthrop. "I am no artist, as you have already mentioned; but, plainly, as a northerner, I must do something, or fall hopelessly below your expectations. There is no mountain here for me to climb, there is no ball at which I can dance. I'm not a Congressman and can't tell you about the 'halls,' and I haven't a diamond to my name, not one. Clearly, therefore, I must sketch; there is nothing else left." And with slow, accurate touch he began to pencil an outline of the flower-starred walls upon his little page. Garda, the handle of her white umbrella poised on one shoulder, watched him from under its shade. He did not look up nor break the silence, and after a while she closed her eyes and sat there motionless in the flower-perfumed air. Thus they remained for fully fifteen minutes, and Winthrop, going on with his work, admired her passiveness, he had never before seen the ability to maintain undisturbed an easy silence in a girl so young. True, the silence had in it something of that same element of indifference which he had noted in her before; but one could pardon her that for her tranquillity, which was so charming and so rare.

"Ah—sketching?" said a voice, breaking the stillness. "Yes—yes—the old mill has, I suppose, become an object of antiquity; we must think of it now as venerable, moss-grown."

Garda opened her eyes. "Jessamine-grown," she said, extending her hand.

The new-comer, whose footsteps had made no sound on the sand as he came round the cape of thorns, now crossed the arena, and made a formal obeisance over the little glove; then he threw back his shoulders, put his hands behind him, and remained standing beside her with a protecting, hospitable air, which seemed to include not only herself and the stranger artist, but the ruin, the sky, the sunshine, and even to bestow a general benediction upon the whole long, warm peninsula itself, stretching like a finger pointing southward from the continent's broad palm into the tropic sea.

But now Miss Thorne laid her white umbrella upon the heap of fallen blocks beside her, and rose; she did this as though it were something of a trouble, but a trouble that was necessary. She walked forward several steps, and turned first towards the new-comer, then towards the younger gentleman. "Let me present to you, Doctor, Mr. Evert Winthrop, of New York," she said, formally. "Mr. Winthrop, this is our valued friend, Mr. Reginald Kirby, surgeon, of Gracias-á-Dios." She then returned to her seat with the air of one who had performed an important task.

Dr. Kirby now advanced and offered his hand to Winthrop. He was a little man, but a little man with plenty of presence; he bore—if one had an eye for such things—a general resemblance to a canary-bird. He had a firm, plump little person, upon which his round, partly bald head (visible as he stood with hat doffed) was set, with scarcely any intervention of neck; and this plump person was attired in nankeen-colored clothes. His face showed a small but prominent aquiline nose, a healthily yellow complexion, and round, bright black eyes. When he talked he moved his head briskly to and fro upon his shoulders, and he had a habit of looking at the person he was addressing with one eye only, his face almost in profile, which was most bird-like of all. In addition, his legs were short in proportion to his body, and he stood on his small, well-shaped feet much as a canary balances himself on his little claws.

"I am delighted to meet you, sir," he said to Winthrop. "I esteem it a fortunate occurrence, most fortunate, which brought me to East Angels this evening to pay my respects to Mistress Thorne, thus obtaining for myself, in addition, the pleasure of your acquaintance. Mistress Thorne having mentioned to me that you were making a little tour of the place with Miss Garda, I offered to bear you company during a portion, at least, of your progress, for Miss Garda, though possessing an intelligence delicately keen, may not (being feminine) remember to present you with the statistics, the—as I may say—historical items, which would naturally be interesting to a northerner of discrimination." The Doctor had a fine voice; his words were borne along on it like stately ships on the current of a broad river.

"Do not praise me too highly," said the possessor of the delicate intelligence, from her block. "I could never live up to it, you know."

"Miss Thorne has said many interesting things," answered Winthrop, "but she has not as yet, I think, favored me with anything historical; her attention has perhaps been turned rather more to the agricultural side."

"Agricultural?" said Kirby, bringing to bear upon Winthrop a bright left eye.

"He is making sport of me," explained Garda, laughing.

"Pooh! pooh!" said the Doctor, raising himself a little, first on his toes, then on his heels, thus giving to his plump person a slightly balancing motion to and fro. "A little more seriousness, Garda, my child; a little more seriousness." Then, with his hands behind him, he turned to Winthrop to present, in his full tones, one of the historical items of which he had spoken. "These walls, Mr. Winthrop, whose shattered ruins now rise before you, once formed part of a large sugar-mill, which was destroyed by the Indians during the Seminole war. This province, sir, has had a vast deal of trouble with her Indians—a vast deal. The nature of the country has afforded them every protection, and clogged pursuit with monstrous difficulties, which, I may add, have never been in the least appreciated by those unfamiliar with the ground. The records of our army—I speak, sir, of the old army," said the Doctor, after a moment's pause, making his little explanation with a courteous wave of the hand, which dismissed, as between himself and the guest of Mistress Thorne, all question as to the army which was newer—

"these records, sir, are full of stories of the most harassing campaigns, made up and down this peninsula by our soldiers, in pursuit—vain pursuit—of a slippery, creeping, red-skinned, damnable foe. Canebrake, swamp, hammock; hammock, swamp, canebrake; ague, sunstroke, everglade; fever, scalping, ambuscade; and massacre—massacre—massacre!—such, sir, are the terms that succeed each other endlessly on those old pages; words that represent, I venture to say, more bravery, more heroic and unrequited endurance, than formed part of many a campaign that shines out to-day brilliantly on history's lying scroll. Yet who knows anything of them? I ask you, who?" The Doctor's fine voice was finer still in indignation.

"As it happens, by a chance, I do," answered Winthrop. "A cousin of my father's was in some of those campaigns. I well remember the profound impression which the Indian names in his letters used to make upon me when a boy—the Withlacoochee, the Caloosahatchee, the Suwannee, the Ocklawaha; they seemed to me to represent all that was tropical and wild and far, far away."

"They represented days of wading up to one's waist in stiff marsh-grass and water, sir. They represented rattlesnakes, moccasins, and adders, sir. They represented every plague of creation, from the mosquito down to the alligator, that great pig of the Florida waters. They represented long, fruitless tramps over the burning barrens, with the strong probability of being shot down at the last by a cowardly foe, skulking behind a tree," declaimed the Doctor, still indignant. "But this cousin of yours—would you do me the favor of his name?"

"Carey—Richard Carey."

"Ah! Major Carey, without doubt," said the little gentleman, softening at once into interest. "Allow me—was he sometimes called Dizzy Dick?"

"I am sorry to say that I have heard that name applied to him," answered Winthrop, smiling.

"Sir, you need not be," responded the other man, with warmth; "Dizzy Dick was one of the finest and bravest gentlemen of the old army. My elder brother Singleton—Captain Singleton Kirby—was of his regiment, and knew and loved him well. I am proud to take a relative of his by the hand—proud!" So saying, the Doctor offered his own again, and the two men went gravely through the ceremony of friendship a second time, under the walls of the old mill.

"Returning to our former subject," began the Doctor again—"for I hope to have many further opportunities for conversation with you concerning your distinguished relative—I should add, while we are still beside this memento, that the early Spanish settlers of this coast—"

"As a last wish," interrupted Garda, in a drowsy voice, "wait for the resurrection."

"As a last wish?" said the Doctor, turning his profile towards her with his head on one side, in his canary-bird way.

"Yes. I see that you have begun upon the history of the Spaniards in Florida, and as I shall certainly fall asleep, I think I ought to protect, as far as possible beforehand, my own especial ancestors," she answered, still somnolent; "they always have that effect upon me—the Spaniards in Florida." And as she slowly pronounced these last words the long lashes drooped over her eyes, she let her head fall back against the block behind her, and was apparently lost in dreams.

In this seeming slumber she made a lovely picture. But its chief charm to Evert Winthrop lay in the fact that it had in it so much more of the sportiveness of the child than of the consciousness of the woman. "I am interested in the old Spaniards, I confess," he said, "but not to the extent of allowing them to put you to sleep in this fashion. We will leave them where they are for the present (of course Elysium), and ask you to take us to the crane; his powers of entertainment are evidently greater than our own." And he offered his hand as if to assist her to rise.

"I am not quite gone yet," replied Garda, laughing, as she rose without accepting it. "But we must take things in their regular order, the magnolias come next; the crane, as our greatest attraction, is kept for the last." And she led the way along a path which brought them to a grove of sweet-gum-trees; the delicately cut leaves did not make a thick foliage, but adorned the boughs with lightness, each one visible on its slender stalk; the branches were tenanted by a multitude of little birds, whose continuous carols kept the air filled with a shower of fine small notes.

"How they sing!" said Winthrop. "I am amazed at myself for never having been in Florida before. The Suwannee River can't be far from here.

"'Way down upon de Suwannee River,
Far, far away—'

I must confess that Nilsson's singing it is the most I know about it."

"Nilsson!" said Garda, envyingly.

"You, sir, are too young, unfortunately too young, to remember the incomparable Malibran," said Dr. Kirby. "Ah! there was a voice!" And with recollections too rich for utterance, he shook his head several times, and silently waved his hand.

"Oh, when shall *I* hear something or somebody?" said Garda.

"We shall accomplish it, we shall accomplish it yet, my dear child," said the Doctor, coming briskly back to the present in her behalf. "Malibran is gone. Her place can never be filled. But I hope that you too may cross the seas some day, and find, if not the atmosphere of the grand style, which was hers and perished with her, at least an atmosphere more enlarging than this. And there will be other associations open to you in those countries besides the musical—associations in the highest degree interesting; you can pay a visit, for instance, to the scenes described in the engaging pages of Fanny Burney, incomparably the greatest, and I fear, from the long dearth which has followed her, the last of female novelists. For who is there since her day worthy to hold a descriptive pen, and what has been written that is worth our reading? With the exception of some few things by two or three ladies of South Carolina, which I have had the privilege of seeing, and which exist, I regret to say, only in manuscript as yet, I know of nothing—no one."

Winthrop glanced at Garda to see if her face would show merriment over the proposed literary pilgrimage. But no, the young girl accepted Miss Burney calmly; she had heard the Doctor declaim on the subject all her life, and was accustomed to think of the lady as a celebrated historical character, as school-boys think of Helen of Troy.

Beyond the grove, they came to the Levels. Great trees rose here, extending their straight boughs outward as far as they could reach, touching nothing but the golden air. For each stood alone, no neighbor near; each was a king. Black on the ground beneath lay the round mass of shadow they cast. Above, among the dense, dark foliage, shone out occasional spots of a lighter green; and this was the mistletoe. Besides these monarchs there were sinuous lines of verdure, eight and ten feet in height, wandering with grace over the plain. Most of the space, however, was free—wide, sunny glades open to the sky. The arrangement of the whole, of the great single trees, the lines of lower verdure, and the sunny glades, was as beautiful as though Art had planned and Time had perfected the work. Time's touch was there, but Art had had nothing to do with it. Each tree had risen from the ground where it and Nature pleased; birds, perhaps, with dropped seeds, had been the first planters of the lower growths. Yet it was not primeval; Winthrop, well used to primeval things, and liking them (to gratify the liking he had made more than one journey to the remoter parts of the great West), detected this at once. Open and free as the Levels were, he could yet see, as he walked onward, the signs of a former cultivation antecedent to all this soft, wild leisure. His eye could trace, by their line of fresher green, the course of the old drains crossing regularly from east to west; the large trees were sometimes growing from furrows which had been made by the plough before their first tiny twin leaves had sprouted from the acorn which had fallen there. "How stationary things are here!" he said, half admiringly. He was thinking of the ceaseless round of change and improvement which went on, year after year, on the northern farms he knew, of the thrift which turned every inch of the land to account, and made it do each season its full share. The thrift, the constant change and improvement, were best, of course; Winthrop was a warm believer in the splendid industries of the great republic to which he belonged; personally, too, there was nothing of the idler in his temperament. Still, looked at in another way, the American creed for the moment dormant, there was something delightfully restful in the indolence of these old fields, lying asleep in the sunshine with the low furrows of a hundred years before stretching undisturbed across them. Here was no dread, no eager speed before the winter. It was, in truth, the absence of that icy task-master which gave to all the lovely land its appearance of dreaming leisure. Growing could begin at any time; why, then, make haste?

"All this ground was once under cultivation," said the Doctor. "The first Edgar Thorne (your great-grandfather, Garda) I conjecture to have been a man of energy, who improved the methods of the Dueros; these Levels probably had a very different aspect a hundred years ago."

"A hundred years ago—yes, that was the time to have lived," said Garda. "I wish I could have lived a hundred years ago!"

"I don't know what we can do," said Winthrop. "Perhaps Dr. Kirby would undertake for a while the stately manners of your Spanish ancestors; I could attempt, humbly, those of the British colonist; I haven't the high-collared coat of the period, but I would do my best with the high-collared language which has been preserved in literature. Pray take my arm, and let me try."

Garda, looking merrily at the Doctor, accepted it.

"Arms were not taken in those days," said the Doctor, stiffly. "Ladies were led, delicately led, by the tips of their fingers." He was not pleased with Garda's ready acceptance; but they had kept her a child, and she did not know. He flattered himself that it would be an easy matter to bring about a withdrawal of that too freely accorded hand from the northerner's arm; he, Reginald Kirby, man of the world and noted for his tact, would be able to accomplish it. In the mean while, the hand remained where it was.

Beyond the Levels they came to the edge of a bank. Below, the ground descended sharply, and at some distance forward on the lower plateau rose the great magnolias, lifting their magnificent glossy foliage high in the air. "The Magnolia Grandiflora," said the Doctor, as if introducing them. "You no doubt feel an interest in these characteristically southern trees, Mr. Winthrop, and if you will walk down there and stand under them for a moment—the ground is too wet for your little shoes, Garda—you will obtain a very good idea of their manner of growth."

Miss Thorne made no objection to this suggestion. But neither did she withdraw her hand from Winthrop's arm.

"I can see them perfectly from here," answered that gentleman. "They are like tremendous camellias."

"When they are in bloom, and all the sweet-bays too, it is superb," said Garda; "then is the time to come here, the perfume is enchanting."

"Too dense," said the Doctor, shaking his head disapprovingly; "it's fairly intoxicating."

"That is what I mean," Garda responded. "It's as near as I can come to it, you know; I have always thought I should love to be intoxicated."

"What is your idea of it?" said Winthrop, speaking immediately, in order to prevent the Doctor from speaking; for he saw that this gentleman was gazing at Garda with amazement, and divined the solemnity his words would assume after he should have got his breath back.

"I hardly know how to describe my idea," Garda was answering. "It's a delicious forgetting of everything that is tiresome, an enthusiasm that makes you feel as if you could do anything—that takes you way above stupid people. Stupid people are worse than thieves."

"You describe the intoxication, or rather, to give it a better name, the inspiration of genius," said Winthrop; "all artists feel this inspiration at times—musicians, poets, painters, sculptors, all who have in them a spark, great or small, of the creative fire; even I, when with such persons—as by good fortune I have been once or twice—have been able to comprehend a little of it, have caught, by reflection at least, a tinge of its glow."

"Oh, if *you* have felt it, it is not at all what I mean," answered Garda, with one of her sudden laughs. She drew her hand from his arm, and walked down the slope across the lower level towards the magnolias.

As soon as her back was turned, Dr. Kirby tapped Winthrop on the back impressively, and raising himself on tiptoe, spoke in his ear. "She has never, sir, been near—I may say, indeed, that she has never *seen*—an intoxicated person in her life." He then came down to earth again, and folding his arms, surveyed the northerner challengingly.

"Of course I understood that," Winthrop answered.

When Garda reached the dark shade under the great trees she paused and turned. Winthrop had followed her. She gave him a bright smile as he joined her. "I wanted to see if you would come," she said, with her usual frankness.

"Of course I came; what did you suppose I would do?"

"I did not know, that was what I wanted to find out. You are so different, I should never know."

"Different from whom? From your four persons about here? I assure you that I am not different, I have no such pretension; your four are different, perhaps, but I am like five thousand, fifty thousand, others—as you will see for yourself when you come north."

"I don't believe it," said Garda, beginning to retrace her steps. She looked at him reflectively, then added, "I don't believe they are like you."

"What is it in me that you dislike so much?"

"Oh, I haven't thought whether I dislike it or not," responded Garda, with what he called in his own mind her sweet indifference. "What I meant was simply that I do not believe there are fifty thousand, or five thousand, or even five hundred other men, who are as cold as you are."

"Do I strike you in that way?"

"Yes; but of course you cannot help it, it is probably a part of your nature—this coldness," said the girl, excusingly. "It was that which made me say that you could never have felt the feeling I was trying to describe, you know—intoxication; it needs a certain sort of temperament; I have it, but you haven't."

"I see you are an observer," said her companion, inwardly smiling, but preserving a grave face.

"Yes," responded Garda, serenely, "I observe a great deal; it helps to pass the time."

"You have opportunities for exercising the talent?"

"Plenty."

"The four persons about here?"

Garda's laugh rippled forth again. "My poor four—how you make sport of them! But I should have said five, because there is the crane, and he is the wisest of all; he is wiser than any one I know, and more systematic, he is more systematic even than you are, which is saying a great deal. His name is Carlos Mateo, and you must be careful not to laugh at him when he dances, for a laugh hurts his feelings dreadfully. His feelings are very deep; you might not think so from a first glance, but that will be because you have not looked deep into his eyes—taken him round the neck and peered in. He has a great deal of expression; you have none at all—what has become of it? Did you never have any, or have you worn it all out? Perhaps you keep it for great occasions. But there will be no great occasions here."

"No, great occasions are at the North, where they are engaged in climbing mountains, walking on frozen lakes, wearing diamonds, and attending the halls of Congress," Winthrop answered.

Dr. Kirby was waiting for them on the bank, he had not stained his brightly polished little boots with the damp earth of the lower level. He had surveyed with inward disfavor the thick-soled walking shoes of the northerner, and the rough material of his gray clothes. The northerner's gloves were carelessly rolled together in his pocket, but the Doctor's old pair were on.

Garda led the way westward along the bank. After they had proceeded some distance, in single file owing to the narrowness of the path, she suddenly left her place, and, passing the Doctor, took Winthrop's hand in hers. "Close your eyes," she commanded; "I am going to lead you to a heavenly wall."

Winthrop obeyed; but retarded his steps.

"How slow you are!" she said, giving his hand a little pull.

"It's a wild country for a blind man," Winthrop answered, continuing to advance with caution. "Please take both hands."

"Let me lead him, Garda," said the Doctor, preferring to join in this child's play rather than have her continue it alone.

But the child's play was over, the bend in the path had been but a short one, and they were now before her "heavenly wall." Winthrop, upon being told to open his eyes—he had perhaps kept them closed longer than was absolutely necessary—found himself standing before a wall of verdure, fifteen feet high, composed of a mass of shining little leaves set closely together in an almost even expanse; this lustrous green was spangled with white flowers widely open, the five petals laid flatly back like a star.

"The Cherokee rose," said Dr. Kirby. He had been greatly vexed by Garda's freak of taking Winthrop's hands and pulling him along, and as he added, explanatorily, "the wild white rose of the South," he glanced at him to see how he, as a northerner and stranger, regarded it.

But the stranger and northerner was gazing at the southern flowers with an interest which did not appear to depend at all upon the southern girl who had brought him thither.

Garda remained but a moment; while they were looking at the roses she walked slowly on, following her heavenly wall.

"She is but a child," said the Doctor, looking after her. "We have perhaps kept her one too long."

"On the contrary, that is her charm," replied Winthrop. "How old is she?"

"Barely sixteen. If her father had lived, it would perhaps have been better for her; she would have had in that case, probably, more seriousness—a little more. Mistress Thorne's ideas concerning the training of children are admirable, most admirable; but they presuppose a certain kind of child, and Garda wasn't that kind at all; I may say, indeed, the contrary. Mistress Thorne has therefore found herself at fault now and then, her precedents have failed her; she has been met by perplexities, sometimes I have even thought her submerged in them and floundering—if I may use such an expression of the attitude of a cultured lady. The truth is, her perceptions have been to blame."

"Yet I have thought her perceptions unusually keen," said Winthrop.

"So they are, so they are; but they all advance between certain lines, they are narrow. Understand me, however—I would not have them wider; I was not wishing that, I was only wishing that poor Edgar, the father, could have lived ten years longer. Too wide a perception, sir, in a woman, a perception of things in general—general views in short—I regard as an open door to immorality; women so endowed are sure to go wrong—as witness Aspasia. It was a beautiful provision of nature that made the feminine perceptions, as a general rule, so limited, so confined to details, to the opinions and beliefs of their own families and neighborhoods; in this restricted view lies all their safety."

"And ours?" suggested Winthrop.

"Ah, you belong to the new school of thought, I perceive," observed the Doctor, stroking his smoothly shaven chin with his plump gloved hand.

The two men had begun to walk onward again, following their guide who was now at the end of the rose wall. Here she disappeared; when they reached the spot they found that she had taken a path which turned northward along a little ridge—a path bordered on each side by stiff Spanish-bayonets.

"Garda's education, however, has been, on the whole, good," said the Doctor, as they too turned into this aisle. "Mistress Thorne, who was herself an instructress of youth before her marriage, has been her teacher in English branches; Spanish, of course, she learned from the Old Madam; my sister Pamela (whom I had the great misfortune to lose a little over a year ago) gave her lessons in embroidery, general deportment, and the rudiments of French. As regards any knowledge of the world, however, the child has lived in complete ignorance; we have thought it better so, while things remain as they are. My own advice has decidedly been that until she could enter the right society, the society of the city of Charleston, for instance—it was better that she should see none at all; she has therefore lived, and still continues to live, the life, as I may well call it, of a novice or nun."

"The young gentleman who has just joined her is then, possibly, a monk?" observed Winthrop.

The Doctor was near-sighted, and not at all fond of his spectacles; with his bright eyes and quickly turning glance, it humiliated him to be obliged to take out and put on these cumbrous aids to vision. On this occasion, however, he did it with more alacrity than was usual with him. "Ah," he said, when he had made out the two figures in front, "it is only young Torres, a boy from the next plantation."

"A well-grown boy," commented the northerner.

"A mere stripling—a mere stripling of nineteen. He has but lately come out from Spain (a Cuban by birth, but was sent over there to be educated), and he cannot speak one word of English, sir—not one word."

"I believe Miss Thorne speaks Spanish, doesn't she?" remarked Winthrop.

CHAPTER II

The Doctor admitted that Garda could converse in Spanish. He suggested that they should walk on and join her; joining her, of course, meant joining Torres. The Cuban proved to be a dark-skinned youth, with dull black eyes, a thin face, and black hair, closely cut, that stood up in straight thickness all over his head, defying parting. He was tall, gaunt, with a great want of breadth in the long expanse of his person; he was deliberate in all his motions; ungainly. Yet he could not have been described as insignificant exactly; a certain deep reticent consciousness of his own importance, which was visible in every one of his slow, stiff movements, in every glance of his dull, reserved eyes, saved him from that. He bowed profoundly when introduced to the northerner, but said nothing. He did not speak after the others came up. When Garda addressed him, he contented himself with another bow.

They all walked on together, and after some minutes the little ridge, winding with its sentinel bayonets across old fields, brought them to the main avenue of the place. This old road, broad as it was, was completely overarched by the great live-oaks which bordered it on each side; the boughs rose high in the air, met, interlaced, and passed on, each stretching completely over the centre of the roadway and curving downward on the opposite side; looking east and looking west was like looking through a Gothic aisle, vaulted in gray-green. The little party entered this avenue; Garda, after a few moments, again separated herself from Winthrop and Dr. Kirby, and walked on in advance with Torres. The Doctor looked after them, discomfited.

"We should have spoken Spanish," said Winthrop, smiling.

"I do not know a word of the language!" declared the Doctor, with something of the exasperation of fatigue in his voice.

For the Doctor was not in the habit of walking, and he did not like to walk; the plump convexes of his comfortable person formed, indeed, rather too heavy a weight for his small feet in their little boots. But he was far too devoted a family friend to be turned back from obvious duty by the mere trifle of physical fatigue; he therefore waved his hand towards the live-oaks, and (keeping one eye well upon Garda and her companion in front) resumed with grace his descriptive discourse. "These majestic old trees, Mr.

Winthrop, were set out to adorn the main avenue of the place, leading from the river landing up to the mansion-house. You will find a few of these old avenues in this neighborhood; but far finer ones—the finest in the world—at the old places on the Ashley and Cooper rivers, near the city of Charleston."

"But there are no trees near the house," said Winthrop; "I noticed that particularly."

"The road goes to the door, the trees stop at the edge of the open space; that space was left, as you have probably divined, as a protection against surprises by Indians."

The younger man laughed. "I confess I was thinking more of the traditional Spanish jealousy than of Indians. You are right, of course; I must not allow my fancies, which are, after all, rather operatic in their origin, to lead me astray down here."

"You will find, I think, very little that is operatic among us," said Kirby, a trace of sombreness making itself felt for the first time through the courteous optimism of his tone. Truly there had been little that was operatic in their life at the South for some years past.

"I don't know," said Winthrop. "Isn't that rather an operatic personage who has just stopped Miss Thorne? The Tenor himself, I should say."

The spectacles were safely in their case, and back in the Doctor's pocket. But he now made haste to take them out a second time, he knew of no Tenors in Gracias. When he had adjusted them, "It's only Manuel Ruiz," he said, with both relief and vexation in his tone. He was relieved that it was only Manuel, but vexed that he should have been led, even for a moment, to suppose that it might be some one else, some one who was objectionable (as though objectionable persons could penetrate into their society!); and he asked himself inwardly what the deuce this northerner meant by calling their arrangement of their land "operatic," and their young gentlemen "Tenors." "Manuel Ruiz is the son of an old friend of ours; their place is on Patricio, opposite," he said, frigidly. "The Ruiz family were almost as well known here in the old Spanish days as the Dueros."

He had no time for more, for, as Garda had stopped, they now came up with the little party in front.

Manuel Ruiz was older than Torres. Manuel was twenty-one. He was a tall, graceful youth, with a mobile face, eloquent dark eyes, and a manner adorned with much gesture and animation. He undoubtedly cherished an excellent opinion of Manuel Ruiz; but undoubtedly also there was good ground for that opinion, Manuel Ruiz being a remarkably handsome young man. That Winthrop should have called him operatic was perhaps inevitable. He wore a short black cloak, an end of which was tossed over one shoulder after the approved manner of the operatic young gentleman when about to begin, under the balcony of his lady-love, a serenade; on his head was a picturesque sombrero, and he carried, or rather flourished, a slender cane, which might have been a rapier; these properties, together with his meridional eyes, his gestures, and the slight tendency to attitude visible in his graceful movements, made him much like the ideal young Tenor of the Italian stage, as he comes down to the foot-lights to sing in deepest confidence, to the sympathetic audience, of his loves and his woes.

That the ideal young Tenor has often encountered wide-spreading admiration, no one would venture to deny. Still, there have been, now and then, those among his audiences who have not altogether shared this feeling. They have generally been men; not infrequently they have been men of a somewhat lighter complexion, with visual orbs paler, perhaps, and not so expressive; a grace in attitude less evident. Evert Winthrop cared nothing for Tenors, real or imitative. But he was a man made with more pretensions to strength than to sinuousness; he had no gestures; his complexion, where not bronzed by exposure, was fair; his eyes were light. They were gray eyes, with, for the most part, a calm expression. But they easily became keen, and they could, upon occasion, become stern. He opposed a short, thick, brown beard to Manuel's pointed mustache, and thick, straight hair, closely cut, of the true American brown, to the little luxuriant rings, blue-black in color, short also, but curling in spite of shortness, which the breeze stirred slightly on the head of the handsome young Floridian as he stood, sombrero in hand, beside Garda Thorne.

Manuel was not another Torres; he was an American, and spoke English perfectly. Upon this occasion, after his introduction, he offered to the northerner with courtesy several well-turned sentences as the beginning of an acquaintance, and then they all walked on together up the old road.

"I believe we have now finished our little tour, Miss Garda, have we not?" said the Doctor, in a cheerful voice. Though very tired, he was walking onward with his usual trim step, his toes well turned out, his shoulders thrown back, his head erect, but having no perception of the fact (plump men never have) that, as seen from behind, his round person appeared to be projected forward into space as he walked with something of an overweight in front, and his little legs and feet to have been set on rather too far back to balance this weight properly, so that there seemed to be always some slight danger of an overthrow.

"Oh no," answered Garda; "I have promised to take Mr. Winthrop over the entire place, and we have still the orange walk, the rose garden, the edge of the swamp, the wild cattle, and the crane."

"I doubt whether Mr. Wintup will find much to amuse him in the wild cattle," remarked Manuel, laughing.

It was certainly a slight offence: Manuel had never been north, and did not know the name; in addition, owing to the mixture of races, much liberty of pronunciation was allowed in Gracias, Manuel himself seldom hearing his own name in proper form, the Spanish names of Florida, like the Huguenot names of South Carolina, having undergone more than one metamorphosis on New World shores. Winthrop walked on without replying, he seemed not to have heard the remark.

"You do want to see the wild cattle, don't you, Mr. Winthrop?" said Garda. "They're beautiful—in glimpses."

"If—ah—somebody should ride one of them—in glimpses—it might be entertaining," answered Winthrop. "Perhaps one of these young gentlemen would favor us?"

Garda's laugh pealed forth; Manuel looked angry, Torres watched the scene, but prudently gave no smile to what he did not understand. Even the Doctor joined in Garda's laugh.

"What in the world are you thinking of?" he said to Winthrop. "Bull-fighting? I am afraid we shall not be able to gratify you in that way just now."

At this moment, round a bend in the road, appeared the small figure of Mrs. Thorne; she was advancing towards them, accompanied by a gentleman in clerical attire.

"Here is mamma, with Mr. Moore," said Garda. She left the others, and went across to Winthrop. "The whole four," she murmured; "my four persons about here."

"So I supposed," Winthrop answered, in the same tone.

The two parties now met, and it was decided that the wild cattle and the swamp should be postponed for the present, and that they would all go together to the rose-garden, where, at this hour, Carlos Mateo was generally to be found disporting himself. Garda explained that he was disporting himself with the roses—he was very fond of roses, he was often observed gazing with fixed interest at unclosing buds. When they were fully opened, he ate them; this, however, was not gluttony, but appreciation; it was his only way of showing his admiration, and a very expressive one, Garda thought.

"Remarkably," observed the Doctor. "Captain Cook was of the same opinion."

The live-oak avenue brought them to the open space which surrounded the house; crossing this space, they took a path that came up to its border from the opposite direction. This second avenue was a green arched walk, whose roof of leaves seemed, as one looked down it, sure to touch the head;

but it never did, it was an illusion produced by the stretching vista of the long aisle. The same illusion made the opposite entrance at the far end—a half-circle of yellow light shining in from outside—seem so low, so near the ground, that one would inevitably be forced to creep through it on one's hands and knees when one had reached it, there would be no other way. This, again, was an illusion, the aisle was eight feet in height throughout its length. This long arbor had been formed by bitter-sweet orange-trees. Not a ray of the sunshine without could penetrate the thick foliage; but the clear light color of the shining leaves themselves, with the sunshine touching them everywhere outside, made a cheerful radiance within, and the aisle was further illuminated by the large, warm-looking globes of the fruit, thickly hanging like golden lamps from the roof of branches. There was an indescribably fresh youthfulness in this golden-green light, it was as different from the rich dark shade cast by the magnolias as from the gray stillness under the old live-oaks.

Through this orange aisle it pleased Miss Thorne to walk with Evert Winthrop. Mrs. Thorne came next, with the Rev. Dr. Moore; Dr. Kirby followed at a little distance, walking alone, and resting, if not his feet, at least his conversational powers. The two younger men were last, and some yards behind the others, Torres advancing with his usual woodenness of joint, not indulging in much conversation, but giving a guarded Spanish monosyllable now and then to his New World compatriot, who, still angry, let his slender cane strike the trunks of the orange-trees as they passed along, these strokes being carefully watched by Torres, who turned his thin neck stiffly each time, like an automaton, to see if the bark had received injury.

"We make quite a little procession," said Winthrop, looking back. "We have four divisions."

"What do you think of them?" inquired Garda.

"The divisions?"

"No; my four persons about here."

"Dr. Kirby is delightful, I don't know when I have met any one so much so."

"Delightful," said Garda, meditatively. "I am very fond of Dr. Reginald, he is almost the best friend I have in the world; but delightful?—does delightful mean—mean—" She paused, leaving her sentence unfinished.

"Does delightful mean Dr. Kirby?" said Winthrop, finishing it for her. "Dr. Kirby is certainly delightful, but he doesn't exhaust the capacity of the adjective; it has branches in other directions."

"And the others?"

"The other directions?"

"No; the other persons about here."

"I have seen Mr. Moore so few times that I have had scarcely opportunity to form an opinion."

"You formed one of Dr. Reginald the first time you saw him. But I was not speaking of Mr. Moore, I meant the others still."

"Those young natives? Really, I have not observed them."

"Now, there, I do not believe you," said Garda; "you have observed them, you observe everything. You say that to put them down—why should you put them down? You are very imperious, why should you be imperious?" And she looked at him, not vexed but frankly curious.

"Imperious," said Winthrop; "what extraordinary words you use? I am not imperious, as you call it, with you."

"No; but you would be if it were allowable," said the girl, nodding her head shrewdly. "Fortunately it isn't."

"Make the experiment—allow it; I might do better than you think."

"There is room for improvement, certainly," she answered, laughing. They had reached the end of the orange aisle, she passed under the green archway (which proved to be quite high enough), and went out into the sunshine beyond, calling "Carlos Mateo? Carlos, dear?" Then, in Spanish, "Angel of my heart, come to me."

The old garden had long been left untended. It was large, but seemed larger even than it was, because it had wandered out into the forest, and wild growths from there had come back with it; these had jumped boldly across the once well-guarded boundaries and overrun the cultivated verdure with their lawless green; oleanders were lost in thickets, fig-trees, pomegranates, and guavas were bound together in a tangle of vines; flower beds had become miniature jungles in which the descendants of the high-born blossoms that had once held sway there had forgotten their manners in the crowd of lusty plebeian plants that jostled against them. Even the saw-palmetto had pushed his way in from the barrens, and now clogged the paths with his rough red legs, holding up his stiff fans in the very faces of the lilies, who, being southern lilies, longed for the sun. A few paths had been kept open, however, round the great rose-tree, the pride of the place, a patriarch fifteen feet high, its branches covered with beautiful tea-roses, whose petals of soft creamy hue were touched at the edges with an exquisite pink. A little space of garden beds in comparative order encircled this tree; here, too, on the right, opened out the sweet-orange grove.

This grove was by no means in good condition, many of its trees were ancient, some were dead; still, work had been done there, and the attempt, such as it was, had been persisted in, though never effectually. The persistence had been due to the will of Mrs. Thorne, the ineffectualness to the will of old Pablo. His mistress, by a system of serene determination, had been able to triumph, to a certain extent, over the ancient and well-organized contrariness of this old man—a dumb opposition whose existence she never in the least recognized, though its force she well knew. Each season the obstinate old servant began by disapproving regularly of everything she ordered; next, he carried out her orders slowly, and with as many delays as possible—this not so much from any reasonable objection to her ideas as from his general principles of resistance, founded upon family pride. For Pablo, who was Raquel's husband—a bent little negro of advanced age—could never forget that "Marse Edgar's wife" was but an interloper after all, an importation from New England, and not "ob de fambly c'nection," not even of southern birth. The memory of majestic "Old Madam," Edgar Thorne's Spanish aunt, kept her "Young Miss" still in the estimation of the two old slaves, though "Ole Miss" had now been for a number of years safely in her coquina tomb—"let us hope enjoying rest and peace—as that poor little Mistress Thorne will now enjoy them too, *at last*," as an old friend of the family, Mrs. Betty Carew, had remarked with much feeling, though some ambiguity of phrase (the latter quite unintentional), the day after the funeral.

"Young Miss 'lows dese yere's *yappul*-trees," Pablo said to Raquel, with a fine scorn, as he dug objectingly round their roots. "An' 'lowing it, *'lowing* it, Raquel, she orders accordin'!"

But the southern trees had lived, and had even, some of them, thrived a little under the unwonted northern methods applied to them; Mrs. Thorne, therefore, was able to rise above old Pablo's disapprovals—a feat, indeed, which she had been obliged to perform almost daily, and with regard to many other things than oranges, ever since her first arrival at East Angels, seventeen years before.

This lady now seated herself on a bench under the rose-tree. She had tied on, over her neat little widow's cap, the broad-brimmed palmetto hat which she usually wore in the garden; this hat had fallen slightly back, and now its broad yellow brim, standing out in a circle round her small face, looked not unlike the dull nimbus with which the heads of the stiff, sweet little angels in the early Italian paintings are weighted down. The clergyman, Mr. Moore, stood beside her.

The Rev. Middleton Moore, rector of St. Philip and St. James's, Gracias-á-Dios, was a tall gentleman, with narrow, slightly stooping shoulders, long thin hands, a long smooth face, and thin dry brown hair which always looked long (though it was not), because it grew from the top of his head down to his ears in straight flat smoothness, the ends being there cut across horizontally. His features were delicately moulded. His long feet were slender and well-shaped. There was a charming expression of purity and goodness in his small, mild blue eyes. He was attired in clerical black, all save his hat, which was brown—a low-crowned, brown straw hat adorned with a brown ribbon. Mrs. Penelope Moore, his wife, profound as was her appreciation of the dignity of his position as rector of the parish, could yet never quite resist the temptation of getting for him, now and then, a straw hat, and a straw hat, too, which was not black; to her sense a straw hat was youth, and to her sense the rector was young. It was in a straw hat that she had first beheld and admired him as the handsomest, as well as the most perfect, of men; and so in a straw hat she still occasionally sent him forth, gazing at the back view of it and him, from the rickety windows of her Gothic rectory, with much satisfaction, as he went down the path towards the gate on his way to some of the gentle Gracias entertainments. For of course he wore it only on such light, unofficial occasions.

Dr. Kirby, meanwhile, was making the circuit of the orange grove. He stopped and peered up sidewise into each tree, his head now on one shoulder, now on the other; then he came back, his hands and pockets filled with oranges, which he offered to all; seating himself on the low curb of an old well, he began to peel one with the little silver knife which he kept for the purpose, doing it so deftly that not a drop of the juice escaped, and looking on calmly meanwhile as the other bird, Carlos Mateo, went through his dance for the entertainment of the assembled company. Carlos Mateo was a tall gray crane of aged and severe aspect; at Garda's call he had come forward with long, dignified steps and stalked twice round the little open space before the rose-tree, following her with grave exactitude as she walked before him. She then called him to a path bordered with low bushes, and here, after a moment, the company beheld him jumping slowly up and down, aiding himself with his wings, sometimes rising several feet above the ground, and sometimes only hopping on his long thin legs; he advanced in this manner down the path to its end, and then back again, Garda walking in front, and raising her hand as he rose and fell, as though beating time. Nothing could have been more comical than the solemnity of the old fellow as he went through these antics; it was as if a gray-bearded patriarch should suddenly attempt a hornpipe.

His performance ended, he followed his mistress back to the company, to receive their congratulations.

"What can we give him?" said Winthrop. "What does he like?"

"He will not take anything except from me," answered Garda; she gathered a rose, and stood holding it by the stem while Carlos Mateo pecked gravely at the petals. The sun was sinking, his horizontal rays shone across her bright hair; she had taken off her hat, which was hanging by its ribbon from her arm; Winthrop looked at her, at the rose-laden branches above her head, at the odd figure of the crane by her side, at the background of the wild old garden behind her. He was thinking that he would give a good deal for a picture of the scene.

But while he was thinking it, Manuel had spoken it. "Miss Garda, I would give a year out of my life for a picture of you as you are at this moment!" he said, ardently. Winthrop turned away.

He went to look at some camellias, whose glossy leaves formed a thicket at a little distance; on the other side of this thicket he discovered a crape-myrtle avenue, the delicate trees so choked and hustled by the ruder foliage which had grown up about them that they stood like captives in the midst of a rabble, broken-hearted and dumb; with some pushing he made his way within, and followed the lost path. It brought him to a mound of tangled shrubbery which rose like a small hill at this end of the garden, decked here and there, in what seemed inaccessible places, with brilliant flowers. But the places had not been inaccessible to Torres. Winthrop met him returning from the thorny conflict with a magnificent stalk of blossoms which he had captured there, and was now bringing back in triumph; it was a long wand of gorgeous spurred bells, each two inches in length, crimson without, cream-color within, the lip of the flaring lower petal lined with purple, and spotted with gold. Torres carried his prize to Garda, and offered it in silence. She thanked him prettily in Spanish, and he stood beside her, his dark face in a dull glow from pleasure.

"Perhaps it is poisonous," murmured Manuel, taking good care, however, to murmur in English.

"Oh, my dearest child! pray put it down," said Mrs. Thorne, anxiously.

"It is quite harmless," said the clergyman, "I know the family to which it belongs. It is not indigenous here; probably the original shrub was planted in the garden many years ago, and has run wild."

Garda took the stalk in her right hand, extended her left rigidly, and, stiffening her light figure in a wooden attitude, looked meekly upward.

"Bravo! bravo!" said the Doctor from his well-curb, laughing, and beginning on a second orange.

She stood thus for a few instants only. But it was very well done—an exact copy of a dark, grim old picture in the little Spanish cathedral of Gracias, a St. Catherine with a stalk of lilies in her hand.

Winthrop, who had returned, was standing on the other side of the open space. Apparently he had not noticed this little pantomime. Garda looked at him for a moment. Then she left her place, went across, and gravely decorated him with her stalk of blossoms, the large stem going through three of the button-holes of his coat before it could hold itself firmly; the brilliant flowers extended diagonally across his breast, past his chin, and above one ear.

"Your hat will break the top buds," said Garda, surveying her handiwork. "Please take it off."

He obeyed. "For what sacrifice am I thus adorned?" he asked.

"It's no sacrifice," answered Garda, "it's a rebellion—a rebellion against your constant objections to everything in the world!"

"But I haven't opened my lips."

"That is the very thing; you object silently—which is much worse. I'm not accustomed to people who object silently. Everybody here talks; why don't you talk?"

This little dialogue went on apart, the others could not hear it.

"I do—when you give me an opportunity," Winthrop answered.

"I'll give you one now," responded Garda; "we'll go back to the house, we'll go through the orange-walk as we came, and the others can follow as *they* came." Without waiting for reply, she went towards the garden gate. Winthrop followed her; and then Carlos Mateo, stalking across the open space, followed Winthrop. He followed him so closely that Winthrop declared he could feel his beak on his back. When they reached the house they paused; Carlos then took up his station a little apart, and stood on one leg to rest himself, watching Winthrop meanwhile with a suspicious eye.

Mrs. Thorne was crossing the level with the Rev. Mr. Moore. Following them, at a little distance, came Dr. Kirby, with his hands behind him. Manuel and Torres, forced to be companions a second time, formed the rear-guard of the returning procession. But as it approached the house, Manuel, raising his hat to Mrs. Thorne, turned away; he went down the live-oak avenue to the river landing, where his skiff was waiting. Manuel had his ideas, he did not care to be one of five. Torres, who also had his ideas, and many more of them than Manuel had, was not troubled by considerations of this sort; in his mind a Torres was never one of five, or one of anything, but always a Torres, and alone. Left to himself, he now took longer steps, passed the others, and came first to the doorway where Garda was standing.

"Why do you always look so serious, Mr. Torres?" she said, in Spanish, as he came up.

"It is of small consequence how I look, while the señorita herself remains so beautiful," answered the young man, bowing ceremoniously.

"Isn't that pretty?" said Garda to Winthrop.

"Immensely so," replied that decorated personage.

"But he does not look half so serious as you look comical—with all those brilliant flowers by the side of your immovable face," she went on, breaking into a laugh.

"It is of small consequence how I look, seeing that the señorita herself placed them where they are," answered Winthrop, in tolerable if rather labored Spanish, turning with a half-smile to Torres as he borrowed his phrase.

"You did not like it? You thought it childish?" said Garda. She drew the stalk quickly from its place. She was now speaking English, and Torres watched to see the fate of his gift; she had taken the flowers with the intention of throwing them away, but noticing that the Cuban's eyes were fixed upon them, she slipped the end of the stem under her belt, letting the long brilliant spray hang down over her dark skirt.

"I am now more honored than ever," said Winthrop.

"But it is Mr. Torres whom I am honoring this time," answered the girl.

Torres, hearing his name in her English sentence, drew the heels of his polished boots together with a little click, and made another low bow.

The rest of the party now came up, and soon after, the visitors took leave; Winthrop rode back across the pine-barrens to Gracias. Dr. Kirby bore him company on his stout black horse Osceola, glad indeed to be there and off his own feet; on the way he related a large portion of that history of the Spaniards in Florida which Garda, their descendant, had interrupted at the mill.

As they left East Angels, and rode out on the barren, this descendant was being addressed impressively by her mother. "That, Garda, is my idea of a cultivated gentleman: to have had such wide opportunities, and to have improved them; to be so agreeable, and yet so kind; so quiet, and yet so evidently a man of distinction, of mark—it's a rare combination."

"Very," replied Garda, giving the crane her gloves to carry in his beak.

They were still standing in the lower doorway; Mrs. Thorne surveyed her daughter for a moment, one of her states of uncertainty seemed to have seized her. "I hope you appreciate that Mr. Winthrop is not another Manuel or Torres," she said at last, in her most amiable tone.

"Perfectly, mamma; I could never make such a mistake as that. Mr. Winthrop inspires respect."

"He does—he does," said Mrs. Thorne, with conviction.

"I respect him already as a father," continued Garda. "Manuel and Ernesto also respect him as a father. Come, Carlos, my angel, let us go down to the landing, and see if we can call Manuel back."

CHAPTER III

Gracias-á-Dios was a little town lying half asleep on the southern coast of the United States, under a sky of almost changeless blue.

Of almost changeless blue. Americans have long been, in a literary way, the vicarious victims, to a certain extent, of the climate of the British Isles. The low tones of the atmosphere of those islands, the shifting veils of fog and rain rising and falling over them, the soft gray light filtered through mist and cloud—all these have caused the blue skies and endless sunshine of Italy to seem divinely fair to visitors from English shores; and as among these visitors have come the poets and the romance writers, this fairness, embalmed in prose and verse, has taken its place in literature, has become classic. The imaginative New World student, eager to learn, passionately desirous to appreciate, has read these pages reverently; he knows them by heart. And when at last the longed-for day comes when he too can make his pilgrimage to these scenes of legend and story, so dominated is he, for the most part, by the spell of tradition that he does not even perceive that these long-chanted heavens are no bluer than his own; or if by chance his eye, accurate in spite of himself, notes such a possibility, he puts it from him purposely, preferring the blueness which is historic. The heavens lying over Venice and her palaces are, must be, softer than those which expand distantly over miles of prairie and forest; the hue of the sky which bends over Rome is, must be, of a deeper, richer tint than any which a New World has attained. But generally this preference of the imaginative American is not a choice so much as an unconscious faith which he has cherished from childhood, and from which he would hardly know how to dissent; he is gazing at these foreign skies through a long, enchanting vista of history, poetry, and song; he simply does not remember his own sky at all.

Only recently has he begun to remember it, only recently has he begun to discover that, in the matter of blue at least, he has been gazing through glasses adjusted to the scale of English atmosphere and English comparisons, and that, divested of these aids to vision, he can find above his own head and in his own country an azure as deep as any that the Old World can show.

When this has been discovered it remains but blue sky. The other treasure of those old lands beyond the sea—their ruins, their art, their ancient story—these he has not and can never have, and these he loves with that deep American worship which must seem to those old gods like the arrival of Magi from afar, men of distant birth, sometimes of manners strange, but bringing costly gifts and bowing the knee with reverence where the dwellers in the temple itself have grown cold.

Compared with those of the British Isles, all the skies of the United States are blue. In the North, this blue is clear, strong, bright; in the South, a softness mingles with the brilliancy, and tempers it to a beauty which is not surpassed. The sky over the cotton lands of South Carolina is as soft as that of Tuscany; the blue above the silver beaches of Florida melts as languorously as that above Capri's enchanted shore. Gracias-á-Dios had this blue sky. Slumberous little coast hamlet as it was, it had also its characteristics.

"Gracias á Dios!" Spanish sailors had said, three hundred years before, when, after a great storm, despairing and exhausted, they discovered this little harbor on the low, dangerous coast, and were able to enter it—"Gracias á Dios!" "Thanks to God!" In the present day the name had become a sort of shibboleth. To say Gracias á Dios in full, with the correct Spanish pronunciation, showed that one was of the old Spanish blood, a descendant of those families who dated from the glorious times when his Most Catholic and Imperial Majesty, King of Spain, Defender of the Church, always Victorious, always Invincible, had held sway on this far shore. To say Gracias without the "á Dios," but still with more or less imitation of the Spanish accent, proved that one belonged among the older residents of the next degree of importance, that is, that one's grandfather or great-grandfather had been among those English colonists who had come out to Florida during the British occupation; or else that he had been one of the planters from Georgia and the Carolinas who had moved to the province during the same period. This last pronunciation was also adopted by those among the later-coming residents who had an interest in history, or who loved for their own sakes the melody of the devout old names given by the first explorers—names now so rapidly disappearing from bay and harbor, reef and key. But these three classes were no longer all, there was another and more recent one, small and unimportant as yet, but destined to grow. This new class counted within its ranks at present the captains and crews of the northern schooners that were beginning to come into that port for lumber; the agents of land-companies looking after titles and the old Spanish grants; speculators with plans in their pockets for railways, with plans in their pockets for canals, with plans in their pockets (and sometimes very little else) for draining the swamps and dredging the Everglades, many of the schemes dependent upon aid from Congress, and mysteriously connected with the new negro vote. In addition there were the first projectors of health resorts, the first northern buyers of orange groves: in short, the pioneers of that busy, practical American majority which has no time for derivations, and does not care for history, and which turns its imagination (for it has imagination) towards objects more veracious than the pious old titles bestowed by an age and race that murdered, and tortured, and reddened these fair waters with blood, for sweet religion's sake. This new class called the place Grashus—which was a horror to all the other inhabitants.

The descendants of the Spaniards, of the English colonists, of the Georgia and Carolina planters—families much thinned out now in numbers and estate, wearing for the most part old clothes, but old prides as well—lived on in their old houses in Gracias and its neighborhood, giving rather more importance perhaps to the past than to the present, but excellent people, kind neighbors, generous and devoted friends. They were also good Christians; on Sundays they all attended service in one or the other of the two churches of Gracias, the Roman Catholic cathedral of Our Lady of the Angels, and the Episcopal church of St Philip and St. James'. These two houses of worship stood side by side on the plaza, only an old garden between them. St. Philip and St. James' had a bell; but its Spanish neighbor had four, and not only that, but a habit of ringing all four together, in a sort of quickstep, at noon on Sundays, so that the Episcopal rector, in that land of open windows, was obliged either to raise his voice to an unseemly pitch, or else to preach for some minutes in dumb-show, which latter course he generally adopted as the more decorous, mildly going back and giving the lost sentences a second time, as though they had not been spoken, when the clamor had ceased. This, however, was the only warfare between the two churches. And it might have been intended, too, merely as a friendly hint from the Angels to the Saints that the latter's sermons were too long. The Episcopal rector, the Rev. Middleton Moore, had in truth ideas somewhat behind his times: he had not yet learned that fifteen or at most twenty minutes should include the utmost length of his weekly persuasions to virtue. It had never occurred to the mind of this old-fashioned gentleman that congregations are now so highly improved, so cultivated and intellectual, that they require but a few moments of dispassionate reminder from the pulpit once a week, that on the whole it is better to be moral, and, likewise, that any assumption of the functions of a teacher on the part of a clergyman is now quite obsolete and even laughable—these modern axioms Middleton Moore had not yet learned; the mistaken man went on hopefully exhorting for a full three-quarters of an hour. And as his congregation were as old-fashioned as himself, no objection had as yet been made to this course, the simple people listening with respect to all he had to say, not only for what it was in itself, but for what he was in himself—a man without spot, one who, in an earlier age, would have gone through martyrdom with the same pure, gentle firmness with which he now addressed them from a pulpit of peace. It was in this little church of St. Philip and St. James' that Evert Winthrop had first beheld Garda Thorne.

The next day he presented a letter of introduction which his aunt, Mrs. Rutherford, had given him before he left New York; the letter bore the address, "Mrs. Carew." Winthrop had not welcomed this document, he disliked the demand for attention which epistles usually convey. How much influence the beautiful face seen in church had upon its presentation when he finally made it, how long, without that accident, the ceremony might have been delayed, it would be difficult, perhaps, to accurately state. He himself would have said that the beautiful face had hastened it somewhat; but that in time he should have obeyed his aunt's wish in any case, as he always did. For Winthrop was a good nephew, his aunt had given him the only mother's love his childhood had known.

Mrs. Carew, who as Betty Gwinnet had been Mrs. Rutherford's roommate at a New York school forty-four years before, lived in one of the large, old, rather dilapidated houses of Gracias; she was a widow, portly, good-natured, reminiscent, and delighted to see the nephew of her "dearest Katrina Beekman." It was not until his second visit that this nephew broached the subject of the face seen in church, and even then he presented it so slightly, with its narrow edge towards her, as it were, that the good lady never had a suspicion that it was more than a chance allusion on his part, and indeed always thereafter took to herself the credit of having been the first to direct a cultivated northern attention to this beautiful young creature, who was being left, "like the poet's flower, you know, to blush unseen and waste her sweetness on the desert air, though of coarse you understand that I am not literal of course, for fortunately there are no deserts in Florida, unless, indeed, you include the Everglades, and I don't see how you can, for certainly the essence of a desert is, and always has been, dryness of course, dryness to a *degree*, and the Everglades are all under water, so that there isn't a dry spot anywhere for even so much as the sole of your foot, any more than there was for Noah's weary dove, you know, and it's water, water, everywhere, and not a drop to drink, that is, if you should *wish* to drink it, which I am sure I hope you wouldn't, for it's said to be *most* unhealthy, and even the Ancient Mariner himself couldn't have stood it long."

Mrs. Carew was fertile in quotations, rich in simile; and if both were rather wanting in novelty, there was at least an element of unexpectedness in her manner of connecting them which amused her present visitor and kept him listening. Not that Winthrop was ever inattentive. On the contrary, he had listening powers of admirable range and calm. He was capable of participating in any amount of conversation upon the weather, he could accept with passiveness those advisers who are always telling their friends what they "ought" to do, he could listen imperturbably to little details from the people who always will tell little details, he could bear without impatience even the narration of dreams; he was able to continue an acquaintance unmoved with those excellent persons who, when they have said a good thing, immediately go back and tell it over again; in short, he betrayed no irritation in the presence of great Commonplace. The commonplace people, therefore, all liked him, he had not an enemy among them. And this was the more amusing, as, in reality, he detested them.

His friends, those who knew him best, told him that he went about most of the time in a mask. "All the world's a stage," he answered; "the only point is that the mask should be an agreeable one. Why should I be obliged to show my true complexion to Tom, Dick, and Harry, when Tom, Dick, and Harry so much prefer the one I have assumed? It's good practice for me—the mask-wearing—practice in self-control; and besides, Tom, Dick, and Harry are right, the borrowed complexion *is* the better one; perhaps I may be able, in time, to really acquire one like it."

To find himself listening, therefore, without his mask, listening for the simple entertainment of it, was always an agreeable variety to this gentleman, who kept at least his outward attention in such strict control; and the first time he heard Mrs. Betty Carew hold forth, he had a taste of it.

"Yes, that was Mistress Thorne and Garda, I reckon; on second thoughts, I am sure of it; for they always come up from East Angels on Sunday mornings to service, with old Pablo to row, as Mistress Thorne *has* succeeded in getting as far as the Episcopal church, though Our Lady of the Angels *was* too much for her, which was quite as well, however, because, of course, all the Thornes, being English, were Church people of course in the old country, though poor Eddie, having been twice diluted, as one may say, owing to his mother and grandmother having been Spanish and Roman Catholic, was not *quite* so strong in the real Episcopal doctrines as he might have been, which was a pity, of course, but could hardly, under the circumstances, have been prevented so far as I can see, for one swallow doesn't make a summer, I reckon, any more than one parent makes a Protestant, especially when the other's a Duero—with the Old Madam *roaring* on the borders, ready to raise Ned on the slightest provocation, to come down like wolf on the fold, you know—or was it the Assyrian? Now at East Angels—perhaps you are wondering at the name? Well, the cathedral, to begin with, is Our Lady of the Angels, and, in the old days, there were two mission-stations for the Indians south of here, one on the east coast, one more to the west, and bearing the same name. These chapels are gone; but as the Duero house stood near one of them, it took the name, or part of it, and has been called East Angels ever since. There was no house near the other chapel—West Angels—and some say the very site is lost, though others again have declared that the old bell is still there, lying at the foot of a great cypress—that hunters have seen it. But I haven't much faith in hunters, have you?—nor in fishermen either, for that matter. Little Mistress Thorne must know a great deal about fish, I suppose she lived on cod before she came down here;

she belongs to Puritan stock, they say, and there *were* good people among them of course, though, for my part, I have always had a horror of the way they treated the witches; not that I approve of witchcraft, which is of course as wicked as possible, and even the witch of Endor, I suppose, could hardly be defended upon moral grounds, whatever you may do upon historical—which are so much the fashion nowadays, though I, for one, can't abide them—making out as they do that everything is a falsehood, and that even Pocahontas was not a respectable person; I don't know what they will attack next, I'm sure; Pocahontas was our *only* interesting Indian. Not that I care for Indians, don't fancy that; the Seminoles particularly; I'm always so glad that they've gone down to live in the Everglades, half under water; if anything could take down their savageness, I should think it would be that. I know them very well, of course—the Thornes, not the Seminoles—though perhaps I was never *quite* so intimate with them as Pamela Kirby was (she's dead now, poor soul! *so* sad for her!), for Pamela used to give Garda lessons; she moulded her, as she called it, taught her to shoot—of course I mean the young idea, and not guns. In fact, they have all had a hand in it—the moulding of Garda; too many, I think, for *I* believe in *one* overruling eye, and if you get round that, there's the good old proverb that remains pretty true, after all, I reckon, the one about too many cooks, though in this case the broth has been saved by the little mother, who is a very Napoleon in petticoats, and never forgets a thing; she actually remembers a thing *before* it has happened; Methuselah himself couldn't do more, though, come to think of it, I suppose very little had happened in the world before *his* day—excepting trilobites, that we used to read about in school. And Mistress Thorne knows all about *them*, you may be sure, just as well as Methuselah did; for she was a teacher, to begin with, a prim little New England school marm whom poor Eddie Thorne met by accident one summer when he went north, and fell in love with, as I have always supposed, from sheer force of contrast, like Beauty and the Beast, you know—not that she was a beast, of course, though poor Eddie *was* very handsome, but still I remember that everybody wondered, because it had been thought that he would marry the sister of Madame Giron, who had hair that came down to her feet. However, I ought to say that poor little Mistress Thorne has certainly done her very best to acquire our southern ways; she has actually tried to make herself over, root, stem, and branch, from her original New England sharpness to our own softer temperament, though I always feel sure, at the same moment, that, in the core of the rock, the old sap burns still—like the soul under the ribs of death, you know; not that I mean that exactly (though she *is* thin), but simply that the leopard cannot change his spots, nor the zebra his stripes, nor," added the good lady—altering her tone to solemnity as she perceived that her language was becoming Biblical—"the wild *cony* her *young*. Just to give you an idea of what I mean, Mr. Winthrop: for a long time after she first came to Gracias that little creature used regularly to parse twenty-four pages of 'Paradise Lost' every day, as a sort of mental tonic, I reckon, against what she thought the enervating tendencies of our southern life here—like quinine, you know; and as she parsed so much, she was naturally obliged to quote, as a sort of safety-valve, which was very pleasant of course and very intellectual, though I never care much for quotations myself, they are so diffuse, and besides, with all your efforts, you cannot make 'Paradise Lost' appropriate to all the little daily cares of life and house-keeping, which no true woman, I think, should be above; for though Eve *did* set a table for the angel, that was merely poetical and not like real life in the least, for she only had fruits, and no dishes probably but leaves, that you could throw away afterwards, which was *very* different from nice china, I can assure you, for you may not know, not being a house-keeper, that as regards china *nowadays*—our old blue sets—our servants are not in the *least* careful not to nick; I don't enter here into the great question of emancipation for the slaves, *but*—nick they *will*! Mistress Thorne speaks like 'Paradise Lost' to this day, and, what is more, she has taught Garda to speak in the same way—just like a book; only Garda's book is her own, you never know what she is going to say next, she turns about in all sorts of shapes, like those kaleidoscopes they used to give us children when I was little, only *she* never rattles (they did, dreadfully)—for I am sure a softer voice *I* never heard, unless it was that of the Old Madam, who used to say in velvet tones the most ferocious things you ever heard. Ah, you should have seen her!—straight as an arrow, and they said she was ninety for over thirty years, which of course was impossible, even if she had wished it, which I doubt, for there is the well-known Bible age of threescore years and ten, and to have exceeded it to *that* extent would have been irreverent. She was poor Eddie Thorne's aunt, the sister of his mother, a Duero and a tremendous one, dyed in ancestors to the core; every one was afraid of her but Garda, and Garda she took complete charge of as long as she lived, though Mistress Thorne did what she could on the outskirts—*not* much, I fancy, for the Old Madam declared that the child was a true Duero and should be brought up as one, which seemed to mean principally that she should swing in the hammock, and not learn verbs. I *think* Mistress Thorne began to teach Garda verbs the day after the funeral; at least when I went down there to pay a visit of condolence I found her with a grammar in her hand, and a good deal of cheerfulness under the circumstances—a good deal! The first Edgar Thorne, the one who came out from England, is said to have been a man of a good deal of force of character, for he kept a coach and four, and at that early day, on these pine-barrens, it almost seemed as if he must have created them by magic, which makes one think of Cinderella and her rats, doesn't it? And indeed, in this case, the horses did turn into rats, as one may say, before their very eyes; the poor Thornes have no horses *now*" said the kind-hearted lady, pausing to shake her head sympathetically, and then speeding on again. "They say that rats desert a sinking ship—though I have always wondered how, since ships are not apt to sink at the piers, are they?—and I never heard that rats could make rafts, though squirrels can, they say—a bit of plank with their tails put up as a sail, though of course rats' tails would never do for that, they are so thin; but if rats *do* desert their ship, Mistress Thorne will *never* desert hers, she will keep the Thorne colors flying to the last, and go down, if down she must, with the silent courage of the Spartan boy—although it was a fox he had gnawing him, wasn't it? and not a rat; but it makes no difference, it's the principle that's important, not the illustration. Garda's name is really Edgarda, Edgarda after all the Thornes, who, it seems, have been Edgars and Edgardas for centuries, which I should think must have been very inconvenient, for, just to mention one thing, they could never have signed their names in initials, because that would have meant fathers and sons and brothers and sisters indiscriminately, in fact all of them except the wives, who, having come in from outside families, would be able, fortunately, to be plain Mary and Jane. I am very fond of Garda, as indeed we all are; and I think she has wonderful beauty, don't you?—though *rather* Spanish perhaps. When she was about twelve years old I was afraid that the tinge of her mother in her was going to make her thin; but Nature fortunately prevented that in time, for you know that once an elbow gets fixed in the habit of being sharp, sharp it remains to the end of the chapter, though you may have pounds and pounds both above and below it, which seems strange, doesn't it? though of course it must serve some good purpose, as we ought all to believe. And that reminds me to say that I hope dear Katrina has gained flesh since she left school, for she used to be rather too slender (though *very* handsome otherwise), so that, in profile view, you couldn't help thinking of a paper-cutter, and you doubted whether she could even cast a shadow—like the man without a shadow, you remember, who used to double his up and put it in his pocket—only of course dear Katrina was never anything horrible like that, and, after all, why we should *wish* to cast shadows I am sure I don't know; certainly there are enough of them, as it is, in this vale of tears. If you like, I will take you down some day to call upon the Thornes; they will be delighted to see us and we shall be like angels' visits, few and far between, or fair as a star when only *one*; I *hope* you like poetry—you modern young gentlemen have such a way of being above it! But Mr. Carew was always very fond of Mrs. Hemans."

The monologues of Mr. Carew's relict could with the utmost ease be regulated, their flowing currents turned aside into another channel (from which they never came back to the first one), or stopped entirely, by any one who wished to accomplish it, the lady's boundless good-nature preventing her from even perceiving that she had been interrupted. But Evert Winthrop had no wish to interrupt, he was enjoying the current's vagaries; upon this occasion, therefore, it pursued its way unchecked to the end—a thing which rarely happened, all Gracias having the habit of damming it temporarily, turning it aside, or stopping it abruptly, in a brisk manner which showed long usage.

To-day, when at last this easy-tempered lady paused of her own accord, Winthrop accepted her invitation promptly; he spoke of coming for her with a carriage the next afternoon; he should enjoy seeing something of the interior, those singular roads across the barrens which were so old and untouched and yet in such perfect condition—so he had been told.

When he had brought his little speech to a close, his hostess gave way to laughter (her laugh was hearty, her whole amplitude took part in it). "But this isn't interior," she said, "this is coast; East Angels is down the river, south of here; when I said I would take you, I meant in a boat."

She had in her mind Uncle Cato, and the broad, safe, old row-boat, painted black and indefinite as to bow and stern, which that venerable negro propelled up and down the Espiritu as custom required. But instead of voyaging in this ancient bark, Winthrop persuaded her to intrust herself to the rakish-looking little craft, sloop-rigged, which he had engaged for his own use among the lagoons during his stay in Gracias, a direct descendant, no doubt, of the swift piratical barks of the wreckers and smugglers who, until a very recent date, had infested the Florida keys. Once on board, Mrs. Carew adjured the man at the helm to "keep the floor straight at any price," and then seating herself, and seizing hold of the first solid object she could find, she tightly closed her eyes and did not again open them, being of the opinion apparently that the full force of a direct glance would infallibly upset the boat. She had postponed their visit for a day, in order that she might have time to send Uncle Cato down to East Angels, with a note saying that they were coming. Stately Raquel, in a freshly starched turban, was therefore in waiting to open the lower door; Mrs. Thorne's best topics were arranged in order in her mind, as well as orange wine and wafers upon her sideboard, and Garda also, neither asleep in the hammock nor wandering afield with the crane, was in readiness, sitting expectant in an old mahogany arm-chair, attired in her best gown. Poor Garda had but two gowns to choose from, both faded, both old; but the one called best had been lately freshened and mended by the skilful hands of the tireless mother.

"When that little woman dies, some of her mendings ought to be enclosed in a glass case and set up over her grave as a monument, I do declare!" said Mrs. Carew, as, again voluntarily blinded, she sailed back to Gracias with Winthrop over the sunset-tinted water. "Did you notice that place on Garda's left sleeve? But of course you didn't. Well, it was a perfect miracle of patience, which Job himself couldn't have equalled (and certainly the Thornes are as poor as Job, and Carlos might well be the turkey); as black silk, or even black thread, would have shone—they *will* shine, you know, in spite of all you can do, even if you ink them—she had actually used ravellings, and *alpaca* ravellings—you know what *they* are! Don't you think it would be nicer to have that sail out sideways, as it was when we came down, and go straight, instead of slanting in this way back and forth across the river?"

Evert Winthrop, thus introduced, had received from the mistress of East Angels an invitation to repeat his visit. He had repeated it several times. It was easy to do this, as, in addition to the piratical little craft already mentioned, he had engaged a saddle-horse, and was now amusing himself exploring the old roads that led southward.

Upon returning from one of these rides he found awaiting him a letter from the North. It was from his aunt, Mrs. Rutherford, and contained the intelligence that she was coming southward immediately, having been ordered to a warmer climate on account of the "threatenings of neuralgia, that tiresome neuralgia, my dear boy, that makes my life such a burden. I am so tired of Pau and Nice that, instead of crossing that cold ocean again, I have suddenly made up my mind to come down and join you under the blue sky you have discovered down there—Egypt, you say, Egypt without the ruins; but as I am a good deal of a ruin myself just now, I shall not mind that lack; in fact, can supply it in my own person. My love to Betty Carew; I shall be delighted to see her again after all these years. Margaret comes with me, of course, and we shall probably follow this letter without much delay."

Winthrop was surprised. He knew that his aunt was fond of what she patriotically called her "own country;" but he should have said that she would not probably consider that there was any of it worth her personal consideration south of Philadelphia, or, at the utmost, south of Baltimore and Washington. This amiably blind lady was, however, a great traveller, in her leisurely way she had taken long journeys across Europe and the East; if she did not know the Mississippi, she knew the Nile; if Shasta was a stranger to her eyes, the Finsteraarhorn and Vesuvius were old friends. Shasta, indeed!—where was Shasta? She had once been to Niagara Falls.

Her nephew smiled to himself as he thought that probably, in her own mind, her present undertaking wore much of the air of an exploring expedition, the kind of tour through remote regions that people made sometimes, and then wrote books about—books with a great many illustrations.

But Mrs. Rutherford would write no books. This lady noticed but slightly the characteristics of the countries through which she passed, she never troubled her mind with impressions, or burdened it with comparisons. She seldom visited "objects of interest," but was always "rather tired" when the appointed hour came, and thought she would lie down for a while; they could tell her about it afterwards. Yet in her easy, irresponsible fashion she enjoyed travelling; she liked new scenes and new people, especially new people. In the evening, after a quiet (but excellent) little dinner, and twenty minutes or so of lady-like tranquillity after it, Mrs. Rutherford was always pleased to see the new people aforesaid; and it could with truth be added that the new people were, as a general thing, equally pleased to see her. She was a handsome, stately woman, with agreeable manners, and so well-dressed that that alone was a pleasure—a pleasure to the eyes; it was an attire rich and quiet, which combined with extraordinary skill the two often sadly dissevered qualities of personal becomingness and adaptation to the fashion of the hour.

Evert Winthrop was much attached to his aunt. Associated with her were the happiest memories of his childhood. He knew that her strongest love had not been given to him, it had been given to her other nephew, his cousin Lansing Harold. But of Lansing she had had entire charge from his birth, he had been to her like her own child, while Andrew Winthrop had kept closely in his own care his motherless little son Evert, allowing him to spend only his vacations with his aunt Katrina—who was spoiling one boy (so thought the New-Englander) as fast as possible, but who should not be permitted to spoil another. These vacations, so grudgingly granted, had been very happy times for the little Evert, and their memory remained with him still. As he grew older he had gradually become conscious of some of the traits and tendencies of his aunt's mind, apart from his boyish idea of her, as we generally do become conscious, by degrees, of the traits (as they are estimated by others) of even those who are nearest and dearest, save in the case of our parents, who remain always, beautifully always, "father" and "mother" to the end, precious beyond all analysis, all comparison. Separating itself, therefore, from the delightful indulgence with which she had sweetened his boyhood days, separating itself from his own unquestioning childish belief in her, there had gradually come to Evert Winthrop (though without any diminution of his affection for her) the consciousness that his aunt's nature was a narrow one. Her narrowness could have been summed up roughly in the statement that her views upon every subject were purely personal ones. It was difficult to realize how personal they were, Winthrop himself, well as he knew her, had only within the past five or six years become fully conscious of the absolute predominance of the principle. No one besides himself had had the opportunity to make the same discovery, save possibly—so he had sometimes thought with a smile—the departed Peter Rutherford, the lady's husband. But Peter Rutherford, among many excellent qualities, had not been endowed with a delicate observation, and indeed having been of a robust and simple nature, he had had small respect for the talent, at least in a man, associating it vaguely with a knowledge of millinery, with a taste for spelling-games and puzzles, for cake and religious novels—things he considered unworthy of the masculine mind. His wife's nephew, however, though not a judge of millinery, and not interested in the mild entertainments and literature referred to, possessed observation in abundance, and with regard to his aunt he had not been able to keep it from exercising itself, at least to a certain degree. He had discovered—he had been unable to help discovering—the secret springs that moved much of her speech; and these springs were so simple that, in a complicated age, they seemed extraordinary. Her opinions of persons (he knew it now) were based entirely upon the narrow but well-defined foundation of their behavior to herself.

Concerning people with whom she had no personal acquaintance, she was utterly without opinions; no matter how eminent they might be, they were no more to her than so much sand of the shore. You might talk to her about them by the hour, and she would listen approvingly, or at least quite without contradiction. People spoke of her, therefore, as very appreciative, and, for a woman, broad-minded. What, in truth, can be more broad-minded in one of the sex most given to partisanship than to be able to listen with unprejudiced attention to the admirers of the Rev. Mr. A., the distinguished High-Church clergyman, and then the very next day to the friends of the Rev. Mr. B., equally eminent, but Low; to the devotees of the C. family, who trace their descent directly from old English barons—passing over, of course, that unimportant ancestor who happened to have been the one to cross to the New World, and who, immediately after his arrival, engaged in blacksmithing, and became in time the best blacksmith the struggling little colony possessed—to listen, I say, to the partisans of this ancient race, and then to hearken the next afternoon with equal equanimity to warm praise of the D.'s, who, having made their great fortune so vigorously in the present generation, are engaged in spending it with a vigor equally commendable—what, indeed, could be broader than this? It never occurred to these talkers that A. and B., the C.'s and the D.'s, alike, were all non-existent bodies, nebulæ, to Mrs. Peter Rutherford so long as she was not personally acquainted with them, so long as their names were not upon her visiting list.

But when once this had been discovered, as Evert Winthrop had discovered it, it made everything clear; it was perfectly easy to understand her, easy to see how simple the opinions appeared to the lady herself, since they had to do merely with a series of facts. If Mr. X. had been polite to her, if he had been attentive, deferential, he was without doubt (if at all presentable) a most delightful and praiseworthy person in every way. If Mr. X. had been civil to a certain extent, yet on the whole rather indifferent, he was a little dull, she thought; a good sort of a man perhaps, but not interesting; tiresome. If Mr. X. had simply left her alone, without either civility or incivility, she was apt to have mysterious intuitions about him, intuitions which she mentioned, confidentially of course, to her friends; little things which she had noticed—indications. Of bad temper? Or was it bad habits? It was something bad, at any rate; she was very ingenious in reading the signs. But if Mr. X. had been guilty of actual rudeness (a quality which she judged strictly by the standard of her own hidden but rigorous requirements), Mr. X. was immediately thrust beyond the pale, there was no good in him; in the way of odious traits there was nothing which she did not attribute to him at one time or another, she could even hint at darker guilt. She wondered that people should continue to receive him, and to her dying day she never forgot to give, upon opportunity, her well-aimed thrust—a thrust all the more effective because masked by her reputation for amiability and frank, liberal qualities.

As, however, people generally were sufficiently attentive, this lady's judgments seldom reached the last-mentioned stage, a condition of things which she herself was the first to approve, because (this was the most curious shade of her disposition) she believed fully in her own opinions, and would have disliked greatly to "have anything to do with unprincipled persons." But the world at large had no suspicion of these intricacies; to the world at large Mrs. Rutherford was a handsome, amiable woman, who, possessing a good fortune, a good house in New York, a good old country-place on the Sound, and much hospitality, was considered to be above petty criticisms—criticisms which would do for people less pleasing, less well-endowed.

But though he read his aunt's nature, Winthrop was none the less attached to her; it might be said, perhaps, with more accuracy, that he was fond of her. He had been a very lonely little boy, his father while loving him deeply had been strict with him, and had permitted him few amusements, few companions; to go, therefore, and spend a month with his aunt Katrina, to taste her indulgent kindness and enjoy the liberty she allowed, to have her come and kiss him good-night, and talk to him about his beautiful mother, to have her take him up on her lap and pet him when he was a tired-out, drooping little fellow after immense exertions with his big cousin Lanse, to hear her stories about his uncle Evert (after whom he had been named)—that wonderful Uncle Evert who had gone down to Central America to see the Aztecs—these things had been deeply delightful at the time to the child, whose nature was reserved and concentrated. And if the details were no longer distinct, now that he was a man, the general remembrance at least was always there, the remembrance of happy hours and motherly caresses. He therefore welcomed the idea of his aunt's coming to Gracias. Though what Mrs. Peter Rutherford would be able to find in that sleepy little hamlet in the way of entertainment, he did not pretend to have discovered.

Five days later the party arrived, his aunt, her niece Mrs. Harold, her maid Celestine.

As he greeted Mrs. Rutherford, Winthrop remarked to himself, as he had remarked many times before, that his aunt was a fine-looking woman. Mrs. Rutherford was sixty years of age, tall, erect, with a well-cut profile, and beautiful gray hair, which lay in soft waves, like a silvery cloud, above her fine dark eyes. The state of her health had evidently not interfered with the arrangement of this aureola, neither had it relaxed in any degree the grave perfection of her attire; her bonnet was a model of elegance and simplicity, her boot, as she stepped from the carriage, was seen to be another model of elegance and good sense. Mrs. Rutherford loved elegance. But Mrs. Rutherford loved indolence as well, and indolence never constructed or kept in order an appearance such as hers; the person (of very different aspect) who followed her, laden with baskets, cushions, and shawls, was the real architect of this fine structure, from the soft waves of hair to the well-shaped boot; this person was Celestine, the maid.

Celestine's real name was Minerva Poindexter. Her mistress, not liking the classic appellation, had changed it to Celestine, the Poindexter being dropped entirely. Mrs. Rutherford was accustomed to say that this was her one deliberate affectation—she affected to believe that Celestine was French; the maid, a tall, lean, yellow-skinned woman, reticent and unsmiling, might have been French or Scotch, Portuguese or Brazilian, as far as appearance went, tall, lean women of unmarried aspect being a product scattered in regular, if limited, quantities over the face of the entire civilized globe. As she seldom opened her lips, her nationality could not be determined by an inquiring public from her speech. There were those, however, who maintained that Celestine knew all languages, that there was a dark omniscience about her. In reality she was a Vermont woman, who had begun life as a country dress-maker—a country dress-maker with great natural talent but no opportunities. The opportunities had come later, they came when she was discovered by Mrs. Peter Rutherford. This tall Vermont genius had now filled for many years a position which was very congenial to her, though it would have been considered by most persons a position full of difficulties. For Mrs. Rutherford required in her personal attendant talents which are generally supposed to be conflicting: esteeming her health very delicate, she wished to be minutely watched and guarded by an experienced nurse, a nurse who should take to heart conscientiously the responsibilities of her charge; yet at the same time she cherished that deep interest in the constantly changing arcana of feminine attire for which it is supposed that only a skilful but probably immoral Parisian can suffice.

But the keen New England eyes of Minerva Poindexter had an instant appreciation of such characteristics of arriving fashions as could be gracefully adopted by her handsome mistress, whose best points she thoroughly understood, and even in a certain way admired, though as regarded herself, and indeed all the rest of womankind, she approved rigidly of that strict neutrality of surface, that ignoring of all merely corporeal points, which is so striking a characteristic of the monastic heavenly paintings of Fra Angelico. At the same moment, however, that her New England eyes were exercising their natural talent, her New England conscience, equally keen, made her a nurse of unmatched qualities, albeit she was perhaps something of a martinet. But with regard to her health Mrs. Rutherford rather liked to be domineered over. She liked to be followed about by shawls (her shawls were always beautiful, never having that niggardly, poverty-stricken aspect which such feminine draperies, when reserved for use in the house, are apt to assume); she liked to be vigilantly watched with regard to draughts; she liked to have her pulse felt, to have cushions, handsomely covered in rich colors, placed behind her well-dressed back. Especially did she like to be presented, at fixed hours, with little tea-spoonfuls of homœopathic medicine, which did not taste badly, but which, nevertheless, it always required some urging to induce her to take; the urging—in fact, the whole system, regularly persevered in—could give variety to the dullest day.

After greeting his aunt, Winthrop turned to speak to Celestine. By way of reply Celestine gave a short nod, and looked in another direction. In reality she was delighted with his notice, but this was her way of showing it. The two boys, Evert Winthrop and Lansing Harold, Mrs. Rutherford's nephews, had been her pets from childhood; but even in the old days her manner towards them had always been so curt and taciturn that they used to consider it a great triumph when they had succeeded in drawing out Minerva's laugh—for they always called her Minerva behind Mrs. Rutherford's back. It may be that this had had something to do with her liking for them; for, in her heart, Miss Poindexter considered her baptismal name both a euphonious and dignified one, and much to be preferred to the French frivolity of the title to which she was obliged to answer.

"But where is Margaret?" said Mrs. Rutherford, turning.

A third person, who had been looking at the new scene about her—the orange-trees, the palmettoes, the blue water of the Espiritu beyond the low sea-wall, and the fringe of tropical forest on Patricio opposite—now stepped from the carriage.

"I was beginning to think that there had been some change of plan, Mrs. Harold, and that you had not come," said Winthrop, going back to the carriage to assist her.

Margaret Harold smiled. Her smile was a very pleasant one; she and Winthrop greeted each other with what seemed like a long-established, though quiet and well-governed, coldness.

CHAPTER IV

Later in the evening Mrs. Rutherford was sitting with her nephew on the piazza of her new residence, the little house he had engaged for her use during her stay in Gracias; they were looking at the moonlight on the lagoon.

The little residence had but one story, and that story was a second one. It had been built above an old passageway of stone, which had led from the Franciscan monastery down to the monks' landing-place on the shore; the passageway made a turn at a right angle not far from the water, and this angle had been taken possession of by the later architect, who had rested his square superstructure solidly on the old walls at the south and west, and had then built a light open arch below to support the two remaining sides, thus securing an elevated position, and a beautiful view of the sea beyond Patricio, at comparatively small expense for his high foundation. An outside stairway of stone, which made a picturesque turn on the way, led up to the door of this abode, and, taken altogether, it was an odd and pleasant little eyrie on a pleasant shore.

Evert Winthrop, however, when he secured it for his aunt, had not been thinking so much of its pleasantness as its freedom from damp, Mrs. Rutherford having long been of the opinion that most of the evils of life, mental, moral, and physical, and even in a great measure the disasters of nations, could be directly traced to the condition of cellars.

"You will observe, Aunt Katrina, that there *is* no cellar," he remarked as she took possession.

The eyrie had but one fault, and that was a fault only if people were disposed to be sentimental: the old walls beneath, built by the monks long before, had the air of performing their present duty with extreme unwillingness. Coming up from the water, they passed under the modern house reluctantly, supporting it under protest, as it were; their cold disapprovals seemed to come through the floors.

Mrs. Rutherford declared that it made her feel "sacrilegious." But the sentiments of Minerva Poindexter were of an entirely different nature. "I *admire* to have 'em there," said this rigid Protestant; "I admire to know they're under my feet, so that I can tromple 'em down!" For though she had been over the entire civilized world, though she could adapt Paris fashions, and was called Celestine, Miss Poindexter had never in her heart abated one inch of her original Puritan principles, and as she now came and went over the old monks' passage, her very soles rejoiced in the opportunity to express their utter detestation of the monastic system, she ground them deeply into the mattings on purpose.

The little plaza of Gracias-á-Dios was near the eyrie. On one side of it stood the rambling old inn, the Seminole House, encircled by a line of stout ancient posts for the use of its patrons, who for the most part had come mounted; for in that country there had been very little driving, all rode. There had been horses of many grades, mules, and the little ponies not much larger than sheep that browsed in the marshes. To walk was beneath the dignity of any one; the poorest negro had his sorry animal of some sort to save him from that. As to walking for pleasure, that crazed idea had not yet reached Gracias.

The Seminole had agreed to send lunches and dinners of its best cooking to the eyrie, and its best cooking, though confined to the local ingredients, was something not to be despised; it owed its being to the culinary intuitions of Aunt Dinah-Jim, a native artist, who evolved in some mysterious way, from her disorderly kitchen, the dishes for which she was celebrated at uncertain hours. But if the hours were uncertain, the dishes were not.

The old black woman sent the results of her labors to the house on the wall, in the charge of Telano Johnson, a tall, slender colored boy of eighteen summers, whose spotless white linen jacket and intense gravity of demeanor gained him the favor of even Celestine. "He has manners like the Governor of Vermont and all his staff, I do declare!" was the secret thought of this good woman. Telano, who had never seen a white servant before, treated Celestine with profound respect; his inward belief was that she was a witch, which would account for her inexplicable leanness, and the conciseness of her remarks, the latter most singular of all to Telano, who had the usual flowery fluency of his race. He carried a Voudoo charm against her, and brandished it when she was not looking; in addition, he often arranged, swiftly and furtively, in a corner of the dining-room when he came to lay the cloth, a little pile of three minute twigs crossed in a particular fashion, and sprinkled with unknown substances which he also took from his pocket, the whole a protection from her supposed incantations against him. Minerva meanwhile had no suspicion of these pagan rites, she continued to be pleased with Telano, and had a plan for teaching him to read. The boy sang with the charming sweetness so common among the Africans, and once, after listening, duster in hand, in spite of herself, for a quarter of an hour, as he carolled over the dishes he was washing in his pantry, she went so far as to appear at his pantry door to ask, briefly, if he knew a favorite song of her youth, "The Draggle-tail Gypsies, Oh!" Telano did not know it. And she said she would sing it to him some day. Whereupon Telano, as soon as possible afterwards, took flight in his long white apron back to the Seminole House for a fresh charm against her; he was convinced that the singing of this strange bony woman would finish him, would be the worst spell of all.

"That's a very good black boy we've got to wait at table and do the chores," Celestine remarked approvingly to her mistress, as she brought a shawl of different thickness, suitable to the dew in the air, to put round her. "He's a deal sight more serious-minded than the rantum-scootum boys one has to put up with in a wanderin' life like this. He's spry, yet he's steady too; and he sings like a bobolink, though his songs are most *dreadful* as to words. There's one, 'O Lord, these *bones* of mine! O Lord, these BONES of mine! O Lord, these BONES of mine!'"—Celestine sang this quotation in a high chanting voice, with her eyes closed and her face screwed up tightly, which was her usual expression when musical. "And I suppose it refers to rheumatism," she added, descending to her ordinary tones; "but it's very irreverent. He doesn't know 'The Draggle-tail Gypsies,' nor yet 'Barbara Allen,' nor yet 'I'll Make You a Present of a Coach and Six;' but I'm going to sing 'em to him some day. I feel that I must do my duty by him, poor neglected African. Have you any objections to my teaching him to read?"

"No, provided he doesn't read my books," Mrs. Rutherford answered.

"He will read in McGuffey's Third Reader," responded Celestine.

Winthrop had retained his bachelor quarters at the Seminole; the house over the old monks' passage was not large, and Mrs. Rutherford was fond of space. She liked open doors in all directions, she liked to have several sitting-rooms; she liked to leave her book in one, her fan in another, her scent-bottle or handkerchief in a third, and have nobody disturb them.

"I don't detect in you, Aunt Katrina, any signs of the ruin you mentioned," her nephew said, as they sat together, that first evening, on the piazza.

The light from the room within shone across Mrs. Rutherford's face and the soft waves of her silvery hair as, with a pink shawl thrown round her, she sat leaning back in an easy-chair. "Celestine repairs the breaches so cleverly that no doubt I continue to present a fair appearance to the world," she answered, drawing the shawl more closely round her shoulders, and then letting her hands drop on its pink fringes.

Mrs. Rutherford's hands always took statuesque positions; but probably that was because they were statuesque hands. They were perfect in shape according to sculptors' rules, full and white, one ringless, its beautiful outlines unmarred, the other heavily weighted with gems, which flashed as she moved.

"But pray don't imagine, my dear boy," she continued, "that I enjoy my ill health, as so many women do. On the contrary, I dislike it—dislike it so much that I have even arranged with Margaret that she is never to ask me (save when we are alone) any of those invalid questions—whether I have slept well, how my cough is, if there isn't a draught, and that sort of thing. I used to think that talking with a mother when her children were in the room, was the most trying thing, conversationally; she listens to you with one ear, but the other is listening to Johnnie; right in the midst of something very pathetic you are telling her, she will give a sudden, perfectly irrelevant smile, over her baby's last crow, and your best story is hopelessly spoiled because she loses the point (though she pretends she hasn't) while she rearranges the sashes of Ethel and Tottie (they are always rearranging them), who are going out to walk with their nurse. Still, bad as this is, I have come to the conclusion, lately, that invalid-questions are worse, because they are not confined to the hours when children are about; and so I have given Margaret my directions."

"Which are to be mine too, I suppose," said Winthrop, smiling. "Mrs. Harold looks well."

"Yes, Margaret always looks the same, I think. She has not that highly colored, robust appearance that some women have, but her health is absolutely perfect; it's really quite wonderful," said the aunt. She paused; then sighed. "I almost think that it has been like an armor to her," she went on. "I don't believe she feels little things as some of us do, some of us who are perhaps more sensitive; she is never nervous, never disturbed, her temper is so even that it is almost exasperating. She thinks as well of everything, for instance, in an east wind as in any other."

"A great gift in some climates; but here it will have less play. Gracias air isn't easterly, it bends towards one—yields, melts."

"I wish Margaret could yield—melt," said Mrs. Rutherford, with another sigh. "You see my mind still broods upon it, Evert; seeing you, my other boy, brings it all back."

"I don't know, but I suppose you do, whether Lanse has made any overtures lately?" said Winthrop, after a moment of silence.

"I know nothing, she is the most reticent woman living. But it would not be like him; with his pride—you know his pride—he would never speak first, never urge."

"A man might speak first to his wife, I should suppose," replied Winthrop, a stern expression showing itself for a moment in his gray eyes. "It need not be urging, it might be a command."

"Lanse would never do that. It would show that he cared, and—well, you know his disposition."

"I used to think that I knew it; but of late years I have doubted my knowledge."

"Don't doubt it, Evert," said Mrs. Rutherford, earnestly, laying her hand on his arm, "he is just what you think, just what he always was. We understand him, you and I—we comprehend him; unfortunately, Margaret cannot."

"I have never pretended to judge Mrs. Harold," answered Evert Winthrop (but he looked as if he might have, if not a judgment, at least an opinion); "I know her too slightly."

"Yet you have seen a good deal of her since you came back from Europe," remarked his aunt.

"I have seen enough to know that she is, at least, a very good niece to you," he answered.

His feeling against Margaret Harold was strong, it was founded upon some of the deepest beliefs of his nature. But these beliefs were his own, in their very essence they were personal, private, he could not have discussed them with any one; especially would he never have discussed them with his aunt, because he thought that she did not, even as it was, do full justice to Margaret Harold, and he had no wish to increase the feeling. On the contrary, he thought that full justice should always be scrupulously awarded to that lady, and the more scrupulously if one did not happen to like her; he himself, for instance, did not like her; on that very account he was careful always, so he would have said, to keep in clear view a just estimate of the many good qualities which she undoubtedly possessed.

In response to his suggestion that Margaret had proved herself a good niece, Mrs. Rutherford answered, in a voice somewhat softened, "Yes, she is very devoted to me." Her conscience seemed to stir a little, for she went on: "Regarding my health, my personal comfort, she is certainly most thoughtful."

Here a door within opened, and she stopped. They heard a light step cross the floor; then a figure appeared in the long window that opened upon the piazza.

"Ah, Margaret, is that you? You have finished the letter?" said Mrs. Rutherford. "She has been writing to my cousins, to tell them of my safe arrival; I did not feel equal to writing myself," she added, to Winthrop.

He had risen to bring forward a chair. But Margaret passed him, and went to the piazza railing, which came solidly up as high as one's elbows, with a broad parapet to lean upon; here she stood looking at the water.

"I believe now all I have heard of this Florida moonlight," she said, her eyes on the broad silvery expanse of the ocean, visible beyond the low line of Patricio. She had turned her head a little as she spoke, and perceiving that a ray from the room within was shining across Mrs. Rutherford's face, she stepped back through the window, changed the position of the lamp, and returned.

"Thank you, my dear; I did not know how much it was teasing me until you moved it," said Mrs. Rutherford. Perhaps she still felt some twinges of conscience, for she added, "Why not go out with Evert and take a look at the little old town by moonlight? It's not yet nine."

"I shall be most happy if Mrs. Harold is not too tired," said Winthrop. He did not rise; but probably he was waiting for her consent.

"Margaret is never tired," said Mrs. Rutherford, making the statement with a wave of her hand—a wave which drew a flash from all her gems.

"Yes, that is one of the things quite understood and settled—that I am never tired," observed Mrs. Harold; she still stood by the parapet, there was no indication in her tone whether she agreed with the understanding or not.

"Do go," urged Mrs. Rutherford. "You have been shut up with me for six days on those slow-moving southern trains, and you know how you enjoy a walk."

"Not to-night, Aunt Katrina."

"You say that because you think I shall not like to be left alone in this strange house on the first evening. But I shall not mind it in the least; Celestine is here, and that black boy."

At this moment the door of the room within was opened by Celestine, and there followed a quick, and what seemed to be, from the sound, a voluminous entrance, and a hurried step across the floor. "My dearest darling Katrina!" said Mrs. Carew, pausing at the long window (which she filled), her arms extended in anticipative welcome, but her eyes not yet certain which of the three figures on the piazza should properly fill them.

Mrs. Rutherford rose, with cordial if less excited welcome. "Is that you, Betty?" she said. And then she was folded in Betty's capacious embrace.

Hand in hand the two ladies went within, to look at each other, they said. Mrs. Harold and Winthrop followed.

"Now, Margaret," said Mrs. Rutherford, after the first greetings were over, "you surely need feel no further scruples about leaving me; Betty and I have enough to say to each other for a half-hour, I am sure."

"For a half-hour, Katrina? For days! weeks! months!" cried Betty, with enthusiasm. And she began upon what was evidently to be a long series of retrospective questions and replies.

"Why not go for a while, if, as you say, you are not tired?" said Winthrop, in pursuance of his system of showing always a careful civility to Margaret Harold.

"It was not I that said it," replied Margaret, smiling a little. "I will go for a quarter of an hour," she added, as though compliance were, on the whole, less trouble than a second refusal. She took a white shawl which was lying on a chair, made a veil for her head of one corner, while the rest of its fleecy length fell over her dark dress. They left the room and went down the outside stairway to the street below.

It was called a street, and had even a name—Pacheco; but in reality it was the open shore.

"It has such an odd effect to me, all this low-lying country on a level with the water," said Margaret; "the whole land is like a sea-beach, a sea-beach with trees growing on it."

"Do you like it? or do you think it ugly?"

"I think it very beautiful—in its own way."

"I will take you to the Benito," said Winthrop.

At the end of Pacheco lane they passed under an old stone archway into the plaza. This little pleasure-ground was shaded by orange-trees, which formed a thick grove; paths ran irregularly through the grove, and there were stone benches here and there. On the north side the gray-white façade of Our Lady of the Angels rose above the trees, conferring architectural dignity upon the town. The main building was low and rather dilapidated, but the front was felt to be impressive, it elevated itself with candid majesty three stories above the roof, quite undisturbed by a thinness of aspect in profile; the first story bore upon its face an old clock and sun-dial, the second, which was narrower, was punctured by three arches, each containing a bell, and the third under the apex had also an aperture, through which the small bell hanging there should have swung itself picturesquely to and fro, far out against the blue; as a matter of fact, however, none of the bells were rung, they were struck ignominiously from behind by a man with a hammer. The point of the apex was surmounted by a broken globe and a cross.

The uncertain Gothic of St. Philip and St. James' came next, much lower as to height, much younger as to age. But the glory of St. Philip and St. James' lay not in its height, it lay in the flying buttresses of which it had no less than eight, four on each side. These flying buttresses were of course a great feature, they showed how much imagination the architect had had;

for they did not support the roof, nor anything else, they appeared indeed to have some difficulty in supporting themselves, so that it was always more or less of a question as to whether, in a northerly gale, they might not take to flying themselves—in fragments and a wrong direction. So far, however, this had not happened; and Mrs. Penelope Moore, the rector's wife, had trained vines over them so thickly that they looked like arbors; Mrs. Penelope, however, had a better name for them than that; she called them "the cloisters."

The west side of the plaza was occupied by the long front of the old Government House, the residence of crown officials during Spanish days. Over its low height, palmetto-trees lifted their ostrich-plumed foliage high in the air from the large garden behind. At one end there rose above the roof a lookout tower, which commanded a view of the harbor; here had floated for two hundred years the flag of Spain, here also had hung the bell upon which the watchman had struck the signal when the beacon on Patricio opposite had flamed forth from its iron cage the tidings that a ship was in sight, a ship from Spain. But the bell had long been gone, and nothing floated from the old staff now save twice a year, when on the Fourth of July and Washington's Birthday the postmaster, who used the old Government House for his post-office, unfurled there, with official patriotism, the Stars and Stripes of the United States.

As Winthrop and his companion on their way across the plaza came out from the shade of the orange-trees, some one spoke Winthrop's name. It was Dr. Kirby, who was entering the grove by another path which intersected theirs. Garda Thorne was with him, and a little behind them appeared the dark countenance of Torres. The Doctor stopped and extended his hand, it was not the Doctor's custom to pass his friends without speech. Winthrop therefore stopped too; and then, as the Doctor seemed to expect it, he presented him to Mrs. Harold. The Doctor paid his respects in his best manner, and introduced his "young friend, Miss Thorne, of Gracias-á-Dios." After that, "Mr. Adolfo Torres, of Cuba." He had been with Miss Thorne (who was spending a day or two with his mother, Mistress Kirby) to pay an evening visit to Mistress Carew. But they had not found Mistress Carew at home.

"She is with my aunt," said Winthrop; "the two ladies having a past of forty years to talk over, Mrs. Harold and I came out for a stroll."

"Ah—a first impression, I conjecture," said the Doctor, standing, hat in hand, before the northern lady. "You find our little town, I fear, rather old-fashioned."

"I like old-fashioned things," replied Margaret. "I have been looking at something more old-fashioned still—the sea."

"If you like to look at the sea, you are going to the Benito, I am sure of it," said Garda in her soft tones, tones that contrasted with those of Mrs. Harold, which were equally low, but much more reserved, and also more clear. She came forward and stood beside the northern lady, scanning her face in the moonlight with her beautiful eyes. "Please let me go with you," she said, urgently; "I want to go so much. It is so long since I have been on the Benito by moonlight!"

Mrs. Harold smiled at her earnestness; and Garda, speaking to the Doctor now, though without turning her head, said, "You will come, won't you, Doctor? Do; oh, please do."

The Doctor hesitated, then sacrificed himself; in the cause of the Thorne family pedestrianism seemed to be required of him. But Benito was long; he made up his mind that he would not go one inch beyond a certain old boat which he remembered, drawn up on the sand at not more than a quarter of the distance to the end of the point.

"We will go ever so far," said Garda, taking Mrs. Harold's arm; "we will go way out to the end!"

"Certainly," replied the Doctor.

They all walked on together through the St. Luz quarter, Torres following. Torres had no idea where they were going, nor why the direction of their walk had been changed. But this was a frequent condition of things with him in Gracias, and, besides, it did not trouble him; a Torres was not curious, he wished to go, therefore he went.

The little streets here were not more than eight feet wide. Garda kept her place beside Mrs. Harold, and Dr. Kirby followed with Winthrop; Torres, joining no one, walked by himself, five or six yards behind the others.

"That young man seems fond of acting as rear-guard," said Winthrop, glancing back as they turned a corner, and noting the solitary figure advancing stiffly in the moonlight.

"Garda is the only one of our present party whose conversation he can really enjoy," answered the Doctor. "When he cannot converse with her, he prefers, I think, to be by himself. At least I have gathered that impression from his manner."

"His manner is his strong point," said Winthrop. "It's very picturesque."

"It strikes you as picturesque?" said the Doctor, looking up at him with his quick bird-glance.

"It's a little feudal, isn't it?" replied Winthrop. "But I am afraid you will think my comparisons fantastic; I have treated you to a good many of them."

"Sir," responded the Doctor, courteously waiving the question of accuracy, "what I notice is your command of language. It would never have occurred to me to say feudal, I admire your affluence."

"And I am ashamed of it," said Winthrop, "I am ashamed of myself for staring about and applying adjectives in this way to the people and scenery here, as though it were a foreign country; it ought to be as much a part of me, and I of it, as though it were Massachusetts Bay."

But this view of the subject was beyond the Doctor's comprehension; to him the difference between New England and the South was as wide, whether considered geographically, psychologically, or historically, as that between the South and Japan. Nothing could have made him, Reginald Kirby, feel a sympathetic ownership in Massachusetts Bay, and he saw no reason why this Mr. Evert Winthrop should be claiming proprietorship in a distinctively Spanish and Carolinian shore. The singular views of these northerners were apparently endless! But in this case, at least, the views could do no harm, Florida would remain Florida, in spite of northern hallucinations.

Beyond the low stone houses of St. Luz, they crossed a common, and gained the open shore. The coast here bent sharply to the east, and went out to sea in a long point, the beach which fringed this point was called the Benito; the party of strollers walked down the Benito's firm white floor, with the sea breaking in little lapping wavelets at its edge, and the moonlight flooding land and water with its wonderful radiance. The beach was forty feet broad; Winthrop and the Doctor joined the ladies. But Garda kept her place beside Mrs. Harold, and talked only to her, she seemed to be fascinated by all the northern lady said. Winthrop could not fail to see that her interest in this new companion was of the same sort as that which she had originally shown regarding himself—curiosity, apparently; and that Margaret Harold excited the feeling in a stronger degree than he had done. Meanwhile it amused him to see how completely this Florida girl did as she pleased. It pleased her now to forget him entirely; but he was not the only one, she forgot the Doctor also, and the patient lonely Torres behind.

It may as well be mentioned here that the Doctor went as far as the old boat he remembered. And that then he went farther; he went to the end of the point, a mile away.

"Surely you have not been gone half an hour?" said Mrs. Carew, as Margaret and Winthrop re-entered the eyrie's little drawing-room.

"Two hours, nearly," answered Winthrop, looking at his watch.

"Betty is *so* demonstrative," said Mrs. Rutherford to her niece, in a plaintive tone, when they were left alone. "I verily believe she has kissed me during this one call at least twenty times. She always had the best heart in the world—poor Betty!"

"She is very stout, isn't she?" she resumed, after a pause. "Her figure is all gone, she's like a meal-sack with a string tied round it."

Her eyes wandered to the mirror, which gave back the reflection of her own shapely person in its rich, perfectly fitting attire. "And how she was dressed!—did you notice! That old-fashioned glacé silk that shines, made with gathers, and a hem—I don't know *when* I've seen a hem before."

She spoke with much seriousness, her eyes were slowly measuring the gulf that separated this friend of her youth from herself. After a while these eyes moved up to the reflection in the mirror of her own silver-gray locks, arranged in their graceful waves above her white forehead.

"She has the old-time ideas, poor Betty!" she murmured. Then, gravely and impartially, as one who chronicles a past historical epoch: "She still colors her hair!"

CHAPTER V

Mrs. Carew's candles, in the old candelabra hung with glass prisms, were all lighted; in addition, her astral lamp was shining on a table in the back drawing-room, and near this lamp she was standing.

The two rooms were large, square, separated by folding-doors which were held open by giant sea-shells, placed upon the carpet as weights. Wide doors led also from each room into the broad hall, which was lighted by a hanging lamp in a pictured porcelain shade. From the back drawing-room a second door led into the dining-room behind, which was also entered by a broader door at the end of the hall.

"Now, Pompey," said the mistress of the house, "are you quite sure you understand? Tell me what it is you are to do."

Pompey, a small, yellow-skinned negro, whose large, orb-like, heavily wrinkled eyelids (underneath which but a narrow line of eye appeared) were the most prominent features of his flat face, replied, solemnly: "W'en eberyting's ready, I fuss slips inter de hall, steppen softly, an' shets *dish* yer do', de back parlo' do' inter de hall. I nex' announces suppah at de *fron'* parlo' do'. Den, wiles de compahny's parsing inter de hall, I hurries roun' tru *dish* yer do'—de do' from de *dinin'*-room—gits out dat ar lamp mighty quick, an' has it onter de middle ob de suppah table befo' de *fuss* head ob de compahny appeahs at de hall do'. An' I follers de same course *ob*wersed w'en de compahny retiahs."

"Very well," said Mrs. Carew. "Now mind you do it."

Hearing the gate-latch fall, she hurried into the front room to be ready to receive her dearest Katrina. But it was only Mrs. Thorne, who, with Garda, entered without knocking; the evening was warm and the hall door stood open, the light from within shining across the broad piazza, and down the rose-bordered path to the gate. Mrs. Carew herself accompanied her friends up-stairs, and stood talking while they laid aside their light wraps; these guests were to spend the night, having come up from East Angels in their boat, old Pablo rowing.

"We shall be ten," said their hostess; "a good number, don't you think so? I shall have whist, of course, later—whist and conversation." Here Mrs. Thorne, having taken from her basket a small package, brought forth from their careful wrappings two pairs of kid gloves, one white, the other lavender; they did not appear to be new.

"You are not going to wear *gloves*?" said Mrs. Carew, interrupting herself in her surprise. "It's only a small tea-party."

"No entertainment given by you, dear friend, can be called small; it is not a question of numbers, but of scope, and your scope is always of the largest," replied the mistress of East Angels, beginning to cover her small fingers with the insignia of ceremony. "Our only thought was to do you honor, we are very glad to have this little opportunity."

Garda put her gloves in her pocket. She had the white ones.

"My daughter," said Mrs. Thorne, admonishingly.

"But, mamma, I don't want to wear them; I don't like them."

"We are obliged, in *this* world at least, my child, to wear many things, gloves included, which we do not especially like," said Mrs. Thorne, with the air of expecting to wear only the choicest garb (gloves included) in the next. "Do not interfere with my plan for doing honor to our dear friend."

Garda, with a grimace, took out the gloves and put them on, while the dear friend looked on with much interest. There was not a trace of jealousy in her glance, a Gwinnet, in truth, could not have cause for jealousy; she was really admiring the little New England woman's inspiration. "Gloves have never been worn here at small tea-parties," she said to Evert Winthrop afterwards. "But she thought that your aunt and Mrs. Harold, coming as they do from New York, would have them, and so she unearthed those two old pairs. There is really *no* limit to that woman's energy; I verily believe that if an East Indian prince should be wrecked off Gracias, she would find an elephant to receive him with! Her courage is inexhaustible, and if she had any money *at all*, she'd move the world—like Archimedes, wasn't it, who only wanted a point for his lever? To be sure, that is the great thing—the point, and Mr. Carew used always to say that I forgot mine. I told him that he could pick them up and put them in himself if he missed them so much, but he said that anybody could put them in, but that it took a real genius to leave them out, as I did." Here the good lady laughed heartily. "It was only his joking way, of course," she added; "you see, Mr. Carew was a lawyer."

The gloves having been duly put on, the three ladies descended to the front drawing-room, where Mrs. Thorne seated herself in an attitude which might have been described as suggesting a cultured expectation. Her little figure remained erect, not touching the back of her chair; her hands, endued with the gloves, were folded lightly; her countenance expressed the highest intelligence, chastened by the memory of the many trials through which she had passed; this, at least, was what she intended it to express.

The fall of the gate-latch was now heard again.

"Had we not better be standing?" suggested their hostess, in a hurried whisper. It was so many years since she had opened her old house for what she called "evening company" that she felt fluttered and uncertain—embarrassed, as imaginative people always are, by the number of things that occurred to her, things she might do.

"I think not, dear friend," answered Mrs. Thorne, with decision. "We are too few, it would have, I fear, the air of a tableau."

Mrs. Thorne was above flutter, a whisper she scorned. As the approaching footsteps drew nearer, the listening silence in the drawing-room, whose long windows stood open, became in her opinion far too apparent; she coughed, turned to her daughter, and, in her clear little voice, remarked, "I have always esteemed the pearl the most beautiful of precious stones. The diamond has more brilliancy, the ruby a richer glow, but the pearl—" Here the steps, entering the hall without ceremony, showed that the new-comers were not the expected northern guests, since they, of course, would have gone through the form of raising the knocker upon the open door. It was Dr. Kirby who entered, followed by the Rev. Mr. Moore.

The Doctor offered his salutations in his usual ceremonious fashion. He made a compact little bow, and a formal compliment, over the hand of each of the ladies in turn; he was dressed in black, but still looked like a canary-bird—a canary-bird in mourning.

After some minutes, again came the sound of the gate-latch. Mrs. Carew, who was talking, stopped short, even Dr. Kirby's attention flew to the gravel-path; there was danger of another pause. But bravely Mrs. Thorne came to the rescue a second time. "The emerald," she observed, to the unlistening Kirby, "is clear, and even one may say translucent. And how profound it is!—how deep the mysterious green which—" The new-comers had crossed the piazza, lifted the knocker, and had then, without waiting for Pompey's appearance, entered the hall; this showed acquaintance, though not the familiar intimacy of the first guests; it proved to be Manuel Ruiz, and with him Adolfo Torres.

But now came the sound of wheels, Mrs. Carew listened eagerly. "A carriage!" she murmured, turning to the Doctor, as the sound stopped before her house. He nodded and twirled his thumbs. This time there could be no doubt, the strangers were coming up the path.

But silence had again attacked the little group, and Mrs. Thorne, feeling that graceful conversation was now more than ever imperative, if the strangers were to be impressed with the ease and distinction of Gracias society, was again about to speak, when Garda, with a merry gleam in her eyes, exclaimed, with sudden enthusiasm, to Manuel, "Sapphires, oh, beautiful sapphires, how I wish I had a tiara of them!" Manuel, though somewhat surprised by the unexpectedness of the topic, gallantly answered that she was worthy to have her floors paved with them if she should wish it; nay, that he himself would become a sapphire for such a purpose. And then by the formal knock and the delay, all felt that the strangers were at last within their gates. A few minutes later they entered the drawing-room, Mrs. Rutherford, Margaret Harold, and Evert Winthrop. Mrs. Thorne's eyes turned towards her daughter with one quick single beam of triumph: the ladies wore gloves.

Mrs. Carew seated herself beside her dearest Katrina, and Dr. Kirby bore them company; the Rev. Mr. Moore and Mrs. Thorne gave their attention to Mrs. Harold. Evert Winthrop took a seat which had the air of being near enough to the first group for conversational purposes, but which was in reality a little apart. Garda and Manuel were on the opposite side of the room, with Torres standing near them; Manuel was talking, but Garda gave him a divided attention, she was looking at Evert Winthrop. At length she rose and went across to his chair.

"Did you have a pleasant ride to-day?" she asked, standing with the simplicity of a child before him, her hands clasped and hanging.

"Yes; I went down the King's Road," he answered, rising. "I like a 'King's Road;' we have no King's Roads at the North."

"Why not?" said Garda.

"We abolished kings more completely than you did perhaps; in 1776."

"What happened then? Something at the North?"

"Oh, a small matter, quite unimportant; it didn't include Gracias-á-Dios."

"It might have, I don't pretend to know the history of Gracias-á-Dios," replied Garda, rather loftily; "all I know is the history of my own family. In 1776 my grandmother Beatriz was five years old, and even then, they say, water could run under her insteps."

"Why did they keep the poor child in such wet places? It must have been very unhealthy. Won't you have this chair?"

"I'm so tired of chairs."

"Have you been asleep in the hammock all the afternoon?"

"Yes," she confessed. "But I hope I don't show it so plainly? It isn't polite to look sleepy at a party."

"Let us walk up and down for a while: that will waken you," he said, offering his arm.

"Do people walk up and down when the party is such a small one? Is that a northern custom?"

"I am a northerner certainly; and it's my custom," he answered. As they entered the back drawing-room, "I did not mean that you looked sleepy," he added, "but the contrary; the walking will be of use as a sedative."

"You need not be afraid, I shall not do anything out of the way; don't you see that I have on white gloves?" And she extended her hands for his inspection. "They are not mine, as you may well imagine, I never had a pair of white gloves in my life; they are mamma's, and ever so many years old, she wore them when she was married."

"I wish I could have seen her; she must have looked like a little blossom of the May."

"Yes," answered Garda, "I am sure that mamma must have been very pretty indeed when she was young." She spoke with seriousness, Winthrop imagined that she had given the subject much consideration. They reached the end of the second room, and turned to come back.

"I should never have asked the señorita to do that," said Torres in Spanish to Manuel.

"Very likely not; but do at least sit down, people don't stand up against the wall all the time at tea-parties, like wooden soldiers."

"It is my method," replied Torres; "I have always my own method about everything."

"Change it, then; at least for this evening," suggested his New World companion.

"If they do not, as you say, stand, it appears that they walk. And continue to walk," remarked the Cuban, after a moment, his eyes still upon Garda and Winthrop.

"Of course they do, if they wish to," replied Manuel, who was at heart as much surprised by Winthrop's proceeding as Torres had been; but, if surprised, quick also to seize and appropriate to his own use any advantages which new codes of manners might offer. "But you cannot walk all alone—don't try that. Take something and look at it, if you won't sit down; a book; daguerreotypes. There's a Chinese puzzle; take that."

Thus adjured, Torres stepped forward, took the puzzle from a table, and returned with it to his place. Here he stood still again, holding his prize solemnly.

"Play with it," said Manuel; "I never saw such a fellow! Move the rings up and down."

"I took it because you wished me to do so," replied the Cuban, with dignity. "But to play with it is impossible; why should I play with an ivory toy?—I am not a child."

Here the gray head of Pompey appeared at the front drawing-room door. The old servant waited respectfully until he had caught his mistress's eye; he then made a low bow, with his hands folded before him—"Miss C'roo am serbed."

Dr. Kirby offered his arm to Mrs. Rutherford, Mr. Moore offered his to Mrs. Harold; Mrs. Carew waved Winthrop towards Mrs. Thorne, while she herself took the arm of Manuel Ruiz. Garda was left to Torres, who, thus unexpectedly made happy, accompanied her into the hall, still bearing his puzzle.

"What in the world are you carrying?" she asked, laughing.

"It is a toy of ivory which Manuel insisted that I should take. With your permission I will now lay it aside." And he deposited it carefully upon a chair.

The little procession now came to a pause, Mrs. Carew having asked her dearest Katrina to look at a portrait upon the wall. "It was taken the year after my marriage," she explained, watching for the increased glow through the dining-room door which should proclaim to her anxious eyes the arrival of the astral lamp in its destined place.

"I do not need a portrait, Betty; I have one in my memory," replied Mrs. Rutherford, graciously. She could not see the picture without her glasses, but she gazed at the gilt frame with an interested air, looking at it with her head now a little on one side, now on the other, as if to get the right light.

"I have never considered this portrait a faithful representation of our friend," observed Dr. Kirby. He could not see even the frame, but he surveyed the wall with disapprobation. "It quite fails to give her vivacity, which is so characteristic a feature. But what painter's brush, what limner's art, can fix upon canvas that delicate, that, I may say, intangible charm which belongs to the fairer portion of our humanity? It is, and must always be, a hopeless task."

Mrs. Rutherford admired the Doctor's way of expressing himself. It was the fine old style. She herself had kept pace with the new, as she kept pace with everything; but the old style was more stately, and she had always preferred it; for one thing, she understood it better. Mrs. Rutherford liked conversations to have a beginning, a middle, and an end; the Doctor's conversations, and even his sentences, had all three.

The increased glow now showed itself through the distant door, and Mrs. Carew moved on; the little company passed down the hall and into the dining-room, where stood a bountifully decked table with the astral lamp radiant in the centre, and Pompey, so dignified under his responsibilities that he actually looked tall, in attendance. It was an old-fashioned repast; they were all seated round the table as though it had been a dinner. But the hostess did not place them in the order in which they had proceeded through the hall; having paid what she considered due acknowledgment to etiquette, she now arranged them for the long repast in the way which she thought would please them best, which is quite another matter. Winthrop found himself between Garda and Mrs. Harold; Mrs. Harold had upon her left hand Manuel Ruiz, and Garda upon her right the happy Torres, who, however, in spite of happiness, looked more rigid and solemn than ever as the soft horizontal light of the lamp, shining above the central plum-cake, illumined his dark face.

"You remember, of course, that he does not speak English," Garda said to Winthrop. She was alluding to her right-hand neighbor.

"Does that mean that you intend to speak Spanish to him?" said Winthrop. "He has quite enough as it is in being next you; you should not give too much."

"I like generosity."

"That wouldn't be generosity, but squandering; you shouldn't give at random."

"Poor Adolfo isn't at random! But I believe you are trying to instruct me?" she said, surveying him frankly.

"Would it displease you if I were?"

Garda paused, as if considering the point. "You might try it," she answered. "It would at least be new, and I generally like new things. That is the reason, you know, that I liked you; you were new."

Manuel, meanwhile, was bringing forward his finest powers for the entertainment of Mrs. Harold, by whose side he had been placed; and if he talked in a somewhat more decorated strain than was prevalent in the colder circles from which she had come, it was carried off easily by his youth, his handsome face, his animated manner. Winthrop overheard occasionally his fervid little speeches, he did not admire them. But it was only occasionally, for he himself was fully occupied, Garda talked to him, or listened to him, during the entire time they remained at the table. And this was over two hours; there were many delicious things to be eaten, or at least tasted, for Mrs. Carew's Cynthy, having been one of the good cooks of the old days before the war, was still in possession of a remnant of her former skill. As these "old days" lay but six years back, it would seem that Cynthy must have worked hard to forget all but a remnant, in so short a time. She had, however, succeeded perfectly, and only upon great occasions, like the present, would she condescend to revert to her ancient knowledge, as a favor to "Miss Betty," whose fortunes were so sadly fallen. Cynthy and Pompey had accompanied their young mistress from her Georgia home to the new one in Florida many years before; they now remained with her for the excellent reason that, owing to age and infirmities, it would have been impossible for them to have found a home or employment elsewhere. This, however, they never acknowledged, they spoke of their fidelity as a weakness of which they were rather ashamed; but "dat poor Miss Betty, she nebber get 'long widout us nohow, Pomp, dat's a fac'." In reality, they adored Miss Betty, and would have pined and died in a month if taken from her kindly, indulgent rule, and from the old Carew kitchen, with its disorder and comfort, where they had reigned so many years.

The superior table manners of Mrs. Thorne were never more apparent than upon this occasion. In this lady's opinion, when one was required to turn from intellectual occupations to the grosser employment of supplying nourishment to the body, one could at least endeavor to etherealize it as much as possible by confining one's self to that refined implement, the fork. In accordance with this theory, she scarcely touched her knife; once, under protest as it were, she delicately divided with its aid the wing of a wild-duck, but that was all. She encountered difficulties; slices of cold tongue betrayed a remarkable tenacity of fibre, portions of broiled chicken manifested a very embarrassing slipperiness under the silver tines, as she tried to divide them or roll them up. But she persevered in her efforts to the end, and succeeded, though her small fingers became deeply dented by the force she was obliged to exert.

When the meal was at length over, Mrs. Carew, with a bow to Mrs. Rutherford as her most distinguished guest, rose. Garda called Winthrop's attention, as they also rose, to the fact that she had scarcely spoken six sentences of Spanish during its entire continuance. "See how well I have obeyed you," she said.

"Surely I did not venture a command?"

"I think you did. At least you came as near it as you dared, and you are very daring."

"I? Never in the world! You are quite mistaken, Miss Thorne, I am the exact opposite of that," he answered, laughing.

"But I should think you would like me to at least believe you so," responded Garda, looking at him with wonder.

"Believe me to be daring? We probably use the word in a different sense; it isn't a word I am fond of, I confess; but I don't think you would find me lacking in any emergency."

"Oh, emergencies!—they never come to Gracias. Now please don't say, like the dear old Doctor, 'May they never come to *you*, my dearest child!'"

"I will say, then—may I be present when they do."

"But you won't be," responded Garda, her tone suddenly changing; "you will go away, Mrs. Harold will go away, everybody will go away, and we shall be left alone again, mamma and I, on this old shore!"

"But you have seemed to me very happy here on this old shore," said Winthrop, in a tone which was indulgent as well as comforting—she had looked so young, so like a child, as she made her complaint.

"So I have been—until now. But now that I have seen you, now that I have seen Mrs. Harold, I—I don't know." She looked at him wistfully.

This little conversation had gone on while they were all returning through the hall to the front drawing-room. Manuel, however, who was with Mrs. Harold, had a plan of his own, he turned boldly aside towards the closed door of the back drawing-room, his intention being to establish himself with the charming northern lady upon a certain sofa which he remembered at the extreme end of that broad apartment; if isolation were a northern fashion, he would be isolated too. But Mrs. Carew (with the returning lamp on her mind) saw his hand upon the knob, and summoned him in haste: "Mr. Ruiz! Mr. Ruiz!"

When he obeyed her call, she begged him fervently to promise to sing for them immediately that "sweet little air" which it seemed was "such a favorite" of hers, though when he asked her to define it more clearly, she was unable to recall its name, the words, or any characteristic by which he could identify it; however, by this effort of the imagination the door of the back drawing-room was kept closed, and all her guests were piloted safely to the front room by the way they had come. The lamp was in position, only the retreating legs of Pompey were visible through the dining-room door; the mistress of the house, unused to strategy, sank into a chair, and furtively passed her handkerchief across her brow.

Manuel was already tuning the guitar.

"Does he like to sing so soon after—after tea?" said Mrs. Rutherford.

But the handsome youth could sing as well at one time as another. He looked about him, found a low ottoman and drew it towards the sofa where Mrs. Harold was sitting, thus placing himself as nearly as possible at her feet; then he struck a chord or two, and began. He had a tenor voice (as Winthrop would have said, "of course"); and the voice had much sweetness. He sang his little love song admirably.

Garda was standing near one of the windows with Winthrop. When the song was ended, "How old is Mrs. Harold?" she asked, abruptly; that is, abruptly as regarded subject, her voice itself had no abrupt tones.

"I don't know," Winthrop answered.

"Isn't she your cousin?"

"She is my aunt's niece by marriage; Mr. Rutherford was her uncle."

"But if you have always known her, you must know how old she is."

"I have not always known her, and I don't know; I suppose her to be about twenty-seven or twenty-eight."

"She is over thirty," said Garda, with decision. "Do you think her handsome?"

"She is considered handsome."

"But do you think her so?"

"That is rather a close question, isn't it?"

"It doesn't seem so to me; people are handsome or not handsome, it's fact—not opinion. And what I wanted to see was whether you had any eye for beauty, that was all. Mrs. Rutherford, for instance, is handsome, Mrs. Carew is not. Manuel is handsome, Adolfo Torres is not."

"And Miss Thorne?"

"She hopes she is, but she isn't sure," replied the girl, laughing; "it isn't 'sure' to be thought so by the four persons about here. And she can't find out from the only stranger she knows, because he hasn't a particle of expression in his face; it's most unfortunate."

"For him—yes. It's because he's so old, you know."

"How old are you?"

"I am thirty-five."

"You look younger than that," said Garda, after scanning him for a moment.

"It's my northern temperament, that keeps me young and handsome."

"Oh, you're not handsome; but in a man it's of little consequence," she added.

"Very little. Or in a woman either. Don't we all know that beauty fades as the leaf?"

"The leaf fades when it has had all there was of its life, it doesn't fade before. That is what I mean to do, have all there is of *my* life, I have told mamma so. I said to mamma more than a year ago, 'Mamma, what are our pleasures? Let us see if we can't get some more;' and mamma answered, 'Edgarda, pleasures are generally wrong.' But I don't agree with mamma, I don't think them wrong; and I intend to take mine wherever I can find them, in fact, I do so now."

"And do you find many?"

"Oh yes," replied Garda, confidently. "There are our oranges, which are excellent; and Carlos Mateo, who is so amusing; and the lovely breeze we have sometimes; and the hammock where I lie and plan out all the things I should like to have—the softest silks, laces, nothing coarse or common to touch me; plenty of roses in all the rooms and the garden full of sweet-bay, so that all the air should be perfumed."

"And not books? Conversation?"

"I don't care much about books, they all appear to have been written by old people; I suppose when I am old myself, I shall like them better. As to conversation—yes, I like a little of it; but I like actions more—great deeds, you know. Don't you like great deeds?"

"When I see them; unfortunately, there are very few of them left nowadays, walking about, waiting to be done."

"I don't know; let me tell you one. The other day a young girl here—not of our society, of course—was out sailing with a party of friends in a fishing-boat. This girl had a branch of wild-orange blossoms in her hand; suddenly she threw it overboard, and challenged a young man who was with her to get it again. He instantly jumped into the water; there was a good deal of sea, they were at the mouth of the harbor and the tide was going out; they were running before a fresh breeze, and, having no oars with them, they could not get back to him except by several long tacks. He could not swim very well, and the tide was strong, they thought he certainly would be carried out; but he kept up, and at last they saw him land, ever so far down Patricio—he was only a black dot. He walked back, came across to Gracias in a negro's dug-out, and just as he was, without waiting to change his clothes, he brought her the wet flowers."

"It is the old story of the Glove. Did he throw them in her face?"

"Throw them in her face!—is that what you would have done?" said Garda, astonished.

"Oh, I should never have jumped overboard," answered Winthrop, laughing.

During this interval, Torres, wishing to show himself a man of conversation, after his own method, had propounded no less than three questions to the Rev. Mr. Moore, who understood something of Spanish. He had first requested information as to the various methods of punishment, other than the whip, which had been in use on the plantations in the Gracias-á-Dios neighborhood before the emancipation, and which of them had been considered the most effective. His next inquiry, made after a meditative silence of some minutes, was whether, in the reverend gentleman's opinion, the guillotine was not on the whole a more dignified instrument for the execution of justice than the noose—one more calculated to improve the minds of the lower classes? Finally, he wished to know whether the clergyman supposed that a person suffered more when an arm was amputated than he did when a leg was taken off, the arm being nearer the vital organs; and whether either of these operations could be compared, as regarded the torture inflicted, with that caused by a sabre wound (such as one might receive in a duel with swords) which had cut into the breast?

"That is a very blood-thirsty young man; his style of conversation is really extraordinary," said the clergyman to Dr. Kirby, when Torres, having exhausted all his topics, and not having understood one word of the rector's Spanish in reply, returned gravely to his place on the other side of the room.

"He is blood-thirsty because he is forced to be so dumb," answered the Doctor, with one of his sudden little grins—grins which came and went so quickly that, were it not for a distinct remembrance of about sixteen very white little teeth which he had seen, the gazer would scarcely have realized that it had been there at all. "No one here (besides yourself and Manuel) can talk Spanish with him but Garda, and Mr. Winthrop has kept Garda talking English every moment since he came; I don't wonder the youth is blood-thirsty, I'm afraid that at his age I should have called the northerner out."

But now Winthrop and Garda joined the others. Winthrop was addressed by Mrs. Thorne.

"I have been begging Mrs. Rutherford and Mrs. Harold to pay us a visit at East Angels some day this week; I hope, Mr. Winthrop, that you will accompany them."

Winthrop expressed his thanks; he put forward the hope in return that she would join them for an afternoon sail, before long, down the Espiritu. Mrs. Thorne was sure that that would be extremely delightful, she was sure that his yacht (she brought out the word with much clearness; no one had ventured to call it a yacht until now) was also delightful; and its name—*Emperadora*—was so charming!

She was perched, by some fatality, on a high-seated chair, so high that (Winthrop suspected) her little feet did not touch the floor. She did not look like a person who could enjoy sailing, one who would be able to undulate easily, yield to the motion of the boat, or find readily accessible in her storehouse of feelings that mood of serene indifference to arriving anywhere at any particular time, which is a necessary accompaniment of the aquatic amusement when pursued in the lovely Florida waters. But "I enjoy sailing of all things," this brave little matron was declaring.

"I am afraid there will be little novelty in it for you. You must know all these waters well," observed Winthrop.

"Even if I do know them well, it will be a pleasure to visit them again in such intelligent society," replied Mrs. Thorne. "We have lived somewhat isolated, my daughter and I; it will be a widening for us in every way to be with you—with Mrs. Rutherford, Mrs. Harold, and yourself. I have sometimes feared," she went on, looking at him with her bright little eyes, "that we should become, perhaps have already become, too motionless in our intellectual life down here, my daughter and myself."

"Motionless things are better than moving ones, aren't they?" answered Winthrop. "The people who try to keep up with everything are apt to be a panting, breathless set. Besides, they lose all sense of comparison in their haste, and don't distinguish; important things and unimportant they talk about with equal eagerness, the only point with them is that they should be new."

"You console me—you console me greatly," responded Mrs. Thorne. "Still, I feel sure that knowledge, and important knowledge, is advancing with giant strides outside, and that we, my daughter and I, are left behind. I have seen but few of the later publications—could you not kindly give me just an outline? In geology, for instance, always so absorbing, what are the latest discoveries with regard to the Swiss lakes? And I should be so grateful, too, for any choice thoughts you may be able to recall at the moment from the more recent essays of Mr. Emerson; I can say with truth that strengthening sentences from Mr. Emerson's writings were my best mental pabulum during all the early years of my residence at the South."

"I—I fancy that Mrs. Harold knows more of Emerson than I do," replied Winthrop, reflecting upon the picture of the New England school-teacher transplanted to East Angels, and supporting life there as best she could, on a diet of Mr. Emerson and "Paradise Lost."

"An extremely intelligent and cultivated person," responded Mrs. Thorne, with enthusiasm. "Do you know, Mr. Winthrop, that Mrs. Harold quite fills my idea of a combination of our own Margaret Fuller and Madame de Staël."

"Yet she can hardly be called talkative, can she?" said Winthrop, smiling.

"It is her face, the language of her eye, that give me my impression. Her silence seems to me but a fulness of intellect, a fulness at times almost throbbing; she is a Corinne mute, a Margaret dumb."

"Were they ever mute, those two?" asked Winthrop.

Mrs. Thorne glanced at him. "I see you do not admire lady conversationalists," she murmured, relaxing into her guarded little smile.

Dr. Kirby, conversing with Mrs. Rutherford, had brought forward General Lafayette. On the rare occasions of late years when the Doctor had found himself called upon to conduct a conversation with people from the North, he was apt to resort to Lafayette.

The Rev. Mr. Moore, stimulated by Mrs. Carew's excellent coffee, advanced the opinion that Lafayette was, after all, "very French."

"Ah! but Frenchmen can be *so* agreeable," said Mrs. Carew. "There was Talleyrand, you know; when he was over here he wrote a sonnet to my aunt, beginning 'Aimable Anne.' And then there was little Dumont, Katrina; you remember him?—how well he danced! As for Lafayette, when he made his triumphal tour through the country afterwards, he grew so tired, they say, of the satin sheets which Gratitude had provided for him at every town that he was heard to exclaim, 'Satan de satin!' Not that I believe it, because there are those beautiful memoirs and biographies of all his lady-relatives who were guillotined, you know, poor things!—though, come to think of it, one of them must have been saved of course to write the memoirs, since naturally they couldn't have written them beforehand themselves with all those touching descriptions of their own dying moments and last thoughts thrown in; well—what I was going to say was that I don't believe he ever swore in the least, because they were all so extremely pious; he couldn't—in that atmosphere. What a singular thing it is that when the French *do* take to piety they out-Herod Herod himself!—and I reckon the reason is that it's such a novelty to them that they're like the bull in the china shop, or rather like the new boy at the grocer's, who is not accustomed to raisins, and eats so many the first day that he is made seriously ill in consequence, for clear raisins *are* very trying."

"The French," remarked Dr. Kirby, "have often, in spite of their worldliness, warm enthusiasms in other directions which take them far, very far indeed. It was an enthusiasm, and a noble one, that brought Lafayette to our shores."

"*Such* a number of children as were named after him, too," said Mrs. Carew, starting off again. "I remember one of them; he had been baptized Marquis de Lafayette (Marquis de Lafayette Green was his full name), and I didn't for a long time comprehend what it was, for his mother always called him 'Marquisdee,' and I thought perhaps it was an Indian name, like

Manatee, you know; for some people do like Indian names *so* much, though I can't say I care for them, but it's a matter of taste, of course, like everything else, and I once knew a dear sweet girl who had been named Ogeechee, after our Southern river, you remember; Ogeechee—do you like that, Katrina?"

"Heavens! no," said Mrs. Rutherford, lifting her beautiful hands in protest against such barbarism.

"Yet why, after all, is it not as melodious as Beatrice?" remarked Mr. Moore, meditatively, his eyes on the ceiling.

Gracias society was proud of Mr. Moore; his linguistic accomplishments it regarded with admiration. Mrs. Carew, divining the Italian pronunciation of Beatrice, glanced at Katrina to see if she were properly impressed.

Garda, upon leaving Evert Winthrop, had joined Mrs. Harold, at whose feet Manuel still remained, guitar in hand. "Do you sing, Mrs. Harold?" the young girl said, seating herself beside the northern lady, and looking at her with her usual interest—an interest which appeared to consist, in part, of a sort of expectancy that she would do or say something before long which would be a surprise. Nothing could be more quiet, more unsurprising, so most persons would have said, than Margaret Harold's words and manner. But Garda had her own stand-point; to her, Mrs. Harold was a perpetual novelty. She admired her extremely, but even more than she admired, she wondered.

"No," Mrs. Harold had answered, "I do not sing; I know something of instrumental music."

"I am afraid we have no good pianos here," pursued Garda; "that is, none that you would call good.—I wish you would go and talk to Mr. Torres," she continued, turning to Manuel.

The young Cuban occupied a solitary chair on the other side of the room, his method apparently having allowed him to seat himself for a while; he had not even his ivory puzzle, but sat with his hands folded, his eyes downcast.

"You ask impossibilities," said Manuel. "What! leave this heavenly place at Mrs. Harold's feet—and yours—for the purpose of going to talk to that tiresome Adolfo? Never!"

"But I wish to talk to Mrs. Harold myself; you have already had that pleasure quite too long. Besides, if you are very good, I will tell you what you can do; cards will be brought out presently, and then it will be seen that there are ten persons present, and as but eight are required for the two tables, I shall be the one left out to talk to Adolfo, as he can neither play nor speak English; in this state of things you can, if you are watchful, arrange matters so as to be at the same table with Mrs. Harold; perhaps even her partner."

"I will be more than watchful," Manuel declared; "I will be determined!"

"I play a wretched game," said the northern lady, warningly.

"And if you should play the best in the world, I should never know it, absorbed as I should be in your personal presence," replied the youth, with ardor.

Mrs. Harold laughed. Winthrop (listening to Mrs. Thorne's remarks upon Emerson) glanced towards their little group.

"People do not talk in that way at the North. That is why she laughs," said Garda, explanatorily.

"And do I care how they talk in their frozen North!" cried Manuel. "I talk as my heart dictates."

"Do so," said Garda, "but later. At present, go and cheer up poor Mr. Torres; he is fairly shivering with loneliness over there in his corner."

Manuel, who, in spite of his studied attitude at the feet of Mrs. Harold, was evidently the slave of whatever whim Garda chose to express, rose to obey. "But do not in the least imagine that Adolfo needs cheering," he explained, still posing a little as he stood before them with his guitar. "He entertains himself perfectly, always; he is never lonely, he has only to think of his ancestors. Adolfo is, in fact, a very good ancestor already. As to his shivering—that shows how little you know him; he is a veritable volcano, that silent one! Still, I obey your bidding, I go."

"What do *you* think of him?" said Garda, as he crossed the room towards the solitary Cuban.

"Mr. Torres?"

"No; Mr. Ruiz."

"I know him so slightly, I cannot say I have formed an opinion."

Garda looked at the two young men for a moment; then, "They are both boys," she said, dismissing them with a little wave of her hand.

"But Mr. Winthrop is not a boy," she went on, her eyes returning to the northern lady's face. "How old is Mr. Winthrop?"

"I don't know."

"Isn't he your cousin?"

"Mr. Winthrop is the nephew of Mrs. Rutherford, who is only my aunt by marriage."

"But if you have always known him, you must know how old he is."

"I have not always known him. I suppose he is thirty-four or five."

"That is just what he said," remarked Garda, reflectively.

"That I was thirty-four or five?"

"No; but he began in the same way. He said that he did not know; that you were not his cousin; that you were the niece of Mr. Rutherford; and that he supposed you to be about twenty-seven or eight."

"I am twenty-six," said Margaret.

"And he is thirty-five," added Garda.

"I suppose they both seem great ages to you," observed Margaret, smiling.

"It's of very little consequence in a man—his age," replied the young girl. "I confess that I thought you older than twenty-six; but it's not because you look old, it's because you look as if you did not care whether people thought you old or not, and generally it's only women who are really old, you know, over thirty, like mamma and Mrs. Carew, who have that expression—don't you think so? And I fancy you don't care much about dress, either," she went on. "Everything you wear is very beautiful; still, I don't believe you care about it. Yet you would carry it off well, any amount of it, you are so tall."

"I think you are as tall as I am," said Margaret, amused by these unconventional utterances.

"Come and see," replied Garda, suddenly. She took Margaret's hand and rose.

"What is it we are to do?" inquired Margaret, obeying the motion without comprehending its object.

"Come," repeated Garda.

They passed into the back drawing-room, and Garda led the way towards a large mirror.

"But we do not wish to survey ourselves in the presence of all this company," said Margaret, pausing.

"Yes, we do. They will not notice us, they are talking; it's about our height, you know," answered the girl. She held Margaret's hand tightly, and drew her onward until they both stood together before the long glass.

Two images gazed back at them. One was that of a young girl with bright brown hair curling low down over wonderful dark eyes. A white rose was placed, in the Spanish fashion, on one side above the little ear. This image in the mirror had a soft warm color in its cheeks, and a deeper one still on its slightly parted lips; these lips were very lovely in outline, with short, full, upward-arching curves and a little downward droop at the corners. The rich beauty of the face, and indeed of the whole figure, was held somewhat aloof from indiscriminate appropriation, by the indifference which accompanied it. It was not the indifference of experience, there was no weariness in it, no knowledge of life; it was the fresh indifference rather of inexperience, like the indifference of a child. It seemed, too, as if it would always be there, as if that face would never grow eager, no matter how much expansion of knowledge the years might bring to it; very possibly, almost certainly, this beautiful girl would demand more of life in every way, year by year, as it passed; but this would not make her strive for it, she would always remain as serenely careless, as unconcerned, as now.

The mirror gave back, also, the second image. It was that of a woman older—older by the difference that lies between sixteen years and twenty-six. This second image was tall and slender. It had hair of the darkest brown which is not black—hair straight and fine, its soft abundance making little display; this hair was arranged with great simplicity, too great, perhaps, for, brushed smoothly back and closely coiled behind, it had an air of almost severe plainness—a plainness, however, which the perfect oval of the face, and the beautiful forehead, full and low, marked by the slender line of the dark eyebrows, with the additional contrast of the long dark eyelashes beneath, could bear. The features were regular, delicate; the complexion a clear white, of the finest, purest grain imaginable, the sort of texture which gives the idea that the bright color will come and go through its fairness. This expectation was not fulfilled; the same controlled calm seemed to hold sway there which one perceived in the blue eyes and round the mouth.

As Winthrop had said, Margaret Harold was considered handsome. By that was meant that she was in possession of a general acknowledgment that the shape and poise of her head were fine, that her features were well-cut, that her tall, slender form was charmingly proportioned, her movements graceful. Winthrop would have stated, as his own opinion, that she was too cold and formal to be beautiful—too restricted; it was true that in one thing she was not restricted (this was also his own opinion), namely, in the high esteem she had for herself.

She had undoubtedly a quiet reserved sort of beauty. But other women were not made jealous by any especial interest in her, by discussions concerning her, by frequent introduction of her name. She was thought unsympathetic; but as she never said the clever, cutting things which unsympathetic women sometimes know how to say so admirably, she was not thought entertaining as well—as they often are. Opinion varied, therefore, as to whether she could say these things, but would not, or whether it was the contrary, that she would have said them if she had been able, but simply could not, having no endowment of that kind of wit; one thing alone was certain, namely, that she continued not to say them.

Her dress, as seen in the mirror, had much simplicity of aspect; but this was owing to the way she wore it, and the way in which it was made, rather than to the materials, which were ample and rich. The soft silk, Quakerish in hue, lay in folds over the carpet which Garda's scanty skirt barely touched; it followed the lines of the slender figure closely, while Garda's muslin, which had been many times washed, was clumsy and ill-fitting. The gray robe came up smoothly round the throat, where it was finished by a little ruff of precious old lace, while the poor Florida gown, its fashion a reminiscence of Mrs. Thorne's youth, ended at that awkward angle which is neither high nor low.

But all this made no difference as regarded the beauty of Garda. Of most young girls it can be said that richness of attire spoils them, takes from their youthfulness its chief charm; but of Garda Thorne it could easily be believed that no matter in what she might be clad, poor garb as at present, or the most sumptuous, she herself would so far outshine whichever it happened to be, that it would scarcely be noticed.

"You are the taller," said Garda. "I knew it!" The outline of the head with the smooth dark hair was clearly above that crowned by the curling locks.

"You are deceptive," said Margaret, "you look tall, yet I see now that you are not. Are there many more such surprises about you?"

"I hope so," answered Garda, "I love surprises. That is, short ones; I don't like surprises when one has to be astonished ever so long, and keep on saying 'oh!' and 'dear me!' long after it's all over. But everything long is tiresome, I have found *that* out."

Winthrop had watched them pass into the second room. He now left his place, and joined them.

"We came to see which was the taller," said Garda, as his face appeared in the mirror behind them. Margaret moved aside; but as Garda still held her hand, she could not move far. Winthrop, however, was not looking at her, his eyes were upon the reflection of the younger face; perceiving this, her own came back to it also.

"You two are always so solemn," said Garda, breaking into one of her sweet laughs; "standing between you, as I do, I look like Folly itself. There was an old song of Miss Pamela's:

"'Reason and Folly and Beauty, they say,
Went on a party of pleasure one day—'

Here they are in the glass, all three of them. Mrs. Harold is Beauty."

"I suppose that means that I am that unfortunate wretch, Reason," said Winthrop. "Didn't he get a good many cuffs in the song? He generally does in real life, I know—poor fellow!"

Garda had now released Mrs. Harold's hand, and that lady turned away. She found herself near an interesting collection of Florida paroquets, enclosed in a glass case, and she devoted her attention to ornithology for a while; the birds returned her gaze with the extremely candid eyes contributed by the taxidermist. Presently Dr. Kirby came to conduct her to the whist-table. Pompey had arranged these tables with careful precision upon the exact figures of the old carpet which his mistress had pointed out beforehand; but though Pompey had thus arranged the tables, the players were not arranged as Garda had predicted. Mrs. Rutherford, Dr. Kirby, Mrs. Thorne, and the Rev. Mr. Moore formed one group. At the other table were Mrs. Harold, Manuel Ruiz, and Mrs. Carew, with a dummy. Evert Winthrop did not play.

This left him with Garda. But Torres was also left; the three walked up and down in the broad hall for a while, and then went out on the piazza. Here there was a hammock, towards which Garda declared herself irresistibly attracted; she arranged it as a swing, and seated herself. Winthrop found a camp-chair, and placed himself near her as she slowly swayed in her hanging seat to and fro. But Torres remained standing, according to his method; he stood with folded arms in the shadow, close to the side of the house, but without touching it. As he stood there for an hour and a half, it is possible that he found the occupation tedious—unless indeed the picture of Garda in the moonlight was a sufficient entertainment; certainly there was very little else to entertain him; Garda and Winthrop, talking English without intermission, seemed to have forgotten his existence entirely.

"Adolfo," said Manuel, on their way home, giving a rapier-like thrust in the air with his slender cane, "that northerner, that Wintup, is unendurable!"

"He is a matter of indifference to me," replied Torres.

"What—when he keeps you out there on the piazza for two hours in perfect silence? I listened, you never spoke one word; he talked all the time to Garda himself."

"*That*—I suffered," said Torres, with dignity.

"Suffered? I should think so! Are you going to 'suffer' him to buy East Angels, too?"

"He may buy what he pleases. He cannot make himself a Spaniard."

"How do you know Garda cares so much for Spaniards?" said Manuel, gloomily. "I suppose you remember that the mother, after all, is a northerner?"

"I remember perfectly," replied the Cuban. "The señorita will always do—"

"What her mother wishes?" (Manuel was afraid of Mrs. Thorne.)

"—What she pleases," answered Torres, serenely.

CHAPTER VI

"I think you very wonderful," said Garda. "And I think you very beautiful too, though no one seems to talk about it. That in itself is a wonder. But everything about you is wonderful." She was sitting on the floor, her hands crossed on Margaret Harold's knee, her chin resting on her hands; her eyes were fixed on that lady's face.

"You are easily pleased," said Margaret.

"No," replied Garda, with the leisurely utterance which took from her contradictions all appearance of opposition; "I am not easily pleased at all, it's the contrary. I see the goodness of all my friends, I hope; I love them very much. But they do not please me, as you please me, for instance, just because they are good, or because I love them; to be pleased as I am now, to admire as I admire you, is a very different thing."

Margaret said nothing, and Garda, as if wishing to convince her, went on; "I love my dear Dr. Reginald, I love him dearly; but don't you suppose I see that he is too stout and too precise? I love my dear Mr. Moore, I think him perfectly adorable; but don't you suppose I see that he is too lank and narrow-shouldered, and that his dear good little eyes are too small for his long face—like the eyes of a clean, thin, white pig? Mrs. Carew is my kindest friend; that doesn't prevent me from seeing that she is too red. Mr. Torres is too dark, Mr. Winthrop too cold; and so it goes. But you—you are perfect."

"You have left out Mr. Ruiz," suggested Margaret, smiling.

"Manuel is beautiful; yes, in his face, Manuel is very beautiful," said Garda, consideringly. "But you have a beautiful nature, and Manuel has only an ordinary one. It's your having a beautiful face and beautiful nature too which makes you such a wonder to me, because people with beautiful natures are so apt to have ugly faces, or at least thin, wrinkled, and forlorn ones, or else they are invalids; and if they escape that, they are almost sure to have such dreadful clothes. But *you* have a beautiful nature, and a beautiful face, and beautiful clothes—all three. I could never be like you, I don't want to be; but I admire you more than any one I have ever known, and I hope you will let me be with you as often as I can while you stay here; I don't know what I shall do when you go away!"

Margaret smiled a second time; the young girl seemed to her very young indeed as she uttered these candid beliefs.

"Mamma too admires you so much," continued Garda; "I have never known mamma to admire any one (outside of our own family) so completely as she admires you; for generally mamma has her reservations, you know. But it is your intellect which mamma admires, and *I* do not care so much for intellect; of course it's all very well for a foundation, but one doesn't want to be all foundation."

"Mrs. Rutherford would like to see you for a moment, Miss Margaret, if you please," said a voice which seemed startlingly near them, though no one was in sight.

It was Celestine; she had opened the door noiselessly the sixteenth part of an inch, delivered her message with her lips close to the crack, and then closed it again with the soundless abruptness which characterized all her actions.

"That is the fourth time Mrs. Rutherford has sent a message since I came, an hour ago," remarked Garda. "She depends upon you for everything."

"Oh no; upon Celestine," said Margaret, as she left the room.

When she came back, fifteen minutes later, "You are mistaken," Garda answered, as though there had been no interruption; "she depends upon Celestine for her clothes, her hair, her medicine, and her shawls; but she depends upon you for everything else."

"Have you been thinking about it all this time?" Margaret asked.

"How good you are! Why didn't you say, '*Is* there anything else?' But I have noticed that you never say those things. Have I been thinking about it all this time? No, it doesn't require thinking about, any one can see it; what I have been thinking about is you." She had taken her former place, her arms crossed on Margaret's knee. "You have such beautiful hands," she said, lifting one and spreading it out to look at it.

"My dear Miss Thorne, your own are much more beautiful."

"Oh, I do very well, I know what I am; but I am not you. I don't believe there is any one like you; it would be too much."

"Too much perfection?" said Margaret, laughing.

"Yes," answered Garda, her seriousness unbroken. "For you take quantities of trouble for other people—I can see that. And the persons who do so are hardly ever happy—thoroughly happy; it seems such a pity, but it's true. Now I am always happy; but then I never take any trouble for any one, not a bit."

"I haven't observed that," said Margaret.

"No one observes it," responded Garda, composedly; "but it is quite true. And I never intend to take any trouble, whether they observe it or not. But with you it is different, you take a great deal; partly you have taught yourself to do it, and partly you were made so."

"Since when have you devoted your attention to these deep subjects, Miss Thorne?" said Margaret, smiling down upon the upturned face of the girl before her.

Garda rose to her knees. "Oh, don't call me Miss Thorne," she said, pleadingly, putting her arms round her companion. "I love you so much—please never say it again."

"Very well. I will call you Garda."

"I like it when you are cold like that—oh, I like it!" said Garda, with enthusiasm. "All you say when I tell you I adore you is, 'Very well; I will call you Garda;' you do not even say 'my dear.' That is beautiful, because you really mean it; you mean nothing more, and you say nothing more."

"Do you praise me simply because I speak the truth?" said Margaret.

"Yes; for nothing is more rare. I speak the truth myself, but my truth is whatever happens to come into my head; your truth is quiet and real, as you yourself are. I could never be like you, I don't want to be; but I admire you—I admire you."

"I don't know that I am much complimented, if you keep on insisting, in spite of it all, that you don't want to be like me," said Margaret, laughing again.

"Well," replied Garda, "I don't; what's the use of pretending? For I wish to be happy, and I mean to be happy. You are a sort of an angel; but I have never heard that angels had very much of a good time themselves, or that anybody did anything especial for *their* pleasure; they are supposed to be above it. But I am not above it, and never shall be." And leaning forward, she kissed Margaret's cheek. "It's because you're so wonderful," she said.

"I am not wonderful at all," answered Margaret, rather coldly, withdrawing a little from the girl's embrace.

"And if you didn't answer in just that way, you wouldn't be, of course," said Garda, delightedly; "that is exactly what I mean—you are so cold and so true. You think I exaggerate, you do not like to have me talk in this way about you, and so you draw back; but only a little, because you are too good to hurt me, or any one. But I don't want to be 'any one' to you, Mrs. Harold. Do let me be some one."

Now came again the ventriloquistic voice at the door, "phaeton's ready, Miss Margaret."

"Why doesn't Mr. Winthrop drive out with Mrs. Rutherford?" said Garda, watching Margaret put on her bonnet.

"He is probably occupied."

"He is never occupied. Do you call it occupied to be galloping over the pine barrens in every direction, and stopping at East Angels? to be exploring the King's Road, and stopping at East Angels? to be sailing up and down the Espiritu, and stopping at East Angels? to be paddling up all the creeks, and stopping at East Angels?"

"I should call that being very much occupied indeed," said Margaret, smiling.

"I don't then," replied Garda; "that is, not in your sense of the word. It's being occupied with his own pleasure—that's all. But the truth is Mrs. Rutherford takes you, always you, because no one else begins to make her so comfortable; you not only see that she has everything as she likes it, but that she has nothing as she doesn't like it, which is even more delightful. Yet apparently she doesn't realize this in the least; I think that so very curious."

"Do you fancy that you understand Mrs. Rutherford on so short an acquaintance?" asked Margaret, rather reprovingly.

"Yes," responded Garda, in her calm fashion, her attention, however, not fixing itself long upon the subject, which she seemed to consider unimportant. "I wish you would get a palmetto hat like mine," she went on with much more interest; "your bonnet is lovely, but it makes you seem old."

"But I *am* old," said Margaret, as she left the room.

She did not apologize for leaving her guest; the young girl was in the habit of bestowing her presence upon her so often now, that ceremony between them had come to an end some time before. She took her place in the phaeton, which was waiting at the foot of the outside stairway, Mrs. Rutherford, enveloped in a rich shawl, having already been installed by Celestine. Telano, in his Sunday jacket of black alpaca, held the bridle of the mild old horse with great firmness. He had put on for the occasion his broad-brimmed man-of-war hat, which was decorated with a blue ribbon bearing in large gilt letters the inscription *Téméraire*. Telano had no idea what *Téméraire* meant (he called it Turmrer); he had bought the hat of a travelling vender, convinced that it would add to the dignity of his appearance—as it certainly did. For there was nothing commonplace or horizontal in the position of that hat; the vender had illustrated how it was to be worn, but Telano, fired by the new ambitions of emancipation, had practised in secret before his glass until he had succeeded in getting the Turmrer so far back on his curly head that it was not on the top at all, but applied flatly and perpendicularly behind, so that the gazer's mind lost itself in possibilities as to the methods of adhesion which he must have employed to keep it in place. His mistresses seated, Telano sprang to the little seat behind them, where, with folded arms, he sat stiffly erect, conscious of the Turmrer, showing the whites of his eyes, happy. Margaret lifted the reins, and smiling a good-bye to Garda, who was standing on the outside stairway, drove down Pacheco Lane into the plaza, and out of sight.

Garda still leaned on the balustrade; though left alone, she did not take her departure. After a while she sat down on a step, and leaned her head back against the railing; her eyes were fixed indolently upon the sea.

"Looking across to Spain?" said Evert Winthrop's voice, ten minutes later. He had come down the lane, his step making no sound on the mat of low, thick green.

"No," Garda answered, without turning her eyes from the water. "If I want Spain, I have only to send for Mr. Torres; he's Spain in person."

"Are you here alone? Where are the others?"

"Gone out to drive; I wish you had never sent for that phaeton!"

Several weeks had passed since the arrival of the northern ladies; but it seemed more like several months, if gauged by the friendship which had been bestowed upon them. The little circle of Gracias society had opened its doors to them with characteristic hospitality—the old-time hospitality of the days of better fortune; its spirit unchanged, though the form in which it must now manifest itself was altered in all save its charming courtesy. Mrs. Rutherford was a friend of Mrs. Carew's, that was enough; they were all friends of Mrs. Rutherford in consequence. Mrs. Kirby, the active little mother of Dr. Reginald, invited them to dine with her. Mrs. Penelope Moore, the rector's wife, though seldom able to leave her sofa, did not on that account consider herself exempt from the present privilege of entertaining them. Madame Ruiz, the mother of Manuel, insisted upon several visits at her residence on Patricio Point. Madame Giron, the aunt of Adolfo Torres, came up the Espiritu in her broad old boat, rowed by four negro boys, to beg them to pass a day with her at her plantation, which was south of East Angels. Mrs. Thorne did what she could in the way of afternoon visits at her old Spanish mansion, with oranges, conversation, and Carlos Mateo. And good Betty Carew moved in and out among these gentle festivities with assiduous watchfulness, ready to fill any gaps that might present themselves with selections from her own best resources; the number of times she invited her dearest Katrina to lunch with her, to spend the day with her, to pass the evening with her, to visit the orange groves with her, to play whist, to go and see the rose gardens, and to "bring over her work" in the morning and "sit on the piazza and talk," could not be counted. Mrs. Rutherford, who never had any work beyond the holding of a fan sometimes to screen her face from the fire or sun, was amiably willing to sit on the piazza (Betty's) and talk—talk with the peculiar degree of intimacy which embroidery (or knitting) and piazzas, taken together, seem to produce. Especially was she willing as, without fail, about eleven o'clock, Pompey appeared with a little tray, covered with a snowy damask napkin, upon which reposed a small loaf of delicious cake, freshly baked, two saucers (of that old blue china whose recent nicks owed their origin to emancipation), a glass dish heaped with translucent old-fashioned preserves, and a little glass pitcher of rich cream. Mrs. Rutherford thought this "so amusing—at eleven o'clock in the morning!" But it was noticed that she never refused it.

If Katrina had no work, Betty had it in abundance. It was not embroidery—unless mending could be called by that name. But Betty did not accomplish as much as she might have done, owing to the fact that about once in ten minutes she became aware of the loss of her scissors, or her spool of thread, and was forced to get up, shake her skirts, or dive to the bottom of her pocket in search of them. For her pocket had a wide mouth, which was not concealed by a superfluous overskirt; it was a deep comfortable pocket going well down below the knee, its rotund outline, visible beneath the skirt of the gown, suggesting to the experienced eye a handkerchief, a battered porte-monnaie, a large bunch of keys, two or three crumpled letters, a pencil with the stubby point which a woman's pencil always possesses, a half-finished stocking and ball of yarn, a spectacle-case, a paper of peppermint drops, and a forgotten pair or two of gloves.

These little entertainments hospitably given for the northern ladies succeeded each other rapidly—so rapidly that Margaret began to fear lest, mild as they were in themselves, they should yet make inroads on Mrs. Rutherford's strength.

"You needn't be scairt, Miss Margaret," was Celestine's reply to this suggestion, a remote gleam of a smile lighting up for a moment her grim face; "a little gentlemen-talk is *very* strengthenin' to yer aunt at times; nothin' more so."

During these weeks Garda Thorne had manifested a constantly increasing devotion to Margaret Harold; that, at least, was what they called it in the little circle of Gracias society, where it was considered an interesting development of character. These good friends said to each other that their little girl was coming on, that they should soon be obliged to think of her as something more than a lovely child.

Mrs. Rutherford had another name for it; she called it curiosity. "That little Thorne girl (who is quite pretty)," she remarked to Winthrop, "seems to be never tired of looking at Margaret, and listening to what she says. Yet Margaret certainly says little enough!" Mrs. Rutherford never went beyond "quite pretty" where Garda was concerned. It was her superlative for young girls, she really did not think they could be more.

"You wish that I had never sent for that phaeton? Would you, then, deprive my poor aunt of her drives?" Winthrop had said, in answer to Garda's remark.

"Do you care much for your poor aunt?" she inquired.

"I care a great deal."

"Then why do you never drive out with her yourself?"

"I do; often."

"I have been here every afternoon for a week, and every afternoon Margaret has had to leave me, because Mrs. Rutherford sends word that the phaeton is ready."

"Well, perhaps for the past week—"

"I don't believe you have been for two; I don't believe you have been for three," pursued the girl. "You are willing to go, probably you suppose you do go; but in reality it is Margaret, always Margaret. Do you know what I think?—you do not half appreciate Margaret."

"I am glad at least that you do," Winthrop answered. "Do you prefer that step to a chair?"

"Yes; for I ought to be going back to the Kirbys, and sitting here is more like it. Not that I mean to hurry, you know."

"It's pleasant, staying with the Kirbys, isn't it?" said Winthrop. He was standing on a step below hers, leaning against the side of the house in the shade.

"No," answered Garda, "it isn't; that is, it isn't so pleasant as staying at home. I like my own hammock best, and Carlos Mateo is funnier than any one I know. But by staying in town I can see more of Margaret, and that is what I care for most; I don't know how I can endure it when she goes away!"

"You had better persuade her not to go."

"But she must go, unless Mrs. Rutherford should take a fancy to stay, which is not at all probable; Mrs. Rutherford couldn't get on without Margaret one day."

"I think you exaggerate somewhat my aunt's dependence upon Mrs. Harold," observed Winthrop, after a pause.

"I was waiting to hear you say that. You are all curiously blind. Mrs. Rutherford is so handsome that I like to be in the same room with her; but that doesn't keep me from seeing how much has to be done for her constantly, and in her own particular way, too, from important things down to the smallest; and that the person who attends to it all, keeps it all going, is—"

"Minerva Poindexter," suggested Winthrop.

"Is Margaret Harold; I cannot imagine how it is that you do not see it! But you do not any of you comprehend her—comprehend how unselfish she is, how self-sacrificing."

Winthrop's attention had wandered away from Garda's words. He did not care for her opinion of Margaret Harold; it was not and could not be important—the opinion of a peculiarly inexperienced young girl about a woman ten years older than herself, a woman, too, whose most marked characteristic, so he had always thought, was the reticence which kept guard over all her words and actions. No, for Garda's opinions he did not care; what attracted him, besides her beauty, was her wonderful truthfulness, her grace and ease. "How indolent she is!" was his present thought, while she talked on about Margaret, her eyes still watching the sea. "On these old steps she has taken the one position that is comfortable; yet she has managed to make it graceful as well; she finds a perfect enjoyment in simply sitting here for a while in this soft air, looking at the water, and so here she sits, without a thought of doing anything else. At home, it would be the hammock and the crane; so little suffices for her. But she enjoys her little more fully, she appreciates her enjoyment as it passes more completely, than any girl of her age, or, indeed, of much more than her age, whom I have ever known. Our northern girls are too complex for that, they have too many interests, too many things to think of, and they require too many, also, to enjoy in this simple old way; perhaps *they* would say that they were too conscientious. But here is a girl who is hampered, or enlarged—whichever you choose to call it—by no such conditions, who tastes her pleasures fully, whatever they may happen to be, as they pass. But though her pleasures are simple, her enjoyment of them is rich, it's the enjoyment of a rich temperament; many women would not know how to enjoy in that way. She's simple from her very richness; but she doesn't in the least know it, she has never analyzed herself, nor anything else, and never will; she leaves analysis to—to thin people." Thus he brought up, with an inward laugh over his outcome. His thoughts, however, had not been formulated in words, as they have necessarily been formulated for expression upon the printed page; these various ideas—though they were scarcely distinct enough to merit that name—passed through his consciousness slowly, each melting into the next, without effort on his own part; the effort would have been to express them.

When Garda, after another quarter of an hour's serene contemplation of the sea, at length rose, he walked with her down the lane and across the plaza to Mrs. Kirby's gate. Then, when she had disappeared, he went over to the Seminole, mounted his horse, and started for a ride on the pine barrens.

CHAPTER VII

He continued to think of this young girl as he rode. One of the reasons for this probably was the indifference with which she regarded him, now that her first curiosity had been satisfied; her manner was always pleasant, but Manuel evidently amused her more, and even Adolfo Torres; while to be with Margaret Harold she would turn her back upon him without ceremony, she had repeatedly done it. Winthrop asked himself whether it could be possible that he was becoming annoyed by this indifference, or that he was surprised by it? Certainly he had never considered himself especially attractive, personally; if therefore, in the face of this fact, he was guilty of surprise, it must be that he had breathed so long that atmosphere of approbation which surrounded him at the North, that he had learned, though unconsciously, to rely upon it, had ended by becoming complacent, smug and complacent, expectant of attention and deference.

The advantages which had caused this approving northern atmosphere were now known in Gracias. And Garda remained untouched by them. But that he should be surprised, or annoyed, by her indifference—this possibility was the more distasteful to him because he had always been so sure that he disliked the atmosphere, greatly. He had never been at all pleased by the knowledge that he inspired a general purring from good mammas, whenever his name was mentioned; he had no ambition to attract so much domestic and pussy-like praise. Most of all he did not enjoy being set down as so extremely safe; if he were safe, it was his own affair; he certainly was not cultivating the quality for the sake of the many excellent matrons who happened to form part of his acquaintance.

But, viewed from any maternal stand-point, Evert Winthrop was, and in spite of himself, almost ideally safe. He was thirty-five years old, and therefore past the uncertainties, the vague hazards and dangers, that cling about youth. His record of personal conduct had no marked flaws. He had a large fortune, a quarter of which he had inherited, and the other three-quarters gained by his own foresight and talent. He had no taste for speculation, he was prudent and cool; he would therefore be sure to take excellent care of his wealth, it would not be evanescent, as so many American fortunes had a way of becoming. He had perfect health; and an excellent family descent on both sides of the house; for what could be better than the Puritan Winthrops on one hand, and the careful, comfortable old

Dutch settlers of New Amsterdam, from whom his mother came, on the other? He had a fair amount of good looks—one did not have to forgive him anything, physically; he had sufficient personal presence to escape the danger of being merely the cup, as it were, for the rich wine of his own good-luck. Though quiet in manner, rather silent, and not handsome, he was a man whom everybody remembered. Those who were not aware of his advantages remembered him as clearly as those who knew them all; his individuality was distinct. He had been a good son, he was now a good nephew; these facts were definitely known and proved; American mothers are not mercenary, and it is but just to add that this good sonship and good nephewship, as well as his good record in other directions, had had as much to do with the high appreciation that many of them had of him, as the amount of his income. He was, in short, a bright example of a person without drawbacks, he was a rare instance whose good points it was a pleasure to sum up; they summed him up, therefore, joyfully; they proclaimed the total; they said everything that was delightful about him. Going deeper, they were sure that he had broken none of the commandments. There had been times when Winthrop had almost felt like breaking them all, in order to get rid of this rampart of approval, which surrounded him too closely, like a wall of down. But there again—he could not be vicious simply to oblige these ladies, or rather to disoblige them; he must be what it seemed good to him to be. But he respectfully wished that they could realize how indifferent he was to their estimation of him, good or bad.

He was a man by no means easily pleased. He could not, therefore, always believe that other people were sincere when they were so unlike himself—so much more readily pleased, for instance, with him, than he was with them. For he was essentially modest at heart; though obstinate in many of his ideas, he had not that assured opinion of himself, that solidly installed self-approbation, which men in his position in America (possessed of large fortunes which they have gained for the most part by their own talent) are apt, though often unconsciously, to cherish. As he was fastidious, it was no pleasure to him to taste the open advantages of his position; they were too open, he did not care for things so easily gained. And when these advantages were presented to him in feminine eyes and smiles, or a feminine handwriting, he could not even take a jocular view of it. For though he was a man of the world, he was not (this was another of his secrets) in the least blasé; he had his ideal of what the best of life should be, and he kept it like a Madonna in its shrine. When, therefore, this ideal was pulled by force from its niche, or, worse still, stepped down of its own accord, he was immensely disgusted, he felt a sense of personal injury, as if the most precious feelings of life had been profaned. He had believed in this woman, perhaps, to the extent of supposing her sweet and womanly; yet here she was thinking—yes, without doubt thinking (either for herself or for some one else) of the benefits which his position could confer. That the little advances she had made had been microscopically small, only made the matter worse; if she had enough of refinement to make them so delicate, she should have had enough to not make them at all. It was characteristic of this man that he never at such times thought that the offender might be actuated by a real liking for himself—himself apart from this millstone of his excellent reputation and wealth; this was a feature of the personal modesty that belonged to him. A man less modest (that is, the great majority of men), placed in a position similar to his, would have been troubled by no such poverty of imagination.

It must, however, be added that this modesty of Winthrop's was strictly one of his inner feelings, not revealed to the world at large. The world never suspected it, and had no reason for suspecting it; it had, indeed, nothing to do with the world, it was a private attribute. To the world he was a cool, quiet man, equally without pretensions and without awkwardnesses. One could not have told whether he thought well of himself—especially well—or not.

Why this man, so fully belonging to this busy, self-asserting nineteenth century, should have preserved so much humility in the face of his successes—success of fortune, of equilibrium, of knowledge, of accomplishment of purpose, of self-control—this would have been, perhaps, a question for the student of heredity. Was it a trait inherited from Puritan ancestors, some Goodman Winthrop of gentle disposition, a man not severe in creed or demeanor, nor firm in exterminating Indians, and therefore of small consequence in his day and community, and knowing it? Or was it a tendency inherited from some Dutch ancestress on the maternal side, some sweet little flaxen-haired great-grandmother, who had received in her maiden breast one of those deadly though unseen shafts—the shaft of slight—from which a woman's heart never wholly recovers?

But mental organizations are full of contradictions; looked at in another way, this deep, unexpressed personal humility in Evert Winthrop's nature, underneath his rather cold exterior, his keen mind and strong will, might almost have been called a pride, so high a demand did it make upon life. For if one has not attractive powers, love, when it does come, when it is at last believed in, has a peculiarly rich quality: it is so absolutely one's own!

The father of Evert Winthrop, Andrew Winthrop, was called eccentric during all his life. But it was an eccentricity which carried with it none of the slighting estimations which usually accompany the term. Andrew Winthrop, in truth, had been eccentric only in being more learned and more original than his neighbors; perhaps, also, more severe. He was a fair classical scholar, but a still better mathematician, and had occupied himself at various times with astronomy; he had even built a small observatory in the garden behind his house. But most of all was he interested in the rapid advance of science in general, the advance all along the line, which he had lived to see; he enjoyed this so much that it was to him, during his later years, what a daily draught of the finest wine is to an old connoisseur in vintages, whose strength is beginning to fail him. He once said to his son: "The world is at last getting into an intelligible condition. My only regret is that I could not have lived in the century which is coming, instead of in the one which is passing; but I ought not to complain, I have at least seen the first rays. What should I have done if my lot had been cast among the millions who lived before Darwin! I should either have become a bacchanalian character, drowning in stupid drinking the memory of the enigmas that oppressed me, or I should have fled to the opposite extreme and taken refuge in superstition—given up my intellect, bound hand and foot, to the care of the priests. The world has been in the wilderness, Evert, through all the ages of which we have record; now a clearer atmosphere is at hand. I shall not enter this promised land, but I can see its shining afar off. You, my son, will enter in; prize your advantages, they are greater than those enjoyed by the greatest kings, the greatest philosophers, one hundred years ago."

This Puritan without a creed, this student of science who used more readily than any other the language of the Bible, brought up his only child with studied simplicity; in all that related to his education, with severity. The little boy's mother had died soon after his birth, and Andrew Winthrop had mourned for her, the young wife who had loved him, all the rest of his life. But in silence, almost in sternness; he did not welcome sympathy even when it came from his wife's only sister, Mrs. Rutherford. And he would not give up the child, though the aunt had begged that the poor baby might be intrusted to her for at least the first year of his motherless life; the only concession he made was in allowing the old Episcopal clergyman who had baptized Gertrude to baptize Gertrude's child, and in tacitly promising that the boy should attend, if he pleased, the Episcopal Church when he grew older, his mother having been a devoted Churchwoman. He kept the child with him in the large, lonely New England house which even Gertrude Winthrop's sweetness had not been able to make fully home-like and warm. For it had been lived in too long, the old house, by a succession of Miss Winthrops, conscientious old maids with narrow chests, thin throats, and scanty little knobs of gray-streaked hair behind—the sort of good women with whom the sense of duty is far keener than that of comfort, and in whose minds character is apt to be gauged by the hour of getting up in the morning. There had always been three or four Miss Winthrops of this pattern in each generation; they began as daughters, passed into aunts, and then into grandaunts, as nieces, growing up, took their first positions from them. Andrew Winthrop himself had spent his childhood among a number of these aunts—aunts both simple and "grand." But the custom of the family had begun to change in his day; the aunts had taken to leaving this earthly sphere much earlier than formerly (perhaps because they had discovered that they could no longer attribute late breakfasts to total depravity), so that when, his own youth past, he brought his Gertrude home, there was not one left there; they were alone.

The poor young mother, when death so soon came to her, begged that the little son she was leaving behind might be called Evert, after her only and dearly loved brother, Evert Beekman, who had died not long before. Andrew Winthrop had consented. But he was resolved, at the same time, that no Beekman, but only Winthrop, methods should be used in the education of the child. The Winthrop methods were used; and with good effect. But the boy learned something of the Beekman ways, after all, in the delightful indulgence and petting he received from his aunt Katrina when he went to visit her at vacation times, either at her city home or at her old country-house on the Sound; he learned it in her affectionate words, in the smiling freedom from rules and punishments which prevailed at both places, in the wonderful toys, and, later, the dogs and gun, saddle-horse and skiff, possessed by his fortunate cousin Lanse.

Andrew Winthrop was not that almost universal thing in his day for a man in his position in New England, a lawyer; he owned and carried on an iron-foundery, as his father had done before him. He had begun with some money, and he had made more; he knew that he was rich (rich for his day and neighborhood); but save for his good horses and his observatory, he lived as though he were poor. He gave his son Evert, however, the best education (according to his idea of what the best education consisted in), which money and careful attention could procure; but he did not send him to college, and at sixteen the boy was put regularly to work for a part of the day in the iron-foundery, being required to begin at the beginning and learn the whole business practically, from the keeping of books to the proper mixture of ores for the furnaces—those furnaces which had seemed to the child almost as much a part of nature as the sunshine itself, since he had seen their red light against the sky at night ever since he was born. In the mean time his education in books went steadily forward also, under his father's eye—a severe one. Fortunately the lad had sturdy health and nerves which were seldom shaken, so that these double tasks did not break him down. For one thing, Andrew Winthrop never required, or even desired, rapid progress; Evert might be as slow as he pleased, if he would but be thorough. And thorough he was. Even if he had not been naturally inclined towards it, he would have acquired it from the system which his father had pursued with him from babyhood; but he was naturally inclined towards it; his knowledge, therefore, as far as it went, was very complete.

In four years he had made some progress in the secrets of several sorts of iron and several ancient languages. In six, he could manage the foundery and the observatory tolerably well. In the ninth year his part of the foundery went of itself, or seemed to, under his clear-headed superintendence, while he ardently gave all his free hours to the studies in science, in which his father now joined, instead of directing, as heretofore. And then, in the tenth year of this busy, studious life, Andrew Winthrop had died, and the son of twenty-six had found himself suddenly free, and alone.

He had never longed for his freedom, he had never thought about it; he had never realized that his life was austere. He had been fond of his father, though his father had been more intellectually interested in him as a boy who would see in all probability the fulness of the new revelation of Science, than fond of him in return. Andrew Winthrop's greatest ambition had been to equip his son so thoroughly that he would be able to take advantage of this new light immediately, without any time lost in bewilderment or hesitation; the 'prentice-work would all have been done. And Evert, interested and busy, leading an active life as well as a studious one, had never felt discontent.

The evening after the funeral he was alone in the old house. Everything had been set in order again, that painful order which strikes first upon the hearts of the mourners when they return to their desolate home, an order which seems to say: "All is over; he is gone and will return to you no more. You must now take up the burdens of life again, and go forward." The silent room was lonely, Evert read a while, but could not fix his attention; he rose, walked about aimlessly, then went to the window and looked out. It was bitterly cold, there was deep snow outside; an icy wind swayed the boughs of a naked elm which stood near the window. Against the dark sky to-night the familiar light was not visible; the furnaces had been shut down out of respect for the dead. For the first time there stirred in Evert Winthrop's mind the feeling that the cold was cruel, inhuman; that there was a conscious element in it; that it hated man, and was savage to him; would kill him, and did kill him when it could. The house seemed in league with this enemy; in spite of the bright fire the chill kept creeping in, and for the life of him he could not rid himself of the idea that he ought to go out and cover his poor old father, lying there helpless under the snow, with something thick and warm. He roused himself with an effort, he knew that these were unhealthy fancies; he made up his mind that he would go away for a while, the under-superintendent could see to the foundery during his absence, which would not, of course, be long. But the next day he learned that he could remain away for as long a time as he pleased—he had inherited nearly a million.

It was a great surprise. Andrew Winthrop had so successfully concealed the amount of his fortune that Evert had supposed that the foundery, and the income that came from it, a moderate one, together with the old house to live in, would be all. Andrew Winthrop's intention in this concealment had been to bestow upon his son, so far as he could, during his youth, a personal knowledge of life as seen from the side of earning one's own living—a knowledge which can never be acquired at second-hand, and which he considered inestimable, giving to a man juster views of himself and his fellow-men than anything else can.

In the nine years that had passed since his father's death Evert had, as has been stated, quadrupled the fortune he had inherited.

It was said—by the less successful—that Chance, Luck, and Opportunity had all favored him. It was perhaps Chance that had led the elder Winthrop in the beginning to invest some hundreds of dollars in wild lands on the shore of Lake Superior—though even that was probably foresight. But as for Luck, she is generally nothing but clear-headedness. And Opportunity offers herself, sooner or later, to almost all; it is only that so few of us recognize her, and seize the advantages she brings. Winthrop had been aided by two things; one was capital to begin with; the other a perfectly untrammelled position. He had no one to think of but himself.

Early in the spring after his father's death he journeyed westward, looking after some property, and decided to go to Lake Superior and see that land also. He always remembered his arrival; the steamer left him on a rough pier jutting out into the dark gray lake; on the shore, stretching east and west, was pine forest, unbroken save where in the raw clearing, dotted with stumps, rose a few unpainted wooden houses, and the rough buildings of the stamping-mills, their great wooden legs stamping ponderously on iron ore. His land was in the so-called town; after looking at it, he went out to the mine from which the ore came; he knew something of ores, and had a fancy to see the place. He went on horseback, following a wagon track through the wild forest. The snow still lay in the hollows, there was scarcely a sign of spring; the mine was at some distance, and the road very bad; but at last he reached it. The buildings and machinery of the struggling little company were poor and insufficient; but few men were employed, the superintendent had a discouraged expression. But far above this puny little scratching at its base rose "the mountain," as it was called; and it was a cliff-like hill of iron ore. One could touch it, feel it; it was veritable, real. To Winthrop it seemed a striking picture—the great hill of metal, thinly veiled with a few trees, rising towards the sky, the primitive forest at its feet, the snow, the silence, and beyond, the sullen lake without a sail. The cliff was waiting—it had waited for ages; the lake was waiting too.

Winthrop took a large portion of his fortune and put it into this mine. A new company was formed, but he himself remained the principal owner, and took the direction into his own hands. It was the right moment; in addition, his direction was brilliant. For a time he worked excessively hard, but all his expectations were fulfilled; by means of this, and one or two other enterprises in which he embarked with the same mixture of bold foresight and the most careful attention to details, his fortune was largely increased.

When the war broke out he was abroad—his first complete vacation; he was indulging that love for pictures which he was rather astonished to find that he possessed. He came home, took a captain's place in a company of volunteers, went to the front, and served throughout the war. Immediately after the restoration of peace, he had gone abroad again. And he had come back this second time principally to disentangle from a web of embarrassments the affairs of a cousin of his father's, David Winthrop by name, whom he had left in charge of the foundery which he had once had charge of, himself. Having some knowledge of founderies, David was to superintend this one, and have a sufficient share of the profits to help him maintain his family of seven sweet, gentle, inefficient daughters, of all ages from two to eighteen, each with the same abundant flaxen hair and pretty blue eyes, the same pale oval cheeks and stooping shoulders, and a mother over them more inefficient and gentle and stooping-shouldered still—the very sort of a quiverful, as ill-natured (and richer) neighbors were apt to remark, that such an incompetent creature as David Winthrop would be sure to possess. This cousin had been a trial to Andrew Winthrop all his life. David was a well-educated man, and he had a most lovable disposition; but he had the incurable habit of postponing (with the best intentions) until another time anything important which lay before him; the unimportant things he did quite cheerily. If it were but reading the morning's paper, David would be sure to not quite get to the one article which was of consequence, but to read all the others first in his slow way, deferring that one to a more convenient season when he could give to it his best attention; of course the more convenient season never came. Mixed with this constant procrastination there was a personal activity which was amusingly misleading. Leaving the house in the morning, David would walk to his foundery, a distance of a mile, with the most rapid step possible which was not a run; the swing of his long arms, the slight frown of preoccupation from business cares (it must have been that), would have led any one to believe that, once his office reached, this man would devote himself to his work with the greatest energy, would make every moment tell. But once his office reached, this man devoted himself to nothing, that is, to nothing of importance; he arrived breathless, and hung up his hat; he rubbed his hands, and walked about the room; he glanced over the letters, and made plans for answering them, pleasing himself with the idea of the vigorous things he should say, and changing the form of his proposed sentences in his own mind more than once; for David wrote a very good letter, and was proud of it. Then he sharpened all the pencils industriously, taking pains to give each one a very fine point. He jotted down in neat figures with one of them, little sums—sums which had no connection with the foundery, however, but concerned themselves with something he had read the night before, perhaps, as the probable population of London in A.D. 1966, or the estimated value of a ton of coal in the year 3000. Then he would do a little work on his plan (David made beautiful plans) for the house which he hoped some day to build. And he would stare out of the window by the hour, seeing nothing in particular, but having the vague idea that as he was in his office, and at his desk, he was attending to business as other men attended to it; what else was an office for?

Evert, as a boy, had always felt an interest in this whimsical cousin, who came every now and then to see his father, with some new enterprise (David was strong in enterprises) to consult him about—an enterprise which was infallibly to bring in this time a large amount of money. But this time was never David's time. And in the mean while his daughters continued to appear and grow. Evert, left master, had had more faith in David than his father had had; or perhaps it was more charity; for his cousin had always been a source of refreshment to him—this humorous, sweet-tempered man, who, with his gray-sprinkled hair and thin temples, his well-known incompetency, and his helpless family behind him, had yet no more care on his face than a child has, not half so much as Evert himself, with his youth and health, his success and his fortune, to aid him. But, curiously enough, David was quite well aware of his own faults; his appreciation of them, indeed, had given him a manner of walking slightly sidewise, his right shoulder and right leg a little behind, as though conscious of their master's inefficiency and ashamed of it. For the same reason he chronically hung his head a little as he walked, and, if addressed, looked off at a distance mildly instead of at the person who was speaking to him. But though thus conscious generally of his failings, David was never beyond a sly joke about them and himself. It was the way in which he laughed over these jokes (they were always good ones) which had endeared him to his younger cousin: there was such a delightful want of worldly wisdom about the man.

Having disentangled David, refunded his losses, and set him going again in a small way, Evert had come southward. He would have preferred to go back to Europe for a tour in Spain; but he felt sure that David would entangle himself afresh before long (David had the most inscrutable ways of entangling himself), and that, unless he were willing to continually refund, he should do better to remain within call, at least for the present. In the early spring another relative on his father's side, a third cousin, was to add himself to the partnership, and this young man, Evert hoped, would not only manage the foundery, but manage David as well; when once this arrangement had been effected, the owner of the foundery would be free.

All this was very characteristic of Evert Winthrop. He could easily have given up all business enterprises; he could have invested his money safely and washed his hands of that sort of care. To a certain extent he had done this; but he wished to help David, and so he kept the foundery, he wished to help two or three other persons, and so he retained other interests. This, at least, was what he said to himself, and it was true; yet the foundations lay deeper—lay in the fact that he had been born into the world with a heavy endowment of energy; quiet as he appeared, he had more than he knew what to do with, and was obliged to find occupation for it. During boyhood this energy had gone into the double tasks of education in books and in iron which his father had imposed upon him; in young manhood it had gone into the scientific studies in which his father had shared. Later had come the brilliant crowded years of the far-seeing conception and vigorous execution which had given him his largely increased wealth. Then the war occupied him; it occupied fifty millions of people as well. After it was over, and he had gone abroad a second time, he had not been an idle traveller, though always a tranquil one.

The truth was, he could not lead a purely contemplative life. It was not that he desired to lead such a life, or that he admired it; it was simply that he knew he should never be able to do it, even if he should try, and the impossibility, as usual, tempted him. There must be something very charming in it (that is, if one had no duties which forbade it), this full, passive, receptive enjoyment of anything delightful, a fine picture, for instance, or a beautiful view, the sunshine, the sea; even the angler's contented quiescence on a green bank was part of it. These pleasures he knew he could never have in their full sweetness, though he could imagine them perfectly, even acutely. It was not that he was restless; he was the reverse. It was not that he liked violent exercise, violent action; he liked nothing violent. But, instead of sitting in the sunshine, his instinct was to get a good horse and ride in it; instead of lounging beside a blue sea, he liked better to be sailing a yacht over it; instead of sitting contemplatively on a green bank, holding a fishing-rod, he would be more apt to shoulder a gun and walk, contemplatively too, perhaps, for long miles, in pursuit of game. In all this he was thoroughly American.

He had a great love for art, and a strong love for beauty, which his studies in mathematics and science had never in the least deadened. As regarded determination, he was a very strong man; but he was so quiet and calm that it was only when one came in conflict with him that his strength was perceived; and there were not many occasions for coming in conflict with him now, he was no longer directing large enterprises. In private life, he was not in the habit of advancing opinions for the rest of the world to accept; he left that to the people of one idea.

On the present occasion he rode over the pine barrens for miles, every now and then enjoying a brisk gallop. After a while he saw a phaeton at a distance, moving apparently at random over the green waste; but he had learned enough of the barrens by this time to know that it was following a road—a road which he could not see. There was only one phaeton in Gracias, the one he himself had sent for; he rode across, therefore, to speak to his aunt.

CHAPTER VIII

She was returning with Margaret from her drive, and looked very comfortable; with a cushion behind her and a light rug over her lap, she sat leaning back under her lace-trimmed parasol.

"I enjoy these drives *so* much," she said to her nephew in her agreeable voice. "The barrens themselves, to be sure, cannot be called beautiful, though I believe Margaret maintains that they have a fascination; but the air is delicious."

"Do you really find them fascinating?" said Winthrop to Margaret.

"Extremely so; I drive over them for miles every day, yet never want to come in; I always long to go farther."

"Oh, well, there's an end to them somewhere, I suppose," remarked Mrs. Rutherford; "the whole State isn't so very broad, you know; you would come out at the Gulf of Mexico."

"I don't want to come out," said Margaret, "I want to stay in; I want to drive here forever."

"We shall wake some fine morning, and find you gone," said Mrs. Rutherford, "like the girl in the 'Dismal Swamp,' you know:

> "'Away to the Dismal Swamp she speeds—'

I've forgotten the rest."

> "'Through tangled juniper, beds of reeds,
> And many a fen where the serpent feeds,
> And man never trod before,'"

said Winthrop, finishing the quotation. "The last isn't true of the barrens, however, for man has trod here pretty extensively."

"You mean Indians?" said Mrs. Rutherford, rather as though they were not men, as indeed she did not think they were. She yawned, tapping her lips two or three times during the process with her delicately gloved hand, as people will, under the impression, apparently, that they are concealing the sign of fatigue. Mrs. Rutherford's yawn, however, was not a sign of fatigue, it was an indication of sheer bodily content; the soft air and the lazy motion of the phaeton were so agreeable to her that, if she had been imaginative, she would have declared that the Lotus-eaters must have yawned perpetually, and that Florida was evidently the land of their abode.

"You look too comfortable to talk, Aunt Katrina," said Winthrop, amused by the drowsy tones of her voice; "I think you would rather be rid of me. I will go off and have one more gallop, and be home before you."

Mrs. Rutherford smiled an indolent good-by; Margaret Harold looked straight before her. Winthrop turned off to the right, and was soon lost to view.

He pulled up after a while, and let his horse walk slowly along the trail; he was thinking of Margaret Harold. He was always seeing her now, it could not be otherwise so long as she continued to live with his aunt. But he said to himself that he should never really like her, and what he was thinking of at present was whether or not she had perceived this.

She was not easy to read. Just now, for instance, when she had begun to speak of the pine barrens, and to speak with (for her) a good deal of warmth, had he not perhaps had something to do with her falling into complete silence immediately afterwards? He had answered, of course; he had done what was necessary to keep up the conversation; still, perhaps she had seen—perhaps— Well, he could not help it if she had, or rather he did not care to help it. Whatever she might be besides, quiet, well-bred, devoted to the welfare of his aunt, she was still in his opinion so completely, so essentially wrong in some of her ideas, and these in a woman the most important, that his feeling towards her at heart was one of sternest disapproval; it could not be otherwise. And she held so obstinately to her mistakes! That was the worst of her—her obstinacy; it was so tranquil. It was founded, of course, upon her immovable self-esteem—a very usual foundation for tranquillity! No doubt Lanse had required forgiveness, and even a great deal of forgiveness; there had, indeed, been no period of Lanse's life when he had not made large demands on this quality from those who were nearest him. But was it not a wife's part to forgive? Lanse could have been led by his affections, probably, his better side; it had always been so with Lanse. But instead of trying to influence him in that way, this wife had set herself up in opposition to him—the very last thing he would stand. She had probably been narrow from the beginning, narrow and punctilious. Later she had been shocked; then had hardened in it. She was evidently a cold woman; in addition, she was self-righteous, self-complacent; such women were always perfectly satisfied with themselves, they had excellent reasons for everything. Of course she had never loved her husband; if she had loved him she could not have left him so easily, within a few months—less than a year—after their marriage. And though seven years had now passed since that separation, she had never once, so far as Winthrop knew, sought to return to him, or asked him to return to her.

The marriage of Lansing Harold and Margaret Cruger had taken place while Winthrop was abroad. When he came home soon afterwards, at the breaking out of the war, he found that the young wife of nineteen had left her husband, had returned to live with Mrs. Rutherford, with whom she had lived for a short time before her marriage. She had come to Mrs. Rutherford upon the death of her grandmother, Mrs. Cruger; this aunt by marriage was now her nearest relative, and this aunt's house was to be her home. To this home she had now returned, and here it was that Evert first made her acquaintance. Lanse, meanwhile, had gone to Italy.

There had been no legal separation, Mrs. Rutherford told him; probably there never would be one, for Margaret did not approve of them. Lanse, too, would probably disapprove; they were well matched in their disapprovals! It was not known by society at large, Mrs. Rutherford continued, that there had been any irrevocable disagreement between the two; society at large probably supposed it to be one of those cases, so common nowadays, where husband and wife, being both fond of travelling, have discovered that they enjoy their travels more when separated than when together, as (unless there happens to be a really princely fortune) individual tastes are so apt to be sacrificed in travelling, on one side or the other. Take the one item of trains, Mrs. Rutherford went on; some persons liked to get over the ground by night, and were bored to death by a long journey by day; others became so exhausted by one night of travel that the whole of the next day was spent recovering from it. Then there were people who preferred to reach the station at the last minute, people who liked to run and rush; and others whose day was completely spoiled by any such frantic haste at the beginning. The most amiable of men sometimes developed a curious obstinacy, when travelling, concerning the small matter of which seat in a railway-carriage the wife should take. Yes, on the whole, Mrs. Rutherford thought it natural that husbands and wives, if possessed of strong wills, should travel separately; the small differences, which made the trouble, did not come up in the regular life at home. It was very common for American wives to be in Europe without their husbands; in the case of the Harolds, it was simply that the husband had gone; this at least was probably what society supposed.

Mrs. Rutherford further added that her listener, Winthrop, was not to suppose that Margaret herself had ever discussed these subjects with her, or had ever discussed Lanse; his name was never mentioned by his wife, and when she, the aunt, mentioned it, her words were received in silence; there was no reply.

"I consider," continued Mrs. Rutherford, warming with her subject—"I consider Margaret's complete silence the most extraordinary thing I have ever known in my life. Living with me as she has done all these years, shouldn't you suppose, wouldn't any one suppose, that at some time or other she would have talked it over with me, given me some explanation, no matter how one-sided—would have tried to justify herself? Very well, then, she *never* has. From first to last, in answer to my inquiries (for of course I have made them), she has only said that she would rather not talk about it, that the subject was painful to her. Painful! I wonder what she thinks it is to me! She makes me perfectly miserable, Evert—perfectly miserable."

"Yet you keep her with you," answered Winthrop, not taking Mrs. Harold's side exactly, but the side of justice, perhaps; for he had seen how much his aunt's comfort depended upon Margaret's attention, though he was not prepared to admit that it depended upon that entirely, as Garda Thorne had declared.

"Yes," responded Mrs. Rutherford, "I keep her with me, as you say. But my house was really her home, you know, before her marriage, and of course it is quite the best place for her now, as things are; if she will not remain with her husband, at least her continuing to live always with her husband's aunt, his almost mother, is the next best thing that could be arranged for her. Appearances are preserved, you know; and Margaret has a great regard for appearances."

"Possibly too great," Winthrop answered. But his sarcasm was not intended to apply to the wife's regard for appearances—he also had a regard for appearances—it was intended to apply to the wife herself. His idea of her was that she had argued it all out carefully in her own mind (she was not a person who acted on impulse), and had taken her stand upon what she considered irrefragable grounds. In other words, she had sat apart and judged her husband. Instead of trying to win him or to keep him, she had made little rules for him probably, and no doubt very good little rules of their kind; but Lanse had of course broken them, he wasn't a man for rules; a man of his age, too, would hardly keep the rules made by a girl of nineteen. After repeated breakage of all her well-regulated little canons, she had withdrawn herself, and kept aloof; she had held herself superior to him, and had let him see that she did. Winthrop could imagine the effect of all this upon Lanse!

But no matter what Lanse had done that annoyed her (and it was highly probable that he had done a good deal), her duty as a wife, in Winthrop's opinion, clearly was, and would to the end of time continue, to remain with her husband—not to leave him, unless her life or the welfare of her children should be in actual danger; that was what marriage meant. The welfare of children included a great deal, of course; he held that a wife was justified in separating them from a father whose influence was injurious. But in this case there had been no questions of the sort, Lanse was not violent, and there were no children to think of. There was, indeed, nothing very wrong about Lanse save that he was self-willed, and did quite as he pleased on all occasions. But what he did was, after all, nothing very terrible; he was willing that other people should do as they pleased, also; he was not a petty tyrant. But this state of things had not satisfied his wife, who wished other people, her husband first of all, to do as *she* pleased. Why? Because she was always sure that she was right! This slender, graceful woman with the dark blue eyes and clear low voice had a will as strong as her husband's. She had found, probably, that her tranquillity and what she called her dignity—both inexpressibly dear to her—were constantly endangered by this unmanageable husband, who paid not the slightest heed to her axioms as to what was "right" and "not right," what was "usual" (Lanse was never usual) and "not usual," but strode through and over them all as though they did not exist. His course, indeed, made it impossible for her to preserve unbroken that serenity of temper which was her highest aspiration; for she was exactly the woman to have an ideal of that sort, and to endeavor to live up to it; it was not improbable that she offered her prayers to that effect every night.

All this was a very harsh estimate. But Winthrop's beliefs on these subjects were rooted in the deepest convictions he possessed. Such a character as the one he attributed to Margaret Harold was to him insufferable; he could endure easily a narrow mind, if with it there was a warm heart and unselfish disposition, but a narrow mind combined with a cold, unmoved nature and impregnable self-conceit—this seemed to him a combination that made a woman (it was always a woman) simply odious.

These things all passed through his thoughts again as he rode over the barrens. He recalled Lanse's handsome face as he used to see it in childhood. Lanse was five years older than the little Evert, tall, strong, full of life, a hero to the lad from New England, who was brave enough in his way but who had not been encouraged in boldness, nor praised when he had been lawless and daring. Mrs. Rutherford had a phrase about Lanse—that he was "just like all the Harolds." The Harolds, in truth, were a handsome race; they all resembled each other, though some of them were not so handsome as the rest. A good many of them had married their cousins. They were tall and broad-shouldered, well made, but inclined to portliness towards middle-age; they had good features, the kind of very well-cut outline, with short upper lip and full lower one, whose fault, if it has a fault, is a tendency to blankness of expression after youth is past. Their hair was very dark, almost black, and they had thick brown beards of rather a lighter hue—beards which they kept short; their eyes were beautiful, dark brown in hue, animated, with yellow lights in them; their complexions had a rich darkness, with strong ivory tints beneath. They had an appearance of looking over the heads of everybody else, which, among many noticeable things about them, was the most noticeable—it was so entirely natural. Because it was so natural nobody had tried to analyze it, to find out of what it consisted. The Harolds were tall; but it was not their height. They were broad-shouldered; but there were men of the same mould everywhere. It was not that they expanded their chests and threw their heads back, so that their eyes, when cast down, rested upon a projecting expanse of shirt front, with the watch-chain far in advance; the Harolds had no such airs of inflated frog. They stood straight on their feet, but nothing more; their well-moulded chins were rather drawn in than thrust out; they never posed; there was never any trace of attitude. Yet, in any large assemblage, if there were any of them present, they were sure to have this appearance of looking over other people's heads. It was accompanied by a careless, good-humored, unpretending ease, which was almost benevolent, and which was strikingly different from the self-assertive importance of more nervous (and smaller) men.

As a family the Harolds had not been loved; they were too self-willed for that. But they were witty, they could be agreeable; in houses where it pleased them to be witty and agreeable, they were the most welcome of guests. The small things of life, what they called the "details," the tiresome little cares and responsibilities, annoyances, engagements, and complications, these they shed from themselves as a shaggy dog sheds water from his coat—they shook them off. People who did not love them (and these were many) remarked that this was all very pretty, but that it was also very selfish. The Harolds, if their attention had been called to it, would have considered the adjective as another of the "details," and would have shaken that off also.

Mrs. Rutherford in her youth never could help admiring the Harolds (there were a good many of them, almost all men; there was but seldom a daughter); when, therefore, her sister Hilda married Lansing of the name, she had an odd sort of pride in it, although everybody said that Hilda would not be happy; the Harolds seldom made good husbands. It was not that they were harassing or brutal; they were simply supremely inattentive. In this case, however, there had been little opportunity to verify or prove false the expectation, as both Lansing Harold and his wife had died within two years after their marriage, the wife last, leaving (as her sister, Mrs. Winthrop, did later) a son but a few days old. The small Lansing was adopted by his aunt. Through childhood he was a noble-looking little fellow, never governed or taught to govern himself; he grew rapidly into a large, manly lad, active and strong, fond of out-of-door sports and excelling in them, having the quick wit of his family, which, however (like them), he was not inclined to bestow upon all comers for their entertainment; he preferred to keep it for his own.

Evert remembered with a smile the immense admiration he had felt for his big cousin, the excited anticipation with which he had looked forward to meeting him when he went, twice a year, to see his aunt. The splendid physical strength of the elder boy, his liberty, his dogs and his gun, his horse and boat—all these filled the sparingly indulged little New England child with the greatest wonder and delight. Most of all did he admire the calm absolutism of Lanse's will, combined as it was with good-nature, manliness, and even to a certain degree, or rather in a certain way, with generosity—generosity as he had thought it then, careless liberality as he knew it now. When Evert was ten and Lanse fifteen, Lanse had decided that his cousin must learn to shoot, that he was quite old enough for that accomplishment. Evert recalled the mixture of fear and pride which had filled his small heart to suffocation when Lanse put the gun into his hands in the remote field behind Mrs. Rutherford's country-house which he had selected for the important lesson. His fear was not occasioned so much by the gun as by the keen realization that if his father should question him, upon his return home, he should certainly feel himself obliged to tell of his new knowledge, and the revelation might put an end to these happy visits. Fortunately his father did not question him; he seldom spoke to the boy of anything that had happened during these absences, which he seemed to consider necessary evils—so much waste time. On this occasion how kind Lanse had been, how he had encouraged and helped him—yes, and scolded him a little too; and how he had comforted him when the force of the discharge had knocked the little sportsman over on the ground rather heavily. A strong affection for Lanse had grown up with the younger boy; and it remained with him still, though now not so blind a liking; he knew Lanse better. They had been widely separated, and for a long time; they had led such different lives! Evert had worked steadily for ten long, secluded years; later he had worked still harder, but in another way, being now his own master, and engaged in guiding the enterprises he had undertaken through many obstacles and hazards towards success. These years of unbroken toil for Evert had been spent by Lanse in his own amusement, though one could not say spent in idleness exactly, as he was one of the most active of men. He had been much of the time in Europe. But he came home for brief visits now and then, when his aunt besought him; she adored him—she had always adored him; she was never tired of admiring his proportions, what seemed to her his good-nature, his Harold wit, his poise of head; she was never so happy as when she had him staying with her in her own house. True, he had his own way of living; but it was such a simple way! He was not in the least a gourmand—none of the Harolds were that; he liked only the simplest dishes, and always demanded them; he wanted the windows open at all seasons when the snow was not actually on the ground; he could not endure questioning, in fact, he never answered questions at all.

Returning for one of these visits at home, Lanse had found with his aunt a young girl, Margaret Cruger, a niece of her husband's. Evert smiled now as he recalled certain expressions of the letter which his aunt had written to him, the other nephew, announcing Lanse's engagement to Miss

Cruger; in the light of retrospect they had rather a sarcastic sound. Mrs. Rutherford had written that Margaret was very young, to be sure—not quite eighteen—but that she was very gentle and sweet. That it was time Lanse should marry, he was thirty-two—though in her opinion that was exactly the right age, for a man knew then what he really wanted, and was not apt to make a mistake. That she hoped the girl would make him the sort of wife he needed; for one thing, she was so young that she would not set up her opinion in opposition to his, probably, and with Lanse that would be important. Mrs. Rutherford furthermore thought that the girl in a certain way understood him; she (Mrs. Rutherford) had had the greatest fear of Lanse's falling into the hands of some woman who wouldn't have the sense to appreciate him, some woman who would try to change him; one of those dreadful Pharisaic women, for instance, who are always trying to "improve" their husbands. There was nothing easier than to get on with Lanse, and even to lead him a little, as she herself (Mrs. Rutherford) had always done; one had only to take him on the right side—his good warm heart. Margaret was almost too simple, too yielding; but Lanse had wit and will enough for two. There was another reason why this marriage would be a good thing for Lanse: he had run through almost all his money (he had never had a very great deal, as Evert would remember), and Margaret had a handsome fortune, which would come in now very well. She was rather pretty—Margaret—in a delicate sort of way. Mrs. Rutherford *hoped* she appreciated her good-luck; if she didn't now, she would soon, when she had seen a little more of the world. And here one of his aunt's sentences came, word for word, into Winthrop's memory: "But it's curious, isn't it, Evert? that such an inexperienced child as she is, a girl brought up in such complete seclusion, should begin life by marrying Lansing Harold! For you know as well as I do how he has been sought after, what his career has been." This was true. Allowance, of course, had to be made for Mrs. Rutherford's partiality; still, Evert knew that even with allowance there was enough to verify her words, at least in part. Lansing Harold had never been in the least what is called popular; he was not a man who was liked by many persons, he took pains not to be; he preferred to please only a few. Whether or not there had been women among those he had tried to please, it was at least well known that women had tried to please him. More than one had followed him about, with due regard, of course, for the proprieties (it is not necessary to include those—who also existed—who had violated them), finding themselves, for instance, in Venice, when he happened to be there, or choosing his times for visiting Rome. Now Lanse had had a way of declaring that June was the best month for Rome; it had been interesting to observe, for a long period, that each year there was some new person who had made the same discovery.

"We were home long before you," said Mrs. Rutherford, when Winthrop, having brought his reflections to a close, and enjoyed another gallop, returned to the eyrie. "Mrs. Thorne has been here," she added; "she came up from East Angels after Garda, and took the opportunity—she generally *does* take the opportunity, I notice—to pay me a visit. She never stopped talking, with that precise pronunciation, you know, one single minute, and I believe that's what makes her so tired all the time; I know *I* should be tired if I had to hiss all my s's as she does! She had ever so many things to say; one was that when her life was sad and painful she was able to rise out of her body—out of the flesh, she called it (there isn't much to rise from), and float, unclothed, far above in the air, in the realm of pure thought, I think she said. And when I asked her if it wasn't rather unpleasant—for I assure you it struck me so—she wasn't at all pleased, not at all. She's such an observer of nature,—I suppose that's because she has always lived where there was nothing but nature to observe; well, I do believe she had seen an allegorical meaning in every single tree on the shore as she came up the river!"

"I rather think she saw her meanings more than her trees," said Winthrop; "I venture to say she couldn't have told you whether they were cypresses or myrtles, palmettoes or gums; such people never can. Tired? Of course she's tired; her imagination travels miles a minute, her poor little body can't begin to keep up with it."

"So foolish," commented Mrs. Rutherford, tranquilly—Mrs. Rutherford, who had never imagined anything in her life. "And do you know she admires Margaret beyond words—if she's ever beyond them! Isn't it odd? She says Margaret *answers* one so delightfully. And when I remarked, 'Why, we think Margaret rather silent,' she said, 'That is what I mean, it is her silence that is so sympathetic; she answers you with it far more effectually than most persons do with their talkativeness.'"

"I'm afraid you talked, Aunt Katrina," said Winthrop, laughing.

"I never do," replied Mrs. Rutherford, with dignity. "And she told me, also," she went on, resuming her gossip in her calm, handsomely dressed tone (for even Mrs. Rutherford's tone seemed clothed in rich attire), "that that young Torres had asked her permission to 'address' Garda, as she expressed it."

"To address Garda? Confound his impudence! what does he mean?" said Winthrop, in a disgusted voice. "Garda's a child."

"Oh, well," replied Mrs. Rutherford, "she's half Spanish, and that makes a difference; they're older. But I don't think the mother favors the Cuban's suit, she prefers something 'more Saxon,' she said so. And, by-the-way, she asked me if you were not 'more recently English' than the rest of us. What do you suppose she could have meant?—I never quite know what she is driving at."

Winthrop burst into a laugh. "More recently English! Poor little woman, with her small New England throat, she has swallowed the British Isles! You don't think the Cuban has a chance, then?"

"Oh, I don't know," replied Mrs. Rutherford, comfortably; "it doesn't concern us, does it? It will depend upon what Garda thinks, and Garda will think what she pleases; she isn't a girl to be guided."

"She hasn't been difficult to guide so far, I fancy," said Winthrop, after a moment's silence.

"She will be, then," responded his aunt, nodding her head with an assured air. "You'll see."

CHAPTER IX

"I am not partial to it myself," said the Rev. Mr. Moore—"this confection of oranges called marmalade. I am told, however, that the English are accustomed to make their breakfast principally of similar saccharine preparations; in time, therefore, we may hope to establish an export trade."

A fresh breeze astern was blowing the *Emperadora* down the lagoon in a course straight enough to please even Mrs. Carew, if that lady could have been pleased by anything aquatic. She was present, in spite of fears, sitting with the soles of her prunella gaiters pressed tightly against the little yacht's side under the seat (the peculiarity of the attitude being concealed by her long skirt), with the intention, probably, of acting as a species of brake upon too great a speed.

The position was a difficult one. But she kept her balance by means of her umbrella, firmly inserted in a crack of the planking before her, and did not swerve.

The broad sails were set wing and wing; the morning was divinely fair. Down in the south the tall trees looming against the sky seemed like a line of hills; owing to the lowness of the shores, on a level with the water, and the smoothness of the sea stretching eastward beyond Patricio, the comparative effect was the same. Above, the soft sky bending down all round them, touching here the even land and there the even water, conveyed nothing of that sense of vastness, of impersonality, which belongs so often to the American sky further north. This seemed a particular sky belonging to this especial neighborhood, made for it, intimate with it; and the yacht, with those on board did not appear like a floating atom, lost in immensity; on the contrary, it was important, interesting; one could not rid one's self of the idea that its little voyage was watched with friendly curiosity by this bending personal sky, and these near low shores.

The Rev. Mr. Moore had been sent upon this pleasure-party by his wife. Mrs. Penelope Moore was sure that a pleasure-party would do him good; the Reverend Middleton therefore endeavored to think the same, though it was not exactly his idea of pleasure. He was not fond of sailing; there was generally a breeze, and a breeze he did not enjoy. There was, indeed, something in his appearance, when exposed to a fresh wind, which suggested the idea that a portion of it was blowing through him, finding an exit at his shoulder-blades behind; his lank vest somehow had that air; and the sensation (so the spectator thought) could hardly have been an agreeable one to so thin a man, even on the warmest day.

Mrs. Penelope Moore was a brave woman. And she knew that she was brave. Not being able, on account of her delicate health, to take part personally in the social entertainments of Gracias, she sent her husband in her place. And this was her bravery; for he was without doubt the most agreeable as well as the handsomest of men, and anybody with sense could foretell what must follow: given certain conditions, and the results all the world over were the same. Other people might say that quiet little Gracias was safe, Mrs. Penelope Moore knew better. Other people, again, might be blind; but Mrs. Penelope Moore was never blind. She knew that such a man as her Middleton passed, must pass, daily through temptations of the most incandescent nature, all the more dangerous because merged inextricably with his priest's office; but he passed unscathed, he came out always, as she once wrote triumphantly to her mother, "without so much as a singe upon the hem of his uttermost garment." And if, on the other hand, it might have seemed that so little (blessedly) that was inflammable had been included in this good man's composition that he might have passed safely through any amount of incandescence, even all that his wife imagined, here again, then, others were most decidedly mistaken; Mrs. Moore was convinced that her Middleton was of the fieriest temperament. Only he kept it down.

Gracias-á-Dios was certainly quiet enough. But Mistress Penelope, like many good women before her, could believe with ease in a degree of depravity which would have startled the most hardened of actual participants. Having no standards by which to gauge evil, no personal experience of its nature, she was quite at sea about it. As Dr. Kirby once said of her (when vexed by some of her small rulings), "If people don't come to Friday morning service, sir, she thinks it but a small step further that they should have poisoned their fathers and beaten their wives."

On the present occasion this lady set her husband's hat straight upon his amiable forehead, and gave him his butterfly net; then from her Gothic windows (the rectory of St. Philip and St. James' was of the same uncertain Gothic as the church), she watched him down the path and through the gate, across the plaza out of sight, going back to her sofa with the secure thought in her heart, "I can trust him—*anywhere*!"

The party on the yacht was composed of the same persons who had taken part in most of the entertainments given for the northern ladies, save that Manuel and Torres were absent. Torres had not been allowed to "address" Garda, after all, Mrs. Thorne having withheld her permission. The young Cuban was far too punctilious an observer of etiquette to advance further without that permission; he had therefore left society's circle, and secluded himself at home, where, according to Manuel, he was engaged in "consuming his soul."

"His cigars," Winthrop suggested.

Whereupon Manuel, who was not fond of the northerner, warmly took up the cause of the absent Adolfo (though ordinarily he declared himself tired to death of him), and with his superbest air remarked, "It is possible that Mr. Wintup does not understand us."

"Quite possible," Winthrop answered.

Mrs. Thorne had consulted him about the request of Torres. Not formally, not (at least it did not appear so) premeditatedly; she alluded to it one afternoon when he had found her alone at East Angels. Winthrop was very severe upon what he called the young Cuban's "presumption."

"Presumption—yes; that is what I have been inclined to consider it," said Mrs. Thorne, with her little preliminary cough. But she spoke hesitatingly, or rather there seemed to be hesitation in her mind behind her words, for her words themselves were carefully clear.

Winthrop looked at her, and saw, or fancied he saw, a throng of conflicting possibilities, contingencies, and alternatives in the back part of her small bright eyes. "Your daughter is too young to be made the subject of any such request at present," he said, curtly. For it seemed to him a moment when a little masculine brevity and masculine decision were needed in this exclusively feminine atmosphere.

Mrs. Thorne accepted his suggestion. "Yes, Garda *is* young," she murmured, emerging a little from her hesitations. "Quite too young," she repeated, more emphatically. Winthrop had given her a formula, and formulas are sometimes as valuable as a life-raft.

Torres, therefore, being engaged in the consumption of his soul, and Manuel having haughtily declined the northerner's invitation, the party on the yacht consisted, besides Winthrop, of Mrs. Rutherford and Margaret Harold, Mrs. Carew, Garda, Dr. Kirby, and the Rev. Mr. Moore, Mrs. Thorne having been detained at home by the "pressing domestic engagements" which Winthrop had been certain would lift their heads as soon as the day for the *Emperadora's* little voyage had been decided upon. Wind and tide were both in their favor; they had a swift run down the Espiritu, and landed on Patricio a number of miles below Gracias, where there was a path which led across to the ocean beach. This path was narrow, and the gallant Dr. Kirby walked in the bushes all the way, suffering the twigs to flagellate his plump person, in order to hold a white umbrella over Mrs. Rutherford, who, arm in arm with her Betty, took up the entire track. Patricio, which had first been a reef, and then an outlying island, was now a long peninsula, joining the main land some forty miles below Gracias in an isthmus of sand; it came northward in a waving line, slender and green, lying like a ribbon in the water, the Espiritu on one side, the ocean on the other. When the ocean beach of the ribbon was reached, Mrs. Rutherford admired the view; she admired it so much that she thought she would sit down and admire it more. Dr. Kirby therefore bestirred himself in arranging the cushions and rugs which Winthrop's men had brought across from the yacht, to form an out-of-door sofa for the ladies; for Betty, of course, decided to remain with Katrina. The Doctor said that he should himself bear them company, leaving the "younger men" to "fume and fluster and explore."

The Rev. Mr. Moore was, in actual years, not far from Dr. Reginald's own age. But the Rev. Mr. Moore was perennially young; slender and light, juvenile in figure, especially when seen from behind, his appearance was not that of an elderly man so much as of a young man in whom the progress of age has been in some way arrested, like the young peaches, withered and wrinkled and yet with the bloom of youth about them still, which have dropped to the ground before their prime. He now stood waiting on the beach, armed with his butterfly net; as his butterfly net was attached to a long green pole, one end of which rested on the ground, he had the air of a sort of marine shepherd with a crook.

The Rev. Mr. Moore always carried this entomological apparatus with him when he went upon pleasure excursions; his wife encouraged him in the amusement, she said it was a distraction for his mind; the butterflies also found it a distraction, they were in the habit of laughing (so some persons declared) all down the coast whenever the parson and his net appeared in sight.

"You are going to explore, aren't you?" said Garda to Margaret Harold; "it's lovely, and we shall not fume or fluster in the least, in spite of the Doctor; we shall only pick up shells. Over these shells we shall exclaim; Mr. Winthrop will find charming ones, and present them to us, and then we shall exclaim more; we shall dote upon the ones he gives us, we shall hoard them away carefully in our handkerchiefs and pockets; and then, to-morrow morning, when the sun comes up, he will shine upon two dear little heaps of them outside our bedroom windows, where, of course, we shall have thrown them as soon as we reached home."

Mr. Moore listened to these remarks with surprise. Upon the various occasions when he had visited Patricio he had always, and with great interest, picked up shells for the ladies present, knowing how much they would value them. He now meditated a little upon the back windows alluded to by Garda; it was a new idea.

"Oh, how *delightful* it is to go marooning!" said Mrs. Carew, who, beginning to recover from the terrors of the voyage, had found her voice again. Her feet were still somewhat cramped from their use as brakes; she furtively extended them for a moment, and then, unable to resist the comfort of the position, left them extended. Her boots were the old-fashioned thin-soled all-cloth gaiters without heels, laced at the side, dear to the comfort-loving ladies of that day; her ankles came down into their loose interiors without any diminishing curves, as in the case of the elephant.

"Are you going, Margaret?" said Mrs. Rutherford, in her amiably patronizing voice. "Don't you think you will find it rather warm?" Mrs. Rutherford inhabited the serene country of non-effort, she could therefore maintain without trouble the satisfactory position of criticising the actions of others; for whether they succeeded or whether they failed, success or failure equally indicated an attempt, and anything like attempt she was above. "People who *try*" was one of her phrases; she would not have cared to discover America, for undoubtedly Columbus had tried.

"I like this Florida warmth," Margaret had answered. "It's not heat; it's only softness."

"It's lax, I think," suggested Mrs. Rutherford, still amiably.

No one disputed this point. It was lax.

"Doesn't he look like a tree?" murmured Garda to Margaret, indicating by a glance the Rev. Mr. Moore, as he stood at a little distance, gazing at the sea—"a tall slim one, you know, that hasn't many leaves; his arms are like the branches, and his fingers like the twigs; and his voice is so innocent and—and vegetable."

Margaret shook her head.

"You don't like it?" said the girl; "you think I am disrespectful? I am not disrespectful at all, I adore Mr. Moore. But you must acknowledge that he's a mild herby sort of man; he's like lettuce—before it's dressed. All the same, you know, he's an angel."

Dr. Kirby meanwhile was entertaining Betty and Katrina, now seated together on the out-of-door sofa he had made. He was arranging at the same time a seat for himself near them by piling together with careful adjustment the scattered fragments of drift-wood which he had found in the vicinity, in a sort of cairn; his intention was to crown this cairn, when finished, with one of the boat cushions, which he had reserved for the purpose. "No," he said, pursuing his theme and the dovetailing of the drift-wood with energy, "I cannot say that I admire these frivolous new fashions which have crept into literature. The other day, happening to turn over the pages of one of these modern novels, I came upon a scene in which the hero and heroine are supposed to be shaken, tortured by the violence of their emotions, stirred to their utmost depths; and yet the author takes *that* opportunity to leave them there, leave them in the midst of their agonies—and the reader's as well—to remark that a butterfly flew in through the open window and hovered for a moment over their heads; now he poised here, now he poised there, now he did this, and now that, and so on through a quarter of a page. I ask you—what if he did?" (Here he finished his cairn, and sat down to try it.) "Who cares? Why should the whole action of the tale pause, and at such a critical moment, in order that the flight and movements of an insignificant insect should be minutely chronicled?"

"But the butterfly," said the Rev. Mr. Moore, who had drawn near, "can hardly, I think, be described as an 'insignificant insect.'"

"Have you read these modern novels?" demanded the Doctor, facing him from his cairn.

"Certainly," replied Mr. Moore; "I am familiar with 'Bracebridge Hall,' 'Swallow Barn,' and several other works of fiction of that type." And he stood there looking at the Doctor with the peculiar mild obstinacy which belongs to light-blue eyes, whose under-lids come up high at the outer corners.

"But, Doctor, you are attacking there one of our most cherished modern novelties," said Winthrop, who had now joined them, "namely, the new copartnership between Nature and Literature. Nature is now a very literary personage and a butterfly can mean a great deal."

"Nature has nothing to do with literature, I mean the literature we call polite," Dr. Kirby protested, still fierily (while Mrs. Rutherford admired his ardor). But the clergyman had nodded his head in approval, a butterfly could certainly mean a great deal; he himself had long been of the opinion that they possessed reasoning powers—he had so seldom been able to capture one.

The explorers now left the sofa and cairn, and started down the beach, Garda and Winthrop first, Mr. Moore and Margaret following. It seemed natural to everybody that Winthrop should be with Garda, he had been with her so much; his manner, however, had in it so little of admiration (as admiration was understood in Gracias) that this had occasioned no remark. Manuel (whose admiration had the local hues) cherished resentment against this northerner, but it was not the resentment of jealousy; Manuel, indeed, did not dream that he had occasion for jealousy. He was sure that Mrs. Thorne yearned for him, that her highest aspirations regarding a son-in-law could go no further; but there need be no haste, he must see something of the world first. He had made a beginning (so he flattered himself) by seeing something of it in that charming though rather silent Mrs. Harold. As for Torres, that dark youth could never have conceived the possibility of admitting any one to a serious rivalry with himself—any one, at least, outside of Spain. Who was this Wintup? Only an American; even Manuel was but an American-Spaniard, as any one could see. But Garda was all Duero, Spanish to the finger-tips; Garda understood him. And this in itself was no small matter—to understand a Torres; many persons, even when thrown with them daily, had lived all their lives without accomplishing that. Garda understood herself also; she might delay, have little freaks; but in the end it was impossible that she should be content with anything less than a Torres, if there were one in attendance upon her graceful steps,—as there certainly would be.

For a time the four pedestrians kept together. "See the pelicans on the bar," said Garda. "The wish of my life has been to go out there and chase them with a stick."

"Why should you wish to do that, my child?" said the clergyman. "Surely there are many occupations more interesting, as well as more instructive."

"Shouldn't you love to be a curlew?" said the girl, going to him and putting her arm in his. "The sickle-bill, you know; he hasn't the least realization of the faults of his profile, and that must be such a comfort."

"Profiles," responded Mr. Moore, with a little wave of his hand, "are quite unimportant; what is a profile, in most cases, but the chance outline of a nose? Handsome is as handsome does, Garda; that is the best view to take."

Winthrop listened to this little dialogue with entertainment, evidently the good rector had no more realization of Garda's beauty than he had of the new short length for sermons; his standard in profiles was probably the long thin nose and small straight mouth of his excellent Penelope.

"The Bermudoes lie off in that direction," continued the clergyman, looking over the blue water. Garda had now left him and gone back to Winthrop. "I mean the Barbagoes," he added, correcting himself. He was silent for a moment. "No, no, not Barbagoes; I am thinking, of course, of the Bahamoes." Again he paused, his face began to wear a bewildered expression; slackening his pace a little, he repeated over to himself softly, as if trying them, "Bahamoes—Bergudas; then there is Tor—no, *Tobaga,* isn't it? Certainly I cannot be wrong in thinking one of the groups to be the Dry Tortugoes?" And yet it did not seem quite certain, after all.

"A butterfly, a splendid one," called Garda.

And then the reverend gentleman, forgetting the tangled islands, brandished his net and leaped forward in pursuit.

Garda was now with Margaret; Winthrop walked on beside them, and they went southward at a leisurely pace, down the broad beach. To the ordinary observer Winthrop and Margaret appeared to be on the usual friendly terms; the only lack which could have been detected was the absence between them of little discussions, and references to past discussions, brief allusions where one word is made to do the work of twenty, which are natural when people have formed part of the same family for some time. Margaret and Winthrop talked to each other, and talked familiarly; but this was always when other persons were present. Garda, though she seldom troubled herself to observe closely, had remarked these little signs. "I think you are horrid to Margaret," she had once said to Winthrop with warmth. "And Margaret is far too good and too gentle to you."

"Yes, Mrs. Harold has always a very gentle manner," he had answered, assentingly.

"That is more horrid still! Of course she has. But I wish she hadn't—at least with you; I wish she would be sharp with you—as I am."

"Are you sharp?" Winthrop had asked, smiling indulgently at the contrast between her allegation and the voice in which it was uttered.

Garda, with her hand on Margaret's arm, was now walking onward, humming lightly to herself as she walked. Her humming was vague, as she had no ear for music. It was a complete lack, however; she was not one of those persons who are haunted by tunes half caught, who afflictingly sing a song all through a semi-note flat, and never know it.

Margaret's eyes were following the sands. "What lovely sea-weeds," she said, as little-branching fibres, like crimson frost-work, began to dot the silver here and there.

"Now how feminine that is!" said Winthrop, argumentatively, as he strolled on beside them. "Instead of looking at the ocean, or this grand beach as a whole, what does Mrs. Harold do? She spends her time admiring an infinitesimal pink fragment at her feet. Fragments!—I am tired of the fragmentary taste. In a picture, even the greatest, you fragmentary people are always admiring what you call the side touches; you talk about some little thing that has been put in merely as a decorative feature, or if for a wonder you do select a figure, it is sure to be one of minor importance; the effect of the whole as a whole, the central idea to which the artist has given his best genius and power, this you don't care for, hardly see. It is the same way with a book; it is always some fragment of outside talk or description, some subordinate character, to which you give your praise; never—no matter how fine it is—the leading motive and its development. In an old cathedral, too, you women go putting your pretty noses close to all the little things, the bits of old carving, an old inscription—in short, the details; the effect of the grand mass of the whole, rising against the sky, this you know nothing whatever about."

"I am glad at least that the noses are pretty," interpolated Garda, amid her humming.

"I think I have met a few men also who admire details," observed Margaret.

"A few? Plenty of them. They are the men of the feminine turn of mind. But don't imagine that I don't care for details; details in their proper place may be admirable, exquisite. What I am objecting to is their being pushed into a place which is not theirs by you fragmentary people, who simply shirk (I don't know whether it is from indolence or want of mental grasp) any consideration of a whole."

"Never mind," said Garda to Margaret; "let's be fragmentary. We'll even pick up the sea-weeds if you like (though generally I hate to pick up things); we'll fill your basket, and make Mr. Winthrop carry it."

"No," said Margaret. "On the contrary, let us abhor the sea-weeds; let us give ourselves to the consideration of a whole." And, pausing, she looked over the sea, then up at the sky and down the beach, with a slow musing sweep of the head which became her well.

"You're not enough in earnest," said Garda; "we can see the edge of a smile at the corners of your lips. Wait—I'll do it better." She stepped apart from them, clasped her hands, and turned her eyes towards the sea, where they rested with a soft, absorbed earnestness that was remarkable. "Is this wide enough?" she asked, without change of expression. "Is it free from details—unfragmentary? In short, is it—a Whole?"

"Yes," said Winthrop; "far too much of one! You are as universal as a Universal Geography. Come back to us—in as many details and fragments as you please; only come back."

"By no means; I have still the beach to do, and the sky." And slowly she turned the same wide, absorbed gaze from the sea to the white shore.

The beach was worth looking at; broad, smooth, gleaming, it stretched southward as far as eye could follow it; even there it did not end, it became a silver haze which mixed softly with the sea. On the land side it was bounded by the sand-cliff which formed the edge of Patricio; this little cliff, though but twelve or fourteen feet in height, was perpendicular; it cut off, therefore, the view of the flat ground above as completely as though it had been five hundred. Great pink-mouthed shells dotted the beach's white floor; at its edge myriads of minute disks of rose and pearl lay heaped amid little stones, smooth and white, all of them wet and glistening. Heaps of bleached drift-wood lay where high tides had left them. Little beach-birds ran along at the water's edge with their peculiar gait—many pauses, intermixed with half a dozen light fleet steps as though running away—the gait, if ever there was one, of invitation to pursue. There were no ships on the sea; the tracks of vessels bound for Cuba, the Windward and Leeward islands, lay out of sight from this low strand. And gentle as the water was, and soft the air, the silence and the absence of all signs of human life made it a very wild scene; wild but not savage, the soft wildness of an uninhabited southern shore. For no one lived on Patricio, save where, opposite East Angels, the old Ruiz house stood on its lapsed land—lapsed from the better tilling of the century before.

The Rev. Mr. Moore had come gambolling back, striking actively hither and thither with his net, still pursuing the same butterfly. The butterfly—at his leisure—flew inland; and then Mr. Moore gave up the chase, and joined Mrs. Harold calmly, seeming not in the least out of breath, his face, indeed, so serious that she received the impression that while his legs might have been gambolling, his thoughts had perhaps been employed with his next Sunday's sermon; he had had an introspective, mildly controversial air as he leaped.

Garcia and Winthrop walked on in advance. The beach waved in and out in long scallops, and when they had entered the second they found themselves alone, the point behind intervening between them and their companions.

"What a dreadfully lonely place this beach is, after all!" said Garda, pausing and looking southward with a half-appreciative, half-disturbed little shudder.

"Not lonely; primeval," answered Winthrop. "Don't you like it? I am sure you do; take time to think."

"Oh, I don't want any time. Yes, I like it in one way, in one way it's beautiful. One could be perfectly lazy here forever, and I should like that. As for the loneliness, I suppose we should not mind it after a while—so long as we could be together."

Before Winthrop could reply to this, "Suppose we race," she went on, looking at him with sudden animation. And she began to sway herself slightly to and fro as she walked, as though keeping time to music.

"I think you mean suppose we dance," he answered. She had soon deserted the mood that chimed in with his own; still, he had not misjudged her, she had it in her to comprehend the charm of an existence which should be primitive, far from the world, that simple free life towards which the thoughts of imaginative men turn sometimes with such inexpressible longing, but to whose attractions feminine minds in general are said to be closed. The men of imagination seldom carry, are seldom able to carry, their aspirations to a practical reality; that makes no difference in their appreciation of the woman who can comprehend the beauty of the dream.

Here was a girl who, under the proper influences, would be able to take up such a life and enjoy it; the vast majority of educated women, no matter what influences they should be subjected to, would never be able to do this in the least; they would long for—silk lamp-shades and rugs.

"Racing or dancing," Garda had replied, "*you* would never win a prize in either; you are far too slow."

"And you too indolent," he rejoined.

He had scarcely spoken the words when she was off. Down the beach she sped, and with such unexpected swiftness that he stood gazing instead of following; the line of her flight was as straight as that of an arrow. He was surprised; he had not thought that she would take the trouble to run, he had not thought her fond of any kind of exertion. But this did not seem like exertion, she ran as easily as a slim lad runs; her figure looked very light and slender, outlined against the beach and sky. As he still stood watching her, she reached the end of the scallop, passed round its point, and disappeared.

He looked back, there was no one in sight; if he had a mind to revive his school-boy feats, he could do so without being observed. It was a beautiful day; but running might make it warmer. At thirty-five one does not run for the pure pleasure of it, as at sixteen; if one is not an acrobat, it seems a useless waste of energy. Garda was probably waiting for him beyond the next point, even her desire to surprise him would not take her farther than that; he walked onward at a good pace, but he did not run; he reached the point, turned it, and entered the next scallop. She was not there.

It was not a very long scallop, she had crossed it, probably, while he was crossing the last; he went on and entered the next. Again she was not there. But this scallop was a mile long, she had certainly not had time to cross it; where, then, could she be? There was nothing moving on the white beach, the perpendicular sand-cliff afforded no footing; he walked on, thinking that there must be some niche which he could not see from where he stood. But though he went farther than she could possibly have gone in the time she had had, he found nothing, and retraced his steps, puzzled; the firm white sand showed no trace of her little feet, even his own heavier tread was barely visible.

Not far from the entrance of the scallop across which he was now returning, there was a pile of drift-wood higher than the other chance heaps, its base having been more solidly formed by portions of an old wreck which had been washed ashore there. Upon this foundation of water-logged timbers, branches and nondescript fragments, the flotsam and jetsam of a Southern ocean, had been flung by high tides, and had caught there one upon the other, until now the jagged summit was on a level with the top of the sand cliff, though an open space, several feet in width, lay between. Could it be that Garda had climbed up this insecure heap, and then sprung across to the firm ground of Patricio beyond? It seemed impossible; and yet, unless she had an enchanted chariot to come at her call, she must have done so, for there was no other way by which she could have escaped. Winthrop now essayed to follow her. But it was not without difficulty that he succeeded in reaching the top; for it was not so much a question of strength (of which he had an abundance) as of lightness; it was not so much a question of a good hold, as of no hold at all; the very place, he said to himself, for feminine climbing, which is generally hap-hazard clutches diversified by screams. At length, not without much fear of bringing the whole pile toppling down upon himself, he reached the summit, and from an insecure foothold looked across to the firm land. Patricio at this point was covered, at a short distance back from the edge, by a grove of wild-myrtle trees. There was no path, but the grove was not dense, Garda could have passed through it anywhere; there was no sign of her visible, but he could not see far. He sprang across, and went inland through the myrtles, his course defined in a measure by the thick chaparral which bordered the grove on each side. Suddenly he heard the sound of voices, he pushed on, and came to a little open space, thickly dotted with large bright flowers. On the farther side of this space an easel had been set up, and a young man was at work sketching; behind this young man, looking over his shoulder, stood Garda.

As Winthrop came out from the myrtles, "How long you have been!" she said. Then, "Come and see this sketch," she went on immediately, her eyes returning to the picture. "I've never seen anything so pretty in my life."

As Winthrop, after a moment's survey of the scene, came towards her over the flowers, "Oh," she said, "I forget that you don't know each other. Mr. Winthrop, Mr. Lucian Spenser, civil engineer, from Washington, the District of Columbia. Mr. Spenser, Mr. Evert Winthrop—he is nothing in particular now, I believe—from the city of New York."

"It's an occupation in itself, isn't it? to be from New York," said the artist, going on with his sketching, after the little motion, half nod, half wave of the hand, with which he had acknowledged Garda's introduction. Winthrop in the mean while had neither spoken nor bowed; he had only, as slightly as possible, raised his hat.

"Why do you stop there?" said Garda. She came to him, took his arm, and led him behind the easel. "The picture—the picture's the thing to look at!"

The sketch—it was in water-colors—represented the little arena, which was in itself a brilliant picture, done by Nature's hand. It was an open oval space about fifteen feet in diameter, entirely bare of trees or bushes, and covered with low green, through which rose lightly slender leafless stalks, each holding up, several inches above the herbage, a single large bright-faced flower; the flowers did not touch each other, they were innumerable spots of gold and bright lavender, which did not blend; on three sides the thick dark chaparral, on the fourth the dark myrtles, enclosed this gayly decked nook, and seemed to have kept it safely from all the world until now. The artist was making a very good sketch, good, that is, in the manner of the new foreign school.

"Isn't it beautiful—wonderful?" insisted Garda.

"Very clever," Winthrop answered.

The artist laughed. "You hate the manner," he said. "Many people do; I think I hate it a little myself, now and then." And he began to sing softly to himself as he worked:

"'Oh, de sun shines bright in my ole Kentucky home,
'Tis summah, de darkies are gay—'"

"'Twas his singing, you know, that attracted my attention," said Garda to Winthrop, under cover of the song. She did not seem to be explaining so much as repeating a narrative that pleased herself. "I had climbed up here to hide myself from you, when I heard singing; I followed the sound, and—here he was!"

"You have met him before, of course?" was Winthrop's reply.

"Never in the world—that is the beauty of it; it's so delightful to meet people you have never met before. And then to find him here in the woods, where I didn't expect to see anybody, save perhaps you, later, coming slowly along. And isn't it nice, too, that we shall have a new person to add to our excursions, and parties! For they were getting to be a little dull,—don't you think so? always the same people. He is a cousin of Mr. Moore's," she added, "or rather his mother was; he has just been telling me about it." She did not bring out this last fact as though it were the most important. Important?—the only important point was that she should be pleased. She had kept Winthrop's arm during this time; now she relinquished it, and turned back to the easel.

"'De corn-tops ripe, an' de meddars all abloom,
In my ole Kentucky home far away,'"

sang the stranger; and this time he let out his voice, and sang aloud. It was a very good voice. But Winthrop did not admire it.

"The others have probably no idea what has become of us," he said to Garda; "shall we go and look for them?"

"Yes," answered Garda; "of course they must be wondering. You go; I will wait here; go and bring Mr. Moore to see his cousin."

"It will be quite easy for Mr.— for this gentleman—"

"Spenser," said the artist, good-humoredly, as he painted on.

"—to see Mr. Moore at any time in Gracias," continued Winthrop, without accepting the name. For the life of him he could not put full confidence in this impromptu relationship which Garda had discovered, any more than he could in this, as one might say, impromptu man, whom she had also unearthed, miles from any inhabited point, on a wild shore. If the stranger were indeed a cousin of the Rev. Mr. Moore's, why had he not made himself known to him before this? He must have come through Gracias; Gracias was not so large a place that there could have been any difficulty in finding the rector of St. Philip and St. James'; nor was it so busy a place that one could have been pressed for time there.

"The truth is," answered Spenser, after he had completed a bit of work which seemed much to his mind—"the truth is," he repeated, looking at it critically, with his head on one side, "that I have, so far at least, rather shirked my good cousin; I am ashamed to say it, but it is true. You see, I only faintly remember him; but he will very clearly remember me, he will have reminiscences; he will be sure to tell me that he knew me when I was a dear little baby! Now I maintain that no man can really welcome that statement, it betokens recollections into which he cannot possibly enter; all he can do is to smirk inanely, and say that he fears he must have been a bad little boy."

"I know Mr. Moore will say it," said Garda, gleefully; "I know he will! Do go and call him," she said to Winthrop; "he will walk down to Jupiter Inlet if you don't stop him."

But Winthrop stood his ground; Mr. Moore's cousin or not Mr. Moore's cousin, he did not intend to leave Garda Thorne alone again with this chance, this particularly chance acquaintance. True, this was a very remote place, to which city rules did not apply; but the very seclusion had been like a wall, probably the girl had never made a chance acquaintance in all her life before.

"I will go myself, then," said Garda, seeing that he did not move. She did not seem annoyed, she was, in truth, very seldom ill-tempered. On the present occasion Winthrop might have been better pleased if she had showed some little signs of irritation; for she was simply not thinking of him at all, she was thinking only of Mr. Moore's cousin.

She crossed the flower-decked space quickly, and entered the myrtle grove; Winthrop followed her. When they reached the verge, "There they are," she said, looking southward.

"I don't know how I am to get you down," said Winthrop. "You could jump across from the drift-wood, but you cannot jump back upon it; it's not steady."

"I don't want to go down," said Garda. "They must come up." And she called, in a long note, "Mar—garet!" "Mar—garet!"

Mrs. Harold heard her and turned.

"There! I've called her Margaret to her face!" exclaimed the girl.

"To her back, you mean."

"I never did it before. But I was sure to do it some time; we always call her Margaret when we talk about her, mamma and I; and we talk about her by the hour."

"Mr. Moore and I together can perhaps get you down," said Winthrop, trying the edge of the sand-cliff to see if a niche could be trodden out.

"How odd you are—when I tell you I'm not going down! The others are to come up. Mr. Moore will be enchanted to see his cousin; I am sure *I* was—though he isn't mine."

Winthrop asked himself whether he should take this opportunity to give this beautiful Florida girl a first lesson in worldly wisdom. Then he reflected that what he had admired the most in her had been her frank naturalness, the freedom with which she had followed her impulses, without pausing to think whither they might lead her. So far, her impulses had all been child-like, charming. As regarded this present one, though it was child-like also, he would have liked, with it, a little more discrimination; but discrimination is eminently a trait developed by time, and time, of course, had not yet had a chance to do much for Edgarda Thorne.

He decided to leave her to herself, and to return for the moment to his old position (from which he had rather departed of late), the position of looking on, without comment, to see what she would do or say next. What she did was simple enough. She directed, with much merriment, the efforts of the Rev. Mr. Moore, as in response to her request he climbed up the jagged pile of drift-wood first, in order to show Mrs. Harold the best footholds, his butterfly pole much in his way, but not relinquished; for had not that butterfly flown inland? When he was safely landed on Patricio, Margaret Harold followed him. Winthrop, in spite of the difficulties of descent, wished to come down and assist her; but this she would not allow, and assistance, indeed, was plainly worse than useless in such a place. Nor did she betray any need of it; she climbed with an ease which showed a light foot and accurate balance, and was soon standing by Garda's side.

When they reached the little flower cove it immediately became apparent that the mother of this singing, painting stranger had really been (she had been dead many years) a cousin of Middleton Moore's, Winthrop himself, unless he was prepared to believe in an amount of plotting for which there seemed no sufficient motive, being forced to acknowledge the truth of the story. The conversation between the clergyman and Spenser went on with much animation. Mr. Moore was greatly interested, he was even excited; and they talked of many things. At last he said, with feeling, "I remember you *so* well, Lucian, as a baby; I was in the same house with you once for a whole week when you were just able to walk alone."

"Ah, yes! I am afraid I was rather a bad little boy," Spenser answered.

"You *were* rather—rather animated," the clergyman admitted, mildly.

Garda, who, as usual, had her arm in Margaret's, leaned her head on Margaret's shoulder and gave way to soft laughter.

Middleton Moore talked, enjoying his adventure greatly. But though he talked, he did not question, he was too complete a southerner for that; he leaned on his butterfly pole, and regarded Lucian with the utmost friendliness, not thinking, apparently, of the fact that he had come upon this interesting young relative quite by chance, and that this same young relative must have passed through Gracias (if indeed he were not staying there) without paying him a visit, though he knew that his cousin was rector of St. Philip and St. James'; he had confessed as much. Lucian, who had left his easel, now moved towards it again, and stood scanning his work with the painter's suddenly absorbed gaze—as though he had forgotten, for the moment, everything else in the world but that; then he sat down, as if unable to resist it, and began to add a touch or two, while (with his disengaged faculties) he was good enough to give to his cousin, of his own accord, a brief account of himself in the present, as well as the past. It seemed that he was by profession a civil engineer (as he had already told Garda), and that the party of which he was chief were engaged in surveying for a proposed railway, which would reach Gracias-á-Dios (he thought) in about seventy-five years. However, that was nothing to him; there was undoubtedly a company (they had got an English lord in it), and he, Lucian, was willing to survey for them, if it amused them to have surveying done; that part of the scheme, at least, was paid for. His party were now some distance north of Gracias, they had reached one of the swamps; it had occurred to him that it was a good time to take a day or two, and come down and see the little old town on the coast; and as he was a dabbler in water-colors, he had not been able to resist doing some of the little "bits" he had found under his hand. "I was coming to see you, sir, to-morrow," he concluded. "The truth is, I had only these rough clothes with me; I have sent back for more."

"To the swamp?" said Garda.

"To the swamp—precisely; I keep them there very carefully in a dry canoe."

"You must not only come and see us, Lucian, you must come and stay with us," said the clergyman, cordially; "Penelope will hear of nothing else," he added, bending in his near-sighted way to look at the picture, and putting his nose close to Lucian's pinks and blues. "Isn't it rather—rather bright?" he asked, blinking a little as he drew back. Mr. Moore's idea of a picture was a landscape with a hill in the background, a brook and willows in front, a church spire peeping out somewhere in the middle distance, and a cow or two at the brook's edge, all painted in a dark, melancholy—what he himself would have called a chaste—green, even the cow partaking in some degree of that decorous hue.

"It's not brighter than the reality, is it?" said Lucian.

"I—don't—know," answered Mr. Moore, straightening himself, and looking about him as if to observe the reality, which he evidently was now noting for the first time. "You have put in a butterfly," he added, returning to his inspection; "that is—if it isn't a bird? There are no butterflies here now; has there been one here?"

"There should have been; it's the very place for them," Lucian declared.

"I don't think, Lucian, that there's any certainty about that; I myself have often searched for them in places where it seemed to me they *should* be; they are never there."

Garda again gave way to merriment, hiding it and her face on Margaret's shoulder.

"Hasn't your sky rather too vivid a blue, Lucian?" Mr. Moore went on, his face again close to the picture.

"Well, sir, that's as we see it; *I* see that color in the sky, you know."

"How can you see it if it is not there?" demanded his relative, with his temperate dwelling upon his point. And he transferred his gaze from the sketch to the young man.

"But it *is* there for me. It's the old question of the two kinds of truth."

"There are not two kinds, I think, Lucian," responded the clergyman, and this time he spoke with decision.

"There are two ways of seeing it, then. We state or believe a thing as we see it, and we do not all see alike; you see the hues of a sunset in one way, Turner saw them in another; he painted certain skies, and people said there were no such skies; but Turner saw them."

"The fault was still there, Lucian; it was in his vision."

"Or take another instance," continued Spenser. "A man has a wife whom he loves. She has grown old and faded, there is no trace of beauty left; but he still sees her as she was; to him she does not merely seem beautiful, she is beautiful."

The eyes of Garda and Margaret met, one of those rapid exchanges of a mutual comprehension which are always passing between women unless they happen to be open enemies; even then they are sometimes forced to suspend hostilities long enough for one of these quick passwords of intelligence;—men are so slow! The mutual thought of the two women now was—Mrs. Penelope. Certainly she was old and faded, and very certainly also her husband regarded her as much of a Venus as it was proper for a clerical household to possess. Their entertainment continued as they saw that the clergyman made no personal application of Spenser's comparison, but merely considered the illustration rather an immoral one.

As if to change the subject, this good man now demanded, in his equable, unresonant voice, "How do you return to Gracias, Lucian?"

"There's a contraband with a dug-out waiting for me over on the Espiritu side," answered Spenser; "I walked across."

"Ah! *we* are sailing," remarked the clergyman, in a gently superior tone; little as he himself enjoyed maritime excursions, he felt that this was the proper tone to take in the presence of his host, the owner of the *Emperadora*. "We shall reach home, probably, much earlier than you will," he went on, looking off at the chaparral with an abstracted air.

Winthrop, smiling at this innocent little manœuvre, invited Spenser to return to Gracias with them; he could send one of his men across to tell the contraband of the change of plan. Spenser accepted the offer promptly. He packed his scattered belongings into small compass, and slung them across his shoulder; his easel, under his manipulation, became a stout walking-stick.

"That is a very convenient arrangement," said the clergyman.

"Yes; I am rather proud of it. I invented it myself."

"Ah, that's your father in you," said Mr. Moore, unconsciously betraying something that was almost disapproval; "your father was a northern man. But your mother, Lucian, was a thorough southerner; *she* had no taste for invention."

"She wouldn't have had it even if she had been a northern woman, I fancy," responded Spenser; "women are not inventors. I don't mind saying it before Mrs. Harold and Miss Thorne, because they haven't the air of wishing to be; it's a particular sort of air, you know."

"Is your invention strong?" asked Winthrop. "I don't know how we are going to get the ladies down to the beach, unless we make a perch for them by driving that stick of yours and Mr. Moore's butterfly pole into the sand-drift half-way down. From there, with our help, they might perhaps jump the rest of the distance; we should have to tread out some sort of footing for ourselves."

Mr. Moore involuntarily glanced at his green pole, and then at Margaret and Garda, as if estimating their weight.

"We shall certainly snap it in two," exclaimed Garda, gayly. "Snip, snap, gone!"

"But there's a descent not so very far above here," said Spenser; "I've found it once, and I think, if you will trust me, I can find it again." He led the way into the chaparral, and the others followed.

The chaparral, a thicket of little evergreen oaks, rose, round the flower cove, to a height of ten feet. But soon it grew lower, and they came out upon a broad stretch of it not much over four or four and a half feet in height, very even on the top, extending unbroken to the south as far as they could see, and rising gently on the west, in the same even sweep, over the small ridge that formed Patricio's backbone; their heads were now well above the surface of this leafy sea.

"There's my track," said Spenser.

It was a line which had been made across the foliage by his passage through it; the leaves had been rippled back a little, so that there was a trail visible on the green surface like that left by a boat which has passed over a smooth pond; they made their way towards this trail.

The little oaks were not thorny, but their small stubborn branches grew as closely at the bottom as at the top, so that it was necessary to push with the ankles as well as with the shoulders in order to get through.

"Deep wading," said Lucian, who led the way.

"Wading?" said Garda. "Drowning! These leaves are like *waves*. And I'm sure that fishes are biting my ankles. Or else snakes! I shall sink soon; you'll hear a gurgle, and I shall have gone."

Spenser, laughing, turned and made his way back to her from the front at the same moment that Winthrop, who was last, pushed his way forward from behind; they reached her at the same moment, and placed themselves, one on each side, so that they could make her progress easier.

The Rev. Mr. Moore, who had been calling back a careful explanation that the Florida snakes, that is, the dangerous ones, were not found in chaparral, was now left at the head of the party, to keep the course for them by the line of rippled leaves. This duty he performed with much circumspection, lifting the long butterfly pole high in the air every now and then, and stretching it forward as far as he could to tap the line of rippled leaves, as much as to say, "There you are; *quite* safe." He had the air of a magician with his wand.

"I shall have to stop for a moment," said Margaret Harold, after a while, speaking for the first time since their entrance into the chaparral; she was next to Mr. Moore in their little procession, but a distance of ten or fifteen feet separated them, while Garda, with Spenser and Winthrop, was at a still greater distance behind. Winthrop waited only an instant after she had spoken (long enough, however, to give Spenser and the clergyman the opportunity, in case they should desire it); he then made his way forward and joined her.

"Here—lean on me," he said, quickly, as soon as he saw her face; he thought she was going to faint.

Margaret, though she was pale, smiled, and declined his help; she only wished to rest for a moment, she said; the chaparral had tired her. She stood still, embosomed in the foliage, her eyes closed, the long dark lashes lying on her checks. Winthrop could see now more clearly how delicate her face was; he remembered, too, that though she was tall, she was a slender woman, with slender little hands and feet; her grace of step, though remarkable, had probably not been of much use in forcing a way through chaparral. But her cheeks were growing whiter, he was afraid she would fall forward among the bristling little branches; he pushed his way nearer and supported her with his arm. Garda meanwhile, her fatigue forgotten, had started to come to her friend, Spenser helping her, while Mr. Moore, his pole carefully held out over the trail (as though otherwise it would disappear), watched them with anxiety from the front.

But now Margaret was recovering, the color had come back to her face in a flood; she opened her eyes, and immediately began to push her way forward again, as if she wished to show Winthrop that he need have no further fears. He stayed to aid her, nevertheless.

"Why didn't you go to her?" said Garda to Lucian Spenser, as they resumed their former pace after Margaret's recovery. "I mean why didn't you start before Mr. Winthrop did? There was time."

"He had the better right; he knows her."

"It wasn't a question of knowing, but of helping. As to knowing—you don't know me."

"Oh yes, I do!" answered Spenser.

"But you have never seen me until to-day. Now please don't tell me that I am so much like some one else that you feel as if you had known me for ages."

"You are like no one else, your type exists only in dreams—the dreams of artists mad on color. It's in my dreams that I have seen you," he went on, surveying her with the frankest, the most enjoying admiration. "Aren't you glad you're so beautiful?"

"Yes," responded Garda, with serene gravity. "I am very glad indeed."

They came before long to the descent of which he had spoken; it was a miniature gorge, which led down to the beach in the scallop where Garda had begun her race. As soon as they reached the lower level, Garda went to Margaret and took her hands. "Do you really feel better!" she said. "We'll stay here a while and rest."

Margaret refused, saying that the feeling of fatigue had passed away.

"You *have* got more color than usual," said Garda, scanning her face.

"A sure sign that I am perfectly well again," answered Margaret, smiling.

"A sure sign that you are very tired," said Evert Winthrop.

Margaret made no reply, she began to walk northward, with Garda, up the beach; Lucian Spenser kept his place on the other side of Garda; but Winthrop joined the Rev. Mr. Moore, who was alone.

Mr. Moore improved the occasion, he related the entire history of the Spenser, or rather the Byrd family, the family of Lucian's mother (connections of the celebrated Colonel Byrd). That is, their history in the past; as to the present and its representative, he seemed quite without information.

The present representative spent several days at the rectory; and probably imparted the information which was lacking. During his visit he formed one, as Garda had anticipated, of the various little parties which Betty still continued to arrange and carry out for the entertainment of her dearest Katrina; then he took leave of the rector and his wife, and returned to the camp in the swamp.

Three days later he came back to remain some time; he took a room at the Seminole, saying that his hours were quite too uncertain for a well-regulated household like that of the Moores.

His hours proved to be uncertain indeed, save that a certain number of them were sure to be spent with Garda Thorne. A few also were spent in bringing Torres out of his seclusion. For Lucian took a fancy to the young Cuban; "I don't think you half appreciate him," he said, in his easy, unattached way—unattached to any local view. "He's a perfect mine of gold in the way of peculiarities and precious oddities; he repays you every time."

"I was not aware that oddities had so much value in the market," remarked Dr. Kirby, dryly.

"My dear sir, the greatest!" said Lucian, still in his detached tone.

The Doctor was not very fond of Lucian. The truth was, the Doctor did not like to be called "my dear sir;" the possessive pronoun and the adjective made a different thing of it from his own Johnsonian mode of address.

"*I* appreciate Mr. Torres," Garda remarked, "I always have appreciated him. He's like a thunder-cloud on the edge of the sky; you feel that he could give out some tremendous flashes if he pleased; some day he will please."

"I'll tell him that," said Spenser, who, among his other accomplishments, had that of speaking Spanish.

Whether he told or not, the young Cuban at any rate appeared among them again. He was tired, possibly, of the consumption of his soul. But there was this advantage about Torres, that though he might consume his own, he had no desire to consume the soul (or body either) of any one else; whereas Manuel appeared to cherish this wish to an absolutely sanguinary degree. The dislike he had had for Evert Winthrop was nothing compared with the rage with which he now regarded Lucian Spenser. To tell the truth, Lucian trespassed upon his own ground: if Manuel was handsome, Lucian was handsomer still. "A finer-looking young man than Lucian Spenser," Mrs. Rutherford had more than once remarked, "is *very* seldom seen." And Kate Rutherford was a judge.

Lucian having no horse, as Winthrop had, could not, as Garda expressed it, ride over the pine barrens in every direction and stop at East Angels; but he had a fisherman's black boat, with ragged sail, and though it was not an *Emperadora*, it could still float down the Espiritu with sufficient swiftness, giving its occupant an opportunity to stop at the same old Spanish residence, where there was a convenient water-landing as well as an entrance from the barrens. The occupant stopped so often, and his manner when he did stop was so different from that of their other visitors, that Mrs. Thorne felt at last that duty demanded that she should "make inquiries." This duty had never been esteemed one of the principal ones of life at Gracias-á-Dios; Mrs. Thorne's determination, therefore, showed that her original New England maxims were alive somewhere down in her composition still (as Betty Carew had always declared that they were), in spite of the layer upon layer of Thorne and Duero traditions with which she had carefully overlaid them. She was aware that it was a great inconsistency on her part to revert, at this late day, to the methods of her youth. But what could she do? The Thornes and Dueros were dead, and had left no precedents for a case like this; and Lucian Spenser was alive (particularly so), and with Garda almost all the time.

"She asked me," said the Rev. Mr. Moore to his wife, "what I knew, that was 'definite,' about Lucian, which seemed to me, Penelope, a very singular question, Lucian being so near and dear a relative of ours. I did not, however, comment upon this; I simply gave her a full account of the

Spenser family, or rather of the Byrds, his mother's side of the house, going back (in order to be explicit) through three generations. Strange to say, this did not appear to satisfy her; I will not say that she interrupted me, for she did not; but she had nevertheless, in some ways, an appearance of—of being perhaps somewhat impatient."

"Oh, *I* know!" said Mrs. Moore, nodding her head. "She coughed behind her hand; and she shook out her handkerchief, holding it by the exact middle between her forefinger and thumb; and she tapped on the floor with the point of her slipper; and she settled her cuffs; and then she coughed again."

"That is exactly what she did! You have a wonderful insight, Penelope," said her husband, admiringly.

"Give me a *woman*, and I'll unravel her for you in no time—in no time at all," answered Penelope. "But men are different—*so* much deeper; you yourself are very deep, Middleton."

The clergyman stroked his chin meditatively; his eyes wandered, and after a while rested peacefully on the floor.

"There! I know just what you're thinking of now," resumed his wife from her sofa; "I can tell you every word!"

Her husband, who at that moment was thinking of nothing at all, unless it might be of a worn place which he had detected in the red and white matting at his feet, raised his eyes and looked at her with amiable expectancy. He had long ago learned to acquiesce in all the discoveries respecting himself made by his clever Penelope; he even believed in them after a vague fashion, and was much interested in hearing the latest. But he was so unmitigatedly modest, he took such impersonal views of everything, including himself, that he could listen to her eulogistic divinations by the hour without the least real appropriation of them, as though they had been spoken of some one else. He thought them very wonderful, and he thought her almost a sibyl as she brought them forth; but no glow of self-appreciation followed, this frugal man was not easily made to glow. At present, when his wife had unrolled before him the interesting thoughts which she knew he was thinking (and the rector himself was always of the opinion that he must be thinking them somewhere, in some remote part of his mind which for the moment he had forgotten), she concluded, triumphantly, as follows: "I can always tell what you are thinking of from the expression of your face, Middleton; it's not in the *least* necessary for you to speak." Which was on the whole, perhaps, fortunate for Middleton.

Mrs. Thorne, not having succeeded in obtaining "definite" information from the Rev. Mr. Moore, addressed herself, at length, to Evert Winthrop. Something that was almost a friendship had established itself between these two; Mrs. Thorne found Winthrop very "satisfying," she mentioned that she found him so; she mentioned it to Margaret Harold, with whom, also, she now had an acquaintance which was almost intimate, though in this case the intimacy had been formed and kept up principally by herself. "Yes, extremely satisfying," she repeated; "on every subject of importance he has definite information, or a definite opinion, and these he gives you—when you ask for them—with the utmost clearness. Touch him anywhere," continued the lady, tapping her delicately starched handkerchief (which she held up for the purpose) with her little knuckle, "anywhere, I say," she went on, still tapping, "and—he *resounds*."

"Dear me, mamma! is he hollow?" said Garda, while Margaret gave way to laughter. But Mrs. Thorne liked even Margaret's laughs; Margaret too she found "very satisfying," she said.

When she spoke to Winthrop about Lucian Spenser, however, she found him perhaps not so satisfying as usual.

"I know nothing whatever about Mr. Spenser," he answered.

"We are seeing a good deal of him at present," remarked the little mother, in a conversational tone, ignoring his reply. "It's rather better—don't you think so?—to know something—*definite*—of those one is seeing a good deal of?"

"That is the way to learn, isn't it—seeing a good deal of them?" Winthrop answered.

Mrs. Thorne coughed in her most discreet manner, and looked about the room for a moment or two. Then, "Do *you* like him, Mr. Winthrop?" she said, her eyes on the opposite wall.

"My dear lady, what has that got to do with it?"

"Much," responded Mrs. Thorne, modestly dropping her eyes to the carpet. "A man's opinion of a man, you know, may be quite different from a woman's."

"There is his cousin, Mr. Moore."

"I have already asked Mr. Moore; he knows only Mr. Spenser's grandfathers," replied Mrs. Thorne, dismissing the clergyman, as informant, with a wave of her dry little hand.

"Dr. Kirby, then."

"Dr. *Kirby*" said the lady, with an especial emphasis on the name, as though there were a dozen other doctors in Gracias—"Dr. *Kirby* speaks well of Mr. Spenser. But we should not count too much upon that, for Dr. *Kirby* looks upon him, as I may say, medically."

"Good heavens! does he want to dissect him?" said Winthrop.

Mrs. Thorne gave her guarded little laugh. "No; but he says that he is such a perfect specimen, physically, of the Anglo-Saxon at his best. He may be; I am sure I am willing. But we are not all ethnologists, I suppose, and something more definite in the way of a background than ancient Saxony, or even Anglia, would be, I think, desirable, when, as I remarked before, one is seeing so much of a person."

There was a short silence, which Winthrop did not break. Then he rose, and took up his hat and whip; he had been paying one of his afternoon visits at the old house. "Don't be uneasy," he said, in the half-protecting tone which he often adopted now when speaking to the little mistress of East Angels; "if you are seeing much of this Mr. Spenser, you and your daughter, you must remember that you are also seeing much of others as well; of Manuel Ruiz, of young Torres, even of myself; there's safety in numbers."

"Mr. Spenser is not in the least like any of you; that is my trouble," Mrs. Thorne declared, with emphasis. "I do not mean," she added, with her anxious particularity, "that *you* are in the least like Manuel or Adolfo, Mr. Winthrop; of course not."

Winthrop did not reply to this beyond a smile. He took leave, and went towards the door.

Mrs. Thorne's gaze followed him; then with her quick step she crossed the room, and stopped him on the threshold. "Mr. Winthrop, do *you* like to see my little girl showing such an interest in this Lucian Spenser?" Her voice was almost a whisper, but her bright eyes met his bravely.

For a moment he returned her gaze. Then, "I like it immensely," he said, and went down the stairs.

Soon after this, however, there was what Mrs. Thorne called "definite" information about Lucian Spenser in circulation in Gracias; it was even very definite. He might have the background of honorable grandfathers which Mr. Moore attributed to him, but for the foreground there was only himself, himself without any of the adjuncts of wealth, or a fixed income of any kind, even the smallest. He was a civil engineer (apparently not a very industrious one); he had whatever emoluments that profession could bring in to a man who painted a good many pictures in water-colors; and he had nothing more. This he told himself, with the utmost frankness.

"Nothing more?" commented Mrs. Rutherford, with appreciative emphasis. "But he has always his wonderful good looks; that in itself is a handsome fortune."

"His good looks, I confess, *I* have never seen," answered Mrs. Thorne, who was paying a morning visit at the eyrie. Garda was at that moment on the eyrie's east piazza with Lucian, and the mother knew it; true, Margaret

Harold, Dr. Kirby, and Adolfo Torres were there also; but Mrs. Thorne had no difficulty in picturing to herself the success with which Lucian was engrossing Garda's attention.

"You've never seen them? You must be a little blind, I should think," said Mrs. Rutherford, pleasantly. Mrs. Rutherford was not fond of Mrs. Thorne.

"I am blind to the mere sensuous delights of the eye," responded the little mother, the old Puritan fire sparkling for a moment in her own blue ones. Then she controlled herself. "I cannot admire his expression," she explained. "His nature is a very superficial one; I am surprised that Mrs. Harold should listen to him as she does."

"Oh, as to that," remarked Mrs. Rutherford, "he amuses her, you know; Margaret and I are both very fond of being amused. However, we do not complain; we find a vast deal of amusement in Gracias; it's a very funny little place," added the northern lady, with much tranquil entertainment in her tone, paying back with her "funny" her visitor's "sensuous." (Mrs. Rutherford could always be trusted to pay back.)

That evening she announced to her niece, "Little Madam Thorne has designs upon Evert."

Margaret looked up from her book. "Isn't she rather old for that sort of thing?"

"*That* sort of thing? Do you mean designs? Or attractions? Attraction is not in the least a matter of age," answered Mrs. Rutherford, with dignity. She disposed her statuesque hands upon her well-rounded arms, and looked about the room as though Margaret were not there.

"I meant her feelings," replied Margaret, smiling. "There's such a thing as age in feelings, isn't there?"

"Yes; and in manner and dress," said Mrs. Rutherford, accepting this compromise. "Certainly Mrs. Thorne is a marked example of all three. I don't think any one of *our* family *ever* looked so old as she does, even at ninety! But how could you suppose I meant that she had designs upon Evert for herself? For Garda, of course."

"Garda is very young."

"Why don't you say she's a child! That is what they all say here, I think they say it too much. To be sure, she is only sixteen, barely that, I believe, and with us, girls of that age are immature; but Garda Thorne isn't immature, she talks as maturely as I do."

"She does—in some ways," admitted Margaret.

"She talks remarkably *well*, if you mean that," responded Mrs. Rutherford, who always felt called upon to differ from her niece. "And she is certainly quite pretty."

"She is more than pretty; she is strikingly beautiful."

"Oh no, she isn't," replied Mrs. Rutherford, veering again; "you exaggerate. It's only because you see her here in this dull little place."

"I think it would be the same anywhere, Aunt Katrina."

"Well, we shall not have to compare, fortunately. She will stay here, of course, where she belongs, she will probably marry that young Torres. But that little ill-bred mother's designs upon Evert—that is too amusing. Evert, indeed! Evert has more coolness and discrimination than any man I have ever known."

The man of discrimination was at that moment strolling slowly through the St. Luz quarter, on his way to the Benito; he reached it, and walked out its silver floor. The tide was coming in. On that low coast there were no rocks, the waves reached the shore in long, low, unbroken swells, like quiet breathing; they had come evenly in from deep water outside, and now flowed softly up the beach a little way and then back again, with a rippling murmurous sound that was peace itself. Warm as was the land, still dreaming of the sun, the ocean was warmer still; the Gulf Stream flowed by not far from shore, and the air that came from the water was soft on the cheek like a caress. From the many orange groves of the town dense perfume was wafted towards him, he walked through belts of it. At last, at the point's end, he found himself bathed in it; he threw the light overcoat he had been carrying down upon the sand, and stretched himself upon it, with his back against an old boat; lying there, he could look down the harbor and out to sea.

He was thinking a little of the scene before him, but more of Garda—her liking for the new-comer. For she had confessed it to him herself; confessed, however, was hardly the term, she had no wish apparently to conceal anything; she had simply told him, in so many words, that she had never met or known any one so delightful as Lucian Spenser. This was innocent enough, Garda was, in truth, very childlike. True, she was not shy, she was very sure of herself; she talked to him and to everybody with untroubled ease. Her frankness, indeed, was the great thing; it had an endless attraction for Evert Winthrop. His idea had been (and a very fixed belief it had grown to be) that no girl was frank after the age of long clothes; that the pretty little creatures, while still toddling about, developed the instinct to be "good" rather than outspoken; and that the "better" they were, the more obedient and docile, the less outspoken they became. He could not say that he did not admire obedience. But the flower of frankness had come to seem to him the most fragrant of the whole bouquet of feminine virtues, as it certainly was the rarest. He had told Mrs. Thorne that he liked to see Garda show her preference for Spenser, and this had been true, to a certain extent; he knew that he had felt a distinct pleasure in the swiftness with which she had turned from him to the younger man as soon as she found that the younger man pleased her more. For it showed that she was not touched by the attractions of a large fortune, that they were not attractions to her; and Winthrop held (he knew that many persons would not agree with him) that young girls are more apt to be influenced by wealth, more apt to be dazzled by it, to covet it, than older women are. The older women know that it does not bring happiness in its train, that it may bring great unhappiness; the young girls do not know, and, from their very ignorance, they do not care, because they have not learned as yet what a cruel, torturing pain unhappiness may be. Garda Thorne was poor, and even very poor; she had a strong natural taste for luxury. Yet her passing amusement was evidently far more to her than anything else; she simply did not give a thought to the fortune that lay near. And even her amusement was founded upon nothing stable; Lucian, though she considered him so delightful, was by no means devoted to her. He openly admired her beauty (Winthrop thought too openly), he preferred her society to that of any one in Gracias; but all could see that Gracias was probably the limit, that in other and larger places he would find others to admire; that he was, in short, a votary of variety. In spite of this, Garda found him supremely entertaining, and that was enough for her; she followed him about, always, however, in her indolent way, in which there was no trace of eagerness. But if she were not eager, she seemed to consider him her own property; she always wished to be near him, so that she could hear all he was saying, she laughed far oftener when with him than she did when with any one else.

Winthrop was always attracted by Garda's laugh; he seemed to hear it again as he lay there in the moonlight, breathing the dense perfume from the groves, and looking at the warm, low, glittering sea. "There isn't a particle of worldliness about her," he said to himself. "What a contrast to Margaret!"

He did not leave the perfumed point until it was midnight and high tide.

CHAPTER X

Lucian Spenser's good looks were of the kind that is conspicuously attractive while the youth, which accompanies them, lasts, his face and figure being a personification of radiant young manhood at its best; the same features, the same height and bearing, would have had quite a different aspect if robbed of the color, the sunniness—if one may so express it—which was now the most striking attribute of the whole. He was tall and broad-shouldered, but slender still, he had a bearing which was graceful as well as manly; his hair of a bright golden color had a burnished look, which came from its thick mass being kept so short that the light could find only an expanse of crisped ends to shine across. His eyes were blue, the deep blue which is distinguishable as blue, and not gray or green, across a room; this clear bright color was their principal beauty, as they were not large. They were charming eyes, which could turn to tenderness in an instant; but though they could be tender, their usual expression was that of easy indifference—an expression which, when accompanied by a becoming modesty and frankness, sits well upon a strong, handsome young man. He had a well-cut profile, white teeth gleaming under a golden mustache, a pleasant voice, and a frequent, equally pleasant laugh. No one could resist a certain amount of admiration when he appeared; and the feeling was not dimmed by anything in his manner, for he was good-humored and witty, and if, as has been said, he was rather indifferent, he was also quite without egotism, and quite without, too, that tendency to underrate others which many excellent persons possess—a tendency which comes oftenest from jealousy, but often, too, from a real incapacity to comprehend that people may be agreeable, and happy, and much admired, and even good, with tastes and opinions, appearance and habits, which differ totally from their own. Lucian Spenser underrated nobody; on the contrary, he was apt to see the pleasant side of the people with whom he was thrown. He took no trouble to penetrate, it was not a deep view; probably it was a superficial one. But it was a question—so some of his friends had thought—whether this was not better than the strict watch, the sadly satisfactory search for faults in the circle of their own families and acquaintances, which many conscientious people keep up all their lives.

A day or two after his midnight musings on the beach, Evert Winthrop was coming down Pacheco Lane towards the eyrie when he heard, in a long, sweet, distant note, "Good-by." It came from the water. But at first he could not place it; there were two or three fishermen's boats passing, but the fishermen of Gracias were not in the habit of calling "good-by" in clear English accents to each other; their English was by no means clear, it was mixed with Spanish and West Indian, with words borrowed from the not remote African of the Florida negro, and even with some from the native Indian tongues; it was a very patchwork of languages. Again came the note, and Winthrop, going forward to the edge of the low bank, looked over the water. The course of one of the boats, the smallest, had brought it nearer, and he now recognized Lucian Spenser in the stern, holding the sail-rope and steering, and Garda Thorne, facing him, seated in the bottom of the boat. Garda waved her hand, and called again "Good-by." They glided past him, and he raised his hat, but did not attempt conversation across the water; in a few minutes more Lucian had tacked, and the boat turned eastward down the harbor, the sail, which had swung round, now hiding their figures from his view. Winthrop left the bank, crossed the green-carpeted lane, and went up the outside stairway to the eyrie's drawing-room. It was inhabited at present by tea-leaves. Celestine, loathing, as Minerva Poindexter, the desultory methods of Cindy, the colored girl who was supposed to act as parlor-maid, was in the habit of banishing her at intervals from the scene, and engaging personally in an encounter with the dust according to her own system. The system of Celestine was deep and complicated, beginning with the pinning of a towel tightly over her entire head in a compact cap-like fashion of much austerity, followed, as second stage, by an elaborate arrangement of tea-leaves upon the carpet, and ending—but no one knew where it ended, no one had ever gone far enough. It was at the tea-leaf stage that Winthrop found her.

"She's gone out with Mrs. Carew," Celestine replied, in answer to his inquiry for Mrs. Rutherford. "You see she got her feet all sozzled last night coming home across the plazzer from *church* with that there Dr. Kirby, and so she took cold, *of course*. And there's nothin' so good for a cold as half an hour outside in this bakin' sun, and so I told her."

"You don't speak as though you altogether approved of evening service, Minerva?" Winthrop answered, amused by her emphasis.

"Well, I don't, and that's a fact, Mr. Evert. In the *mornin'* it's all very well; but in the *evenin'*, I've noticed, the motive's apt to be mixed, it's pretty generally who you come home with. My mother used to say to Lovina (that was my sister) and me, 'Girls, in the evenin's I *don't* like to have you go loblolloping down to meetin' and straddlin' up the aisle. It ain't real godliness; it's just purtense, and everybody knows it.' And she was quite right, Mr. Evert—quite." And having thus expressed herself at much greater length than was usual with her, Celestine resumed her labors, and raised such a dust that the man (whom she still considered quite a young lad) was glad to beat a retreat.

He went to the east piazza, and seated himself with a book in his hand; but his eyes followed the sail which was moving slowly down the harbor towards Patricio. Fifteen minutes later Margaret Harold, coming through the long window, found him there. By this time the sail was gone, only the bare mast could be seen; Lucian and his companion had landed on Patricio.

"They are going to see Madam Ruiz," said Margaret.

"No," replied Winthrop; "if they had been going there, they would have stopped this side, at the landing."

"It would amuse Garda more to stop on the ocean side. It's the only thing she plans for—amusement."

"I can see no especial entertainment in it; it will simply be that he will have hard work to get the boat off."

"That is what will amuse her—to see him work hard."

"He won't enjoy it!"

"But she will."

"You knew they were going?" said Winthrop, taking up his book again.

"I was passing the plaza landing, and happened to see them start."

"Did they tell you they were going to see Madam Ruiz?"

"They were too far off to speak to me, they were just passing the end of the pier. No; but when I saw they had landed (I have been watching them from my window) I knew of course that they were going there."

"There's no 'of course' with Lucian Spenser!" answered Winthrop. He got up, took the glass which was hanging on a nail behind him, and turned it towards the point of Patricio. "They're not going towards the Ruiz plantation at all," he said; "they're walking southward, down the beach." He put the glass back in its case, closed it, replaced it on the nail, and sat down again.

"I am surprised that Mrs. Carew should have allowed Garda to go," he went on, after a moment. "She's staying with Mrs. Carew, isn't she?—she's always staying with some one now."

"She is staying with Mrs. Carew till to-morrow only. Mrs. Carew likes Lucian Spenser immensely, she tells every one how much she likes him."

"I don't think that has anything to do with it—Mrs. Carew's admirations," responded Winthrop. "He's an irresponsible sort of fellow," he added, speaking with moderation. He was not moderate, but he often spoke with moderation. On the present occasion he felt that he might have said much more.

"Yes, I think he is rather irresponsible," assented Margaret. "I suppose he would say why shouldn't he be, if it pleases him."

"No reason in the world, I don't imagine any one cares. But they ought not to permit Edgarda Thorne to go about with him as she does; she has never been in the habit of walking or sailing with Manuel Ruiz, or that young Cuban—I mean walking or sailing with them alone."

"Probably they have never asked her."

"That is very likely, I suppose they wouldn't dream of it. And that is what I am referring to; she has been brought up here under such a curious mixture of freedom and strictness that she is not at all fitted to understand a person like Spenser."

"Shall I speak to Mrs. Thorne?" said Margaret. She was standing by the piazza's parapet, her hand resting on its top, her eyes fixed on Patricio, though the two figures were no longer in sight. Winthrop's chair being behind her and on one side, he could see only her profile, outlined against the light.

"Mrs. Thorne is already awakened to it," he answered; "she has spoken to me on the subject."

"There was your opportunity. What did you say?"

"I told her—I told her not to be uneasy," he replied, breaking into a laugh over his own inconsistencies. "But it isn't Mrs. Thorne who is to blame—I mean Mrs. Thorne alone; it is Mrs. Carew, the Kirbys, the Moores, and all the rest of them."

"In other words, the whole society of Gracias. Do you think we ought to corrupt them with our worldly cautions?"

"We're not corrupting, it's Spenser who's corrupting; we should never corrupt them though we should stay here forever. They're idyllic, of course, it's an idyllic society; but we can be idyllic too."

Margaret shook her head. "I'm afraid we can only be appreciative."

"It's the same thing. If we can appreciate little Gracias, with its remoteness and simplicity and stateliness, its pine barrens and beaches and roses, I maintain that we're very idyllic; what can be more so?"

Margaret did not reply. After a while she said, "If you will take Aunt Katrina to drive to-morrow afternoon, I will have Telano row me down to East Angels."

"You think you will speak in any case? I suppose you know with what enthusiastic approval Mrs. Thorne honors all you say and do?"

"Yes, something of it."

"But you don't care for her approvals," he said, half interrogatively.

"Yes, I care," Margaret answered. "In this case I care a great deal, as it may give me some influence over her."

"What shall you say to her?—not that I have any right to ask."

"I am very willing to tell. I had thought of asking whether she would let Garda go back with me when we go home—back to New York; I had thought of having her go to school there for six months."

"I can't imagine her in a school! But it's very kind in you to think of it, all the same."

"She could stay with Madame Martel, and take lessons; it wouldn't be quite like a school."

"That might do. Still—I can hardly imagine her away from Gracias, when it comes to the point."

"Neither can I. But, as you say, irresponsible people have made their way in here, they will do so again; we shall not be able to keep the place, and Garda, idyllic simply to please ourselves."

"Well, then, I wish we could!" responded Winthrop. "But I don't believe the little mother could stand the separation," he went on.

"I shouldn't ask her to, at least not for long; I should ask her to come herself, later. New York might amuse her."

"Never in the world, she wouldn't in the least approve of it," said Winthrop, laughing. "It wouldn't be Thorne and Duero; it wouldn't even be New Bristol, where she spent her youth. She would feel that she ought to reform it, yet she wouldn't know how; she would be dreadfully perplexed. She has a genius for perplexity, poor little soul. But I can't express how good I think it is of you to be willing to give them such a delightful change as that," he went on—"to take a whole family on your shoulders for six long months."

"A family of two. And it would be a pleasure."

"I suppose you know that people don't often do such things, except for their relatives. Not very often for them."

"I know it perfectly; I have always wondered why they did not—provided, of course, that they had the ability," answered Margaret.

Winthrop in his heart had been much astonished by her plan. He looked at her as if in search of some expression that should throw a gleam of light upon her motives. But she had not moved, and he could still see only her profile. After a while she lifted her eyes, which had been resting with abstracted gaze upon the water, and, for the first time, turned them towards him. A faint smile crossed her face as she met his inquiring look, but her expression under the smile seemed to him sad; she bent her head slightly without speaking, as if to say good-by, and then she went back through the long window into the house. Winthrop, left behind, said to himself that while he had no desire as a general thing for long conversations with Margaret Harold, he wished this time that she had not gone away so soon. Then it came to him that she almost always went away, that it was almost always she who rose, and on some pretext or other left him to himself; she left him—he did not leave her; on this occasion she had gone without the pretext; she had not taken the trouble to invent one, she had simply walked off. Of course she was quite free to come and go as she pleased. But he should have liked to hear more about her plan for Garda.

The next day she did not go down to East Angels. Her proposed visit had had to do with Lucian Spenser, and Lucian Spenser had taken his departure from Gracias that morning—a final departure, as it was understood; at least he had no present intention of returning. It was very sudden. He had had time to say good-by only to his cousin, Mr. Moore. To Mr. Moore he had intrusted a little note of farewell for Edgarda Thorne, who had returned to East Angels at an earlier hour, without seeing Lucian or knowing his intention. Mr. Moore said that Lucian had not known his intention himself until that morning; he had received a letter, which was probably the cause of his departure (this "probably" was very characteristic of the clergyman). He, Lucian, intended to go directly north to Washington, and from there to New York; and then, possibly, abroad.

"Dear me!—and his surveying camp, and the swamp, and those interesting young bears he had there?" said Mrs. Rutherford, who, having once arranged this very handsome young man's background definitely in her mind, was loath to change it, "even," as she remarked, with an unusual flight of imagination,—"even for the White House!"

"It would hardly be the Executive Mansion in any case, I fancy," explained Mr. Moore, mildly, "Lucian has, I think, no acquaintance with the President. But Washington is in reality his home; though it is perhaps apparent that he has not been there very often of late years."

These rather vague deductions regarding his young cousin's movements were satisfactory to Middleton Moore; he had evidently asked no more questions of Lucian on the occasion of his unexpected departure than he had upon the occasion of his equally unexpected arrival; his interest in him (which was great) had no connection with the interrogation point.

"What shall you do now?" said Winthrop to Margaret, after the clergyman had taken leave. They were alone in the little drawing-room, Mrs. Rutherford having gone to put herself in the hands of Celestine for the elaborate change of dress required before her daily drive.

Margaret had risen; but she stopped long enough to answer: "Of course now I need not speak to Mrs. Thorne about Mr. Spenser."

"No. But about Garda's going north? Do you still think of that?"

"Yes; that is, I should like very much to take her. But I don't think I shall speak of it immediately, there need be no hurry now." She paused. "I should like first to talk it over more clearly with you," she said, as if with an effort.

"Whenever you please; I am always at your service," replied Winthrop, with a return of his formal manner.

That afternoon he rode down to East Angels. Mrs. Thorne received him; there was excitement visible in her face and manner—an excitement which she held in careful control; but it manifested itself, in spite of the control, in the increased brightness of her eyes, which now fairly shone, in the round spot of red on each little cheek-bone, and in the more accentuated distinctness of her speech, which now came as nearly as possible to a pronunciation of every letter. She asked him how he was; she inquired after the health of Mrs. Rutherford, after the health of Mrs. Harold; she even included Celestine. She spoke of her own health, and at some length. She then branched off upon the weather. All her T's were so preternaturally acute that they snapped like a drop of rain falling into a fire; when she said "we" or "week," she brought out the vowel-sound so distinctly that her thin lips widened themselves flatly over her small teeth, and her mouth became the centre of a sharp triangle whose apex was the base of the nose, and the sides two deep lines that extended outward diagonally to the edge of the jaws. So far, she was displaying unusual formality with the friend she had found so satisfying. The friend betrayed no consciousness of any change, he saw that she wished to keep the direction of the conversation in her own hands, and he did not interfere with her desire; he was sure that she had something to say, and that in her own good time she would bring it forth. And she did. After treating him to twenty minutes of pronunciations, she folded her hands closely and with the same crisp utterance remarked: "My daughter is in the rose garden, I should like to have you see her before you go. I shall not accompany you, I shall ask you to do me the favor of seeing her alone."

He could not help smiling a little, in spite of the repressed tragedy of the tone. "Favor?" he repeated.

"Yes, favor," responded Mrs. Thorne, in a slightly higher key, though her voice remained musical, as it always was. "Favor, indeed! Wait till you see her. Listen, Mr. Winthrop; I want you to be very gentle with Edgarda now." And, leaning forward, she touched his arm impressively with her finger.

Winthrop always felt an immense pity for this little mother, she was racked by so many anxieties of which the ordinary world knew nothing, the comfortable world of Mrs. Rutherford and Mrs. Carew; that these anxieties were exaggerated, did not render them any the less painful to the woman who could not perceive that they were.

"Of course I shall be gentle," he said, taking her hand cordially. As he held it he could feel the hard places on the palm which much household toil, never neglected, though never mentioned, had made there.

"But when you see her, when you hear her talk, it may not be so easy," responded Mrs. Thorne, looking at him with an expression in her eyes which struck him as containing at the same time both entreaty and defiance.

"It will always be easy, I think, for me to be gentle with Garda," responded Winthrop; and his own tone was gentle enough as he said it.

Tears rose in Mrs. Thorne's eyes; but she repressed them, they did not fall. "I depend greatly upon you," she said, with more directness than she had yet used. She drew her hand from his, took up his hat, which was lying on a chair near her, and gave it to him; she seemed to wish him to go, to say no more.

He obeyed her wish, he left the house and went to the rose garden. Here, after looking about for a moment, he saw Garda.

CHAPTER XI

She was under the great rose-tree. Dressed in an old white gown of a thick cotton material, she was sitting on the ground, with her crossed arms resting on the bench, and her head laid on her arms; her straw hat was off, the rose-tree shading her from the afternoon sun. Carlos Mateo, mounting guard near, eyed Winthrop sharply as he approached. But though Garda of course heard his steps, she did not move; he came up and stood beside her, still she did not raise her head. He could see her face in profile, as it lay on her arm; it was pale, the long lashes were wet with tears.

"Garda," he said.

"Yes, I know who it is," she answered without looking up;—"it is Mr. Winthrop. Mamma has asked you to come and talk to me, I suppose; but it is of no use." And he could see the tears drop down again, one by one.

"I should be glad to come on my own account, without being asked, if I could be of any use to you, Garda."

"You cannot," she murmured, hopelessly.

His speech had sounded in his own ears far too formal and cold for this grieving child—for the girl looked not more than fourteen as she sat there with her bowed head on her arms. He resisted, however, the impulse to treat her as though she had been indeed a child, to stoop down and try to comfort her.

"I am very sorry to find you so unhappy," he went on, still feeling that his words were too perfunctory.

"I don't believe it; I wish I did," answered Garda, who was never perfunctory, but always natural. "If I did, perhaps I could talk to you about it, and then it wouldn't be *quite* so hard."

"Talk to me whether you believe it or not," suggested Winthrop.

"I cannot; you never liked him."

A frown showed itself on Winthrop's face; but Garda could not see it, and he took good care that his voice should not betray irritation as he answered: "But as I like you, won't that do as well? You ought to feel safe enough with me to say anything."

"Oh, why won't you be good to me?" said the girl, in a weeping tone, abandoning the argument. "I shall die if everybody is so cruel when I am suffering so."

"I am not cruel," said Winthrop. He had seated himself on the bench near her, he put out his hand and laid it for a moment on her bright brown hair.

The touch seemed very grateful to Garda; instantly she moved towards him, put her arms on his knee, and laid her head down again, in much the same attitude she often assumed when with Margaret Harold, save that she did not look up; her eyes remained downcast, the lashes heavy with tears. "I cannot bear it—he has gone away," she said, letting her sorrow come forth. "I liked him so much—so much better than I liked any one else. And now he has gone, and I am left! And there was no preparation—it was so sudden! Only yesterday we had that beautiful walk on Patricio beach (don't you remember?—I called to you as we passed), and he said nothing about going. I can never tell you how long and dreadful the time has been since I got his note this morning."

"Don't try," said Winthrop. "Think of other things. Some of us are left, make the best of us; we are all very fond of you, Garda." He felt a great wrath against Lucian Spenser; but he could not show any indication of it lest he should lose the confidence she was reposing in him, the confidence which made her come and lay her crossed arms on his knee and tell him all her grief. This confidence had other restrictive aspects, it showed that she regarded him as a species (somewhat younger, perhaps) of Mr. Moore or Dr. Kirby; Winthrop was acutely conscious that he could not play that part in the least; it certainly behooved him, therefore, to do the best he could with his own.

"Yes, you are all kind, I know," Garda had answered. "But Lucian was different, Lucian *amused* me so."

"Amused? Was that it?" said Winthrop, surprised by the word she had chosen.

"Of course," answered Garda, in the same dejected tone. "Is there anything better than to be amused? I am sure I don't know anything. I was so dull here, and he made everything delightful; but now—" Her tears rose again as the contrast came over her.

"Perhaps, now that you have called our attention to it, the rest of us might contrive to be more amusing," said Winthrop, with a tinge of sarcasm in his tone.

But Garda did not notice the sarcasm. "No," she answered, seriously, "you could not. You might try; but no, you could not," she repeated, with conviction. "For it wasn't anything he did, it was Lucian himself. Besides, I liked so much to look at him—he was so beautiful. Don't you remember the dimple that came when he threw back his head and laughed?" She moved a little so that she could rest her chin on her clasped hands, and look up into Winthrop's face; her eyes met his dreamily; she saw him, but she was thinking of Spenser.

"Torres has a dimple too," answered Winthrop, rather desperately. For between the beauty of the girl herself, made more appealing as it was now by her sorrow, her confiding trust that he was prepared to play on demand the part of grandfather or uncle—between this and her extraordinary, frank dwelling upon the attractive points of Lucian Spenser, together with the wrath he felt against that accomplished young engineer—he was not, perhaps, so fully in possession of his accustomed calmness as usual. But she was a child, of course; he always came back to that; she was nothing but a child.

It was true that poor Torres had a dimple, as Winthrop had said. It was in his lean dark cheek, and everybody was astonished to see it there; once there, everybody wondered where it found space to play. It did not find it in depth, and had to spread itself laterally; it was a very thin dimple on a bone.

But Garda paid no attention to this attempt at a diversion. "Did you ever see such eyes as Lucian's, such a deep, deep blue?" she demanded of Winthrop's gray ones.

"Very blue," he answered. He was succeeding in keeping all expression out of his face (if there had been any, it would not have been of the pleasantest). He felt, however, that his tone was dry.

But acquiescence was enough for Garda, she did not notice his tone; she continued the expression of her recollections. "When the light shone across his hair—don't you remember the color? It was like real gold. He looked then like—like a sun-god," she concluded, bringing out the word with ardor.

"What do you know of sun-gods?" said Winthrop, endeavoring to bear himself agreeably in these intimate confidences. "How many of the warm-complexioned gentlemen have you known?"

"I mean the Kirbys' picture," answered Garda, with much definiteness, rejecting sun-gods in general as a topic, as she had the dimple of poor Torres; "you must remember the one I mean."

Winthrop did remember; it was a copy of the Phœbus Apollo of Guido's "Aurora" at Rome.

"Oh," continued Garda, without waiting for reply, "what a comfort it is to talk to you! Mamma has been so strange, she has looked at me as though I were saying something very wrong. I have only told her how much I admired him—just as I have been telling you; is that wrong?"

"Not the least in the world," answered Winthrop, who had at last decided upon the course he should pursue. "But it won't last long, you know, it's only a fancy; you have seen so few people, shut up in this one little place. When you have been about more, your taste will change."

Garda did not pay much heed to these generalities arrayed before her, nor did he expect that she would. But this was the tone he intended to take; later she would recall it. All she said now was, "Oh, please stay ever so long, all the evening; I cannot let you go, now that you are so good to me." And taking his hand with a caressing little motion, she laid her soft cheek against it.

"Suppose we walk a while," suggested Winthrop, rising. He said to himself that perhaps he should feel less like a grandfather if he were on his feet; perhaps, too, she would treat him less like one.

Garda obeyed him directly. She was as docile as possible. When they were a dozen yards off, Carlos Mateo began to follow them slowly, taking very high steps with his thin legs, and pausing carefully before each one, with his upheld claw in the air, as if considering the exact point in the sand where he should place it next. They went to the live-oak avenue. "How long do you think it will hurt me so, hurt me as it does now—his going away?" the girl asked, sadly.

"Not long," replied Winthrop, in a matter-of-course tone. "It's always so when we are parted from our friends; perhaps you have never been parted from a friend before?"

"That is true, I have not," she answered, a little consoled. "But no," she went on, in a changed voice, "it's not like that, it's not like other friends; I cared so much for him! You might all go away, every one of you, and I shouldn't care as I do now." And with all her figure drooping, as though it had been struck by a blighting wind, she put her hand over her eyes again.

"Take my arm," said Winthrop; "we will go down to the landing, where you can rest on the bench; you are tired out, poor child."

Again she obeyed him without opposition, and they walked on; but her breath came in long sobs, and she kept her little hand over her eyes, trusting to his arm to guide her. He felt that it was better that she should talk of Spenser than sob in that way, and, bracing himself with patience, he began.

"How was it that he entertained you so? what did he do?" he asked. There was no indefiniteness about that "he;" there was only one "he" for Garda.

She took the bait immediately. "Oh, I don't know. He always made me laugh." Then her face brightened as recollection woke. "He was always saying things that I had never thought of—not like the things that other people say," she went on; "and he said them, too, in a way that always pleased me so much. Generally he surprised me, and I like to be surprised."

"Yes, I see; it was the novelty."

"No," answered Garda, with a reasonable air, "it couldn't have been the novelty alone, because, don't you see, there were you. You were novel—nothing could have been more so; and yet you never *began* to give me any such amusement as Lucian did."

Evert Winthrop remarked to himself that a girl had to be very pretty, very pretty indeed, before a man could enjoy such comparisons as these from her lips. But Garda Thorne's beauty was enchanting, sometimes he had thought it irresistibly so; to be wandering with this exquisite young creature on his arm, in this soft air, on this far southern shore—yes—one could put up with a good deal for that.

They reached the landing; she seated herself on the bench that stood at the bank's edge, under the last oak, and folded her hands passively. A little dilapidated platform of logs, covered with planks, ran out a few yards into the water; the old boat of the Thornes lay moored at its end. Winthrop took a seat on the bench also. "Tell me, Garda," he said, "have you ever thought of going north?"

"I have thought of it to-day. But there's no use, we cannot go."

"Don't you remember that you wanted to see snow, and the great winter storms?"

"Did I?" said Garda, vaguely. "I should like to go to Washington," she added, with more animation. "But what is the use of talking about it? We cannot go." And she relapsed again. "We cannot ever go anywhere, unless we should be able to sell the place, and we shall never be able to sell it, because nobody wants it; nobody *could* want it."

"It's a pleasant old place," remarked Winthrop.

A sudden light came into Garda's eyes. "Mr. Winthrop," she said, eagerly, "I had forgotten your odd tastes; perhaps you really do like East Angels? I remember I thought so once, or rather mamma did; mamma thought you might buy it. I told her I did not want you to feel that it was urged upon you; but everything is different to me now, and I wish you *would* buy it. I suppose that you are so rich that it wouldn't matter to you, and it would make us so happy."

"Us?"

"Oh yes, to sell it has long been mamma's hope. I won't say her only one, because mamma has so many hopes; but this has been the principal one, the one upon which everything else hung. So few people come to Gracias—people of our position, I mean (for of course we wouldn't sell it to any one else)—that it has seemed impossible; there have been only you and Lucian, and Lucian, you know, has no money at all. But you have a great deal, they all say, and I almost think you really do like the place, you look about you so when you come."

"I like it greatly; better than any other place I have seen here."

"He likes it greatly; better than any other place he has seen here," repeated Garda, in a delighted tone. She rose and began to walk up and down the low bank, clapping her hands softly, and smiling to herself. Then, laughing, she came back to him, her pretty teeth shining beneath her parted lips. "You are the kindest man in the whole world," she announced, standing before him. Winthrop laughed also to see how suddenly happy and light-hearted she had become. "Let us go and tell mamma," continued Garda. "Poor mamma—I haven't been nice to her. But now I will be; I shall tell her that you will buy the place, there's nothing nicer than that. *Then* we can go to Washington."

"It will take some time, you know," Winthrop suggested.

Her face fell. "Much?" she asked.

"I hardly know; probably a good deal could be done in the course of the summer. There may be difficulty about getting a clear title; complications about taxes, tax claims, or the old Spanish grants." He thought it was as well she should comprehend, in the beginning, that there would be no going to Washington, for the present at least.

"But in our case there can be no complications, we are the old Spaniards ourselves," said Garda, confidently.

He was silent.

"It would be very hard to have to wait long," she went on, dejected by his manner.

"Yes. But it's something to have it sold, isn't it?"

"Of course it is, it's everything," she responded, taking heart again. "And even if it is long, I am young, I can wait; Lucian is young too; and—I don't think he will forget me, do you?"

"I want to advise one thing—that you should not talk so constantly about Spenser," suggested Winthrop.

"Not talk about him? It's all I care for." She drew her arm from his, and moved away. Stopping at a little distance, she gazed back at him with a frown.

"I know it is," answered Winthrop, admiring the beauty of her face in anger. "My suggestion is that you talk about him only to me."

"Then I shall have to see you *very* often," she answered, breaking into smiles, and coming to take his arm again of her own accord. They went back through the avenue towards the house.

They found Mrs. Thorne in the drawing-room. She appeared to have dressed herself afresh from head to foot, her little black gown was exquisitely neat, her hair under her widow's cap was very smooth; she had a volume of Emerson in her hand. She looked guardedly at Winthrop and her daughter as they came into the room; her face was steady and composed, she was ready for anything.

Garda kissed her, and sat down on the edge of her chair, with one arm round her small waist, giving her a little hug to emphasize her words.

"Oh, mamma, think of it! Mr. Winthrop wants to buy the place."

Mrs. Thorne turned her eyes towards Winthrop. They still had a guarded expression, her face remained carefully grave.

"I have long admired the place, Mrs. Thorne," he began, in answer to her glance. "I have thought for some time that if you should ever feel willing to sell it—"

"Willing? Delighted!" interpolated Garda.

"—I should be very glad to become the purchaser," he concluded; while Garda laughed from pure gladness at hearing the statement repeated in clear, business-like phrase.

Mrs. Thorne gave her little cough, and sat looking at the floor. "It would be a great sacrifice," she answered at last. "There would be so many old associations broken, so many precious traditions given up—"

"Traditions?" repeated Garda, in her sweet, astonished voice. "But, mamma, we cannot live forever upon traditions."

"We have done so, or nearly so, for some time, and not without happiness, I think," replied Mrs. Thorne, with dignity. "Take one thing alone, Edgarda, one thing that we should have to relinquish—the family burying-ground; it has been maintained here unbroken for over two hundred years."

"Mamma, Mr. Winthrop would leave us that."

"Even if he should, there's not room for a house there that I am aware of," replied Mrs. Thorne, funereally.

Winthrop with difficulty refrained from a laugh. But he did refrain. He saw that the relief of having her daughter returned to her, freed from the incomprehensible grief that had swept over her so strangely, this, combined with the suddenly expanding prospect of a fulfilment of her long-cherished dream of selling the place, had so filled her constantly anxious mind with busy plans, pressing upon each other's heels, that beyond them she had only room for a general feeling that she must not appear too eager, that she must, as a Thorne, say something that should seem like an objection—though in reality it would not be one.

But if Winthrop refrained from a laugh, Garda did not. "Oh, mamma, how funny you are to-day!" she said, embracing her again with a merry peal.

"I am not aware that I am funny," replied Mrs. Thorne, with solemnity.

"Why, yes, you are, mamma. Do we *want* to live in the burying-ground?" said Garda, with another peal.

But Mrs. Thorne preserved her composed air. It almost seemed as if that indeed might be her wish.

Winthrop took leave soon afterwards, in spite of Garda's entreaty that he should stay longer. He had administered a good deal of comfort, it may have been, too, that he had come to the end of his capacity to hear more, that day at least, about Lucian Spenser. He had reached the bottom of the old stairway, and gone some distance down the stone-flagged corridor towards the door, when he heard Garda's voice again:

"Mr. Winthrop?" He looked up. She had come half-way down the stairs, and was standing with one hand on the carved balustrade, her white figure outlined against the high dark panelling of the other side. "I shall never be able to keep silence as you wish, unless I see you *very* soon again," she said.

He smiled, without making answer in words, for Raquel had now appeared, coming from her own domain to open the lower door. Raquel always paid this attention, though no one asked her to do it. Mrs. Thorne, indeed, disapproving of it and her, never rang to let her know that her guests were departing. This made no difference to Raquel, or rather it gave her the greater insistence; when guests were in the house she now made a point of giving up all work while they remained, in order to be in readiness for this parting ceremonial. Raquel had a high regard for ceremonials; she had been brought up by the Old Madam.

Winthrop carried out his project. Asking the good offices of Dr. Kirby as appraiser, he took the first steps towards the purchase of East Angels. It soon became apparent that the steps would be many. The Dueros having been, as Garda had said, "the old Spaniards" themselves, there was no trouble in this case about the Spanish grants; theirs was a *bona fide* one. But there were other intricacies, and in studying them Winthrop learned the history of the place almost back to the landing of Ponce de Leon. The lands had been granted in the beginning by the crown of Spain (of course over the heads of the unimportant natives) to Admiral Juan de Duero in 1585. They had been regranted (over the heads of the Dueros), seventy years later, by the crown of England, to an English nobleman, who, without taking possession, had sold his grant, and comfortably enjoyed the profits; the buyer meanwhile had crossed the ocean only to lose his life by shipwreck off the low Florida coast, and his descendants had, it appeared, sent an intermittent cry across from England that they should assuredly come over, and take possession. They never did, however; and the Dueros of course considered their claim as merely so much unimportant insanity. Later, at the beginning of the British occupation in 1763, the Dueros themselves had transferred part of their domain to other owners. Then, upon the return of the Spaniards, twenty years afterwards, they had calmly taken possession of the property again, without going through the form of asking permission, the new owners meanwhile having gone north, to cast their fortunes with the raw young republic called the United States; the descendants of these new owners had also at intervals sent up a cry, which echoed through the title rather more clearly than the earlier one from England. The place had been three times pillaged by buccaneers, who at one period were fond of picnic-parties on Florida shores; it had been through several attacks by Indians, in one of which the stone sugar-mill had been destroyed. Since the long warm peninsula had come into the possession of the United States these same lands had suffered several partitions (on paper) from forced sales (also on paper), owing to unpaid taxes, the confusion having been much increased by the late war. Tax claims in large numbers lifted their heads, like a crop of quick-growing malodorous weeds, at the first intimation that a *bona fide* purchaser had appeared, a man from the North who had the eccentricity of wishing, in the first place, for such a worn-out piece of property as East Angels, and, in the second, for a clear title to it; this last seemed an eccentricity indeed, when the Dueros themselves had lived there so long without one. Evert Winthrop persevered; he persevered with patience, for he was amused by the local history his researches unearthed. Dr. Kirby persevered also, but he persevered with impatience; he was especially incensed against the attorney who represented a portion of the later tax titles. This attorney, a new-comer in Gracias, was a tall, narrow-chested young man from Maine, who had hoped to obtain health and a modest livelihood in the little southern town; it was plain that he would obtain neither, if long opposed to Reginald Kirby.

"Sir," said the Doctor, who had been especially exasperated by a tax title which stood in the name of a certain Increase Kittredge, described as a resident, "there is collusion in this evidently. There is no such person in

Gracias-á-Dios, and I venture to say there is no such person in the State; it is some northern *freebooter* who is acting through you. Kittredge," he repeated, putting on his spectacles to read the name again. "And Increase!" he added, throwing back his head and looking about the room, as if calling the very furniture to witness. "No southerner, high or low, sir, had ever such a name as that since the universe was created; it's Yankee, Yankee to the core, as—if you will kindly allow me to mention it—is your own also."

The youthful attorney, whose name was Jeremiah Boise, sat looking at his pen-holder with a discouraged air; he was very young, and he admired the Doctor profoundly, which made it worse.

"And I am surprised," continued the Doctor, changing his tone to one of simple gravity, "that you should be willing to lend yourself to these plots and jobs" (the Doctor brought out these two words with rich round utterance), "which must, of course, act more or less upon the nerves, you who are so far from robust, who have so evidently a tendency"—here the Doctor paused, surveying Jeremiah from head to foot—"a tendency to weakness of the breathing powers."

The poor young man, who knew that he had, looked so pallid, nevertheless, under this professional statement of his case that the kind-hearted Doctor instantly repented. He put out his hand, "There, there," he said; "don't look so disheartened. Come to my office and let me see you, I venture to say I can set you up in no time—in no time at all. I presume you haven't the least idea how to take care of yourself, it's extraordinary how people go about the world one mass of imprudence. Have the kindness to stand up for a moment. Now draw a long breath. Hum—hum—I thought so; no absolute harm done as yet." And the Doctor tapped and listened, and tapped and listened again, with as much interest as though the suspected chest had belonged to a southern Kirby instead of to a Jeremiah from Maine. "That will do; thank you. You must come and see me this very afternoon; come about five. I shall give you some rules to follow. One of the first will be that you live more generously, enjoy yourself more (you northerners don't seem to know how). Never fear, man; we'll build you up in a few months so that you won't know yourself!" And cordially shaking his hand, the Doctor took leave—only to come back and remark, standing upon the threshold, with a full return of his majestic manner, "But I should advise you, sir—I should most seriously advise you to relinquish all connection with the scandalous claims masquerading under that fraudulent name—that name of Increase Kittredge!"

He departed, and returned again briskly, to say in his pleasantest voice: "Oh, by-the-way, I'm going to send you some sound wine—port; I have a little left. Be good enough to take it according to the directions." And this time he was really gone.

In the mean while all Gracias congratulated Mrs. Thorne. That lady bore herself with much propriety under the altered aspect of her affairs. There were advantages in it, she said with a sigh, which of course she appreciated; still, it was impossible for her to think without sadness of "the severing of old associations" which such a change must bring about. Gracias agreed with her there—the severing would be difficult; old associations, indeed, had always been Gracias's strong point. Still, a good deal of breakage could be borne—it was, indeed, a duty to bear it—when such an equivalent was to be rendered ("equivalent" was the term they had decided upon). The equivalent—that is, the sum which Winthrop was to pay for the plantation—was not large. But to Gracias in its reduced state it seemed an ample fortune; Gracias wondered what Mrs. Thorne would do with it. That lady kept her own counsel; but in private she covered sheets of paper with her small careful figures, and pondered over them.

To Garda the hoped-for sum represented but one word—Washington! Winthrop had again dwelt upon the advice that she should not speak that word too audibly. "So long as I can whisper it to you, I can be dumb to the others," she answered, laughing.

But it did not seem to him that she whispered.

The conditions of their friendship at present were remarkable. Garda was restless unless she could see him every day; if he came on horseback, she had espied him from afar, and was at the edge of the barren to meet him; if he sailed down the lagoon in the *Emperadora*, she had recognized the sail, and was in waiting on the landing. Once there, she wished to have him all to herself, she grudged every moment he spent with her mother. This did not prevent him from spending a good many with the little mistress of East Angels, who now received him with a subdued resignation which was his delight. This was the man who was about to dispossess them of their home, the home of her daughter's forefathers; he meant no harm, he wished for the place, sad misfortune compelled them to part with it; but naturally, naturally, they could not quite welcome him with undiluted feelings; naturally their feelings were, must be, charged with—retrospect. All this, especially the retrospect, was so reluctantly yet perfectly expressed in her voice and manner that Winthrop was never tired of admiring it, and her; she was practising the tone she intended to take about him; he could not deny that it was a very perfect little minor note. Garda's feelings, however, did not seem to be diluted with anything; she received him with unmixed joy. As soon as she could get him to herself she carried him off to the live-oak avenue, whose high arches and still gray shade had now become her favorite resort; here she strolled up and down with him and talked of Lucian, being contented with his mere presence as reply. Often Carlos Mateo stalked up and down behind them; for he lived in the live-oak avenue now, Garda declared that he danced by himself there on moonlight nights. Sometimes Adolfo Torres performed similar sentinel duty. For Garda had become almost tender in her manner to the young Cuban since her own interest in Lucian had developed itself. "He feels as I do," she said to Winthrop, with conviction.

"Never mind *his* feeling. What is yours for him?" suggested Winthrop, who was perhaps rather tired of the sentinels, bird and man.

"Pity," answered Garda, promptly. "A nice, kind pity."

"He must be a poor stick to keep coming here for that."

"Oh, he doesn't think it's pity, he would never comprehend that, though you should tell him a dozen times. He's satisfied; Adolfo is always satisfied, I think."

"Couldn't he enjoy his satisfaction at home, then?—it doesn't seem to depend at all upon your talking to him?"

"I talk to him when you are not here. You cannot always be here, you know, but he almost can, he lives so near. Lucian was always going to see him—don't you remember? He said he was like a mediæval finger-post; you must remember that."

Winthrop felt that he was sometimes required to remember a good deal.

He did not, however, have to remember Manuel, at least at present; Lucian not having discovered mediæval qualities in that handsome youth, Garda was content to let him remain where he was; this was the San Juan plantation, twenty miles away. He had been there some time. His mother said he was hunting.

"Yes, there are a number of pretty girls about there," remarked Dr. Kirby.

But Torres, who was jealous of no one, and whose patience and courteous certainty remained unmoved, continued to accompany Garda and Winthrop in their strolls up and down the live-oak avenue. He generally walked a little behind them; that gave him his sentinel air. Several yards behind him came Carlos Mateo; but Carlos affected not to belong to the party, he affected to be taking a stroll for his own amusement, like any other gentleman of leisure; he looked about him, and often stopped; he appeared to be admiring the beauties of nature.

And Garda talked on, never rapidly, her topic ever the same. Torres, of course, understood nothing of her monologues. And Winthrop? Winthrop suffered them.

CHAPTER XII

Of his reasons for pursuing this course, Margaret Harold knew more than any one else. For as Garda's devotion to Margaret remained unchanged, she talked to her as freely as she talked to Winthrop. She saw Winthrop oftener; but whenever she could pay a visit to Margaret, or whenever Margaret came down to East Angels, Garda's delight was to sit at her feet and talk of Lucian. The girl, indeed, had made an express stipulation with Winthrop that Margaret should be excepted from his decree of silence. "I must talk to Margaret," she said, "because I am so fond of her. The reason I like to talk to you is because you are a man, and therefore you can appreciate Lucian better."

"I should think it would be just the other way," observed Winthrop.

"Oh no; Margaret doesn't even *see* how beautiful he is, much less talk about it."

"And I like to talk about it so much!"

"You do it to please me," said Garda, gratefully. "I appreciate that."

"She tells me she talks to you—I mean, of course, about Lucian Spenser—just as she does to me," he said to Margaret one day; "she has chosen to confide her little secrets to you and me alone." Margaret was standing by a table in the eyrie's dining-room, arranging in two brown jugs a mass of yellow jessamine which she had brought in from the barrens. "Rather a strange choice," he went on, smiling a little as he thought of himself, and then of Margaret, reserved, taciturn, gentle enough, but (so he had always felt) cold and unsympathetic.

"Yes," assented Margaret. "What do you think the best way to receive it?" she added, going on with her combinations of green and gold.

"Not to bluff her off—to let her talk on. It is only a fancy, of course, a girl's fancy; but it needs an outlet, and we are a safe one, because we know how to take it—know what it amounts to."

"What does it amount to?"

"Nothing."

"Oh," murmured the woman at the table, rather protestingly.

"I mean that it will end in nothing, it will soon fade. But it shows that the child has imagination; Garda Thorne will love, some of these days; a real love."

"Yes; that requires imagination."

"My sentences were not connected, they did not describe each other. What I meant was that the way the child has gone into this—this little beginning—shows that she will be capable of deep feelings later on."

Margaret did not reply.

"There are plenty of excellent women who are quite incapable of them," pursued Winthrop, conscious that he had, as he expressed it to himself, taken the bit in his teeth again, but led on by the temptation which, more and more this winter, Margaret's controlled silences (they always seemed controlled) were becoming to him. "And the curious point is that they never suspect their own deficiencies; they think that if they bestow a prim, well-regulated little affection upon the man they honor with their choice, that is all that is necessary; certainly it is all that the man deserves. I don't know what we deserve; but I do know that we are not apt to be much moved by such affection as that. They are often very good mothers," he added, following here another of his tendencies, the desire to be just—a tendency which often brought him out at the end of a remark where people least expected.

"Don't you think that important?" said Margaret.

"Very. Only let them not, in addition, pretend to be what they are not."

"I don't think they do pretend."

"You're right, they're too self-complacent. They're quite satisfied with themselves as they are."

"If they are satisfied, they are very much to be envied," began Margaret.

"She's going to defend herself," thought Winthrop. "It's a wonder she hasn't done so before; to save my life, I don't seem to be able to resist attacking her."

But Margaret did not go on. She took up the last sprays and looked at them. "Then you think I had better let her talk on, without checking her," she said, returning to the original topic between them. "You think I had better not try to guide her?"

"Refused again!" thought Winthrop. "Guide her to what?" he said, aloud.

"Not *to* anything. Away—away from Lucian Spenser."

"Then you don't like him?" he said, questioningly.

"He is very handsome," answered Margaret, smiling.

"But that isn't what we're discussing, that isn't advice."

"Let her talk as she pleases—that is my advice; let her string out all her adjectives. My idea is that, let alone, it will soon exhale; opposition would force it into an importance which it does not in reality possess. Are you going?"

"Yes, I have finished. But I shall remember what you say." And she left the room, carrying the flowers with her.

Mrs. Thorne came up to Gracias, and called upon Mrs. Rutherford at the eyrie. Her visits there had always been frequent, but this one had the air of a visit of ceremony; it seemed intended as a formal expression of her chastened acquiescence in the northern gentleman's projects concerning East Angels.

"I have reserved the memories," she said, with expression.

"Yes, indeed; fond Memory brings to light, and so it will be with you, Mistress Thorne," said Betty, who was spending the afternoon with her Katrina; "you can always fall back on that, you know."

"Have you reserved old Pablo?" inquired Mrs. Rutherford. "He is a good deal of a memory, isn't he?"

"I have reserved Pablo, and also Raquel; they will travel with us," replied Mrs. Thorne. "Raquel will act as my maid, Pablo as my man-servant."

"They're *very* southern," remarked Betty, shaking her head. "I doubt whether they would get on well, living at the North. Raquel, you know, has no system; she would as soon leave her work at any time and run and make a hen-coop—that is, if you should happen to have hens, and I am sure I hope you would, because at the North, they tell me—"

But here Mrs. Thorne bore down upon her. "And did you suppose, Betty—were you capable of supposing—that Edgarda and I were thinking of *living* at the North?"

"I don't know what I'm capable of," answered Betty, laughing good-humoredly; "Mr. Carew never knew either. But you're really a northerner after all, Mrs. Thorne; and so it didn't seem so unlikely."

Mrs. Thorne had called her Betty, but she did not address Mrs. Thorne as Melissa in return. No one had called Mrs. Thorne Melissa (Melissa Whiting had been the name of her maiden days) since she had entered the manorial family to which she now belonged. Her husband had called her "Blue-eyes" (he had admired her very much, principally because she was so small and fair); the Old Madam had unfailingly designated her by the Spanish equivalent for "madam my niece-in-law," which was very imposing—in the Old Madam's tone. To every one else she was Mistress Thorne, and nothing less than Mistress Thorne; the title seemed to belong to every inch of her straight little back, to be visible even in the arrangement of her bonnet-strings.

Madam my niece-in-law now addressed herself to answering Betty. "When I married my dear Edgar, Betty, I became a Thorne, I think I may say, without affectation, a thorough one; no other course was open to me, upon entering a family of such distinction; Edgarda, therefore is Thorne and Duero, she is nothing else. Gracias-á-Dios will continue to be our home; we could not permanently establish ourselves anywhere, I think, save on the—the strand, where her forefathers have lived, and died, with so much eminence and distinction."

"Well, I'm sure I am very glad to hear it," answered Betty, cordially. "We are all so fond of Garda that we should miss her dreadfully if she were to be away long, though of course we can't expect to monopolize her so completely as we have done; she'll be going before long, you know, to that bourne from which—"

"Oh, Betty," interrupted Mrs. Rutherford, throwing up her white hands, "what horrors you *do* say!"

"I didn't mean it," exclaimed Betty, in great distress, the tears rising in her honest eyes; "I didn't mean anything of the sort, dear Mistress Thorne, I beg you to believe it; I meant 'She stood at the altar, with flowers on her brow'—indeed I did." And much overcome by her own inadvertence, Betty produced her handkerchief.

"Never mind, Betty; *I* always understand you," said Mrs. Thorne, graciously.

But it soon became evident that though she might understand Betty she did not understand Melissa, at least not so fully as she supposed she did, for, not long after her visit at the eyrie, she fell ill. On the fifth day it was feared that her illness had taken a dangerous turn; the delicate little cough with which they had been acquainted so long, in the various uses she put it to, that they had almost come to consider it a graceful accomplishment, this cough had all the time had its own character under the assumed ones, and its own character was simply an indication of a bronchial affection, which had now assumed a serious phase, sending inflammation down to the lungs.

"Her lungs have never been good," said Dr. Kirby to Winthrop; the Doctor was much affected by the danger of his poor little friend. "She has never had any chest to speak of, none at all." And the Doctor tapped his own wrathfully, and brought out a sounding expletive, the only one Winthrop had ever heard him use; he applied it to New-Englanders, New-Englanders in general.

The Doctor went back to East Angels. And in the late afternoon Winthrop himself rode down there. The little mistress of the house was very ill; besides Garda, the Doctor, his mother, and Mrs. Carew were in attendance. He saw only Mrs. Carew. She told him that Mrs. Thorne was very much disturbed mentally, as well as very ill, that she seemed unable to allow Garda out of her sight; when she did not see her at the bedside, she kept calling for her in her weak voice in a way that was most distressing to hear; Garda therefore now remained in the room day and night, save for the few moments, now and then, when her mother fell into a troubled sleep. The Doctor was very anxious. They were all very anxious.

Winthrop rode back to Gracias, he went to the eyrie. Mrs. Rutherford was out, she was taking a short stroll with the Rev. Mr. Moore. Margaret was on the east piazza; she was bending her head over some fine knitting.

"I'll wait for Aunt Katrina," said Winthrop, taking a chair near her. "Knitting for the poor, I suppose. Do you know, I always suspect ladies who knit for the poor; I suspect that they knit for themselves—the occupation."

"So they do, generally. But this isn't for the poor; don't you see that it's silk?"

"You could sell it. In the Charity Basket."

"What do you know of Charity Baskets?" said Margaret, laughing. "But I'm afraid I am not very good at working for the poor; the only thing I ever made—made with my own hands, I mean—was a shirt for that eminent Sioux chieftain Spotted Tail, and he said it did not fit."

"They don't want shirts, they want their land," said Winthrop. "We should have made them take care of themselves long ago, but we shouldn't have stolen their land. I'm not thinking of Lo, however, at present, I am thinking of that poor little woman down at East Angels. I am afraid she is very ill. Do you know, I cannot help suspecting that the sudden change in her prospects has had something to do with her illness; I mean the unexpected vision of what seems to her prosperity. She has kept up unflinchingly through years of struggle, and I think she could have kept up almost indefinitely in the same way, for Garda's sake, if she had had the same things to encounter; but this sudden wealth (for, absurd as it is, so it seems to her) has changed everything so, has buried her so almost over her head in plans, that the excitement has broken her down. You probably think me very fanciful," he concluded, realizing that he was speaking almost confidentially.

"Not fanciful at all; I quite agree with you," answered Margaret, her head still bent over her knitting.

"She has asked for you a number of times, Mrs. Carew tells me," he said, after a moment or two of silence.

"Has she?" said Margaret, this time raising her eyes. "I should have gone down to East Angels before this if I had not feared that I should be only in the way; all their friends have been there, I know; it is a very united little society."

"Yes, Madam Ruiz and Madam Giron were there yesterday taking care of her; Mrs. Kirby and Mrs. Carew are there to-day. Everything possible is being done, of course. Still—I don't know; from something Mrs. Carew said, I fear the poor woman is suffering mentally as well as physically; she is constantly asking for Garda, cannot bear her out of her sight."

"If I thought I could be of any service," said Margaret.

"I am sure you could; the greatest," he responded promptly, his voice betraying relief. "Mrs. Thorne is an odd little woman; but she has a very genuine liking for you; I think she feels more at home with you, for some reason or other, than she does with any of these Gracias friends, long as she has known them. And as for Garda, I am sure you could do more for her than any other person here could—later, I mean—she is so fond of you." He paused; what he had said seemed to come back to him. "Both of them, mother and daughter, appear to have selected you as their ideal of goodness," he went on; "I hope you appreciate the compliment." This time the slight, very slight indication of sarcasm showed itself again in his tone.

"Is it possible that you think the poor mother really in danger?" said Margaret, paying no heed, apparently, to his last remark.

"She has evidently grown very weak, and I have never thought she had any strength to spare. But it is only my own idea, I ought to tell you, that she is—that she may not recover."

"I will go as soon as possible; early to-morrow morning," said Margaret. "But if I do—" She hesitated. "I am afraid Aunt Katrina will be lone—I mean I fear she might feel deserted if left alone."

"Alone—with Minerva and Telano and Cindy, and the mysterious factotum called Maum Jube?"

"There would still be no companion, no one for her to talk to."

"How you underrate the conversation of Celestine! I should, of course, come in often."

"I think that if you should stay in the house, while I am gone, it would be better," answered Margaret.

"To try and make up, in some small degree, for what she loses when she loses you?"

"Whatever you please, so long as you come," she responded.

The next morning she went down to East Angels. Garda received her joyously. "Oh, Margaret, mamma is better, really better."

It was true. The fever had subsided, the symptoms of pneumonia had passed away; the patient was very weak, but Dr. Kirby was now hopeful. He had taken his mother back to Gracias, but the kind-hearted Betty remained, sending by the Kirbys a hundred messages of regret to her dearest Katrina that their separation must still continue.

Later in the day Margaret paid her first visit to the sick-room. Mrs. Thorne was lying with her eyes closed, looking very white and still; but as soon as she perceived who it was that had entered, a change came over her; she still looked white, but she seemed more alive; she raised herself slightly on one arm, and beckoned to the visitor.

"Now don't try to talk, that's a dear," said Mrs. Carew, who was sitting on the other side of the bed, fanning the sick woman with tireless hand.

Mrs. Thorne slowly turned her head towards Betty, and surveyed her solemnly with eyes which seemed to have grown during her illness to twice their former size. "Go—away," she said, in her whispering voice, which preserved even in its faintness the remains of her former clear utterance.

"What?" said the astonished Betty, not sure that she had heard aright.

"I wish—you would go—away," repeated Mrs. Thorne, slowly. And with her finger she made a little line in the air, which seemed to indicate, like a dotted curve on a map, Betty's course from the bed to the door.

Betty gave her fan to Margaret. Incapable of resentment, the good soul whispered to Garda, as she passed: "They're very often so, you know—sick people; they get tired of seeing the same persons about them, of course, and I am sure it's *very* natural. I'll come back later, when she's asleep."

"I was not tired of seeing her, that wasn't it," murmured Mrs. Thorne, who had overheard this aside. "But I wanted to see Margaret Harold alone, and without any fuss made about it; and the first step was to get *her* out of the room. Now, Edgarda, you go too. Go down to the garden, where Mrs. Carew will not see you; stay there a while, the fresh air will do you good."

"But, mamma, I don't think I ought to leave you."

"Do as I tell you, my daughter. If I should need anything, Margaret will call you."

"You need not be afraid, Garda, that I shall not know how to take care of her," said Margaret, reassuringly. "I am a good nurse." She arranged Mrs. Thorne's pillows as she spoke, and gently and skilfully laid her down upon them again.

"Of course," whispered Mrs. Thorne. "Any one could see that." Then, as Garda still lingered, "Go, Garda," she said, briefly. And Garda went.

As soon as the heavy door closed behind her, Mrs. Thorne began to speak. "I have been so anxious to see you," she said; "the thought has not been once out of my mind. But I suppose my mind has not been perfectly clear, because, though I have asked for you over and over again, no one has paid any attention, has seemed to understand me." She spoke in her little thread of a voice, and looked at her visitor with large, clear eyes.

Margaret bent over her. "Do not exert yourself to talk to me now," she answered. "You will be stronger to-morrow."

"Yes, I may be stronger to-morrow. How long can you stay?"

"Several days, if you care to have me."

"That *is* kind. I shall have time, then. But I mustn't wait too long; of one thing I am sure, Margaret: I shall not recover."

"That is a fancy," said Margaret, stroking the thin little hand that lay on the white coverlet; "Dr. Kirby says you are much better." She spoke with the optimism that belongs to the sick-room, but in her heart she had another opinion. A change had come over Mrs. Thorne's face, the effect of which was very striking; it was not so much the increase of pallor, or a more wasted look, as the absence of that indomitable spirit which had hitherto animated its every fibre, so that from the smooth scanty light hair under the widow's cap down to the edges of the firm little jaws there had been so much courage, and, in spite of the constant anxiety, so much resolution, that one noticed only that. But now, in the complete departure of this expression (which gleamed on only in the eyes), one saw at last what an exhausted little face it was, how worn out with the cares of life, finished, ready for the end.

"Yes, I am better, it is true, for the present," whispered Mrs. Thorne. "But that is all. My mother and my two sisters died of slow consumption, I shall die of the rapid kind. I shall die and leave Garda. Do you comprehend what that is to me—to die and leave Garda?" Her gaze, as she said this, was so clear, there was such a far-seeing intelligence in it, such a long experience of life, and (it almost seemed) such a prophetic knowledge of death, that the younger woman found herself forced to make answer to the mental strength within rather than to the weakness of the physical frame which contained it. "Why am I taken now, just when she will need me most?" went on the mother's whisper, which contrasted so strangely in its feebleness with the power of her gaze. "Garda had only me. And now I am called. What will become of her?"

"You have warm friends here, Mrs. Thorne; they are all devoted to Garda. It has seemed to me that to each one of them she was as dear as an own child."

"Yes, she is. They would do anything in the world they could for her. But, I ask you, what can they do? The Kirbys, the Moores, Betty Carew, and Madam Giron, Madam Ruiz—what can they do? Nothing! And Garda—oh, Garda needs some one who is—different."

Margaret did not reply to this; and after a moment Mrs. Thorne went on.

"When Mr. Winthrop buys the place," she said, with the touching Gracias confidence that a few thousands would constitute wealth, "my child need not be a charge, pecuniarily. But of course I know that in other ways she might be. And I cannot leave her to them, these people here; I *cannot* die and do that. Garda is not a usual girl, Margaret—you must have seen it for yourself. I only want a little oversight of the proper kind for her; that would be all that I should ask; it would not be a *great* deal of care. From the very first, Margaret, I have liked you so much! You have no idea how much." Her voice died away, but her eyes were full of eloquence. Slowly a tear rose in each, welled over, and dropped down on the white cheek below, but without dimming the gaze, which continued its fixed, urgent prayer.

Margaret had remained silent. Now she covered her face with her hand, the elbow supported on the palm of the other. Mrs. Thorne watched her, mutely; she seemed to feel that she had made her appeal, that Margaret comprehended it, was perhaps considering it; at any rate, that her place now was to wait with humility for her answer.

At length Margaret's hand dropped. She turned towards the waiting eyes. "Before your illness, Mrs. Thorne," she said, in her tranquil voice, "I had thought of asking you whether you would be willing to let me take Garda north with me for some months. I have a friend in New York who would receive her, and be very kind to her; she could stay with this lady, and take lessons. I should see her every day, it would not be quite like a school."

"That is what I long for—that she should be with you," said Mrs. Thorne, not going into the details of the plan, but seizing upon the main fact. "That *you* should have charge of her, Margaret—that is now my passionate wish." She used the strongest word she knew, a word she had always thought wicked in its intensity. But it was applicable to her present overwhelming desire.

"And I had thought that perhaps you would follow us, a little later," pursued Margaret; "I hope you will do so still."

Mrs. Thorne made a motion with her hand, as if saying, "Why try to deceive?" She lay with her eyes closed, resting after her suspense. "You are so good and kind," she murmured. "But not kinder, Margaret, than I knew you would be." Her voice died away again, and again she rested.

"I have asked and accepted so much—for of course I accept instantly your offer—that I feel that I ought not to ask more," she began again, though without opening her eyes. "But I have got to die. And I *trust* you so, Margaret—"

"Why do you trust me?" interposed Margaret, abruptly. "You have no grounds for it; you hardly know me. It makes me very uncomfortable, Mrs. Thorne."

But Mrs. Thorne only smiled. She lifted her hand, and laid it on Margaret's arm. "My dear," she said, simply (and it was rare for Mrs. Thorne to be simple; even now, though deeply in earnest, she had had the old appearance of selecting with care what she was about to say), "I don't know why any more than you do! I only know that it is so; it has been so from the beginning. I think I understand you," she added.

"Oh no," said the younger woman, turning away.

"At any rate, I understand your steadfastness, Margaret. You have steadfastness in the supreme degree. Many women haven't any, and they are much the happiest. But you, Margaret, are different. And it is your steadfastness that attracts me so—for my poor child's sake I mean. Yes, for hers I must say a little more—I must. If you could only see your way to letting her remain under your care as long as she is so young—you see I mean longer than the few months you spoke of just now,—it would make my dying easier. For it's going to be very hard for me to die. Perhaps you think I'm not going to. But I know that I am. All at once my courage has left me. It never did before, and so I know it is a sign."

Margaret sat listening, she looked deeply troubled. "You wish to intrust to me a great responsibility," she began.

"And it seems to you very selfish. Of course I know that it is selfish. But it is desperation, Margaret; it is my feeling about Garda. Let me tell you one thing, I am relying a little upon your having suffered yourself. If you had not, I should never have asked you, because people who haven't suffered, women especially, are so hard. But I saw that you had suffered, I saw it in the expression of your face before I had heard a word of your history."

"What do you know of my history?" asked Margaret, the guarded reserve which was so often there again taking possession of her voice and eyes.

"In actual fact, very little. Only what Mrs. Rutherford told Betty Carew."

"What did she tell her?"

"That her nephew, your husband, was travelling abroad—that was all. But when I learned that the travelling had lasted seven years, and that nothing was said of his return or of your joining him, of course I knew that inclination, his or yours, was at the bottom of it. And I imagined pain somewhere, and probably for you. Because you are good; and it is the good who suffer."

"In reality you know nothing about it," replied Margaret to these low-breathed sentences. "I think I ought to tell you," she went on, in the same reserved tone, "that both Mrs. Rutherford and Mr. Winthrop think I have been much to blame; it may make a difference in your estimation of me."

"Not the least. For Mrs. Rutherford's opinions I care nothing. As to Mr. Winthrop, Mr. Winthrop—"

"Agrees with Mrs. Rutherford."

"He will live to change his opinion; I think very highly of Mr. Winthrop, but on this subject he is in the wrong. Do you know why I think so highly of him?"

But Margaret's face remained unresponsive.

"I think highly of him because he has had such a perfect, such a delicate comprehension of Garda—I mean lately, through all this fancy of hers—such a strange one—for that painter." Mrs. Thorne always called Lucian a "painter," very much as though he had been a decorator of the exterior of houses. His profession of civil engineer she steadily ignored; perhaps, however, she did not ignore it more than Lucian himself did.

"Mr. Winthrop likes Garda so much that it is easy for him to be considerate," Margaret answered.

"On the contrary," murmured Mrs. Thorne; "on the contrary. While I am most grateful to him for his consideration, I have feared that it was in itself a proof that he did not really care for her. If he had cared, would he have been so patient with her—her whim? Would he have let her talk on by the hour, as I know she has done, about Lucian Spenser? Men are jealous, extremely so; far more so than women ever are. They don't call it jealousy, of course; they have half a dozen names for it—weariness, superiority, disgust—whatever you please. You don't agree with me?"

"It's a general view, and I've given up general views. But of one thing I am certain, Mrs. Thorne—Evert admires Garda greatly."

The mother raised herself so that she could look at Margaret more closely. "Do you think so?—do you really think so?" she said, almost panting.

"Yes, I think so."

"Then, Margaret, I will have no concealments from you, not one. If Mr. Winthrop should ever care enough for my poor child—some time in the future—to wish to make her his wife, I should be *so* happy, I am sure I should know it wherever I was! I could trust her to him, he is a man to trust. He is much older. But if she should once begin to care for him, that would make no difference to her, nothing would make any difference; she will never be influenced by anything but her own liking, it has always been so. And if—she could once—begin to care—" The short sentences, which had been eager, now grew fainter, stopped; the head sank back upon the pillows again. "If she were to be with you, Margaret, she would have—more opportunity—to begin."

"About that I could promise nothing," said Margaret, with decision. "I could take no step to influence Garda in that way."

"I don't ask you to. I myself wouldn't *do* anything, that would be wrong; on such subjects all must be left to a Higher Power," replied Mrs. Thorne, with conviction. For, in spite of her efforts to be Thorne and Duero, she had never departed a hair's-breadth from her American belief in complete liberty of personal choice in marriage. Love, real love, was a feeling heaven-born, heaven-directed; it behooved no one to meddle with it, not even a mother. "I could never scheme in that way," she went on, "I only wanted you to know all my thoughts. The great thing with me, of course, is that she is to be in your charge."

Here the door at the other end of the large room opened, and Dr. Kirby came in; he had returned as soon as possible, putting off all other engagements. "You look better," he said to his patient, with his hand on her pulse. "Come, this is doing well."

"I am better," murmured Mrs. Thorne, looking gratefully at Margaret. Mrs. Carew soon followed the Doctor; Margaret went down to the garden to find Garda, the girl who was to become so unexpectedly her charge. For she shared the mother's feeling; the illness might advance slowly, but it would conquer in the end.

Garda was in the garden, lying at full length under the great rose-tree, on a shawl which she had spread upon the ground; her hands were clasped under her head, and she was gazing up into the sky. Carlos, standing near, with his neck acutely arched, his breast puffed out and his beak thrust in among the feathers, looked like a gentleman of the old school in a ruffled shirt, with his hand in the breast of his coat.

"Does mamma want me?" asked Garda, as Margaret came up.

"Dr. Kirby and Mrs. Carew are there. No, I do not think she wants you at present."

"Come down on the shawl, then, and look up into the sky," pursued Garda. "I've never tried it before—looking straight up in this way—and I assure you I can see miles!"

"I'm not such a sun-worshipper as you are," answered Margaret, taking a seat on the bench in the shade.

"The sun's almost down. No, it isn't the sun, it's because you never in the world could stretch yourself out full length on the ground, as I'm doing now. The ground's nice and warm, and I love to lie on it; but you—you have always sat in chairs, you have been drilled."

"Yes, I have been drilled," answered Margaret, sombrely, looking at the graceful figure on the shawl.

Garda did not notice the sombre tone, her attention was up in the sky. After a while she said, "Mr. Winthrop hasn't been here to-day; I wonder why?"

"He won't be able to come so often while I am here, he will have to see to Aunt Katrina."

"Mist' Wintarp desiahs to know whedder you's tome, Miss Gyarda," said the voice of old Pablo. "I tole him I *farnsied* you was in de gyarden." Pablo recognized Garda as a Duero; he treated her therefore with respect, and benignant affection.

Winthrop now appeared at the garden gate, and Margaret rose.

"Perhaps I had better go in, too?" said Garda.

"No, stay as long as you like; I will send word, if your mother asks for you," Margaret responded.

She left the garden by another way. When she had gone some distance, she looked back. Garda had changed her position; she was still looking at the sky, though she was no longer lying at length; she had curled herself up, and was leaning against a dwarf tree. Winthrop was in Margaret's place on the bench, and Garda had evidently spoken to him of the sky, for he, too, was looking up.

But he did not look long; while Margaret stood there, his eyes dropped to the figure at his feet. This was not surprising. There was nothing in the sky that could approach it.

CHAPTER XIII

Mrs. Thorne improved. She was still very weak, confined to her bed, and the cough continued at intervals to rack her wasted frame. But there was now no fever; she slept through the nights; she had always been so delicate in appearance that she did not seem much more fragile now. These at least were the assertions of her Gracias friends; her Gracias friends were determined to believe that time and good nursing would restore her. The nursing they attended to themselves, and with devoted care, one succeeding the other day after day. Mrs. Thorne appreciated their good offices; but she no longer concealed her preference for the companionship, whenever it was to be obtained, of Margaret Harold.

"I have pretended so long!" she said to Margaret, when they were alone together. "I am so tired of pretending! and with you I can be myself. It isn't really necessary now to be any one else—now that I shall so soon have to go; but I have got into such a habit of it with the others that I shouldn't know how to stop. With you I can talk freely, and you are the only one."

"So long as it doesn't tire you," Margaret answered.

"It tires me a great deal more to be silent," responded Mrs. Thorne.

Often, therefore, when Margaret came down to East Angels, Mrs. Thorne would send Garda into the open air to stroll about, or rest under the rose-tree, and then, while Madam Ruiz, or Mrs. Carew, or whoever happened to be in attendance, was sleeping to make up for the broken rest of the coming night, she would talk to her northern friend, talk with an openness which was in itself a sign that the many cautions of a peculiarly cautious life were drawing to a close. One reason for this freedom was that in spite of the apparent improvement, there were no illusions between these two regarding the hoped-for recovery. "We are northerners, Margaret, and *we* know," Mrs. Thorne had said one day, when Margaret had raised her so that she could cough with less difficulty. "Consumption—*our* kind—these southerners cannot grasp!" She did not wish to die, poor woman; she clung to life with desperation; nevertheless, she found a momentary satisfaction in a community of feeling with Margaret over this southern lack.

"Oh, these southern lacks—how Garda would have been part of them!" she went on. "If I had had to leave her here, if you had not promised to take her, how inevitably she would have been sunk in them, lost in them! she would never have got out. Oh! I so hate and loathe it all—the idle, unrealizing, contented life of this tiresome, idle coast. They amounted to something once, perhaps; but their day is over, and will never come back. They don't know it; you couldn't make them believe it even if you should try. That is what makes you rage—they're so completely mistaken and so completely satisfied! Every idea they have is directly contrary to all the principles of the government under which they exist But what is that to them? They think themselves superior to the government. I'm not exaggerating, it's really true; I can speak from experience after my life with that"—she paused, then chose her word clearly—"with that devilish Old Madam!"

It seemed to Margaret as if this poor exile were imbibing a few last draughts of vitality from the satisfaction which even this late expression of her real belief gave her; she had been silent so long!

Her Thorne and Duero envelope was dropping from her more and more. "Oh yes, I have stood up for them," she said, another time. "Oh yes, I have boasted of them, I knew how! I knew how better than any of them; I made a study of it. The first Spaniards were blue-blooded knights and gentlemen, of course; *they* never worked with their hands. But the Puritans were blacksmiths and ploughmen and wood-choppers—anything and everything; I knew how to bring this all out—make a picture of it. 'Think what their *hands* must have been!' I used to say" (and here her weak voice took on for a moment its old crispness of enunciation)—"'what great coarse red things, with stiff, stubby fingers, gashed by the axe, hardened by digging, roughened and cracked by the cold. Estimable men they were, no doubt; heroic—as much as you like. But *gentlemen* they were not.' I have said it hundreds of times. For those idle, tiresome, wicked old Dueros, Margaret (the English Thornes too, for that matter), were Garda's ancestors, and the right to talk about them was the only thing the poor child had inherited; naturally I made the most of it. They were the feature of this neighborhood, of course—those Spaniards, I knew that; I had imagination enough to appreciate it far more, I think, than the very people who were born here. I made everything of it, this feature; I learned the history and all the beliefs and ideas. I always hoped to get hold of some northerners to whom I could tell it, tell it in such a way that it would be of use to us, make a background for Garda some time. That's all ended; I have never had the proper chance, and now of course never shall. But at least I can tell *you*, Margaret, now that it is all over, that in my heart I have always hated the whole thing—that in my heart I have always ranked the lowest Puritan far, far above the very finest Spaniard they could muster. They didn't work with their hands, these knights and gentlemen; and why? Because they caught the poor Indians and made them work for them; because they imported Human Flesh, they dealt in negro slaves!" It was startling to see the faded blue eyes send forth such a flash, a flash of the old abolitionist fire, which for a moment made them young and brilliant again.

Margaret tried to soothe her. "It is nothing," said Mrs. Thorne, smiling faintly and relapsing into quiet.

But the next day Melissa Whiting blazed forth anew. "I detest every vestige of those old ideas of theirs; I hate the pride and shiftlessness of all this land. I am attached to our friends here, of course; they have always been kind to me. But—it is written! They will go down, down, they and all who are like unto them; already they belong to the Past. Their country here will be opened up, improved; but not by them. It will be made modern, made rich under their very eyes; but not by them. It will be filled with new people, new life; but they will get no benefit from it, their faces will always be turned the other way. They will dwindle in numbers, but they will not change; generations must pass before the old leaven will be worn out. *Could* I leave Garda to that? Could I die, knowing that she would live over there on Patricio, on that forlorn Ruiz plantation, or down the river in that tumble-down house of the Girons—that Manuel with his insufferable airs, or that wooden Torres with his ridiculous pride, would be all she should ever know of life and happiness—my beautiful, beautiful child? I could not, Margaret; I could not." Her eyes were wet.

"But she is not to be left to them," said Margaret.

"No; you have saved me from that," responded the mother, gratefully. She put out her hand and took Margaret's for a moment; then relinquished it. The brief clasp would have seemed cold to their southern friends; but it expressed all that was necessary between these two northerners.

Another day the sick woman resumed her retrospect, she spoke of her early life. "I was a poor school-teacher, you know; I had no near relatives, no home, I was considered to have made a wonderful match when I married as I did. Everybody was astonished at my good luck—perfectly astonished; they couldn't comprehend how it had happened. When they knew, in New Bristol, that I was to marry Mr. Edgar Thorne, of Florida; that I was to be taken down to an old Spanish plantation which had been in his family for generations; that I was to live there in luxury, and 'a tropical climate'—they all came to see me again, to look at me; they seemed to think that I must have changed in some way, that I couldn't be the same Melissa Whiting who had taught their district school. At New Bristol the snow in the winter is four feet deep. At New Bristol everybody is busy, and everybody is poor. But I was to live among palm-trees in a place called Gracias-á-Dios; I was to go down by sea; roses bloomed there at Christmas-time, and oranges were to be had for the asking. Gracias-á-Dios *is* very far from New Bristol,

Margaret," said Melissa Whiting, pausing. "It's all the distance between a real place and an ideal one. I know how far that is!"

She was silent for some minutes; then she went on. "My elevation—for it seemed that at New Bristol—was like a fairy story; I presume they are telling it still. But if I hadn't you behind me, Margaret, I would put Garda back there in all the snow, I would put her back in my old red school-house on the hill (only she wouldn't know how to teach, poor child!)—I would do it in a moment, I say, if I had the power, rather than leave her here among the 'roses,' the 'oranges,' and the 'palms.'" (Impossible to give the accent with which she pronounced these words.) "I don't say my husband wasn't kind to me; he was very kind; but—the Old Madam was here! He only lived a short time; and then, more than ever, the Old Madam was here! Well, I did the best I could—you must give me that credit: there was Garda to think of, and I had no other home. It's so unfortunate to be poor, Margaret—have you ever thought of it?—unfortunate, I mean, for the disposition. So many people could be as amiable and agreeable and yielding as any one, if they only had a little more money—just a little more! I could have been, I know. But how could I be yielding when I had everything on my hands? Oh! you have no idea how I have worked! We had no income to live upon, Garda and I, there hasn't been any for a long time; we have had the house and furniture, the land, Pablo and Raquel,—that's all. We have lived on the things that we had, the things that came off the place, with what Pablo has been able to shoot, and the fish and oysters from the creeks and lagoon. The few supplies which one is obliged to buy, such as tea and coffee, I have got by selling our oranges; I have taken enormous pains with the oranges on that account. The same way with Garda's shoes and gloves; I couldn't make shoes and gloves, though I confess I did try. Then, if any one broke a pane of glass, that took money; and there were a few other little things. But, with these exceptions, I have tried to do everything myself, and manage without spending. I have kept all the furniture in repair; I have painted and varnished and cleaned with my own hands; I learned to mend the crockery and even the tins. I have made almost everything that Garda and I have worn, of course; I braid the palmetto hats we both wear; I have dyed and patched and turned and darned—oh! you haven't a conception! Some of the table-cloths are nothing *but* darns. I could put in myself the new panes of glass, after they were once bought. And, every month or two, I have had to mend the roof, to keep it from leaking; generally I did that at sunrise, but I have done it, too, on moonlight nights, late, when no one was likely to come. Then, every single day, I have had to begin all over again with Pablo and Raquel. Three times every week I have had to go out myself and stand over Pablo to see that he did as I wished about the orange-trees. Always the very same things; but we have been at it in this way for years! Every day of my life I have had to go out and see with my own eyes whether Raquel had wiped off the shelves; three hundred and sixty-five times each year, for seventeen years, she has pretended to forget it."

She lay silent, as if reviewing it all. "Perhaps I have been over-thorough," she resumed. "But somehow I couldn't help it, thoroughness has always been my mania. It has taken me to great lengths—I see it now; it has made burdens where there needn't have been any. Still, I couldn't have helped it, Margaret; I really don't think I could. After sweeping, I always used to go down on my hands and knees and dust the carpets with a cloth. And I used to pick up every seed that Dick, my canary, had dropped. Dear little Dick, how I cried when he died!—he was the last northern thing I had left; yet, would you believe it? I pretended I didn't care for him, that I was tired of his singing. I pretended I preferred the mocking-birds. Mocking-birds!" repeated Melissa Whiting, with whispered but scathing contempt.

She came back to the subject of her thoroughness when Margaret paid her next visit. "It has been a hard task-master; I have been thinking it over," she said. "Still, without it, should I have got on as well even as I have? I don't believe I should. Take the way I have made myself over—made myself a Thorne. I couldn't have lived here at all as I was, there was no room for Melissa Whiting. I saw that; and so, while I was about it, I made the change complete. Oh yes, I was very complete! I swallowed everything. I even swallowed slavery,—I, a New England girl,—what do you say to that?—a New England girl, abolitionist to the core! It was the most heroic thing I ever did in my life. Very likely you don't think so, but it was. For, never for one instant were my real feelings altered, my real beliefs changed—I couldn't have changed them if I had tried. And I could have died for them at any moment, if I had been called upon to do so, though I *was* playing such a part. But I wasn't called upon, and so I made them stay down; I covered every inch of myself with a southern skin. But if any one thinks that it was easy or pleasant, let him try it—that's all!"

"When the war began," she went on, "I remember how much more clearly reasoned out were *my* views of the southern side of the question than were those of the southerners themselves about here. They were as warm as possible in their feelings, of course, but they hadn't studied the subject as I had, got their reasons into shape; so it ended in their borrowing my reasons! But every night through all that time, Margaret, on my knees I prayed for my own people, and I used to read the accounts of the northern victories—when I could get them—with an inward shout; never once, never once, had I a doubt of the final success."

"It's a curious story, isn't it?" Margaret said to Winthrop, when she repeated to him some of these confidences. "She wished me to tell you, she asked me to do so; she said she should like to have *you* understand her life."

"Does she expect me to admire it?" said Winthrop, rather surprised himself to feel how quickly the old heat could rise in his throat again when confronted with a tale like this. For the southern women, who had everywhere suffered so much, given so much, and lost their all, he had nothing but the tenderest pity. But a northern woman who had joined their cause—that seemed to him apostasy. That the apostasy had been but pretence only made it worse.

"She expects you to remember her motive for it, after she is gone," Margaret answered.

"Her motive can't make me like it. Even in the midst of her mistakes, however, she has been a wonderful little creature. But you say 'after she is gone'—do you think her worse, then? I thought she was so much better."

"So she is better. But she will fail again; at least that is what she thinks herself, and I cannot help fearing she is right."

"I am very sorry to hear it." He seemed to have the idea that she would say more; and he waited. But she did not speak.

"I suppose, then, you have had some further talk about Garda?" he said at last, breaking the pause.

"Yes."

"You would rather not tell me?"

"I will tell you later."

At this moment Mrs. Rutherford came into the room. But her nephew remained silent so long, his eyes resting absently on Margaret's dusky hair as she bent her head over a long seam (she seemed to like long seams!), that at last the aunt asked him if he knew that he was growing absent-minded.

"Absent-minded—impossible! No one has ever accused me of that before. I have always been too present-minded; viciously so, they say."

"People change," remarked Mrs. Rutherford, with dignity. "There have been many changes here lately."

Her voice had an undertone that suggested displeasure; the lady was indeed in the fixed condition of finding nothing right. The state appeared to have been caused by the absences of her niece at East Angels. The household wheels had apparently moved on with their usual smoothness during that interval; Mrs. Rutherford herself had appeared to be in the enjoyment of her usual agreeably weak health; her attire had been as becoming as ever, her hair as artistically arranged. But in spite of all this there was the undertone. Nothing was as it should be—that might have been the general summing up. If she leaned back in her chair, that was not comfortable; if she sat erect, that was not comfortable either; there were draughts everywhere, it was insupportable—the draughts; the floors were cold; they were always cold. She was convinced that the climate was damp; it must be, "with all this water" about. Then, again, she was sure that it was "feverish;" it must be, "with all this sand." The eyrie had become "tiresome," the fragrance of the orange flowers "enervating;" as for pine barrens, she never wished to see a pine barren again.

These things were not peevishly said, Mrs. Rutherford's well-modulated voice was never peevish; they were said with a sort of majestic coldness by a majestic woman who was, however, above complaints. She was as handsome as ever; but it was curious to note how her inward dissatisfactions had deepened lines which before had been scarcely visible, had caused her fine profile to assume for the first time a little of that expression to which regular profiles, cut on the majestic scale, are liable as age creeps on—a certain hard, immovable appearance, as though the features had been cut out of wood, as though the changing feelings, whatever they might be, would not be able to affect their rigid line.

"She's missed you uncommon," Celestine confided to Margaret, when she returned; "*nothin's* ben right. 'Most every mornin' when she was all dressed I sez to her, 'Mrs. Rutherford,' sez I, 'what's the preposition for now?' And there never warn't any preposition, or, ruther, there was so many we couldn't begin to manage 'em! Mr. Evert—he's ben down to the Thornes' a good deal, you know, an' Dr. Kirby—*he* hasn't ben in at all. Even Mrs. Carew's ben gone. An' so she's rather petered out. Glad you're back, Miss Margaret; dear me suz! yes. A person needn't be a murderer to make a house almighty uncomfortable by just sheer grumpiness. But she'll pick up now."

Celestine had been right when she said that the lady's mental condition would improve now that her niece had returned. Gradually, as Margaret's touch on the helm brought the household back into the atmosphere she loved, the atmosphere of few questions and no suggestions, suggestions as to what she had "better" do (Mrs. Rutherford hated suggestions as to what she had "better" do), of all her small customs silently furthered, her little wishes remembered without the trouble of having to express them, her remarks listened to and answered, and conversation (when she wished for conversation) kept up—all this so quietly done that she could with ease ignore that it was anything especial to do, maintain the position that it was but the usual way of living, that anything else would have been unusual—gradually, as this congenial atmosphere re-established itself, Mrs. Rutherford recovered her geniality, that geniality which had been so much admired. Her majestic remarks as to the faults of Gracias and everything in Gracias became fewer, the under-note of cold displeasure in her voice died away; her profile grew flexible and personal again, it was less like that of a Roman matron in a triumphal procession—a procession which has been through a good deal of wind and dust.

This happy revival of placidity at the eyrie (to which possibly the reappearance of Dr. Kirby had added something) was sharply broken one morning by bad news from East Angels. Mrs. Thorne was worse—"sinking" was the term used in the note which Betty Carew had hastily scribbled; she was anxious to see Mrs. Harold.

It had come, then, the end, and much sooner than even she herself had expected. She had suffered severely for twenty-four hours; the suffering was over now, but she had not the strength to rally.

"It's because she's always worked *so* hard—I can't help thinking of it," said Betty, who sat in the outer room, crying (she had been up all night, but did not dream of taking any rest); "she *never* stopped. We all knew it, and yet somehow we didn't half realize it, or try to prevent it; and it's too late now."

All the Gracias friends were soon assembled at East Angels; even Mrs. Moore, invalid though she was, made the little journey by water, and was carried up to the house in an arm-chair by her husband and old Pablo. Recovering, if not more strength, then at least that renewed command of speech which often comes back for a time just before the end, Mrs. Thorne, late in the afternoon, opened her eyes, looked at them all, and then, after a moment, asked to be left alone with Garda, Margaret, and Evert Winthrop. Margaret thought that she had spoken Winthrop's name by mistake.

"She doesn't mean you, I think," she said to him, in a low tone.

"Yes, I mean Mr. Winthrop," murmured Mrs. Thorne, with a faint shadow of her old decision.

Her Gracias friends softly left the room. Even Dr. Kirby, after a few whispered words with Winthrop, followed them.

When the door was closed, Mrs. Thorne signified that she wished to take Margaret's hand. Then, her feeble fingers resting on it, "Garda," she said, in her husky voice, "Margaret—whom I trust entirely—has promised—to take charge of you—for a while—after—I am gone. Promise me—on your side—to obey her—to do as she wishes."

"Do not make her promise that," said Margaret. "I think she loves me; that will be enough."

Garda, crying bitterly, kissed Margaret, and then sank on her knees beside the bed, her head against her mother's arm. The sight of her child's grief did not bring the tears to Mrs. Thorne's eyes—already the calm that precedes death had taken possession of them; but it did cause a struggling effort of the poor harassed breath to give forth a sob. She tried to stroke

Garda's hair, but could not. "How can I go—and leave her?" she whispered, looking piteously at Margaret, and then at Winthrop, as he stood at the foot of the bed. "She had—no one—but me." And again came the painful sound in the throat, though the clogged breast had not the strength to rise.

"If I could only know," she went on, desolately, to Margaret, the slow turning of the eyes betraying the approach of that lethargy which was soon to touch the muscles with numbness. "You have said—for a while; but you did not promise for longer. If I could only know, Margaret, that she would be under your care as long as she is so alone in the world, then, perhaps, it would be easier to die."

These words, pronounced with difficulty one by one, separated by the slow breaths, seemed to Winthrop indescribably affecting. It was the last earthly effort of mother-love.

Margaret hesitated. It was only for a moment that she was silent. But Evert took that moment to come forward, he came to the side of the bed where she was standing. "Give *me* your permission, Mrs. Thorne," he said to the dying woman. "Trust *me*, and I will fill the trust. Garda shall have every care, my aunt shall take charge of her." He was indignant with Margaret for hesitating.

But Margaret hesitated no longer. "I think I am the better person," she interposed, gently. Then, bending forward, she said, with distinctness, "Mrs. Thorne, Garda shall live with me, or near me under my charge, as long as she is so young and alone, as long as she needs my care. You have given me a great trust, I hereby accept it; and I will keep it with all the faithfulness I can." Her voice took on an almost solemn tone as the last words were spoken.

Winthrop, glancing at her as she bent forward beside him, perceived that though she was holding herself in strict control, she was moved by some deep emotion; he could feel that she was trembling. Again, even then and there, he gave an instant to the same conjecture which had occupied his thoughts before. Why should she show emotion? why should her voice take on that tone? She was not excitable; he had had occasion to know that she was not afraid of death, she had stood beside too many death-beds in her visits among the poor (not that he admired her philanthropy); it could not be that she had suddenly become so fond of poor Mrs. Thorne. But he left his conjectures unsolved. A faint but beautiful smile was passing strangely over the mother's face, strangely, because no feature stirred or changed—she was beyond that—and yet the smile was there; the eyes became so transfigured that the two who were watching stood awe-struck; for it seemed as if she were beholding something, just behind or above them, which was invisible to them, something which had lifted from her all the pains and cares of her earthly life, and set her free. For some moments longer the beautiful radiance shone there. Then the light departed, and death alone was left, though the eyes retained a consciousness. They seemed to try to turn to Garda, who was still kneeling with her head hidden against her mother's shoulder.

"Take her in your arms, Garda," whispered Margaret; "your face is the last she wishes to see."

Winthrop had summoned Dr. Kirby; the other friends came softly in. For twenty minutes more the slow breaths came and went, but with longer and longer intervals between. Garda, lying beside her mother, held her in her arms, and the dying woman's fixed eyes rested on her child's for some time; then consciousness faded, the lids drooped. Garda put her warm cheek against the small white face, and, thus embraced, the mother's earthly life ebbed away, while in the still room ascended, in the voice of the clergyman, the last prayer—"O Almighty God, with whom do live the spirits of men after they are delivered from their earthly prisons, we humbly commend to Thee the soul of this thy servant, our dear sister—" Our dear sister; they were all there, her Gracias friends—Mrs. Kirby, Mrs. Carew, Mrs. Moore, Madam Giron, Madam Ruiz—and they all wept for her as though she had been a sister indeed. In the hall outside, at the open door, stood handsome Manuel, not ashamed of his tears; and near him, more devout as well as more self-controlled, knelt Torres, reverently waiting, with head turned away, for the end.

Dr. Kirby laid the little hand he had been holding, down upon the coverlet. "She has gone," he said, in a low voice. And, with a visible effort to control his features, he passed round to the other side of the bed, and lifting Garda tenderly, tried to draw her away. But Garda clung to the dead, and cried so heart-brokenly that all the women, with fresh tears starting at the desolate sound—that sound of audible sobbing which first tells those outside the still room that the blow has fallen—all the women came one by one and tried to comfort her. But it was not until Margaret Harold took her in her arms that she was at all quieted.

"Come with me, Garda," she said. "You are not leaving your mother alone, your mother is not here; she has gone home to God. Come with me; remember she wished it." And Garda yielded.

They buried Mrs. Thorne in the family burying-ground at East Angels (the one of which she had spoken), her daughter and her friends following, on foot, the coffin, borne on the shoulders of eight of their former slaves. Thus the little procession crossed the Levels to the secluded enclosure at the far end, Mr. Moore in his surplice leading the way. A high hedge of cedar-trees set closely together like a wall, their dark branches sweeping the ground, encircled the place; across the narrow opening which had been left for entrance, was a low paling-gate. Within, ranged in a circle, were a number of oblong coquina tombs, broad and low, without inscriptions; here slept all the Dueros, the first Englishman, Edgar Thorne, and the few American-born Thornes who had succeeded him. Into the presence of this company was now borne Melissa Whiting.

Her coffin was covered with the beautiful flowers of the South; but within, hidden on her breast, there was a faded spray of arbutus, the last "May-flowers" which had been sent to her, years before, from her northern home; she had given them to Margaret, and asked her, when the time came, to place them there. Thus was she lowered to her rest. All who were present came one by one, according to Gracias custom, to cast into the deep grave the handful of white sand which, in Florida, represents the "earth to earth"—that sound which, soft though it be, breaks the heart. Garda, shivering, clung to Margaret and hid her face. Then rose Mr. Moore's voice among them: "I heard a voice from heaven saying unto me, 'Write. From henceforth blessed are the dead—for they rest from their labors.'"

Beautiful words, unmeaning to the young and happy, more and more do they convey to many of us a dear comfort, for ourselves as well as for those already gone—blessed are the dead, for they rest from their labors. For they *rest*.

That evening the negroes of the neighborhood assembled at East Angels, and, standing outside in the darkness, under the windows, sang their own funeral hymn; their voices rose with sweetness in the wildly plaintive minor strains; then grew softer and softer, as, still singing sweetly, they marched quietly away.

And so night closed down over the old southern house. But the little mother, who had toiled there so long, was gone. She was away in that far country where we hope we shall no more remember the cares and pain, the mysteries and bitter griefs of this.

CHAPTER XIV

The next day it was arranged that Garda should, for the present, remain where she was; she wished to do this, and Mrs. Carew, unselfish always, had offered to close her own house (so far as Cynthy and Pompey would permit), and stay with her for a while.

It was known now that Mrs. Harold was to have charge of Garda. The Gracias friends were grieved by this tidings; they had supposed that Garda would be left to them. But they all liked Margaret, and when, a little later, they learned that she had asked Dr. Kirby to fill the office of guardian, they welcomed with gladness this guarantee that they were not to be entirely separated from the child whom they had known and loved from her birth, that one of them was to have the right, in some degree, to direct her course, and watch over her. These unworldly people, these secluded people, with their innocently proud, calm belief in their own importance, never once thought of its being possibly an advantage to Garda, this opportunity to leave Gracias-á-Dios, to have further instruction, to see something of the world. They could not consider it an advantage to leave Gracias-á-Dios, and "further instruction," which, of course, meant northern instruction, they did not approve; as for "the world," very little confidence had they in any world so remote from their own. That, indeed, was the Gracias idea of New York—"remote." Nor did the fact that Mrs. Harold had a fortune (a very large one it would have seemed to them had they known its amount) make any especial impression. They would each and all have welcomed Garda to their own homes, would have freely given her a daughter's share in everything they possessed; that, from a worldly point of view, these homes were but poor ones, and a daughter's share in incomes which were in themselves so small and uncertain, a very limited possession—these considerations did not enter much into their thoughts. Their idea was that for a fatherless, motherless girl, love was the great thing; and of love they had an abundance.

Before he had had his interview with Margaret, before he knew of her intention to ask him to be guardian, Dr. Kirby had gone about silent; with a high color; portentous. Much as he admired Mrs. Rutherford, he did not present himself at the eyrie; his mirror told him that he had not the proper expression. But Margaret did not delay; on the third day she made her request; and then the Doctor went home stepping with all his old trimness, his toes well turned out, his head erect.

"It's very fortunate, ma" (the Doctor's *a* in this word had a sound between that of *a* in "mare" and in "May"), "that she *has* asked me," he said to his mother; "I doubt whether I could have kept silence otherwise. I admire Mrs. Rutherford highly, as you know; she is a lady of the finest bearing and presence. And I admire Mrs. Harold too. But if they had attempted—if Mrs. Harold had attempted to take Garda off to the North, and keep her there, without any link, any regularly established communication with us, I *fear*" (the Doctor's face had grown red again)—"I fear, ma, I should have balked; I should have just set my feet together, put down my head, and—raised the devil behind!"

"Why, my son, what language!" said his mother, surprised; though she felt, too, the force of his comparison, as she lived in the country of the mule.

"Excuse me, ma; I am excited, or rather I have been. But Garda is one of us, you know, and we could not, *I* could not, with a clear conscience allow them to separate her from us entirely, hurry her off into a society of which we know little or nothing, save that it is totally different from our own—modern—mercantile—hurrying" (the Doctor was evidently growing excited again)—"all that we most dislike. You are probably thinking that there are Mrs. Rutherford, Mrs. Harold, yes, and Mr. Winthrop too (if he would only dress himself more as a gentleman should), to answer for it, to serve as specimens. Those charming ladies would grace, I admit, any society—any society in the world! But I am convinced that they are not specimens, they are exceptions; I am convinced that society at the North is a very different affair. And, besides, Garda belongs here. Her ancestors have been men of distinction,—among the most distinguished, indeed, of this whole coast; I *may* be mistaken, of course, ma; I *may* be too severe; but still I cannot help thinking that at the North this would fall on ignorant ears; that the people there are too—too ignorant of such matters to appreciate them."

"I reckon you are right," replied Mrs. Kirby. "Still, Reginald, we must not forget that it was the mother's own wish that Mrs. Harold should take charge of Garda."

"Yes, ma, I know. Poor little Mistress Thorne, to whom I was most sincerely attached"—here the Doctor paused to give a vigorous cough—"was, we must remember, a New-Englander by birth, after all; and in spite of her efforts (most praiseworthy they were too), she never *quite* outgrew that fact. It couldn't, therefore, be expected that she should comprehend fully the great advantages (even taking merely the worldly view of it) of having her daughter continue to live here—here where such a descent is acknowledged, and proper honor paid to ancestors of distinction."

"True, my son," said the neat little old lady, knitting on. "But still a mother has a good deal to do with the 'descent!' I'm not sure that she hasn't even more than an ancestor—ahem."

On the whole, as matters were now arranged, with Dr. Kirby appointed as guardian, it could be said that Gracias accepted the new order of things regarding Garda's future. Not thankfully or gratefully, not with inward relief; it was simply an acquiescence. They felt, too, that their acquiescence was magnanimous.

The only discordant element was Mrs. Rutherford. And she was very discordant indeed. But as she confined the expression of her feelings to her niece, the note of dissonance did not reach the others.

"It's beyond belief," she said. "What possible claim have these Thornes upon you? The idea of her having tried to saddle you with that daughter of hers! She took advantage of you, of course, and of the situation; I am really indignant for you, and feel that I ought to come to your rescue; I advise you to have nothing to do with it. You can be friendly, of course, while we are here; but, afterwards, let it all drop."

"I can hardly do that when I have promised, Aunt Katrina," answered Margaret. And she answered in the same way many times.

For Mrs. Rutherford could make a very dexterous use of the weapon of iteration. She was seldom betrayed into a fretful tone, there was always a fair show of reason in what she said (its purely personal foundation she was skilful in concealing); her best thrust was to be so warmly on the side of the person she was trying to lead, to be so "surprised" for him, and "angry" for him (as against others), that he was led at last to be "surprised" and "angry" himself, though in the beginning he might have had no such idea. By these well-managed reiterations she had gained her point many times during honest Peter's lifetime; he never failed to be touched when he saw how warmly she was taking up "his side," though up to that moment, perhaps, he had not been aware that he had a "side" on that particular subject, or that anybody was on the other.

But if she gained her point with Peter, she did not gain it with Peter's niece.

"Garda, I hope, will not be a trouble to you, Aunt Katrina. For the present she is to remain at East Angels; when we go north, I shall place her with Madame Martel."

"It's really pitiful to think how unhappy she will be," said Mrs. Rutherford, the next day, shaking her head prophetically. "Poor child—poor little southern flower—to take her away from this lovely climate, and force her to live at the cold North—to take her away from a real home, where they all love her, and put her with Madame Martel! You must have a far sterner nature than *I* have, Margaret, to be able to do it."

To this Margaret made no answer.

"I really wish you would tell me why you rate your own influence over that of everybody else," remarked Mrs. Rutherford on another occasion. She spoke impersonally, as though it were simply a curiosity she felt. "Have you had some experience in the management of young girls that I know nothing about?"

"No," replied Margaret.

"Yet you undertake it without hesitation! You have more confidence in your powers than I should have in mine, I confess. How do you know what she may do? Depend upon it, she won't have our ideas at all. You are a quiet sort of person, but she may be quite the reverse, and then what a prospect! She will be talked about, such girls always are; she may even get into the papers."

"Not for a year or two yet, I think," answered Margaret, smiling.

The next day, "It would be so *easy* to do it now," observed the handsome aunt; "it almost seems like a tempting of Providence to neglect such an opportunity." (Mrs. Rutherford always lived on intimate terms with Providence.) "You could keep up your interest in her, send her down books, and even a governess for six months or so, if you wished to be very punctilious; all the people here want Garda to stay—they cannot bear to give her up; you would be doing them a kindness by yielding. They are really fond of her, and she is fond of them; of course you can't pretend that she cares for *you* in that way?"

"Oh no, I don't pretend," replied Margaret.

"You carry her off without it!"

The next advance was on another line. "What are you going to do when she is through school, Margaret?" demanded the inquirer, with interested amiability. "She'll have to see something, go somewhere—you can't shut her up; and who is going to chaperon her? I am an invalid, you know, and you yourself are much too young. You must remember, my dear, that you are a young and pretty woman." (Aunt Katrina had evidently been driven to her best shot.)

But though this, or a similar remark, would have been certain to bring down Peter, and place him just where his wife wished him to be, it failed to bring down Peter's niece.

Mrs. Rutherford saw this. And concluded as follows: "However, it doesn't make much difference; with the kind of beauty Garda Thorne has, no one would look at *you*, you might be any age; she has the sort of face that simply extinguishes every one else."

"Having no radiance of my own to look after, I can see her all the better, then," replied Margaret. "She'll be the lighted Bank, and I the policeman with the dark lantern."

Mrs. Rutherford did not like this answer, she thought it flippant. It was true, however, that Margaret was very seldom flippant.

"It does seem to me so *weak* to keep an extorted promise," she began another day. "I suppose you won't deny that it was extorted?"

"It was very much wished for."

"And you gave it unwillingly."

"Not unwillingly, Aunt Katrina."

"Reluctantly, then."

"Yes, I was reluctant."

"You were reluctant," repeated Mrs. Rutherford, with triumph. "Of course I knew you must be. But whatever possessed you to do it, Margaret—induced you to consent, extortion or no extortion—that passes me!"

Margaret gave no explanation. So the aunt attempted one. "It *almost* seems as though you were influenced by something *I* am ignorant of," she went on, making a little gesture of withdrawal with her hand, as if she found herself on the threshold of mysterious regions of double motive into which she should prefer not to penetrate.

This was a random ball. But Margaret's fair face showed a sudden color, though the aunt's eyes did not detect it. "She is alone, and very young, Aunt Katrina; I have promised, and I must keep my promise. But I shall do my best to prevent it from disturbing you, with me you will always be first; this is all I can say, and I do not think there is any use in talking about it more." She had risen as she said these words, and now she left the room.

In addition to her niece's obstinacy, this lady had now to bear the discovery that her nephew Evert did not share her views respecting Garda Thorne—views which seemed to her the only proper and natural ones; he not only thought that Mrs. Harold should keep her promise, but he even went further than she did in his ideas as to what that promise included. "She ought to keep Garda with her, and not put her off at Madame Martel's," he said.

"I see that *I* am to be quite superseded," remarked Mrs. Rutherford, in a pleasant voice, smoothing her handkerchief, however, with a sort of manner which seemed to indicate that she might yet be driven to a use—lachrymose—of that delicate fabric.

"My dear aunt, what can you be thinking of?" said Winthrop. "Nobody is going to supersede you."

"But how *can* I like the idea of sharing you with a stranger, Evert?" Her tone continued affectionate; she seldom came as far as ill temper with her nephew; she seldom, indeed, came as far as ill temper with any man, a coat seemed to have a soothing effect upon her.

"There's no sharing, as far as I am concerned," Winthrop answered. "*I* have nothing to do with Garda; it's Margaret."

"Yes, it *is* Margaret. And very obstinate, too, has she been about it. Now, if the girl had been left to me," pursued the lady, in a reasonable way, "there would have been some sense in it. I have had experience, and *I* should know what to do. I should pick out an excellent governess, and send her down here with all the books necessary—perhaps even a piano," she added, largely; "in that way I should keep watch of the child's education. But I should never have planned to take her away from her home and all her friends; that would seem to me cruelty. My idea would have been, and still is, that she should live here, say with the Kirbys; then she would have the climate and life which she always has had, to which she is accustomed; and in time probably she would marry either that young Torres, or Manuel Ruiz, both quite suitable matches for her. But what could she do in *our* society, if Margaret should persist, later, in taking her into it? It would be quite pitiable, she would be so completely out of her element, poor little thing!"

"So beautiful a girl is apt to be in her element wherever she is, isn't she?" remarked Winthrop.

"Is it possible, Evert, that you really admire her?"

"I admire her greatly."

The tears rose in Mrs. Rutherford's eyes at this statement. They were only tears of vexation, but the nephew did not know that; he came and stood beside her.

She had hidden her face in her handkerchief. "If you should ever marry that girl, Evert, my heart would be broken!" she lamented from behind it. "She isn't at all the person for you to marry."

Winthrop burst into a laugh. "I'm not at all the person for *her* to marry. Have you forgotten, Aunt Katrina, that I am thirty-five, and she—barely sixteen?"

"Age doesn't make any difference," answered Mrs. Rutherford, still tearful. "And you are very rich, Evert."

"Garda Thorne doesn't care in the least about money," responded Winthrop, shortly, turning away.

"She ought to, then," rejoined Mrs. Rutherford, drying her eyes with a soft pressure of the handkerchief, so that the lids should not be reddened.

"In fact, that is another of her lacks: she seems to have no objection to imposing herself upon Margaret in a pecuniary way as well as in others. She has nothing, there isn't literally a cent of income, Betty Carew tells me; only a pile of the most extraordinarily darned old clothes and house-linen, a decayed orange grove, and two obstinate old negro servants, who don't really belong to anybody, and wouldn't obey them if they did. That you should buy the place, that has been their one hope; it was very clever of them to give you the idea."

"Garda didn't give it, I wanted the place as soon as I saw it. She *is* ignorant about money; most girls of sixteen are. But what is it that really vexes you so much in this affair, Aunt Katrina? I am sure there is something."

"You are right," replied Mrs. Rutherford, with dignity. "But 'vexes' is not the word, Evert. It is a deeper feeling." She had put away her handkerchief, and now sat majestically in her chair, her white hands extended on its cushioned arms. "*Hurt* is the word; I am hurt about Margaret. Here I have done everything in the world for her, opened my home and my heart to her, in spite of *all*; and now she deserts me for a totally insignificant person, a stranger."

"Margaret has always been very devoted to you, and I am sure she will continue to be—she is conscientious in such things—no matter what other responsibilities she may assume," said Winthrop, with warmth.

Mrs. Rutherford noticed this warmth (Winthrop noticed it too); but, for the moment, she let it pass. "That is just it—other responsibilities," she answered; "but why should she assume any? Before she promised to give that girl a home, she should have remembered that it was *my* home. Before she promised to take charge of her, she should have remembered that she had other things in charge. I am an invalid, I require (and most properly) a great deal of her care; not to give it, or to give it partially, would be, after all I have done for her, most ungrateful; she should have remembered that she was not free—free, that is, to make engagements of that sort."

Winthrop had several times before in his life come face to face with the evidence that his handsome, agreeable aunt was selfish. He was now face to face with it again.

"As regards what you say about a home, Aunt Katrina, Margaret could at any time have one of her own, if she pleased," he answered; "her income fully permits it."

Mrs. Rutherford now gave way to tears that were genuine. "It's the first time, Evert, I've known you to take *her* part against me," she answered, from behind her shielding handkerchief.

Winthrop recalled this speech later—after he had made his peace with his afflicted relative; it *was* the first time. He thought about it for a moment or two—that he should have been driven to defend Lanse's wife. But that was it, he had been driven. "She was so confoundedly unjust," he said to himself, thinking of his aunt. He knew that he had a great taste for justice.

A few days after this he came to the eyrie one morning at an hour much earlier than his accustomed one; he sent Celestine to ask Mrs. Harold to come for a moment to the north piazza, the one most remote from Mrs. Rutherford's rooms. Margaret joined him there immediately; her face wore an anxious expression.

"I see you think I bring bad news—sending for you in this mysterious way," he said, smiling. "It isn't bad at all; under the circumstances I call it very good, the best thing that could have happened. Mr. Moore has had a letter; Lucian Spenser was married last week. Something sudden, I presume; probably it was that that took him north."

Margaret's eyes met his with what he called their mute expression. He had never been able to interpret it, he could not now.

"It hasn't, of course, the least interest for us, except as it may touch Garda," he went on. "I don't apprehend anything serious; still, as we are the only persons who have known her little secret—this fancy she has had—perhaps it would be better if one of us should go down to East Angels and tell her before any one else can get there—don't you think so? And will you go? or shall I?"

"You," Margaret answered.

"I don't often ask questions, you must give me that credit," he said, looking at her. "But I should really like to know upon what grounds you decide so quickly."

"The grounds are unimportant. But I am sure you are the one to go."

Winthrop, on the whole, wished to go. He now found himself telling his reasons. "I can go immediately, that is one thing; you would have to speak to Aunt Katrina, make arrangements, and that would take time. Then I think that Garda has probably talked more freely to me about that youth than she has to you; it's a little odd that she should, but I think she has."

"It's very possible."

"On that account it would come in more naturally, perhaps, if she should hear it first from me."

Again Margaret assented.

"And then it won't make her think it's important, my stopping there as I pass; your going would have another look. I'm a little curious to see how she will take it," he added.

"That is your real reason, I think," said Margaret.

"She has just lost her mother," he went on, without taking up this remark. "Perhaps the real sorrow may make her forget the fictitious one; I am sure I hope so. I will go down, then. But in case I am mistaken, in case she should continue to—fancy herself in earnest, shall I come back and tell you?"

"I suppose so, she is in my charge. But if I should have to go down there myself, Aunt Katrina would take it rather ill, I am afraid,—that is just now."

"You are very good to Aunt Katrina, I want to tell you that I appreciate it; I am afraid she has rather a way of treating you as an appendage to herself, not as an independent personage."

"That is all I am—an appendage," said Margaret. She paused. "Feeling as she does," she continued, "she yet allows me to stay with her. That has been a great deal to me."

Winthrop's face changed a little; up to this time his expression had been almost warmly kind. "Feeling as she does!" Yes, Aunt Katrina might well feel as she did, with her favorite nephew, her almost son, wandering about the world (this was one of the aunt's expressions, he used it in his thoughts unconsciously), without a home, because he had a wife so Pharisaic, so icily unforgiving.

"You make too much of it," he answered, coldly; "the obligation is by no means all on one side." Then he finished what he had begun to say before she made her remark. "I had occasion to remind my aunt, only the other day, that if at any time you should wish to have a home of your own, she ought not to object. She would miss you greatly, of course; I, however—and I am glad to have this opportunity of saying it—should consider such a wish very natural, and I should be happy to do everything possible towards furthering it."

"I have no such wish; but perhaps you think—perhaps you prefer that I should leave Mrs. Rutherford?" She had turned away, he could not see the expression of face that accompanied the words.

"It would be impossible that I should prefer such a thing; I don't think you can be sincere in saying it," responded Winthrop, with a tinge of severity. "We both know perfectly well what you are to Aunt Katrina; what is the use of pretending otherwise?" His voice softened. "Your patience with her is admirable; as I said before, don't think I don't see it. I spoke on your own account, I thought you might be tired."

"I am tired—sometimes. But I should be tired just the same in a house of my own," answered Margaret Harold.

He left her, and rode down to East Angels.

But his visit was short; before three o'clock he was again at the eyrie. "I think you had better go down," he said to Margaret, as soon as he could speak to her unheard. "She is taking it most unreasonably; she is crying almost convulsively, and listens to nothing. So far, Mrs. Carew thinks it the old grief for her mother; a revival. But she won't think so long; for Garda, you know, never conceals anything; as soon as she is a little calmer she will be sure to say something that will let out the whole."

"You do not want it known?"

"I thought we were agreed about that. How can any one who cares for the girl want it known? It's so"—he hesitated for a word, and then fell back upon the useful old one—"so childish," he repeated.

"I will go down, then," said Margaret.

"The sooner the better. I hope that you will be able to bring her to reason."

"But if you didn't—"

"I didn't because I lost my temper a little. It seemed to me that the time had come to speak to her plainly."

"Plainly generally means severely. I think severity will never have much effect upon Garda; if you are severe, you will only lose your influence."

"My influence!—I don't know that I have any. What is your idea of Edgarda Thorne?" he said, suddenly. "I don't know that I have ever asked you. Very likely you won't tell."

"I will tell exactly, so far as I know it myself—my idea," replied Margaret. "One cannot have a very definite idea of a girl of sixteen."

"I beg your pardon; to me she seems a remarkably definite person."

"She is, in one way. I think she is very warm-hearted. I think she is above petty things; I have never seen any girl who went so little into details. Mentally, I think her very clever, though she is also indolent. Her frankness would be the most remarkable thing about her were it not for her beauty, which is more remarkable still; it is her beauty, I think, that makes her, young as she is, so 'definite,' as you call it."

"We seem to have much the same idea of her," said Winthrop. "I shouldn't have thought it possible," he added.

"That we should agree in anything?" said Margaret, with a faint smile.

"No, not that; but a woman so seldom has the same idea of another woman that a man has. And—if you will allow me to say it—I think the man's idea often the more correct one, for a woman will betray (confide, if you like the term better) more of her inner nature, her real self, to a man, when she knows him well and likes him, than she ever will to any woman, no matter how well she may know and like her."

Margaret concurred in this.

"So you agree with me there too? Another surprise! What I have said is true enough, but women generally dispute it."

"What you have said is true, after a fashion," Margaret answered. "But the inner feelings you speak of, the real self, which a woman confides to the man she likes rather than to a woman, these are generally her ideal feelings, her ideal self; what she thinks she feels, or hopes to feel, rather than the actual feeling; what she wishes to be, rather than what she is. She may or may not attain her ideal; but in the mean time she is judged, by those of her own sex at least, according to her present qualities, what she has already attained; what she is practically, and every day."

"So you think it is her ideals that Garda has confided to me? What sort of an ideal was Lucian Spenser!"

"Garda is an exception; she has no ideals."

"Oh! don't make her out so disagreeable."

"I couldn't make her out disagreeable even if I should try," answered Margaret. "All I mean is that her nature is so easy, so sunny, that it has never occurred to her to be discontented; and if you are contented you don't have ideals."

"Now you are making her out self-complacent."

"No, only simple; richly natural and healthy. She puts the rest of us (women, I mean) to shame—the rest of us with our complicated motives, and involved consciences."

"I hope you don't mean to say that Garda has no conscience?"

Margaret looked up; she saw that he was smiling. "She has quite enough for her happiness," she answered, smiling too.

But in spite of the smile he detected a melancholy in her tone. And this he instantly resented. For he would never allow that it was owing to her conscientiousness—her conscience, in short—that Margaret Harold's married life had been what it was; that sort of conscientiousness was odious.

"Don't imagine that I admire conscience," he remarked. "Too much of it makes an arid desert of a woman's life. A woman of that sort, too, makes her whole family live in the desert!"

Margaret made no reply to this. She left him and went to find Mrs. Rutherford.

"Of course if it is Garda, little Garda," that lady replied, with a sort of sardonic playfulness which she had lately adopted, "I couldn't dream of objecting." She had given up open opposition since Winthrop's suggestion that Margaret could have, if she should wish it, a home of her own. The suggestion had been very disagreeable, not only in itself (the possibility of such a thing), but also because it cut so completely across her well-established position that it was an immense favor on her part to give Margaret a home. The favor implied, of course, a following gratitude; and Margaret's gratitude had been the broad cushion upon which Mrs. Rutherford had been comfortably seated for seven years. Take it away, and she would be reduced to making objections—objections (if it should really come to that) to Margaret's departure; and what objections could she make? She would never admit that her niece's presence had become necessary to her comfort; and to say that she was too young and attractive to be at the head of a house of her own, this would not accord at all with her accustomed way of speaking of her—a way which had carried with it the implication (though not in actual words) that she was neither. For some reason, the youth of other women was always an offence to Mrs. Rutherford.

However, she was skilful in reducing that attraction. Up to twenty, girls, of course, were "silly," "uninteresting." After that date, they all sprang immediately, in her estimation, to be "at least twenty-five," and well on the road, both in looks and character, to old-maidhood. If they married, it was even easier; for in a few months they were sure to become "so faded and changed, poor things," that one would scarcely know them; and, with a little determination, this stage could be kept along for fifteen or twenty years. Only when they were over forty did Mrs. Rutherford begin to admit the possibility of their being rather attractive; in this lady's opinion, all the really "superb" women were several years even beyond that.

"I shall not be long away this time," Margaret had responded.

"Oh, enjoy your new plaything; it won't last!" said the aunt, still sportive.

Margaret reached East Angels before sunset. Mrs. Carew told her that Garda was down at the landing.

"I've been down there three times myself; in fact, I've just got back," said Betty, who looked flushed by these excursions. "The truth is, I fancy she doesn't want to talk—she's cried so; and so of course I don't stay, of course. And then, no sooner do I get back here, than I think perhaps she's lonely, and down I go again. I don't mind the walk in the *least*, though it *is* a little warm to-day, but Carlos Mateo seems to have taken a spite against me, for every single time, both going and coming, he has chased me the whole length of the live-oak avenue—just as soon as we were out of Garda's sight; and I'm *so* afraid he'll reach down and nip my ankles, that I *run*. However, I don't mind it at all, *really*; and when I came up this last time I thought the best thing I could do would be to try and get up something nice for Garda's supper; she's touched nothing since morning, and so much crying is dreadfully exhausting, of course. I'm right glad you've come, you'll be such a comfort to her; and now *I* will devote my time (I reckon it'll take it all) to that Raquel, who certainly is the most tiresome; the only manner of means, Mrs. Harold, by which I can get what I want this evening is to keep going out to the kitchen and pretend to be merely looking in for a moment or two in a friendly sort of way, as though she were an old servant of my own, and talk about other matters, and then just allude to the supper at the end casually, as one may call it; by keeping this up an hour and a half *more* (I've already been out three times) I *may* get some faint approach to what I'm after. You see I'm only a Georgian, not a Spaniard! And to think of what poor little Mistress Thorne must have gone through with her—she, not even a Southerner! Oh dear! she must have suffered. But a good many of us have suffered," continued Betty, suddenly breaking down and bursting into tears. "I'm sure I don't know why I cry now, Mrs. Harold, any more than any other time; I'm ashamed of myself, really I am. But—sometimes—I—cannot—help it!" And for a few moments the stout, ruddy-faced woman sobbed bitterly. In truth she had suffered; she had seen her brothers, her husband's brothers, her young nephews, her own fortune and theirs, swept off by war, together with the hopes and beliefs which had been as real to her as life itself. She had never reasoned much, or argued, but she had felt. The unchangeable sweetness of her disposition, which had kept her from growing bitter, had not been a sign of quick forgetfulness; poor Betty's heart ached often, and never, never forgot.

"I didn't think you could be so sympathetic, my dear," she said, naïvely, to Margaret, as she wiped her eyes. "Thank you; I can see now why Garda's so fond of you." She pressed Margaret's hand, kissed her, and, still shaken by her sudden emotion, went out for another encounter with Raquel.

Margaret found Garda on the bench at the landing. She looked pale and exhausted, and was glad to lay her head on her northern friend's shoulder and tell her all her grief. It was a surprising sort of sorrow—she expressed it freely as usual; there was no manifestation of wounded pride in it, no anger that she had been so soon forgotten, or jealousy of the person whom Lucian had married; she seemed, indeed, scarcely to remember the person whom Lucian had married. All she remembered was that now she should probably not see him again, or soon again; and this was the cause of all her tears—disappointment in the hope of having the pleasure, the entertainment, of his presence. For it all came back to that, her amusement; the rich share of enjoyment that had been taken from her; even Lucian himself she did not dwell upon save as he was associated with this, save as he could give her the delight of looking at him (she announced this as a great delight), could charm her with the versatility of his talk. "I have never seen any one half so beautiful"—"Nobody *ever* made me laugh so"—these two declarations she repeated over and over again; Margaret could have laughed herself had the grief which accompanied them been less real. But there was nothing feigned in the heavy eyes, and the sobs which came every now and then, shaking the girl's whole frame.

She remained at East Angels two days. During this time, while she was very gentle with Garda, she did not try to "bring her to reason," as Winthrop had suggested; but she did try the method of simple listening, and found it very efficacious.

Garda, unrebuffed, unchilled, and frank as always, let out all her thoughts, all her feelings; she said some very astonishing things—astonishing, that is, to her hearer; but then she was herself an astonishing girl, an unusual girl. The end of it was that the unusual girl clung more closely than ever to her friend, and that she soon became calmer, passive if not happy. Winthrop, coming down to East Angels on the second day, found her so, and took counsel with Margaret, after she had returned home, over the change; he expressed the opinion that very soon she would have forgotten all about it. In this he was mistaken; the days passed, and Garda remained in the same passive condition. She was gentle with every one; to Margaret and Winthrop she was affectionate. But in spite of her bloom—for her color came back as soon as the tears ceased—in spite of her rich youthfulness, she had the appearance of a person who has stopped, who does not care, who has lost interest and lets the world go by. This could not make her look older; but it did give her a strange expression.

"A mourning child is worse than a mourning woman," said Winthrop to Margaret, emphatically. "It's unnatural."

"Garda isn't a child," she answered.

"Since when have you come to that conclusion?"

She hesitated. "I think, perhaps, I have never fully understood her. I don't know that I understand her even now."

"Oh, 'understand'—as if she were a sphinx, poor little girl! One thing is certain," he added, rather contradictorily, "if she loses her simplicity, she loses all her charm."

"Not all, I think."

"Yes, all to me."

"You cannot see what she finds to admire in Lucian Spenser; that is what vexes you."

"I am not in the least vexed. She fancied her own fancy, her own imagination; that was all."

"Garda has very little imagination."

"How you dislike her!" said Winthrop, looking straight into her eyes.

To his surprise he almost thought he saw them falter. "On the contrary, I am much attached to her," she answered, letting her glance drop; "I shall grow very fond of her, I see that. It was nothing against her to say that she has little imagination. If she had had more, would she have been so contented here? I think it has been very fortunate."

"Yes, she has certainly been contented," said Winthrop. "I like that."

"As to what you say about her losing her simplicity, I don't think she has lost it in the least. Why, what could be a greater evidence of it than the open way in which she has shown out to me, but more especially to you, all she has felt about Mr. Spenser?"

"Yes, to me—I should think so! I might have been her grandfather," responded Winthrop, flapping his hat with his gloves, which he had just discovered in some unremembered pocket.

In the mean time the dark Torres, lean and solemn, had haunted East Angels ever since Mrs. Thorne's death. Twice a day, with deep reverence for affliction, he came to inquire after Garda's health; twice a day, walking almost on tiptoe, he withdrew. His visits never exceeded ten minutes in length. So great was his respect that he never sat down. But underneath all this quietude the feelings, which Manuel had described as volcanic, were surging within; if they did not show on the surface, that was the misfortune (or advantage) of having a profound sense of dignity, and a yellow skin. Garda was now alone in the world, and she was in great trouble; like the other Gracias friends, Torres believed that all the recent grief, together with the change in her, had been caused by her mother's death—Margaret and Winthrop had at least succeeded in that. But even if all Gracias had known the truth, Torres would never have known it; he would never have known it because he would never have believed it. A Torres believed only what was credible, and such a tale about a Duero would be incredible. In the same way, he had never given the least credit to the story that Garda was going north—to New York. Why should Garda go to New York, any more than he, Torres, to Japan? No; what Garda needed now was not wild travelling about the world with promiscuous people, but safeguards that were not promiscuous; safeguards that should be embodied in a single and distinct

Arm, a single and distinguished Name; in short, what he himself could give her—an Alliance; an Alliance suited to her birth.

So when the visits of affliction had been all accomplished, he started one morning in his best attire, and his aunt's black boat, rowed by eight negroes, for Gracias-á-Dios, to ask permission from Reginald Kirby, guardian, to "address," with reference to an Alliance, the Dueros' daughter.

The Giron fields, meanwhile, lay idle and empty behind him; he had swept them of every man.

"Dear Adolfo," said his aunt, who, as a widow with six little children, was trying hard (for a Giron) to raise something on her plantation that year, "must you have them all? They are very much needed to-day, we are so behindhand with everything."

"My aunt, what is sugar compared with our name?"

Madam Giron immediately agreed that it was nothing, nothing.

"Look out, my aunt, as we start; that will be compensation," said Adolfo.

Madam Giron not only looked out, but she came down to the landing. She was a handsome woman still, though portly; she had dark eyes of a charming expression, and shining black hair elaborately braided. When she was dressed for a visit she had a waist. On ordinary occasions it lapped over the band more or less. She was good-nature itself, and now stood on the bank smiling, wearing a gown of rather shapeless aspect, which was, however, short enough to show a pair of very pretty Spanish feet incased in neat little black slippers. She had already forgotten the idle fields in her pride at the fine appearance of the rowers. "A good voyage!" she said.

The boat, with the eight negroes sitting close together, was low in the water as it started off. The stern seemed higher; any place where Torres sat always seemed higher.

Reaching Gracias, he landed at the water-steps of the plaza, and leaving the boat waiting below, went to the residence of the Kirbys—an old white house in a large garden. Dr. Reginald, for the moment, was out. Torres signified that he would return, and making his way with his stiff gait to one of the side streets, he walked up and down for twenty minutes, beguiling the time (as all his phrases for the interview were definitely arranged, and he did not wish to disturb them) by trying to translate a sign which was nailed on a low coquina house near.

CHRISTOBAL REY, TONSORIAL ARTIST.

N.B.—Clean Towels. Satisfaction guaranteed.

Having thus employed the interval (and still at "Tonsorial" in his attempted translation), he returned to the Kirby homestead.

The Doctor was now in, and received him courteously. Torres, standing in the centre of the room, hat in hand, his feet drawn together at the heels, made (after several opening sentences of ceremony which he had constructed with care at home) his formal demand.

The Doctor had always got on very well with Torres by replying to him in English; any chance remark would do. Torres listened to the remark with respect, understanding no more of it than the Doctor had understood of the Spanish sentence which had preceded it. Then, after due pause, the Cuban would say something more in his own tongue. And the Doctor would again reply in English. In this way they had had, when they happened to meet, quite long conversations, which appeared to be satisfactory to both. The Doctor now reverted to this method; the boy had evidently come to pay him a visit of ceremony in acknowledgment of several invitations; he would not probably stay long. So, in answer to Torres' request for permission to "address" Garda, with reference to an "Alliance," he replied that on the whole he thought the oranges would be good this year, though—and here followed a little disquisition on the effects respectively of wet and dry seasons, to which Torres listened with gravity unmoved. He then advanced to his second position: he hoped the Doctor, as guardian, cherished no personal objections to his suit; this was the courtesy of ceremony on his part, of course; the Doctor naturally could cherish no objection.

The Doctor replied that he had never cared much for mandarins; for his own part, he preferred the larger kinds. However, that was a matter of taste—each one to his own; he believed in letting everybody have what he liked. And, having the third time pushed a chair in vain towards his visitor, he waived further ceremony and seated himself; he had already been kept standing unconscionably long.

Torres, who had understood at least the gesture, responded with deference, pointing out that to be seated would not accord with his present position as most humble of suitors for the Doctor's favor.

And then the Doctor responded that, to please his mother, he had planted a few mandarins after all.

So they went on. The Doctor thought his visitor would never go. From his comfortable chair he watched him standing in his fixed attitude, producing his Spanish phrases, one after the other, with grave regularity, whenever there was a pause. Finally the Doctor, who had a gleam of fun in him, folded his arms and recited to him two hundred lines from "The Rape of the Lock," which was one of his favorite poems; he emphasized the parts which he liked, and even gesticulated a little as he went on, not hurrying at all, but finishing the whole in round full tones, with excellent taste and elocution. "There!" he said to himself; "let us see how he likes that."

But Torres, apparently, liked it as well as anything else; he listened to the whole without change of expression, and then, after the proper pause, brought out another of his remarks. The Doctor glanced at the clock; the visitor had been there over half an hour. "Look here, Torres, what *is* it you are talking about?" he said, convinced at last that the Cuban had really something to say, and that their usual tactics would not do this time. He had understood not a word of the long Spanish sentences, for Garda's name, which might have thrown some light upon them, had been scrupulously left unspoken by this punctilious suitor, who had used the third person throughout, alluding to her solely as the descendant of her ancestors, and, as such, a "consort" who would be accepted by his own.

Torres watched while the Doctor walked about the room, trying to think of something which should act as interpreter; he paused at pen and paper on the writing-table; but written Spanish was no clearer to him than spoken. At last, with a sudden inspiration, he took down a dictionary. "Here," he said, "find the words you want." And he thrust the Spanish half upon the grave young man.

But Torres recoiled; he could not possibly make a "school exercise," he declared, of his most sacred aspirations.

The Doctor, exasperated, pried the words out of him one by one, and then himself, with spectacles on, looked them out, or tried to, in the dictionary. But progress was slow; Torres' sentences contained much circumlocution, and he would not give the infinitives of his verbs when the Doctor asked for them, considering it beneath his dignity to lend himself in any way to such a childish performance. At length, after much effort, suddenly the Doctor got at his meaning. "You ridiculous idiot!" he said, throwing the dictionary down with a slam (for he had had to work hard, and the print was fine), "you make 'an Alliance,' indeed! Alliance! Why, you're two years under age yourself, and haven't done growing yet, not to speak of your having nothing in the world to offer a wife that I know of—except your impudence, which is colossal, I grant! Go home and play with your top. When you're a man, you can come back and talk of it—if you like; at present face about, go home and play with your top!"

Torres, of course, could not comprehend these injunctions. But he could comprehend the Doctor's opening the door for him; and, with respect unbroken, he formally took leave. He walked down the side street, and looked mechanically at the sign again; but he could not translate it any more than he could the Doctor's last sentence, whose words he carried carefully in his memory. He went back to his boat, and was rowed in state again down the shining water.

"My aunt," he said, when he had arrived, drawing Madam Giron apart from the small Girons who encompassed her, "what is 'Co—ome—oonplay—weetyer—torp?'"

But Madam Giron could not tell him; her English was not imaginative enough to enable her to comprehend her nephew's pronunciations. Torres decided that he would go and ask Manuel, and rowed himself across to Patricio for the purpose; this not being a state occasion, it was allowable to ply the oars.

"Manuel, what is 'Co—ome—oonplay—weetyer—torp?'" he said, appearing on the piazza of Manuel's room, which formed one of the wings of the rambling old house.

But Manuel was in a desperate humor; he was putting on his hat, then dragging it off again, and rushing up and down the room with a rapid step; he glared at his friend, but would not reply.

"I asked you, Manuel, what is 'Co—ome—oonplay—weetyer—torp?'" repeated Torres. "It is what the Gracias-á-Dios doctor said to me, as answer, when (after very long stupidity on his part; I can say it to you, Manuel—doltishly long) he at last comprehended that I was requesting his permission to address the Señorita Duero. Naturally, as you will now understand, I desire a careful translation."

Manuel laughed bitterly. "So you've got it too! But *I* went to the girl herself, as you would have done if you hadn't been such a ninny; but you're always a ninny. What do you suppose she said to me—yes, Garda herself?" he went on, furiously, dropping, in the recital of his wrongs, even the pleasure of abusing his friend. "Here I only went to her because she is so alone now, so unhappy, it was pure compassion on my part; I made sacrifices, *sacrifices,* I tell you, and poignant ones!—I intended to see the world first. Am I not in the flower of my youth—I ask you that? Am I not keenly pleasing? But—everybody knows! Well, was she grateful? I leave you to judge! She deliberately said—yes, in so many words—that she had never cared for me, when the whole world knows she has cared to distraction, to frenzy. And she had the effrontery to add that the only person she cared for—and for him she cared 'day and night'—was that—that—" In his rage

Manuel could not speak the name, but he seized a great knife with a sharp edge, and cut straight through a book which was lying on the table. "There!" he cried, throwing the severed leaves in handfuls about the room, "that is how I will serve him—Spenser-r-r-r! Let him come on!" And he continued to throw the papers wildly.

Torres was shocked. Not at the sight of his friend displaying his vengeance in that childish fashion; he had long considered Manuel hopelessly undignified. His shock came from the idea of a Señorita Duero having been spoken to on such a subject, spoken to directly! Of course she had rejected Manuel (it would always be of course that she should reject Manuel), but the idea of her having been forced to do so by word of mouth—being deprived of the delicate privilege of expressing herself through her proper guardian! As to the story that she was thinking of some one else, "day and night," he paid no heed to it; that was plainly Manuel's fiction. No one could for a moment believe that the señorita thought of any one long after sunset—say half-past seven or eight; anything else would be clearly improper.

"If you had given the subject a deeper consideration, Manuel—" he began.

But Manuel was still engaged with the book; he was now slicing the cover. "Spenser-r-r-r!"

Torres went towards him, and put out his forefinger with an impressive gesture. "I say if you had given the subject a deeper consideration, Manuel—"

"Scat!" said Manuel.

"What?" said the Cuban.

"Scat! scat! You're no better than an old tabby."

Torres looked at him solemnly. Then he put up his finger again. "It was *not* the proper course, Manuel," he began, a third time. "If you had given—"

"Oh, *go* to the devil!" cried Manuel, with a sort of howl, leaping towards him with the knife.

Torres thought he had better go.

He was not in the least afraid of Manuel; Torres had never been afraid in his life. But Manuel was a little excited (he had the bad habit of excitement); it was, perhaps, better to leave him to himself for a while. So he went back to the main-land; and meditated upon the Doctor's words. They remained mysterious, and the next day he made another progress up the Espiritu to Gracias, having decided to intrust his secret to the good rector of St. Philip and St. James', and profit by his knowledge of both languages.

The Rev. Mr. Moore was not only good, but he had not been troubled by nature with too large an endowment of humor—often an inconvenient possession. He listened to his visitor's story and the quoted sentence with gravity; then, after a moment's meditation, he put his long hands together, the tip of each delicately finished finger accurately meeting its mate, and made a discreet translation as follows: "You are still young; it would be better, perhaps, to remain at home until you are somewhat older." "Somewhat" was Mr. Moore's favorite word; everything with him was somewhat so; nothing (save wickedness) entirely so. In this way he escaped rashness. Certainly Reginald Kirby had put no "somewhat" of any sort in his answer to the Cuban. But Mr. Moore was of the opinion that he intended to do so (being prevented, probably, by that same rashness), and so he gave his guest the benefit of the doubt.

Torres reflected upon the translation; he had accepted a chair this time, but sat hat in hand, his heels drawn together as before. "With your favor, sir," he said at last, raising his eyes and making the clergyman a little bow, "this seems to me hardly an acceptance?"

"Hardly, I think," replied the clergyman, with moderation.

"At the same time, it is not a rejection. As I understand it, I am advised—for the present at least—simply to wait?" And he looked at the clergyman inquiringly.

"Exactly—very simple—to wait," assented Mr. Moore.

The Cuban rose; and made ceremonious acknowledgments.

"You return?" asked the clergyman, affably.

"I return."

"There is, no doubt, much to interest you on the plantation," remarked Mr. Moore, in a general way.

"What there is could be put upon the point of the finest lance known to history, and balanced there," replied Torres, with a dull glance of his dull dark eyes.

"I fear that young man has a somewhat gloomy disposition," thought the clergyman, when left alone.

Torres went down the lagoon again; and began to wait.

CHAPTER XV

"Man alive! of all the outlandish!" This was the unspoken phrase in Minerva Poindexter's mind as she watched a little scene which was going on near by. "I suppose it's peekin', but I don't care. What in the name of all *creation* are they at?"

Behind one of the old houses of Gracias there was a broad open space which had once been a field. On the far edge of this sunny waste stood some negro cabins, each brilliant with whitewash, and possessing a shallow little garden of its own, gay with flowers; in almost every case, above the low roof rose the clear green of a clump of bananas. A path bordered by high bushes led from the town to this little settlement, and here it was that Celestine, herself invisible, had stopped to look through a rift in the foliage. A negro woman was coming down the dusty track which passed in front of the cabins; on her head she carried a large bundle tied up in a brightly colored patchwork counterpane. As she drew near the first house she espied her friend Mrs. Johnson sitting on her front step enjoying the air, with the last young Johnson, Nando, on her knee. The first woman (Celestine knew that she was called Jinny) stopped, put one arm akimbo, and, steadying her bundle with the other hand, began to sway herself slightly from side to side at the hips, while her bare feet, which were visible, together with a space of bare ankle above, coming out below her short cotton skirt, moved forward in a measured step, the heel of the right being placed diagonally against the toes of the left, and then the heel of the left in its turn advanced with a slow level sweep, and placed diagonally across the toes of the right. There was little elevation of the sole, the steps, though long, being kept as close as possible to the ground, but without touching it, until the final down pressure, which was deep and firm. There seemed to be no liberty allowed, it was a very exact measure that Jinny was treading; the tracks made by her heel, the broad spread of her foot, and the five toes in the white dust, followed each other regularly in even zigzags which described half circles. Thus swaying herself rhythmically, turning now a little to the right, now a little to the left, Jinny slowly approached Mrs. Johnson, who regarded her impassively, continuing to trot Nando without change of expression. But when Jinny had come within a distance of fifteen feet, suddenly Mrs. Johnson rose, dropped her offspring (who took it philosophically), and began in her turn to sway herself gently from side to side, and then, with arms akimbo, her bare feet performing the same slow, exact evolutions, she advanced with gravity to meet Jinny, the two now joining in a crooning song. They met, circled round each other three times with the same deliberate step and motion, their song growing louder and louder. Then Mrs. Johnson shook her skirts, flung out her arms with a wild gesture, and stopped as suddenly as she had begun, walking back to her door-step and picking up Nando, while Jinny, advancing and taking up a comfortable position on one broad foot (idly stroking its ankle meanwhile with the dust-whitened sole of the other), the two fell into conversation, with no allusion either by word or look to the mystic exercises of the moment before.

"Howdy, Mis' Johnson?" said Jinny, as though she had just come up. "How's Mister Johnson dis mawnin'? Speck he's bettah; I year he wuz."

"Yessum, Miss Jinny More, yessum. He's bettah, dat's a fac'; he's mighty nigh 'bout well agin, Mister Johnson is, tank de Lawd!"

"Save us! what mistering and missussing!" said Celestine to herself. She watched them a moment longer, the colored people being still a profound mystery to her. Then she emerged from her bush-bordered path, and making her way to Mrs. Johnson, hurriedly delivered her message: Mrs. Harold would like to have her come to the eyrie for a while, to act as nurse for Mrs. Rutherford.

For that lady had met with an unfortunate accident; while stepping from her phaeton she had fallen, no one knew how or why, and though the phaeton was low and the ground soft, she had injured one of her knees so seriously that it was feared that she would not be able to walk for some time. Once fairly in bed and obliged to remain there, other symptoms had developed themselves, so that she appeared to have, as the sympathetic Betty (who had hurried up from East Angels) expressed it, "a little, just a *little*, you know, of pretty much everything under the sun." In this condition of affairs Katrina Rutherford naturally required a good deal of waiting upon. And after the time had been divided between Margaret and Celestine for several days and nights, Dr. Kirby peremptorily intervened, and told Margaret to send for Looth Johnson, "the best nurse in Gracias—the best, in fact, south of the city of Charleston." Looth was Telano's mother: this was in her favor with Celestine. But when the poor Vermont spinster was actually face to face with her, it was difficult to believe that a person who danced with bare black legs in the dusty road in the middle of the day could be either the mother of the spotlessly attired Telano, or the sort of attendant required by Mrs. Peter Rutherford. Dr. Kirby's orders, peremptory as they were, Celestine would have freely disobeyed; but she did not dare disobey them when they had been repeated by Margaret Harold.

"It's where your son is," she explained, desperately, forcing herself to think of Telano's snowy jackets as she caught another glimpse of his mother's toes.

"I knows whar 'tis," replied Looth, who had risen and dropped a courtesy. And then, as Celestine departed, hurrying away with an almost agitated step, "Telano 'lows she's a witch," she said to Jinny, in a low voice, as the two looked after the spare erect figure in its black gown. "*I* 'lows, howsumebber, it's juss ribs an' bones an' all knucklely up de back; nubbuddy 'ain't nebber *seed* so many knucklelies! I say, Jinny, 'tain't much honeyin' roun' *she's* eber been boddered wid, I reckon." And the two women laughed, though restraining themselves to low tones, with the innate civility of their race.

Meanwhile it was taking Minerva Poindexter the entire distance of the walk home to compose herself after that dancing, and more especially after the unseemly amplitude of the two large, comely black women, an amplitude which she would have confined immediately, if she had had the power, in gowns of firm fibre made after a straight fashion she knew, in which, by means of a system of restrictive seams in unexpectcd places, the modeller was able to neutralize the effect of even the most expansive redundancy.

At present Mrs. Rutherford was absorbing the time of Margaret, Celestine, Evert Winthrop; of Betty Carew, who, sending Garda to stay with the Moores, remained with dear Katrina; of Dr. Kirby, who paid three visits a day; of Telano, Cyndy, Maum Jube, and Aunt Dinah-Jim, who had transferred herself and her disorderly skill to the kitchen of the eyrie. During the only other serious illness Katrina Rutherford had known, one of her friends had remarked, "Oh, she's *such* a philanthropist!"

"Philanthropist?" said another, inquiringly.

"Yes; she has such a wonderful talent for employing people. That's philanthropy nowadays, you know, and I *think* Katrina could employ the whole town."

Looth arriving, still redundant but spotlessly neat in a loose white linen short-gown over a brilliant yellow cotton skirt, a red handkerchief arranged as a turban, white stockings, and broad, low shoes (which were soundless), supplied an element of color at the eyrie, as well as abundant tact, a sweet, cooing voice, and soft strong arms for lifting. She called Mrs. Rutherford "honey," and changed her position skilfully and sympathetically twenty times a day. Mrs. Rutherford liked the skill; even better she liked the sympathy; she had often complained that there was very little true sensibility in either Margaret or Celestine. To hear and see Looth persuade her patient to eat her dinner was a daily entertainment to Winthrop. It was the most persuasive coaxing ever heard, and Mrs. Rutherford, while never once losing her martyr expression, greatly enjoyed it; there was some different method of tender urging for each dish. Celestine, who was not a jealous person, looked on with deep though concealed interest, never failing to be in the room, apparently engaged with something else, when Looth appeared with the tray. Though she understood her mistress's foibles perfectly, she was at heart fond of her (she had dressed her too long not to be), and would have felt her business in life at an end if separated from her; yet she could no more have called her "my dove," and cooed over her with soft enthusiasm when she had eaten a slice of venison, than she could have danced at noon barelegged in the dusty road.

But in spite of all these helpers, Mrs. Rutherford did not improve; if she did not grow worse, she did not grow better. At last she declared that she should never grow better so long as she must hear, day and night, the wash of the water on the beach; now it was only a teasing ripple, which still she must listen for, now a long regular swell, to which she found herself forced mentally to beat time. As they could not take away the sea—even Looth could not coo it away—there was some uneasiness at the eyrie as to what the result would be; they decided that it was but a fancy, and that she would forget it. But Katrina Rutherford did not forget. At length there came three nights in succession during which she did not sleep "a moment;" she announced to Winthrop that she should soon be in need of no more sleep, "save the last long one." Dr. Kirby, who still profoundly admired her—she continued to look very handsome after Celestine had attired her for the day in a dressing-gown of delicate hue, covered with white lace, a dainty little lace cap lightly resting on her soft hair—Dr. Kirby said to Winthrop that unstrung nerves were a serious matter; and that though her idea about the water was a fancy, of course, the loss of three nights' sleep was anything but fanciful. They could not move the sea; but they could move her, and they must. The next question was—where? The Seminole being as near the water as the eyrie, there was nothing to be gained by going there. Betty promptly offered her house, she was full of plans for taking in their whole party under her hospitable roof. But Mrs. Rutherford confided to her nephew that the constant sighing of the pines round Betty's domicile would be as "maddening" as the water, if not worse. "I'd much rather they'd howl!" she said.

Then came old Mrs. Kirby in her black silk visite, her parasol held high above her head, and with mathematical precision directly over it, though the afternoon sun, slanting from the west, shone steadily into her eyes underneath, so that she was kept winking and blinking all the way. She came to offer their residence; the full half of it stood empty, and, needless to say that she and Reginald would be "right glad" if the ladies would accept it. But Mrs. Rutherford confided, to Margaret this time, that nothing would induce her to go there. "She would be sure to come in every day with cookies hidden somewhere about her, and then *nibble*."

"They're wafers, I think," said Margaret, laughing.

"Wafers or cookies, she crunches when she eats them; I've heard her," Mrs. Rutherford declared. "It's all very well for you to laugh, Margaret; *you* have no sensitiveness. I wish I had a cooky now," she went on, irrelevantly—"a real one; or else a jumble, or a cruller, or an oley-koek. But there's no getting anything in this desolate place; their one idea is plum-cake—plum-cake!"

Mrs. Kirby was followed by Mr. Moore, who brought a note from his wife, cordially placing at the disposal of the northern party "five pleasant rooms at the rectory," which could be made ready for them at any time upon shortest notice.

"They haven't more than six in all," commented Winthrop. "Does this mean, do you suppose, that they intend to shut themselves up into one, and give up to us all the rest?"

"Very probably," Margaret answered.

But the Moores were not obliged to make good their generous offer. Mrs. Rutherford said that she could not possibly live in the house with an invalid. "Always little messes being carried clinking up-stairs on waiters, or left standing outside of doors for people to tumble over;—cups, with dregs of tea in them, set into each other. Horrid!"

"But there are no stairs at the rectory," suggested Winthrop.

"Don't be owlish, Evert; one is even more apt to step into them on a ground-floor," replied the aunt.

Meanwhile the sea still washed the beach under the eyrie, and now, too, the nerves of almost everybody in it, for neither Margaret nor Celestine could sleep when Mrs. Rutherford could not; even Winthrop, at the Seminole, found himself wakeful, listening to the little soft sound, and thinking of his suffering aunt. For in spite of her fancies and her fairly good appetite, in spite of her rich dressing-gowns and carefully arranged hair, Aunt Katrina undoubtedly did suffer. Already her eyes had begun to have something of a sunken look; to Margaret and Winthrop she appeared sometimes to be seeing them through a slight haze, and to be trying, though ineffectually, to pierce it. "That dreadful water on the beach! that dreadful water!" was still her constant complaint.

"Do you think she would like to go down to East Angels?" suggested Dr. Kirby to Margaret one morning. "The motion of a carriage she couldn't bear at present, but she could go down very well in the *Emperadora*."

But Margaret thought she would not like it at all.

"How do you know, without asking, what I shouldn't like at all?" Aunt Katrina demanded when Margaret repeated to her this little conversation. Aunt Katrina liked to have the little conversations repeated. "Don't imagine, Margaret, I beg, that you know all my feelings by intuition."

Later in the day came Evert. "Dr. Kirby has a fantastic plan for your going down to East Angels to stay for a while, Aunt Katrina. But I told him that you didn't like East Angels."

"Where did you get that idea? But of course from Margaret, who thinks she knows everything. East Angels is a charming old place."

"Oh!" said her nephew, rather astonished, remembering various adjectives she had applied to it; "decayed" had been a favorite one.

"I have always thought it charming," pursued the lady. And then she began to enumerate its good points. It was too far from the lagoon to be troubled by that tiresome sound of the water; it had no pines near it to tease people to death with their sighing; there would be no old ladies to drop in with cookies, and nibble; and there were no invalids, with teacups being sent clinking up-stairs (Mrs. Rutherford herself drank chocolate). The one objection was that Dr. Reginald would have a long ride every morning to get to her. But Dr. Reginald, coming in at this moment, gallantly volunteered, in case she should go down there, to spend a week with them by way of beginning; in the evenings they could play cribbage until she should feel drowsy, for she certainly would feel drowsy down there among the—he had almost said "pines," but stopped in time; then he thought of live-oaks, but remembered that she considered them "dreary." Among the—he had nearly brought out "magnolias," but recollected that she disliked their perfume. "Among the andromedas," he concluded at last, pronouncing the word firmly, determined not to abandon it.

"Oh, andromedas. Aromatic?" inquired the patient, languidly.

"Immensely so," replied the Doctor. "Im—*mensely*!"

The next day, coming in again and finding that the poor lady had passed another bad night, and that at half-past nine in the morning she had burst into tears, and called Looth her "only friend," as that turbaned handmaid was feeding her with toast and the softest sympathy, he took Winthrop to the north piazza and seriously advised the change.

"But East Angels is still Garda's," said Winthrop. "I don't see how we can go there."

"She will be delighted to have you. I don't think Garda is happy at present when long separated from Mrs. Harold," went on the speaker, candidly; "Mrs. Harold has had a wonderfully cheering influence over her, poor child, since her mother's death. Garda has been so unlike herself—I hardly know what to call it—passive, perhaps; I presume you have not noticed the change, but ma and I have."

Winthrop thought he had noticed. But all he said was: "We should have to send down the servants, and—and a good many other things, I'm afraid. The party would be large, it would be like taking possession—so many of us."

"Don't let that trouble you," said the Doctor, balancing himself in his old way. "In the matter of guests, our feeling here has always been that the more we had under our roof the better; yes, the better."

"It is true that the place is to be mine as soon as I can get a title. You are the guardian; perhaps you will allow us to rent it until then?"

"Sir," said the Doctor, stopping his balancing, "we will not speak of rent." (And in truth rent was not a word esteemed in Gracias. Nobody "rented" there, and nobody "boarded;" each man lived in his own house, and sat at his own table; the roof might be in need of repairs, and the table bare, but they were at least his own.) "As you have remarked, I am Miss Thorne's guardian, and as such I can assure you that she will be right glad to entertain you all at East Angels, and for as long a time as it will be agreeable to you to so favor her."

Thus it was arranged; they were all to pay Garda a visit. It was to be ignored that workmen were to be sent down to the old house, and the resources of Gracias-á-Dios strained to the utmost to make the rooms accord with the many requirements of Mrs. Rutherford; it was to be ignored that six servants and supplies of all kinds were to be added. Garda appeared at the eyrie and gave her invitation. She seemed to think of it in the same way that the Doctor did—it was a visit; she had all the air of a hostess, though rather a listless one.

Nothing in this young girl had Margaret Harold admired more than the untroubled way in which she had accepted her new friend's assistance. Mrs. Rutherford, who was industrious in prodding for motive (she considered it a praiseworthy industry), had long ago announced that Garda's affection for Margaret was based upon her own pennilessness and Margaret's fortune. If this were so, there was at least no eagerness about it; the girl accepted all that Margaret did, simply; sweetly enough, but as a matter of course. The funeral expenses had been paid by the Gracias friends, they had claimed this as their privilege; but since then Margaret had provided for everything, from Garda's new mourning garb to the money for the daily house-keeping at East Angels—sums which Betty Carew had disbursed with her nicest care, which was yet a mad expenditure when compared with the economies of Mrs. Thorne. The lean, clean larder of East Angels had had a sense of repletion that was almost profligate, and had felt itself carried wildly back to the days of Old Madam—who had spent the last of the Duero capital in making herself comfortable, smiling back wickedly at the blue eyes of Melissa Whiting when the latter had tried to save some of it.

Margaret could not but contrast Garda's simple way with the scruples, the inward distress, which she herself should have been a victim to if she had been placed at that age in such a situation, thrown entirely upon the care of a comparative stranger, at best a new friend. But here was a nature which could accept unreservedly; it seemed to her a noble trait; she said this to Mrs. Rutherford in answer to one of that lady's attacks.

"If the positions were to be reversed, Aunt Katrina, I am sure she would be just the same, she would give in the way in which she now accepts; she would share everything with me with the same unreserve, and without a second thought."

"Give *me* the second thoughts, then!" said Aunt Katrina. "I must say I cannot see the nobility in it that you and Evert see." (This was quite true; Aunt Katrina never saw nobility.) "The girl has always had what she wanted, and she's got it now; that's all there is of it. Evert talks about her being so contented; most of us are contented, I suppose, when every wish is gratified, and if you would look at it fairly, without all this decoration you have added to it, you would see that hers have always been. Evert brings up their poverty—it has all come out, of course, since the mother's death. But, poor or not poor, *Garda* at least always had what she wanted; there were always honey-cakes and oranges for her, and those old servants would wait upon her when they would not speak to her mother. She has never lifted her hand to do anything in her life but swing in her hammock, smell her roses, and play with that crane. Evert keeps harping—what simple things they were to give her so much pleasure. But *somebody* had to work to keep up even the 'simple things;' and that somebody was her mother. Simple—of course they were simple, she has been brought up in the country, and she is only sixteen; she has had no opportunity to see anything else. But it seems to me that the laziness which is shown by that hammock, and the epicureanism which comes out in the honey-cakes and oranges, yes, and the roses too, and the frivolity which makes her find amusement by the hour in playing with that dreadful crane—all these are a very pretty development of temperament in a girl of that age."

Over this dark picture Margaret was unable to resist a laugh.

"Laugh on," said Aunt Katrina, ominously. "You will live to come to my opinion."

But Margaret continued to think Garda's free acceptance the sign of a generous nature; the girl judged her benefactress by herself; if she had been the one to bestow the kindness, she would not have liked effusive thanks; Margaret therefore would not like them either.

But if Garda did not turn the conversation towards Margaret's material gifts, she did turn it, and warmly, upon the delight it was to her that her friend was to be at East Angels; upon that point she was effusive enough. "*Now* I can live," she said.

"There's something so tiresome in being with Aunt Betty Carew day after day," she added, meditatively. "Don't you think so?"

"She has been extremely kind to you," Margaret answered.

"Yes, she's very kind, there's nobody kinder. That doesn't make her any the less wandering in her conversation, does it? or any the less flushed. Do you remember how pretty my dear little mother was? She had such a nice straight little nose it was a pleasure to look at her. You have a lovely nose too, Margaret; I wonder if I should have liked you so well without it? Oh, won't you stay at East Angels until it is time to go north? In that way, as I am to go with you, we shouldn't be separated at all."

"Aunt Katrina may tire of East Angels in two days," Margaret answered.

"We won't allow it We'll amuse her!" Garda declared, with soft energy.

But something else was to amuse poor Aunt Katrina. She made the little journey comfortably, one beautiful morning, on the *Emperadora,* surrounded by her retinue, of which Betty was one; she enjoyed her installation, and the novelty of the new rooms; she enjoyed the congratulations of Dr. Kirby, when, later in the day, he came down for his week's visit; and she played cribbage with him for a little while in the evening. Her nephew too was there; she had required his presence. "You must come, of course, Evert," she said; "I couldn't possibly stay way down in that lonely place without you." So Evert had been obliged to install himself as well as his aunt; he took up his abode not unwillingly in the old house which he expected some day to own.

After the cribbage, Aunt Katrina went to bed, and passed a night of blessed oblivion, unteased by the whining water: that had been her latest term for it—that it whined. But after a few days of this delightful rest, a fresh assortment of pains lifted their heads. The Doctor at first alluded to them as rheumatic. But Aunt Katrina would not accept that suggestion. He then called them "suppressed gout." This was better; Aunt Katrina had always had a certain esteem for gout. Besides, suppressed gout had no fixed habitation; Aunt Katrina, having very shapely feet, took the opportunity, the very day she accepted the name, to have herself lifted to the sofa, where these same members, in delicate slippers, reposed upon a bear-skin, only half concealed by an India shawl.

But these little vanities could be forgiven, they could even be encouraged (and were by the quick-witted Looth), if they had the power to make her forget her pain. This pain was of the kind she herself described as "wearing." Fortunately it was not constant, there were many free intervals; but during these intervals she was often tired, and Katrina Rutherford had lived such an easy, comfortable life that she had almost never been tired before. This fatigue after pain sometimes extended to her mind, and made her irritable. On these days no one could soothe her but Margaret, and it was soon discovered that no one must try. Margaret must read to her, read her to sleep; Margaret must sit in a certain place, and sit still; she must not leave the room; nobody must speak to her but Margaret—the others could say what was necessary through her. During one of her free intervals she explained to Winthrop that it was Margaret's voice that soothed her; "it's so hard," she said.

"I shouldn't think that quality would be particularly soothing," Winthrop answered.

"On the contrary, it's the very one—that is, for me. I only need her when I've been reduced to a pulp—like the pulp in the paper mills—by pain; at such times that hard voice of hers is the first firm thing I can take hold of; I crystallize round it by degrees, don't you know, and gradually get back *some* shape again."

Margaret's voice was not in the least hard; it was low and clear; when it took on certain intonations, very sweet. But Winthrop did not remind his aunt of this. She could crystallize round any adjectives that pleased her in her moments of rest; her nephew's usual championship of justice was postponed until she should be better.

During this time Celestine and Looth were often obliged to be companions; there were certain things they each did which no one else could do as well, and therefore neither one could be spared. To Celestine it was a weird experience, this sitting up at night in the large bare room of a strange old Spanish house (a house which had been inhabited for generations by Papists), opposite a great black woman in a red turban, who was in the habit of dancing barelegged in the roads in the middle of the day; and all this on a winter night with roses blooming outside in the garden, and the perfume of orange blossoms coming in through the half-closed windows—a winter night which seemed to have gone astray from some other world. The absence of cold in winter climates abroad Celestine had accepted without opposition; it was only part of their general outlandishness. But that such foreign eccentricities should exist in the United States of America, under the Stars and Stripes, this she by no means approved; like many other persons, she could not help believing that frost-tipped noses were an accompaniment of republican simplicity and virtue, and that a good conscience and east wind could not be long separated without danger to morals.

She had never alluded to the dance. But one night Looth herself alluded to it. "Specks yer seen us, Miss Selsty, dat day you wuz firs' down dar fur to ax me to come up yer to nuss—specks yer seen me an' Jinny?"

Celestine nodded grimly: a confession was evidently on the way.

"Yessum, Miss Selsty, I reckoned yer seen us. We wuz *shoutin'*," Looth went on, with gentle satisfaction. "I's a very rilligeous 'oman, Miss Selsty, yessum. An' so's Jinny too."

All the Gracias friends came down often to East Angels to inquire after Mrs. Rutherford; Madam Ruiz and Madam Giron came over from their respective plantations. Adolfo Torres, however, did not come; he remained at home, and sent his respectful inquiries by his aunt. Neither the Doctor nor Mr. Moore had betrayed his secret; these two gentlemen were not in the habit of betraying anybody. Torres did not altogether like their reticence upon this particular occasion, he could not see that it was a subject upon which reticence was required. In the old days (the only days he cared about) the position of suitor, devoted suppliant for his lady's hand, was an honorable one, one distinctly recognized; he should like to be recognized as occupying it now. But if these friends would not tell, he could not; to tell would not accord with his present posture. "Posture" was his own word, no one else would have dreamed of applying it to anything connected with this self-controlled young man. Gracias, too, was having veritable postures of another kind to look at. These were the attitudes of Manuel Ruiz, which were very new and surprising. After that first burst of fury (which Torres had witnessed) he had taken to riding over the barren at headlong speed on his large, thin black horse, with several knives stuck in his belt—a belt whose presence (in itself brigandish) he had further emphasized by tying over it a crimson sash. Next he had suddenly appeared as a man of dissipations, a scoffer; he haunted the two small, rather sleepy bar-rooms of Gracias, smoking large cigars, wearing his sombrero much on one side, and in public places—the plaza for instance—made cynical remarks about "the fair sex." This was worse even than the knives and the galloping, and Gracias was considering what had better be done, when, lo! Manuel appeared among them playing a third part. He was not only himself, but more mellifluous even than he had ever been before; his manner, indeed, when he met any of these ladies, had in it such a delicate yet keenly personal admiration, such an appreciation of what they had been as well as of what they were, that all of them, even stout, honest Betty, and little Mrs. Kirby herself, under her high-held parasol, were set to blushing a little, without knowing why, and to vaguely adjusting their front hair with a touch or two, only to become conscious of it later, and say to themselves, angrily, that that boy ought to have a good horsewhipping! Manuel called upon all his friends and all his mother's friends (except Garda at East Angels), and could hardly sit in a chair. Upon seeing him, the idea was that he had been accustomed to a divan; he seemed to have come from the sipping of nectar, and to have touched nothing but rose-leaves. Having thus thrown dust in the eyes of the town, he took his departure; as he had long threatened, he was going to see the world. He mentioned to Mrs. Harold that he should try to "take in" New York; and then he sailed on a coasting schooner for Key West, with four dollars and twenty five-cents in his pocket.

Gracias knew nothing of the real cause of all this. Madam Ruiz, Manuel's broad-shouldered and martial-looking, but in reality sighingly gentle, sentimental step-mother, was not in his confidence with regard to Garda. But she would not have credited the story, even if she had been, for she firmly believed her handsome step-son to be invincible from the Everglades to the Altamaha. During the long, warm, mid-summer afternoons, when flat Patricio, low in the blue sea, had not a shadow, this lady, in her thick white house, the broad rooms darkened by the closed shutters, was in the habit of amusing herself with many romances about this; for your warm, still countries are ever the land of the storyteller. Madam Ruiz now and then told her stories to her husband.

"Yes, yes," said that gentleman; "he inherits it all from me." He was partially paralyzed, and sat all day in his chair; he did not like to have Manuel about much, he envied him so. He took more comfort in the children of this second marriage—a flock of brown-skinned, chattering little girls, who would be sure to grow up dark, lovely, and gentle, with serene, affectionate eyes, and the sweetest voices in the world, in which to call him their "dearest papa."

Adolfo Torres meanwhile kept his friend's secret punctiliously, as it was not to his credit; it was terribly against his credit to have gone as he did to Garda herself,—so Adolfo thought.

As for Garda, she said, afterwards, that she did not mention it because it was so much trouble; she did not like to tell things, she was not a narrator (one of her mother's phrases); besides it was not interesting. The girl had a very decided idea about what was and what was not interesting. But she stopped there, she did not explain her idea to others; she had the air of not even explaining it to herself.

CHAPTER XVI

Evert Winthrop was very fond of the pine barrens. They seemed to him to have a marked character of their own; their green aisles were as unlike the broad roll of the prairie as they were unlike the usual growth of the American forest farther north. The pines of the barren stood apart from each other, they were not even in clusters or pairs. To a northerner, riding or walking for the first time across the broad sun-barred spaces under them, the feeling was that this separated growth was the final outer fringe of some thick forest within, that it would soon come to an end, widen out, and disappear. But it never did disappear, the single trees went on rising in the same thin way from the open ground, they continued to rise for miles; and when the new-comer had once got rid of the idea that they would soon stop, when he had become accustomed to the sparse growth, it seemed beautiful in a way of its own; as slender girls will sometimes seem more exquisite in their fair meagreness than the maturer women about them with their sumptuous shoulders and arms.

For one thing, the barrens were the home of all the breezes; winds from the four quarters of the heavens could sweep through their aisles as freely as though no trees were there, the foliage was so far above. But though the winds could blow as they liked, they yet had to take something of the influences of the place as they passed, and the one they took oftenest was the aromatic odor, odor sun-warmed through and through, never chilled by ice or snow. These odors they gathered up and bore along, so that if it was a breeze from the south, one felt like sitting still and breathing the soft fragrance forever; and if it was a north wind, careering down the vistas, the resinous tang it carried gave a sort of excitement which could find its best expression in the gallop of a fast horse over the levels. At least so Winthrop thought. And he had often been guilty of riding for miles at a speed which he would not have acknowledged at the North; it seemed boyish to ride at that rate for the mere sake of the glow and the spicy wind in one's face.

The barrens were always green. But it was not the green of the northern forest; it was the dark, tranquil, unchanging hue of the South. The ground was covered thickly with herbage and little shrubs. Here and there flower stalks made their way through, pushing themselves up as high as they could in order to get their heads out in the sunshine; there they swung merrily to and fro, and looked about them—violets so broad and bright that one could recognize their blueness at a distance, red bells of the calopogon, the yellow and lavender of pinguiculas rising from their prim little rosettes of leaves down below; near the pools the pitcher-plants; nearer still, hiding in thickets, the ferns. These pools were a wonder. How came they there in so dry a land? For the barrens were pure white sand; each narrow road, where the exterior mat of green had been worn away, was a dry white track in which the foot sank warmly. The pools were there, however, and in abundance. Though shallow, their clear water had a rich hue like that of dark red wine. Those on horseback or in a cart went through them, the little silver-white descent on one side to get to them, and the ascent on the other, forming the only "hills" the barrens knew; for those on foot, a felled pine-tree sometimes served as a bridge.

The trails, crossing in various directions, were many, they all appeared to be old. One came upon them unexpectedly, often they were not visible in the low shrubbery three feet away. Once found, they were definite enough; they never became merged in the barren, or stopped; they always went sleepily on and on, they did not appear themselves to know whither. And certainly no one else knew, as Winthrop found when occasionally, he being more lost than usual (on the barrens he was always lost to a certain degree, and liked it), he would stop his horse to ask of a passing cracker in what direction some diverging trail would take him, in case he should follow it. The cracker, astride his sorry pony, would stare at him open-mouthed; but he never knew. Packed into the two-wheeled cart behind him, all his family, with their strange clay-colored complexions and sunburnt light hair, would stare also; and they never knew. They were a gentle, mummy-like people, too indolent even to wonder why a stranger should wish to know; they stared at him with apathetic eyes, and then passed on, not once turning their heads, even the children, for a second look. But as a general thing Winthrop rode on without paying heed to the direction he was taking; he could always guide himself back after a fashion by the pocket-compass he carried.

One afternoon Winthrop, out on the barren, saw in the distance a horse and phaeton. There was no phaeton in all that country but his aunt's. He rode across to see who was in it. To his surprise it was Garda; she was leaning indolently back on the cushioned seat, the reins held idly in her hand, an immense bunch of roses fastened in her belt. The horse was one he did not know.

"Garda!—this you!" he said.

"Yes," she answered, laughing at his astonishment. "Everything was so dull at the house that I thought I *must* do something. So I did this."

"I wasn't aware that you knew how to drive?"

"This isn't driving."

"No, I hardly think it is," he answered, looking at her reclining figure and the loose reins. "Where are you going?"

"Oh, I don't know."

"Whose horse have you?—if I may ask another question."

"Madam Giron's; I sent Pablo to borrow it, as I did not like to take your aunt's."

"Then they know what you are doing?"

"Pablo knows."

"And Margaret?"

"No, Margaret doesn't know. I should have told her, of course, if I could have seen her, or rather, if I could have seen her, I should not have come out at all. But that was the trouble—I couldn't see her; she has been shut up in Mrs. Rutherford's room ever since early this morning, and there's no prospect, according to Looth, of seeing her until to-morrow."

"Yes, I feared my aunt was going to have one of her bad days."

"Of course I'm sorry, but that doesn't make the hours any shorter, that I know of; there was no one to speak to; even you were away. *You* have the advantage of being able to leave the house whenever you like, and staying out forever."

"Well, I've turned up now."

"I don't want you now; I've 'turned up' myself. Where are you going, may I ask in my turn?"

"Going to drive you home."

"Not if you intend to tie that horse of yours at the back of the phaeton, where he will nibble my shoulders all the way. But I'm not going home yet; haven't I told you how dull it was there? I'm going on."

"I don't know about letting you go on; I'm not satisfied with the look of that horse."

"Yes, he's the wildest one Madam Giron has; but that isn't very wild," said Garda, in a tone of regret.

"You are already over four miles from East Angels—"

"Delightful!"

"—and if you won't turn round, I shall have to follow you on horseback; I shouldn't have a clear conscience otherwise."

"Oh, have a clear conscience, by all means."

But she did not long like this arrangement; the sound of another horse behind made Madam Giron's horse restless, so that she could not keep the reins lying idle, as she liked.

"Let your horse go, and come and drive me," she said.

"Let him go? Where?"

"Home, I suppose."

"He wouldn't go; he's an animal of intelligence, and of course has observed that he could lead a nomadic life here perfectly, with constant summer, and water, and—but I can't say much for the grass. I think, however, that I can arrange it so that he shall not trouble you." And dismounting, he changed and lengthened some straps; then seating himself in the phaeton beside her, he took the reins, his own horse trotting along docielly at his side of the phaeton, fastened by a long line.

"It's caravanish," said Garda. "But I'll allow it because I want you to drive; it's more amusing than driving myself."

"More lazy, you mean."

"Yes; I ran away to be lazy."

"For a variety?"

She did not take this up, but, leaning back still further, half closed her eyes.

"Have you often been out in this way on the barrens, driving yourself?" he went on.

"This is the first time I have ever driven—on the barrens or anywhere else."

"Yet you come out alone, and with this restless horse! I never knew you to do such a thing before."

"That only shows how short a time you have known me; I always like to do things I have never done before."

The phaeton rolled on towards the west—on and on, as she would not let him turn. But he did not wish to turn now; they had reached a part of the barren which he had not visited, though he had ridden to much greater distances both towards the north and the south. Here were wider pools; and here also was a sluggish narrow stream; far off on the left rose the long dark line of the great cypresses on the edge of a swamp. The sluggish stream at length crossed their road, or rather their road essayed to cross the sluggish stream; but the dark water looked deep, there were no tracks of wheels on the little descent to show that any one had tried the ford lately—say within the last twenty years. Winthrop hesitated.

"Go on," said Garda.

"But I might have to swim with you to the other shore."

"Nothing I should like better."

"To see me soaked?"

"To see you excited."

"That wouldn't excite me; I should only be wet and depressed. In any case it is time for us to turn back."

"No, I've set my heart upon going at least as far as that ridge." And she indicated a little rise of land on the other side of the stream, whose summit was covered thickly with Dr. Kirby's andromedas, and shining laurel, sprays of yellow jessamine, bright with flowers, pushing through the darker green and springing into the air. "There's a bridge," she added.

Winthrop turned; a felled pine-tree, roughly smoothed, crossed the stream a short distance below the ford.

"You can tie the horses here, and we will walk over," pursued Garda.

"Then will you come back?" he asked, amused by her taking it as a matter of course, always, that she was to have her own way.

"Then I will come back."

He tied the horses to two pine-trees, some distance apart from each other. Then he tried the bridge. It seemed firm. Garda, refusing his offers of assistance, crossed lightly and fearlessly behind him. Some of the twigs still remained on the old trunk, and she lifted her skirt so that they should not catch upon it and cause her to stumble; when they had gone nearly three-quarters of the distance, Winthrop, turning his head to speak to her, saw that she wore low slippers, thin-soled papery little shoes fit only for a carpeted floor. "You must not go among the bushes in those shoes," he said. "The bushes over there are sure to be wet; all that ground is wet."

"Don't stop on the bridge," said Garda, laughing.

But he continued to bar the way. "I will bring you the flowers," he said.

"I don't want the flowers, I want to go myself to the top of that ridge, and look down on the other side."

"There's nothing to see on the other side."

"That makes no difference. Go on. Go on."

He turned round; cautiously, for the bridge was slippery and narrow. They were now face to face.

"I shall never yield," Garda declared, gayly. "But I shall make *you* yield. Easily."

"How?"

"By telling you that if you do not go on, I shall jump into the water, and get to the other bank in that way."

He laughed. But as he did so he suddenly felt a conviction come over him, owing to an expression he saw in her eyes, that she was capable of carrying out her threat. He seized her hands; but she wrested them from his grasp; and as she did so he had a vision of her figure in the water below. He could easily rescue her, of course; but it would be a situation whose pleasures he should fail to appreciate, both of them wet through, and many miles from home. She had no sooner freed her hands, therefore, than he took a firmer hold of her, so that she could not stir.

But she still openly exulted; her face, close to his, was brilliant with light and mirth. "That's of no use," she said. "You cannot possibly walk backward on this narrow tree, even if you could carry me—which I doubt."

It was true that his back was towards the bank which was near, the one they had been approaching, and that he could not make his way thither on that narrow surface without seeing where he was going. He had flushed a little at her taunt. "I can carry you back to the side we started from," he said.

"No, you cannot do that, either. For I could easily blind you with my hands, and make you stumble."

"Garda!—how absurd!"

"Yes; but it's *you* who look so," she answered, bursting into a peal of irrepressible glee.

Winthrop had the feeling that she might be right. He knew that he was flushed and angry; no man likes to be laughed at, even by a girl of sixteen. Her eyes, though over-flowing with mirth, had still an unconquerable look in them. Suddenly he released her. "Your actions are ridiculous," he said; "I can only leave you to yourself." And turning, he crossed to the near bank. He had successfully resisted his impulse, which had been to take her, mocking and mirthful as she was, and carry her back to the bank from which they had started; he felt sure that he could have done it in spite of any resistance she might have offered.

Garda ran after him, and put her arm in his. "Are you vexed with me?" she said, looking up coaxingly in his face.

"Don't you think you are old enough now, Garda, not to act so much like a child?"

"It isn't a child," she answered, as it seemed to him rather strangely. "I shall always be like this."

"Do you mean that you never intend to be reasonable?"

"Oh, I don't know what I intend, I don't think I intend anything; intending's a trouble. But don't be angry with me," she went on; "you and Margaret are all I have now." And she looked up at him still coaxingly, but this time through a mist of tears.

"I am not vexed," answered Winthrop, quickly. "Will you have the kindness to glance at your feet?" he added, by way of diversion into another channel.

They had been standing among the low bushes on the further shore, and Garda was again holding her skirt slightly lifted; her thin slippers were seen to be as completely drenched as though they had been in the stream. "Yes, they're wet," she assented, lifting first one, and then the other, so as to get a good view; "they're quite wet through, soles and all. And, do you know, my feet are already very cold."

"And we have still the long drive home! You must acknowledge that you are wise."

At this moment they heard a sound, and turned; Madam Giron's horse had broken his fastenings, and started down the barren, the phaeton gently rolling along behind him. Winthrop ran across the pine-tree bridge and after him, as swiftly yet as noiselessly as he could, so that the sound of pursuit should not increase his speed. But Madam Giron's horse enjoyed a run on his own account, and after trotting for a while, he broke into the pace which suited him best, a long-stepped easy gallop; thus, with the phaeton bounding at his heels, he took his way down the broad green vista, faster and faster, yet still with a regular motion, which was doubly exasperating because it seemed so much more like an easy gait for the saddle (which it was) than a demoralized running away. At length, when Winthrop himself had run half a mile, in the vain hope that he would stop or turn, Madam Giron's steed disappeared in the distance, having reached and gone down, Garda said, the curve of the earth, as a ship does at sea.

"Isn't it funny? What are we going to do now?" she asked. She had come back across the bridge while he was vainly pursuing the chase.

"If it were not for your wet feet I should put you on my horse and start towards home, hoping to meet some one with a cart. As it is, I think you had better try to walk for a while."

"It would be very uncomfortable in these wet things. No; I couldn't."

"I hardly know what we can do, then, unless you will take off your stockings and those silly slippers, and wrap your feet up in something dry. Then I could put you on the horse."

"But there's nothing to wrap them up in."

"Yes; my coat."

Garda laughed. "To think of seeing *you* without one!"

But at length this was done; the pretty little feet, white and cold, she dried with her handkerchief, and then wrapped up as well as she could in his coat, securing the wrapping with the black ribbon which had been her belt. Thus protected he lifted her, laughing at her own helplessness, on the horse, where she sat sidewise, holding on; she had fastened all the roses which had been in her belt on her palmetto hat, so that she looked like a May-queen. Winthrop walked on in advance, leading the horse by the bridle, and carrying her slippers dangling from his arm by a string, in the hope, he said, of at least beginning the drying. For some time Garda amused herself making jests at their plight. But after a while the uneasy posture in which she was obliged to sit began to tire her; she begged him to stop and let her rest.

"We shouldn't reach home then until long after dark," he answered. "As it is, at this rate, it will be very late before we can get there."

"Never mind that; of what consequence is it? I'm *so* tired!"

He came back, and walking by her side, guiding the horse by the rein, he told her to put her hand on his shoulder, and steady herself in that way; this bettered matters a little, and they got over another long slow mile. The sun had sunk low in the west; his horizontal rays lit up the barren with a flood of golden light. "My poor slippers are no drier," said Garda, lifting the one that hung near her.

"If we had had time we could have made a fire, and dried them with very little trouble."

"Oh, let us make a fire now! I love to make a fire in the woods. You could get plenty of dry cones and twigs and it wouldn't take fifteen minutes; then, if they were once dry, I could walk, you know."

"Your fifteen minutes would be an hour at least, and that is an hour of daylight very precious to us just now. Besides, I am afraid I doubt your walking powers."

"Yes," answered Garda, with frankness; "I hate to walk."

"Yet you can run," he suggested, referring to her escapade on Patricio beach.

Garda took up this memory, and was merry over it for some time. Then, growing weary again, she told him despotically that he must stop. "I cannot bear this position and jolting a moment longer, with my feet fettered in this way," she said, vehemently. "You couldn't either."

He turned; though she was smiling, he saw that she had grown pale. "I shall have to humor you. But I give you fifteen minutes only." He lifted her down, and mounting the horse, rode off to a distance, first in one direction, then in another, hoping to discover some one whom he could send in to Gracias for a carriage or wagon. But the wide barren, growing rapidly dusky, remained empty and still; there was no moving thing in sight.

When he came back he found that Garda had put on her stockings and slippers again, wet as they were. She was trying to walk; but the soft sand of the track clung to each soaked shoe so that she lifted, as she said, a mountain every time she took a step. In spite of this, "I'm going on," she announced.

"You must, now that you have put on those wet things again; it's the only way to keep from taking cold."

So they started, Garda leaning on his arm, while he held the bridle with his other hand. "I might ride, and carry you behind me," he suggested. "Like Lochinvar."

"Who's Lochinvar? See; there's somebody!"

He looked towards the point she indicated, and saw the figure of a man going in another direction, and at a good distance from them. He jumped on his horse again, and rode across to speak to him. The man proved to be a tall young negro of eighteen or nineteen; he was ready to do anything that Winthrop should desire, but he had also the disappointing tidings to communicate that they were even farther from East Angels and Gracias than they had supposed; they were still ten miles out.

"Why, it's Bartolo," said Garda, as they came back together. She had seated herself, and was looking at her clogged feet gravely.

"Yessum," said Bartolo, removing his fragmentary straw hat.

"He's Telano's cousin," pursued Garda, inspecting the wrinkled kid at the heel of the left slipper. "Do you know, they are beginning to shrink; and they hurt me."

Winthrop stood still, deliberating. There was no house or cabin of any kind within a number of miles, Bartolo said; if he should send the boy in to Gracias on foot for a carriage, and keep on advancing with Garda in the same direction at their present slow rate, they should not probably reach East Angels until midnight; to go in himself on horseback, and leave Garda with only Bartolo as protector—no, he could not do that. This last would have been the southern way, and Garda herself suggested it. "Ride in to Gracias as fast as you can, and come back with a carriage, or something, for me; I shall not be afraid if Bartolo can stay."

Bartolo showed his white teeth. "I ken stay, sho," he said. He was blacker and jollier than his cousin Telano, he had not the dignified manners of a Governor of Vermont; he was attired in a light costume of blue cotton shirt and butternut trousers, his sleeves rolled up, his feet bare.

Winthrop still deliberated. "Perhaps it would be better," he said at last, "if Bartolo should go in, on my horse; I could wait here with you." And he looked at Garda with eyes which asked the question—was Bartolo to be trusted so far as that?

She understood. "Bartolo will carry your message as well as any one could, I know," she answered.

Bartolo gave his head a lurch to one side in acknowledgment of her compliment. He slapped his leg resoundingly;—"I *tell* yer!" he said. It was his way of affirming his capabilities.

There was really nothing else to be done, unless Winthrop should essay to ride, as he had suggested, with Garda behind him; and Garda had declined to try this mode of progression. Bartolo offered the statement that he could reach Gracias, and have a carriage back, before dark.

"That's impossible," said Winthrop, briefly.

"'Twon' be more'n de edge of de ebenin', den, marse," said Bartolo, with his affable optimism.

"Be off, in any case; the sooner you are back, the more dimes you will have."

Bartolo flung himself in a heap upon the saddle, disentangling his legs after the horse was in motion; then, his bare feet dangling and flapping without use of the stirrup, he galloped across the barren, not by the road, but taking a shorter cut he knew. Winthrop stood watching him out of sight; but he could not see far, as the light was nearly gone.

"Now make a fire," said Garda.

"Don't you think you could walk on—if we should go very slowly? We might shorten the distance by a mile or two."

"I don't think I could take a step. These slippers are tightening every minute, in the wrong places; they hurt me even as I sit still."

"Try my shoes."

"I couldn't carry them, my feet would slip out at the top."

This was true; her little feet looked uselessly small, now that they were needed for active service. "You are very inconvenient," he said, smiling.

"The next thing—you will be asking me to go in to Gracias barefoot," continued Garda. "But I never could, never; one step on this sand would make me all creepy."

"Well," said Winthrop at last, accepting his fate, "I suppose I might as well make a fire."

"It's what I wanted you to do in the first place," answered Garda, serenely.

He made a fire that leaped high towards heaven. He made it systematically, first with twigs and pine cones which he collected and piled together with precision before applying the match; then he added dry branches, which he searched for and hauled in with much patience and energy.

"When I asked you to make a fire, I did not suppose you would be away all night," remarked Garda, as he returned from one of these expeditions, dragging another great load behind him.

"All night? Twenty minutes, perhaps."

"At least an hour."

He looked at his watch by the light of the blaze and found that she was right; he had been at work an hour. As he had now collected a great heap of branches for further supply, he stood still, watching his handiwork; Garda was sitting, or rather half reclining, on his coat, her back against a pine, her slippers extended towards the glow.

"You look sleepy," he said, smiling to see her drowsy eyes. "But I am glad to add that you also look warm."

"Yes, I am extremely comfortable. But, as you say, I am sleepy; would you mind it if I should really fall asleep?"

"The best thing you could do."

She put her head down upon her arm, her eyes closed; it was not long before he could perceive that sleep had come. He took off his soft felt hat, and, kneeling down, raised her head gently and placed it underneath as a pillow. She woke and thanked him; but fell asleep again immediately. He drew the little mantle she wore—it was hardly more than a scarf—more closely round her shoulders, added to it the only thing he had, his silk handkerchief. And then, coatless and hatless, he walked up and down beside the fire and her sleeping figure, keeping watch and listening for the distant sound of wheels. But it was too early to listen, he knew that. Night had darkened fully down upon the barren, the fire, no longer leaping, burned with a steady red glow; a warm breeze stirred now and then in the pine-trees; but except that soft sound it was very still. And the aromatic odors grew stronger.

CHAPTER XVII

The next morning, about eight o'clock, the only covered carriage of which Gracias could boast drove up to the door of East Angels. From it descended (it really was a descent, for the carriage had three folding steps) Evert Winthrop, then Garda, then Mrs. Carew, to meet, gathered in the lower hall near the open door, Dr. Kirby and his mother, the Rev. Middleton Moore, Madam Ruiz, Madam Giron, and, in the background, Pablo and Raquel. Margaret was not there, nor Celestine; but Looth's head peeped over the old carved railing at the top of the stairway, and outside, gathered at the corner of the house, were Telano, Aunt Dinah-Jim, Maum Jube, and Cyndy, furtively looking on. Dr. Kirby's face was dark. Mr. Moore, who always preferred that everything should be as usual, was doing his best (in opposition to the Doctor) to keep it usual now; of course they had been anxious; but Garda was found, he did not see why they should continue to be distressed. Little Mrs. Kirby, in her neat brown bonnet with little brown silk cape, looked apprehensive. Madam Giron (with some hastily donned black lace drapery over her head) and Madam Ruiz appeared much more reserved than was usual with them.

The arriving Betty alone was radiant; but she shone for all. She half fell out of the carriage in her haste, and almost brought Evert Winthrop, who was assisting her, to the ground. Garda, while waiting a moment for these two to disentangle themselves, glanced at the assembled group within, and, smiling at their marshalled array, waved a gay little salutation to the Doctor, who was advancing to meet them. But the Doctor was in no mood for such light greetings; in majestic silence he came forth, representing the others, representing Gracias-á-Dios, representing himself.

Winthrop detested scenes, he was much annoyed that these people had (as he said to himself) thought it necessary to make one. But he saw that he could not prevent it, they had made up their minds to take it in that way; if he did not speak, the Doctor would, and it was better to speak first and speak lightly, and by ignoring their solemnity, break it up, than be put through a catechism on his own account.

"Ah, Doctor," he said, "good-morning; we have had an accident, as you see, and are rather late. But it isn't of as much consequence as it might have been, because Garda has given me the right to take care of her; she has promised to be my wife."

It was out—the great news! Betty Carew fell to kissing everybody in her excitement, and saying, tearfully, "Isn't it—*isn't it* beautiful?" Old Mrs. Kirby walked back, and meekly sat down on the bottom stair; she was pleased, but she was also extremely tired, in the reaction she was becoming conscious of it; though deeply interested, her principal hope now was that somebody would think of breakfast. Madam Giron (generously unmindful of her missing horse) and Madam Ruiz came forward together to offer their congratulations; at heart they were much astonished, for they both thought Winthrop far too old for Garda; they tried not to show their surprise, and said some very sweet things. But Mr. Moore was the most startled person present, Winthrop's speech had seemed to him the most unusual thing he had ever heard. He walked up and down several times, as if he did not quite know what to do. Then he tried to present a better appearance in the presence of all these friends, and stood still, rubbing his hands and saying every now and then, in a conciliating tone (apparently as much to himself as to any one else), "Why yes, of course. Why yes."

These little flurries of words, movement, and embraces had gone on simultaneously; and Winthrop had all the time been trying to lead the way towards the stairs. Dr. Kirby had not spoken a syllable, either in answer to Winthrop's first speech, or Betty's tearful "*Isn't* it beautiful?" or Mr. Moore's "Why yes." But now he found his voice, and drawing Garda—who had kept on laughing to herself softly—away from the women who were surrounding her, "Come up-stairs, Garda," he said; "this open hall is no place for a serious conversation."

It occurred to Winthrop that he might have thought of this before.

Meanwhile the large heavy Looth had gone on a thunderous run through the whole length of the upper hall, on her way to a back staircase, in order to get down first and tell the news to Telano, Aunt Dinah, and the others. For Pablo and Raquel held themselves aloof from the new servants (though kindly allowing them to do the work of the household), and it gave Looth joy to forestall them. Pablo and Raquel were of the old *régime*, they held their heads high because they were not receiving wages, but "b'longed to de place;" they had small opinion of "free niggahs" still, and were distinctly of the belief that "man's payshin" was an invention of the Yankees, which would soon come to an end. "*Den* we'll see squirmin'—ki!"

When the friends were re-assembled in the drawing-room up-stairs, Dr. Kirby said, with gravity, "Let some one inform Mrs. Harold."

Winthrop repressed a movement of impatience; the little Doctor with his magisterial air, the tall, lank clergyman trying to conciliate his own surprise, Mrs. Carew with her ejaculations and handkerchief, the two Spanish ladies, who, as it was a sentimental occasion, stood romantically holding each other's hands, even poor tired little Mrs. Kirby, folded up quiet and small as a mouse in her chair—they all seemed to him tedious, unnecessary. Then his glance reached Garda, who was looking at him over the low bulwark of the Doctor's shoulder. His face softened, and he smiled back at her, evidently they must let these good people have their way.

But Garda was less patient. "I shall go myself to find Margaret," she said; and slipped from the room before the Doctor could stop her.

"I don't think she will come back immediately," said Winthrop, smiling a little with recovered good-humor at the solemn face the Doctor turned towards him. "If these friends will kindly excuse me, I should like to go to my room for a while, as I have been up all night; perhaps you will come with me?" he added to the Doctor;—"for a moment or two."

It was not at all the Doctor's idea, this easy "moment or two," of the formal interview which should take place between the suitor and the guardian. But neither had it been at all to his taste—Winthrop's first remark that they were "rather late." Rather late—he should think so, indeed! About fifteen hours. However, his genuine fondness for Garda induced him to waive ceremony, and he prepared to follow the northerner who, with a courteous bow to the others, was turning to leave the room.

But they would not let him go so, they must all shake hands with him again. Madam Ruiz and Madam Giron turned their lovely eyes upon him, and said some more enchanting things; Betty, taking his hand in both of hers, gave him her blessing. Mr. Moore's clasp was more limp; he was a very sincere man, and did not know yet whether he was pleased or not. He did not think Penelope would know. When Winthrop and Dr. Kirby had left the room, he took leave of the ladies, mounted his pony, and started on his return to Gracias; perhaps, after all, Penelope *would* know. Madam Ruiz and Madam Giron went next, not aware that the tidings they carried would bring another access of that terrific rage to Manuel when he should hear it (in Key West), and a heavy conviction that the world's last days were certainly near to poor stiff Torres. Betty Carew was to remain; to her, when they were alone together, Mrs. Kirby, waiting for Reginald, confided her need for breaking her fast.

"And *I'm* famished too," said Betty, wiping her eyes decisively for the last time, and putting away her handkerchief; "only one doesn't remember it now, of course, at such a time as *this*." (But Mrs. Kirby thought she did remember.) "We had a little something before we started, at my house—where dear Evert in the *sweetest* way brought Garda, as soon as they reached Gracias; but it was only a little, and I'll go directly out now myself and speak to Aunt Dinah, as Mrs. Harold and Garda are talking, I reckon—yes, *indeed*, they've got something to talk about, haven't they? and *what* a comfort this will be to Mrs. Harold, coming so *soon* after her taking charge of the dear, dear child, and making her more than ever one of the family, of course; and Katrina too, what a comfort it will be to her to have her dear nephew so *delightfully* married! But there, I'll go out and speak to Aunt Dinah; 'twon't be long, Mistress Kirby; 'twon't be long."

Mrs. Kirby hoped it would not be; she sat very still in her low chair, it seemed to help her more if she sat still. She was seventy-five years old, and a very delicate little woman; her last meal had been taken at five o'clock of the afternoon, or, as she would have said, of the evening, before. She had been up all night, having started with her son for East Angels soon after Telano had appeared at their door late in the evening, saying that Garda had not come home, and Mrs. Harold wished to know if she were with them; Reginald, though in his mental perceptions so keen, was very blind at night as regarded actual vision; in consequence they had missed their way, and after long meandering wanderings over the level country in various directions through the soft darkness, behind their old horse June on a slow walk (her white back was the only thing they could either of them see), they had found themselves at dawn far away from East Angels, so that they had only been able to arrive there half an hour before Garda herself appeared. They had found several of their friends already assembled, and had learned from them that word had been sent down from Gracias that Garda had reached Mrs. Carew's house in safety, with Evert Winthrop; and that all three would soon be at East Angels.

This news had occasioned much relief. Also some conjecture. But Reginald Kirby did not conjecture when they told him the tale, he maintained an ominous silence. Too ominous, Mr. Moore thought: let ominousness be kept for one's attitude towards crime. The truth was that Mr. Moore, much as he admired Dr. Reginald (and he admired him sincerely), thought that he had just one little fault: he was disposed at times to be somewhat theatrical. So he spoke in his most amiable way of Garda's adventure being "idyllic," and turning to the Doctor, added, pleasantly, "Why so saturnine?" And then again (as it seemed to him a good phrase), "Why so saturnine?" And then a third time, and more playfully, as though it were a poetical quotation, "Why?—tell me why?"—which was indeed imitated from one of Penelope's songs, "Where, tell me where,"—referring to a Highland laddie.

The Doctor glared at him. Then he took him by the button and led him apart from the others. "Sir," he said, frowning, "you can take what stand you like in this matter, *you* are a clergyman, and a certain *oatmealish* view of things becomes your cloth; but I, sir, am a man of the world, and must act accordingly!" And leaving the parson to digest that, he returned to his post at the door.

When Betty came back from her interview with Aunt Dinah she brought with her a piece of hot corn-bread; "I thought you might like a taste of it," she said. Mrs. Kirby was very glad to get it; she sat breaking off small fragments and eating them carefully—Mrs. Rutherford would have said that she nibbled. "Yes, the *sweetest* thing!" continued Betty, seating herself broadly in an arm-chair, and searching again for her handkerchief. "Let me see—you and the Doctor started down here about midnight, didn't you? Well, of course we didn't feel like going to bed, of course, not knowing *where* our poor dear child might be, and so I went over and sat with Penelope Moore; and Mr. Moore *very* often went down to the gate, and indeed a good deal of the time he stayed out on the plaza; Telano's coming up from here had let everybody know what had happened, and many others sat up besides ourselves, and some of the servants got together with torches and went out on the barren to look, only Mr. Moore wouldn't organize a *regular* search, because he supposed that was being done here under the Doctor's directions, he never dreamed you hadn't got here at all! At length, when it was nearly three, Mr. Moore came in and said that he thought we had better go to bed and get what sleep we *could*; that we should only be *perfectly* useless and exhausted the next day if we sat up all night" (here little Mrs. Kirby heaved a noiseless sigh); "and so I went home, and *did* go to bed, but more to occupy the time than anything else, for of course it was simply *impossible* to sleep, anxious as I was. But I must have dropped off, after all, I reckon, because it was just dawn when Cynthy came up to tell me that Mr. Moore was down-stairs; I *rushed* down, and he said that Marcos Finish, the livery-stable man, had been to the rectory to say that Bartolo Johnson had come to his house a short time before, knocked him up, and told him that the northern gentleman and Garda were ten miles out on the barren, and that he had been sent in to bring out a carriage for them. He confessed—Bartolo—that he ought to have been there *hours* before, as the gentleman had sent him in on his own horse not much past eight in the evening. But, on the way, he had to pass the cabin of one of his *friends*, he said—a nice friend, that wild, drinking Joe Tasteen!—and Joe stopped him, and he intended to stay only a moment, of course, which soon became many minutes as the foolish boy lay on the floor in a drunken sleep, while two of Joe's hangers-on, though not actually Joe himself, I believe, made off with the horse. Of course it was a regular plot, and I'm afraid Mr. Winthrop will never see *that* horse again! When Bartolo *did* at last wake up, he came in to Gracias as fast as he could scamper, and went straight to Marcos's place and told all about it—the only redeeming feature in *his* part of the affair—and Marcos got out his carriage, and sent one of his best men as driver, with Bartolo as guide, and then he went over to your house to tell the Doctor, and not finding him, came on to the rectory, and Mr. Moore told him that he did wrong not to come to him *before* sending the carriage (but Marcos said Bartolo wouldn't wait), because he himself would have gone out in it after Garda, of course. This was the first *we* knew, in Gracias, of Mr. Winthrop's being with the dear child, and it *did* seem so fortunate that if they were to be lost at all, they should happen to be lost *together*. Mr. Moore thought, and so did Marcos Finish, that they would drive directly here, without stopping in Gracias, and so he rode down at once; and I was coming down myself, later, only they did that *sweet* thing, they stopped after all, and came to *me*. There they were in the drawing-room when I hurried down, Garda laughing, oh, *so* pretty, the dear! As soon as I knew, I took her in my arms and gave her a true *mother's* blessing. Oh, Mistress Kirby, how such days as this take us back to our *own* spring-time, to the first buddings and blossomings of our *own* dear days of love! I am sure—I am sure," continued Betty, overcome again, and lifting the handkerchief, "that we *cannot* but remember!"

Mrs. Kirby remembered; but not with her lachrymal glands; it was not everybody who was endowed with such copious wells there, suitable for every occasion, as Betty had been endowed with. She nodded her head slowly, and looked at the floor; she had finished the corn-bread, and now sat holding the remaining crumbs carefully in the palm of her hand, while, in a secondary current of thought (the first was occupied with Garda and her story), she wished that Betty had brought a plate. "Do what I can," she said to herself, "some of them *will* get on the carpet."

Garda, escaping from the Doctor, had gone to Margaret's room; she had not much hope of finding her; her not having been present to greet them seemed to indicate that she was with Mrs. Rutherford, and "with Mrs. Rutherford" was a hopeless bar for Garda. But Margaret was there.

Garda ran up to her and kissed her. "The only thing I cared about, Margaret, was you—whether *you* were anxious."

"How could I help being anxious?" Margaret answered. "It was the greatest relief when we heard that you had reached Gracias." She was seated, and did not rise; but she took the girl's hand and looked at her.

Garda sat down on a footstool, and rested her elbows on Margaret's knee. "You are so pale," she said.

"I am afraid we are all rather pale, we haven't been to bed; we were very anxious about you, and then Aunt Katrina has had one of her bad nights."

But Garda never had much to say about Aunt Katrina. She looked at Margaret with an unusually serious expression in her dark eyes; "I have something to tell you, Margaret. You know how wrong you have thought me in liking Lucian as I did; what do you say, then, to my liking somebody who is very different—Mr. Winthrop? What do you say to my marrying him? Not now; when I am two or three years older. He has always been so kind to me, and I like people who are kind. Of course you are ever so much surprised; but perhaps not more so than I am myself. I hope you won't dislike it; one of the pleasantest things about it to me is that it will keep me near you."

Margaret did not say whether she was surprised or not. But she took the girl in her arms, and held her close.

"How much you care about it!—I believe you care more than I do," said Garda, putting her head down on Margaret's shoulder contentedly.

"No," answered Margaret, "that is impossible, isn't it? It is only that those who are older always realize such things more."

"Well, I don't want to realize anything more just at present," said Garda. She left her friend, and standing long enough to lift her rounded arms above her head in a long stretch, she threw herself down on a low couch. "*Oh*, I'm so sleepy! And I'm hungry too. I wish you would let me have my coffee in here, Margaret; then I could talk to you and tell you all about it. Don't you want to hear all about it?"

Margaret had risen to ring for Telano. "Of course," she said, as she crossed the room.

"Let me see," began Garda, in a reviewing tone. "I went to sleep. Then I woke up; and after a while I got frightened." She put her hands under her head and closed her eyes. Presently she began to laugh. "That's all there is to tell; yes, really. I got frightened—the barren was so dark and so large behind me."

She said no more. As she had once remarked of herself, she was not a narrator.

Margaret did not question her; she was clearing one of the tables for the coffee.

After a while Garda, still with her eyes closed, spoke again: "Margaret."

"Well?"

"You will have to tell me all the things I mustn't say and do."

"You will know them without my telling."

"Never in the world."

A few minutes more of silence, and then Garda's voice a second time: "Margaret."

"Well?"

"Tell me you are pleased, or I won't go on with it."

"Oh, Garda, that's not the tone—"

"Yes, it is. The very one! Don't be afraid, we like each other, he likes me in his way, and that will do; that is, it will do if you will tell me how to please him."

"You must ask him that."

"Oh, *he'll* tell; his principal occupation for a long time is going to be the discovery of my faults." But as she looked up at Margaret, re-awakened and laughing, it did not seem to the latter woman that he would be able to find many.

In any case, he had not set about it yet. As he went through the hall towards his room, accompanied by the Doctor, "I take it that it's hardly necessary, Doctor," he said, "to formally ask your consent."

The Doctor waited until they had reached the room, and the door was closed behind them. "I think it *is* necessary, Mr. Winthrop," he answered, gravely.

"Very well, then. I ask it," said the younger man. And his voice, as he spoke, had a pleasant sound.

The Doctor had liked Evert Winthrop. There were two or three things which he should have preferred to see changed; still, faults and all, he had liked him. And he liked his present demand (though by no means the manner of it); the Northerner was taking the proper course, he had taken it promptly. Nevertheless the idea was impossible, perfectly impossible, that Garda, the child whom they all loved, the daughter of Edgar Thorne and all the Dueros, could be carried off by this stranger without any trouble to himself, at an hour's notice! And that he, Reginald Kirby, should be asked to give his consent to it in that light way! Give his consent? Never!

The Doctor's feelings were conflicting. And growing more so. He looked at Winthrop, and thought of twenty things; at one instant he felt a strong desire to knock him down; the next, he was grateful. He said to himself, almost with tears, that at least it should not be so easy, there should be obstacles, and plenty, of them; if there was no one else to raise them, he, Reginald Kirby, would raise them. He found it difficult to know what he really did think with any clearness.

But Winthrop was waiting, he must say something. "Edgarda is very young," he began, in rather a choked voice.

"I know it. I should, of course, wait until she was older—at least eighteen."

"Two years," said the Doctor, mechanically.

"Yes, two years."

"And in the mean time?"

"In the mean time we should, I hope, go on much as we are going now; she is in Mrs. Harold's charge, you know."

The southerner thought that this also was spoken much too lightly. "Would your intention be to—to educate her further?" he asked, bringing out the question with an effort. It seemed to him that he never could consent to that, to have their child carried off, while still so young and impressible, and subjected to the radical modern processes that passed as education for girls at the high-pressure North.

"No," Winthrop answered, divining the Doctor's thought, and smiling over it, "I have no intentions of that kind, how could I have? If Garda should choose to study for a while, that would be her own affair, and Mrs. Harold's. She will be entirely free."

"Do you mean that you will exercise no authority?"

"None whatever."

"Then you do not consider it an engagement?" said the Doctor, drawing himself up belligerently.

"As much of an engagement as this: she has said that she would be my wife at the end of two years, if, at the end of two years, she should find herself in the same mind."

"For God's sake, sir, don't smile, don't take it in that way! At what are you laughing? It cannot be at Garda, it must be therefore at myself; I am not aware in what respect I am a subject for mirth." The Doctor was suffocating.

"You don't do me justice," said Winthrop, this time seriously enough. "I ask you, and with all formality, since you prefer formality, for your permission, as guardian, to make Edgarda Thorne my wife, if, at the end of two years, she should still be willing."

"And if she shouldn't be? She is a child, sir—a child."

"That is what I am providing for; if she shouldn't be, I should not hold her for one moment."

"And in the mean time do you hold yourself?" The Doctor was still fiery.

"I hold myself completely."

"Do I understand, then, that you consider yourself engaged to her, but that she is not to be engaged to you?"

"That is what it will amount to. And it should be so, on account of the difference in our ages."

There was a silence. Then, "It is an honorable position for you to take," said Kirby.

He had forced himself to say it. For, now that he was sure of this man (he had really in his heart been sure of him all along, but now that he had it in so many words), and his anxieties of one sort were set at rest, he could allow himself the pleasure of freely hating him, at least for a few moments. It was not a violent hate, but it was deep—the jealous dislike, the surprised pain, which a father who loves his young daughter has to surmount before he can realize that she is willing to trust herself to another man, even the man she loves; what does she know of love? is his thought—his fair little child.

Winthrop did not appear to be especially impressed by the Doctor's favorable opinion of him—of him and his position. He went on to define the latter further. "I think it would be more agreeable for us all now, Garda herself included, if she could be made independent, even if only in a small way, as regards money. I had not intended, as you know, to buy all the outlying land of East Angels; but now I will do so; it is just as well to have it all. The money will be in your charge, of course; but perhaps you will allow me to see to the investment of it, as I have good opportunities for that sort of thing? I think it is probable that we can secure for her, between us, a tolerable little income."

"As you please," said the Doctor. Then he tried to be more just. "Very proper," he said.

This was the only allusion between them to the fact that the suitor was a rich man. And Winthrop, often as Kirby's unnecessary (as he thought) ceremonies had wearied him, forgave it all now in the satisfaction it was to him to be considered purely for himself—himself alone without his wealth; yes, even by an unknown little doctor down in Gracias-á-Dios. He felt quite a flush of pleasure over this as he realized that the interview was coming to an end without one word more on this subject, apparently not one thought. He shook hands with the Doctor warmly; and he felt that all these people would talk and care far more about what he was personally than about what he possessed. It was very refreshing.

The Doctor allowed his hand to be shaken; but his feeling of dislike was still enjoying its season of free play. He looked at the younger man and felt that he detested him, he had a separate (though momentary) detestation for his gray eyes, for his white teeth, his thick hair, his erect bearing, he wanted to strike down his well-shaped hands. This stranger (stranger, indeed; a few months ago they had never heard of him) was to have Garda, carry her off, and make what he chose of her; for that was what it would come to. He, as guardian, might raise as many obstacles as he pleased; but if the child herself consented, what would they amount to? And the child had consented—this stranger! A mist rose in his eyes. He turned quickly towards the door.

"I am afraid you have had no breakfast," said Winthrop, courteously, as he followed him.

The Doctor had not thought of this, he seized it as an excuse. "I will go and ask for something now," he said, and, with a brief bow, he left the room. In the hall outside, in a dark corner, he was obliged to stop and wipe his eyes. Poor Doctor! Poor fathers all the world over! They have to, as the phrase is, get over it.

Before Gracias had been formally apprised of Garda's engagement, Mr. and Mrs. Moore came down to East Angels to see Margaret; they came, indeed, the morning after Winthrop's interview with Dr. Kirby, and explained that they should have come on the previous afternoon if they had been able to secure old Cato and his boat. It was no small thing for Mrs. Moore to make such a journey; and Margaret expressed her acknowledgments.

"It is, in fact, an especial matter that has brought me down to-day," answered Penelope. "*Would* you allow Middleton to go out and look at the roses? It is a long time since he has had an opportunity of seeing them." When Middleton had departed, his wife, who was established in an easy-chair with her own rubber cushion, disguised in worsted-work, behind her, went on as follows: "I have come, Mrs. Harold, about this reported engagement between our little Garda and your cousin Mr. Winthrop" (Winthrop and Margaret had ceased to disclaim this relationship which Gracias had made up its mind to establish between them). "When Middleton returned from here yesterday, he told me what Mr. Winthrop had said—when they first reached here, you know—and we talked it over. Middleton was pleased, of course" (Penelope *had* known, then)—"I mean with the general idea; as he has the highest esteem for your cousin. But while we were still talking about it—for anything that so nearly touches Garda touches us too—we thought of something, which, I confess, troubled us. Edgarda is lovely, but Edgarda is a child, or nearly so; what is more, we remember that your cousin has always treated her as one. Now a man doesn't care for a child, Mrs. Harold, in the way he cares for a wife, and Middleton and I are both firmly of the opinion that only a love that is inevitable, overwhelming" (Penelope emphasized these adjectives with her black-gloved forefinger), "should be the foundation of a marriage. Look at us; *we* are examples of this. I couldn't have lived without Middleton; Middleton couldn't have lived without me—I mean after we had become aware of the state of our feelings towards each other. And we both think this should be the test: can he *live* without her?—can she *live* without him? If they can, either of them, they had better not marry. Of course, as to what may happen *afterwards*" (Penelope had suddenly remembered to whom she was talking), "that is another matter; things may occur; we may not be responsible for differences. But, as a *beginning*, this overmastering love is, we are convinced, the only real foundation. Now, does your cousin care for Garda in this way? That is what we ask. And if he does not, is there any reason that could have influenced him in making such an engagement? At this point of our conversation, Middleton repeated to me a remark of Dr. Kirby's—which I will not particularize further than to say that it contained the *Kirbyly* coined word—*oatmealish*. But it was that very epithet that made us think that he had the—the *worldly* idea that what had happened would cause remark in Gracias, unless it could be said, by authority, that the two persons concerned were formally engaged to each other. Now, Mrs. Harold, that is a complete mistake. You and your cousin, all of you, in fact, are strangers, you do not know either Gracias-á-Dios, or Reginald Kirby, as we do. Gracias will *not* remark; Gracias has no such habits; and Reginald Kirby's views must not be taken in such a serious matter as this. Much as we like Reginald Kirby, indisputable as is his talent—and we consider him, all Gracias considers him, one of the most brilliant men of the time—he is in some of his judgments—I regret to say it—but he *is* light! When he speaks on certain subjects, one might almost think that he was" (here Penelope lowered her voice) "*French!* And so Middleton and I have come down to-day to say that your cousin must not be in the least influenced by anything he may have suggested. Gracias will *not* comment; Middleton, speaking (through me) as rector of the parish, assures you of this; and he knows our people. I hope you will not think us forward; but we could not possibly stand by and see Garda so terribly sacrificed—married to a man who does not love her in the only *true* way. And all on account of a misconception!"

"I don't think Evert was influenced by anything Dr. Kirby said," Margaret answered.

"Or would say?"

"Or would say."

"You think, then, that the idea of possible comment in Gracias had nothing to do with it?"

"I don't know anything about that, Mrs. Moore. But I do think that Evert has long been interested in Garda."

"Oh, interested. We are all interested."

"I mean he has cared for her."

Mrs. Moore shook her head, and folded her hands decisively. "That is not enough," she answered. "The question is—does he *love* her?" And she drew in her small lips so tightly that there was scarcely any mouth visible; only a puckered line.

"You'll have to ask him that," said Margaret, rising. "I am going to get you a glass of wine."

"Now that is the only unkind thing I have ever heard you say, Mrs. Harold. Of course we cannot ask him; his position forces him to say yes, and we should know no more than we did before. But *could* you sit by—I ask you as a woman—and see Garda sacrificed?"

"It wouldn't be such a sacrifice—marrying Evert Winthrop," said Mrs. Harold, in a tone which was almost sharp.

"It makes no difference *who* it is, if he doesn't love her," responded Penelope, solemnly; and she believed with all her heart in what she said. She looked at Margaret; but Margaret's back was towards her. She rose, and with her weak step crossed the room to where Margaret was standing, taking some cake from Mrs. Thorne's shining old mahogany sideboard.

This champion of love, as she made her little transit, was seen to be attired in a gown of figured green delaine, the plain untrimmed skirt, which was gathered at the waist, touching the floor. The upper part of this garment had the appearance of being worn over a night-dress. But this was because Penelope believed in all persons presenting themselves "exactly as Nature made them." She therefore presented herself in that way; and it was seen that Nature had made her with much shoulder-blade and elbow, a perfectly flat chest, over which the green gown was tightly drawn, to expand below, however (with plenty of room to show the pattern), over one of those large, loose, flat waists concerning which the possessors, for unexplained reasons, always cherish evident pride. In the way of collar, Penelope had a broad white ruffle, which, however, in spite of broadness, was loose enough in front (though fastened with a large shell-cameo breastpin) to betray, when she turned, two collar-bones and an inch of neck below. An edge of black lace, upon which bugles had been sewed, adorned her sleeves; she wore a black silk bonnet with a purple flower, and black kid gloves with one button. Her black shawl, with a stella border, lay on a chair.

"Dear Mrs. Harold," she said, when she reached the sideboard, "we are thinking only of Garda. Do content us if you can,—relieve our anxiety; we have the most complete confidence in you."

"There's no reason why you should have it."

But the southern woman took her hands. "Something has vexed you, of course I don't know what; we should be very fond of you, Margaret, if you would let us; perhaps some day you will let us. But this, meanwhile, is another matter, *this* is about Garda."

"Yes, it's another matter," answered Margaret. She drew her hands away, but her voice took on its old sweetness again. "Don't feel in the least troubled, Mrs. Moore; there's no cause for it. If you want my opinion, here it is: I think he loves her; I think he has loved her, though possibly without knowing it, for some time."

And, ringing for Telano, she gave her orders about the wine, and sent for Mr. Moore—in case he had completed his inspection of the roses.

CHAPTER XVIII

One beautiful morning towards the last of November three skiffs were making their way up a tide-water creek which led into Patricio towards its southern end. The little boats were each propelled by one person, who stood erect facing the prow, and using, now on one side, now on the other, a single light paddle; the stream, though deep, was not wide enough to allow the use of two oars, and it wound and doubled so tortuously upon itself that the easiest way to guide it was to stand up and paddle in the Indian fashion. At the stern of each boat, seated on the bottom on cushions, leaning back in the shade of a white parasol, was a lady; Margaret Harold, Garda Thorne, Mrs. Lucian Spenser.

Mr. Moore was propelling the boat in which Mrs. Spenser was reclining; Lucian's skiff held Garda; Torres had the honor of piloting Mrs. Harold. The skiffs were advancing together, though in single file, and the voyagers talked.

"How delightful it is that one never has to speak loud here!" said Margaret; "the air is so still that the voice carries—all out-doors is like a room. I believe it's our high skies at the North, as much as the clatter of our towns, that make us all public speakers from our cradles."

"I don't agree with you; that is, I don't if you mean that you prefer the southern articulation," said Mrs. Spenser.

"Yet I'm sure you prefer mine, Rosalie," said her husband, laughing.

"You're not a real southerner, Lucian."

"Oh yes, I am. But even if I'm not, here's Miss Thorne; she certainly is."

"Miss Thorne is Spanish," answered Mrs. Spenser, briefly; "she doesn't come under the term southerner, as I use it, at all; she is Spanish—and she speaks, too, like a New-Englander." Then feeling, perhaps, that this statement had been rather dry, she turned her head and gave Garda a little bow and smile.

"You have described it exactly," said Garda, who was letting the tips of her fingers trail in the water over the skiff's low side. "Try this, Margaret; it makes you feel as if you were swimming."

"The southern pronunciation," went on Mrs. Spenser, in a general way, "*I* do not admire." (She spoke as though combating somebody.) "And they have, too, such a curious habit, especially the women, of talking about their State. 'We Carolinians,' 'We Virginians,' they keep saying; and when they are excited, they will call themselves all sorts of names—'daughters of Georgia,' for instance. Imagine northern women speaking of themselves seriously (and the southern women are as serious as possible about it) as 'We daughters of Connecticut,' 'We daughters of Nebraska.' We care about as much, and think about as much of the especial State we happen to live in, as the county."

"The more's the pity, then," said Lucian. "That State-feeling you criticise, Rosalie, is patriotism."

"The northern women are quite as patriotic, I think," said Margaret. "But it's for their country as a whole, not for the State. And for their country as a whole, Mrs. Spenser, haven't you heard them use fine language, occasionally? I have; 'Columbia,' and the 'Starry Mother,' the 'Home of the Free,' and so forth."

Margaret had made remarks of this sort a good many times since the arrival of Lucian and his wife, three weeks before; she compared them in her own mind to the cushions in bags of netting which sailors are accustomed to let down by ropes over a ship's side as she enters port, to prevent too close a grazing against other ships. Not that Lucian and his wife quarrelled, a quarrel requires two persons, and Lucian quarrelled with no one; he had possessed a charming disposition when he first visited Gracias, he possessed a charming disposition still. Nor did it appear that his wife thought otherwise, or that she wished to quarrel with him; on the contrary, any woman could have detected immediately that she adored him, that she had but the one desire, namely, to please him; her very irritations—and they were many—came from the depth of this desire.

She was a tall woman, rather heavy in figure, though not ill made; she had a dark complexion, a good deal of color, thick low-growing dark hair, heavy eyebrows that almost met, very white teeth, and fairly good, though rather thick, features. With more animation and a happier expression—an occasional smile, for instance, which would have revealed the white teeth—she might have passed as handsome in a certain way. As it was, she was a woman who walked with an inelastic tread, her eyes had a watchful expression, her brow was often lowering; her rather long upper lip came down moodily, projecting slightly over the under one, which was not quite so full. She had stout white hand, with square fingers. Her large shoulders stooped forward a little. She was always too richly dressed.

When Rosalie Bogardus had insisted upon marrying Lucian Spenser the winter before, all her relatives had shaken their heads; they were shaking them still. The sign of negation had signified that, to their minds, Lucian was a fortune-hunter. Not that they had meant to insinuate that Miss Bogardus had not sufficient personal charm to attract for herself; on the contrary, they all thought Rosalie a "handsome woman;" but the fact still remained that she had a good deal of money, while the young engineer had not one cent—a condition of things which they could have pardoned, perhaps, if he had shown any activity of mind in relation to obtaining the lacking coin. But here was where Lucian, so active (unnecessarily) in many other matters, seemed to them singularly inert. The truth of the case was not what the relatives supposed; money had had nothing to do with this marriage, and love had had everything.

Rosalie had been a silent, rather dull-looking girl, with a brooding dark eye which had a spark slumbering at the back of it; she had a deep-seated pride which never found its outlet in speech, and she had led always a completely repressed life among her relatives, who were kind enough in their way, but who did not in the least understand her. The girl had the misfortune to be an orphan. Her disposition was reserved, jealous in the extreme; but, as is often the case with reserved women, there was an ocean of pent-up tenderness surging below, which made her sombre and unhappy; for indiscriminate friendship she had no taste, while as to the more intimate ones, she had always found herself forced, sooner or later, to share them with some one else, and the pain her jealousies had given her upon these occasions had been so keen that she had learned to abstain from them entirely; it was easier to live quite alone. When, therefore, at last she believed that she was loved, loved for herself, these long-repressed feelings burst forth; like the released spirit of the magician's vial, they expanded and filled her whole life, they could never be put back in their prison again.

Five years before, Miss Bogardus had met Lucian Spenser at the White Mountains. For a number of weeks they had been thrown together almost daily in excursions and mountain walks, and the young engineer, with his easy, happy temper, his wit and his kindness, had seemed to her the most agreeable person she had ever met. There happened to be no one else there at the moment whom Lucian cared to talk to; still, it was really his good qualities rather than this mere accident of there being no one else that led him on. For he had divined the unhappiness under the pride, he could not resist the charity (as well as the small entertainment to himself, perhaps, in the absence of other diversions) of drawing a smile from that dark reserved face, a look of interest from those moody eyes; yes, it even gave him pleasure to put some animation into that inert figure, so that the step grew almost light beside his. For Lucian had endless theories about the possible good points of the people he met; he was constantly saying of plain women that if they would only be a little more this or a little less that, they would be positively handsome. And he fully believed in these possibilities; perhaps that was one of the reasons why he was so agreeable; it is such a charming talent—the divining the best there is in everybody. At any rate, he was so genuinely kind-hearted, so proselytingly so, if the phrase may be used, that it gave him real pleasure to make people happy, even if it were only for the moment. Of possible reactions he never thought, because he never had reactions himself; if one thing had come to an end, was it not always easy to find another? Easy for him.

He cared nothing about Miss Bogardus's money, as in reality he cared nothing for Miss Bogardus herself. But when the weeks of their mountain life were over, Miss Bogardus found that she was caring for him, though (as he would have honestly and earnestly maintained if he had known it) he had never in the least tried to make her. He had only tried to make her happier; but with Rosalie Bogardus that was the same thing, she had passed, owing to him, the one interesting summer of her dull rich life. She did not know that she could be so light-hearted, she did not know that any one could be; she had had the vague idea that all persons must go more or less unsatisfied, and that this was the reason why so many women (if they had not children to bring up) took to good works and charitable societies, and so many men to horses and wine. Her life had been extremely dull because the people she lived with and those she saw frequently (as has been said, she had never been a woman who made many acquaintances) were all dull; and she had not had among them even the secondary importance which money often bestows, because they were all rich themselves. In addition, there were in the same circle younger cousins much handsomer than she had ever been. The summer she had first met Lucian she was twenty-seven years old; her relatives had become accustomed to the unexciting round of her life—at home in the winter, at the mountains in the summer; a few concerts, some good works; they looked for nothing new from her; she was "only Rosalie" to them. She had every comfort, of course, every luxury; it never occurred to their minds that she might like also a taste of the leading *rôle* for a time, a taste of life at first hand; families are very apt to make this mistake regarding the left-over sisters and daughters whom they shelter so carefully, perhaps, but also so monotonously, under their protecting wing.

That summer Lucian was twenty-three; but, tall, handsome, and in one way very mature, he had looked quite as old as he did now, five years later. He was always sunny, always amusing; he had not been in the least afraid of her, of her age, her moodiness, or her money, but had joked with her and complimented her with an ease which had at first disconcerted her almost painfully. He had noticed and criticised her reserve; he had discovered and praised her one little talent, a contralto voice of smallest possible compass, but some sweetness in a limited range of old English songs; he had teased her to make him a pocket pin-cushion, and then when her unaccustomed hands had painfully fashioned one (on her own behalf she never touched a needle), he had made all manner of sport of it and of her. He had helped her dry-shod over brooks (unexpectedly she had a pretty foot), standing ankle-deep in water himself; he had gone miles for some dark red roses, because one of them would "look so well" (as it did) in her hair; he had laughed at her books, and made her feel, though without the least approach to saying so, that she was ignorant; made her realize, simply through her own quickened sense of comparison, that she, Rosalie Bogardus, who belonged among the "best people," and who had enjoyed what is vaguely but opulently summed up as "every advantage," was yet an uncultivated and even a stupid sort of person, by the side of a certain young idler, one who had no background whatever (so her relatives would have said), no connections, no ambitions or industry of the tangible sort, and no money; no appreciable baggage, in short, with which to go through life, save a graceful little talent for painting in water-colors, and the most delightful disposition in the world. Her relatives would have added—an immense assurance. But Rosalie did not call it that; to her it seemed courage—courage indomitable, was the term in her mind.

She over-estimated this trait in Lucian, as she did one or two other traits; he himself would never have dreamed of being so brave as she supposed him to be. He was brave enough, physically he had never known a fear; but that it was indomitable courage which made him smile so light-heartedly in the face of fortunes so modest—that it was a splendid defiance—this was where the slow, silent, passionate-hearted Rosalie was entirely mistaken. It was temperament more than anything else. But it was natural that she should fall into this error, brought up as she had been among people who were immovably set in all their ideas, proud of their mediocrity (they called it conservatism), who had inherited their wealth through several generations, and who, while close and careful in all their ways, enemies to everything in the least like extravagance, were yet fully of the opinion that respectability as well as happiness depended upon an unassailable foundation of fixed income; having always lived in this atmosphere, and possessing small talent for remarking anything outside of her own narrow little world, it was impossible for Rosalie Bogardus to grasp at once a plan of life which differed so widely from the only one she knew. She could not conceive the idea at first of a person like Lucian living on with contented enjoyment, day after day, without any fortune, any hope of inheriting one, or any effort towards obtaining one. She knew people, of course, who had no fortunes; but if young, as he was, they were all engaged in either planning for them, waiting for them, or working for them, with more or less eagerness and energy. Lucian appeared to be neither waiting nor working, and the only plan he had with regard to such matters was to go back to the office of the company that employed him (because he must), when his summer should be ended; so long as he was earning his mere living from year to year (not a difficult task, as he had no very extravagant tastes, and only himself to provide for), he seemed to think that he was doing sufficiently well as regarded material things—always to him subordinate: a state of mind which Rosalie's relatives, if they had known it, would have deemed either a negligence that was almost criminal, or downright idiocy, one or the other. Rosalie herself, not conceiving such an unambitious creed in a nature so rich, idealized what she did not understand. She dressed up this lack of energetic acquisitiveness, and made of it fortitude; in her long reveries she grew at last to think of it in unspoken words which, if written down, would have been almost poetry.

But though she thus idealized his bravery, she did not have to idealize his kindness; that had been real. He had not cared about her money, she had divined that; what he did had been done for herself alone. When, therefore, they met again, as they did in the winter, the acquaintance continued to grow because she fostered it; she had had time to think everything over, to realize what it would be to live without it, during the four months that had passed since they parted. Lucian, responsive and delightful as ever, and never so conceited (this is what he would have called it) as to bring that pretentious thing, conscience, into such a simple matter as this, lent himself, as it were, to her liking for the time being, whenever he happened to see her. With him it was a temporary and even a local interest, and he supposed it to be the same on her side; when he thought of the part of the city in which she lived, he thought of her: "Second Avenue—oh yes, Miss Bogardus;" but he did not think of it or of her for days together, he was a man who had a thousand interests, who roamed in many and widely differing fields. Meanwhile Miss Bogardus thought of him without ceasing; she lived upon his visits, going over in her own mind the last one, and all that he had said, or failed to say, upon that occasion, until he had come again; she dwelt upon every look and gesture, and made the woman's usual mistake of giving a significance to little acts and phrases which they were very far from having. Lucian did not in the least realize that he was the subject of so much reverie; nor did he in the least realize the absorbed, concentrated nature with which he had to do. His life moved on with its usual evenness; for three-quarters of the day he occupied himself in a third-story office, then he sallied forth to see what the remaining hours held for him in the way of entertainment. It is but just to say that generally they held an abundance; other people liked him besides Rosalie Bogardus, he was a man who, from first to last, was dear to very many. About once in so often he went to see his friend of the summer; he no longer thought of her as a person who needed his help especially; but he knew that a visit pleased her, and, when other things were not over-amusing, he would go for a while and give her that trifling pleasure. He never dreamed that it was a great one.

Long afterwards the character of Lucian Spenser was summed up as follows by a man of his own age who had a taste for collecting and classifying characteristics; he even ventured to think such collections almost as interesting as old china. "He was the most delightful and lovable fellow I have ever known; and a great many persons thought so besides myself. But he never was hampered with, he never took, a grain of responsibility in his whole life. This not from selfishness, or any particular plan for evading it; he simply never thought about *that* at all."

This was true. Even in the case of so serious a thing as his marriage, the responsibility was all assumed by Rosalie.

How she came to have the idea that he loved her, she herself alone could have told. Probably she was deceived by his manner, which was often intangibly lover-like simply through the genius for kindness that possessed him; or by the tones which his voice fell into now and then when he was with any woman he liked, even in a small degree. All this was general, for women in general; but poor concentrated Rosalie, who seldom saw him with other women, thought that it was for one. However her belief had been obtained, it was a sincere one; and she accounted for his silence by saying to herself that he would not speak on account of her fortune. Here again she completely misjudged him; southerner as he was, Lucian's thoughts did not dwell upon money; southerner as he was, too, twenty fortunes would not have kept him from the woman he loved. But, once convinced in her own heart, Rosalie no longer fought against her love for him—why should she? It was the one bright spot of her life. It was possible, after all, then, for life to be happy!

She worshipped every glance of his eye, every word that he spoke; it was pathetic to see the adoration which that repressed nature was lavishing upon a nature so different from its own. But no one saw the adoration save Lucian, she concealed it from all the world besides. For a long time even he did not see it—he was so accustomed to being liked. When suddenly he did become aware of it (long after the evil was done), he left her and left New York. There had never been a word of explanation between them.

Rosalie did not yield; she knew her own heart, she knew that she loved him, she believed that he loved her; she trusted to time. And meanwhile she kept up the acquaintance.

Here, again, Lucian's invincible habit of kindness kept him from telling her the truth, his invincible habit of not taking responsibility made him avoid the responsibility of telling her. He, too, trusted to time.

And there was time enough, certainly; that is, it would have been enough for any one but Rosalie Bogardus. Five years passed, five years of all the torture intermixed with delight which a woman who loves goes through. Now and then they met, and she always wrote to him; she tried to write lightly, as she knew he liked that; she anathematized herself for taking everything in such a ponderous way. She composed long letters about books, about Spanish and Italian, both of which she was studying, about music, and about pictures; she went to see every picture she could hear of, because he painted, not realizing, poor soul, that those who paint themselves, especially those who paint "a little," do not as a general rule care much for pictures, or at least care only for those of a few of their immediate contemporaries, that interest being principally curiosity. Who fill the great galleries of Europe day after day? Who are the people that go again and again? Almost without exception the people who do not paint; for the people who do, it is noticed that one or two visits amply suffice.

But nature will out—at least some natures will. At the end of these five years of a fictitious existence Rosalie Bogardus fell seriously ill; her life was threatened. Then she wrote three trembling lines to Lucian, at Gracias-á-Dios. Her one wish now was to marry him, in order to be able to leave him her fortune; she did not allude to this, but she said that she was probably dying, and hoped to see him soon. Lucian, kind as always, hurried north to Washington, where she was staying with some friends—much more independent now, as regarded her relatives, than she had been before the growth of her love. He married her; it was as well that he had been perfectly sincere, when he did so, in not thinking about her money, because her money did not come to him; she did not die, but improved rapidly; in two months she was well.

Mrs. Lucian Spenser, as has been said, was not a quick or a clever woman, but she had the clairvoyance of love. A year had not passed since her marriage; but it does not take a year for a wife to discover that her husband is not, and never has been, in love with her, and this wife had no longer any illusions on that subject. Lucian's manner towards her was invariably gentle, his temper was always sweet; she could say to herself, miserably enough, but truthfully too, that he did not in the least dislike her. If she had known it, this was something, as things stood. But she did not know it; how should she, without a grain of experience, and with her passionate nature, comprehend and endure the necessity, as well as the great wisdom, of holding on simply to the fact that she was his wife, and that no one on earth could rout her from that position, and that in time his heart might come round to her? She did know, however, she had learned, that such love as their marriage was to have at present must be supplied principally by herself, and she had accustomed her mind to accept this idea; if she was ever discontented, she had only to recall the dreary void of her life before she knew him, and she was reconciled. But while she was still arranging her existence upon these foundations, a new element rose; her jealousy was excited, and it was the strongest passion she had. She discovered that

Lucian was very apt to be more or less in love with every attractive woman, every lovely young girl, he happened to meet. True, it was only a temporary absorption; but it was real enough while it lasted. To this the jealous wife could not accustom herself, this she found herself unable to take "lightly." All the moodiness came back to her eyes, she grew suspicious and sharp; such good looks as she had were obscured, in her unhappiness she seemed larger and more round-shouldered than ever.

She was too proud to appeal to her husband, to tell him that he was torturing her. So they lived on. He was wholly unconscious of the extent of her sufferings, though he knew that she had a jealous nature; he felt that he was a good husband, he had really married her more to please her than to please himself; she had not so much as one unkind word, one unkind look, with which to reproach him. He never neglected her, she could not say that he did. She did not say it; her only wish was that he would neglect some other persons. She preferred this condition of things, however, racked though she often was, to any open discussions between them, any explanations; her instinct warned her that explanations might be worse than the reality. A woman who loves is capable of any cowardice; or is it—any courage?

Margaret's little conversational cushion had brought to Mrs. Spenser's mind the thought that she had perhaps been speaking acrimoniously. She did not mean to be acrimonious; but she was not a southerner, as Lucian was, by birth at least, and he was making a great deal of this southern origin of his whenever he was with Garda Thorne. He was with her every day; true, his wife was present, and other persons; and Garda herself was engaged to Mrs. Rutherford's nephew, Evert Winthrop, who had gone north for three weeks or so on business just before they came. But there might be fifty wives and five hundred other persons present, poor Rosalie thought, Lucian would look at that beautiful girl and talk to that beautiful girl, engaged or not engaged, whenever he pleased. She accused him in her heart of not having told her that there was any such person in Gracias. But the truth was (and she knew it) that, as she had never been able to respond with sympathy to allusions on his part to such acquaintances, much less to any recitals concerning them, he had learned (as he had not a grain of malice) not to make them. As for Gracias, she herself had proposed their coming there; she had not cared to spend the winter in New York or Washington, and see her husband cajoled by society; she had never loved society, and now she hated it; Lucian's content was not in the least dependent upon it, fortunately. He had described this little Florida town to her with a good deal of amusing decoration, she had thought that she should like to see it for herself; in her painstaking, devoted way she had studied the sketches he had made while there until she was much better acquainted with them than he was himself. There had been no sketch of Garda Thorne, no sketch in words or water-colors; but perhaps if her jealousies had been less evident, there might have been. She knew that her jealousies were a weakness. That did not make them any the less hard to bear; it was, each separate time, as if Lucian and the person he was for the moment admiring were engaged in stabbing her to the heart; only, in some miraculous way, she lived on.

On the present occasion she said no more about southern patriotism, but gazed in silence at the near shores as the skiffs glided round the next bend. They were in a wide salt-marsh, a flat reedy sea; the horizon line, unbroken by so much as a bush, formed an even circle round them. It was high tide, the myriad little channels were full, the whole marsh was afloat; the breeze fanning their faces had a strong salty odor, the sedges along shore were stiff with brine. Tall herons waded about, or, poised on one leg among the reeds, gazed at them, as they passed, with high-shouldered indifference; now and then a gray bird rose from the green as they approached, and with a whir of wings sped away before them, sounding his peculiar wild cry. The blue seemed to come down and rest on the edge of the marsh all round them, like the top of a tent; it was like sailing through a picture of which they could always see (though they never reached it) the frame.

The stream they were following was not one of the marsh channels; it was a tide-water creek which penetrated several miles into Patricio, and after a while they came to the solid land.

"The odor of Florida—I perceive it," said Lucian; "the odor of a pitch-pine fire! And I don't know any odor I like better." The stream wound on, the banks grew higher, palmettoes began to appear; they all leaned forward a little in the golden air, they formed the most graceful groups of curiosity. At length as the skiffs turned the last bend, a house came into sight. It was a ruin.

But the pitch-pine fire was there, all the same; it had been made on the ground behind a small out-building. This out-building had preserved three of its sides and the framework of its roof; the roof had been completed by a thatch of palmetto, the vanished façade had been gayly replaced by a couple of red calico counterpanes suspended from the thatch. Here lived a family of "poor whites"—father, mother, and six children; their drawing-room was the green space before the kitchen; their bedchambers were behind the calico façade; their kitchen was an iron pot, at this moment suspended over the fragrant fire. The father had just come home in his roughly made cart, drawn by the most wizened of ponies, with a bear which he had killed in a neighboring swamp; the elder boys were bringing up fish from their dug-out in the creek; the mother, her baby on her arm, lifted her bed-quilt wall to smile hospitably upon the visitors. They did not own the land, these people; they were not even tenants; they were squatters, and mere temporary squatters at that. They had nothing in the world beyond the few poor possessions their cart could hold; they were all brown and well, and apparently perfectly happy.

"They look contented," said Margaret, as, after accepting the hospitalities of the place, which the family hastened to offer—the best in their power—a clean gourd with water from the mansion's old well, a look at the bear, the baby, and the pet alligator of tender years confined in a pen near by, they took their way along an old road leading down the island towards the south.

"They *are* contented," said Lucian. "For one thing, they are never cold; poor people can stand a great deal when winter is taken out of their lives. Here, too, they can almost get their food for the asking—certainly for the hunting and fishing. Yes, yes: if I had to be very poor—if *we* had to be very poor, Rosalie—I should say, with all my heart, let it be in Florida!"

These sallies of Lucian's fancy were always rather hard for his wife; she admired them, of course—she admired everything Lucian said; but she could not see any reasonable connection between their life, under any emergencies that could come to it, and the life of people who lived behind a façade of counterpane, who caught bears, and ate them from an iron pot. However, there must be one, since Lucian saw it; she smiled assent, therefore, and did her best to answer warmly, "Oh *yes*, in Florida!"

"But I suppose they have very little chance to improve here—to rise," began Margaret.

"I don't want them to rise," said Lucian, in his light way; "too much 'rising,' in my opinion, is the bane of our American life. The ladder's free to all, or rather the elevator; and we spend our lives, the whole American nation, in elevators."

Rosalie fully agreed with her husband here. This was a subject upon which she had definite opinions. She thought that every one should be as charitable as possible, and she herself lived up to this belief by giving away a generous sum in charity every year. Her ideas were liberal; she thought that "the poor" should have plenty of soup and blankets in the winter, as well as coals (somehow, in charity, it seemed more natural to say "coals"); there should be a Christmas-tree for every Sunday-school, with a useful present for each child; she would have liked, had it been possible, to reintroduce May-poles on May-day; May-day would come at the North about the last of June. She had a dislike for the free-school system; she thought school-girls should not have heels to their shoes; she thought there should be a property qualification attached to the suffrage. She looked at Torres, who was by her side, wondering if he would understand these ideas if she should explain them; and she thought that perhaps he might. She was doing her best, as Lucian's wife—she had been doing it ever since she arrived in Gracias—to discover the "gold mine" which he saw in this young man; so far (as she had but little sense of humor) she had not succeeded. Once she asked Lucian what it was that he found so amusing in the Cuban.

"Oh, well, he has so many fixed ideas, you know," Lucian answered.

His wife said nothing, she, too, had fixed ideas; she could not see, though she tried to, humbly enough, how any one could help having them. Torres could now speak a little English; but as Rosalie could talk in Spanish in a slow, measured sort of way, their conversations, which were never lively, were carried on in the last-named language; it was understood in Gracias that they were "great friends."

Torres had been brought from his retirement by Lucian. Lucian, who told everybody that he delighted in him, had gone down to the Giron plantation to find him on the very day of his arrival in Gracias; and Torres, yielding to his friend's entreaties, had consented to appear again in "society."

In his own estimation, the Cuban had never swerved from his original posture, of waiting. He had not believed one word of his aunt's story of Garda's engagement; women were credulous where betrothals were concerned; they were, indeed, congenitally weak in all such matters. Manuel—a masculine mind though unregulated—was still absent, engaged in seeing the world (at Key West); but he had been able to obtain a good deal of consolation from the society of the Señor Ruiz, who had not credited the ridiculous tale any more than he himself had.

He had first heard of the señor's disbelief through Madam Giron; he immediately went over to Patricio to pay his respects to him. Since then he had paid his respects regularly on Wednesdays and Fridays, just before sundown. The two never alluded to the story when they were together, they would have considered it ill-bred to speak familiarly of such private matters. True, the Señor Ruiz, having been confined for a long time to his arm-chair, had grown a little lax in the strict practice of etiquette, and it may have been that he would have enjoyed just a trifle of conversation upon the rumor in question. But Torres was firm, Torres kept him up to the mark; the subject had never once been put into actual words, though the Señor Ruiz skirted all round it, talking now about Winthrop, now about East Angels, now about the detention of the northern party all summer, owing to the long illness of Mrs. Rutherford, "that majestic and distinguished lady."

The Señor Ruiz had had time to skirt round every subject, he knew, Torres having paid his biweekly respects regularly now for eight long months. Torres said that there was much "hidden congeniality" between them; on the Señor Ruiz's side the congeniality was extremely well hidden, so much so, indeed, that he had never been able to discover it. But on Torres' side it was veritable, he had found that he could think of Garda with especial comfort over there on quiet Patricio, in the presence of a masculine mind so much resembling his own; and think of her he did by the hour, answering with a bow and brief word or two now and then the long despairing monologues of the Señor Ruiz, who, impelled by his Spanish politeness to keep up the conversation, was often driven into frenzy (concealed) by the length of time during which his visitor remained seated opposite to him, stiff as a wooden statue, and almost equally silent.

Because the poor señor could not move his legs very easily, Torres (on much the same principle which induces people to elevate their voices when speaking to a foreigner, as though he were deaf) always sat very near him, so that their knees were not more than two inches apart. This also enraged the Señor Ruiz, and on more than one occasion, when fingering the cane which always stood beside him, he had come near to bringing it down with violence upon the offending joints; the unconscious Adolfo little knew how near he had come to a bone-breaking occurrence of that sort.

"Two years," Torres was in the habit of saying to himself during these Patricio meditations; "they were safe enough in putting off the verification of their impossible gossip until then." The matter stood arranged in his mind as follows: Mr. Wintup was an old man, he was older than they knew; he was probably nearly forty. It was a pastime for him, at that dull age, to amuse himself for a while with the *rôle* of father. And he filled it well, Torres had no fault to find with him here; to the Cuban, Winthrop's manner fully took its place in the class "parental;" it was at once too familiar and too devoid of ardor to answer in the least to his idea of what the manner of "a suitor" should be. The most rigid and distant respect covering every word and look, as the winter snow covers Vesuvius; but underneath, all the same, the gleam of the raging hidden fires below—that was his idea of the "manner." Owing to the strange lack of discrimination sometimes to be observed in Fate, Garda had had a northern mother (an estimable woman in herself, of course); on account of this accident, she had been intrusted for a while to these strangers. But this would come to an end; these northerners would go away; they would return to their remote homes and Gracias would know them no more. Garda, of course, would never consent to go with them; it was but reasonable to suppose, therefore (they being amiable people), that they would be pleased to see her make a fit Alliance before their departure; and there was but one that could be called fit. It was not improbable, indeed, that the whole had been planned as a test of his own qualities; they wished to see whether he had equanimity, endurance. One had to forgive them their ignorance—the doubting whether or not he possessed these qualities—as one had to forgive them many other things; they should see, at any rate, how triumphantly he should issue from their trial.

He now walked down the old road with his usual circumspect gait; he was with Lucian's wife, whom he always treated with the respect due to an elderly lady.

Lucian was first, with Garda; he had gathered for her some sprays of wild blossoms, and these she was combining in various ways as she walked. She scarcely spoke. But her silence seemed only part of a supreme indolent content.

Mrs. Spenser was behind with Torres—close behind. Margaret, too, did not linger; Mr. Moore, who was with her, would have preferred, perhaps, a less direct advance, a few light expeditions into the neighboring thickets, for instance; he carried his butterfly pole, and looked about him scrutinizingly. They were going in search of an old tomb, which Lucian was to sketch. It was a mysterious old tomb, no one had any idea who lay there; the ruined mansion they had passed had its own little burial-ground, standing in a circle of trees like the one at East Angels; but this old tomb was alone in the woods, isolated and unaccounted for; there was no trace of a house or any former cultivation near. Its four stone sides were standing, but the top slab was gone, and from within—there was no mound—grew a cedar known to be so ancient that it threw back the lifetime of the person who lay beneath to unrecorded days; for he must have been placed at rest there before the old tree, as a baby sapling, had raised its miniature head above the ground.

They had advanced about a mile, when Mrs. Spenser stopped, she found herself unable to go farther; she made her confession with curt speech and extreme reluctance. They all looked at her and saw her fatigue; that made her more curt still. But it could not be helped; she was flushed in an even dark red hue all over her face from the edge of her hair to her throat; she was breathing quickly; her hands shook. The heat had affected her; she was always affected by the heat, and it was a warm day; she had never been in the habit of walking far.

"You must not go another step, Rosalie," said Lucian, who had come back to her; "the others can go on, and I will wait here with you. When you are quite rested we will go slowly back to the shore; there will still be time, I presume, for me to get in my sketch."

But Rosalie never could bear to give her husband trouble. "I will wait here," she said, "but you need not. Please go with the others, as you first intended; you will find me here on your way back."

"I shall stay with you," repeated Lucian.

She looked so tired that they all busied themselves in preparing a seat for her; they made it of the light mantles which the ladies had been carrying over their arms, spreading them on the ground under a large tree where there was a circle of shade. Here she sat down, leaning against the tree's trunk. "If you don't go on with the others, Lucian, I shall be perfectly wretched," she said. "There's nothing in the world the matter with me; you have seen me in this way before, and you know it is nothing—I have only lost my breath."

"Yes, I know it's nothing," Lucian answered, kindly. "But I cannot leave you here alone, Rosalie; don't ask it."

Mr. Moore, who had been standing with his hands patiently folded over his butterfly pole, now had an inspiration; it was that he himself should remain with "Cousin Rosalie." "I have no talent for sketching," he said, looking round upon them; "really none whatever, I assure you; thus it will be no deprivation. And I *have* observed some interesting butterflies in this neighborhood, which I should like to obtain, if possible."

"Why shouldn't we all desert Mr. Spenser?" said Margaret. "I have no doubt his sketch will be much more picturesque than the reality. It's very warm; I don't think any of us (those not inspired by artistic intentions) care to go farther."

Mrs. Spenser watched her husband's face, she was afraid he would not be pleased. But under no circumstances was Lucian ever ill-natured. He now made all manner of sport of their laziness, singling out Torres especially as the target for his wit. Torres grinned—Lucian was the only person who could bring out that grin; then he repressed his unseemly mirth by passing his hand over his face, the thumb on one side, all the fingers on the other, and letting them move downward and come together at the chin, thus closing in the grin on the way. Restored to his usual demeanor, he bowed and was ready for whatever should be the ladies' pleasure. Their pleasure, after Lucian's departure, was simply to recline under the large tree; Mr. Moore had already begun his search in the neighboring thickets, and was winding in and out, now in sight, now gone again, with alert step and hopeful eye.

The three ladies sat idly perforating the ground with the tips of their closed parasols. "What are we going to do to amuse ourselves?" said Garda.

"You think a good deal of your amusement, don't you, Miss Thorne?" said Rosalie. She spoke in rather an acid tone; Lucian, too, thought a good deal of his amusement.

But Garcia never noticed Rosalie's intonations; acid or not, they never seemed to reach her. "Yes; I hate to be just dull, you know," she answered, frankly. "I'd much rather be asleep."

Torres was standing at the edge of their circle of shade in his usual taut attitude.

"Oh, Mr. Torres, do either sit down or lie down," urged Garda; "it tires me to look at you! If you won't do either, then go and lean against a tree."

Torres looked about him with serious eyes. There was a tree at a little distance which had no low branches; he went over and placed himself close to it, his back on a line with the trunk, but without touching it.

"You're not leaning," said Garda. "Lean back! Lean!"

Thus adjured, Torres stiffly put his head back far enough to graze the bark. But the rest of his person stood clear.

"Oh, how *funny* you always are!" said Garda, breaking into a peal of laughter.

Torres did not stir. He was very happy to furnish amusement for the señorita, inscrutable as the nature of it might be; it never occurred to Torres that his attitudes were peculiar.

But Garda was now seized with another idea, which was that they should lunch where they were, instead of at the shore; it was much prettier here, as the shore was sandy; the squatter's boys would be delighted to bring the baskets. Torres, no longer required to make a Daphne of himself, was detached from the bark and sent upon this errand, he was to convoy back baskets and boys; obedient as ever, he departed. And then Garda relapsed into silence; after a while she put her head down on Margaret's lap, as if she were going to try the condition that was better than being "just dull, you know." It was true that they were a little dull. Mr. Moore had entirely disappeared; Rosalie was never very scintillant; Garda was apparently asleep; Margaret, whatever her gifts might have been, could not very well be brilliant all alone. After a while Garda suddenly opened her eyes, took up her hat, and rose.

"I think I will go down, after all, and join Mr. Spenser," she said. "I like to watch him sketch so much; I'll bring him back in an hour or so."

Rosalie's eyes flashed. But she controlled herself. "Aren't you afraid of the heat?" she asked.

"Don't go, Garda," said Margaret. "It's very warm."

"You forget, you two, that I was born here, and like the heat," said Garda, looking for her gloves.

"Surely it cannot be safe for you to go alone," pursued Rosalie. "We are very far from—from everything here."

"It's safe all about Gracias," answered Garda. "And we're not very far from Lucian at least; I shall find him at the end of the path, it goes only there."

It was a simple slip of the tongue; she had talked so constantly of him, and always as "Lucian," to Margaret and Winthrop the winter before, that it was natural for her to use the name. She would never have dreamed of using it merely to vex Mrs. Spenser; to begin with, she would not have taken the trouble for Mrs. Spenser, not even the trouble to vex her.

"I fear Lucian, as you call him, will hardly appreciate your kindness," responded Rosalie, stiffly. "He is fond of sketching by himself; and especially, when he has once begun, he cannot bear to be interrupted."

"I shall not interrupt him," said Garda. "I hardly think he calls *me* an interruption."

She spoke carelessly; her carelessness about it increased Mrs. Spenser's inward indignation.

"Do you sanction this wild-goose chase, Mrs. Harold?" she said, turning to Margaret, with a stiff little laugh.

"No, no; Garda is not really going, I think," Margaret answered.

"Yes, Margaret, this time I am," said Garda's undisturbed voice.

Mrs. Spenser waited a moment. Then she rose. "We will all go," she said, with a good deal of dignity; "I could not feel easy, and I don't think Mrs. Harold could, to have you go alone, Miss Thorne."

"I don't know what there is to be afraid of—unless you mean poor Lucian," said Garda, laughing.

Mrs. Spenser rested her hands upon her arms with a firm pressure, the right hand on the top of the left arm, the left hand under the right arm as a support. In this pose (which gave her a majestic appearance) she left the shade, and walked towards the path.

"I'm afraid you will suffer from the heat," said Garda, guilelessly. It really was guileless—a guileless indifference; but to a large, dark, easily flushed woman it sounded much like malice.

They had gone but a short distance when Garda's prophecy came true; the deep red hue re-appeared, it was even darker than before. Margaret was alarmed. "Do go back to the shade," she urged.

Mrs. Spenser, who had stopped for a moment, glanced at her strangely. "I am perfectly well," she answered, in a husky whisper.

Margaret looked at Garda, who was standing at a little distance, waiting. The girl, who was much amused by this scene, mutely laughed and shook her head; evidently she would not yield.

"I will go on with Garda," Margaret said; "but I beg you not to attempt it, Mrs. Spenser."

"Oh, if *you* are going," murmured Rosalie, her eyes still shining strangely from her copper-colored face.

"Yes, I am going," answered Margaret, with decision.

Rosalie said something about its being "much better," as the road was "so lonely;" and then, turning, she made her way back to the tree.

"It's not like you, Garda, to be so wilful," said Margaret, when was out of hearing.

"Why, yes, it is. *Your* will is nice and beautiful, so I don't come into conflict with it; hers isn't, so I do. *I* don't weigh one hundred and eighty pounds, and *I* don't mind the heat; why, then, should I sit under a tree forever because she has to?"

"I wish you would sit under it to oblige me."

"It isn't to oblige you, it's to oblige Mrs. Rosalie; I can't possibly take the trouble to oblige Mrs. Rosalie. You don't really mind the sun any more than I do, you slim fair thing! it's all pretence. Let red people sit under trees; you and I will go on." She put her arm round Margaret and drew her forward. "Don't be vexed with me; you know I love you better than anything else on earth."

"Yet never wish to please me."

"Yes, I do. But I please you as I am. Is that impertinent?"

"Yes," said Margaret, gravely.

"It's your fault, then; you've spoiled me. When have you done one thing or said one thing through all this long summer which was not extraordinarily kind? Nobody in the world, Margaret, has ever dreamed of being as devoted to me as you have been. And if that's impertinent too—the saying so—I can't help it; it's true."

Margaret made no reply to this statement, which had been made without the least vanity; it had been made, indeed, with a detached impartiality which was remarkable, as though the girl had been speaking of some one else.

Rosalie watched their two figures go down the path out of sight. A few minutes later Mr. Moore made a brief appearance, flying with extended pole across the glade like a man possessed. But he had seen that she was alone, and he therefore returned, after he had not succeeded in catching his prey; he sat down beside her, and asked her if she had read the Westover Manuscript.

Margaret and Garda reached the path's end—it ended in a wood—and found Lucian sketching.

"Ah-h-h! curiosity!" he said, as they came up.

"Yes," answered Garda, seating herself on the ground beside him, and, as usual, taking off her hat; "I never was so curious in my life. Show me your sketch, please."

He held it towards her.

She looked at him as he bent from his camp-stool, she did not appear to be so curious as her previous statement had seemed to indicate. She smiled and fell into her old silence again as he returned to his work, that silence of tranquil enjoyment, leaving Margaret to carry on the conversation, in case she should wish for conversation.

Apparently Margaret wished for it. She, too, was resting in the shade; she spoke of various things—of the white bird they had seen sitting on its nest, which had been constructed across the whole top of a small tree, so that the white-bosomed mother sat enthroned amid the green; of the song of the mocking-birds, which had made a greater impression upon her than anything in Florida; and so on.

"Excuse my straying answers," said Lucian, after a while. "However, painting is not so bad as solitaire; did you ever have the felicity of conversing with a friend (generally a lady) while a third person is engaged at the same table with that interesting game? Your lady listens to you with apparent attention, you are led on, perhaps, to talk your best, when suddenly, as you least expect it, her hand gives a swoop down on her friend's spread-out cards, she moves one of them quickly, with a 'There!' or else an inarticulate little murmur of triumph over his heedlessness, and then transfers her gaze back to you again, with an innocent candor which seems to say that it has never been abstracted. I don't know anything pleasanter than conversation under such circumstances."

Margaret laughed. "Come, Garda, let us go and have a nearer look." For Lucian had placed himself at some distance from the tomb; he was giving a view of it at the end of a forest vista.

But Garda did not care for a nearer look. She had seen the old tomb many times.

"Let us make a wreath for it, then, while Mr. Spenser is sketching. So that it can feel that for once—"

"It's too old to feel," said Garda.

Margaret gathered a quantity of a glossy-leaved vine which was growing over some bushes near. "I shall make a wreath, even if you don't," she said. And she sat down and began her task.

"I think this will do," said Lucian, after another ten minutes, surveying his work. "I can finish it up at home."

Margaret threw down her vines, and began to help him collect his scattered possessions.

"Don't go yet; it's so lovely here," said Garda. "Make a second sketch for me."

"I will copy you one from this," he answered.

"No, I want one made especially for me, even if it's only a beginning; and I want it made here."

"But we really ought to be going back, Garda," said Margaret.

"I *never* want to go back," Garda declared. She laughed as she said it. But she looked at Lucian with the same serene content; it was very infectious, he sank down on his camp-stool, and began again.

Margaret stood a moment as if uncertain. Then she sat down beside Garda, and went on with her wreath.

"How perfectly still it is here!" said Lucian. "Florida's a very still land, there are no hot sounds any more than cold ones; what's your idea of the hottest sound you know, Mrs. Harold?"

Margaret considered. "The sound—coming in through your closed green blinds on a warm summer afternoon when you want to sleep—of a stone-mason chipping away on a large block of stone somewhere, out in the hot sun."

"Good! Do you know the peculiar odor made by summer rain on those same green blinds you speak of? Dusty ones?"

"They needn't be dusty. Yes, I know it well."

"I'm afraid you're an observer; I hope you don't turn the talent towards nature?"

"Why not?"

"Because people who observe nature don't observe their fellow-man; the more devoted you are to rocks and trees, and zoophytes and moths, the less you care for human beings; bless you! didn't you know that? You get to thinking of them in general, lumping them as 'humanity.' But you always think of the zoophytes in minutest particulars."

"Never mind sketching the tomb; sketch me," said Garda.

Margaret and Lucian looked up; she appeared to have heard nothing that they had been saying, she was sitting with her hands clasped round one knee, her head thrown back.

"Sketch you?" Lucian repeated.

"Yes," she answered. "Please begin at once."

"In that attitude?"

"You may choose your attitude."

"Oh, if I may choose!" he said, springing up. He stood for a moment looking at her as she sat there. Unrepressed admiration of her beauty shone in his eyes.

"I didn't know you could paint portraits, Mr. Spenser," remarked Margaret.

"I can now; at least I shall try," he answered, with enthusiasm. "Will you give me all the sittings I want, Miss Thorne?"

"Yes. This is the first."

"To-morrow—" began Margaret.

"Do you want me to keep this position?" said Garda.

"Yes—no. It shall be an American Poussin—'I too have been in' Florida! Come over to the tomb, please." In his eagerness he put out his hands, took hers, and assisted her to rise; they went to the tomb. Here he placed her in two or three different positions; but was satisfied with none of them.

Margaret had made no further objections. She followed them slowly. Then her manner changed, she gave her assistance and advice. "She should be carrying flowers, I think," she suggested.

"Yes; branches of blossoms—I see them," said Lucian.

"But as for the attitude—perhaps we had better leave it to her. Suppose yourself, Garda, to be particularly happy—"

"I'm happy now," said the girl. She had seated herself on the old tomb's edge, and folded her hands.

"Well, more joyous, then."

"I'm joyous."

"I shall never finish my legend if you interrupt me so," said Margaret, putting her hand on Garda's shoulder. "Listen; you are on your way home from an Arcadian revel, with some shepherds who are playing on their pipes, when you come suddenly upon an old tomb in the forest. No one knows who lies there; you stop a moment to make out the inscription, which is barely legible, and it tells you, 'I too lived in—'"

"Florida!" said Lucian.

"I am to do that?" asked Garda, looking at him.

He nodded. She went back, took Margaret's nearly finished wreath and all the rest of the gathered vines, and returning to the tomb, one arm loaded with them, the long sprays falling over her dress, she laid her other hand on Lucian's shoulder, and drawing him near the old stones, clung to him a little as if half afraid, bending her head at the same time as though reading the inscription which was supposed to be written there. The attitude was extremely graceful, a half-shrinking, half-fascinated curiosity. "This it?" she asked.

"Not the least in the world! What has Mr. Spenser to do with it?" said Margaret.

"He's the Arcadian shepherds."

"Let me place you." And Margaret drew her away.

Garda yielded passively. Nothing could have been sweeter than the expression of her face when Margaret had at length satisfied herself as regarded position. The girl stood behind the tomb, which rose a little higher than her knees; she rested one hand on its gray edge, holding the wreath on her other arm, which was pressed against her breast.

"You ought to be looking down," said Margaret.

But Garda did not look down.

"She is supposed to have read the inscription, and to be musing over it," suggested Lucian.

He fell to work immediately.

"We have been here an hour and a half, and we promised to be back in an hour—remember that, Mr. Spenser," said Margaret, who had seated herself near him.

"The bare outlines," murmured Lucian.

He did not appear to wish to speak. As for Garda, she looked as though she should never speak again; she looked like a picture more than a real presence—a picture, but not of nineteenth-century painting. She did not stir, her eyes were full of a wonderful light. After a while it seemed to oppress Margaret—this glowing vision beside the gray tomb in the still wood. She rose and went to Lucian, watching him work, she began to talk. "It's fortunate that you have already sketched the tomb," she said; "you can use that sketch for the details."

He did not reply, Garda's softly fixed eyes seemed to hold him bound.

Margaret looked at her watch; then she went to Garda, took the wreath from her, and, putting her arm in hers, led her back towards the path. "I am obliged to use force," she said. "The sitting is declared over."

"Till the next, then," said Garda to Lucian.

As he began to pack up his sketching materials, Margaret went back and hung her wreath upon the old stones. "In some future world, that shade will come and thank me," she said.

Then they left the wood, and started down the path on their way back to the shore.

They found Mrs. Spenser with both complexion and temper improved; her greatest wish always was to hide her jealousies from Lucian, and this time she succeeded. Mr. Moore had made a fire at a distance, and boiled their coffee; he was now engaged in grilling their cold meat by spearing each slice with the freshly peeled end of one of the long stiff leaf-stalks of the saw-palmetto. These impromptu toasting-forks of his, four feet in height, he had stuck in the ground in an even circle all round the fire, their heads bending slightly towards the flame; when one side of the range of slices was browned, he deftly turned each slice with a fork, so as to give the other side its share.

Torres had made no attempts as regarded grilling and boiling, he and Rosalie had spent the time in conversation. Rosalie had, in fact, detained him, when, after bringing the boys and baskets safely to her glade, he had looked meditatively down the road which led to the old tomb. "What do you think of the Alhambra?" she asked, quickly.

The Alhambra and the Inquisition were her two Spanish topics.

"I have not thought of it," Torres mildly replied.

"Well, the Inquisition, then; what do you think of the Inquisition? I am sure you must have studied the subject, and I wish you would give me your *real* opinion." (She was determined to keep him from following Garda.)

Torres reflected a moment. "It would take some time," he observed, with another glance down the road.

"The more the better," said Rosalie. This sounded effusive; and as she was so loyal to Lucian that everything she did was scrupulously conformed to that feeling, from the way she wore her bonnet to the colors she selected for her gloves, she added, immediately and rather coldly, "It is a subject in which I have been interested for years."

Torres looked at her with gloom. He wished that she had not been interested in it so long, or else that she could be interested longer, carrying it over into the future. The present he yearned for; he wanted to follow that road.

But Rosalie sat there inflexible as Fate; and he was chivalrous to all women, the old as well as the young. He noticed that she was very strongly buttoned into her dress. And then he gave her the opinion she asked for; he was still giving it when the sketching party returned.

Lucian was in gayest spirits. He seized the coffee-pot. "No one should be trusted to pour out coffee," he said, "but a genuine lover of the beverage. See the people pour out who are not real coffee-drinkers themselves; they pour stingily, reluctantly; they give you cold coffee, or coffee half milk, or cups half full; they cannot understand how you can wish for more. Coffee doesn't agree with them very well; they find it, therefore, difficult to believe—in fact they never do believe—that it should really agree with you. It may have been all talked over in the family circle, and a fair generosity on the part of the non-loving pourer guaranteed; but I tell you that in spite of guarantees, she *will* scrimp."

Mr. Moore, a delicate pink flush on his cheeks, now came up with his grilled slices, which proved to be excellent.

"My cousin, you are a wonderful person," said Lucian.

Mr. Moore made a little disclaiming murmur in his throat; "Er-um, er-um," he said, waving his hand in a deprecatory way.

"—But you ought to have been a Frenchman," pursued Lucian.

Mr. Moore opened his eyes.

"Because then your goodness would have been so resplendent, my cousin. As it is, it shines on an American background, and eight-tenths of native-born Americans are good men."

"Yes, we have, I think, a high standard of morality," said Mr. Moore, with approbation.

"And also a high standard of splendor," continued Lucian; "we are, I am sure, the most splendid nation in the world. Some years ago, my cousin, a clergyman at the West was addressing his congregation on a bright Sunday morning; he was in the habit of speaking without notes, and of preaching what are called practical sermons. Wishing to give an example of appropriate Christian simplicity, he began a sentence as follows: 'For instance, my friends, none of you would think of coming to the house of the Lord in'—here he saw a glitter from diamond ear-rings in several directions—'of coming to the house of the Lord, I say, in'—here he caught the gleam from a number of breastpins—'in'—here two or three hands, from which the gloves had been removed, stirring by chance, sent back to him rays from wrists as well as fingers—'in *tiaras* of diamonds, my friends,' he concluded at last, desperately. His congregation had on there, before his eyes, every other known arrangement of the stone."

Mr. Moore smiled slightly—just enough not to be disagreeable; then he turned the conversation. Mr. Moore was strong at that; he thought it a great moral engine, and had often wondered (to Penelope) that it was not employed oftener. For instance, in difficult cases: if violent language were being used in one's presence—turn the conversation; in family quarrels and disagreements—the same; in political discussions of a heated nature—surely there could be no method so simple or so efficacious.

It proved efficacious now in the face of Lucian's frivolity. "Our next course will consist of oysters," he remarked.

"Where are they?" demanded Lucian, hungrily.

"For the present concealed; I conjectured that the sight of two fires might prove oppressive. The arrangements, however, have been well made; they are in progress behind that far thicket, and the sons of the squatter are in charge."

The sons of the squatter being summoned by what Mr. Moore called "yodeling," a pastoral cry which he sounded forth unexpectedly and wildly between his two hands, brought the hot rocks to the company by the simple process of tumbling them into a piece of sackcloth and dragging them over the ground. They were really rocks, fragments broken off, studded with small oysters; many parts of the lagoon were lined with these miniature peaks. Mr. Moore produced oyster-knives; and, with the best conscience in the world, they added another to the shell-heaps of Florida for the labors of future antiquarians.

And then, presently, they embarked. The sun was sinking; they floated away from the squatter's camp, down the winding creek between the leaning palmettoes, across the salt-marsh, over which the crows were now flying in a long line, and out upon the sunset-tinted lagoon. The *Emperadora* was waiting for them; it was moonlight when they reached home.

CHAPTER XIX

The next afternoon Margaret was strolling in the old garden of East Angels. The place now belonged to Evert Winthrop; but it had not pleased him to make many changes, and the garden remained almost as much of a blooming wilderness as before. When at home (and it was seldom that she was absent for any length of time, as she had been the previous day) Margaret was occupied at this hour; it was the hour when Mrs. Rutherford liked to have "some one" read to her. This "some one" was always Margaret.

Poor Aunt Katrina had been a close prisoner all summer; an affection of the hip had prostrated her so that she had not been able to leave East Angels, or her bed. Everything that care or money could do for her had been done, Winthrop having sent north for "fairly *ship-loads* of every known luxury," Betty Carew declared, "so that it makes a *real* my ship comes from India, you know, loaded with everything wonderful, from brass beds down to verily *ice-cream*!" It was true that a schooner had brought ice; and many articles had been sent down from New York by sea. The interior of the old house now showed its three eras of occupation, as an old Roman tower shows its antique travertine at the base, its mediæval sides, and modern top. In the lower rooms and in the corridors there remained the original Spanish bareness, the cool open spaces empty of furniture. Then came the attempted prettinesses of Mrs. Thorne, chiefly manifested in toilet-tables made out of wooden boxes, covered with paper-cambric, and ruffled and flounced in white muslin, in a very large variety of table mats, in pin-cushions, in pasteboard brackets adorned with woollen embroidery. Last of all, incongruously placed here and there, came the handsome modern furniture which had been ordered from the North by Winthrop when Dr. Kirby finally said that Mrs. Rutherford would not be able to leave East Angels for many a month to come.

The thick walls of the old house, the sea-breeze, the spaciousness of her shaded room, together with her own reduced condition, had prevented the invalid from feeling the heat. Margaret and Winthrop, who had not left her, had learned to lead the life which the residents led; they went out in the early morning, and again at nightfall, but through the sunny hours they kept within-doors; during the middle of the day indeed no one stirred; even the negroes slept.

The trouble with the hip had declared itself on the very day Winthrop had announced his engagement to the group of waiting friends at the lower door. The news, therefore, had not been repeated in the sick-room; Mrs. Rutherford did not know it even now. Her convalescence was but just beginning; throughout the summer, and more than ever at present, Dr. Kirby told them, the hope of permanent recovery for her lay in the degree of tranquillity, mental as well as physical, in which they should be able to maintain her, day by day. Winthrop and Margaret knew that tranquillity would be at an end if she should learn what had happened; they therefore took care that she should not learn. There was, indeed, no occasion for hurry, there was to be no talk of marriage until Garda should be at least eighteen. In the mean time Aunt Katrina lived, in one way, in the most complete luxury; she had now but little pain, and endless was the skill, endless the patience, with which the six persons who were devoted to her—Margaret, Winthrop, Dr. Kirby, Betty Carew, Celestine, and Looth—labored to maintain her serenity unbroken, to vary her few pleasures. Betty, it is true, had to stop outside the door each time, and press back almost literally, with her hand over her mouth, the danger of betraying the happiness of "dear Evert" and "darling Garda" through her own inadvertence; but her genuine affection for Katrina accomplished the miracle of making her for the time being almost advertent, though there was sure to be a vast verbal expansion afterwards, when she had left the room, which was not unlike the physical one that ensued when she released herself, after paying a visit, from her own tightly fitting best gown.

To-day Aunt Katrina had felt suddenly tired, and the reading had been postponed; Margaret had come out to the garden. She strolled down a path which had recently been reopened to the garden's northern end; here there was a high hedge, before which she paused for a moment to look at a sensitive-plant which was growing against the green. Suddenly she became conscious that she heard the sound of low voices outside; then followed a laugh which she was sure she knew well. She stepped across the boundary ditch, full of bloom, and looked through the foliage. Beyond was an old field; then another high hedge. In the field, a little to the right, there was a thicket, and here, protected by its crescent-shaped bend, which enclosed them both in its half-circle, were Garda and Lucian; Lucian was sketching his companion.

Only the sound of their voices reached Margaret, not their words. She looked at them for a moment; then she stepped back over the ditch, passed through the garden, and returned to the house, where she seated herself on a stone bench which stood near the lower door. Here she waited, she waited nearly an hour; then Garda appeared, alone.

Margaret rose, went to meet her, and putting her arm in hers, turned her towards the orange walk. "Come and stroll a while," she said.

"You are tired, Margaret; I wish you didn't have so much care," said Garda, affectionately, as she looked at her. "Mrs. Rutherford isn't worse, I hope?"

"No; she is sleeping," Margaret answered. After a pause: "You heard from Evert this morning, I believe?"

"Yes; didn't I show you the letter? I meant to. I think it's in my pocket now," and searching, she produced a crumpled missive.

Margaret took it. Mechanically her fingers smoothed out its creases, but she did not open it. "You have been out for a walk?" she said at last, with something of an effort.

But Garda did not notice the effort; she was enjoying her own life very fully that afternoon. "No," she answered. Then she laughed. "You could not possibly guess where I have been."

"I am afraid I couldn't make the effort to-day."

"And you shall not—I'll tell you; I've been in the green studio. Fortunately you haven't the least idea where that is."

"Have you taken to painting, then?"

"No; painting has taken to me. Lucian has been here."

"When did he come?"

"About two hours ago, I should say. You didn't see him because he did not come to the house; I met him in—in the green studio, of course; I gave him another sitting."

"Then you expected him?" said Margaret, looking at her.

"Yes; we made the arrangement in the only instant you gave us yesterday—when you went to hang your wreath on that old tomb."

"Why was it necessary to be so secret about it? Am I such an ogre?"

"No; you're a fairy godmother. But you would have objected to it, and spoiled it all beforehand; you know you would," said Garda, with gay accusation.

Margaret's eyes were following the little inequalities of the ground before them as they advanced.

"Perhaps you could have brought me round," she answered. "At any rate, you must admit me to the next sitting."

"No, that I cannot do, Margaret; so don't ask me. I love to be with you, and I love to be with Lucian. But I don't love to be with you two together—you watch him so."

"I—watch Mr. Spenser? Oh no!"

"Well, then—and it's the same thing—you watch me."

"Is that the word to use, Garda? You are under my charge—I have hoped that it was not disagreeable to you; I have tried—"

Garda stopped and kissed her. "It isn't disagreeable; it's beautiful," she said, with impulsive warmth. "But there's no use in your trying to keep me from seeing Lucian," she added, as they walked on; "I can't imagine how you should even think of it, when you know so well how much I have always liked him. Oh, what a comfort it is just to *see* him here again!"

"You must remember that he has other things to think of now."

"Only his wife; he needn't take long to think of her."

"He took long enough to leave Gracias last winter and go north and marry her."

"Yes; and wasn't it good of him? I couldn't bear to have him go at the time; but I've forgotten all about that, now that he's back again."

"But not alone this time."

"Lucian's always alone for me," responded Garda. "But why do you keep talking about Mrs. Rosalie, Margaret? Isn't it enough that we have to talk *to* her? She isn't an object of pity in the least; she's got everything she wants, and six times more than she deserves; I detest people who, when they're cross, are all upper lip."

A vision of Rosalie's face rose in Margaret's mind. But she did not at present discuss its outlines with Garda, she simply said, "I must come to the next sitting. And don't choose for it the exact hour when I'm reading to Aunt Katrina."

"I chose that hour on purpose, so that you shouldn't know."

"Yes, because you thought I should object. But if I don't object—"

"You do," said Garda, laughing; "you're only pretending you don't. Very well, then. Only—you mustn't keep stopping me."

"Stopping you? What do you mean?"

"Oh, stopping, stopping—I mean just that; there's no other word. I want to look at Lucian and talk to him exactly as I please."

"I'm not aware that I've blinded or gagged you," said Margaret, smiling.

"No, but you have a way of saying something that makes a change; you make him either get up, or turn his head away, or else you stop what he's saying. You see, *he* follows your lead."

"Though you do not."

"He does it from politeness—politeness to you," Garda went on.

"Yes, he has very good manners," said Margaret, dryly.

"Haven't I good manners too?" demanded the girl, in a caressing tone, crossing her hands upon her friend's arm.

"Very bad ones, sometimes. Now, Garda, don't you really think—"

"I never really think, I never even think without the really. What is the use of getting all white with thinking?—you can't set anything straight by it. *You* are sometimes so white that you frighten me."

"Never mind my whiteness; I never have any color," said Margaret, a nervous impatience showing itself suddenly. Then she controlled herself. "Are you thinking of having another sitting to-morrow?"

"Perhaps; it isn't quite certain yet. I don't know whether you know that Lucian is trying to persuade Madam Giron to take him in for a while?"

"To take *him* in?"

"Them-m-m," said Garda, "since you insist upon it."

"I can't imagine Madame Giron consenting," said Margaret. She was much surprised by this intelligence.

"She wouldn't unless it were to please Adolfo; if he should urge her to do it. And I think he will urge her, because—because he and Mrs. Spenser are such great friends."

"They're nothing of the sort. You know as well as I do that she only talks to him because her husband likes him."

"Well, then, Adolfo will urge because I told him to."

"You told him?"

"Yes," said Garda, serenely; "I told him we could make so many more excursions if they were staying down here. And so we can, I hope—Lucian and I, at any rate; *we're* light on our feet."

"If Madam Giron should consent, when would the Spensers come down?" said Margaret, pursuing her investigations.

"To-morrow at twelve," Garda answered, promptly.

"Mrs. Spenser knew nothing of it yesterday."

"Oh yes, she did; a little."

"She didn't speak of it."

"She didn't speak of it because she's not pleased with the idea. At least not much."

"Then it's Mr. Spenser who is pleased?"

"Yes; still, I am the most pleased of all; I suggested it to him, he would never have thought of it himself. You see, he was losing so much time in coming and going. If he were at Madam Giron's, too, I could hope to see him sometimes in the evening; for instance, to-morrow evening."

"Do you mean that he is coming to see us then?"

"He is coming to see me; that is, if they are down there. I shall not let him see any of the rest of you. It isn't a sitting, you know, we don't have sittings by moonlight; I shall send him word where to come, and then I shall slip out and find him."

Margaret stopped. "Garda," she said, in a changed tone, "you told me yesterday that I had been very kind to you—"

"So you have been."

"Then I hope you won't think me unkind—I hope you will yield to my judgment—when I tell you that you must not send any such message to Mr. Spenser."

"Didn't I tell you you would try to stop it?" said Garda, gleefully.

"Of course I shall try. And I think you will do as I wish."

Garda did not answer, she only looked at her friend with a vague little smile. She seemed not to be giving her full attention to what she was saying; and at the same moment, singularly enough, she seemed to be admiring her, taking that time for it—admiring the delicate moulding of her features, her oval cheeks, which had now a bright flush of color. The expression of her own face, meanwhile, remained as soft as ever, there was not a trace of either opposition or annoyance.

"Isn't there some one else, too, who would not like to have you do such—such foolish thing?" Margaret went on. "Shouldn't you think a little of Evert?"

"Evert's too far off to think of. He's a thousand miles away."

"What difference does that make?"

"You're right, it doesn't make any," said Garda. "I should do just the same, I presume, if he were here." She spoke in a matter-of-fact tone.

Margaret looked at her, and seemed hardly to know what to say next.

In the position in which they were standing, Garda was facing the entrance of the orange walk. Her eyes now began to gleam. "Isn't this funny?" she said. "Here he is himself!"

Margaret turned, expecting to see Lucian. But it was Evert Winthrop who was coming towards them.

"You didn't expect me?" he said as he took their hands, Garda's in his right hand, Margaret's in his left, and held them for a moment. "But I told you in the postscript of my last letter, Garda, that I might perhaps follow it immediately."

"I haven't had time to get to the postscript yet," Garda answered. "The letter only came this morning; and Margaret has it now."

"You know I haven't opened it, Garda," said Margaret, hastily returning it.

"No; but I meant you to," said the girl. Something in this little scene seemed to strike her as comical, for she covered her face with both hands and began to laugh. "What a bad account you will give of me!" she said.

"You will have to give it yourself," replied Margaret. "I must go; Aunt Katrina must be awake by this time."

"Isn't she well?" said Winthrop, looking after her as she left them.

"She had color enough before you came," said Garda, smiling, then laughing at recollections he could not share. "Have you come back as blind as you went away?"

"How blind is that?"

"Blind to all my faults," she responded, swinging her hat by its ribbons.

"Don't spoil your hat. No, I'm not blind to them, but we're going to cure them, you know."

"I'm so glad!"

He had taken a case from his pocket, and was now opening it; it held a delicate gold bracelet, exquisitely fashioned, which he clasped round her arm.

"How pretty!" said Garda. Her pleasure was genuine, she turned her hand so that she could see the ornament in every position.

"You prefer diamonds, I know," said Winthrop, smiling. "But you're not old enough to wear diamonds yet."

She continued to look at her bracelet until she had satisfied herself fully. Then she let her hand drop. "Will you give me some very beautiful diamonds by-and-by?" she asked, turning her eyes towards him.

"To be quite frank, I don't like them much."

"But if *I* like them?" She seemed to be curious as to what he would reply.

"You may not like them yourself, then."

She regarded him a moment longer. Then her eyes left him; she looked off down the long aisle. "I shall not change; no, not as you seem to think," she said, musingly. And she stood there for a moment very still. Then her face changed, her light-heartedness came back; she took his arm, and, as they strolled slowly towards the house, talked her gayest nonsense. He listened indulgently.

"Why don't you ask me what I have been doing all these weeks while you have been away?" she said at last, suddenly.

"I suppose I know, don't I? You have written."

"You haven't the least idea. I have been *amused*—really amused all the time."

"Is that such a novelty? I've always thought you had a capital talent for amusing yourself."

"That's just what I mean; this time I've *been* amused, I didn't have to do it myself. Oh, promise me you won't stop anything now you've come. We've had some lovely excursions, and I want ever so many more."

"When did I ever stop an excursion in Florida?" said Winthrop.

"Yes, you've been very good, very good always," answered Garda, with conviction. "But this time you must be even better, you must let me do exactly as I please."

"Oh, I don't pretend to keep you in order, you know; I leave that to Margaret."

"Poor Margaret!" said Garda, laughing.

The next day Lucian and his wife came down to the Giron plantation; Madam Giron had consented to take them in.

Three nights afterwards, Margaret, awake between midnight and one o'clock, thought she heard Garda's door open; then, light steps in the hall. She left her bed, and opening the door between their two rooms, went through into Garda's chamber. It was empty, the moonlight shone across the floor. She returned to her own room, hastily threw on a white dressing-gown, twisted up her long soft hair, and put on a pair of low shoes; then she stole out quietly, went down the stone staircase and through the lower hall, and found, as she expected, the outer door unfastened; she opened it, closed it softly after her, and stood alone in the night. She had to make a choice, and she had only the faintest indication to guide her—a possible clew in a remembered conversation; she followed this clew and turned towards the live-oak avenue. Her step was hurried, she almost ran; as she drew the floating lace-trimmed robe more closely about her, the moonlight shone, beneath its upheld folds, on her little white feet. She had never before been out alone under the open sky at that hour, she glanced over her shoulder, and shivered slightly, though the night was as warm as July. Her own shadow, keeping up with her, was like a living thing. The moonlight on the ground was so white that by contrast all the trees looked black.

The live-oak avenue, when she entered it, seemed a shelter; at least it was a roof over her head, shutting out the sky. The moonlight only came at intervals through the thick foliage, making silver checker-work on the path.

There were two or three bends, then a long straight stretch. As she came into this straight stretch she saw at the far end, going towards the lagoon, a figure—Garda; behind Garda, doubly grotesque in the changing shade and light, stepped the crane.

Margaret's foot-falls made no sound on the soft sand of the path; she hurried onward, and passing the crane, laid her hand on the girl's shoulder. "Garda," she said.

Garda stopped, surprised. But though surprised, she was not startled, she was as calm as though she had been found walking there at noonday. She was fully dressed, and carried a light shawl.

"Margaret, is it you? How in the world did you know I was here?"

Margaret let her head rest for a moment on Garda's shoulder; her heart was beating with suffocating rapidity. She recovered herself, stood erect, and looked at her companion. "Where are you going?" she asked.

"I am going to try and find Lucian; but it may be only trying. He was to start from the Giron landing at one, when the tide would serve, he said; but you heard him, so you know as much as I do."

"No. For I don't know what *you're* going to do."

"Why, I've told you; I'm going to try to go with him, if I can. I'm going to stand out at the edge of the platform, and then, when he comes by, perhaps he will see me—it's so light—and take me in. I want to sail through that thick soft fog he told us about (when it comes up later), with the moonlight making it all queer and white, and the gulls fast asleep and floating—don't you remember?"

"Then he doesn't expect you?"

"Oh no," said Garda; "it's my own idea. I knew he would be alone, because Mrs. Rosalie can't go out in fogs, she's afraid of rheumatism."

"And you see nothing out of the way in all this?"

"No."

"—Stealing out secretly—"

"Only because you would have stopped it if you had known."

"—At night, and by yourself?"

"The night's as good as the day when there's moonlight like this. And I shall not be by myself, I shall be with Lucian; I'd rather be with him than anybody."

"And Evert?"

"Well," said Garda, "the truth is—the truth is I'm *tired* of Evert."

"You'd better tell him that," said Margaret, with a quick and curious change in her voice.

"I will, if you think best."

"No, don't tell him; you're not in earnest," said Margaret, calming himself.

"Yes, I am in earnest. But I shall miss Lucian if I stay here longer."

"Garda, give this up."

"I don't see how you happened to hear me come out," said the girl, laughing and vexed.

"Have you been out in this way before?"

"No; how could I? Lucian has only just come down here. I should a great deal rather tell you everything, Margaret, as fast as I think of it, and I would—only you would be sure to stop it."

"I want to stop this. Give it up—if you care at all for me; I make it a test."

"You know I care; if you put it on that ground, of course I shall have to give it up," said Garda, disconsolately.

"Come back to the house, then," said Margaret, taking her hand.

"No, I'm not going back, I'm going down to the landing," answered the girl. She appeared to think that she had earned this obstinacy by her larger concession.

"But you said you would give up—"

"If we keep back under the trees he cannot see us; I mean what I say—he *shall* not. But I want to see him, I want to see him go by."

She drew Margaret onward, and presently they reached the shore. "There he comes!" she said—"I hear the oars." And she held tightly to Margaret's hand, as if to keep herself from running out to the platform's edge.

The broad lagoon, rippling in the moonlight, lay before them; the night was so still that they heard the dip of the oars long before they saw the boat itself; Patricio, opposite, looked like a country in a dream. The giant limbs of the live-oak under which they stood rose high in the air above them, and then drooped down again far forward, the dark shade beneath concealing them perfectly, in spite of Margaret's white robe. Now the boat shot into sight. Its sail was up, white as silver, but as there was no wind, Lucian was rowing. It was a small, light boat, almost too small for the great silver sail; but that was what Lucian liked. He kept on his course far out in the stream; he was bound for the mouth of the harbor.

Garda gave a long sigh. "I ought to be there!" she murmured. "Oh, I ought to be there!" She stood motionless, watching the boat come nearer, pass, and disappear; then she turned and looked at Margaret in silence.

"We can go out to-morrow evening, if you like," said Margaret, ignoring the expression of her face.

"Yes, at eight o'clock, I suppose, with Evert, and Mrs. Rosalie!"

"Would you prefer to go in the middle of the night?"

"Infinitely. And with Lucian alone."

"I should think that might be a little tiresome."

"Oh, come, don't pretend; you don't know how," said Garda, laughing. "At heart you're as serious as death about all this—you know you are. Tiresome, did you say? Just looking at him, to begin with—do you call *that* tiresome? And then the way he talks, the way he says things! Oh, Margaret, I give you my word I *adore* being amused as Lucian amuses me." She turned as she said this and met Margaret's eyes fixed upon her. "You can't understand it," she commented. "You can't understand that I prefer Lucian to Evert."

Margaret turned from her. But the next instant she came back. "There are some things I must ask you, Garda."

"Well, do stay here a little longer then, it's so lovely; we'll sit down on the bench. But perhaps you'll be chilled—you're so lightly dressed. What have you on your feet? Oh Margaret! only those thin shoes—no more than slippers?" She took her shawl, and kneeling down, wrapped it round Margaret's ankles. "What little feet you have!" she said, admiringly. "It reminds me of my wet shoes that night on the barren," she added, rising; and then, standing there with her hands clasped behind her, she appeared to be meditating. "Now that time I was in earnest too!" she said, with a sort of wonder at herself.

"What do you mean?" asked Margaret.

"Oh, nothing of consequence. Are you sure you're not cold?"

"I'm quite warm; it's like summer."

"Yes, it's warm," said Garda, sitting down beside her. "Oh, I wish I were in that boat!" And she put her head down on Margaret's shoulder.

After a moment Margaret began her interrogatory. "You consider yourself engaged to Evert, don't you?"

"Yes, after a fashion. He doesn't care about it."

"Yes, he does. You don't comprehend him."

"Don't you think he ought to *make* me comprehend, then? It seems to me that that's his part. But no, the real trouble is that he doesn't in the least comprehend *me*. He has got some idea of his own about me, he has had it all this time. But I'm not like his idea at all; I wonder how long it will be before he will find it out?"

"Don't you care for him, Garda?"

"No, not any more. I did once; at least that night on the barren I thought I did. But if I did, I am sure I don't know what has become of the feeling! At any rate it has gone, gone entirely; I only care for Lucian now."

"And would you give up Evert, engaged to him as you are, with your own consent and the consent of all your friends, for a mere fancy like this?"

"Mere fancy? I shall begin to think, Margaret, that you don't know what 'mere fancies,' as you call them, are!"

"And what view do you take of the fact that Lucian is a married man?" Margaret went on, gravely.

"A horribly melancholy one, of course. Still, it's a great pleasure just to see him; I try to see him as often as I can."

"And you're willing to follow him about as you do—let him see how much you like him, when, in reality, he doesn't care in the least for you? If he had cared he would never have left you, as he did last winter, at a moment's notice and without a word."

"No, I know he doesn't care for me as I care for him," said Garda. "But perhaps he will care more in time; I have thought that perhaps he would care more when he found out how I felt towards him; that is what I have been hoping."

Margaret got up, she made a motion with her hands almost as if she were casting the girl off. "Garda," she said, "you frighten me. I have tried to speak with the greatest moderation, because I have not thought you realized at all what you were saying; but you are so calm, you speak in such a tone!—I cannot understand it."

"Well, Margaret, I've never tried to understand it myself. Why, then, should you try?" said Garda, in her indolent way.

Then, as she looked at Margaret, she became conscious of the marked change in her face, and it seemed to startle her. She rose and came to her. "One thing I know," she said, quickly, "if you are vexed with me, so vexed that you will have nothing more to do with me, I don't know what will become of me. You are the only woman I care for. *Don't* throw me over, Margaret. There's one thing that may happen," she added, looking at her friend with luminous gaze, "I may stop caring for Lucian of my own accord before long; you know I stopped caring for Evert."

"Oh, Garda! Garda!" murmured Margaret, putting her hand over her eyes.

"You are shocked because I tell you the exact truth. I believe you would like it better if I should dress it up, and pretend to have all sorts of reasons. But I never have reasons, I only know how I feel; and you can't make me believe, either, that it isn't better to be true about your feelings whatever they are, than to tell lies just to make people think well of you."

"Garda, promise me not to see Lucian in this way again; that is, not to plan to see him," said Margaret, with a kind of desperation in her tone.

"Why, how can you suppose I would ever promise that?" asked Garda, astonished.

"Very well. Then I shall speak to him myself." And as she stood there, her tall slender figure outlined in white, her dark blue eyes fixed on the girl, Margaret Harold looked almost menacing.

"No, I don't think you would do that," answered Garda; "because as he doesn't care for me, it would be like throwing me at his head; and that you wouldn't like because you have a pride about it—for Evert's sake, I mean. Why don't you tell Evert instead of Lucian? I've thought of telling Evert myself. The idea of his needing to be told!"

"It's because he has such a perfect belief in you," began Margaret. "He would never dream that you could—" She stopped, her lips had begun to tremble a little.

But Garda was not paying heed to what Margaret was saying. "No, you'll never speak to Lucian," she repeated, "I know you never will; you couldn't."

"You're right, I couldn't. And the reason would be because I should be ashamed—ashamed for you."

But Garda was not moved by this. "I don't see why we should be ashamed of our real feelings," she said again, with a sort of sweet stolidity.

"We go through life, Garda, more than half of us—women, I mean—obliged always to conceal our real feelings."

"Then *that* I never will do;" said Garda, warmly. "And you shall see whether I come out any the worse for it in the end."

"You intend to do what you please, no matter who suffers?"

"They needn't suffer, it's silly to suffer. They'd better go and do what *they* please."

"And you think that right? You see nothing wrong in it?"

"Oh, right, wrong—I think it's right to be happy, as right as possibly can be; and wrong to be unhappy, as wrong as possibly can be; I think unhappy people do a great deal of harm in the world, besides being so very tiresome! I was a goose to be as unhappy as I was last winter; I might have known that I should either get over caring for him, or else that I should see him again. In this case both happened."

After this declaration of principles the girl walked down the slope and out to the edge of the platform, where she stood in the moonlight looking northward up the lagoon.

"I can just make out his sail," she said, calling back to Margaret, excitedly, and evidently having entirely forgotten her reasoning mood of the moment before. "The fog is rising. Come quick and look."

But Margaret did not come. When the sail finally disappeared, Garda came back, bright and happy. Then, as she saw her friend's face, her own face changed to sudden sympathy.

"Margaret," she said, taking her hands, "I cannot bear to see you so distressed."

"How can I help it?" murmured Margaret. She looked exhausted.

"You wouldn't care about all this as you do—care so deeply, I mean—if it were not for Evert," Garda went on; "it's that that hurts you so. Don't care so much about Evert; throw him over, as I have done."

"It's true that I care about Evert—about his happiness," answered Margaret, in the same lifeless tone; "I have missed happiness myself, I don't want him to miss it." Here she raised her eyes, she looked at Garda for a long moment in silence.

The girl smiled under this inspection; she leaned forward, and put her soft cheek against Margaret's, and her arm round Margaret's shoulders with a caressing touch.

A revulsion of feeling swept over the elder woman, she took the girl's face in both her hands, and looked at it.

"Promise me to say nothing to Evert, not one word—I mean about this renewal of fancy you have for Lucian," she said, quickly.

"You call it fancy—"

"Never mind what I call it. Promise."

"Why, that's as you choose, I left it to you," Garda answered.

"I choose, then, that you say nothing. You're not really in earnest, you don't know what you're talking about. It's a girl's foolishness; you will come to your senses in time."

"Is that the way you arrange it? Any way you like. Perhaps you really do know more about me than I know about myself," said Garda, with a momentary curiosity as to her own characteristics.

"We must go back," said Margaret, her fatigue again showing in her voice.

Garda put her arm round her as a support, and, thus linked, they walked back through the long avenue over the silver lace-work cast by the moon upon the path. Carlos Mateo, who had been off on unknown excursions, joined them again, issuing in a ghostly manner from the Spanish-bayonet walk, and falling into his usual place behind them. The linked figures crossed the open space, which was again as white as snow with black trees at the edges, and went softly in through the unfastened door.

"I'm going to get you a glass of wine," Garda whispered.

Margaret declined the wine, and they separated, each going noiselessly to her own room.

But, half an hour later, Garda stole in and leaned over her friend. "You're crying," she said—"I knew it! Oh, Margaret, Margaret, why do you suffer so?"

"Don't mind," said Margaret, controlling herself. "I have my own troubles, Garda, and must bear them as I can. Go back to your room."

But Garda would not go. As there was no place for her in Margaret's narrow white bed, she got a coverlet and pillows and lay down on a lounge that was near; here, almost immediately, though she said she should not, she fell asleep. The elder woman did not sleep, she lay watching the moonlight steal over the girl, then fade away. Later came the pink flush of dawn; it touched the lounge, but Garda slept on; she slept like a little child; her curling hair fell over her shoulders, her cheek was pillowed on her round arm.

"So much truthfulness—such absolute truthfulness!" the elder woman was thinking; "there must be good in it, there *must*."

CHAPTER XX

"It's the most absurd thing—my being caught here in this way," said Lucian Spenser. "But who would ever have imagined that Madam Giron could turn into a tourist! As well imagine Torres a commercial traveller."

"I think he felt rather like one," answered Margaret, smiling; "he seemed to consider it an extraordinary state of affairs to be closing houses and taking journeys at a lawyer's bidding."

It was the 19th day of December. The thermometer outside stood at sixty-eight Fahrenheit. In the drawing-room of East Angels were Mrs. Carew, Margaret, Garda, Lucian Spenser, and Dr. Kirby. Lucian and his wife had left Gracias within a week after that sail through silver fog which had tempted Garda. Their departure had been sudden, it was due to a telegraphic despatch which had come to Rosalie from her uncle in New York; he was seriously ill, and wished to see her. This was the uncle under whose roof she had spent her childhood and youth. She had not been especially attached to him, she had never supposed that he was attached to her. But all who bore the Bogardus name (save perhaps Rosalie herself) reserved to themselves the inalienable right of being as disagreeable to each other personally, year in, year out, as they chose to be, while remaining, nevertheless, as a family, indissolubly united; that is to say, that though as Cornelia and John, Dick and Alida, they might detest each other, and show not the slightest scruples about evincing that feeling, designated by their mutually shared surname their ranks closed up at once, like a line of battle under attack, presenting to the world an unbroken front. Dying, old John Bogardus had wished to see Rosalie—Rosalie, his brother Dick's child, who had made that imprudent marriage; he felt it to be his duty to advise her about certain investments. In answer to his despatch, Lucian had taken his wife north.

When they reached New York, Rosalie found her uncle better; the physicians gave no hope of recovery, but they said that he might linger in this way for two months or more. In this state of affairs Lucian suggested to his wife that he should leave her there, and take a flying trip to New Orleans; he had always wished to make that journey in the winter, and this seemed as good an occasion as any, since, naturally, "Uncle Giovanni" could have no very burning desire to see him, Lucian, day after day. Rosalie, anxious always to put herself in accord with her husband's ideas, gave her consent; the separation, even for a few weeks, would be hard for her, but that she would bear to give Lucian entertainment.

He left her, therefore, a little before the middle of December. And if he arrived at Gracias-á-Dios instead of at New Orleans, this was because he was taking in Gracias on the way; was it not as easy to come first to Florida, and then cross the southern country westward to the beautiful city on the Louisiana shore, as to follow the long course of the Mississippi down? If it was not as easy, in any case he preferred it, and the course Lucian Spenser preferred he generally followed.

It was fortunate, therefore, that he preferred nothing very evil. In the present instance his preference held intentions quite without that element; he should spend four or five days in Gracias; he should collect various small possessions, which, owing to his hasty departure, he had left scattered about there, at East Angels, at Madam Giron's, at the rectory; he should finish two or three sketches in which he felt an interest; and he should say good-by in a more leisurely way to his relatives, the Moores, as well as to the other people there whom he liked so well, for he had the feeling that a long time might elapse before he should see the little coast hamlet again. He had hoped to stay with Madam Giron, as before. But when he arrived at her door, late in the afternoon of the 19th, he found it barred and that lady absent: evidently his letter had not reached her.

Madam Giron had seemed to him like one of those barges which lie moored far up some quiet bay, with their masts removed and a permanent plank walk made from the deck to the shore. The idea that this stationary craft could have gone to sea, that this sweet-tempered lady, with her beautiful eyes, redundant figure, many children, and complete non-admiration for energy, could have started suddenly on her travels, had never once occurred to him.

Until five days before, it had never occurred to Madam Giron herself.

At that date she had received a letter from Cuba telling her that a share in some property was awaiting her there; a long-contested lawsuit having at length been decided in favor of her mother's family. Madam Giron consulted her friends: was it an occasion when duty demanded that she should make the great effort of going in person to Cuba for the sake of "these dear angels," her children (the lawyer having written that her presence would be necessary), or was it not? Gracias discussed this point. It *was* an effort for a lady to make; a lady was not in the habit of leaving the cherished seclusion of her own circle, to rush about the world at a lawyer's request, exposing herself in public conveyances to association with all sorts of people; some of her friends, notably the Señor Ruiz and her own nephew, Adolfo Torres, were decidedly of the opinion that she should not go.

"It's so characteristic—their discussing it as they are doing," Winthrop remarked to his aunt—"discussing whether or not to take a short journey in order to secure an inheritance."

"It's a very small inheritance, isn't it!" asked Aunt Katrina, languidly.

"About fifteen hundred dollars, I believe. But you must remember that without it those children, probably, will have nothing but that mortgaged land."

"I don't think the people here know or care whether they've got money or not," said Aunt Katrina, in a disgusted tone.

"No, they don't. Probably that is one of the reasons why I like them so well."

"Yet *you* have a clear idea of the value of property, Evert."

"I should think I had! I've worked for it—my idea."

"Tell me one thing," pursued Aunt Katrina, whose mind was now on her nephew's affairs. "When you went north last month, wasn't it on account of something connected with that cousin of yours, or rather of your father's, David Winthrop?"

"Well, David has great capacity: he is really wonderful," answered Winthrop, coming out of his reverie to smile at the remembrance of the ineffectual man. "In spite of the new partnership, he *had* managed to tangle up everything almost worse than before."

"Yet people call you hard!" commented Aunt Katrina, plaintively.

"I am hard, I spend half my time trying not to be," responded her nephew, in what she called one of his puzzling tones. Aunt Katrina sometimes found Evert very puzzling.

Madam Giron had finally decided to follow the advice of Dr. Kirby, which was, and had been unwaveringly from the beginning, to go. For she could not but be aware that the Doctor had a very extensive acquaintance with life, that he was more truly a man of the world than any one they had in Gracias; she mentioned this during a confidential interview she had with his mother. The Doctor, of course, was not surprised by her statement; he could not help knowing that he was.

Madam Giron, therefore, had left her children with Madam Ruiz, closed her house, and started, accompanied by the disapproving Torres, three days before Lucian's arrival at her locked door.

The wagon which had brought him was well on its way back towards Gracias; he had walked up the long, winding path which led to the house, leaving his luggage piled at the distant gate. He turned and stood a moment on the piazza, meditating upon what he should do. Then he left the piazza and went towards the branch, where was the cabin of old Cajo, Madam Giron's factotum. Cajo's wife, Juana, was cook at the "big house," and the two old servants were delighted to extend the hospitality which their mistress, they knew, would have immediately ordered had she been at home. In half an hour, therefore, the guest was seated at the "big house" table, before an impromptu but excellent meal, his old room was ready for him up-stairs, and there were even lights in the drawing-room, which, however, he extinguished as he passed by on his way to the hall door. He locked this door behind him, and put the key in his pocket; the two servants were not to wait for him, they were to go back to their cabin as soon as their work was done, taking with them the key of another entrance.

Lucian was going to East Angels. He went through the fields, still lighted by the after-glow, then passed into the dimness of the wood; reaching East Angels' border, he crossed the Levels, and approached the house through the orange walk. As he had written only to Madam Giron, and the letter had followed her to Cuba, no one knew that he was coming. He entered the drawing-room. And there was a cry of surprise.

The evening that followed was enlivened by animated conversation, Dr. Kirby thought it almost a brilliant occasion. The brilliancy without doubt had been excited by Lucian's unexpected arrival, and he had brought his own gay spirits with him; still, they had all contributed something, the Doctor felt; his own sentences, for instance, had displayed not a small degree of "perspicuity." The Doctor had his own descriptive terms, he had no idea that they had grown old-fashioned. Garda's remarks he designated as "sprightly," Margaret's way of talking he characterized as "most engaging;" the Doctor still praised a young man for possessing "sensibility;" he could even restore the lost distinction to that fallen-from-grace word "genteel." When, after one of his visits at East Angels, he said to his little mother—he described everything to her, partly because he liked to describe, but principally because he was a devoted son, and did all he could to entertain her—"The conversation, ma, during the evening was easy, animated, and genteel," it must have been a coarse-grained person indeed who could not appreciate the delicate aroma of that last word as used by him.

On the present occasion the conversation had been even more than this; and when at last it was brought to a close, and the Doctor, having indulged in a general mental review of it (especially his own share), which made him, as glory is apt to do, extraordinarily thirsty, was compounding a glass of orangeade to drink before going to bed, he could not resist remarking to Winthrop, as the latter passed through the empty room on his way to the balcony for a final cigarette, "Quite a brilliant little occasion, wasn't it?"

"Thanks to you," Winthrop answered.

"Softly, softly," said the Doctor, much pleased, but still considerate. "I am old, and can no longer be a leader. But that young Spenser, now—"

"Yes, that young Spenser now—thanks to him too," said Winthrop, disappearing.

The Doctor could not but think that his host was sometimes a little dry.

The next day Lucian finished one of his sketches, went up to Gracias to pay some visits, and returned at sunset; he again spent the evening at East Angels. He announced, when he came in, that he had decided to remain a week longer in his solitary quarters; after that he should spend a day with the Moores, and then start westward towards New Orleans.

"Eight days more," said Garda, counting.

"Yes. See how agreeable you will have to be! Everything fascinating you know, I beg you to say, so that my last hours may be made harrowingly delightful; for it's very uncertain whether I ever see Gracias again."

"I don't care about 'evers,'" said Garda; "'evers' are always far off. What I care about is to get every instant of those eight days." She left her chair and went across to Winthrop. "Are you going to be nice?" she asked, in a coaxing tone. "*Do* be nice; arrange so that we can go somewhere every day." She spoke so that he alone could hear her.

"Do you call that being nice? I thought you did not like to go out."

"When there's nobody but ourselves I don't; that is, not often, for it's always the same people, the same thing. But when there's somebody else, somebody I *really* want to talk to, that's different; there are a great many more chances to talk and say what you like when everybody is walking about in the woods or on beaches, than you ever get in a parlor, you know."

Winthrop had never lost his enjoyment of Garda's frankness. He did not admire Lucian Spenser, but he did admire the girl's coming to ask him to secure for her as many opportunities as possible for being with that fascinating guest.

"All very well for the present," he answered. "But we cannot forever keep you supplied with a new Punch and Judy."

"What's Punch and Judy?"

He altered his sentence. "With new Lucian Spensers."

"Let me have the old one, then, as long as I can," responded Garda.

They made two or three excursions from East Angels. And she probably had the "chances" which she had so appreciatively outlined. Nevertheless, early in the afternoon of the fourth day, Lucian came over to say good-by to them, he had made up his mind to start westward sooner than he had at first intended; he should not go again to Gracias, he had been up that morning to take leave of the Moores; he should drive from Madam Giron's directly across to the river. There was a moon, he should probably start about nine that night.

"On Christmas-eve?" said Betty, in astonishment. "And be travelling on Christmas-day? Why, Mr. Spenser, that seems to *me* downright heathenish."

Lucian did not contradict Betty's view of the case; and he gave no reason for his sudden departure. There was no change in him in any way, no appearance of determination or obstinacy; yet they could not make him alter his decision, though they all tried, Betty with remonstrance, Dr. Kirby with general Christmas hospitality, Winthrop and Mrs. Harold with courtesy. Garda did not say much.

Dr. Kirby was again at East Angels, Mrs. Rutherford having sent for him on account of a peculiar sensation she felt in a spot "about as large as a dime" under her collar-bone. She had improved since his arrival—she always improved after the Doctor's arrivals; but it had been arranged that he should spend his Christmas there, his mother coming down the next morning to join the party.

Lucian remained an hour; then he bade them all good-by, left his farewells for Mrs. Rutherford, and departed; he had still his packing to do, he said. It was not yet four o'clock; it seemed as if he had reserved for that process a good deal of time.

Garda had received the tidings of his going with dilated eyes. But the startled expression soon left her, she laughed and talked, and, under the laughter, her mood was a contented one; Margaret, watching her, perceived beyond a doubt that the contentment was real. After Lucian had gone, the little party in the drawing-room broke up, and Margaret went to give Lucian's good-by to Aunt Katrina. Aunt Katrina was only "so-so," she was inclined to find fault with her niece for not having brought Lucian in person to take leave of her instead of his message; she was lying on a lounge, and there was an impression of white lace and wood-violets. No, she did not care for any reading that afternoon; Dr. Kirby was coming to play backgammon with her. Betty now entered, and Margaret went to her own room. Presently Garda, who had heard her step, called; Margaret opened the door of communication between their two chambers and looked in. The girl was swinging in her hammock.

"Going out?" she said, as she saw Margaret's garden-hat.

"Yes."

"To the garden?"

"Farther; out on the barren."

"I know where,—to take the medicine to that sick child. Why don't you send somebody?"

"I like to go."

"No, you don't," said Garda, laughing. "You're as good as gold, Margaret, but you don't really like to go, you don't really like the negroes, personally, one bit. You would do anything in the world for them, give them all your money and all your time, teach school for them, make clothes for them, and I don't know what all; but you would never understand them though you should live among them all the rest of your life, and never see a white face again. Now *I* wouldn't take one grain of the trouble for them that you would, because I don't think it's in the least necessary. But, personally, I *like* them, I like to have them about, talk to them and hear them talk; I am really attached to all the old servants about here. And I venture to say, too, that they would all prefer me forever, though I didn't lift a finger for them, prefer me to you, no matter what sacrifices you might make to help them, because they would see and feel that *I* really liked them, whereas *you* didn't. But I really think you like to be busy just for the sake of it; when there's nothing else you can do, you go tramping all over the country until I should think your feet would spread out like a duck's. I should like to know when you have given yourself an hour or two of absolute rest—such as I am taking now?"

"I can't sleep in the daytime," was Margaret's answer to this general southern remonstrance; "and a duck's feet are very useful to the duck."

"Oh, of course I know your feet are lovely. But I shouldn't think they could stay so, long."

"There seems to be no end at least to *your* powers of 'staying so,' especially when you get into a hammock," remarked Margaret. But she spoke with a smile on her lips, she was well satisfied to see the girl swinging there contentedly, her eyes already misty with sleep.

"Good-by," she said, closing the door. Then she put on her hat and gloves, and started on her mission. The sick child, for whom Dr. Kirby had prepared the medicine, lived in a cabin two miles and a half from East Angels, on the barren. In addition to the taste for unnecessary philanthropy which Garda had attributed to her, as well as that for unnecessary exercise, Margaret appeared to have a taste for solitude: she generally took her long walks alone. That is, she took them whenever she had the opportunity. This was not so often as it might have been, because of Aunt Katrina's little wishes, which had a habit of ramifying through all the hours of the day. It was not that Aunt Katrina expected you to occupy yourself in her behalf the whole afternoon, she would have exclaimed at the idea that she made such exactions as that; she only wished you to do some one little thing for her at two; and then something else "a little before three;" and then again possibly she might "feel like" this or that later, say, "any time" (liberally) "between half-past four and five." In this way she was sure that you had almost the whole time to yourself.

In addition Margaret was house-keeper, and with the heterogeneous assemblage of servants at East Angels, the position required an almost hourly exercise of diplomacy. Celestine, so excellent in her own sphere, could not be relied upon in this, because, pressed by her desire to "educate the black man," she was constantly introducing primers "in words of one syllable" into the sweeping, dusting, and bed-making; she had even been known to suspend one open on the crane in the kitchen fireplace for the benefit of Aunt Dinah-Jim during the process (for which she was celebrated) of roasting wild-turkey. But "the black man," including Aunt Dinah, would have been much more impressed by primers in words of six.

For the rest of this afternoon, however, Margaret was free; she had several hours of daylight still before her. She walked on across the barren, and had gone about half the distance, when she was overtaken by Joe, the elder brother, the sixth elder brother, of the little Jewlyann for whom the medicine was intended. Joe, a black lad in a military cap, and a pair of his father's trousers which were so well strapped up over his shoulders by fragmentary braces that they covered his breast and back, and served as jacket as well, took the vial from the lady who was so kind to them; and then Margaret, promising to pay her visit another day, turned back. As she approached East Angels again, she made a long detour, and entered on the southern side at the edge of the Levels. Here, pausing, she looked at her watch; it was not yet half-past five, she turned and entered the south-eastern woods, which came up at this point to the East Angels border. Once within the shaded aisles, she walked on, following no path, but wandering at random. Any one seeing her then would have said that the expression of her face was singularly altered; instead of the composure that usually held sway there, it was the expression of a person much agitated mentally, and agitated by unhappiness. She walked on with irregular steps, her hands interlocked and hanging before her, palms downward, her eyes on the ground. After some time she paused, and seemed to make an effort to press back her troubles, not only a mental effort, but a physical one, after the manner of people whose sensibilities are keen; she placed her hands over her forehead and eyes, and held them there with a firm pressure for several minutes; then she let them drop, and looked about her.

She had wandered far, she was near the eastern boundary of the wood; Madam Giron's house was in sight—only a field lay between. She was sufficiently acquainted with the forest to know that one of the paths must be near; three paths crossed it, leading from East Angels to the Giron plantation and beyond, this should be the most easterly of the three; she turned to look for it.

It was not distant, and before long she came upon it. But at the moment she did so she caught a glimpse of Evert Winthrop's figure; he was on the other side of the path, at some distance from her; in the wood, but nearer its edge than she was. Seated on a camp-stool, he was apparently using the last of the daylight to finish a sketch. For he had taken to sketching during his long stay at East Angels, producing pictures which were rather geometrical, it is true; but he maintained that there was a great deal of geometry in all landscape.

Margaret had now entered the path, and was walking towards home.

It happened that Winthrop at this moment looked up; but he did not do so until her course had carried her so far past him that it was not necessary for her to give sign of having seen him. He was too far off to speak; there was, in fact, a wide space between them, though they could see each other perfectly. But though, by the breadth of a second, he had failed to look up in time to bow to her, he was in time to see that she had observed him—her eyes were in the very act of turning away. In that same instant, too, Margaret perceived that he saw she had observed him.

She passed on; a minute later a sharp bend in the path took her figure out of his sight. He looked after her for a moment, as though hesitating whether he would not follow her. Then he seemed to give up the idea; he returned to his sketch.

Margaret, meanwhile, walking rapidly along the path on the other side of the bend, came upon some one—Garda.

"Garda! you here?" she said, stopping abruptly.

"I might rather say *you* here," answered Garda. "I thought you were out on the barren." She spoke in her usual tone.

"I didn't go far on the barren," Margaret answered; "I met one of the boys and gave him the vial, then I came round this way for a walk. But it's late now, we must both go home."

Garda gave a long sigh, which, however, ended in a smile. "Oh *dear*! it's too bad I've met you at this moment of all others, for of course now I shall have to tell you, and you'll be sure to be vexed. I'm not going home, I'm going over to Madam Giron's to see Lucian."

Margaret looked at her, her eyes for one brief instant showed uncertainty. But the uncertainty was immediately replaced by a decision: no, it was, it must be, that this girl did not in the least realize what she was doing. "It is foolish to go, Garda," she said at last, putting some ridicule into her tone; "Lucian has said good-by to you, he doesn't want to see you again."

Garda did not assert the contrary. And she remained perfectly unmoved by the ridicule. "But *I* want to see him," she explained.

"We can send for him, then—though he will laugh at you; there is plenty of time to send."

"No," replied Garda. "For I want to see him by myself, and that I couldn't do at the house; there'd be sure to be somebody about; you yourself wouldn't be very far off, I reckon. No, I've thought it all over, and I would rather see him at Madam Giron's."

"Absurd! You cannot have anything of the least importance to say to him," said Margaret, still temporizing. She took the girl's hand and drew it through her arm.

"Oh, the important thing, of course, is to *see* him," answered Garda.

Winthrop was so far from the path that the low sound of their voices, speaking their usual tones, could not reach him. But the bend was near; let Garda once pass it, and he would see her plainly; he would not only see her pass through the wood, but, from where he sat, he commanded the field which she would have to cross to reach Madam Giron's. All this pictured itself quickly in Margaret's mind, she tightened her hold on the girl's hand, and the ridicule left her voice. "Don't go, Garda," she said, beseechingly.

"I must; it's my last chance."

"I shouldn't care much for a last chance which I had had to arrange entirely myself."

"Well, that is the difference between us—*I* should," Garda answered.

"I shall have to speak more plainly, then, and tell you that you must not go. It would be thought extremely wrong."

"Who would think so?"

"Everybody."

"You know you mean Evert," said Garda, amused.

"I mean everybody. But if it should be Evert too!"

"I shouldn't care."

"If he were somewhere about here now, and should see you, shouldn't you care for that?" asked Margaret, a change of expression, in spite of her effort to prevent it, passing over her face.

But Garda did not see the change; her eyes had happened to fall upon a loosened end of her sash, she drew her hand away in order to retie the ribbons in a new knot, while she answered: "Do you mean see me going into Madam Giron's? No, provided he didn't follow me. I give you my word, Margaret, that I should really like to have Evert see me, I believe I'd go half a mile out of my way on purpose; he is so exasperatingly sure of—"

"Of what?"

"Of everything," answered Garda, making a grimace; "but especially of me." Having now adjusted the knot to her satisfaction, she raised her eyes again. "But *you* are the one that cares," she said, looking at her friend. "I can't tell you how sorry I am that you have met me here," she went on, in a tone of regret. "But how was I to imagine that you would change your mind, and come way round through this wood? It's too late now." And she walked on towards the bend.

Margaret stood still for a moment. Then she hurried after her. "Garda," she said, "I beg you not to go; I beg you here on my knees, if that will move you. Your mother left you to me, I stand in her place; think what she would have wished. Oh, my dear child, it would be very wrong to go, listen to me and believe me."

Garda, struck by her agitation, had stopped; with a sort of soft outcry she had prevented her from kneeling. "Margaret! *you* kneel to *me*?—you dear, good, beautiful Margaret! You care so much about it, then?—so *very* much?"

"More than anything in the world," Margaret answered, in a voice unlike her own.

With one of her sudden impulses, Garda exclaimed, "Then I won't go! But somebody must tell Lucian," she added.

"Do you mean that he expects you?"

"Not at the house. When he came over to say good-by, of course I made up my mind at once that I should see him again in some way before he started; so when you had gone out on the barren (as I supposed), I wrote a note and sent Pablo over with it."

"Oh, Garda! trust a servant—"

"Why, Pablo would let himself be torn to pieces before he would betray a Duero; I verily believe he thinks he's a Duero himself—a Duero a little sunburnt! To show you how much confidence I have in him—in the note I asked Lucian to take this path, and come as far as the pool, where I would meet him at a certain hour. Then, after it was scaled, I remembered that I had not said clearly enough which path I meant (there are three, you know), and so I told Pablo to say to Mr. Spenser that I meant the eastern one. If I hadn't been afraid he would forget some of it, I should have trusted the old man with the whole message, and not taken the trouble to write at all. Well, after the note had gone I went to sleep. And then, when I woke, it came over me suddenly how much nicer it would be to see Lucian in the house instead of in the woods—for one thing, we could have chairs, you know—and so I came over earlier than I had at first intended, in order to get to Madam Giron's before he would be starting for the pool. But you have kept me so long that he must be starting now."

"Let us go home at once," said Margaret.

"No, I can't let him go to the pool, and wait and wait there all for nothing.—Who's that?" she added, in a startled voice.

They both looked westward. In this direction, the direction of East Angels, the path's course was straight for a long distance; the wood had grown dimmer in the slowly fading light, and the figure they now saw at the far end of this vista, coming towards them, was not yet clearly outlined; yet they both recognized it.

"Dr. Kirby!" whispered Garda. "He *knows*—he is coming after *me*. He would never be here at this hour unless it were for that." She seized Margaret's hands. "Oh, what shall I do? It isn't for myself I care, but he mustn't meet Lucian."

"Come into the woods. This way." And Margaret hurried her from the path, in among the trees on the south side of it.

But Garda stopped. "No—that leaves him to meet Lucian. And he *mustn't* meet Lucian. He *mustn't* meet Lucian."

From the point in the forest to which Margaret had brought her, the southern end of Madam Giron's house was in sight. At this instant Lucian himself appeared; he opened the door, walked across the piazza, and stood there looking about him.

The sight of him doubled Garda's terror. "I must go and warn him," she said; "there's time."

"What is it you are so afraid of?" Margaret asked.

"The Doctor will shoot him."

"Nonsense! The Doctor won't do anything of the sort." The idea struck the northern woman as childish.

"That only shows how little you know him," responded Garda, still in a whisper. "He thinks, of course, that Lucian has been to blame."

Her white lips convinced Margaret even against her own beliefs; she knew that the girl had not a grain of the coward in her nature.

"I can't wait." And Garda broke from her friend's hold, and ran towards the path and the bend.

Margaret was almost as quick as she was, she stopped her before the bend was reached. But though she stopped her, she felt that she could not detain her for more than an instant; the girl was past restraint now, her eyes had flashed at Margaret's touch.

"Listen, Garda: go back up the path, and meet Dr. Kirby yourself. Tell him anything you like to keep him away from here, while *I* warn Lucian." The bend was now not more than three yards distant, and, as she spoke, she looked at it, her eyes had a strange expression.

"Will you go to the very house and take him in?" Garda demanded. "Because if you won't do that, I shall go myself."

"Yes, I will take him in."

"And will you stay there?"

"As long as it's necessary."

The implicit confidence which Garda had in her friend's word prevented her from having any misgivings; she turned and ran up the path towards Dr. Kirby, who was still at some distance (for these words and actions of the two women had been breathlessly swift), and who, owing to his near-sightedness, could not yet see her. When she thought he might be able to distinguish her figure she stopped running, and walked forward to meet him with her usual leisurely grace. The running had brought the color to her cheeks, and taken away the unwonted look of fear; all that was left of it was the eager attention with which she listened to what he said.

This was harmless enough. "Ah! you have been out taking the air?" he remarked, pleasantly.

In the mean while Margaret had passed the bend with rapid step, and followed the path down to the wood's border; reaching it, she did not pause, and soon her figure was clearly outlined crossing the open field towards Madam Giron's. She opened the gate in the low hedge, and went up to the door; as it happened, Lucian had gone within for a moment, leaving the door open; now he re-appeared, coming out. But at the same instant Margaret, crossing the piazza, laid her hand on his arm and drew him in. As he came forth in his strong youth and sunny beauty, she had felt herself unexpectedly and singularly seized by Garda's terror; she had never liked him, but now it rose before her, horrible and incredible—the vision of so much splendid physical life being suddenly brought low. She forgot that she had not believed in the reality of this danger, she was possessed by a womanish panic; swayed by it, she quickly drew him within and closed the door. Yet though with a sudden shiver she had done this, in reality her whole soul was at the moment absorbed by another feeling compared with which the dread was as momentary as a ripple passing over a deep lake; it lasted no longer.

She had drawn Lucian within, and she had closed the door. But from where Evert Winthrop sat in the shade, with his eyes fixed upon their two figures, it looked as though Lucian had played the active part in this little scene; as though Lucian had taken her hand and led her within; and had then closed the door behind them.

CHAPTER XXI

Mrs. Rutherford had dismissed Margaret for the remainder of that afternoon, saying that Dr. Kirby was coming to play backgammon with her. Soon after Margaret had started to cross the barren with the vial of medicine for the sick child, the Doctor came. They played a number of games, Mrs. Rutherford liked backgammon; and certainly nothing could be better for a graceful use of beautiful hands. After the board had been put away, "there was conversation," as Betty would have said; Betty herself was present and took part in it. Then the Doctor left the two ladies and went to his own room.

On the way he was stopped by Pablo, who had come up-stairs for the purpose. "Please, sah, ter step down en see Sola; seems like he look mighty kuse."

Osceola had a corner of his own in his master's heart. At the first suggestion that any ill had befallen him, the Doctor seized his hat and hastened out to the stables, followed by the old negro, who did not make quite so much haste. The stout black horse, comfortable and glossy, seemed to be in the possession of his usual health. "There's nothing the matter with him, Pablo," the Doctor said.

"Looks sorter quare ter me," Pablo answered; "'pears dat he doan git nuff exercise. Might ride 'em little ways now, befo' dark; I done put de saddle on on puppus." And Osceola in truth was saddled and bridled.

"I don't want to ride now," said the Doctor.

He had a great regard for Pablo, and humored him as all the former masters and mistresses of Gracias-á-Dios humored the decrepit old family servants who had been left stranded among them behind the great wave of emancipation. Pablo, on his side, had as deep a respect for the Doctor as he could have for any one who was not of the blood of the Dueros.

"Do Sola lots er good ter go," he persisted, bending to alter one of the straps of the saddle; "he *not* well, sho. Might ride 'em long todes Maddum Giron's, cross de Lebbuls en troo de wood by de eastymose nigh-cut."

The Doctor was listening now with attention. Pablo went on working at the strap. "De *eastymose* nigh-cut," he repeated, as if talking to himself.

"Perhaps you are right," said the Doctor, after a moment, his eyes sharply scanning the withered black face which was bending over the strap. "And I suppose if I go at all, I might as well go at once, eh? So as not to have him out in the dew?"

"Yes, sah," answered Pablo. "De soonah de bettah, sah."

"Very well," said the Doctor.

Pablo led out the horse, and the Doctor mounted. "Mebbe, sah, if you's *gwine* as fur as Maddum Giron's, you'd be so good as ter kyar' dish yer note, as I wuz gwine fer ter kyar it myse'f, on'y my rheumatiz is so bad," said the old man. He held up an envelope, which he had carefully wrapped in brown paper, so that it should not become soiled in his pocket.

The Doctor's face showed no expression of any kind; and Pablo's own countenance remained stolidly dull. "I hope you'll skuse me, sah, fer askin'," he said, respectfully; "it's my bad rheumatiz, sah."

"Yes, Pablo, I know; I can as well carry the note as not," said the Doctor, carelessly.

Pablo made a jerk with his head and hand, which was his usual salutation, and the Doctor rode off.

When at a distance from the house, and among the trees where no one could see him, he took out the package and opened it. It contained a sealed envelope with an address; holding it out at a distance from his eyes in order to be able to read it without his glasses, he found that the name was Lucian Spenser; and the handwriting was Garda's. The Doctor sat for a moment staring at it; then he put the note back in his pocket and rode on; even there, where there was no one to see him but the birds, his face betrayed nothing.

He went towards the Levels. Reaching them, he crossed to the point where the south-eastern wood came up to their border, and, dismounting, tied his horse and entered the wood by the easterly path. Passing the pool, which glimmered dimly in the shade, he came to the long straight vista which led to the bend; here, when half-way across, he saw a figure coming towards him, and a moment later he recognized it—Garda.

He doffed his hat with his usual ceremony. "Ah, you have been out taking the air?" he said, pleasantly.

"Yes," replied Garda. "But I'm going back now."

"Did you go far?" He spoke with his customary kindly interest. While speaking he put on his glasses and looked down the path; there was no one in sight.

"No," Garda answered; "only a little way beyond here. I had thought of going over to Madam Giron's to bid a second good-by to Lucian Spenser;

then I changed my mind. I'm going home now without seeing him; that is, I've *started* for home," she added, half smiling, half sighing; "I don't know whether I shall get there!"

"We will go together," said the Doctor, offering her his arm; "I shall give myself the pleasure of accompanying you, if you will permit it, I think I have had walk enough for to-day." He stopped a moment, however, to admire the size of the oaks, he delivered quite an eloquent apostrophe to Nature, as she reveals herself "in bark;" then he turned, and they went back towards East Angels, walking slowly onward, and talking as they went.

That is, the Doctor talked. And his conversation had never been more delightful. He spoke of the society of the city of Charleston in colonial times; he described the little church at Goose Greek, now buried in woods, but still preserving its ancient tombs and hatchments; he enumerated the belles, each a toast far and wide, who had reigned in the manor-houses on the Ashley and Cooper rivers. Coming down to modern times, he even said a few words about Lucian Spenser. "You find him agreeable; yes—yes; he *has* rather an engaging wit of the light modern sort. But it's superficial, it has no solidity; it has, as I may say, no proper *form*. When you have seen more of the world, my child, you will know better how to estimate such qualities at their true worth. But I can well understand that they amuse you for the present—the young man is, in fact, very amusing; in the old days, Garda, your ancestors would have enjoyed having just such a person for their family jester."

Garda looked off through the woods to hide her smile. If the Doctor could have seen that smile, he might not have been so well content with his jester comparison; but he could not see it, and he remained convinced that his idea had been a particularly happy one. "A feather's-weight touch," he said to himself, with almost grateful self-congratulation; "but masterly! I doubt whether even Walpole could have done it better."

As they approached the Levels he made a little turn through the wood in order to look at a tree with a peculiarly curved trunk—another form of Nature as manifested in bark—and this brought Garda out at some distance from Osceola, who was hidden by an intervening thicket. They walked across the Levels, and at length reached the house, the Doctor going in with his ward, accompanying her up-stairs, still talking cheerfully, and leaving her at her door; he then went on with leisurely step to his own room. But this apartment possessed two entrances; coming in at the first, the Doctor, after closing this door behind him, merely crossed his floor and went out through the second, which opened upon a corridor leading to another stairway; in two minutes he was on his way back to the Levels.

Having crossed them again, he found Osceola standing meditatively where he had left him; Osceola was a patient beast. He mounted him, and rode into the wood, following the same path which he had just traversed with Garda; he intended to follow it to the end. On the way he met no one. At the house he found no one. His two long journeys on foot across the Levels had taken time; he was not a rapid walker, he could not be with such neatly finished steps. When, therefore, he drew rein at Madam Giron's, all was closed and dark, there was no one about.

The moon was rising; by its light he made his way back to Cajo's cabin near the branch.

"Cajo?"

Cajo came out. He was astonished to see the Doctor.

"I came over to speak to Mr. Spenser a moment, Cajo. Has he gone, then?"

"Yes, sah; went haffen 'nour ago."

"Ah, earlier than he intended, I conjecture. But I dare say some one else has been over from East Angels this evening?" The Doctor used the word "evening" as "afternoon."

"No, sah; no one." And Cajo spoke the truth; neither he nor Juana had been at the "big house" when Margaret came, and they had not seen her go away. But the Doctor of course was not thinking of Margaret.

"Ah,—very possibly Mr. Spenser strolled over again in our direction, then; I was occupied, and shouldn't have seen him."

"No, sah, he ain't gwine nowhar; he come home befo' fibe, en here he stay twel he start."

"It's of no consequence, though I thought I should have been in time. I hope you have persevered, Cajo, in the use of that liniment I sent you for your lame arm?"

And after a few more words with the old couple, who stood bowing and courtesying at their low door, the Doctor rode Osceola on a walk down the winding path which led from Madam Giron's to the water road. This water road ran southward from East Angels, following the edge of the lagoon; it was comparatively broad and open, and, though longer, the Doctor now preferred it to that dark track through the wood, since it had become evident that there was no one in the wood at present with whom it was necessary that he should hold some slight conversation.

Reaching East Angels in safety, he entered the drawing-room half an hour later, very tired, but freshly dressed, and repressing admirably all signs of his fatigue. He found Mrs. Carew engaged in telling Garda's fortune in solemn state with four packs of cards, as an appropriate rite for Christmas-eve; the cards were spread upon a large table before her, and Garda and

Winthrop were looking on. Upon inquiring for Margaret (the Doctor always inquired for the absent), he was told that she was suffering from headache, and would not be able to join them.

Garda was merry; she was merry over the fact that a certain cousin of Madam Ruiz, whom they had never any of them seen, kept turning up (the card that represented him) through deal after deal as her close companion in the "fortune," while the three other named cards—Winthrop, Manuel, and Torres—remained as determinedly remote from her as the table would allow.

"I don't see what ever induced me to put him in at all," said Betty, in great vexation, rubbing her chin spitefully with the card she was holding in her hand. "I suppose it's because Madam Ruiz has kept talking about him—Julio de Sandoval, Julio de Sandoval—and something in his name always reminded me of sandal-wood, you know, which is so nice, though some people *do* faint away if you have fans made of it, which is dreadful at concerts, of course, because then they have to be carried out, and that naturally makes everybody think, of course, that the house is on fire. Well, the *real* trouble was, Garda, that I had to have four knights for you, of coarse, because that's the rule, and there are only *three* unmarried men in Gracias—Mr. Winthrop, Manuel (*he's* away), and Adolfo (*he's* away too)—which I must say is a *very* poor assortment for anybody to choose from!"

This entirely unintended disparagement made Winthrop smile. In spite of his smile, however, the Doctor thought he looked preoccupied. The Doctor had put on his glasses to inspect Betty's spread-out cards, and, having them on, he took the opportunity to glance across, two or three times, at their host, who had now left the table, and was seated with a newspaper near a lamp on the opposite side of the room. Their host, for such in fact he was, though everything at East Angels went on in Mrs. Rutherford's name, seemed to the furtively watching Kirby to be at present something more than preoccupied; his face behind the paper (he probably thought he was not observed) had taken on a very stern expression. Having established this point beyond a doubt, the Doctor felt his cares growing heavier; he crossed the room to a distant window, and stood there looking out by himself for some time.

It troubled him to see Winthrop with that expression, and the reason it troubled him was because he could not tell what sternness with him might mean. It might mean—and then again it might not mean—he confessed to himself that he had not the least idea what interpretation to give it, he had never really understood this northerner at all. Garda was engaged to him, of course, there was no doubt of that; he wished with all his heart that the engagement had never been formed. But he recognized that wishes were useless, the thing was done; to the Doctor, an engagement was almost as binding as a marriage. He stared out into the darkness in a depressed sort of way, and his back, which was all of him that could be seen by the others, had a mournful look; the Doctor's back was always expressive, but generally it expressed a gallant cheerfulness that met the world bravely. Winthrop's purchase, at a high price, not only of East Angels with its empty old fields, but also of all the outlying tracts of swamp and forest land owned by the Dueros, to the very last acre, had made Garda's position independent as regarded money; but in his present mood the Doctor cursed the independence as well as the wealth that had produced it. Independence? what does a young girl want with independence? Garda had needed nothing; they were able to take care of her themselves, and they wanted no such gross modern fortunes invading and deteriorating Gracias-á-Dios! But it was too late now; their little girl was not their own any more, she was engaged.

As to her imprudence of to-day—that was owing to her taste for amusement, or rather for being amused; they had not, perhaps, paid sufficient attention to this trait of hers. But, in any case, it was, on her side, nothing but thoughtlessness. The person who had been to blame was Lucian Spenser! He (the Doctor) had been too late in his pursuit of Lucian. But perhaps Winthrop would not be too late. For of course Winthrop would wish— But there, again—would he wish?—the Doctor felt, with bewildered discomfiture, that he had not sufficient knowledge of this man's opinions to enable him to form any definite conclusions on this subject, plain and simple as the matter appeared to his own view.

And then, in order to wish anything, Winthrop must first know; and who was to tell him? And when he had been told, would he take their view, his (the Doctor's) view—the only true one—of Garda's taste for being amused? The Doctor felt that he should like to see him take any other! Still, he did not own Evert Winthrop, and he could not help asking himself whether any of that sternness now visible on the face behind the newspaper would be apt to fall upon Garda, in case the possessor of the face should have a different opinion from theirs as to her little fancies. He clinched his fist at the mere thought.

Garda's voice broke in upon his reverie, she summoned him to the table to see the conclusion of her "fortune." And as he obeyed her summons, his cares suddenly grew lighter: a girl with such a frank voice as that could not possibly have a secret to guard. In the midst of this reasoning, the Doctor would have knocked down anybody (beginning with himself) who had dared to suggest that she had.

That night, before going to bed, the Doctor burned upon the hearth of his own room Garda's sealed note just as it was; and he took the precaution, furthermore, to wrap it in an old newspaper, in order that he should not by chance see any of its written words in the momentary magnifying power of the flames. A limp flannel dressing-gown of orange hue, and an orange silk handkerchief in the shape of a tight turban, formed his costume during this rite. But no knight of old (poet's delineation) was ever influenced by a more delicate sense of honor than was this flannel-draped little cavalier of Gracias, as he walked up and down his room, keeping his eyes turned away from the hearth until the dying light told him that nothing was left but ashes.

Then he sat down and meditated. If he should make up his mind to speak to Winthrop, there must be of course some mention of Garda, even if but a word. To the Doctor's sense it was supremely better that there should be no mention. There was no reason for mentioning her on her own account—not the slightest; it was on account of Lucian. Yes, Lucian! If he had met that young man in the woods, or if he had found him at Madam Giron's, he could not tell; he might—he *might*— And now, in case he did not speak to Winthrop, Lucian would escape, he would escape all reckoning for his misdeeds, a thing which seemed to the Doctor insupportable! Still, he was gone, his place among them was safely empty at last; and here the thinker could not but realize that it was better for everybody that the place should be empty from a voluntary departure than from one which might have resounded through the State, and been termed perhaps—involuntary! And with a flush of conscious color over his own past heat, the fiery little gentleman sought his bed.

The next morning it was discovered that Mrs. Harold's headache had meant an attack of fever. The fever was not severe, but it kept her confined to her bed for eight days; Mrs. Carew took her place at the head of the household, and Mrs. Carew's dear Katrina had a course of severer mental discipline than she had been afflicted with for many months, finding herself desperately uncomfortable every hour without Margaret and Margaret's supervision of affairs.

Garda did all she could for Margaret. But there was something in illness that was extremely strange to her; she had never been ill for a moment in all her recollection; and her delicate little mother had held illness at bay for herself by sheer force of determination all her life, until the very last. Though Garda, therefore, could not be called a good nurse, she was at least an affectionate one; she came in often, though she did not stay long, and she was so radiant with life and health when she did come that it seemed as if the weary woman who looked at her from the pillow must imbibe some vigor from the mere sight of her.

The fever was soon subdued by Dr. Kirby's prompt remedies. But Margaret's strength came back but slowly, so slowly that Mrs. Rutherford "could not understand it;" Aunt Katrina never "understood" anything that interfered with her comfort. However, on the eleventh day her niece came in to see her for a few moments, looking white and shadowy, it is true, but quite herself in every other way; on the fourteenth day she took her place again at the head of the house, and Betty, with her endless kind-heartedness and her disreputable old carpet-bag, with a lion pictured on its sides, no lock, and its handles tied together with a piece of string, returned to her home.

That night—it was the 7th of January—there was a great storm; a high wind from the north, with torrents of rain. Mrs. Rutherford, having, as she complained, "nothing to amuse her," had fallen asleep just before it began, and, strange to say, slept through it all. When she said she had "nothing," she meant "nobody," and her "nobody" was Dr. Reginald. For the Doctor was not at East Angels that night; he had remained there constantly through the first five days of Margaret's illness, and he now felt that he must give some time to his patients in Gracias. Winthrop also was absent.

For to the astonishment and indignation of Betty, Winthrop had started early on Christmas morning on a journey up the St. John's River; when she and Garda had come in to breakfast he was not there, and Dr. Kirby, entering later, had informed them that Telano had given him a note which said that he (Winthrop) had suddenly decided to take this excursion immediately, instead of waiting until the 1st of February, his original date.

"Suddenly decided—I should think so!" said Betty. "Between bedtime and daylight—that's all. And on Christmas morning too! I never heard of such a thing! Lucian went off on Christmas-eve. All the men have gone mad." But here her attention was turned by the entrance of Celestine with the tidings of Margaret's fever.

Before he had joined the ladies at the breakfast-table that morning, the Doctor, contrary to his usual custom, had been out. He had been greatly startled by Winthrop's note, which Telano had brought to him as soon as he was up; hurrying his dressing, he had hastened forth to make inquiries. The note had stated that its writer was going to the Indian River. But the Doctor did not believe in this story of the Indian River. He learned that Winthrop had started at six o'clock, driving his own horses (he had a pair besides his saddle-horse), and taking his man Tom, who was to bring the horses back. The Doctor began to make estimates: Lucian had got off about eight the evening before, he was therefore ten hours in advance of Winthrop; still, if he had been kept waiting at the river (and the steamers were often hours behind time), Winthrop, with his fast horses, might reach the landing before he (Lucian) had left. In any case Winthrop could follow him by the next boat; the Doctor had visions of his following him all the way to New Orleans!

How it was possible that Winthrop could have known of an intention of Garda's which she had not carried out (for of course it was that intention which had made him follow Lucian), how it was possible that Winthrop could have known of a note which he himself had reduced, unread, to ashes upon his own hearth, the Doctor did not stop to ask; neither did he stop to reflect that if Winthrop had been bent upon following Lucian, it was probable that he would have started at once, instead of waiting uselessly ten hours. He prescribed for Margaret; then he rode hastily over to Madam Giron's to make further inquiries.

The horse and wagon that had taken Lucian across the country had returned, and the negro boy who had acted as driver said that Mr. Spenser had not been delayed at all at the landing; the *Volusia* was lying there when they drove up, and Mr. Spenser had gone on board immediately, and then, five minutes later, the boat had started on her course down the river—that is, northward. But, in spite of this intelligence, the Doctor remained a prey to restlessness; he battled all day with Margaret's fever, almost in a fever himself; he was constantly thinking that he heard the gallop of a messenger's horse coming to summon him somewhere; but nothing came, save, late in the afternoon, Winthrop's own horses, and they went modestly round to the stables without pausing. The Doctor went out to see Tom.

Tom said that his master had been obliged to wait two hours at the landing; he had then taken the slow old *Hernando* when she touched there on her way up the river, going, of course, southward. The Doctor went off to the garden, and walked up and down with a rapid step; he was passing through a revulsion of feeling. He knew those two boats and their routes, he knew that one had as certainly taken Lucian northward as that the other had carried Evert Winthrop in precisely the opposite direction. And this was not a country of railways, neither man could make a rapid detour or retrace his steps by train; there was only the river and the same deliberate boats upon which they were already voyaging—in opposite directions! He was relieved, of course (he kept assuring himself of this), that there was to be no encounter between the two men. But he could not keep back a feeling of anger against himself—hot, contemptuous anger—for ever having supposed for one moment that there could be; could be—with Evert Winthrop for one of the men! Or, for that matter, with Lucian Spenser for the other. The present generation was a very poor affair; he was glad, at least, that nobody could say *he* belonged to it. And then the Doctor, who did not know himself exactly what it was he wanted, kicked a fragment of coquina out of his path so vindictively that it flew half-way across the garden, and, taking out his handkerchief, he rubbed his hot, disappointed face furiously. Since then a letter had come from Winthrop; he was hunting on the Indian River.

When, therefore, the storm broke over East Angels on the evening of the day upon which Margaret had taken again the reins of the household, she and Garda were alone. After her visit to Mrs. Rutherford, whom she had found quietly sleeping, with Celestine keeping watch beside her, Margaret came back to the drawing-room, closing the door behind her. Garda had made a great blaze of light-wood on the hearth, so that the room was aglow with the brilliant flame; she was sitting on the rug looking at it, and she had drawn forward a large, deep arm-chair for Margaret.

"I am pretending it's a winter night at the North," she said, "and that you and I have drawn close to the fire because it's so *cold*. Come and sit down. I wonder if you're really well enough to be up, Margaret?"

"I am perfectly well," Margaret answered, sinking into the chair and looking at the blaze.

The rain dashed against the window-panes, the wind whistled. "Isn't it like the North?" demanded Garda.

Margaret shook her head. "Too many roses." The room was full of roses.

"They might have come from a conservatory," Garda suggested.

"It isn't like it," said Margaret, briefly.

"Margaret, what did you say to Lucian? It's two whole weeks; and this is the very first chance I've had to ask you!"

Margaret's face contracted for an instant, as though from a sudden pain. "Yes, I know," she said; "you have had to wait."

"You don't want to talk about it—is that it?" said Garda, who had noticed this. "Because you think it was so dreadful for me to be going there?"

Margaret did not tell what she thought on this point. "Of course you want to know what I said," she answered. "For one thing, I said nothing whatever about you, I made no allusion to your proposed meeting at the pool, or—"

"That's fortunate, since Lucian knew nothing about it."

"Nothing about it? Didn't you ask him in your note—?"

"He never got the note. I've been thinking about it, and I'm convinced of that. I'll tell you afterwards; please go on now about what you said."

"I said as little as I could, I had no desire for a long conversation. I told Mr. Spenser that it would be well if he could start immediately, as I had reason to fear that Dr. Kirby, who, as he knew, had many old-fashioned ideas, might think it necessary to come over, and take him to task in— in various ways. It would be better, of course, to avoid so absurd a proceeding."

"And then did he go?"

"Yes. He said, 'Anything you think best, Mrs. Harold, of course,' and made his preparations immediately."

"Didn't he ask any questions?"

"No; as I told you, I had no desire to talk, and I presume he saw it. I waited until he was ready, and it was time to call Cajo and order the wagon; then I slipped out through one of the long windows on the east side of the house, as I didn't care to have the servants see me. I went through the grove that skirts the water, and as I came into the main avenue again, just at the gate, the wagon passed me, and he was in it; he did not see me, as I had stepped back among the trees when I heard the sound of wheels. Then I came home."

"Yes—and went to bed and had a fever!"

"It's over now."

"Didn't Lucian think it odd—your coming?" Garda went on.

"Very likely. I don't know what he thought."

"And you don't care, I suppose you mean. Well, Margaret, I know you don't think there was any real danger; but I can assure you that there was. You may call Dr. Kirby absurd. But absurd or not, *I* was horribly frightened when I saw him coming, and you cannot say that I am frightened easily; I don't think there is any doubt as to what he would have done if he had met Lucian!"

"I can't agree with you about that, Garda, though I confess that for a moment, when I first came upon Mr. Spenser at the door, I was as frightened as you were. But it didn't last, there was no ground for it."

Garda shook her head. "You don't understand—"

"Perhaps I don't," answered Margaret, with rather a weary intonation. "If Lucian didn't get your note, where is it?"

"The Doctor got it. That is the way he knew, don't you see? Pablo gave it to him."

"Pablo—the servant who could not betray you?"

"You mean that for sarcasm; but there's no cause," Garda answered. "Poor old Pablo was never more devoted to me, according to his light, than when he went to the Doctor; he knew he could trust the Doctor as he trusted himself. You don't comprehend our old servants, Margaret; you haven't an idea how completely they identify themselves with 'de fambly,' as they call it. Well, Pablo didn't tell the Doctor anything in actual words, and in fact he had nothing to tell except 'the eastern path;' I told him that myself, you remember. I presume he suggested in some roundabout way that the Doctor should take an evening walk through that especial 'nigh-cut.'" And Garda laughed. "And of course he gave him the note—nothing less than that would have brought the Doctor out there at that hour; Pablo probably pretended that he couldn't take the note himself on account of his rheumatism, and asked the Doctor to send somebody else with it; and then the Doctor said he would take it himself. And, through the whole, you may be sure that neither of them made the very least allusion to *me*. The Doctor had the 'eastern path' to guide him, and the certainty that I had written to Lucian—for of course he saw the address; with that he started off."

"You think that he did not open the note?"

"Open it? Nothing could have made him open it."

"But he is your guardian, and as such, under the circumstances—"

"He might be twenty guardians, and under a thousand circumstances, and he would never do it," said Garda, securely. "I presume he burned it just as it was; I have no doubt he did. Margaret, I wonder if you remember how strange and cold you were to me that night when you came home? Of course I knew that the Doctor would go straight back to Madam Giron's as soon as he had seen me safely inside my own door, and I couldn't help being dreadfully anxious. I waited, and waited. And at last you came. But you were so silent! you scarcely spoke to me; you wouldn't tell me anything except that Lucian was safely gone."

"I couldn't; I was ill," Margaret answered. She put her hand over her eyes.

"Yes, I understood; or if I didn't that night, I did the next morning, when the fever appeared. You are a wonderful woman, Margaret," the girl went on. She had clasped her hands round her knees, and was looking at the blaze. "How you did go and do that for me without a moment's hesitation, when you hated to, so! I was going to tell you something more," she went on. "But I don't dare to; I am afraid." And she laughed.

Margaret's hand dropped. "What is it you were going to say?" She sat erect now. Her eyes showed a light which appeared like apprehension.

"I should like you to know it first," said Garda, her gaze still on the hearth. "Evert is coming home to-morrow, and I want to tell you beforehand: I am going to break my engagement. I don't care for him; why, then, should I stay engaged?"

"You mean that you think it's wrong?"

"I mean that I think it's tiresome. I have only let it go on as long as it has to please you; you must know that. I should have told him long ago, only you wouldn't let me—don't you remember? You have made me promise twice not to tell him."

"Because I thought you would come to your senses."

"I have come to them—now! The difficulty with you is, Margaret, that you think it will hurt him. But it won't hurt him at all, he doesn't care about it. He never did really care for me in the least."

"And if you don't care for him, as you say, may I ask how your engagement was formed?"

Garda laughed. "I don't wonder you ask! I'll tell you, I *did* care for him then. For some time before that night on the barren I had been thinking about him more and more, and I ended by thinking of nothing but just that one idea—how queer it would be, and how—how exciting, if I could only make him change a little; make him do as *I* wanted him to do. You know how cool he is, how quiet; I think it was that that tempted me, I wanted to see if I could. And, besides, I *did* care for him then; I liked him ever so much. I can't imagine what has become of the feeling; but it was certainly there at the time. Well, when you're lost on a barren all night, everything's different, you can say what you feel. And that's what I did; or at least I let him see it, I let him see how much I had been thinking about him, how much I liked him. I am afraid I told him in so many words," added the girl, after a moment's pause. "I only say 'afraid' on your account; on my own, I don't see any reason why I shouldn't say it if it was true."

Then, in answer, not to any words from Margaret, but to some slight movement of hers, "You don't believe it," she went on; "you don't believe I cared for him. *He* believed me, at any rate; he couldn't help it! At that moment I cared for him more than I cared for anybody in the world, and he saw that I did; it was easy enough to see. So that was the way of it. We came back engaged. And I *did* like him so much!—isn't it odd? I thought him wonderful. I don't suppose he has changed. But I have. He is probably wonderful still; but I don't care about him any more. And that is what I cannot understand—that he has not seen in all this time how different I am, has not seen how completely the feeling, whatever it was, that I had for him has gone. It seems to me that anybody not blind ought to have seen it long ago, for it didn't last but a very little while. And then, too, not to have seen it since Lucian came back!"

"He wouldn't allow himself to think such things of you."

"Now you are angry with me," said Garda, not turning her head, but putting up one hand caressingly on Margaret's arm. "Why should you be angry? What have I done but change? Can I help changing? *I* don't do it; it does itself; it *happens*. You needn't try to tell me that one love, if a true one, lasts forever, because it's nothing of the kind. Look at second marriages. I really cared for Evert. And now I don't care for him. But I don't see that I am to blame for either the one or the other; people don't care for people because they *try* to, but because it comes in spite of them; and it's the same way when it stops. I acknowledge, Margaret, that *you* are one of the kind to care once and forever. But there are very few women like you, I am sure."

She turned as she said this, in order to look up at her friend; then she sprang from her place on the rug and stood beside her, her attitude was almost a protecting one. "Oh," she said, "how I hate the people who make you so unhappy!"

"No one does that," said Margaret. She rose.

"Are you going?"

"Yes; I am tired."

"I suppose I oughtn't to keep you," said Garda, regretfully, "Well,—it's understood, then, that I tell Evert to-morrow."

Margaret, who was going towards the door, stopped. She waited a moment, then she said—"Even if you break the engagement, Garda, it isn't necessary to say anything about Lucian, is it?—this feeling that you think you have for him; I wish you would promise me not to speak of Lucian at all."

"Think I have!" said Garda. "*Know* is the word. But I'm afraid I can't promise you that, because, don't you see" (here she came to her friend, who was standing with one hand on the door)—"don't you see that I shall *have* to speak of Lucian?—I shall have to say how much I like him. Because, after what I let Evert think that night on the barrens, nothing less will convince *him* that I don't care for *him* any more, that I've got over it. For he believed me then—as well he might! and he has never stopped believing. And he never will stop—he wouldn't know how—until I tell him in so many words that I adore somebody else; perhaps he will stop then; he knew what it was when I adored *him*."

Margaret looked at her without speaking.

"Dear me! Margaret, don't *hate* me," said Garda, abandoning her presentation of the case and clinging in distress to her friend.

"Promise me at least not to tell Evert anything about that last afternoon before Lucian left—your plan for meeting him at the pool, your going on towards the house and coming upon me, our seeing Dr. Kirby, and your fear—in short, all that happened. Promise me faithfully."

"I suppose I can promise that, if you care about it. But you mustn't hate me, Margaret."

"What makes you think I hate you?" asked Margaret, forcing a smile.

"A look 'way back in your eyes," Garda answered, the tears shining in her own.

"Never mind about looks 'way back; take those that are nearer the front," responded Margaret. She drew herself away, opened the door, and went down the hall towards her own room.

Garda followed her. But at her door Margaret stopped; "Good-night," she said.

"Are you going to shut yourself up? Mayn't I go through your room to mine? Mayn't I have the door open between?" said Garda. "I'm so afraid of the storm!" The rain was still beating against the windows, the wind was now a gale. "I shall keep thinking of the sea."

"The sound of the storm is as loud in my room as in yours."

"Well, I won't tease," said Garda; "I see you want to be alone." She kissed her friend, and went mournfully down the hall towards her own door. Then her mood seemed to change, for she called back, "I shall keep my lamp burning all night, then."

This was a small hanging lamp of copper, of which Garda was very fond. It had once been thinly coated over with silver, and it had every appearance of having been made to hang before a shrine; there was a tradition, indeed, that though it had been at East Angels longer than even the Old Madam could remember, it had come originally from that East Mission of Our Lady of the Angels which had given the Duero house its name; the lamp remained, though the little coquina shrine, built for the red-skins, had vanished.

Raquel knew how to make a particular kind of oil, highly perfumed with fragrant gums; she made this, in small quantities at a time, for Garda, who burned it in this lamp in her own room, and greatly enjoyed the aromatic odor it gave out. Margaret had remonstrated with her for the fancy. "I cannot think it is wholesome," she said, "to sleep in such a heavily perfumed atmosphere."

"I sleep a great deal better in it than I ever do in your plain, thin, *whitewashed* sort of air," Garda had responded, laughing.

To-night, after lighting her candle, she lighted this lamp also.

"It's burning!" she said, calling through the closed door between their two rooms with childlike defiance. But she got no answer.

CHAPTER XXII

That same evening Evert Winthrop was watching the storm on the St. John's River. It had begun to darken the north-western sky before sunset; rising higher and higher, at length it had come sweeping down the broad stream. First the broken lurid edge (like little puffs of white smoke) of the blackness that followed behind; and that was the wind. Then the blackness itself, pierced here and there by lightning. Then, last, in perpendicular columns extending from the sky to the smooth water below (water that had been pressed flat by wind that had gone on before), the rain falling straight downward densely and softly; the line across the river made by the advancing drops on one side and the smooth water which they had not yet reached on the other, was as distinct as one made across a piece of velvet when one half of its nap has been turned sharply back, while the other remains undisturbed.

The old white house, once a private residence, where Winthrop was spending the night, was now a reluctant hotel; that is, inmates were received there, and allowed to find their way about, to sit round a brilliant light-wood fire on the broad hearth of the pleasant old parlor on cold evenings, to bask in the sunshine on the piazzas during the day, or wander under the magnificent trees, which, draped in silver moss, formed long avenues on the river-bank north and south. They were also allowed to partake of food in the dining-room, where the mistress of the house, a dignified old lady, poured out her coffee herself at the head of her table, the cups being carried about by half-grown negro boys, whose appearance was not in the least an indication of the quality of the beverage, that quality being excellent. This old house, when it had thus changed itself, rather half-heartedly, into a hotel after the war, had been obliged to put out a dock; a sign it could dispense with; it could dispense with many things; but an inn of any sort it could not be on the St. John's without a dock, since the river was the highway, and its wide shallows near shore made it necessary for the steamers to land their passengers far out in the stream. All these "docks" on the St. John's were in reality long narrow piers, formed by spiles driven into the bed of the stream, over whose tops planks had been nailed down; and if a plank was missing here and there, was it not always easy to jump over.

Near the end of the pier belonging to Winthrop's present abode there was a little building about six feet square. This was the United States post-office; any one who should doubt its official character, had only to look at the legal notices written in ink and tightly tacked up on the outside. Generally these notices had been so blurred by the rain that all the "men" who were required to "know" the various matters written underneath by this proclamation thereof, could have made out a good defence for themselves in case of prosecution for failure to comply, since how could they "know" what they could not decipher? But even if the notices had been printed in fairest type, it is hardly probable that the inhabitants would have "known" them any better; they had always hunted and fished wherever and whenever they pleased; it was not likely that a piece of paper tacked up on a shanty a quarter of a mile out in the St. John's was going to change these rights now. The only proclamation they felt any interest in was that which offered bounties for the scalps of wild-cats, a time-honored and sensible ordinance, by which a little money could always be secured.

Winthrop had come down the river that afternoon; his steamer had left him here, as she did not touch at the Gracias landing, which was farther down-stream on the opposite shore; the next morning a boat would pass which did touch there, he must wait for that. The steamer that brought him had also brought the United States mails from the up-river country; the postmaster, a silent man in a 'coon-skin cap, received the bag with dignity; Winthrop watched the distribution of its contents; one limp yellow-enveloped letter and a coffee-pot. When he came down to the pier's end again at sunset the 'coon-skin-crowned official had gone home; but, in a friendly spirit, he had left the post-office unlocked—there was a chair there which some one might like to borrow. Winthrop borrowed it now—of the United States; he brought it outside and sat there alone, watching the approach of the storm. The beautiful river with its clear brown water lay before him, wide as a lake; on the opposite shore the soft foliage of palmettoes, like great ostrich plumes, rose against the sky. But he was not thinking of the river, he was not even thinking of the black cloud, though his eyes were apparently fixed upon it; he did not stir until the wind was fairly upon him, then he retreated to the post-office, placed his chair inside, and sat there under cover at the open door. For a moment he did think of the storm, for it seemed as if the little house over him would be carried off the pier, and sent floating up the stream like a miniature ark; but after the wind had passed on, his mind returned to the old subject, the subject which had engrossed him ever since he left East Angels fourteen days before.

His brief letters had stated that he was hunting, fishing, and sailing, that he had been through the Dummit orange grove. It was true that he had been engaged in all the ways he described, and it was probable also that his various guides and chance companions had not perceived any lack of interest, or at least of energy, in the northerner who had accompanied them; an active life was necessary to Winthrop, and never more necessary than when he was perplexed or troubled; not once during those two weeks had he sat down to brood, as he was apparently brooding now.

But though he had thus occupied himself from daylight to bedtime, though he had talked and listened to the talk of others, there had been always this under-consciousness, which had not left him. At times the consciousness had taken form, if not in actual words, then at least in thoughts and arguments that followed each other connectedly. Generally, however, it had been but a dull realization, like an ache, vivified at intervals by sudden heats of anger, which, he was sure—though he might be talking on other subjects at the moment—must bring the color to his face. Man-like, he preferred the anger, it was better than the ache; he should have liked to be angry all the time.

The ache and the anger had been caused by what he had with his own eyes beheld, namely, the secret visit of Margaret to Lucian Spenser. For it was secret. Lucian had said good-by to her before them all, it had been left clearly to be supposed that they were not to see each other again; this, then, had been a clandestine meeting. Margaret was no school-girl, she was not ignorant of the rules of the world. And she was not an exception, like Garda Thorne, full of sudden impulses, with an extraordinary openness in following them; he had never thought Margaret impulsive in the least. Yet there she was; she had slipped away without the knowledge of any one, to go over to that solitary house for a farewell interview with its occupant. Of course her being there at that last moment, woman of deliberate intentions as she was, proved that an acquaintance which she had not acknowledged existed between them; for she had never shown any especial interest in Lucian in the presence of others; on the contrary, she had appeared indifferent to him, she had acted a part; they had both acted a part, and they had acted it so well that he (Winthrop) had never once suspected them. A wrath rose within him as he thought of this.

He had always disapproved of Margaret in one way; but at least—so he kept telling himself—at least he had thought her entirely without traits of this kind. He had thought her cold; but he had thought, too, that she had principles, and strong ones. It was probably her principles, more than anything else, that had made her leave Lanse in the beginning; she might even be said to have been something of a martyr to them, because, with her regard for appearances, she would have infinitely preferred, of course, to have remained under the same roof with Lanse, had it been possible, to have avoided the comment which is roused by any long separation between a husband and wife, even though but that comparatively mild degree of it which follows a separation as carefully guarded and as undefined in duration as hers had been. For nothing was ever said about its being a permanent one; people might conclude, and they easily did conclude, that before long they should see Lansing Harold back again, and established somewhere with his wife as docilely as though he had never been away; this had happened in a number of cases when the separation had been even longer. Europe was full of American wives spending winters here and summers there, wives whose husbands had remained at home; it might almost be called an American method for infusing freshness into the matrimonial atmosphere, for of course they would be doubly glad to see each other, all these parted ones, when the travels should at last be over, and the hearth-fire re-established again. In this instance it was the husband who had gone. And in the mean while how well-ordered was the life led by Mrs. Harold! there was not, there never could be, a breath of reproach or comment concerning her.

Thus the world. And the world's opinion had been Winthrop's in so far that he had fully shared its belief in the irreproachableness of Margaret's life as regards what is sometimes defined as "a taste for society," or, arranged in another form, as "a love of gayety," or, with more frankness, "a love of admiration." Of course he had approved of this. But he had not realized how deeply he had approved of it (underneath disapprovals of another sort) until now, when, like a thunder-clap, the revelation had come upon him: he and the world had been mistaken! This Margaret, with her fair calm face, with her studiedly quiet life, had a capacity for the profoundest deceptions; she had deceived them all without the slightest difficulty, she was deceiving them now. The very completeness with which she had disguised her liking for Lucian showed what an actress she must be; if she had allowed her liking to come out in a natural way, if she had even let it be known that she intended to see him again, instead of going through that form of bidding him good-by before them all, it would have had another aspect; the present one, given the manner she had always maintained with him in public, and given the fact that she was the most unimpulsive of women, was ominous. In the moment of discovery it had given him a sick feeling,—he had been so sure of her!

The sick feeling had come back often during the two weeks that followed. Each time he had taken himself sharply to task for caring so much. But it was because he had cared that he had left East Angels.

As he sat there in the wood, staring at Madam Giron's house after she had entered it—as it seemed to him drawn in by Lucian—his first feeling, after the shock of surprise, had been one of indignation, he had started up with the intention of following her. Then he remembered that he had no possible authority over her, even though she was his cousin's wife; if he should go over there and confront her, could she not very well turn and ask him what any of it was to *him*? It would make a scene which could now benefit no one; for it was too late to prevent imprudences on her part; and with Lucian he should prefer to deal alone. Then, in another minute, he felt that he could not in any case endure seeing her openly discomfited; for of course if he and Lucian should exchange words in her presence, no matter how few, it would amount to publicity of a certain sort, publicity which it had not yet attained. At present Lucian had no idea that he, Winthrop, had discovered their meeting; of her own accord Margaret would never tell him, and it would be easier for her through all the future if Lucian should never know; it was this thought that made him go homeward instead of crossing the field to Madam Giron's, it drove him away. It was not until he was safe in his own room that his vision grew clearer, that he remembered that he need not have been so considerate of Margaret's feelings, since (what he had not thought of with any distinctness in the first shock of surprise) had she not deliberately braved him? For she had seen him sitting there when she passed the first time, he had clearly perceived that she had seen him. Yet, knowing that he was there, she had passed him that second time in full view; she had crossed the field knowing that he could see her plainly, had met Lucian on the piazza and entered the house with him, without the least attempt at concealment or disguise. It was true that no one else had seen her. But he had seen her; and she had known it, and had not cared.

This last reflection gave his mood a sharp turn in the other direction; he thought—he thought a thousand things. Chief among them came now the remembrance that he should see her at table, she would be obliged to appear there, she would be obliged to speak to him. But when in answer to Telano's summons he went to the dining-room, hardly knowing how he should bear himself towards her, she was not present; Garda brought word that she was suffering from headache, and could not appear.

That night Winthrop was awake until a late hour, he found himself unable to sleep. He was conscious of the depth of the disturbance that swayed him, but though he did his best to conquer it, he made no progress; dawn found him still under its influence. He decided to go away for a few days; he had been shut up at East Angels too long, the narrow little round of Gracias life was making him narrow as well. The evening before, he had felt a strong wish to see Margaret, to note how she would appear; but now his one desire was to get away without seeing her, if possible. Curiosity—if curiosity it had been—had died down; in its place was something that ached and throbbed, which he did not care to analyze further.

Lucian had really gone—he had ascertained that; East Angels was therefore safe for the present, as far as he was concerned. Winthrop remained very indifferent to Lucian personally, even now; he consigned his good looks to the place where the good looks of a strikingly handsome man are generally consigned by those of his less conspicuously endowed brethren who come in contact with him, and he felt that immense disgust which men of his nature are apt to feel in such cases, with no corresponding realization, perhaps, of the effect which has been observed to be produced sometimes by—item, a pair of long-lashed eyes; item, a pink young cheek; item, a soft dimpled arm—upon even the most inflexible of mankind. No, he did not care about Lucian. He said to himself that if it had not been Lucian, it would have been somebody else; he made himself say that.

Now, as he sat there at the end of the long pier, with the dense rain falling all round him, he went over again in his own mind all these things. Two states of feeling had gradually become more absorbing than the rest; one of these was a deep dumb anger against Margaret for the indifference with which she had treated him, was still treating him. What rank must he hold in her mind, then?—one which could leave her so untroubled as to his opinion of her. What estimation must she have of him that made her willing to brave him in this way? She had not written during his absence, expressing—or disguising—apprehension; making excuses; she had not even written (a woman's usual trick) to say that she knew it was not necessary to write, that she was safe with him, and that she only wrote now to assure him that she felt this. Was he such a nonentity in every way that she could remain unconcerned as to any fear of danger from him? Did she suppose him incapable of action?—too unimportant to reckon with, too unimportant to trouble, even if he should try, the well-arranged surface of her unperturbed life? Very possibly she might not like him, but he was at least a man; it seemed to him that she ought to have some regard for any man's opinion; even some fear of it, in a case of this kind.

Yes, he was very angry. And he knew that he was.

Then, adding itself to this anger, there came always a second, came against his will; this was a burning resentment against her personally, for falling so far below the idea he had had of her. He had thought her narrow, self-righteous,—yes; but he had also thought her life in other respects as pellucid (and cold) as a mountain brook; one of those brooks, if one wanted a comparison, that flow through the high valleys of the Alps, clear, cold, and dreary; he had had time to make comparisons in abundance, if that were any entertainment!

But it was not. And he found it impossible, too, to think of Margaret in any other than this his first way; the second, in spite of what he had with his own eyes beheld, remained unreal, phantasmagoric. This seemed to him folly, and he was now going back to East Angels to break it up; it would break it up to find her defiant. And it would amount to defiance—her looking at him and talking to him without giving any sign, no matter how calmly or even timidly she might do it; in his actual presence perhaps she would be timid. In all cases, in any case, he now wished to see her; the desire to find himself face to face with her had taken possession of him again.

He reached East Angels the next day at two o'clock. Betty Carew was the first to greet him, she had herself arrived from Gracias only an hour before. She was full of the intelligence she brought, and immediately repeated it to the new-comer: Mr. Moore had that morning received a letter, or rather a note of six lines; Rosalie Spenser was dead. Her illness had been brief, and she had not suffered; they thought it was the heart. Fortunately Lucian had been able to get to her; he had found the despatch at New Orleans, and had started immediately; they had had the last three days together, and she was conscious to the end. And then followed the good Betty's regrets, which were sincere; she had always liked Lucian, and, when he married, her affectionate, easily expanding heart had made room for Rosalie as well; "Lucian's wife" would have had to be a very disagreeable person indeed to have made Betty dislike her. For Betty's liking included the relatives of all her friends, simply because they were relatives. The relationship made them a whole, she accepted them in a body as one accepts "the French," "the Portuguese;" they did not present themselves to her as objects for criticism.

Winthrop had lunch alone, the others had had theirs. While he was still at the table, Garda came in. He had already seen her, as well as Betty, and he had been in to say a word of greeting to his aunt; but Margaret he had not yet seen.

"I should like to speak to you," Garda said. "Could you come out after lunch to the orange walk for a few moments?" There was nothing unusual in her tone.

When he entered that leafy aisle, later, she came to meet him.

"I am sorry to have made you take this trouble," she said, "when you are only just back from your journey. But I wanted to tell you at once, it seems unfair to wait; I wonder if you will be surprised? I don't care for you any more; don't you think it would be as well, then, to break our engagement?"

CHAPTER XXIII

Winthrop had literally made no answer to Garda's speech; he only looked at her.

After a moment the girl went on, gently enough: "If I don't care about you, I think I ought to tell you; you will feel more free. Don't you think it is better that I should tell you?"

"Certainly; if it is true."

After her first greeting, Garda had moved away a step or two; she now stood leaning back against the firm little trunk of one of the orange-trees, playing with a small spray of the bright leaves as she talked. At this answer of his, her gentleness turned to exasperation. "If it is true! And why shouldn't it be true?—do you think it impossible for anybody to stop caring for you? *I* have stopped, and very completely. I care no more for you now than I do for that twig." And she tossed it away with a little gesture of disdain.

Winthrop's eyes followed the motion. But he did not speak.

"*Still* don't you believe it?" she asked, in surprise; "you look as though you didn't. I think that rude."

"On the contrary, it seems to me that my being slow to believe it, Garda, is the best honor I can pay you."

"Oh, how could I ever have liked you!—how disagreeable you can be when you try!" Tears shone in her eyes. "Everybody in the world seems to tell lies but me," she went on, hotly. "And everybody else seems to prefer it. You yourself would like it a great deal better, and think it nicer in me, if I should tell lies now, pretend that this was the beginning of a change instead of the end, make it more gradual. Whereas I tell you simply the truth; and then you are angry."

"I am not angry."

"You are ever so much surprised, then, and that's worse. I call it almost insulting for you to be so much surprised by what seems to me perfectly natural. Have you never heard of people's changing? That is what has happened to me—I have changed. And I tell you the truth about it, just as I told you the truth when it was different—when I cared for you. For I did care for you once, ever so much; didn't you believe it? Didn't you *know* that I cared for you that night on the barren?"

A red rose in Winthrop's cheeks. After a moment he answered, humbly enough, "Yes, I thought you did."

"Of course you thought I did. And why? Because I *did*; that night, and for some time afterwards, I adored you, Evert. But I don't see why you should color up about it; wasn't it natural that I should be delighted to be engaged to you when I adored you? and isn't it just as natural that I should wish to break it off when I don't? You can't want me to *pretend* to care for you when it's all over?"

"No, no," said Winthrop, his eyes turning from her.

"I do believe you are embarrassed," said Garda, reverting to her usual good temper again. Then she broke into smiles. "You ought to thank me, for, really, you never cared for me at all." She leaned back against her tree again, and folded her arms. "I dare you to tell me that you ever really cared for me, even when I cared so much for you," she continued, in smiling challenge. "What you would answer if you spoke the truth (as I do), would be—'I did my duty, Garda.' As though I wanted duty! You ought to fall down on your knees in the sand this moment and thank me for releasing you; for you are much too honorable ever to have released yourself, you are the soul of honor. Just supposing we had been married—that we were married now—where should we be? I should have got over caring for you, probably (you see I have got over it without being married), and you never did really care for me at all; I think we've had a lucky escape."

"Perhaps we have," Winthrop answered.

"No 'perhaps,' it's a certainty. And yet," she went on, slowly, looking at him with musing eyes, "it might have had a different termination. For I adored you, and you could perhaps have kept it along if you had tried. But you never did try, the only thing you tried to do was to 'mould' me; you made me read things, or, if you didn't, you wanted to; you have treated me always as if I were a child. You have had an idea of me from the first (I don't know where you got it) that wasn't like me, what I really am, in the very least. And you never found out your mistake because you never took the trouble to study me, myself; you only studied your Idea. Your Idea was lovely, of course," pursued the girl, laughing; "so much the worse for me, I suppose, that I am not like her. Your Idea would have been willing to be moulded; and she would have read everything you suggested; and then in due course of time—*when she should be at least eighteen*"—interpolated the girl, with another burst of laughter, "she would have gratefully thanked you for admitting her to the privileges of being 'grown up.' Why—you didn't even want me to care for you as much as I did, because your Idea wouldn't have cared so much for anybody, of course, 'when she was only sixteen.'"

Winthrop flushed fiercely, as her mocking eyes met his, full of mirth. Then he controlled himself, and stopped where he was; he did not answer her.

"You are the best man in the world," said Garda, coming towards him and abandoning her raillery. "With your views (though I think them all wrong, you know), you could say the most dreadful things to me; yet you won't, because—because I'm a woman. You engaged yourself to me in the first place because you thought I cared for you (I did, then); and now, when I tease you because you have made the mistake of not understanding me—of having, that is, a higher idea of me than I deserve—you don't answer back and tell me that, or anything else that would be true and horrid. That's very good of you. I *wish* I could have gone on caring for you! But I don't, I can't; isn't it a pity?" She spoke with perfect sincerity.

Winthrop burst into a laugh.

"Don't laugh in that way," Garda went on; "I assure you I know perfectly that—that the person I care for now isn't what you are in many ways. But if I do care for him (as I cared for you once—you know what that was) shouldn't I be true to it and say so?"

"The—the person?" said Winthrop, looking at her inquiringly, a new expression coming into his face.

"Yes, Lucian, of course."

"Lucian!"

"Oh, very well, if you take *that* tone! And after I have said, too, that I knew he wasn't as—that he wasn't like you. It seems to me that I have been very honest."

"Very," replied Winthrop. Then his voice changed, it grew at once more serious and more gentle. "I hardly know, Garda, how to take what you say, I don't think you know what you are saying. You stand there and tell me that you care so much for Lucian Spenser—a married man—"

"He isn't married now," said Garda.

Winthrop gave her a look which made her rush towards him. "I didn't mean it—that is, I didn't mean that I was thinking about Rosalie's death; I wasn't thinking about that at all, I have never thought about Rosalie. Very likely I shall not see Lucian for ever and ever so long, and very likely he won't care for me when I do. He has never given the least sign that he cared—don't think that." And, clasping her hands round his wrist, she looked up in his face in earnest appeal. "Nothing has ever been said between us—not one word; it is only how *I* have felt."

"Whom are you defending now?" asked Winthrop, as coldly as a man may when a girl so beautiful is clinging to him pleadingly.

"Lucian," responded Garda, promptly.

The mention of his name seemed to give her thoughts a new direction; disengaging herself, she came round to stand in front of her companion in order to have a good position while she told her story. "Don't you remember that I began caring for Lucian first of all? you must remember that? Then I got over it. Next I cared for you. Then, when he came back, I began to care for him again—you have no idea how delightful he is!" she said, breaking off for a moment, and giving him a frank smile. "Well, I should have told you all about it long ago, only Margaret wouldn't let me; she has made me promise her twice, and faithfully, not to tell you. You see, Margaret thinks you care for me; therefore it would hurt you to know it. I have told her over and over again that you don't care at all, and that I don't care any longer for you. But it doesn't make any difference, she can't understand it; she thinks that if I cared once, it must last still; because that is the kind that Margaret is herself; if *she* cared, it *would* last. So she can't believe that I have really changed, she thinks (isn't it funny?) that I am mistaken about myself, that I don't know my own mind. And then, too, to change from you to Lucian—*that* she could never understand in a thousand years."

Winthrop had had his hands deep in the pockets of his morning-coat during this history. He stood looking steadily down, perhaps to keep her from seeing his expression.

But she divined it. "You needn't have such a stern face, I am sure everybody's very good to *you*. Here I've released you from an engagement you didn't desire, and Margaret, the sweetest woman in the world, cares so much for your feelings—what she supposes them to be—that she has done her best to hold me to you just because she thinks *you* would mind. Of course, too, on my own account a little—because she thinks it would be well for me to marry you, that it would be safe. Well, you know you *are* safe, Evert." And the rippling laugh broke forth again, meeting this time decided anger in Winthrop's gray eyes as he raised them to meet hers.

"There, you needn't crush me," Garda resumed. "And you needn't mind me, either me, or my laughing. For, of course, I know that if I could have cared for you, that is, gone on caring, and if in the end you could have cared for me, it would have been better for me than anything that could possibly happen; you ought not to be angry with a girl who tells you that?" And taking his arm, she looked up in his face very sweetly. "But the trouble was that you didn't care for me, you don't now. Yet you kept to your engagement, you took me and made the best of me; and I think that was very good. Well, it's over now." She had kept his arm, and now she began to stroll down the aisle towards the rose-garden. "There's something else I want to speak to you about, now that we've got through with our own affairs; and that's Margaret. Why have you such a wrong idea of her?—she is so noble as well as so sweet. She promised my mother to be like a sister to me; but, Heaven knows, few real sisters would have been as patient as she has been. I have never seen any one that could approach her. I didn't know a woman could be like that—so unchangeable and true. For we are not true to each other—women, I mean; that is, not when we care for somebody. Then we pretend, we pretend awfully; we tell things, or keep them back, or tell only half, just as we choose; and we always think that we have a perfect right to do it. But Margaret's different, Margaret's *wonderful*. Yet none of you, her nearest relatives, do her the least justice; it is left to *me* to appreciate her. Leaving Mrs. Rutherford out, this is more stupidity than I can account for in *you*."

"Men are all stupid, of course," Winthrop answered.

"What makes all she has done for me the more remarkable," Garda went on, not heeding his tone, "is the fact that she doesn't really like me, she cannot, I am so different. Yet she goes on being good to me just the same."

Winthrop made an impatient movement. "Suppose we don't talk any more about Mrs. Harold," he said.

"I must talk about her, when I love her and trust her more than anything."

"Don't trust her too much."

She drew her arm from his, indignantly. "One night she came way down the live-oak avenue after me, with only slippers on her poor little feet, to keep me from going out in the fog with Lucian—sailing, I mean. What do you think of that?"

"I don't think anything."

"Yes, you do; your face shows that you do."

"My face shows, perhaps, what I think of the extraordinary duplicity of women," said Winthrop.

"Duplicity? Do you call it duplicity for me to be telling you every single thing I think and feel, as I have done to-day?"

"I was speaking of Mrs. Harold."

"Duplicity and Margaret!" exclaimed Garda.

They had reached the end of the orange aisle, and she no longer had his arm. "I can't discuss her with you, Garda," he said. And he went out into the sunshine beyond.

But Garda followed him. She came round, placed her hands on his shoulders, and pushed him with soft violence back into the shade. "Why do you speak so of her? you *shall* tell me. Why shouldn't I trust her? But I do and I will in spite of you!"

"Do you mean to marry that man, Garda?" asked Winthrop, at last, as she stood there holding him, her eyes on his, thinking of her no longer as the young girl of his fancy, but as the woman.

"I don't know," answered Garda, her tone altering; "perhaps he won't care for me."

"But if he should care?"

"Oh!" murmured the girl, the most lovely, rapturous smile lighting up her face.

Winthrop contemplated her for a moment. "Very well, then, I think I ought to tell you: she cares for Lucian herself."

Garda's hands dropped. "It isn't possible that you believe that—that you *have* believed it! Margaret care for Lucian! She doesn't care a straw for him, and since *I* have begun to care for him again, I verily believe that she has detested him; he knows it too. Margaret care for him! What are you thinking of? *I* care, not Margaret; I've done nothing but try to be with him, and meet him, and I've seen him more times than she knows. Why—it gave her that fever just because she had to do something for him; that last afternoon before he went away (I promised her I wouldn't tell you; but I don't care, I shall), I had asked Lucian to meet me at the pool in the south-eastern woods, and then I thought that I should rather see him at the house after all, and so I started a little earlier, and was on my way to Madam Giron's, when I came upon Margaret. I had to tell her, because she wanted me to go home with her and of course I couldn't. And then, suddenly, we saw Dr. Kirby coming, and I knew it must be for me—he had found out in some way my plan—and I knew, too, that it would be dreadful if he should meet Lucian; I was sure he would shoot him! And I was going to run over and warn Lucian—there was just time—when Margaret said she would do it, and that *I* had better go back up the path and stop the Doctor, keep him away from there entirely, if possible, which was, of course, much the best plan. So I did. And she went to Madam Giron's. And I am convinced that it was the cause of her illness—it was so disagreeable to her to be mixed up in *anything* connected with Lucian."

Garda had poured out this narrative with all the eloquence of the warm affection she had for her friend. Now she stopped. "She doesn't like Lucian because she doesn't understand him," she said. Then she repented. "No, it isn't that, he isn't the person for *her*. Lucian will do for me; but not for Margaret." And she looked at Winthrop with one of her sudden comprehending glances, clear as a beam of light.

But he did not respond to this. "When you met her that afternoon, Garda, where was she?" he asked; he seemed to be thrusting Garda and her affairs aside now.

"I told you; in the south-eastern woods."

"Yes. But where?"

"In the eastern path, at the end of that long straight stretch beyond the pool—just before you get to the bend."

"And then?"

"Then I went back up the path to meet the Doctor. And Margaret went down the path and across the field to Madam Giron's."

At this instant appeared Celestine. She had gone to the entrance of the aisle which was nearest the house, and looked in; then, seeing that they were at the far end, she had left it and come round on the outside.

For something forbade Celestine to walk down that long vista alone. They would probably hear her and turn; and then there would be the necessity of approaching them for fully five minutes step by step, with the consciousness that they were looking; she could not stare back at them, and yet neither could she look all the time at the sand at her feet—which would be dizzying. Celestine always took care of her dignity in this way; she had a fixed regard for herself as a decent Vermont woman; you could see that in the self-respecting way in which her large neat shoes lifted themselves and came down again when she walked.

"Mrs. Rutherford would like to see you, Mr. Evert, if you please; she isn't so well, she says."

"Nothing serious, Minerva, I hope?"

"I guess there's no occasion to be scairt, Mr. Evert. But she wants you."

"I will come immediately."

Celestine disappeared.

Garda and Winthrop turned back towards the house through the orange aisle.

"Mrs. Rutherford has never known, has she, that we have been engaged?" asked Garda.

"No."

"There is no need that she should ever know, then; she isn't fond of me as it is, and she would detest me forever if she knew there had been a chance of my becoming in reality her niece. I don't want to trouble her any longer with even my unseen presence; I want to go away."

"Where?"

"It doesn't make much difference where. It is only that I am restless, and as I have never been restless before, I thought that perhaps if I should go away for a while, it would stop."

"Yes, you wish to see the world," said Winthrop, vaguely. His mind was not upon Garda now.

"I don't care for 'the world,'" the girl responded. "*I* only care for the people in it."

Then, in answer to a glance of his as his attention came back to her, "No, I am not going after Lucian," she said; "don't think that. I am almost sure that Lucian will go abroad now; he was always talking about it,—saying that he longed to spend a summer in Venice, and paint everything there. No—but I think I might go to Charleston—the Doctor could take me; he has a cousin there, Mrs. Lowndes; I could stay with her. Margaret will oppose it. But the Doctor is my guardian too, you know; and I hope *you* will take my part. Of course I should rather go with Margaret anywhere, if she could only go; but she cannot, you know Mrs. Rutherford would never let her. So she will feel called upon—Margaret—to oppose it."

They had now come to the end of the aisle. "Promise me to take my part," said Garda. Then, perceiving that his attention had left her again, "See what I am reduced to!" she confided to the last orange-tree.

Winthrop brought himself back. "I don't see any reason why you shouldn't go to Charleston if the Doctor will take you," he said; "you must speak to him about it."

"Well, I won't keep you; I see you want to go.—All the same, you know, I liked you," she called after him as he went out in the sunshine.

He glanced back, smiling.

But Garda looked perfectly serious. She stood there framed in the light green shade; "I should like *ever* so much to go back to the time when I first cared for you!" she said, regretfully.

Winthrop found Mrs. Rutherford much excited. Betty, tearful and distressed, met him outside the door, and in whispered words confessed that she had inadvertently betrayed the fact of his engagement, to dear

Katrina; "I can't imagine, though, why she should feel about it as she does—as though it was something terrible," concluded the friend, plucking up a little spirit at the end of her confession, and wiping her eyes.

"She won't feel so long," said Winthrop,—"you can take comfort from that; my engagement is broken."

"BROKEN?"

"Yes; by Garda herself, ten minutes ago." And leaving Betty to digest this new intelligence, he went in to see his aunt.

His aunt had had herself put into an arm-chair: an arm-chair was more impressive than a bed. "I feel very ill, Evert," she began, in a faint voice; "I never could have believed that you would deceive me in this way."

"Let me undeceive you, then. My engagement—for I presume it is that you are thinking of—is broken."

"Did *you* break it, Evert?" pursued Aunt Katrina, still in affliction.

"No, Miss Thorne broke it. Ten minutes ago."

"A forward minx!" said the lady, veering suddenly to heat.

"It is done, at any rate. I suppose you are glad."

"Of course I am glad. But I should be gladder still if I thought I should never see her face again!"

"That is apropos—she is anxious to go to Charleston."

"Let her go," said Aunt Katrina, with majesty.

"She is afraid Margaret will object."

"*I* shall object if she stays! But oh, Evert, how could you have been caught in such a trap as that, by a perfectly unknown, shallow, mercenary girl?"

"Unknown—for the present, yes; shallow—I am not prepared to say; but mercenary? If she were mercenary, would she have let me off? Would she have broken the engagement herself, as she did ten minutes ago?"

"I wish you wouldn't keep repeating that 'ten minutes,'" said Aunt Katrina, irritably. "Who cares for ten minutes? I wish it were ten years." Then her mind reverted to Garda. "She has some plan," she said.

"I don't think she plans. And now that this trouble is off your mind, my dear aunt, will you excuse me if I leave you? I have still only just arrived, and I was up at dawn. Shall I send Celestine to you?"

"Celestine is busy; she is refolding some lace—Flemish church."

"Your Betty, then."

"My Betty has behaved in the most *traitorous* way."

"When she was the one to tell you?"

"She should have told me long before."

"Why she, more than any of the rest of us?" asked Winthrop, rising.

"Because *she* must have made a superhuman effort not to; because *she* must have fairly kept herself in a strait-jacket to prevent it—in a strait-jacket night and day; for eight long months has Elizabeth Gwinnet done that!"

"Don't you think, then, that you ought to have some pity for her?" suggested Winthrop.

He went out. And then Betty, who was sitting, dazed and dejected, on the edge of a chair outside the door, hurried in, handkerchief in hand, to make her peace with dearest Kate, her long limp black skirt (all Betty's skirts were long) trailing in an eager, humble way behind her.

Winthrop had said that he wished to go to his room. The way to it was not through the drawing-room; yet he found himself in the latter apartment.

Margaret sat there near one of the windows sewing, sewing with that even motion of hand, and absorbed gaze bent on the long seam, which he had told himself more than once that he detested. The heavy wooden shutter was slightly open, so that a beam of light entered and shone across her hair; the rest of the room was in shadow.

Winthrop came towards her; he had closed the door upon entering. She gave him her hand, and they exchanged a few words of formal greeting—inquiry and reply about his journey and kindred matters.

"Garda has broken her engagement to me; I presume you know it," he said.

"I knew she intended to do it."

"She tells me that you have tried to dissuade her?"

"Yes; I thought she did not, perhaps, fully know her own mind."

"We must give up the idea that she is a child," he said. "We have been mistaken, probably, about that all along."

Margaret sewed on without answering.

"You are very loyal to her; you don't let me see that you agree with me."

"I didn't suppose that you meant any disparagement, when you said it."

"She tells me that she doesn't care for me any more." He took a book from the table beside him, and looked absently at its title. "We must allow that she has a great facility as regards change."

"She has a great honesty."

Winthrop sat down—until now he had been standing; he threw aside the book. "You certainly can't approve of it," he said,—"such a disposition?"

He did not pay much heed to what he was saying, he was absorbed in the problem before him; face to face with Margaret, he was asking himself, and with more inward tumult than ever, why she had been so willing to have him think of her, as, after what he had seen, he must think? During his two weeks of absence—the evening before on that long pier in the rain—he had felt a hot anger against her for the unconcern with which she was treating him. But now that he knew the real history of that last afternoon, now that he knew that it was Garda who had planned the meeting with Lucian, Garda, not Margaret, who had been on her way to that solitary house, the problem was more strangely haunting even than before. She had saved Garda from compromising herself in the eyes of the man to whom she was engaged—yes; but she had done it at the expense of compromising herself, Garda, meanwhile, remaining ignorant of the greatness of the sacrifice, since she did not know, as Margaret did, that he, Winthrop, was sitting there in the wood beyond the bend.

Certainly it was an immense thing for one woman to have done for another; you might say, indeed, that there was nothing greater that a woman could do.

Then came again the galling thought that Margaret had not found the task so difficult, simply because she was indifferent as to what his opinion of her might be; *she* knew that she had not been in any sense of the word to blame—that was enough for her; what he knew, or thought he knew, troubled her little.

But no, that could not be. Margaret Harold was a proud woman—you could see that, quiet as she was, in every delicate line of her face; it was not natural, therefore, that she should willingly rest in the eyes of any one under such an imputation as that. Surely, now that Garda had, of her own accord, broken off her engagement, and confessed (only Garda never "confessed," she merely told) that her old liking for Lucian had risen again, surely *now* Margaret would throw off the false character that rested upon her, would hasten to do so, would be glad to do so; there was no necessity to shield Garda further. She had made the girl promise not to tell him the real version of the events of that last afternoon; didn't this mean that, if the circumstances should ever change so that it was possible to give the real version, she wished to give it to him herself? The circumstances had changed; and now, wouldn't she take advantage of it? Wouldn't she be glad to explain, at last, the reasons that took her to Madam Giron's that day? Of course she supposed that still he did not know; it would not occur to her that Garda might break her promise.

But still her hand came and went above the white seam. And still she said nothing.

He waited a long time—as long as it was possible to sit there without speaking. Then he went back to his last remark—which she had not answered; annoyed by her silence, he went from bad to worse. "I shall be surprised if you approve of it;—you have such a regard for appearances."

She colored. "I am not very successful in preserving them then, even if I have a regard."

"Oh, you don't mind *me*," answered Winthrop, in a tone which in spite of himself was openly bitter.

She looked up, he could see that she was much moved. "We must do everything we can for Garda now," she said, rather incoherently, her eyes returning to her work.

"You have done altogether too much for her as it is; I don't think you need trouble yourself so constantly about Garda, you might think for a moment of your other friends."

He was absolutely pleading—he could scarcely believe it of himself. But he wanted so to have her set him right! He wanted her to do it of her own accord—show that she was glad to be able to do it at last. There was no longer any question of saving Garda; Garda had, in her own eyes at least, saved herself. He waited for his answer.

She had given him a frightened glance as he spoke, the expression of his face seemed to take her by surprise, and break down her self-possession. She rose, murmuring something about being obliged to go.

"You are sure you have nothing to say to me, Margaret?" he asked, as she went towards the door.

"Say? What do you mean?"

"I am giving you a chance to explain, I long to have you explain. I find myself unable to believe—" He stopped. Then he began again. "I am sure there is some solution—If I have not always liked your course in other matters, at least I have never thought *this* of you. You know what I witnessed that afternoon, as I sat there in the woods; one word will be enough—tell me what I must think of it—and of you." He was trying her to the utmost now.

A painful red flush had darkened her face, but, except for that, she did not flinch. "You must think what you please," she answered.

Then she escaped; she had opened the door, and now she went rapidly down the hall towards her own room.

He stood gazing. If he had not known she was innocent, he should have set down her tone to defiance; it was exactly the sort of low-voiced defiance which he had expected from her when he had supposed—what he *had* supposed.

But his suppositions had been entirely false. Did she still wish him to believe that they were true!

It appeared so.

CHAPTER XXIV

Garda Thorne went to Charleston. Margaret gave her consent only after much hesitation; but Dr. Kirby was from the first firmly in favor of the plan. He himself would take his ward to the South Carolina city (for Garda, the Doctor would draw upon his thin purse whether he were able to afford it or not), she should stay with his accomplished cousin Sally Lowndes; thus she would have the best opportunity to see the cultivated society of that dear little town.

This last sentence was partly the Doctor's and partly Winthrop's; the Doctor had spoken thus reverentially of Charleston society, and Winthrop thus admiringly of Charleston itself, which had seemed to him, the first time he beheld it, the prettiest place on the Atlantic coast, a place of marked characteristics of its own, many of them highly picturesque; his use of the word "little" had been affectionate, not descriptive. He had found a charm in the old houses, gable end to the street; in the jealous walls and great gardens; in St. Michael's spire; in the dusky library, full of grand-mannered old English authors in expensive old bindings; in the little Huguenot church; in the old manor-houses on the two rivers that come down, one on each side, to form the beautiful harbor; in the rice fields; in the great lilies. The Battery at sunset, with Fort Moultrie on one hand, the silver beaches round Wagner and the green marsh where the great guns had been on the other, and Sumter on its islet in mid-stream—this was an unsurpassed lounging-place; there was nothing fairer.

The Doctor had been much roused by the breaking of Garda's engagement. Garda had told him that Evert had not been to blame. But the Doctor was not so sure of that. He felt, indeed, that he himself had been to blame, they had all been to blame; ma, Betty Carew, the Moores, Madam Ruiz and the Señor Ruiz, Madam Giron—they had all been asleep, and had let this worst of modern innovations creep upon them unawares. For surely the foundations of society were shaken when the engagement of a young lady of Garda's position could be "broken." "And broken, ma," as he repeated solemnly to his little mother a dozen times, "*without cause*."

"Well, my son, would you rather have had it broken *with*?" asked ma at last.

The Doctor had had an interview with Winthrop. And he had been obliged to confess (still to ma) that the northerner had borne himself with courtesy and dignity, had given him nothing to take hold of; he had simply said, in a few words, that Garda had asked to be released, and that of course he had released her.

The Doctor himself had fervently desired that she should be freed. But this made no difference in his astonishment that the thing could really be done, had already been brought about. Garda had wished it; he himself had wished it; and Winthrop had obeyed their wish. Nevertheless, Reginald Kirby was a prey to rage, he was sure that somebody ought to be severely handled. In the mean while it seemed a wise course to take Garda to other scenes.

Adolfo Torres returned from Cuba before Garda's departure. He bade her good-by with his usual gravity; then, exactly three hours later, he started for Charleston himself. He kept punctiliously just that amount of time behind her, it was part of his method; on this occasion the method caused some discomfort, since, owing to the small number of trains in that leisurely land, it obliged him to travel with the freight all the way.

A week later a letter came to Evert Winthrop. It was a letter which gave him a sharp surprise.

It bore the postmark of the little post-office out in the St. John's where he had sat in the rain, and the contents were as follows:

> "Dear old Lad,—I am here—on the river. Could you come over for a day? I am very anxious to see you.
>
> "Lansing Harold."

At the last intelligence, Lanse had been in Rome.

There was a scrawled postscript:

"Say nothing, I write only to you."

Winthrop's relations with Margaret since they had parted, on the day of his return, at the drawing-room door, had been of the scantiest; they had scarcely exchanged a word. She avoided him; he said to himself that she had turned into ice; but this was not a truthful comparison, for ice does not look troubled, and Margaret looked both troubled and worn. When he was present she was impassive; but her very impassiveness showed—but what did it show? He could think of no solution that satisfied him any more than he could think of a solution of the mystery of her apparent desire that he should continue to believe of her what he had believed.

And now, to make things more complicated, Lanse had dropped down upon them!

Winthrop made a pretext of another hunting expedition, drove over to the river, and embarked again upon the slow old *Hernando*, which brought him in due course to the long pier; here, sitting in the United States chair, was Harold.

It was a long time since Winthrop had seen Lanse. He thought him much altered. His figure had grown larger; though he was still but forty-one, none of the outlines of youth were left, there was only an impression of bulk. His thick dark hair was mixed with gray, as also his short beard; and the beard could not conceal the increased breadth of the lower part of the face, the slight lap-over of the cheeks above the collar. His dark eyes, with the yellow lights in them, were dull; his well-cut mouth was a little open, giving him a blank expression, as though he were half asleep.

But when this expression changed, as it did when the silent postmaster suggested, by a wave of the hand, that his guest should move the government chair a little in order not to be in the way of the passengers who might land, the alteration was so complete, though not a feature stirred, that Winthrop laughed; Lanse serenely stared at the 'coon-skin-hatted man as though he did not exist; his gaze restored perfectly, for himself at least, the space of light and air which that public servant was mistakenly filling.

All this Winthrop witnessed from the deck, as the *Hernando* was slowly swinging her broad careening side towards the pier. Lanse had not recognized his figure among the motley crowd of voyagers collected at the railing; it was not until the ropes had been made fast by the postmaster (who was also wharf-master, showing much activity in that avocation), and the plank put out, that the lessening crowd brought Winthrop's figure more into relief. He waved his hand again to Lanse; and then Lanse, springing up, responded, and all the old look came back; the dulness vanished, the heaviness became subordinate to the brightening eyes and the smile, he waved his hand in return. They met with gladness; Lanse seemed delighted to see his cousin, and Winthrop had never forgotten his old affection for the big, good-natured, handsome lad of his boyhood days.

The pier was soon left to them; every one else departed, and the two men, strolling up and down, talked together.

At length Lanse said: "Well, I'm glad Margaret's as you describe" (but Winthrop had not described her); "for I might as well tell you at once what I'm down here for—I want her to come back."

"Come back?"

"Yes. I have her promise to come; but women are so insufferably changeable."

"She isn't."

"Isn't she? So much the better for me, then; for she knew the worst of me when she made that promise, and if by a miracle she *has* remained in the same mind, my road will be easy."

"I don't mean to push myself into your confidence, Lanse," said Winthrop, after a moment's silence; "but I think I will say here that I have always as strongly as possible disapproved of her course in leaving you." He made himself say this. It was true, and say it he would.

Lanse laughed, and turned down the brim of his soft hat to keep the sun from his eyes. "I'm not going to lie about it," he answered. "I would have told you at any time if you had asked me; she couldn't help leaving me."

Winthrop stared.

"It's a funny world," Lanse went on. "Come along up and get something to eat; then we'll go off in the canoe, and I'll tell you the whole story; you've got to hear it if you're to help."

An hour later the two men were floating away from the pier in a small boat built upon the model of the Indian's birch-bark canoe. Lanse, an expert in this as in almost all kinds of out-door exercise, wielded the paddle with ease, while Winthrop faced him, reclining in the bottom of the boat; it could only hold two. Lightly it sped out towards deep water, the slightest motion sent it forward; its sides were of such slender thickness that the two men could feel the breathing of the great soft stream, which had here a breadth of three miles, though in sight, both above and below, it widened into six. These broad water stretches were tranquil; from shore to shore the slow, full current swept majestically on; and even to look across the wide, still reaches, with the tropical forests standing thickly on their low strands, was a vision of peace for the most troubled human soul.

Kildee plover flew chattering before the canoe while they were still near land. Far above in the blue a bald-headed eagle sailed along. Lanse chose to go out to the centre of the stream—Lanse never skirted the edge of anything; reaching it, he turned southward, and they voyaged onward for nearly an hour.

He did not appear disposed to begin his narrative immediately; and Winthrop asked no questions. Every now and then each indulged in a retrospective remark; but these remarks concerned themselves only with the days of their boyhood, they brought up the old jokes, and called each other by the old names. Winthrop, after a while, branching off a little, suggested that this warm brown tide, winding softly through the beautiful low green country, was something to remember—on a January day, say, in a manufacturing town at the North, when a raw wind was sweeping the streets, when the horse-cars were bumping along between miniature hills of muddy ice, when all complexions were dubious and harassed, and the constantly dropping flakes of soot from myriad chimneys failed to convey a suggestion of warmth, but rather brought up (to the initiated) a picture of chill half-heated bedrooms, where these same harassed complexions must undergo more torture from soap and water in the effort to remove the close-clinging marks of the "black snow."

"Oh, confound your manufacturing town!" Lanse answered.

"I can't; I'm a manufacturer myself," was Winthrop's response.

At length Lanse turned the canoe towards the western shore. A creek emptied into the river at this point, a creek which had about the breadth of the Thames at Westminster; Lanse entered the creek. Great ragged nests of the fish-hawks crowned many of the trees here, making them resemble a group of light-houses at the creek's mouth. They met an old negro on a raft, who held up a rattlesnake which he seemed to think they would admire. "Fibe foot en eight inch, boss, en ferteen rattles."

"That's African Joe," said Lanse. "I've already made his acquaintance; he was born in Africa.—You old murderer, what do you want for showing us that poor reptile you have put an end to?"

Old Joe, a marvel of negro old age, grinned as Lanse tossed him a quarter. "'Gater, massa," he said, pointing.

It was a black lump like the end of a floating log,—an alligator submerged all but that inch or two of head.

"That's the place I'm looking for, I think," said Lanse; "I was up here yesterday."

And with two or three strong strokes of the paddle he sent the canoe round a cape of lily-pads, into the mouth of a smaller creek which here came, almost unobserved, into the larger one. It was a stream narrow but deep, which took them into the forest. Here they floated over reflections so perfect of the trees draped in silver moss on shore that it was hard to tell where reality ended and the picture began. Great turtles swam along down below, water-moccasins slipped noiselessly into the amber depths from the roots of the trees as the canoe drew near; alligators began to show themselves more freely; the boat floated noiselessly over one huge fellow fifteen feet long.

Lanse was aroused. "I tell you, old lad, this isn't bad," he said.

"I don't care about it," Winthrop answered; "it's sensational."

Over this remark Lanse indulged in a retrospective grin. "Old!" he said. "You've been getting that off ever since you were twenty. Who was it that called Niagara 'violent?' The joke is that, at heart, you yourself are the most violent creature I know."

"Oh—talk about hearts!" said Winthrop.

The trees now began to meet overhead; when their branches interlaced so that the shade was complete, Lanse tied the boat-rope to a bough, stretched himself out in his end of the boat, lit a cigarette, and looked at his companion. "Now for the story," he said. "I tell you because I want your help; I am sure that Margaret has the highest opinion of you."

"She has none at all. She detests me."

"No!" said Lanse, using the word as an exclamation. "How comes that? You must have been very savage to her?"

"I have always been against her about you."

"Has Aunt Katrina been savage too?"

"She has given her a home, at any rate."

"And a pretty one it must have been, if she has looked, while about it, as you look now," Lanse commented.

"Never mind my looks. I don't know that your own are any better. What have you to say?"

"One thing more, first. How much has Margaret told?"

"Nothing. That is, nothing to me."

"I meant Aunt K."

"How should I know?" said Winthrop, shortly. Then he made himself speak with more truth. "Aunt Katrina complains that Margaret has never said a word."

"Yet you've all been disapproving of her all this time! Now I call that a specimen of the fixed injustice so common among nice people," said Lanse, musingly. He was sorry for the nice people.

"Before you criticise, let us see how well *you* have behaved," suggested his companion.

"Oh, *I* don't pretend to be a well-regulated character. Let me see—I shall have to go back to the beginning to make you understand. I don't know whether you know how Margaret was brought up? She had always lived in the country; not a village—the old Cruger place was three miles from everywhere; there she lived with her grandmother and her grandmother's friends, not a young person among them; she hadn't even been to school—always a governess at home. She was only seventeen when I first saw her; we were there in the house together—Aunt Katrina's—and I was at the time more in the dumps than I had ever been in my life. I had just come back from abroad, as you know; and the reason I had come back, which you don't know, was because some one (never mind who—not an American) had gone off and married under my nose a man with a million—several of them if you count in French. As I had expected to marry her myself, you may imagine whether I enjoyed it. Feeling pretty well cut up, smarting tremendously, if I must confess it, it seemed to me, after a while, that it wouldn't be a bad idea to marry Margaret Cruger. I couldn't feel worse than I did, and maybe I might feel better, she was very sweet in her way; I don't pretend that I was ever in love with her, but I liked her from the first. I have always had a fancy for young girls," pursued Lanse, taking off his hat and putting it behind his head as a pillow; "when they're not forward (American girls are apt to be forward, though without in the least knowing it), they're enchanting. The trouble is that they can't stay young forever; they don't know anything, and of course they have to learn, and *that* process is tiresome; it would be paradise if a girl of seventeen could sit down like a woman of thirty, and paradise isn't intended, I suppose, to come just yet."

"Don't talk your French to me," said Winthrop; "I don't admire it."

"That's another of your shams. Yes, you do. But it's perfectly true that a young girl can no more sit down with grace than she can listen with grace."

"Yes; you want to talk."

"On the contrary, I don't want to, I want to be silent; but I want them to know how to listen to my silence. Well, I won't go into the details. She was so young—Margaret—that I easily made her believe that I couldn't live without her, that I should go to the bad direct unless she would take charge of me—a thing that is apt to succeed with young girls when they're conscientious (as Margaret was), unless they happen to care for some one else; Margaret didn't care for any one else, and so she was caught. We were married; and I give you my word I fully intended to treat her as well as I knew how. But—ill luck got mixed with it."

Here Lanse changed his position again, and clasping his hands under his head, gazed up at the dense green above. "Let's hope a moccasin won't take a walk out on one of those branches and fall down; they do it sometimes, I know. We had not been married long, Margaret and I, when the other one wrote to me."

"Nice sort of person."

"Precisely. But I cared more about her than I did about any one in the world, and that makes a difference. I thought she wrote to me because she couldn't help it—in short, because she cared so much for me. That's taking. And now here's where ill luck took a hand. Did I intend to let any of this in the least touch Margaret—interfere with *her*? As far as possible from it; my intention was that she should never know or dream of it, it was all to be kept religiously from her. Why—I wouldn't have had her know it for anything, first on her own account, then on mine; the wife of Lansing Harold," went on Lanse, smiling a little at himself, yet evidently meaning exactly what he said, "must be above suspicion, by which I intend the verb, not the noun; up to thirty, she must be too innocent to suspect. But what do you suppose came next? By the most extraordinary chance in the world Margaret herself got hold of one of my letters to—to the other person. She came upon the loose sheets by accident, and thought it was something that I must have been writing some time to her; she never imagined that it was to any one else, or she wouldn't have read it, she was punctiliousness itself in such matters; but her eyes happened to fall first upon the middle sheet, where there was no name, and the—'the language,' as she afterwards expressed it, made her believe that it was addressed to herself; a man could only write in that way to his wife, she supposed. But at the end she was undeceived, for there she found the other name. Of course we had a scene when I came home. I was horribly annoyed by what had happened, but I did my best to be nice to her. I told her that it was a miserable accident in every way, her coming upon that letter, that I could never forgive myself for having left it where I did; I told her that I could perfectly understand that it had been a great shock to her—a shock that I was more sorry for than she could possibly be. But as it had happened, we must both make the best of it, and her 'best' was simply to forget all about it as soon as she could,—it was wonderful how much one could forget if one tried; I could assure her that nothing should ever touch her position as my wife, there should be no breath upon that; always I should give her in the eyes of all the world the first honor, the first place. You see, it was the best I could do. I couldn't deny the letter; it was in my own handwriting, it even had a date; and it wasn't a letter, either, that you could explain away. But I couldn't do anything with her. I don't mean that she argued or combated, she seemed all broken to pieces; she sat there looking at me with a sort of wonder and horror combined. Before night she was ill—a fever. She was ill three weeks, and I was as nice to her all that time as I possibly could be, I brought her lovely flowers every day. As she grew better, I hoped we were going to go on in peace; certainly the last thing I wanted was a quarrel with her. But—women are bound to be fools! no sooner was she able to sit up than she took the first chance to ask me (there had been a nurse about before) whether I had abandoned that dreadful affair. I suppose I could have lied to her, if I was going to do it, that was the time. But, as it happens, I don't lie, it has never been one of my accomplishments. So I told her that she ought to treat such things as a lady should,—that is, not descend to them; and I told her furthermore that she ought to treat this one as *my wife* should. When I said that, I remember she looked at me as if she were in a sort of stupor; you see, to *her* sense, she *was* treating it as my wife should," commented Lanse, telling his own story, as he felt himself, with much impersonal fairness. "All this time, of course, I had had to postpone everything; she continued to improve, and I took the ground of saying nothing. When another month had passed, and she was perfectly well again, I mentioned one day, carelessly, and before some one else, that I thought I should try a little summer trip of thirty days or so across the ocean and back; I shouldn't take her, because she wasn't as fond of the sea as I was, and twenty of the thirty days would be spent afloat; she would be much more comfortable at home—we had taken a pretty house at New Rochelle for the year. She didn't make any especial comment then, but as soon as she could get me alone I saw that it had all been of no use—my patience and my waiting; she was determined to talk. Her point was that I must not go. I am not very yielding, as you know; but she was even more obstinate than I was; it was owing to the ideas she had about such things, she wasn't a Roman Catholic, but she thought marriage a sacrament—almost. I got in a few words on that side myself, I told her that she seemed to have a singular idea of a wife's duties; one of them was generally supposed to be to guard her husband's name, which was also her own; but, that while *I* wished to occasion no talk, no scandal, she was doing her very best to stir up both by having an open quarrel with me. And then I asked her what she proposed to do? I suppose I looked ugly. She got up and stood there, holding on to the back of a chair; 'I must go with you,' she said. 'I can't take you,' I told her. And then she said that she could *follow* me. That, I confess, put me in a rage, I was never angrier in my life. I imagined her appearing upon the scene there in Paris! A pretty spectacle I should be, followed about and tracked down by a wife of that age—a wife, too, who was acting solely from a sense of duty; with her school-girl face, that was a combination rather too ridiculous for any man to stand. To cut the story short, I left her then and there. That night I slept at a hotel, and the next day I sailed; I had changed my plan of travel, in order that she should not know for some time where I was; but I think I frightened her sufficiently about following me before I left her. I not only expressly forbade it, but I told her that she wouldn't be received in case she should try it; there would be standing orders to that effect left with the servants. I should never touch any more of her money, I told her (I never have to this day); she could set going any story she pleased about me, and I wouldn't contradict it; that would leave her very easy; on my side I should simply say nothing, and I should cause no scandal, she might be sure of that So I went off. On the other side I found a letter from her—she didn't know my address, but she had sent it to my lawyer; I've brought that letter along for you to see, it will give you a better idea of her, as she was at the time, than any of my descriptions." And he took from his pocket-book an old envelope, and tossed it across.

Winthrop opened the envelope; it contained a small sheet of paper, upon which, in a youthful immature handwriting, these words were written:

"My Dear Lanse,—I have stayed here by myself all day. And I have been very unhappy. I have not let anybody know that you were gone.

"I feel as though I must have done wrong, and yet I don't know how.

"Perhaps you will come back. I shall hope that you will. I will wait here for your answer.

"I will come to you at any time if—you know what. And I hope you will soon send for me.

"Your affectionate wife,
"Margaret."

"You see there's no trace of jealousy," Lanse commented, in his generalizing way; "she wasn't jealous, because she wasn't in love with me—never had been. Of course she *thought* she loved me—she never would have married me otherwise; but the truth was that at that time she had no more conception of what real love is than a little snow image: that was one of the reasons why I had first liked her. I've no doubt she *was* horribly miserable when she wrote that letter, as she says she was. But there was no love in her misery, it was all duty; I grant you that with her that was a tremendously strong feeling. Well, I answered her letter, I told her she had better go and live with Aunt Katrina as before, that that was the best place for her. I told her that I should stay where I was for the present, and on no account was she to try to follow me; that was the one thing I would not endure; I had to frighten her about that, because she had so much obstinacy—steadfastness if you like—that if I had not done so, and effectually, she would certainly have started in pursuit—prayer-book in hand, poor child! She wrote to me once more, repeating her offer to come whenever I should wish it; but I didn't wish it then, and didn't answer. Eight years have passed, and I haven't answered yet. But now I think I shall try it."

Winthrop had sat gazing at the little sheet, with the faded girlish handwriting. Hot feelings were surging within him, he felt that he must take a firm hold of himself; this made his manner calm. "What do you want of her?" he said. "Aunt Katrina couldn't get on a day without her."

"Aunt Katrina would give her up to me," said Lanse, securely. (And Winthrop knew that this was true.) "What do I want of her? I want to have a home of my own again, a place where I can be comfortable; I want to have a place where I can keep all my shoes. I am not as young as I once was; I don't mind telling *you* that I've had one or two pretty serious attacks—rheumatism threatening the heart. It's time to be old, to take in sail; I'm a reformed character, and I don't see why Margaret shouldn't come and carry on the good work—especially as she has promised. The one danger is that she may have begun to—But I hardly think that."

"That she may have begun to hate you?" said Winthrop. "Yes, I should think that highly probable." He still held the poor little letter, the childlike, bewildered appeal of the deserted young wife.

"No, I didn't mean that," Lanse answered; "I meant that she might have begun to care for some one else; really care, you know. But I don't believe it. If it were only that she had begun to hate me, that would be nothing; she would think it very wrong to hate me (though she might not be able to help it), and that would make her come back to me all the quicker."

Winthrop looked at him from under his tilted hat—he had tilted it forward over his eyes. "I should think it would make you sick to ask her," he said—"sick with shame!"

"It isn't the least shameful, it's the right thing to do," responded Lanse. "But which side are you on, Ev? You seem to be all over the field."

"Never mind which side I'm on. You can't take her up and drop her in that way."

"You've got it mixed. I dropped her eight years ago; *now* I'm taking her up again. And if she is as I think she is, she will be glad to come."

"Oh!" said Winthrop, with angry scorn.

"She'll be glad, because she's my wife—she's a stickler for that sort of thing. She is a very good woman; that's the advantage of having a really good woman for your wife—you can rely upon her whether she likes you or not—likes you very much, I mean. But I begin to think you don't know her as well as I do, in spite of the time you have had."

"Know her? I don't know her in the least! I have never known her—I see that now."

At this moment they heard the dip of an oar, and stopped. Coming down the narrow stream behind them, appeared a rude craft manned by a very black boy and a very white baby. The boat was a long, rough dug-out, and the boy was paddling; his passenger, a plump child of about three, had the bleached skin of the Florida cracker, and flaxen hair of the palest straw-color. An immense calico sun-bonnet lay across its knee, and, after a slow stare with twisted neck at the two strangers, it lifted and put on this penthouse; to put it on was probably its idea of "manners." The penthouse, in fact, represented the principal part of its attire, there was nothing else but a little red petticoat.

But if the passenger was dignified, the oarsman was not; delighted to see anybody, the little darky had showed his white teeth in a perpetual grin from the moment the canoe had appeared in sight.

Lanse always noticed children. "Where have you been, Epaminondas?" he said, with pretended severity. "What are you doing here?"

Epaminondas, at the first suggestion of conversation, had stopped paddling. He accepted with cheerfulness the improvised name. "Ben atter turkles, boss. But I 'ain't fin' none."

"What is the name of that young lady you have with you?"

"Gin," answered Epaminondas, with an even more extensive smile than before.

"The whole of it, I mean; I know there's more."

"Trufe, boss, der sholy is," responded Epaminondas, impressed by this omniscience. "Gin's wat dey calls her mosely; but Victoryne John Mungumry Gin—dat's de hull ob it. Victoryne en John Mungumry is folks wat her ma knew whar she come fum, up in Alabawm, en she wanted to membunce 'em someways, so she called Gin atter 'em. En Gin—dat's *Virginny*—wuz de name ob her daddy's folks, dey tole me."

"I am surprised that her family should allow Miss Montgomery to be out without her nurse," Lanse went on.

"She 'ain't got no nuss," Epaminondas answered. "En *I* hev to tote her mos' er der time, en she's hebby—she am dat! En so *ter-day* I 'lowed I'd rudder take her in de boat a wiles." He looked anxiously at Lanse as he made this explanation; he was a thin little fellow of about ten, and Miss Montgomery was decidedly solid.

"I'm inclined to think, my man, that you're out without leave; I advise you to go home as fast as you can. And mind you keep the boat straight."

"Yas, boss," answered Epaminondas, glad to escape, and plying his paddle again.

He gave a "Ki!" of delight as a silver coin fell at his feet. "Don't stop to pick it up now," said Lanse. "Go on with Miss Montgomery; restore her to her parents as soon as possible."

Epaminondas bent to his oar; the two men looked after him as the boat went on its way towards the outer creek.

Suddenly, "Good God!" cried Lanse, springing to his feet.

He had to unloose the rope; but he did that in an instant, and, seizing the paddle, he sent the canoe flying down-stream after the dug-out.

Epaminondas, toiling at his oar, had not gone thirty feet when Lanse had seen a large moccasin drop from a branch above directly into the long narrow boat as it passed beneath; the creature fell midway between the children, who occupied the two ends.

Quick as a flash the little negro had jumped overboard. But that was instinct; he would not desert the white child, and swam on, holding by the boat's side and screaming shrilly.

Meanwhile Miss Montgomery sat composedly in her place; she did not appear at all disturbed.

Winthrop had no oar, so he could not help. Lanse, standing up, forced the canoe through the water rapidly; but before he could bring it up where he could seize the child, the little darky, who had not ceased to swim round and round the drifting craft, announced with a yell, as his curly black head peered for one instant over the side, that the snake was coiling for a spring.

Then Lanse gave a mighty plunge into the stream, and, keeping himself up with one hand, snatched the girl and dragged her overboard by main force with the other, handing her in safety to Winthrop, who had taken the paddle and kept the canoe along. Lanse and the little darky then swam ashore, and stepped into the canoe again from the roots of a large tree, which served them for a landing.

They were both wet through, of course. But Epaminondas was amphibious, his single garment, a pair of trousers, could be as well dried upon his small person as upon a bush. With Lanse it was different. But at present Lanse was excited, nothing would do but to go after that snake which was now luxuriously voyaging down the stream in a boat of its own; taking the paddle, he sent the canoe in chase.

Standing up as he drew near, he announced that the moccasin was motionless in the bottom of the dug-out.

His next announcement was that it was "rather a pretty fellow."

Then, still standing up and gazing, "*I* can't kill the poor creature," he said; "I don't suppose he meant any harm when he dropped—had no idea there was a boat there." Sending the canoe towards the land again, he went ashore and found, after some search, a long branch; with this he paddled back, and then, brandishing it at arm's-length, he tilted the dug-out, by its aid, so far over on one side, that the moccasin, perceiving that the element he preferred was conveniently near, with silent swiftness joined it. Through all this scene, Miss Montgomery, plump and dry—Lanse had held her above the water—remained serenely indifferent; she sat in her sun-bonnet on Winthrop's knee, and preserved her dignity unbroken.

"Shucks!" said Epaminondas (now that the enemy had departed), expectorating, with an air of experience, into the stream; "I is seed 'em twicet ez bigger lots er times!"

Lanse, resuming his seat, wiped his forehead. His leap had been a strong exertion, and already his face showed the fatigue; he was a heavy man, and out of practice in such gymnastics.

"Have you any more notions to carry out?" inquired Winthrop. "I've been spinning back and forth in this boat about as long as I care for."

"Come, now, wasn't that a good deed?" asked Lanse (Lanse always wanted praise). "I call it brutal to kill a poor creature simply because he's got no legs."

"You didn't happen to have your revolver with you, I suppose," Winthrop answered, refusing to bestow the applause.

"Never carried one in my life; cowardly things!" responded Lanse, in a disgusted tone. He was hard at work paddling, in order to keep off a chill.

Epaminondas was put ashore at his own landing on the outer creek, and departed up a sandy path, leading Miss Montgomery, his pockets unwontedly heavy with coin. He looked back as long as he could see them, throwing up and waving his ragged straw hat.

But Miss Montgomery never turned; she plodded steadily homeward on her fat white legs—all of her that could be seen below the sun-bonnet.

Lanse's efforts to avoid a chill were apparently successful that night. But the next morning he sent for Winthrop at an early hour. Winthrop found him with a strange pallor on his face, he said he was in great pain. A physician staying in the house was summoned; it was the rheumatism Lanse had spoken of; but this time it did not merely threaten the heart, it had attacked it.

For twelve hours there was danger. Then there was a lull. The lull was followed by something which had the appearance of a partial paralysis of the lower limbs. Lanse's head was now clear, but he was helpless. The physician said that he could not be moved at present; in two weeks or so he should be better able to name a day for that.

To Winthrop, in confidence, he said that in two weeks or so he should be better able to tell whether there was a chance that the present benumbed condition would wear off; it *might* be that Lanse would never be able to sit erect again.

"A pretty fix, isn't it?" Lanse said, on the morning of the second day, as, opening his eyes, he found himself alone with his cousin. "Apparently I'm in for it this time; not going to die, but laid up with a vengeance. Well, the ship's fast in port at last. I suppose *now* you've no objection to bringing Margaret over—provided, of course, she will come?"

Great was Katrina Rutherford's joy and triumph when she heard that her "boy," her Lanse, was so near her; "only over on the river, a short day's journey from here." She had "always known" that he would come, and now it was proved that she had been right; she *hoped* they appreciated it (Her "they" meant Winthrop and Margaret.) Spare Margaret? Of course she could spare her. Margaret's place was with her husband; and especially now was it her place if he were not well (Aunt Katrina had not been told how ill Lanse was). It was a great mistake, besides, to suppose that Margaret was so necessary to her; Margaret was not in the least necessary, that was one of their fancies; Celestine was much more useful; Looth too. But the point now was, not to talk about who was useful, the point was to have Margaret *go*; what was she waiting for, Aunt Katrina would like to be informed.

Winthrop, upon reaching East Angels, had asked for Margaret.

"I want to speak to you," he said; "it won't take long, but we mustn't be interrupted. Any empty room will do."

His manner had changed; he did not wait for her answer, but led the way himself across the hall to the "boudoir" of the Old Madam, now never used; nothing had been altered there since the Old Madam's departure, even Mrs. Thorne, with her persistent desire to make everything serve some present use, had left this room untouched.

Winthrop closed the door, they stood there among the Old Madam's stiff chairs; everything was covered with embroidery, her own work; there was a fierce-looking portrait of her on the wall.

"Lanse is here," said Winthrop; "I mean over on the river. He is ill. He wants you to come to him."

At his first words Margaret had given a great start. For a moment she did not speak. Then she stammered, "Did you say—did you say he was ill?" She spoke almost inaudibly.

"It's something like paralysis. I don't know whether it's really that; but at any rate he's helpless."

"Has he asked for me?"

"He has sent me to bring you."

"Did he give you a letter—a note?"

"No; he told me to bring you."

"Are you *sure* he told you that?"

"Good heavens! if I were *not* sure I should be a great deal better off. Why do you keep asking me? Isn't it bad enough for me to have to say it at all? But he *is* ill, and that makes everything different. I couldn't have stood it otherwise."

"Stood—"

"Stood your going to him."

"I must go to him if he is ill."

"Ill—yes; that's the only thing that—" He stopped, and stood looking at her.

"I am afraid he is very ill."

"Yes, he is very ill. But I'm not thinking about Lanse now. I know everything, Margaret—everything except why you have wished, why you have been determined, that I should think of you in the way I have,—that is, with such outrageous, such cruel wrong. Lanse has told me the whole story of his leaving you, *not* your leaving him. And before that, Garda had told me what really happened that afternoon in the woods. Why have you treated me in this way! Why?"

Margaret, whiter than he had ever seen her, stood before him, her hands tightly clasped. She looked like a person strained up to receive a blow.

"If you could only know how I feel when I think what you have been through, and what the truth really was," Winthrop went on; "when I remember my own stupidity, and dense obstinacy, all those years. I can never atone for that, Margaret; never."

Lanse's wife put out her hand, like a person who feels her way, as she went towards the door. "Don't stop me," she said; "I cannot talk now."

Her voice was so strained and husky that he hardly knew it.

She went hastily out.

CHAPTER XXV

Lansing Harold was unable to move from his bed, or in his bed, for a number of weeks. During much of this time, also, he suffered from severe pain.

Dr. Kirby assured Aunt Katrina that the pain was a favorable symptom; it indicated that there was no torpor; and with time, patience, and self-denial, therefore, there would be hope of a cure.

"Lanse isn't patient," Aunt Katrina admitted. "But I have always thought him extremely self-denying; see how he has allowed Margaret, for instance, to do as she pleased." For Aunt Katrina now regarded the Doctor as an intimate personal friend.

The Doctor went over to see Lanse three times a week, Winthrop's horses taking him to the river and bringing him back. On the other days the case was intrusted to the supervision of the local practitioner, or rather to his super-audition, for as Lanse, after the first interview, refused to see him again (he called him a water-wagtail), Margaret was obliged to describe as well as she could to the baffled man the symptoms and general condition of his patient—a patient who was as impatient as possible with every one, including herself.

But save for this small duty, Margaret had none of the responsibilities of a nurse; two men were in attendance. She had sent to Savannah for them, Lanse having declared that he infinitely preferred having men about him—"I can swear at them, you know, when the pain nips me. I can't swear at you yet—you're too much of a stranger." This he brought out in the scowling banter which he had used when speaking to her ever since her arrival. The scowl, however, came from his pain.

He was able to move only his head; in addition to the suffering, the confinement was intolerably irksome to a man of his active habits and fondness for out-door life. Under the course of treatment prescribed by Dr. Kirby he began to improve; but the improvement was slow, and he made it slower by his unwillingness to submit to rules. At the end of two months, however, he was able to use his hands and arms again, they could raise him to a sitting position; the attacks of pain came less frequently, and when they did come it was at night. This gave him his days, and one of the first uses he made of his new liberty was to have himself carried in an improvised litter borne by negroes, who relieved each other at intervals, to a house which he had talked about, when able to talk, ever since he was stricken down. This house was not in itself an attractive abode. But Lanse violently disliked being in a hotel; he had noticed the place before his illness, and thinking of it as he lay upon his bed, he kept declaring angrily that at least he should not feel "hived in" there. The building, bare and solitary, stood upon a narrow point which jutted sharply into the river, so that its windows commanded as uninterrupted a view up and down stream as that enjoyed by the little post-office at the end of the pier; it had the look of a signal-station.

It had not always been so exposed. Once it was an embowered Florida residence, shaded by many trees, clothed in flowering vines.

But its fate was to be purchased at the close of the war by a northerner, who, upon taking possession, had immediately stripped the old mansion of all its blossoming greenery, had cut down the stately trees which stood near, had put in a dozen new windows, and had then painted the whole structure a brilliant, importunate white. This process he called "making it wholesome."

This northerner, not having succeeded in teaching the southern soil how to improve itself, had returned to the more intelligent lands of colder climates; he was obliged to leave his house behind him, and he contemplated with hope the possibility of renting it "for a water-cure." Why a water-cure no one but himself knew. He was a man haunted by visions of water-cures.

Lansing Harold had no intention of trying hydropathy, unless the wide view of the river from all his windows could be called that. But he said that if he were there, at least he should not feel "jostled."

Jostled he certainly was not, he and his two attendants, Margaret and the colored servants she had with some difficulty obtained, had much more the air of Robinson Crusoes and Fridays on their island; for the hotel, which was the nearest house, was five miles distant, and not in sight, and the river was so broad that only an occasional smoke told that there were abodes of men opposite on the low hazy shore.

Once established in his new quarters, Lanse advanced rapidly towards a more endurable stage of existence. He was still unable to move his legs; but he could now bear being lifted into a canoe, and, once in, with a cushion behind him, he could paddle himself over the smooth water with almost as much ease as ever. He sent for a canoe which was just large enough to hold him; boat and occupant seemed like one person, so perfectly did the small craft obey the motion of his oar. One of his men was always supposed to accompany him; the two boats generally started together from the little home pier; but Lanse soon invented a way of ordering his follower to "wait" for him at this point or that, while he took "a run" up some creek that looked inviting. The "run" usually proved the main expedition of the day, and the "waiting" would be perhaps five hours long,—the two attendants could not complain of overwork; they soon learned, however, to go to sleep comfortably in the bottom of the boat. Oftenest of all, Lanse and his canoe went up the Juana; the Jana came from the Monnlungs Swamp; as the spring deepened, and all the flowers came out, Lanse and his little box went floating up to the Monnlungs almost every day.

Mrs. Rutherford had not seen her "boy;" he could not yet endure the motion of any carriage, even the easiest, across the long miles of pine-barren that lay between the river and East Angels, and it would require a brigade or two of negroes, so he said, to carry him all that distance in his litter. As soon as he should feel himself able to undertake so long a journey, he promised to go by steamer to the mouth of the St. John's; here the *Emperadora* could meet him and take him southward by sea to the harbor of Gracias, thence down the lagoon to the landing of East Angels itself.

Aunt Katrina was therefore waiting. But this was a condition of things which somebody was very apt to be enjoying where Lanse was concerned. Lanse had a marked contempt for what he called a "panting life." Under these circumstances, as he never panted himself, there was apt to be somebody else who was panting; by a little looking about one could have found, almost every day, several persons who had the reverse side of his leisurely tastes to bear.

Aunt Katrina, in bearing hers, at least had her Betty; now that Margaret was absent, this good soul remained constantly at East Angels, not returning to her home at all. She led a sort of camping-out existence, however, for dear Kate never asked her to bring down a trunk and make herself comfortable; dear Kate always took the tone that her friend would return home, probably, "about the day after to-morrow." Betty, therefore, had with her only her old carpet-bag, which, though voluminous, had yet its limits; she was constantly obliged to contrive secret methods of getting necessary articles down from Gracias. She lived in this make-shift manner for a long stretch of weeks, heroically wearing her best gown all the time, because to have sent for the second best would have appeared to dear Kate like preparation for a longer visit than she seemed to think she should at present require.

Every day dear Kate wrote a little note of affectionate inquiry to Lanse. These notes were piled up in a particular place in the house on the river; after the first three or four, Lanse never read them. About twice a week Margaret would take it upon herself to reply; and then Mrs. Rutherford would say, "As though I wanted Margaret *Cruger's* answers!" She explained to Betty that Margaret purposely kept Lanse from writing. And then Betty would shake her head slowly with her lips pursed up, but without venturing further answer; for she had already got herself into trouble with Katrina by expatiating warmly upon the "great comfort" it must be to "poor Mr. Harold" to have his wife with him once more.

"Nothing of the sort!" had been Katrina's brief response.

"Such a comfort to *her*, then, poor dear, to be *able* to devote herself to him in this time of trial."

"*Margaret* devote herself!"

"Well, at least, dear Kate, it must be a great comfort to *you* to have them together again, as they ought to be, of course," pursued Betty, hopefully. "It may be—who knows?—probably it *will* be without doubt, the beginning of a *true* reconciliation, a *true* home."

"True fiddle-sticks! It shouldn't be, then, in my opinion, even if it could be; Margaret Cruger has been *much* too leniently dealt with. After deserting her husband as she has done entirely all these years, she shouldn't have been taken back so easily, she should have been made to go down on her *knees* before he forgave her."

"Dear me! do you really think so?" said Betty, dismayed by this picture. "And Mrs. Harold has so much sweet dignity, too."

"It should be stripped from her then, it's all hum; what right has Margaret *Cruger* to such an amount of dignity? Is she Alexandra, Princess of Wales, may I ask?"

"Do you know, I have *always* thought she looked quite a *deal* like her," exclaimed Betty, delighted with this coincidence.

But Katrina's comparison had been an impersonal one, she was not thinking of the fair graceful Princess of the Danes. "My patience! Elizabeth Gwinnet, how dull you are sometimes!" she exclaimed, closing her eyes with a groan.

Elizabeth Gwinnet agreed that she was dull, agreed with an unresentful laugh. Katrina's epithets were a part of the vagaries of her illness, of course; if she, Betty, was sure of anything in this world, she was sure that she was an enormous comfort to her poor dear Kate. And under those circumstances one could agree to anything.

While helpless and in pain, Lansing Harold had been entirely absorbed in his own condition; even Margaret's arrival he had noticed but slightly. This strong, dark man took his illness as an extraordinary dispensation, a tragic miracle; he was surprised that Dr. Kirby was not more agitated, he was surprised that his two attendants, when they came, did not evince a deeper concern. Surely it was a case unprecedented, terrible; surely no one had ever had such an ordeal before. Not once did he emerge from his own personality and look upon his condition as part of the common lot; Lanse, indeed, had never believed that he belonged to the common lot.

He announced to everybody that Fate was treating him with frightful injustice. Why should *he* be maimed and shackled in this way—he, a man who had always led a wholly simple, natural life? *He* had never shut himself up in an office, burned his eyes out over law papers, or narrowed his chest over ledgers; *he* had never sacrificed his liberty in the sordid pursuit of money-getting. On the contrary, he had admired all beautiful things wherever they were to be found, he had breathed the fresh air of heaven, had seen all there was of life and nature, and enjoyed it all in a full, free, sane way. It was monstrous, it was ridiculous, to strike at *him*; strike, and welcome, at the men who kept their windows down! Thus he inveighed, thus he protested, and all in perfectly good faith; Lanse believed of himself exactly what he said.

But once established in a house of his own, and able to float about on the river, promptly his good-humor came back to him; for Lanse, while not in the least amiable, had always had an abundance of good-humor. He began to laugh again, he began to tell Margaret stories connected with his life abroad; Lanse's stories, though the language was apt to be as condensed as that of telegraphic despatches, were invariably good.

There had been no formal explanations between these two, no serious talk. Lanse hated serious talk; and as for explanations, as he had never in his life been in the habit of giving them, it was not likely that he was going to begin now. When Margaret first arrived, and he could scarcely see her from pain, he had managed to say, "Oh, you're back? glad to see you"—as though she had left him but the week before—and this matter-of-course tone he had adhered to ever since; it was the easier since his wife showed no desire to alter it.

He required no direct services from her, his men did everything. As he grew better, he gave her the position of a comrade whom it was a pleasure to meet when he came (in his wheeled chair) to the parlor in the evening; he thanked her gallantly for being there. In this way they lived on, Margaret had been for nine or ten weeks under the same roof with him before he made any allusion to their personal relations; even then it was only a remark or two, uttered easily, and as though he had happened to think of it just then. The remarks embodied the idea that the "interruption" (that was what he called it) which had occurred in their life together should be left undiscussed between them; it had happened, let it therefore remain "happened;" they couldn't improve it by chattering about it (an illusion of weak minds), but they could take up the threads again where they had left them, and go on without any "bother."

Later, he added a few words more; they were not taking up the threads, after all, just where they had left them, but in a much better place; for now they were relieved from any necessity for being sentimental. He admired her greatly, he didn't mind telling her that she had grown infinitely more interesting, as well as handsomer; but his having remained away from her as long as he had, and of his own accord, debarred him, of course, from expecting personal affection from her, at least at present; he certainly didn't expect it, she might rest secure about that; on the other hand, he didn't believe, either—no, not in the least—that she had broken her heart very deeply about *him*. There was no better foundation than this state of affairs for the most comfortable sort of years together, if she would look at it in the right way. What was the cause of most of the trouble between husbands and wives nowadays?—by "nowadays" he meant in modern times, since women had been allowed to complain. Their being so foolish, wasn't it? on one side or the other, as to wish to absorb each other, control each other, in a petty, dogmatic, jealous sort of way. Now in their case there would not be any clashing of that sort; when people had lived apart as they had, voluntarily and contentedly, for eight years, they must at least have got out of the habit of asking prying questions, of expecting a report of everything that happened, of trying to dictate and govern; as to jealousy, it would be rather late in the day to begin that.

These were the only approaches Lanse had made towards a discussion of intimate topics. The reserve was not so remarkable in him as it might have been in another man, for Lanse seldom talked on intimate topics with anybody; his principle, so far as it could be gathered from his life, appeared to have been to allow himself, in actual fact (quiet fact), the most radical liberty of action, while at the same time in speech, in tastes, in general manner, he remained firmly, even aggressively, a conservative; Lanse's "manner" had been much admired. Always, so he would have said, he behaved "as a gentleman should," which had seemed to mean (according to his own idea of it) that he had no local views of anything, that he was fond of the fine arts and good guns, that he had a taste for ablutions and fresh air, for laced shoes and shooting-jackets, and that he never (it had not happened since his early youth, at least) lost control of himself through drink. All this went perfectly with his apparent frankness. It also went perfectly with his real reserves.

On the occasions when he had said his few words to Margaret, he had given her no chance to reply; he had made his remarks as he took up a book. Lanse was sure that he read a great deal, that he was very fond of reading; in reality he read almost nothing, he only turned to reading as a last resort; he was barbarically ignorant regarding the authors of his day, he liked best personal memoirs and letters of the last century; when these failed him, he reread Fielding—fortunately Fielding was inexhaustible.

He was in the habit of saying this. But one evening even Fielding palled.

It was when they had been for nearly two months in the house on the river. He had been out during most of the afternoon in his canoe; his two attendants had now established him upon his sofa, placed everything which they thought he might want within his reach, had adjusted his reading lamp (he had announced that he was going to read), and had then left him. They were to return at ten o'clock and help him to bed; for Lanse was obliged to keep early hours, the night was the dangerous time, and one of the men always slept on a cot bed in the room with him, so as to be within call.

Margaret was sitting near the larger table, where there was a second lamp; she was sewing. Having thrown down his volume, with the sudden realization (it came to him occasionally) that he knew every word of it before beginning, Lanse sat among his cushions, watching her hand come and go.

"You are always sewing on such long things!" he said. "What is the use of your doing that sort of work nowadays, when there are sewing-machines?"

"That's like the American who asked, in Venice, what was the use of people's sketching there nowadays, when there were photographs?"

"Oh, your seam is a work of art, is it?" said Lanse. He was silent for a moment. Then he took up an old grievance. "Evert is abominably selfish not to come over here oftener. He might just as well come over and stay; do you know any earthly reason why he shouldn't?"

"I suppose he thinks he ought not to leave Aunt Katrina—I mean for any length of time."

"He comes for no length, long or short. Aunt Katrina? I thought you said she'd got a lot of people?"

"Only Mrs. Carew."

"Mrs. Carew and five or six servants; that's enough in all conscience. I shouldn't care in the least about Evert if it weren't for the evenings, they're confoundedly long, you must admit that they are—for a person who doesn't sew seams; if I had Ev here I could at least beat him at checkers,—that would be something."

Checkers was the only game Lanse would play, he hated games generally. His method of playing this one was hopelessly bad. That made no difference in his being convinced that it was excellent. He blustered over it always.

Margaret had not answered. After a while, still idly watching her hand come and go, Lanse began to laugh. "No, I'll tell you what it really is, Madge;

I know it as well as if he had drawn up a formal indictment and signed his name; he's all off with me on account of the way I've treated you."

She started; but she kept on taking her stitches.

"Yes. What do you say to my having told him the whole story—just what really happened, and without a shade of excusing myself in any way? Don't you call that pretty good of me? But I found out, too, what I didn't know before—that you yourself have never said a word all this time either to him or to Aunt Katrina; that you have told nothing. I call that pretty good of *you*; I dare say, in the mean while, Aunt Katrina has led you a life!"

"I haven't minded that—she didn't know—"

"It was really very fine of you," said Lanse, appreciatively, after a moment or two of silence, during which he had seemed to review her course, and to sincerely admire it. "It would have been so easy to have considered it your duty to tell, to have called the telling 'setting yourself right;' everybody would have been on your side—would have taken your part. But I can't say, after all, that I'm surprised," he went on. "I have always had the most perfect confidence in you, Madge. If I hadn't, I shouldn't have been so easy, of course, about going away; but I knew I could leave you, I knew I could trust you; I knew you would always be the perfect creature you have shown yourself to be."

"I'm not perfect at all," answered Margaret, throwing her work down with a movement that was almost fierce. "Don't talk to me in that way."

"There! no need to flash out so; remember I'm only a cripple," responded Lanse, amiably. He sat there stroking his short beard with his strong, well-shaped hand, looking at her, as he did so, with some curiosity.

She rose. "Is there anything I can do for you before I go?" And she began to fold up her work.

"Oh, don't go! that's inhuman; it's only a little after nine—there's nearly an hour yet before the executioners come. I didn't mean to vex you, Madge; really I didn't. I know perfectly that you have done what you did, behaved as you have—so admirably (you must excuse my saying it again)—to please yourself, not me; you did it because you thought it right, and you don't want my thanks for it; you don't even want my admiration, probably you haven't a very high opinion of my admiration. I don't condole with you—you may have noticed that; the truth is, you have had your liberty, you have been rid of me, and there has been no disagreeable gossip about it. If you had loved me, there would have been the grief and all that to consider. But there has been no grief; you probably know now, though you didn't then, that you never seriously cared for me at all; of course you *thought* you did."

Margaret was standing, her folded work in her hand, ready to leave the room. "I should—I should have tried," she answered, her eyes turned away.

"Tried? Of course you would have tried, poor child," responded Lanse, laughing. "I should have had that spectacle! You were wonderfully good, you had a great sense of duty; you really married me from duty—because I told you that I should go to the bad without you, and you believed it, and thought you must try; and you mistook the interest you felt in me on that account for affection—a very natural mistake at your age. Never mind all that now, I only want you to admit that I might have been worse, I might have been brutal, tyrannical, in petty ways, I might have been a pig; instead of leaving you as I did, I might have stayed at home—and made you wish that I *had* left! Even now I scarcely touch your personal liberty; true, I ask you to keep house for me, set up a home and make me comfortable again; but outside of that I leave you very free, you shall do quite as you please. Luckily we've got money enough—that is, you have—not to be forced to sacrifice ourselves about trifles; if you want your breakfast at eight o'clock, and I mine at eleven, why, we can have it in that way; it won't be necessary for us to change our customs in the very least for each other, and I assure you in the long-run that tells. It's possible, of course, that you may hate me; but I don't believe you do; and, in case you don't, I see no reason why we shouldn't lead an easy life together. Really, looking at it in that way, it's a very pretty little prospect—for people of sense."

As he concluded with these words, genially uttered, Margaret dropped suddenly into a chair which was near her and covered her face with her hands.

Lanse looked at her, there was genuine kindness in his beautiful dark eyes with the yellow lights in them. "There's one question I might ask you, Margaret—but no, I won't; it's really none of my business. You will always *act* like an angel; your thoughts are your own affair."

Margaret still sat motionless, her face covered.

"I'm very sorry you feel so; I meant to be—I want to be—as considerate as possible. Great heavens!" Lanse went on, "what a fettered, restricted existence you women—the good ones—do lead! I have the greatest sympathy for you. When you're wretched, you can't do anything; you can't escape, and you can't take any of the compensations men take when they want to balance ill luck in other directions; all you can do is—sit still and bear it! I wonder you endure it as you do. But I won't talk about it, talking's all rot; short of killing myself, I don't know that there's anything I can do that would improve the situation; and that wouldn't be of any use either, at least to you, because it would leave you feeling guilty, and guilt you could never bear. Come, hold up your head, Madge; nothing in this stupid life is worth feeling so wretched about; life's nothing but rubbish, after all. Get the checker-board and we'll have a game."

Margaret had risen. "I can't to-night."

"But what am I to do, then?" began Lanse, in a complaining tone. He was as good as his word, he had already dismissed the subject from his mind. "Well, if you must go," he went on, "just hand me that book of poor Malleson's, first."

This was a book of sketches of the work of Mino da Fiesole, the loving, patient studies of a young American who had died in Italy years before, when Lanse was there. Lanse had been kind to him, at the last had closed his eyes, and had then laid him to sleep in that lovely shaded cemetery under the shadow of the pyramid outside the walls of Rome—sweet last resting-place that lingers in many a traveller's memory. The book of sketches had been left to him, and he was very fond of it.

As Margaret gave it to him he saw her face more clearly, saw the traces of tears under the dark lashes. "Yes, go and rest," he said, compassionately; "go to bed. I should reproach myself very much if I thought it was waiting upon me, care about me, that had tired you so."

"No, I have very little to do; the men do everything," Margaret answered. "I haven't half as much to attend to here as I have at home." She seemed to wish to reassure him on this point.

"At home?" said Lanse, jocularly. "What are you talking about? This is your home, isn't it?—wherever I happen to be."

But evidently his wife's self-control had been rudely shaken when her tears had mastered her, for now she could not answer him, she turned and left the room.

"Courage!" he called after her as she went towards the door. "You should do as I do—not mind trifles; you should shake them off."

She went with a swift step to her own room, and threw herself face downward upon a low couch, her head resting upon her clasped hands; the sudden movement loosened her hair, soon it began to slip from its fastenings and drop over her shoulders in a thick, soft, perfumed mass; then, falling forward, lock by lock, the long ends touched the floor.

As she lay thus behind her bolted doors, fighting with an unhappiness so deep that her whole heart was sobbing and crying, though now she did not shed outwardly a tear, her husband, stroking his brown beard meditatively, was getting a great deal of enjoyment out of poor Malleson's book. Lanse had a very delicate taste in such matters; he knew a beautiful outline when he saw it, from a single palmetto against the blue, on a point in the St. John's, to these low reliefs of the sweetest sculptor of the Renaissance. Long before, he had told Margaret that he married her for her profile; slim, unformed girl as she was, there had been, from the first moment he saw her, an immense satisfaction for his eyes in the poise of her head and the clearness of her features every time she entered the room.

Whether he would have found any satisfaction in these same outlines, could he have seen them prone in their present abandonment, only himself could have told.

He would have said, probably, that he found no satisfaction at all. Lansing Harold, as has been remarked before, had a great deal of benevolence.

CHAPTER XXVI

"I don't know how to tell you, Mrs. Harold, what has happened," began Dr. Kirby. "I cannot explain it even to myself." The Doctor was evidently very unhappy, and much disturbed.

He was in the sitting-room of the house on the river—a place not so desolate after eight months of Margaret's habitation there. She could not restore the blossoming vines to the stripped exterior, she could not bring to life again the old trees; but within she had made a great change; the rooms were fairly comfortable now, green blinds gave a semblance of the former leafy shade.

But more than the rooms was the mistress of them herself transformed. The change was not one of manner or expression; it was the metamorphosis which can be produced by a complete alteration of dress. For Lanse had objected to the simplicity of his wife's attire, and especially to the plain, close arrangement of her hair. "You don't mean it, I know," he said, "but it has an appearance of affectation, a sort of 'holier than thou' air. I hate to see women going about in that way; it looks as if they thought themselves so beautiful that they didn't mind calling attention to it—with sanctimonious primness, of course; it's the most conspicuous thing a woman can do."

"It's not a matter of principle with me; it's only my taste," Margaret answered. "I have always liked simplicity in others, and so I have dressed in that way myself."

"Alter it, then; with your sort of face you couldn't possibly look flashy; and you might look prettier—less like a saint. There, don't be enraged, I know you haven't a grain of that kind of pose. But it seems to me, Margaret, that you might very well dress to please me, since I regard you as a charming picture, keeping my hands off." And he laughed.

The next steamer that touched at the long pier (it was not two hours afterwards) took from there half a dozen hastily written letters to carry north.

"What in the world—why, I hardly *knew* you," Aunt Katrina said, ten days later, when her niece came over to East Angels to see her; now that Lanse was better, she could come oftener.

"Lanse wished it," Margaret answered as she took her seat.

"And very properly. You certainly had a most tiresome way of having your things made—so deadly plain; it looked as if you wanted people to think you either very Quakerish or very miserable, I never knew which."

"If I had been miserable I shouldn't have paid so much attention to it, should I? It takes a great deal of attention to dress in that way." She spoke, if not smilingly, then at least in the even tone which people now called "always so cheerful."

"Oh, I don't know what you really *were*, I only meant how you looked. I am glad, at least, that you acknowledge that it takes a great stock of vanity to go against all the fashions. Well, you don't look Quakerish now!"

"You like the dress, then?"

"It's *lovely*," said Aunt Katrina, scanning every detail from the hat to the shoe. "Expensive, of course?"

"Yes."

"And Lanse likes that?"

"He wishes me to dress richly; he says it's more becoming to me."

"I think that's so nice of him, he wants you to look, I suppose, as well as you *can*" said Aunt Katrina, magnanimously. "And certainly you do look a great deal better."

Whether Margaret looked better was a question whose answer depended upon the personal taste of those who saw her; she looked, at least, very different. The sumptuous wrap with its deep fringes, the lace of the scarf, the general impression of costly fabrics and of color in her attire, brought out the outlines of her face, as the curling waves of her hair over her forehead deepened the blue of her eyes. On her white arms now, at home in the evenings, bracelets gleamed, the flash of rings came from her little hands; her slender figure trailed behind it rich silks of various light hues.

"You are a beautiful object nowadays, Margaret," Lanse said more than once. "Fancy your having known how, all this time, without ever having used your talent!"

"It's my dress-maker's talent."

"Yes; she must have a great deal to carry out your orders."

He was especially pleased one evening. She came in, bringing his newspaper, which had just arrived by the steamer; she was dressed in a long gleaming gown of satin, with long tight sleeves; she wore a little ruff of Venetian lace, there was a golden comb in her dark-hair. A fan made of the bright plumage of some tropical bird lay against the satin of her skirt; it hung by a ribbon from the broad satin belt, which, fastened by a golden buckle, defined her slender waist.

"You look like a fine old engraving," he said.

She stood holding the paper towards him. But for a moment he did not take it, he was surveying her critically; then he lifted his eyes to her face, there was a smile in them. "You did it—do it—to please me?" he said.

She did not answer.

"Because you think it your duty to do what I wish. And because, too, you are a trifle afraid of me!" He laughed. "It would have an even better effect, though, if you wouldn't take it quite so seriously; couldn't you contrive to get a little pleasure out of it on your own account?—I mean the looking so handsome."

She gave him the paper, and went across to her work-table. "I am delighted to look handsome," she said.

"No, you're not. It was probably easier for you to dress as you used to—plainly; more in accordance with your feelings, women like to be in accordance. When they're completely satisfied, or very unhappy, they brush their hair straight back from their faces. Well, yours curls enough now!"

"The truth is, Madge, you're too yielding," he resumed after a short silence. "I take advantage of it, of course—I always shall; but you would get on a great deal better yourself, you might even have had more influence over me (if you care about that), if you had been, if you were now, a little less—patient."

"I suppose there's no use in my repeating that I'm not patient at all," answered Margaret. She was taking some balls of silk from the drawer.

"You want me to think it's self-control. Well, perhaps it is. But then, you know, unbroken self-control—"

"Would you mind it if I should ask you not to discuss it—my self-control?" Her hands were beginning to tremble.

"Put your hands in your pocket if you don't want me to see them," said Lanse, laughing; "they always betray you—even when your voice is steady. What a temper you've got—though you do curb it so tightly! At least you're infinitely better off than you would have been if you had happened to care for me. That's been the enormous blessing of your life—your not caring; just supposing you *had* cared! You ought to be very thankful; and you ought to reckon up your blessings every now and then, for fear of forgetting some of them; we ought all to do that, I think."

He said this with great gravity. Not that he felt in the least grave; but it was a way Lanse had of amusing himself, once in a while,—to make remarks of this sort with a very solemn face.

He looked at her for a moment or two longer as she sat with her eyes bent upon her knitting. "You're in the right chair," he said at length, "but you're sitting too straight. Won't you please take that footstool, put your feet on it, and then lean back more? You long lithe women look better that way."

She did not move.

"Come," he said, "you're furious; but you know you ought to humor me. It's only that I want my picture more complete—that's all."

And then, with nervous quickness, she did what he asked.

It was upon the morning following this little conversation that Dr. Kirby made his appearance at the house on the river and declared that he could not "explain."

"Tell me without explaining," Margaret suggested.

But this at first seemed to the Doctor even more difficult than the other alternative; it would have been so much more in accordance with his sense of the fitness of things to ascend this stumbling-block which had fallen in their path by means of a proper staircase, carpeted steps of probabilities, things he had foreseen—intuitions. But in fact he had foreseen nothing; he felt that he could not make a staircase. So he gave one great hard bound.

"Garda is engaged," he announced. "To Lucian Spenser."

Margaret was greatly astonished. "I didn't know he was back," she said.

"He has only just come. She went up to Norfolk with my cousin, Sally Lowndes"—here the Doctor stopped, gazing at Margaret inquiringly.

"Yes, I left it to you to decide about her going—don't you remember?"

"I decided wrongly. Sally was obliged to go, and anxious to take Garda—I was in Charleston, and I allowed it. I had no business to!" said the Doctor, slapping his knee suddenly and fiercely. "I distinctly disapprove of much travelling for young girls—mere aimless gadding about. But I have been corrupted, to a certain degree, by the new nor—the new modern ideas that are making their way everywhere at present; I could bury my head in a hay-stack! When did you hear from her last?"

"I had a letter from Norfolk immediately after her arrival."

"Before she had met him. And nothing since?"

"Nothing."

"Yes, she said she should rather have me tell you than write herself."

"She thought you would be on her side."

"No, madam, no; she couldn't have thought that—that would be impossible. But she was good enough to say that I should, in the telling, be certain to make you laugh. And that was what she wanted."

Moisture glittered suddenly in his eyes as he brought this out. He pretended it was not there, and searching for his handkerchief, he coughed gruffly, complaining of "a cold."

"I certainly don't laugh," said Margaret. "But perhaps we need not be so—so troubled about it, Doctor. The first thing now is to have her come home."

"She's back in Charleston."

"Oh!"

"Yes. As soon as I received Sally's letter—she wrote at once—I started immediately for Norfolk. I saw Mr. Spenser—in my quality of guardian it was proper that I should see him. And I brought the two ladies home."

"And not Mr. Spenser too?"

"I don't know anything about Mr. Spenser!" Then, after a moment, "I reckon he will follow," the Doctor murmured, dejectedly.

"And I—who thought he was in Venice!"

"He was in Venice until a few weeks ago. I don't know in the least what brought him home. And I don't know in the least what brought him to Norfolk, unless it was, as I was told, some insane fancy for sketching the Dismal Swamp;—of all places in the world the miry old Dismal! And to think that I should have let Garda go there, at just that moment! It's a combination of fortuitous chances which seems to me absolutely infernal!—I beg your pardon, madam"—here the Doctor rose, bowing ceremoniously, with his hand on the broad expanse of beautifully starched linen, which kept its place unmoved over his disturbed breast. "It is not often that I am betrayed into language unsuited to a lady's presence. I ask you to excuse me."

"You do not like Mr. Spenser," said Margaret.

The Doctor stared. "Do you?"

"I suppose it is not so much whether we like him, as whether we approve of him for Garda. But I am afraid she would not listen to us even if we should disapprove."

"I think you are in error there," said the Doctor, beginning to walk to and fro with quick short steps. Much as he liked Margaret, it was with anger that he answered her now.

"I must tell you what I think, mustn't I?" said the other guardian, gently. "And I think she has cared for him a long time."

"It is impossible for me to agree with you. Long time? Permit me to ask how long you mean? In the mean while she has been engaged to another man—Evert Winthrop. Do you forget that?"

"I don't think she realized fully—she was very young; she is extremely impulsive always," answered his colleague, wandering rather helplessly for a moment among her phrases. Then she spoke more decidedly. "But now she knows, now she is sure; she is sure it is Lucian she cares for."

"She is fanciful, and this is only another fancy. Sally, too, has been much to blame."

"I do not think Garda is fanciful," said Margaret. "And—it is not a childish feeling, her liking for Lucian Spenser."

The Doctor stopped on the other side of the room. Then he came back and stood gazing at Margaret in silence. "You are a woman, and you are good," he said at last. "She is very fond of you, she tells you everything, and you *must* know. If therefore you say that she—"

"Yes," answered Margaret, "I do know. I am sure she cares for him very, very much." Here some of Garda's extraordinarily frank expressions about Lucian, and the delight it gave her to even look at him, coming suddenly into her memory, over all her fair face there rose a sweet deep blush.

The Doctor turned away and dropped into a chair.

"There is nothing against Mr. Spenser, I believe," Margaret began again, after a short pause.

"It isn't that. No, I believe there is nothing." He sat there, his figure looking unusually small, his eyes turned away.

Margaret asked some questions. By degrees the Doctor answered them. He said that Lucian was possessed of "a genteel income." He had not accepted his wife's large fortune; she had left everything to him, but he had immediately given the whole back to her relatives, retaining only the profits of some investments which she had made, since their marriage, under his advice; this sum the Doctor described as "a competence."

"When is Garda coming home?" Margaret asked.

"She says she isn't coming; she says she knows you have no place for her here—no time; and she doesn't wish to stay with any one but you."

"She does not mean that. I think she should come, she has been in Charleston a long time; Mrs. Lowndes has been wonderfully kind."

"Oh, as to that, Sally likes to have her there. She says it has made her 'young again' to see Garda. And to admire (I don't know what she meant by that) Adolfo Torres."

"Is he there still?"

"He is there still. He doesn't believe in the least in Garda's engagement."

"He didn't believe in the other one," said Margaret. And then she was sorry she had said it, for the Doctor jumped up and seized his hat; it was still insupportable to him, the thought of those two engagements.

"He's a hallucinated idiot!" he said, violently. Then, controlling himself, he took leave of Margaret, bowing over her hand with his old stately ceremony. Mr. Harold was in the garden? He would go out and see him there. It was most satisfactory, certainly, the improvement in Mr. Harold.

On the present occasion the Doctor found Lanse on a couch which he had had carried out to the garden; here he lay contentedly smoking, and looking at the river. Lanse liked the Doctor; it was an ever-fresh amusement to him to realize that his large, long, muscular self was committed to the care of that "pottering little man." The Doctor was not in the least "pottering." But Lanse really thought that all short men with small hands, who were without an active taste for guns, were of that description. The sad Doctor made but a brief visit this time; then he started homeward. He had still the news about Garda to tell in Gracias. At present it was known only to ma.

Garda did not comply with the wish of her friends, and return to them. She wrote a dozen letters about it, but in actual presence she remained away. Most of these epistles were to Margaret. As time went on she wrote to Margaret every day.

But her letters were not letters at all, in the usual sense of the word; they were brief diaries, rapidly jotted down, of the feelings of the moment; they were pæans, rhapsodies, bubbling exclamations of delight; none of them ever exceeded in length a page.

They seemed to Margaret very expressive. She did not know what Garda might be writing to the Kirbys, the Moores, and Mrs. Carew; but what Garda wrote to her she kept to herself.

This was the girl's first letter after Margaret's note urging her to return:

> "Margaret, I *can't* come—don't ask me; for none of them there would sympathize with me—not even you. It isn't that I want sympathy—I never even think of it. But I don't want the least disagreeable thing now when I am so *blissful*—bliss is the only word. Lucian comes in every morning on the train. The Doctor said that of course he would not stay all the time in Charleston. So to satisfy him Lucian stays four miles out.
>
> "Oh, Margaret, everything is so enchanting!

"Garda."

"Dear Margaret,—Every morning I watch until he opens the gate" (she wrote a day later), "and then I run down to meet him in the hall. We don't stay in the house, we go into the garden. Mrs. Lowndes says she loves to have him come, because he reminds her so much of Mr. Lowndes—'Roger,' she calls him. And she says it makes her young again in her heart to see us. And perhaps it does in her heart, but the change hasn't reached the outside yet. I am expecting him every minute, there he comes now.

"Garda."

"Dear Margaret,—If I could stay with you, I would come back to-morrow," she wrote in answer to a second letter from Margaret, which urged her strongly to return. "But I know you don't want me now—that is, you can't have me—and where else could I stay? The Doctor *hates* Lucian—he may pretend, but he *does*. If I should stay at the rectory, Mrs. Moore would be sure to say, how *pleasant* for Lucian and I to read poetry on the veranda, because that is what she and Middleton used to do when they were engaged. But Lucian and I don't want to read any poetry on verandas.

Garda."

"Dear Margaret,—Lucian has gone for the night, and there's nothing else to do, so I thought I would write to you. Mrs. Lowndes has just been in. She brought a daguerreotype of Mr. Lowndes, taken when he was young, and she says she knows exactly how I feel, because she used to feel just the same; when she was at the window, and saw 'Roger' coming down the street, the very calves of her legs used to quiver, she says. Roger must have been stout—at least he is in the daguerreotype, and he wore glasses.

"Lucian is painting me; but I only wish I could paint *him*. Oh, Margaret, he *is* so beautiful!

Garda."

"Dearest Margaret,—I'm so glad I am alive, it's so nice to be alive. People say life's dreadful, but to me it's perfectly delicious every single minute. I thought I would tell you how happy I was before going to bed,—I love to *write it down*.

Garda."

The Doctor went up to Charleston again. He was much displeased with the course things were taking, he spoke with a good deal of severity to Sally Lowndes.

Sally, who was soft-bodied as well as soft-hearted (her figure was a good deal relaxed), shed tears. Then, recovering some spirit, she wished to know what the Doctor had expected *her* to do? It was true that that sweet Garda had left off her lessons (up to this time she had "had instruction," that is, teachers had arrived at fixed hours); but Sally was decidedly of the opinion that a girl who was so soon to be married should be relieved at least of "*school-room* drudgery."

"Nothing of the sort," said the Doctor; "she should be kept even more closely to her books. Your ideas are provincial and ridiculous, Sally; I don't know where you obtained them."

"From my mother," answered Sally, with a pink flush of excitement in her faded cheeks. "From my grandmother too—who was yours also. It is *you* who are changed, Reginald; it has never been the custom in our family to keep the girls down at their books after sixteen."

This was true. But the very truth of it made the Doctor more angry. "I shall take her back with me," he said.

"She doesn't wish to go."

"That makes no difference."

And then Sally "supposed" that it was not his intention to drag her back "in chains?" Mrs. Lowndes was evidently much displeased with Cousin Reginald.

The Doctor took Garda to a remote part of the garden. Here he placed before her in serious words the strong wish he had that she should return with him to Gracias.

Garda laughed out merrily. Then she came and kissed him. "Don't ask me to do anything so horribly disagreeable," she said, coaxingly.

"Would it be disagreeable?" asked the Doctor, his voice changing to pathos.

"Of course. For you're not nice to Lucian, you know you're not; how can I like that?"

"I will be—nice," said the Doctor, borrowing her word, though the use of it in that sense was to him like turning a somersault.

"Would you really try?" said Garda. She came behind him, putting her arms round his neck and resting her head on his shoulder. "You never could," she said, fondly. And then, as though he were some big good-natured animal, a magnanimous elephant or bear, she let him feel the weight of her little dimpled chin.

"I am weak because I have loved you so long, my child. I might insist; you are my ward. But it seems to me that you ought to care more about doing a little as we wish, Mrs. Harold agrees with me in thinking this."

"Margaret is *sweet*; I love her dearly. But, do you know"—here she disengaged herself, and began with a sudden inconsequent industry to gather flowers—"it's so funny to me that you should think, either of you, for one moment, that I would leave Lucian now."

"He could come too. A little later." The Doctor was driven to this concession.

"But I shouldn't see him as I do here, you know I shouldn't. Here we do quite as we please; no one ever comes to this part of the garden but ourselves; we might be on a desert island—only it would have to be an island of flowers."

"And you care more for this than for our wishes?" began the Doctor. Then he took a lighter tone. "Of course you don't; you will come home with me, my child; we will start this afternoon." Watching her move about among the bushes as she gathered her roses, he had fallen back into his old belief; this young face where to him were still so plainly visible the childish outlines of the little girl he had been used to lead about by the hand—even of the dimpled baby he remembered so well—he could not bring himself to realize that it had gained older expressions, expressions he did not know.

"I'm very sorry, dear," Garda answered, generally. And then she knelt down to peer through a bush which might perhaps be holding its best buds hidden.

The Doctor, completely routed by the word which she had without the least effort used—the maturity of that "dear," addressed her at last, though unconscious that he was doing so, in the tone of equality. "It isn't as though you had anything to bear, like the prospect of a long engagement, as though there were any difficulties in the way; your marriage is to come so soon," he pleaded.

"Soon?" said Garda. "Six long months! Do you call that 'soon?'" She stopped gathering roses, and sat down on a garden bench. "Six months! I must see him every day, and for a long while every day; that will be the *only* way to bear it." Then her words ceased; but her splendid eyes, meeting the Doctor's (she had forgotten that he was there), grew fuller and fuller of the loveliest dreaming expression, until the poor guardian—he realized that she would not perceive his departure—could not stand there and watch it any longer. He turned abruptly and went away.

> "Dear Margaret,—The Doctor has gone" (Garda wrote the next day). "And I am afraid he is displeased. Apparently we please no one but ourselves and Sally Lowndes! Margaret, when my wedding-day really comes at last, nobody must touch me but you; you must dress me, and you must put on my veil, and the orange-blossoms (from the old East Angels grove—I won't have any others). And then, just before we go down-stairs, you must say you are *pleased*. And you must forgive me all I have done—and been too—because I *couldn't* help it. I shall come over from Gracias, and go down on my knees to Mr. Harold to beg him to let me be with you, or rather to let *you*; he must, he shall say yes."

But Lanse was not called upon to go through this ordeal.

He had already said, "*You* go!" in rather a high-noted tone of surprised remonstrance when Margaret suggested, some time before, that she should go herself to Charleston and bring Garda back. "And leave me shut up alone here!" he added, as if to bring home to her the barbarity of her proposal.

"The servants do very well at present."

"They don't look as you do," Lanse answered, gallantly. "I must have something to look at."

"But I think I ought to go."

"You can dismiss that 'ought' from your mind, there are other 'oughts' that come nearer. In fact, viewing the matter impartially, you should never have consented in the beginning, Madge, to take charge of that girl, without first consulting me." Lanse brought out this last touch with much judicial gravity. "Fortunately your guardianship, such as it is, will soon be over," he went on; "she will have a husband to see to her. Apparently she needs one."

"That won't be for six months yet."

"Call it two; as I understand it, there's nothing but dogmatic custom between them, and as Florida isn't the land of custom—"

"Yes, it is."

"Well, even grant that; the girl is, from all accounts, a rich specimen of wilfulness—"

"Of naturalness."

"Oh, if they're guided by naturalness," said Lanse, "they won't even wait two."

And it was not two, when early one morning, in old St. Michael's Church in Charleston, with Sally Lowndes, excited and tearful, as witness—their only one save an ancient little uncle of hers, who had come in from his rice plantation to do them the favor of giving the bride (whom he had never seen before) away, Edgarda Thorne and Lucian Spenser were married.

The Rev. Batton Habersham, as he came robed in his surplice from the vestry-room, could not help being conscious, even then and there, that he had never seen so beautiful a girl as the one who now stood waiting at the chancel-rail—not in the veil she had written about, or the orange-blossoms from East Angels, but in an every-day white frock, and garden hat covered with roses. The bridegroom was very handsome also. But naturally the clergyman was not so much impressed by Lucian's good points as by Garda's lovely ones. Sally Lowndes was impressed by Lucian, she gazed at him as one gazes at a portrait; Lucian looked very handsome, very manly, and very much in love—a happy combination, Sally thought. And then, with fresh sweet tears welling in her eyes, she knelt down for the benediction (though it was not given to her), and thought of "Roger," and the day when she should see him again in paradise.

The Rev. Batton Habersham, who was officiating in St. Michael's for a week only, during the absence of the rector, was a man unknown to fame even in his own diocese. But it is possible to do a great deal of good in the world without fame, and Batton Habersham did it; his little mission chapel was on one of the sea islands. Always thereafter he remembered the early morning marriage of that beautiful girl in the dim, empty old Charleston church as the most romantic episode of his life. Fervently he hoped that she would be happy; for even so good a man is more earnest (unconsciously) in his hopes for the happiness of a bride with eyes and hair like Garda's than he is for that of one with tints less striking. Though the relation, all the same, between the amount of coloring matter in the visual orbs or capillary glands, and the degree of sweetness and womanly goodness in the heart beneath, has never yet been satisfactorily determined.

An hour later the northward-bound train was carrying two supremely happy persons across the Carolinas towards New York—the Narrows—Italy.

"Well, we have all been young once, Sally," the little old rice planter had said to his weeping niece, as the carriage drove away from the hospitable old mansion of the Lowndes'. Garda had almost forgotten that they were there, Sally and himself, as they had stood for a moment at the carriage door; but she had looked so lovely in her absorbed felicity that he forgave her on the spot, though of course he wondered over her choice, and "couldn't imagine" what she could see in that "ordinary young fellow." He went back to his plantation. But he was restless all the evening. At last, about midnight, he got out an old miniature and some letters; and any one who could have looked into the silent room later in the night would have seen the little old man still in his arm-chair, his face hidden in his hand, the faded pages beside him.

"It is perhaps as well," said Margaret Harold. She was trying to administer some comfort to Dr. Kirby, when, two days later, he sat, a flaccid parcel of clothes, on the edge of a chair in her parlor, staring at the floor.

Mrs. Rutherford was triumphant. "A runaway match! And *that* is the girl you would have married, Evert. What an escape!"

"*She* has escaped," Winthrop answered, smiling.

"What do you mean? Escaped?—escaped from what?"

"From all of us here."

"Not from me," answered Aunt Katrina, with dignity. "*I* never tried to keep her, *I* always saw through her perfectly from the very first. Do you mean to say that you understand that girl even now?" she added, with some contradiction.

"Yes, I think I do—*now*," Winthrop answered.

"I don't envy you your knowledge! *Poor* Lucian Spenser—what could have possessed him?"

"He? He's madly in love with her, of course."

"I'm glad at least you think he's a fool," said Aunt Katrina, applying her vinaigrette disdainfully to her well-shaped nose.

"Fool? Not at all; he's only tremendously happy."

"The same thing—in such a case."

"I don't know about that. The question is, is it better to be tremendously happy for a little while, and unreasonable; or to be reasonable all the time, and never tremendously happy?"

"Oh, if you're going to talk *rationalism*—" said Aunt Katrina.

Immediately after her return from Norfolk, in the interval before Lucian came, Garda sent for Adolfo Torres. When he appeared she begged him to do her a favor, namely, to leave Charleston for the present.

"Is it that you wish me to return to Gracias?" asked Adolfo. "The place is a desperation without you."

"You need not go to Gracias if you don't want to; but please go away from here. Go to the Indian River," she suggested, with a sudden inspiration.

"I will go to the Indian River certainly—if that is your wish," replied the Cuban; "though I do not know"—this he added rather longingly—"what harm I do here."

"No harm at all. But I want you to go." She smiled brightly, though there was also a good deal of sympathy in her eyes as she surveyed his lack-lustre countenance.

"That is enough—your wish. I go—I go at once." He took leave of her.

She called him back, and looked at him a moment. Then she said, "Yes, go. And I will write to you."

This was a great concession, Adolfo felt it to be such.

The letter was long in coming; and when it did come at last, it dealt him, like an actual hand, a prostrating blow. It was dated several days after that morning which had seen the early marriage in St. Michael's, and the signature, when his dazed eyes reached it, was one he did not know—Edgarda Spenser.

The Cuban had received this note at dusk. He went out and wandered about all night. At daylight he came in, dressed himself afresh and carefully, and had his boots polished—a process not so much a matter of course on the Indian River at that day as in some other localities. Next he said a prayer, on his knees, in his rough room in the house where he was lodged. Then he went out and asked the old hunter, his host, for the favor of the loan of one of his guns for the morning.

With this gun he departed into the woods. He was no sportsman; but this did not matter, since the game he had in view was extremely docile, it was so docile that it would even arrange itself in the best possible position for the ball.

But the desperate young man—his manner was calm as he made his way through the beautiful southern forest—was not permitted to end his earthly existence then. A hand seized his shoulder. "Are you mad, Adolfo?" said Manuel Ruiz, tears gleaming in his eyes as he almost threw his friend to the ground in the quick, violent effort he made to get possession of the gun. Then, seeing that Adolfo was looking at him very strangely, "If you come another step nearer, I'll shoot you down!" he shouted.

The Cuban did not say, "That is what I want;" he did not move or speak.

Manuel immediately began to talk. "They sent me down here, Adolfo; they had heard, and they were afraid for you. I had just got home, and they asked me to come—your aunt asked me."

"My aunt asked you," repeated Torres, mechanically.

"Yes, Adolfo, your aunt. You must care something for *her*," said Manuel. He looked uneasily about him.

And then hurrying through the wood, came Madam Giron.

The loving-hearted, sweet-tempered woman was much moved. She took her dead sister's unhappy boy in her arms, and wept over him as though he had been her own child; she soothed him with motherly caresses; she said, tenderly, that she had not been kind enough to him, that she had been too much taken up with her own children; "But now—*now*, my dearest—" This all in Spanish, the sweetest sound in the world to poor Torres' ears.

A slight convulsion passed over his features, though no tears came. He was young enough to have felt acutely the loneliness of his suffering, the solitude of the death he was on his way to seek. He stood perfectly still; his aunt was now leaning against him as she wept, he put one arm protectingly round her; he felt a slow, slow return towards, not a less torturing pain, but towards greater courage in bearing it, in this sympathy which had come to him. Even Manuel had shown sympathy. "I feel—I feel that I have been—rather cowardly," he said at last in a dull tone.

"No, no, dear," said his aunt, putting up her soft hand to stroke his dark hair. "It was very natural, we all understand."

And then a mist did show itself for an instant in the poor boy's eyes.

That same evening, Garda, far at sea, sitting with her head on Lucian's shoulder under the brilliant stars, answered a question he asked. She did not answer it at first, she was too contented to talk. Then, as he asked it again, "What ever became of that mediæval young Cuban of mine?"

"Oh, Adolfo?" she said. "I sent him down to the Indian River."

"To the Indian River? What in the world did you do that for?"

"He was in Charleston, and you were coming; I didn't want him there."

"Were you afraid he would attack me?" asked Lucian, laughing.

"I was afraid he would suffer,—in fact, I knew he would; and I didn't want to see it. He can suffer because he is like me—*he* can love."

"Poor fellow!"

"Yes. But I never cared for him; and he *wouldn't* see it."

"And ''way down there in the land of the cotton,' I don't suppose he knows yet what has happened, does he?" said Lucian.

"Oh yes; I wrote to him from New York."

"You waited till then? Wasn't that rather hard?"

"Are you finding fault with me?" she murmured, turning her head so that her lips could reach and rest against his bending face.

"*Fault!*" said Lucian, taking her in his arms.

Adolfo passed out of their memory.

CHAPTER XXVII

"I cannot let you go alone," said Evert Winthrop, decidedly.

He was speaking to Margaret. They were in the East Angels drawing-room, Betty Carew hovering near, and agreeing with perfect sincerity now with one, now with the other, in the remarkable way which was part of the breadth of her sympathy.

"But it's not in the least necessary for you to go," Margaret repeated. "Even if the storm should break before I reach the river, the carriage can be made perfectly tight."

"From the look of the sky, I am almost sure that we shall have a blow before the rain," Winthrop responded; "in the face of such a probability, I couldn't allow you to start across the barrens alone—it's absurd to suppose I should."

Margaret stood hesitating. "You want me to give it up—postpone it. But I cannot get rid of the idea that something has happened—I have had no letter for so long; even if Lanse had not cared to write himself, one of the men, Elliot or Dodd, would have done so, it seems to me, under any ordinary circumstances."

"Lanse probably keeps them too busy."

"They always have their evenings."

But Winthrop showed scanty interest in the evenings of Elliot and Dodd. "For myself, I can't pretend to be anxious," he said—"I mean about Lanse; I am only anxious about you."

"But if I don't go now, I can't go until to-morrow noon; before that time I shouldn't meet a boat that stops at our landing. That would make a delay of twenty-four hours." She looked at him as she said this, with a sort of unconscious appeal.

"I doubt whether anything very exciting could happen over there in twice twenty-four; it isn't an exciting place."

"Of course you think me obstinate. But I cannot help feeling that I ought to go."

"*Perfectly* natural," said Betty. "I should feel just the same in your place—I know I should—not hearing for *so* long."

"It's that—the silence," said Margaret. "I have been disturbed about it for several days."

"Go, by all means, if you feel in that way," said Winthrop. "I haven't the least desire to prevent it—as you seem to think; I only say that I shall go too."

"Yes; and that is what I don't want." She turned away and stepped out on the balcony to scan the sky.

A dark haze edged the eastern horizon. It was far away at present, lying low down on the sea, but it would come, it was already coming, westward; a clear, empty-looking space of cold pearl-hued light preceded it. Here on the lagoon the atmosphere was breathlessly still, not a sound of any kind stirred the warm silence. "Perhaps it will be only a rain," said Margaret, rather helplessly. She looked very uncomfortable.

"Yes, I reckon that's all it *will* be," said Betty, who had followed her to the balcony door. "And then, too, if it *should* be anything more, Mr. Winthrop will be with you, of course; that is, in case you decide to go; and if you don't go, why then he won't, you know; so either way, it's all for the best."

Margaret turned and came back into the drawing-room. Winthrop was standing by the table where she had left him; his eyes met hers, she saw that he would not yield. "I don't dare give it up, I don't dare wait," she broke out with sudden agitation. "Something has happened, nothing less could have kept both of the men from writing, when I gave them my express orders. I don't understand why you don't agree with me."

"You see probabilities, and Lanse isn't a devotee of probabilities, as a general thing. Didn't the last letter say that he had begun to walk a little?—with the aid of two canes? By this time it is one cane, and he is camping out. And he has carried off the whole force of the house to cook for him."

Betty thought this an excellent joke, and laughed delightedly over it.

"If he is camping out, it is quite time I was back," answered Margaret, trying to speak lightly. She took up her gloves. "Good-by, Aunt Betty; you will write to me?"

"Yes, indeed, I will," said Betty, kissing her. "Poor dear, you're like Mahomet's coffin, aren't you? suspended between heaven and—and the other place. And I'm *so* glad you've decided as you have, because you will be *much* easier in your mind, though of course, too, Mr. Winthrop was *quite* right of course, about being afraid for you in case you were alone, for sometimes we *do* have the most dreadful gusts, and the pine-trees are blown down all *over* the barrens and right across the roads; but then, all the same, if you *hadn't* decided, you would be *so* uncomfortable, like the old man and his son and the donkey, who never got anywhere, you know, because they tried to please too many people, or was it that they had to carry the donkey at last? at any rate, certainly, there's no donkey *here*. Well, good-by, dear; I shall be so *dreadfully* anxious about you."

"I am quite sure"—this was called down the stairs after Margaret had descended—"I'm quite sure, dear, that it will be *nothing* but a rain."

A carriage was waiting at the lower door; Winthrop's man was to drive; but the horses were not his; they were a pair Margaret had sent for. Margaret took her place, and Winthrop followed her; Betty, who had now hurried out to the balcony, waved her handkerchief in farewell as long as she could see them.

Margaret had been at East Angels for nearly a month, called there by a sudden illness which had attacked Mrs. Rutherford. It was not a dangerous illness; but it was one that entailed a good deal of suffering, and Margaret had been immediately summoned.

By this time everybody in Gracias knew how dependent "dear Katrina" was in reality upon her niece, in spite of her own majestic statements to the contrary. No one was surprised therefore, when, after the new illness had declared itself, and Mrs. Rutherford had said, plaintively, that she should think Margaret would feel that she *ought* to be there, Betty immediately sat down and wrote a note.

After two weeks of suffering, Mrs. Rutherford had begun to improve. She had now almost attained her former comparatively comfortable condition, and Margaret was returning to the house on the river.

The light carriage crossed the barren rapidly; the same hushed silence continued, the pine-trees which Betty had seen in a vision, prostrate, did not stir so much as one of their green needles. Margaret and Winthrop spoke occasionally, but they did not talk; anything they should say would necessarily be shared by the man who was driving. But conversation between them was not much more free when the steamer was taking them up the river. They sat on the deck together at some distance from the other passengers, but their words were few; what they said had even a perfunctory sound. They exchanged some remarks about Garda which contained rather more of animation.

Garda's last letter to Margaret had borne at the head of the page the magic word "Venice." Garda had appeared to think life there magical indeed. "She admires everything; she is delightfully happy," was Margaret's comment.

"How does she say it?"

"You have heard her talk."

"Not as Mrs. Lucian Spenser. And from Venice!"

"I shall tell her to write her next letter to you."

"I have no doubt she would. I see you are afraid to quote."

"Afraid?" said Margaret, in a tone of cold inquiry. And then, with the same cold intonation, she repeated two or three of Garda's joyous phrases.

"Yes, she is happy! Of course it's magnanimous in me to say so, but I owe her no grudge; on the contrary, it has been refreshing to see, in this nineteenth century, a girl so frankly in love. She would have married Lucian Spenser just the same if they neither of them had had a cent; she would have made any sacrifice for him—don't you think so?"

"Yes; but it wouldn't have been a sacrifice to her."

"Bravo! I gave you such a chance to say insidious things."

Margaret smiled a little at this suggestion. Then, in the silence that followed, the old look came back to her face—a look of guarded reserve, which, however, evidently covered apprehension.

She had, indeed, been in great dread. The dread was lest the agitation which had overpowered her during that last conversation she had had with Winthrop before she went back to her husband, should reappear. This brief journey of theirs together was the first perfect opportunity he had had since then to call it forth again; up to to-day there had been no opportunity, she had prevented opportunity. But now she was at his mercy; any one of a hundred sentences which he could so easily say, would suffice to bring back that emotion which suffocated her, and made her (as she knew, though he did not) powerless. But, so far, he had said none of these things. She was grateful to him for every moment of the respite.

Thus they sat there, appearing no doubt to the other passengers a sufficiently happy and noticeably fortunate pair.

For Winthrop had about him a certain look which, in America, confers distinction—that intangible air that belongs to the man who, well educated to begin with, has gone forth into the crowded course, and directed and carried along his fortunes by his own genius and energy to the goal of success. It is a look of power restrained, of comprehension; of personal experience, personal knowledge; not theory. The unsuccessful men who met Winthrop—this very steamer carried several of them—were never angry with him for his good-fortune; they could see that he had not always been one of the idle, though he might be idle now; they could see that he knew that life was difficult, that he had, as they would have expressed it, "been through it himself," and was not disposed to underrate its perplexities, its oppressions. They could see, too, not a few of them, poor fellows! that here was the man who had not allowed himself to dally with the inertia, the dilatoriness, the self-indulgent weakness, folly, or worse, which had rendered their own lives so ineffectual. They envied him, very possibly; but they did not hate him; for he was not removed from them, set apart from them, by any bar; he was only what they might themselves have been, perhaps; at least what they would have liked to be.

And the women on board all envied Margaret. They thought her very fair as she sat there, her eyes resting vaguely on the water, her cheeks showing a faint, fixed flush, the curling waves of her hair rippling back in a thick mass above the little ear. Everything she wore was so beautiful, too—from the hat, with its waving plume, and the long soft gloves, to the rich shawl, which lay where it had fallen over the back of her chair. They were sure that she was happy, because she looked so fortunate; any one of them would have changed places with her blindly, without asking a question.

The steamer stopped at the long pier which was adorned with the little post-office. The postmaster had made a dim illumination within his official shanty by means of a lantern, and here Margaret waited while the boat was made ready by the negroes who were to row them down the five additional miles of coast which Lanse had considered the proper space between himself and the hotel, to keep him from feeling "hived in." The night was very dark, the water motionless, the men rowed at a good speed; the two passengers landed at the little home-pier in safety, and the negroes turned back.

As soon as Margaret had ascended the winding path far enough to come within sight of the house, "No lights!" she said.

"That's nothing," Winthrop answered; "Lanse is probably outside somewhere, smoking." Then, as the path made another turn, "If there are no lights in front, there are enough at the back," he said.

From the rear of the house light shone out in a broad glare from an open door. Margaret hurried thither. But the kitchen was empty; Dinah, the old cook, her equally ancient cousin Rose, and Primus, the black boy, all three were absent. Rapidly Winthrop went through the house, he found no one; Lanse's room, as well as the parlor and dining-room, appeared not to have been used that day, while the smaller rooms occupied by the two men who were in attendance upon him had an even more deserted air.

"Their trunks are gone," said Margaret, who met Winthrop here. "It is all so strange!" she murmured, looking at him as if for some solution, her eyes dark in the yellow light of the lamp she held.

Winthrop agreed with her in thinking it strange; but he did not tell her so. They went back to the kitchen, none of the servants had returned.

"They are probably somewhere about the grounds; but you must sit down and rest while I go and look for them; you are tired."

"No, I'm not tired," answered Margaret, contradicting this statement.

"Come," he said, authoritatively. Taking the lamp from her, he led the way towards the parlor which she had made so pretty.

She followed him, and sank into the easy-chair he drew forward. "Don't wait," she said.

"But if you feel ill—"

"It's nothing, I'm only nervous."

"I shall probably bring them back in five minutes."

But twenty minutes passed before he returned with Dinah and Rose, whom he had found some distance down the shore. The two old women were much excited, and voluble. Their story was that "Marse Horrel" must be "lorse;" he had started early that morning in his canoe to go up the Juana, and had not returned; when it grew towards evening, as he had never before been out so long, they had become alarmed, and had sent Primus over to East Angels; the steamer that had carried him, and the one that had brought "Mis' Horrel" back, must have passed each other on the way. They did not send Primus to the hotel, because "Marse Horrel," he "'spizes monstons fer ter hev de hotel fokes roun';" they evidently stood in awe of anything "Marse Horrel" should "'spize." And they did not send Primus up the Juana, because "Prime, he sech a borned fool," they "dassent" trust only to that. So not knowing what else to do, they had sent him to East Angels for orders; of course they had no idea that "Mis' Horrel" was on her way back.

Where were the two men? Dodd had been gone a week, "Marse Horrel" had dismissed him; he said he was so well now that he did not need the two. And Elliot? "Marse Horrel" had sent him "day befo' yesserday" up the river on an "arr'nd," they did not know what; he was to return, they did not know when.

"Something has happened to Lanse," said Margaret, drawing Winthrop away a few paces when at last she had extracted these facts from the mass of confusing repetitions, ejaculations, and long, unintelligible phrases in which Dinah and Rose had enveloped them. The little old creatures, who were of exactly the same height, wore scarlet handkerchiefs bound round their heads in the shape of high cones; as they told their story, standing close together, their skinny hands clasped upon their breasts, their great eyes rolling, they might have been two African witches, just arrived on broomsticks from the Cameroons.

"The nearest house is the hotel," said Winthrop; "of course that boat is beyond call." But there was a chance that it might not be, and he hurried down to the landing; Margaret followed.

There was no sound of oars. He hailed loudly, once, twice; no one answered. "I shall have to go to the hotel myself," he said.

"That would take too long, it's five miles; it would be at least two hours before a boat and men from there could get here, and in that two hours you could find Lanse yourself, and bring him in."

"You speak as though you knew where he was."

"So I do, he is in the Monnlungs swamp. For a long while he has been in the habit of going up there every day; I have been with him a number of times, that is, I have followed in the larger boat with one of the men to row. Lanse is there now, and something has happened to him; either the canoe has been wrecked, or else he has hurt himself in some way so that he can't paddle; the great thing is to get him in before the storm breaks; we can't possibly wait to send to the hotel."

The two negresses who had left them, now returned, each carrying a light; apparently they supposed that great illumination would be required, for they had brought out the two largest parlor-lamps, and now stood holding them carefully.

"Bring your lamps this way, since you've got them," said Winthrop. He went towards the boats.

"That is the best," said Margaret, touching the edge of one of them with the tip of her slender boot.

The negresses stood on the low bank above, by the light of the great globes they held, Winthrop examined the canoe. It was in good order, the paddle was lying within.

"Now tell me how to get there," he said.

"Oh, I forgot, you don't know the way!" Margaret exclaimed, a sudden realization that was almost panic showing itself in her voice.

"No, I don't know it. But probably you can tell me."

She stood thinking. "No, it's impossible. Dark as it is, you might not even find the mouth of the Juana, there are so many creeks. And all the false channels in the swamp—No, I shall have to go with you; I will take Rose, possibly she can be of use."

But quickly old Rose handed her great lamp to Dinah, and jerked herself down on her thin knees. "Please, missy, *no*. Not inter de Munloons in de *night, no*! *Ghossesses* dar!" She brought this out in a high shrill voice, her broad flat features working in a sort of spasm, her great eyes fixed beseechingly on her mistress's face.

"You, then, Dinah," said Margaret, impatiently. But in spite of her rheumatic joints, Rose was on her feet in an instant, and had taken the lamps, while Dinah, in her turn, prostrated herself.

"You're perfectly absurd, both of you!" Margaret exclaimed.

"Poor old creatures, you're rather hard on them, aren't you?" said Winthrop from the boat.

"Yes, I'm hard!" She said this with a little motion of her clinched hand backward—a motion which, though slight, was yet almost violent.

"We must lose no more time," she went on. "Go to the house, Rose—I suppose you can do that—and bring me the wraps I usually take when I go out in the canoe, the lantern and some candles—"

"No," said Winthrop, interposing; "let her bring pitch-pine knots, or, better still, torches, if they happen to have them."

It appeared that "Prime" always kept a supply of torches ready, and old Rose hurried off.

Margaret stepped into the boat; she stood a moment before taking her seat "I *wish* I could go by myself," she said.

"You know how to paddle, then?" Winthrop asked, shortly.

"No, that's it, I don't; at least I cannot paddle well. I should only delay everything, it would be ridiculous." She seated herself, and a moment later Rose appeared with the wraps and a great armful of torches.

Both of the old women were quivering with wild excitement; agitated by gratitude at being spared the ordeal of the haunted swamp by night, they were equally agitated by the thought of what their mistress would have to encounter there; they shuffled their great shoes against each other, they mumbled fragments of words; they seemed to have lost all control of their mouths, for they grinned constantly, though their breath came almost in sobs. As Winthrop pushed off, suddenly they broke out into a loud hymn:

> "Didn't my Lawd delibber Dan-yéll, Dan-yéll?
> Didn't my Lawd delibber *Dán*-yell?"

For a long distance up the stream this protective invocation echoed after the voyagers, and the two grotesque figures holding the lamps remained brightly visible on the low shore.

"Turn in now, and coast along close to the land," said Margaret; "it's so dark that even with that I am almost afraid I shall miss the mouth."

But she did not miss it. In ten minutes she said, "Here it is;" and she directed him how to enter.

"I should never have found it myself; it's so narrow," Winthrop commented, as he guided the canoe towards an almost imperceptible opening in the near looming forest.

"That was what I couldn't guard you against."

But the mouth was the narrowest part; inside the stream widened out, and was broad and deep. Winthrop sent the boat forward with strong strokes, the pine torch which Margaret had fastened at the bow cast a short ray in advance.

"I think we shall escape the storm," she said.

"It's holding off wonderfully. But don't be too sure."

They did not speak often. Winthrop was attending to the boat's course, Margaret had turned and was sitting so that she could scan the water and direct him a little. Her nervousness had disappeared; either she had been able to repress it, or it had faded in the presence of the responsibility she had assumed in undertaking to act as guide through that strange water-land of the Monnlungs, whose winding channels she had heretofore seen only in the light of day. Even in the light of day they were mysterious; the enormous trees, thickly foliaged at the top, kept the sun from penetrating to the water, the masses of vines shut out still further the light, and shut in the perfumes of the myriad flowers. Channels opened out on all sides. Only one was the right one. Should she be able to follow it? the landmarks she knew—certain banks of shrubs, a tree trunk of peculiar shape, a sharp bend, a small bay full of "knees"—should she know these again by night? There came to her suddenly the memory of a little arena—an arena where the flowering vines hung straight down from the tree-tops to the water all round, like tapestry, and where the perfumes were densely thick.

"Are you cold?" said Winthrop. "You can't be—this warm night." The slightness of the canoe had betrayed what he thought was a shiver.

"No, I'm not cold."

"The best thing we can do is to make the boat as bright as possible," he went on. "But not in front, that would only be blinding; the light must be behind us." He took the torch from the bow, lighted three others, and stack them all into the canoe's lining of thin strips of wood at the stern. Primus had made his torches long; it would be an hour before they could burn down sufficiently to endanger the boat.

Thus, casting a brilliant orange-hued glow round them, lighting up the dark water vistas to the right and left, as they passed, they penetrated into the dim sweet swamp.

CHAPTER XXVIII

They had been in the Monnlungs half an hour. Margaret acted as pilot; half kneeling, half sitting at the bow, one hand on the canoe's edge, her face turned forward, she gave her directions slowly, all her powers concentrated upon recalling correctly and keeping unmixed from present impressions her memory of the channel.

The present impressions were indeed so strange, that a strong exertion of will was necessary to prevent the mind from becoming fascinated by them, from forgetting in this series of magic pictures the different aspect of these same vistas by day. Even by day the vistas were alluring. By night, lighted up by the flare of the approaching torches, at first vaguely, then brilliantly, then vanishing into darkness again behind, they became unearthly, exceeding in contrasts of color—reds, yellows, and green, all of them edged sharply with the profoundest gloom—the most striking effects of the painters who have devoted their lives to reproducing light and shade.

Lanse had explored a part of the Monnlungs. He had not explored it all, no human eye had as yet beheld some of its mazes; but the part he had explored he knew well, he had even made a map of it. Margaret had seen this map; she felt sure, too, that she should know the channels he called the Lanes. Her idea, upon entering, had been to follow the main stream to the first of these lanes, there turn off and explore the lane to its end; then, returning to the main channel, to go on to the second lane; and so on through Lanse's part of the swamp. They had now explored two of the lanes, and were entering a third.

She had taken off her hat, and thrown it down upon the cloak beside her. "It's so oppressively warm in here," she said.

It was not oppressively warm—not warmer than a June night at the North. But the air was perfectly still, and so sweet that it was enervating.

The forest grew denser along this third lane as they advanced. The trees stood nearer together, and silver moss now began to hang down in long, filmy veils, thicker and thicker, from all the branches. Mixed with the moss, vines showed themselves in strange convolutions, they went up out of sight; in girth they were as large as small trees; they appeared to have not a leaf, but to be dry, naked, chocolate-brown growths, twisting themselves about hither and thither for their own entertainment.

This was the appearance below. But above, there was another story to tell; for here were interminable flat beds of broad green leaves, spread out over the outside of the roof of foliage—leaves that belonged to these same naked coiling growths below; the vines had found themselves obliged to climb to the very top in order to get a ray of sunshine for their greenery.

For there was no sky for anybody in the Monnlungs; the deep solid roof of interlocked branches stretched miles long, miles wide, like a close tight cover, over the entire place. The general light of day came filtering through, dyed with much green, quenched into blackness at the ends of the vistas; but actual sunbeams never came, never gleamed, year in year out, across the clear darkness of the broad water floor.

The water on this floor was always pellucid; whether it was the deep current of the main channel, or the shallower tide that stood motionless over all the rest of the expanse, no where was there the least appearance of mud; the lake and the streams, red-brown in hue, were as clear as so much fine wine; the tree trunks rose cleanly from this transparent tide, their huge roots could be seen coiling on the bottom much as the great vines coiled in the air above. These gray-white bald cypresses had a monumental aspect, like the columns of a Gothic cathedral, as they rose, erect and branchless, disappearing above in the mist of the moss. The moss presently began to take on an additional witchery by becoming decked with flowers; up to a certain height these flowers had their roots in the earth; but above these were other blossoms—air-plants, some vividly tinted, flaring, and gaping, others so small and so flat on the moss that they were like the embroidered flowers on lace, only they were done in colors.

"I detest this moss," said Margaret, as it grew thicker and thicker, so that there was nothing to be seen but the silver webs; "I feel strangled in it,—suffocated."

"Oh, but it's beautiful," said Winthrop. "Don't you see the colors it takes on? Gray, then silver, then almost pink as we pass; then gray and ghostly again."

For all answer she called her husband's name. She had called it in this way at intervals ever since they entered the swamp.

"The light we carry penetrates much farther than your voice," Winthrop remarked.

"I want him to know who it is."

"Oh, he'll know—such a devoted wife! Who else could it be?"

After a while the lane made a bend, and led them away from the moss; the canoe, turning to the right, left behind it the veiled forest, white and motionless. Margaret drew a long breath, she shook herself slightly, like a person who has emerged.

"You have on your jewels again," he said, as the movement caused the torch-light to draw a gleam from something in her hair.

She put up her hand as if she had forgotten what was there. "Jewels? Only a gold arrow." She adjusted it mechanically.

"Jewels enough on your hands, then. You didn't honor *us* with a sight of them—while you were at East Angels, I mean."

"I don't care for them; I put them on this morning before I started, because Lanse likes them."

"So do I. Unwillingly, you also please me; of course I never dreamed that I should have so much time to admire them—parading by torch-light in this way through a great morass."

She did not answer.

"They bring you out, you know, in spite of yourself—drag you out, if you like better; they show what you might be, if you would ever—let yourself go."

"Let myself go? You use strange expressions."

"A man isn't responsible for what he says in here."

"You say that a second time! You know there was no other way; the only hope of getting Lanse home before the storm was to start at once."

"The storm—to be sure. I don't believe it ever storms in here."

She turned towards him. "You *know* I had to come."

"I know you thought so; you thought we should find Lanse sitting encamped on two cypress knees, with the wreck of his canoe for a seat. We should dawn upon him like comets. And he would say, 'How long you've been! It's precious damp in here, you know!'"

She turned impatiently towards the channel again.

"Don't demand too much, Margaret," he went on. "Jesting's safe, at any rate. Sympathy I haven't got—sympathy for this expedition of yours into this jungle at this time of night."

She had now recovered her composure. "So long as you paddle the boat, sympathy isn't necessary."

"Oh, I'll paddle! But I shall have to paddle forever, we shall never get out. We've come to an antediluvian forest—don't you see? a survival. But *we* sha'n't survive. They'll write our biographies; I was wondering the other day if there was any other kind of literature so completely composed of falsehoods, owing to half being kept back, as biographies; I decided that there *was* one other—autobiographies."

On both sides of them now the trees were, in girth, enormous; the red light, gleaming out fitfully, did not seem to belong to them or to their torches, but to be an independent glow, coming from no one knew where.

"If we had the grace to have any imagination left in this bicycle century of ours," remarked Winthrop, "we should certainly be expecting to see some mammoth water creature, fifty feet long, lifting a flabby head here. For my own part, I am afraid my imagination, never very brilliant, is defunct; the most I can do is to think of the thousands of snakes there must be, squirming about under all this water,—not prehistoric at all, nor mammoths, but just nice natural every-day little moccasins, say about seven feet long."

Margaret shuddered.

He stopped his banter, his voice changed. "Do let me take you home," he urged. "You're tired out; give this thing up."

"I am not tired."

"You have been tired to the verge of death for months!"

"You know nothing about that," she said, coldly.

"Yes, I do. I have seen your face, and I know its expressions now; I didn't at first, but now I do. There's no use in your trying to deceive me Margaret, I know what your life is; remember, Lanse told me everything."

"That was long ago."

"What do you mean?" He leaned forward and grasped her arm as though he would make her turn.

For a moment she did not reply. Then, "A great deal may have happened since then," she said.

"I don't believe you!" He dropped her arm. "You say that to stop me, keep me back; you are afraid of me!" He took up his paddle again.

"Yes, I am afraid." Then, putting a little note of contempt into her voice: "And wasn't I right to be afraid?" she added. She drew the arm he had touched close to her waist, and held it there.

"No!" answered Winthrop, loudly and angrily; "you were completely wrong." He sent the canoe forward with rapid strokes.

They went to the end of the lane, then returned to the main channel, still in silence. But here it became necessary again for Margaret to give directions.

"Go as far as that pool of knees," she began; "then turn to the right."

"You are determined to keep on?"

"I must; that is, I must if you will take me."

He sat without moving.

"If anything should happen to Lanse that I might have prevented by keeping on now, how could I ever—"

"Oh, keep on, keep on; bring him safely home and take every care of him—he has done so much to deserve these efforts on your part!"

They went on.

And now the stream was bringing them towards the place Margaret had thought of upon entering—a bower in the heart of the Monnlungs, or rather a long defile like a chink between two high cliffs, the cliffs being a dense mass of flowering shrubs.

Winthrop made no comment as they entered this blossoming pass, Margaret did not speak. The air was loaded with sweetness; she put her hands on the edge of the canoe to steady herself. Then she looked up as if in search of fresher air, or to see how high the flowers ascended. But there was no fresher air, and the flowers went up out of sight.

The defile grew narrower, the atmosphere became so heavy that they could taste the perfume in their mouths. After another five minutes Margaret drew a long breath—she had apparently been trying to breathe as little as possible. "I don't think I can—I am afraid—" She swayed, then sank softly down; she had fainted.

He caught her in his arms, and laid her on the canoe's bottom, her head on the cloak. He looked at the water, but the thought of the dark tide's touching that fair face was repugnant to him. He bent down and spoke to her, and smoothed her hair. But that was advancing nothing, and he began to chafe her hands.

Then suddenly he rose, and, taking the paddle, sent the canoe flying along between the high bushes. The air was visibly thick in the red light of the torches, a miasma of scent. A branch of small blossoms with the perfume of heliotrope softly brushed against his cheek, he struck it aside with unnecessary violence. Exerting all his strength, he at last got the canoe free from the beautiful baleful place.

When Margaret opened her eyes they were outside; she was lying peacefully on the cloak, and he was still paddling vehemently.

"I am ashamed," she said, as she raised herself. "I suppose I fainted? Perfumes have a great effect upon me always. I know that place well, I thought of it before we entered the swamp; I thought it would make me dizzy, but I had no idea that it would make me faint away. It has never done so before, the scents must be stronger at night."

She still seemed weak; she put her hand to her head. Then a thought came to her, she sat up and looked about, scanning the trees anxiously. "I hope you haven't gone wrong? How far are we from the narrow place—the place where I fainted?"

"I don't know how far. But we haven't been out of it more than five or six minutes, and this is certainly the channel."

"Nothing is 'certainly' in the Monnlungs! And five minutes is quite enough time to get lost in. I don't recognize anything here—we ought to be in sight of a tree that has a profile, like a face."

"Perhaps you wouldn't know it at night."

"It's unmistakable. No, I am sure we are wrong. Please go back—go back at once to the narrow place."

"Where is 'back?'" murmured Winthrop to himself, after he had surveyed the water behind him.

And the question was a necessary one. What he had thought was "certainly the channel" seemed to exist only in front; there was no channel behind, there were only broad tree-filled water spaces, vague and dark. They could see nothing of the thicker foliage of the "narrow place."

Margaret clasped her hands. "We're lost!"

"No, we're not lost; at least we were not seven minutes ago. It won't take long to go over all the water that is seven minutes from here." He took out one of the torches and inserted it among the roots of a cypress, so that it could hold itself upright. "That's our guide; we can always come back to that, and start again."

Margaret no longer tried to direct; she sat with her face towards him, leaving the guidance to him.

He started back in what he thought was the course they had just traversed. But they did not come to the defile of flowers; and suddenly they lost sight of their beacon.

"We shall see it again in a moment," he said.

But they did not see it. They floated in and out among the great cypresses, he plunged his paddle down over the side, and struck bottom; they were out of the channel and in the shallows—the great Monnlungs Lake.

"We don't see it yet," she said. Then she gave a cry, and shrank towards him. They had floated close to one of the trees, and there on its trunk, not three feet from her, was a creature of the lizard family, large, gray-white in hue like the bark, flat, and yet fat; it moved its short legs slowly in the light of their torches; no doubt it was experiencing a sensation of astonishment, there had never been in its memory a bright light in the Monnlungs before.

Winthrop laughed, it did him good to see Margaret Harold cowering and shuddering over such a slight cause as that. The boat had floated where it listed for a moment or two while he laughed, and now he caught sight of their beacon again.

"That laugh was lucky," he said, as he paddled rapidly back towards the small light-house. "Now I shall go in exactly the wrong direction—I mean what seems such to me."

"Oh, *must* we go again?"

"I don't suppose you wish to remain permanently floating at the foot of this tree?" He looked at her. "You think we're lost, you're frightened. We're not lost at all, and I know exactly what to do; trust yourself to me, I will bring you safely out."

"You don't know this swamp, it's not so easy. I'm thinking of myself."

"I know you are not. But *I* think of nothing else." He said this impetuously enough.

They started on their second search. And at the end of five minutes they had again lost sight of their beacon. He paddled to the right and back again; then off to the left and back; he went forward a little way, then in the opposite direction; but they did not see the gleam of their guide, nor did they find the defile of flowers.

Suddenly there rose, close to them, a cry. It was not loud, but it was thrilling, it conveyed an impression of agonized fear.

"What was that?" said Margaret. She did not speak the words aloud, but syllabled them with her lips; involuntarily she drew nearer to him.

"I don't know what it was myself, exactly," he answered; "some bird or other small creature, probably, caught by a snake or alligator. It only sounded strange because it is so still here, our nerves are affected, I presume."

"You mean that mine are. I know they are, I will try to be more sensible."

He pursued his tentative course. But the watery vistas seemed only to grow wilder. They never had a desolate appearance; on the contrary there was something indescribably luxuriant, riotously so, in the still lake with its giant trees, its scented air, its masses of flowers. At length something dark, that was not a tree trunk, nor a group of tree trunks, loomed up on their right. Their torches outlined it more plainly; it was square and low.

"It's a *house*" Margaret said, in the same repressed whisper. "Oh, don't go near it!"

"Why—it's deserted, can't you see that? There's no living thing there, unless you count ghosts—there may be the ghost of some fugitive slave. The door, I suppose, is on the other side." And he paddled towards it.

The cabin—it was no more than a cabin—had been built upon the great roots of four cypresses, which had happened to stand in a convenient position for such a purpose; the planks of the floor had been nailed down across these, and the sides formed of rough boards braced by small beams which stretched back to the tree trunks; the roof was a network of the large vines of the swamp, thickly thatched with the gray moss, now black with age and decay. The door was gone; Winthrop brought the boat up towards the dark entrance; the sill was but an inch or two above the water.

They looked within, the light from their torches illuminating the central portion. And as they looked, they saw a slight waving motion on the floor. Were the planks oscillating a little, or was it dark water flowing over the place?

At first they could not distinguish; then in another instant they could. It was not water; it was the waving, squirming bodies of snakes.

Winthrop had given the canoe a quick swerve. But before they could have counted one, the creatures, soundlessly, had all disappeared.

"Men are queer animals," he said; "I should have liked one more good peep. But of course I won't go back."

"Yes—go."

"You are prepared to humor me in everything? Well, it won't take an instant." They were but ten feet away; he gave a stroke with his paddle and brought the canoe up to the entrance again.

Within there was now nothing, their torch-light shone on the bare glistening boards of the floor. But stay—yes, there was; something white in one corner; he took one of the torches, and held it within for a moment. Margaret gave a cry; the light was shining on bones—a white breastbone with the ribs attached, and larger bones near.

He threw the torch into the water, where it went out with a hiss, and sent the canoe rapidly away. This time he did not stop.

Margaret had hidden her face in her hands. "Well," he said, still urging the light boat along, "the last hunter who occupied that cabin was not as tidy in his habits as he might have been; he left the remains of the last bear he had had for dinner behind him."

"Are you sure?" she asked, without looking up, still shuddering.

"Perfectly."

Winthrop held that in some cases a lie was right.

He paddled on for a few minutes more.

"Here's your reward for humoring me. Isn't this the 'narrow place?'"

And it was.

"Now that we've found it, hadn't we better try to go back?" he suggested.

"I will do as you think best."

"You're thoroughly cowed, aren't you? By the skeleton of a bear."

"I think I am tired," she answered.

"Think? You mean you know you are." The mask of jesting had dropped again. "How much more of this horrible place is there—I mean beyond here?"

"We are a good deal more than half-way through; three quarters, I think."

"Can we get out at the other end? Is there an outlet?"

"Yes—a creek. It takes you, I believe—I have never been so far as that—to Eustis Landing, a pier on the St. John's beyond ours."

"If we try to go back we shall have to go through that damnable aisle of miasma again."

"Perhaps I should not faint this time," she said, humbly.

"You don't know whether you would or not; I can't take any risks."

He spoke with bluntness. She sat looking at him; her eyes had a pathetic expression, her womanish fears and her fatigue had relaxed her usual guard.

"You think I'm rough. Let me be rough while I can, Margaret!"

He sent the boat forward towards the outlet, not back through the aisle of flowers. "We'll go on," he said.

After a while she called her husband's name again.

"What's the use of doing that?" he asked. "He isn't here."

"Oh, but I am sure he is. Where else could he be?"

"How should I know?—Where he was for eight years, perhaps."

Presently they came to a species of canebrake, very dense and high; there was no green in sight, only the canes. The channel wound tortuously through the rattling mass, the slight motion of the water made by the canoe caused the canes to rattle.

"Keep watch, please," he said; "it's not so wet here. It wouldn't be amusing to set such a straw-stack on fire."

While they were making their way through this labyrinth, there came a crash of thunder.

"The storm at last, and we haven't heard the least sound of the tornado that came before it! That shows what a place this is," he said. "We might as well be in the heart of a mountain. Well, even if we *do* suffocate, at least we're safe from falling trees; if the lightning has struck one, it can't come down, wedged in as it is in that great tight roof overhead."

There came another crash. "I believe it grows hotter and hotter," he went on, throwing down his hat. "I am beginning to feel a little queer myself; I have to tell you, you know, in order that you may be able to act with—with discrimination, as Dr. Kirby would say."

She had turned quickly. "Do you feel faint?"

"Faint?" he answered, scoffingly. "Never in the world. Am I a woman? I feel perfectly well, and strong as an ox, only—I see double."

"Yes, that is the air of the swamp."

She took off the black lace scarf she was wearing, dipped it into the stream, and told him to bind it round his forehead above the eyes.

"Nonsense!" he said, impatiently.

But she moved towards him, and kneeling on the canoe's bottom, bound the lace tightly round his forehead herself, fastening it with her little gold pin.

"I must look like a Turk," he exclaimed when she released him.

But the wet bandage cleared his vision; he could see plainly again.

After another five minutes, however, back came the blur. "Shall we ever get out of this accursed hole?" he cried, pressing his hands on his eyes.

"I can paddle a little; let me take the oar."

But he dashed more water on his head, and pushed her hands away. "Women never know! It's much better for me to keep on. But you must direct me,—say 'one stroke on the right,' 'two on the left,' and so on."

"Oh, why did I ever bring you in here?" she moaned, giving no directions at all, but looking at his contracted eyes with the tears welling in her own.

"See here, Margaret,—I really don't know what would happen if I should put this oar down and—and let you pity me! I can tell you once. Now be warned." He spoke with roughness.

Her tears were arrested. "Two strokes on the right," she said, quickly.

They went on their course again, he putting his oar into the water with a peculiar deliberation, as though he were taking great care not to disturb its smoothness; but this was because he was guiding himself by sense of touch. It was not that all was dark before him, that he saw nothing, it would have been much easier if there had been nothing to see; but whether his eyes were open or closed he looked constantly and in spite of himself into a broad circular space of vivid scarlet, in the centre of which a smaller and revolving disk of colors like those of peacocks' feathers, continually dilating and contracting, wearied and bewildered him. In spite of this visual confusion he kept on.

Their progress was slow. "I think I'll stop for a while," he said, after a quarter of an hour had passed. They were still among the rattling canes, his voice had a drowsy tone.

"Oh, don't stop now; we're nearly out."

But he had stopped.

"If I had had any idea you would tire so soon— Of course if I *must* take the oar—and blister my hands—"

"Keep back in your place," he cried, angrily, as she made a movement as though she were coming to take the paddle from him.

She went on giving the directions, she could scarcely keep the tremor from her voice, but she did keep it. When she looked at his closed eyes, and saw the effort he was making—every time he lifted his arms it was like lifting a gigantic weight, his fancy made it so—she longed to take the oar from him and let him rest. But she did not dare to, he must not sleep now. She put out her hand and touched an edge of his coat furtively, where he would not perceive it; the gentle little touch seemed to give her courage to say, in a tone of sarcastic compassion, "If, after all, you *are* going to faint, though you assured me—"

"Faint!" said Winthrop,—"what are you talking about?" He straightened himself and threw back his head. Her taunt had answered its purpose, it had made him angry and in his anger he sent the boat forward with more force.

Another anxious ten minutes, and then, "We're out!" she said, as she saw wide water in front. "Now it will be cooler." The channel broadened, they left the rattling canes behind.

Water was coming slowly down the trees, not in drops but in dark streaks; this was rain that had made its way through the roof of foliage, scanty fringe of the immense torrent now falling upon the drenched ground outside.

"I shall go through to that place you spoke of—Eustis Landing, wasn't it?" said Winthrop.

"Oh, you *are* better!"

Her relief showed itself in these words. But much more in her face; its strained tension gave way, her tears fell. She dried them in silence.

"Because I can speak of something outside of this infernal bog? Yes, I shall get you safely through now. And myself also. But—it hasn't been easy!"

"Oh, I know that."

"I beg your pardon, no, you don't; not the half."

In a moment or two more he announced that he was beginning to see "something besides fireworks." She still continued, however, to direct him.

The swamp had been growing more open. At length the channel brought them to a spectral lake, with a few dead trees in it here and there hung with white moss. "I remember this place, the creek opens out just opposite. *At last* it's over!"

"And at last I can see. But I must take this thing off; it binds me." And he unloosed and threw off her lace scarf.

They found the creek and entered. "It seems strange to see solid ground again, doesn't it?" he said.

"Then you *can* see it?"

"As well as ever."

The creek brought them to a waste that was open to the sky.

"Now we can breathe," he said; "I feel as though I should never want to be under a tree branch again!"

It was not very dark; there was a moon somewhere behind the gray clouds that closely covered the sky. The great storm had gone westward, carrying with it the tornado and the rain, and now a cool, moderate, New-England-feeling wind was beginning to blow.

Winthrop glanced back. The great trees of the Monnlungs loomed up in a long dark line against the sky; from the low level of the boat in the flat waste they looked like a line of mountains.

"All the same, you know," he said, contradictorily, "it was very beautiful in there."

The creek was wide; he went on rapidly. He was quite himself again. "You look fearfully worn," he said, after a while.

"Must we have all these torches now?" She spoke with irritation, she could not get away from their light.

"Not if you object to them." He extinguished all but one. "Now put on some of those wraps; it's cold."

"I do not need them."

"Don't be childish." (There was no doubt but that he was himself again.) "Here, let me help you on with this cloak."

She submitted.

It took them three-quarters of an hour to reach the landing.

"This is it, I presume," he said, as he saw the dim outlines of two white houses at a little distance on the low shore. "I will knock them up, and get some sort of a place where you can rest."

"If there is any one to row, I should much rather go directly home."

"Always unreasonable. Give me your hands." He leaned forward and took them. "Cold as ice,—I thought so. You must come up to the house and go to bed."

"I could not sleep. Let me go home; it is the only place for me."

He still held her hands. "Very well," he said.

"Perhaps they have found Lanse," she went on.

"Old Dinah and Rose? Very likely."

In a few minutes he returned, followed by two negroes, one of whom carried a lantern. They got out their own boat. Winthrop helped Margaret into it, and took his place beside her; their canoe was taken in tow. With strong regular strokes the men rowed down the creek, and out on the broad St. John's.

When they came in sight of the house on the point it was gleaming with light; Margaret gave an exclamation.

Dismissing the men, Winthrop went up the path after her. "I am sure he has come," she said, hurrying on.

"Who? Lanse? Oh no, it's those old goblins of yours who have illuminated in this way; it's their idea of keeping watch for you."

The doors had been left unfastened, they entered. Inside, everything was as brilliant as though the house had been made ready for a ball. But there was not a sound, no one stirred. They went through to the kitchen; and there, each on her knees before a wooden chair, with her head resting upon it on her folded arms, appeared the little Africans, sound asleep; the soles of their shoes, turned up behind them, seemed almost as long as they were.

Winthrop roused them. "Here," he said; "we're back. Make some coffee for your mistress as quickly as you can; and you, Rose, light a fire in the sitting-room."

The queer little old women ran about like frightened hens. They tumbled over each other, and let everything drop. Winthrop stood over them sternly, he took the pitch-pine from the distracted Rose and lighted the fire himself. "Now go and put out all those lights," he said; "and bring in the coffee the moment it's ready."

He had made Margaret sit down in a low easy-chair, still wrapped in her cloak, and had placed a footstool for her feet; the fire danced and sparkled, she sat with her head thrown back, her eyes closed.

"Are you warmer?" he asked. "You were chilled through all the way down the river; every now and then I could feel you shiver."

"It was more fatigue than cold." His voice had roused her, she sat up. "Oh, I ought to be doing something—trying—"

"You can do no more now; you must have some coffee, and then you must go to bed. But, in the mean while, I will do everything possible."

"But you don't believe—I don't know *what* you believe!" She rose.

He put her back in her chair. "I will believe nothing if you will go and rest—I mean my beliefs shall not interfere with my actions; I will simply do everything I can—all I should do if I were sure he was lost, somewhere about here."

She remained where he had placed her. After a while she said, "I was so certain he was in the swamp!" Her tired eyes, beginning to glisten a little with tears, had a childlike look as she raised them to his.

Old Rose now came hurrying in with the coffee, its fragrant aroma filled the room. Winthrop poured it out himself, and made Margaret swallow it, spoonful by spoonful, until the cup was empty.

"You have a little color now," he said.

She put the cup down, and rose.

"You're going? Yes, go; go to bed, and sleep as long as you can, it must be near dawn. I will meet you here for a late breakfast at eleven."

She still stood there. "But will you—will you really—"

"Haven't I given you my word?" he said. "Are you afraid that I shall not be tender enough to him? Don't you comprehend that no matter how much I may hate him myself, his being your husband protects him perfectly, because, so long as you persist in continuing so subservient, he could visit anything else upon you?"

She went out without reply.

He sank into the chair she had left vacant to rest for a moment or two; he was desperately tired.

When he came back to the room at eleven, she was already there. It was a dark day, with the same New-England-feeling wind blowing over river and land; there had been spurts of rain, and he was wet. "Why have you no fire?" he asked.

"It did not seem cold enough."

"It's not cold, but it's dreary. I don't believe you have slept at all?" he continued, looking at her. Opening the door, he called Rose, and told her to light the fire. When the old woman had finished her task—it was but a touch, and again the magic wood was filling the room with its gay light and faint sweet odor of the pine—he repeated his question. "I don't believe you have slept at all?"

"How could I sleep!"

He sat down before the fire. "You are wet. And you must be very tired," she went on.

"I am glad you have thought of it—I like sympathy. Yes, I am tired; but the room is cheery now. Let us breakfast in here?"

"You have found no trace?" Her nervousness showed itself in her tone.

"No."

She went to the door, and gave Rose an order. Then she closed it, and walked first to one window; then to another.

"Do come and sit down. You wander about like a ghost."

"I will step softly." She began to walk up and down the room with her light, rather long-paced step. "*You* are not afraid," she said at last.

"No, I am not afraid; if he were wrecked in mid-ocean, he would make the whales cook his dinner for him, and see to it, too, that it was a good one."

"Oh, don't speak in that tone; don't jest about him when we cannot tell—Here we are safe at home, safe and comfortable, when perhaps he—" she stopped.

"You are haunted by the most useless terrors. 'Safe,' are we? How 'safe' were we last night, for his sake too, in that deadly swamp?—how safe were *you*? And 'comfortable'—I sitting here wet and exhausted, and you walking up and down, white as a sheet, eating your heart out with anxiety! 'And home,' did you say? I like that! Pretty place it was to bring you to—hideous barrack miles from every living thing. Of course you've made it better, you would make a cave better; he knew you would do it when he brought you here!"

He changed his bitter tone into a laugh, "Instead of abusing him, I ought rather to admire him—admire him for his success—he has always done so entirely as he pleased! If one wishes to be virtuous or heroic, I don't know that it is the best way; but if one wishes simply to be comfortable, it most certainly is. You can't philosophize?" he went on, turning his head to look at her as she continued her walk.

"No, no. Would you mind telling me what you have done?"

"I have three parties out; one has gone up the shore, and one down; the third is across the river."

"You are very good. For I know you don't believe he is here."

"No, I don't."

"But where, then, can he be?"

"You have asked me that before. This time I will answer that he is probably where he intended to be when he left here early yesterday morning—after ridding himself of Eliot and Dodd."

"You think he planned it. But why should he have been so secret about it? No one could have prevented him from taking a journey if he wished to take one."

"You would have prevented it; you wouldn't have thought him strong enough."

"That would not have deterred him."

"You're right, it wouldn't. Probably he didn't care even to explain that he did not intend to be deterred, Lanse was never fond of explanations."

"I am not at all convinced."

"I didn't expect to convince you. You asked me, and I had to say something."

After breakfast—she could eat nothing—he said, "I have sent for a little steamer; it is to take me to all the landings within ten miles of here. I shall not be back until late, probably; don't sit up." He left the room.

Fifteen minutes later, he appeared again.

"I was waiting for the steamer down by the water, when I saw the boy who brings the mail going away; you have had a letter?"

She did not answer. Her hands were empty.

"You heard me coming and concealed it."

"I have nothing to conceal." She rose. "Yes, I have had a letter, Lanse is on his way to New York; he is taking a journey—for a change."

"You will let me see the letter?"

"Impossible." She was trembling a little, but she faced him inflexibly.

"Margaret, I beg you to let me see it. Show me that you trust me; you seem never to do that—yet I deserve—Tell me, then, of your own accord, what he says. If he has left you again, who should help you, care for you, if not I?"

"You last of all!" She walked away. "Of course now that I know, I am no longer anxious,—I was foolish to be so anxious. We are very much obliged to you for all you have done."

"Very well, if you take that tone, let me tell you that I too have had a letter—Primus has just brought it from East Angels—it was sent there."

She glanced at him over her shoulder with eyes that looked full of fear—a fear which he did not stop to analyze.

"It is possible that Lanse has written to me even more plainly than he has to you," he went on. "At any rate, he tells me that he is going to Italy—it is the old affair revived—and that he has no present intention of returning. What he has said in his letter to you, of course I don't know; but it can hardly be the whole, because he asks me to 'break' it to you. 'Break' it,—he has chosen his messenger well!"

"O my God," said Margaret Harold.

Her words were a prayer. She sank down on her knees beside the sofa, and buried her face in her clasped arms.

CHAPTER XXIX

Evert Winthrop had felt that her words were a prayer, that she was praying still.

Against what especial danger she was thus invoking aid, he did not know; before he could speak, old Rose had opened the door, and Margaret, springing up, was going forward to meet the Rev. Mr. Moore, who with his usual equable expression entered, hat in hand, to pay Mrs. Harold a short visit; he had been obliged to come over to the river that morning on business, and had thought that he would take the occasion for a little social pleasure as well.

Margaret put out her hands eagerly; "It's wonderful—your coming now! You will stay with me, won't you?—I am in great trouble."

Mr. Moore took her hand; all the goodness of his nature came into his long narrow face, making it lovely in its sympathy as he heard her appeal. She was clinging to him—she had put her other hand on his arm. "You will stay?" she repeated urgently.

"If I can be of any use to you, most certainly I will stay."

Upon hearing this, she made an effort to recover herself, to speak more coherently. "I shall need your advice—there are so many things I must decide about. Mr. Winthrop will tell you—but why should I leave it to him? I will tell you myself. My husband has gone north, he is going abroad again. You will understand—it was so sudden. I did not know—" She made another effort to steady her voice. "If you will stay with me for a day or two, I will send over to Gracias for anything you may need."

"I will stay gladly, Mrs. Harold."

"Oh, you are good! But I always knew you were. And now for a few minutes—if you will excuse me—I have only just heard it—I will come back soon." And with swift step she hastened from the room.

Mr. Moore, his face full of sympathy, turned to Winthrop.

But Evert Winthrop's expression showed only anger; he walked off, with his back turned, and made no reply.

"Is it true, then?" said Mr. Moore, infinite regret in his mild tones.

Winthrop was standing at the window, he bit his lips with impatience; he was in no mood for what he would have called "the usual platitudes," and especially platitudes about Lansing Harold.

It could not be denied that Mr. Moore's conversation often contained sentences that were very usual.

"Perhaps he will return," pursued the clergyman, hopefully. "Influences might be brought to bear. We may be able to reach him?" And again he looked at Winthrop inquiringly.

But Winthrop had now forgotten his presence, at this very moment he was leaving the room; he was determined to see Margaret and speak to her, if but for a second. He found Rose, and sent her with a message; he himself followed the old woman up the stairs, and stood waiting in the upper hall as she knocked at Margaret's closed door.

But the door did not open; in answer to Rose's message delivered shrilly outside the door, Margaret replied from within, "I can see no one at present."

Rose came back. "She can't see nobody nohow jess *dis* minute, marse," she answered, in an apologetic tone. Then, imaginatively, "Spec she's tired."

"Go back and tell her that I'm waiting here—in the hall, and that I will keep her but a moment. There is something important I must say."

Rose returned to the door. But the answer was the same. "She done got *mighty* tired, marse, sho," said the old servant, again trying to clothe the refusal in polite terms, though unable to think of a new apology.

"Her door is locked, I suppose?" Winthrop asked. Then he felt that this was going too far; he turned and went down the stairs, but with a momentary revival in his breast all the same of the old despotic feeling, the masculine feeling, that a woman should not be allowed to dictate to a man what he should say or not say, do or not do; in refusing to see him even for one moment, Margaret was dictating.

He walked down the lower hall, and then back again. Happening to glance up, he saw that old Rose was still standing at the top of the stairs; she dropped one of her straight courtesies as he looked up—a quick ducking down of her narrow skirt; she was much disturbed by the direct refusal which she had had to give him.

"I can't stay here, if they are going to watch me," he thought, impatiently. He turned and re-entered the sitting-room.

Mr. Moore was putting more wood on the fire. His mind was full of Margaret and her troubles; but the fire certainly needed replenishing, it would do no one any good to come back to a cold room, Mrs. Harold least of all; Winthrop therefore found him engaged with the coals.

Mr. Moore went on with his engineering feats. He cherished no resentment because Winthrop had left him so suddenly. Still, he had observed that such sudden exits were sometimes an indication of temper; in such cases there was nothing better than an unnoticing, and if possible an occupied, silence; so he went on with his fire.

"It's most unfortunate that there's no one who has any real authority over her," Winthrop began, still smarting under the refusal. Margaret had chosen the clergyman as her counsellor; it would be as well, then, to indicate to that gentleman what course should be pursued.

"You have some plan to recommend to her?" said Mr. Moore, putting the tongs away and seating himself. He held out his long hands as if to warm them a little by the flame, and looked at Winthrop inquiringly.

"No, I don't know that I have. But she is sure to be obstinate in any case." He too sat down, and stared moodily at the flame.

"You think it will be a great grief to her," observed the clergyman, after a while. "No doubt—no doubt."

"No grief at all, as far as that goes. Lanse has always treated her abominably." He paused. Then continued, as if there were now good reasons for telling the whole tale. "Before he had been married a year, he left her, she did not leave him, as my aunt supposes; he went abroad, and would not allow her to come to him. There had never been the least fault on her side; there hasn't been up to this day."

"I cannot understand such fickleness, such dark tendencies towards change," said Mr. Moore, in rebuking wonder.

"As far as regards change, I ought to say, perhaps, that there hasn't been much of that," Winthrop answered. "What took him abroad was an old interest—something he had felt long before his marriage, and felt strongly; he has never changed in that respect."

"Do you allude—is it possible that you are alluding to an interest in a *person*?" asked Mr. Moore, in a lowered tone.

"It certainly wasn't a thing; I hardly think you would call a beautiful French woman of rank that, would you?"

Mr. Moore looked at him with a stricken face. "A beautiful French woman of rank!" he murmured.

"That's what is taking him abroad now, this second time. She threw him over once, but she has evidently called him back; in fact, he admits it in his letter to me."

"Oh, sin! sin!" said Middleton Moore, with the deepest sadness in his voice. He leaned his head upon his hand and covered his eyes.

"I suppose so," answered Winthrop. "All the same, she is the only person Lanse has ever cared for; for her and her alone he could be, and would be if he had the chance, perhaps, unselfish; I almost think he could be heroic. But, you see, he won't have the chance, because there's the husband in the bush."

"Do you mean to say that this wretched creature is a *married* woman?" demanded the clergyman, aghast.

"Oh yes; it was her marriage, her leaving him in the lurch, that made Lanse himself marry in the first place—marry Margaret Cruger."

"This is most horrible. This man, then, this Lansing Harold, is an incarnation of evil?"

"I don't know whether he is or not," Winthrop answered, irritably. "Yes, he is, I suppose; we all are. Not you, of course," he added, glancing at his companion, and realizing as he did so that here was a man who was an incarnation of good. Then the opposing feeling swept over him again, namely, that this man was good simply because he could not be evil; it was not that he had resisted temptation so much as that he had no capacity for being tempted. "An old woman," he thought.

He himself was very different from that, he knew well what temptation meant! A flush crossed his face. "Perhaps Lanse can't help loving her," he said, flinging it out obstinately.

"A man can always help a shameful feeling of that sort," the clergyman answered, with sternness. He drew up his tall figure, his face took on dignity. "We are not the beasts that perish."

"We may not be altogether beasts, and yet we may not be able to help it," Winthrop answered, getting up and walking across the room. Margaret's little work-table stood there, gay with ribbons and fringes; mechanically he fingered the spools and bright wools it held.

"At least we can control its manifestations," replied Middleton Moore, still with a deep severity of voice and eyes.

"You would like to have all sinners of that disposition (which doesn't happen to be yours) consumed immediately, wouldn't you? for fear of their influencing others," said Winthrop, leaving the work-table and walking about the room. "In the days of the burnings, now, when it was for strictly wicked persons of that tendency, I suspect you would have brought a few fagots yourself—wouldn't you?—even if you hadn't taken a turn at the bellows."

Mr. Moore turned and surveyed him in unfeigned astonishment.

"I beg your pardon," said the younger man, "I don't know what I'm saying. I'll go out for a while, and try the fresh air."

When he came back half an hour later, Margaret had returned.

"Ah! you have had a walk? The air is probably pleasant," said the clergyman, welcoming him kindly. He wished to show that he had forgotten the bellows. "I was on the point of saying to Mrs. Harold, as you came in, that in case she should be thinking of leaving this house, I will hope most warmly that she will find it consistent with her plans to return to us at Gracias."

"I should much rather stay here," responded Margaret. "I could have Dinah's son Abram to sleep in the house, if necessary."

"You could never stay here alone, you ought not to think of it," said Winthrop. "We know better than you do about that." He had seated himself at some distance from her. Mr. Moore still kept his place before the fire, and Margaret was beside him; she held a little fan-shaped screen in her hand to shade her face from the glow.

"I am sure Mr. Moore will say that it is safe," she answered.

"I included him; I said 'we,'" said Winthrop, challengingly.

Mr. Moore extended his long legs with a slightly uneasy movement. "I regret to say that I fear Mr. Winthrop is right; it would not be safe at present, even with Abram in the house. The river is no longer what it was" (he refrained from saying "your northern steamers have made the change;") "the people who live in the neighborhood are respectable, but the increased facilities for traffic have brought us dangerous characters."

"Of course you will go back to East Angels," Winthrop began.

"I think not. If I cannot stay here, I shall go north."

"North? Where?"

"There are plenty of places. There is my grandmother's old house in the country, where I lived when I was a child; it is closed now, but I could open it; I should like to see the old rooms once more." She spoke quietly, her manner was that she was taking it for granted that the clergyman knew everything, that Winthrop had told him all. She was a deserted wife, there was no need for any of them to go through the form of covering that up.

"That would be a perfectly crazy idea," began Winthrop. Then he stopped.

"We should be exceedingly sorry to lose you, Mrs. Harold—Penelope would be exceedingly sorry," said Mr. Moore, in his amiable voice. "I can understand that it would afford you much pleasure to revisit your childhood's home. But East Angels, too—after so long a stay there, may we not hope that it presents to you a friendly aspect?"

"I prefer to go north," Margaret answered.

Mr. Moore did not combat this decision; he did not, in truth, know quite what to advise just at present; it required thought. Here was a woman who had been cruelly outraged by the scandalous, by the incredibly abandoned conduct of the worst of husbands. She had no mother to go to (the clergyman felt this to be an unspeakable misfortune), but she was not a child; they could not dictate to her, she was a free agent. But women—women of refinement—were generally timid (he glanced at Margaret, and decided that she was timid also); she might talk a little about her house at the north, but probably it would end in her returning to East Angels after all.

"If I find that I don't care for the country-house, the life there, I can go abroad," Margaret continued. She rose and went out.

This was not much like returning to East Angels!

"Is she thinking, do you suppose, of going to him?" asked the clergyman, in a cautious voice, when the door was closed.

"I don't know what she is thinking of. She is capable of the most mistaken ideas!" Winthrop answered.

"She is possessed of a wonderful sense of duty, if she does go; I mean, in case she is acquainted with the cause of his departure?"

"She is acquainted with everything."

Margaret came back and sat down again. "You decidedly think, then, that I cannot stay here?" she said to the clergyman.

"Do you wish to stay so very ranch?" he asked, kindly.

"Yes, I should much rather stay, much rather make no change; this is my home."

"How can you talk in that way?" said Winthrop. He had risen again, and begun to walk up and down the room; as he spoke, he stopped his walk and stood before her. "You came here against your will; you disliked the place intensely; you said so of your own accord, I heard you." "I know I have said so. Many times. Still, I should like to stay now."

"You cannot. Even Mr. Moore tells you that."

"Yes," said the clergyman, conscientiously, "I must say it though I do not wish to; the place is unusually lonely, it stands quite by itself; it would be unwise to remain."

"I must give it up, I see," Margaret answered; "I am sorry. But at least I can retain the house; I should like to keep it open, too; the servants could stay here, I suppose."

Winthrop turned and looked at her, a quick surprised suspicion in his glance.

"I could do that, couldn't I?" she repeated, addressing Mr. Moore.

Again the clergyman looked uncomfortable. He crossed his legs, and extending the pendent foot a little in its long, thin-soled boot, he looked at it and moved it to and fro slightly, as if he had been called upon to give an opinion upon the leather. "I fear," he said, as the result of his meditation, "that it might not be altogether prudent. The negroes have much hospitality; with a large house at their command, and nobody near, I fear they might be tempted to invite their friends to visit them."

"The place would swarm with them," said Winthrop.

"At any rate, I shall keep the house even if I close it," said Margaret. "It must be ready for occupancy at any time."

"Then you are thinking of coming back?" Winthrop asked. His face still showed an angry mistrust.

"I may come back. At present, however, I shall go north; and as I prefer to go immediately, I shall set about arranging the rooms here so that I can leave them. It will not take long, two days, or three at most; it would be a great kindness, Mr. Moore, if you would stay with me until I leave—by next Saturday's steamer, probably."

"I hardly think you will be able to accomplish so much in so short a time," answered the clergyman, a good deal bewildered by this display of energy. To Mr. Moore's idea, a woman who had been deserted by her husband, even though that husband had been proved to be abnormally vicious, could not well be in the mood for the necessary counting of chairs, for the proper distribution of gum-camphor among carpets and curtains, all so important.

Then, reading again the deep trouble in Margaret's face, under all the calmness of her manner, he dismissed his objections, and said, heartily, "In any case, I will stay with you as long as you wish."

"Possibly one of your difficulties is that I am here," said Winthrop to Margaret. "You cannot expect me to leave you entirely, as long as you are still in this house, I am, after all, your nearest relative; but of course I could stay at the hotel." He spoke with extreme coldness.

Margaret, however, did not try to dissipate it by asking him to remain.

He showed that he felt this, for he said, "Perhaps I had better go up at once and see to getting quarters there."

She did not answer. He walked about aimlessly for a moment or two, and then left the room.

"Will you go over the house with me now, Mr. Moore—I mean this afternoon?"

"Certainly. It would be better, I think, to make a list," Mr. Moore answered, in an interested voice. Mr. Moore enjoyed lists; to him an index was an exciting object; in devising catalogues, or new alphabetical arrangements, he had sometimes felt a sense of pleasure that was almost dissipation.

"You will have three enemies to encounter," he began with much seriousness. "They are, first, the Mildew. Second, the Moth. Third, the Damp; the Mouse, so destructive in other climates, will trouble you little in this. We shall need red pepper."

CHAPTER XXX

A week later, Margaret was still in the house on the point, she had not been able to complete as rapidly as she had hoped the arrangements necessary for leaving it in safe condition behind her. This was not owing to any lingering on her own part, or to any hesitation of purpose; it was owing simply to the constitutional inability of anybody in that latitude, black or white, to work steadily, to be in the least hurried. The poorest negro engaged to shake carpets could not bring himself, though with the offer of double wages before him, to the point of going without a long "res'" under the trees after each (short) "stent." Mr. Moore, with his lists, made no haste—Mr. Moore had never been in a hurry in his life.

But now at last all was completed; the house was to be closed on the morrow. No one but the clergyman was to sleep there on this last night; the negroes, generously paid and rejoicing in their riches, were going to their own homes; in the morning one of them was to return to dismantle Mr. Moore's room, and then the clergyman himself was to bar the windows, lock the doors, and carry the keys to the hotel, where they were to be kept, in accordance with Margaret's orders. She herself was to sleep at the hotel, in order to be in readiness to take the sea-going steamer, which would touch at that pier at an early hour the next morning.

Evert Winthrop had returned to East Angels. Five days he had stayed at the hotel, coming down every morning to the house on the point; not once had he been able to see Margaret alone. Mr. Moore was always with her, or if by rare chance he happened to be absent, she was surrounded by the chattering blacks, who with the jolliest good-humor and aimless wandering errands to and fro, were carrying out, or pretending to, the orders of "Mis' Horrel."

Winthrop chafed against this constant presence of others. But he would not allow himself to speak of it, pride prevented him. Why should he be kept at a distance, and a comparative stranger like Mr. Moore consulted about everything? Mr. Moore! He looked on with impatience while the clergyman gave explanations of Penelope's excellent methods of vanquishing the Mildew, the Damp, the Moth; with impatience grown to contempt he heard him read aloud to Margaret and check off carefully the various items of his lists. Mr. Moore had even made a list of the inhabitants of the poultry-yard, though Margaret intended to present them in a body to Dinah and Rose.

"One brown hen spotted with white," he read; "one yellow hen, spotted with brown. A black hen. A duck."

He had never seemed to Winthrop so narrow, so given up to little details, as now.

On the fourth day Winthrop (perhaps having found pride, in spite of the dignity it carried with it, rather unfruitful) suddenly resolved to overpower the dumb opposition, make himself master of this ridiculous situation—"ridiculous" was his own term for it. Margaret was evidently determined not to see him alone; after their long acquaintance, and their relationship (he insisted a good deal upon this rather uncertain tie), she should not be allowed to treat him in that way; *he* would not allow it. Of what, then, was she afraid?

It came across him strongly that he should like to ask her that question face to face.

He rode down to the house on the point. He found her in the sitting-room, the blacks coming and going as usual.

"Go away, all of you," he said, authoritatively. "Find some work to do in another room for half an hour; I wish to speak to your mistress."

Margaret looked up as she heard this imperative command. She did not contradict it, she could not come to an open conflict with him before her own servants. He knew this.

Closing the door after the negroes, who, in obedience to the thorough master's voice which had fallen upon their ears, had shuffled hurriedly out in a body, Winthrop came over to the writing-table where she was seated. She had kept on with her writing.

"You don't care any more about that list, about any of these trifling things, than I do," he began; "why do you pretend to care? And why do you make it so impossible for me to speak to you? What are you afraid of?"

She did not answer. And he did not get the satisfaction he had anticipated from his question, because her face was bent over her paper.

"Why are you going north?" he went on, abruptly.

"I need a change."

"You cannot live all alone in New York."

"I shall not be in New York. And I could easily have a companion."

"Your best companion is Aunt Katrina. I admit that she is selfish; but she is growing old, and she is ill. Who, after all, is nearer to you?"

"No one is nearer. I have always been alone."

"That is cynical—and it is not true." He paused. "Every one likes you."

"Well they may! When have *I* been—permitted myself to be disagreeable? When have *I* ever failed to be kind? I have always repressed myself. What is the result? I have been at everybody's beck and call, I have been expected to bear everything in silence; to listen, always to listen, and never to reply." She spoke with bitterness, keeping on with her writing meanwhile.

"It is perfectly true—what you say, and I think you have done too much of it. Are you getting tired of the *rôle*?"

"I am tired at least of East Angels; I cannot go back there."

"You think Aunt Katrina will talk about Lanse in her usual style—about this second going away of his? I myself will tell her the whole story—it is time she knew it! She will talk about him no more."

"It isn't that." She threw down her pen and rose. "I need a complete change, I must have it. But I shall arrange it myself. The only thing *you* can do for me is to leave me free; I should like it if you would go back to East Angels—if you would go to-day; you only trouble me by staying here, and you trouble me greatly."

"Margaret, it's outrageous the way you treat me. What have I done that I should be thrust off in this way? And it's a very sudden change, too; you were not so that night in the swamp."

"It's kind to bring that up. I was tired—nervous; I wasn't myself—"

"You're yourself now, never fear," he interpolated, angrily.

—"Will you do what I ask?"

"You really wish me to go?" His voice softened. "You don't want me to see you off? It's very little to do—see you off."

"I should be grateful if you would go now."

"You are throwing us overboard together, I see—all Lanse's relatives; you think we are all alike," he commented, in a savage tone. "And you, well rid of us, free, and determined to do as you please, are going north alone—you do not even say where?"

"There will be no secret about that; I will write. You talk about freedom," she said, breaking off suddenly, "what do *you* know of slavery? That is what I have been for years—a slave. Oh, to be somewhere!"—and she threw up her arms with an eloquent gesture of longing,—"*anywhere* where I can breathe and think as I please—as I really am! Do you want me to die without ever having been myself—my real self—even for one day? I have come to the end of my strength; I can endure no longer."

Winthrop had been thrilled through by this almost violent cry and gesture. Coming from Margaret, they gave him a great surprise. "Yes, I know," he began; "it has been a hard life." Then he stopped, for he felt that he had not known, he had not comprehended; he did not fully comprehend even now. "I am only harsh on account of the way you treat me," he said; "it galls me to be so completely set aside."

"You can help me only by leaving me, I have told you that."

"But where is the sense—"

"I cannot argue. There may be no sense, but your presence oppresses me."

"You shall not be troubled with it long." He went towards the door. But he came back. "Give me *one* reason."

"I have no reason; it is instinct."

He still stood there.

She waited a moment, looking at him. "If you do not leave me, I shall leave you," she said, "I shall refuse to see you again. You are the best judge of whether you believe me or not."

"Women *are* absurd," exclaimed Winthrop; "they must always have vows, renunciations, eternal partings—nothing less contents them. Oh, I believe you! you would keep a vow or die for it, no matter how utterly senseless it might be. Of course I want to see you again; so I will go now—that is, for a while; I will go back to East Angels."

He took her hand, though she did not extend it. "You have been extremely unreasonable," he said. Though he obeyed, she should feel that he had the mastery still.

He left her, and rode back to the hotel. Mr. Moore learned a few hours later, that he had returned to East Angels.

This had happened three days before. It was now late in the afternoon of the third day, and the house was prepared for "Mis' Horrel's" departure. Mr. Moore, standing on the low bank, waved his hand in farewell as the boat, rowed by two old negroes, carried her down the river.

The five miles seemed short. When the men turned in towards the hotel, twilight had fallen, the river had a veil of mist. Margaret's eyes rested vaguely on the shore; suddenly, in a low voice, she said, "Stop!"

The men obeyed. She strained her eyes to see more clearly a figure under the trees near the landing; it was a man, dressed in gray clothes, he was walking up and down; they could see him as he moved to and fro, but he could not see their low boat, pausing out there in the fog.

Margaret appeared to have satisfied herself. "Row out now into the stream," she said, briefly.

And in a few minutes the shore, left behind them, was but a dark line.

"I have changed my mind, I shall not sleep at the hotel, after all. You can take me back home—to the house on the point. Then, to-morrow morning, you can be there again at dawn, and bring me up in time for the steamer; it will do quite as well."

The old men, without comment either of mind or tongue, patiently rowed her back down the river.

When they reached the point, Margaret, after charging them to be punctual, dismissed them, and walked up the path alone towards the house. No lights were visible anywhere. There was a young moon, and she looked at her watch, it was not yet nine o'clock; Mr. Moore had apparently gone to bed at a very early hour.

The truth was that during all this visit of his on the river Mr. Moore had kept much later hours than he was in the habit of keeping at home. At home Penelope, who believed that he needed a great deal of sleep, was in the habit of saying, about ten o'clock, "Now, Middleton—" And Middleton, as Dr. Kirby once expressed it, always "now'd."

On the present occasion, after partaking of the supper which Dinah had prepared for him, he had sent the old woman to her home; then, remembering that he had a week of arrears to make up, he had gone to his room, though there was still a gleam of sunset in the west.

Margaret understood what had happened, she determined that she would not disturb him; probably it would not be difficult to find a way into the house. As she had expected, among the numerous windows on the ground-floor she found one which she could raise; light and lithe, she easily effected an entrance, and stole on tiptoe to a room up-stairs in the south wing, where she knew there was a lounge whose pillows had been left in place. She had her travelling-bag with her, but she did not intend to undress; she would take what sleep she could on the lounge until dawn, covered by her travelling shawl. But she was more weary than she knew, and nature was kind that night at least; very soon she fell asleep.

The figure she had seen on the shore, was, as she had thought, that of Evert Winthrop. He had come back.

It might have been that he did not consider a return to the river prohibited, so long as he did not go down to the house on the point; there was no law, certainly, against a man's travelling where he pleased. He had not been down to the house on the point, he had stayed at the hotel all day. He had seen her trunks when they arrived, and he knew from their being there that she must be expecting to take the next morning's steamer, northward-bound; was she coming herself to the hotel to sleep? After a while he made the inquiry; his tone was careless, he asked at what hour they expected her.

"I will be surprised if she is not here by supper-time," was the answer he received.

At sunset he went down to the shore and strolled to and fro. But though he thus kept watch, he did not see the boat that stole up in the fog, floated off-shore for a moment, and then disappeared.

That night, at three o'clock Middleton Moore woke with the feeling that he had been attacked by asthma, and that Penelope was trying to relieve him with long smoking wisps of thick brown paper, her accustomed remedy. Then consciousness became clearer, and he perceived that there was no Penelope and no candle; but that there was smoke. He sprang up and opened the door, there was smoke in the hall also. "The house is on fire," was his thought; "how fortunate that there is no one here!" He threw on his clothes, drew on his boots, and seizing his coat and hat, ran down the hall. His room was on the ground-floor, he looked into the other rooms as he passed; there was smoke, but no flame; yet he could distinctly perceive the odor of burning wood. "It must be up-stairs," he said to himself. He unlocked the house door, and ran across the lawn in order to see the upper story.

Yes, there were the flames. At present only little tongues, small and blue, creeping along under the cornice; they told him that the fire had a strong hold within, since it had made its way outward through the main wall. It would be useless for him to attempt to fight it, with the water at a distance and no one to assist. The old mansion was three stories high. "It will go like tinder," he thought.

His next idea was to save for Margaret all he could; jamming his clerical hat tightly down on his forehead, he began to carry out articles from the lower rooms, and pile them together at the end of the lawn. He worked hard; he ran, he carried, he piled up; then he ran again. He lifted and dragged ponderous weights, the perspiration stood in drops on his face. But even then he made a mental list of the articles he was saving: "Six parlor chairs. One centre table of mahogany. A work-table with fringe. A secretary with inlaid top. A sofa." In the lower rooms the smoke was blinding now. Outside, the tongues of flame had grown into a broad yellow band.

Presently the fire burst through the roof in half a dozen places, and, freed, rose with a leap high in the air; heretofore there had been but little noise, now there was the sound of crackling and burning, and the roar of flames under headway; the sky was tinged with the red glow, the garden took on a festal air, with all its vines and flowers lighted up.

Mr. Moore did not stop to look at this, nor to call the flames "grand." In the first place, he did not think them grand, eating up as they were a good house and a large quantity of most excellent furniture. In the second, he had not time for adjectives, he was bent upon saving a certain low bookcase he remembered, which stood in the upper hall. He had always admired that bookcase, he had never seen one before that was unconnected with associations of step-ladders, or an equally insecure stepping upon chairs.

He jammed his hat hard down upon his forehead again (he should certainly be obliged to have a new one), and ran back into the house. But the flames had now reached the lower hall, they had burned down as well as up; he was obliged to content himself with a hat-stand near the door. As he was dragging this out he heard shouts, and recognized the voices as those of negro women; when he had reached the lawn, there they were, Dinah and Rose and four other women; they had seen the light, and had come running from their cabins, half a mile down the shore. They were greatly excited; one young girl, black as coal, jumped up and down, bounding high like a ball each time; she was unconscious of what she was doing, her eyes were on the roaring flames, every now and then she gave a tremendous yell. Old Rose and Dinah wept and bewailed aloud.

"Dar goes de settin'-room winders—*ow*!"

"Dar goes de up-steers chimbly—*ow*!"

Another of the women, a thin old creature, clapped her hands incessantly on her legs, and shouted, "De glory's a-comin', de glory's a-comin', a-comin'!"

Mr. Moore deposited his hat-stand under a tree, and standing still for a moment, wiped his hot forehead. He did not attempt to stop their shouting, he knew that it would be useless; he thought with regret of that bookcase.

And now there came a shout louder, or at least more agonized, than any of the others, and round the corner of the house appeared the boy Primus; he ran towards them, shouting still, with each step he almost fell—"She's *dar*—Mis' Horrel!"

He too had seen the light, and, approaching the place from the south, he had passed, in running towards the front, the narrow high south wing; here at a window he had seen a face—the face of Margaret Harold.

Mr. Moore was gone at the boy's first cry. The others followed.

The south wing was not visible from the front. Its third story was in flames, and the back and sides of the ground-floor had caught, but at a second-story window (which she had opened) they all saw a face—that of Margaret Harold; the glare of the main building showed her features perfectly. They could not have heard her, even if she had been able to call to them, the roar of the fire was now so loud.

"She cannot throw herself out, it's too high; and we have no blanket. There's a door below, isn't there? And stairs?" It was Mr. Moore's voice that asked.

"Yes, passon, yes. But it's all *a-bu'nin'*!"

Mr. Moore clasped his hands and bowed his head, it did not take longer than a breath. Then he started towards the wing.

"Oh, passon, yer dassent!"

"Oh, passon, yer can't help her now, de sweet lady, it's too late. Pray for her *yere*, passon; she'll go right straight up, she's wunner der Lawd's *own* chillun, de dove!"

"Oh, passon! de Lawd ain't willin' fer *two* ter die."

The negro women clung about him, but he shook them off; going hastily forward, he broke in the door and disappeared. His moment's prayer had been for his wife, in the case—which he knew was probable—that he should not come from that door alive.

The gap he had made revealed the red fire within; behind the stairs the back of the wing was a glowing furnace.

The negroes now all knelt down, they had no hope; they began to sing their funeral hymn.

The fire had reached the second story; Margaret's face had disappeared.

A bravery which does not reason will sometimes conquer in the teeth of reason. One chance existed, it was one amid a dozen probabilities of a horrible death; it lay in swiftness, and in the courage to walk, without heeding burned feet, directly across floors already in a glow.

Middleton Moore crossed such floors; he went unshrinkingly up the scorching stairs. He found Margaret by sense of touch in the smoke-filled room above, and tearing off his coat, he lifted her as she lay unconscious, wrapped her head and shoulders in it, and bore her swiftly down the burning steps, and through the fiery hall, and so out to the open air. His eyebrows, eyelashes, and hair were singed, his face was blistered; brands and sparks had fallen like hail upon his shoulders and arms, and scorched through to the skin; his boots were burned off, the curled leather was dropping from his burned feet; his breath was almost gone.

He gave Margaret to the women, and sank down himself upon the grass; he could not see, he felt very weak; something was tightening in his throat. The boy Primus, with great sobs, ran like a deer to the well for water, and bringing it back, held a cupful to the lips of the blinded man.

Margaret, though still unconscious, appeared to be unhurt. The skirt of her dress was burned in several places. The women chafed her hands, and bathed her face with the fresh water; once she opened her eyes, but unconsciousness came over her again.

With a crash the northern wing fell in.

"De front'll go nex'," said Primus. "We mus' git 'em 'way from dish yer."

The women lifted Margaret tenderly, and bore her to the end of the lawn. Mr. Moore rose on his burned feet, and, leaning on the boy's shoulder, slowly made his way thither also; their forlorn little group, assembled near the piled-up furniture, was brightly illuminated by the flame.

Presently the front fell in. And now, as the roar was less fierce, they could hear the gallop of a horse, in another minute Evert Winthrop was among them. He saw only Margaret, he knelt by her side and called her name.

"De *passon* done it," said Primus,—"de passon! He jess walk right straight inter de bu'nin', *roarin'* flameses! En brung her out."

Mr. Moore had not seen Winthrop, he could see nothing now. He seemed besides, a little bewildered, confused. As Winthrop took his hand and spoke to him, he lifted his face with its scorched cheeks and closed eyes, and answered: "There was some furniture saved, I think. I think I saved a little. Six parlor chairs—if I am not mistaken; and a centre table—I was sorry about that bookcase."

"Hear de lamb!" said one of the negro women, bursting into fresh tears.

CHAPTER XXXI

Margaret Harold was sitting on a bench at the East Angels landing. She was in walking dress; her large hat, with its drooping plumes, made her face look like that of a Gainsborough portrait. A bunch of ferns which she had gathered had slipped from her lap to her feet. Carlos Mateo, very stiff, stood near. It was sunset; a mocking-bird was pouring forth a flood of notes, rioting in melody, it was marvellous to realize that such a little creature could produce from his tiny throat matchless music like this.

Coming down the live-oak avenue appeared the figure of Celestine.

"If you please, Miss Margaret, Mrs. Rutherford has sent me to look for you."

"Yes, I know; I am late to-night, I will come in now."

"There's no occasion for haste," Celestine answered, bestowing a short glance of general inspection upon the lagoon, the tinted sky, and the stiff figure of the crane. "What a pagan bird that crane is!"

"You hear, Carlos?" said Margaret.

But Carlos was never conscious of the existence of Celestine, he kept his attentions exclusively for his southern friends; the only exception was Margaret, whose presence he was now beginning to tolerate.

"You don't call that mocking-bird a pagan, do you?" Margaret asked.

"I don't care much for mocking-birds *myself*," Celestine responded. "Give me a bobolink, Miss Margaret! As for them leaves you've got there—all the sweet-smelling things in Florida—I'd trade the whole for one sniff of the laylocks that used to grow in our backyard when I was a girl."

"Why, Minerva, you're homesick."

"No, Miss Margaret, no; I've got my work to attend to here; no, I ain't homesick: you get home knocked out of you when you've traipsed about to such places as Nice, Rome, Egypt, and the dear knows where. But if anybody was really going to *live* somewheres (I don't mean just *staying*, as we're doing now), talk about choosing between this and New England—my!"

Margaret rose.

"There's no occasion for haste if you don't want to go in just yet," said Celestine; "she isn't alone, I saw Dr. *Kirby* ride up just as I came away. Well—she's got on that maroon silk wrapper."

"Nobody has such taste as you have, Celestine," said Margaret, kindly. "My aunt is always becomingly dressed."

There was a little movement of the New England woman's mouth, which was almost a grimace. In reality it expressed her pride and pleasure—though no one would have suspected it. It was the only acknowledgment she made.

Dr. Kirby was sitting with his esteemed friend when Margaret entered.

His esteemed friend's feeling for Margaret now seemed to be always a tender compassion.

"My dear child, I fear you have been out too long, you look pale," was the present manifestation of it.

"I have often thought what a variation it would make in the topics of my friends," said Margaret, as she drew off her gloves, "if I should take to painting my cheeks a little; think of it—a touch of rouge, now, and the whole conversation would be altered."

"I am sure that, for artistic purposes at least," said Dr. Kirby, gallantly, "rouge would be totally misapplied. We all know that Mrs. Harold's complexion has always the purest, the most natural, the most salubrious tint; it is the whiteness of Diana."

"Pray give those—those green things to Looth," Aunt Katrina went on, languidly; "I hope they are not poison-ivy?" (Aunt Katrina lived under the impression that everything that came from the woods was poison-ivy.) "And do go to my room, dear child, and sit down there a while before the fire—there's a little fire—and let Looth change your shoes, and make you a nice cup of tea. Later—*later*," Aunt Katrina went on, more animatedly, "we'll have some whist." She spoke as though she were holding out something which Margaret would be sure to enjoy.

There were very few evenings now when Aunt Katrina did not expect her niece to make one at the whist-table drawn up at her couch's side, the other players being Dr. Kirby, Betty, or occasionally Madam Ruiz or Madam Giron. The game had come to be her greatest pleasure, she had therefore established and set going in her circle of friends the idea that it was an especial pleasure to Margaret also; Aunt Katrina was an adept in such tyrannies.

"How is Mr. Moore to-day?" Margaret inquired, not replying to the change of shoes.

"He improves every hour, it's wonderful! He is getting well in half the time that any one else would have taken. He will walk as lightly as ever before long—or almost as lightly. He is rather uncomfortably comfortable just now, however," the Doctor went on, laughing, "he doesn't know how to adapt himself to all his new luxuries; he took up an ivory-handled brush this morning almost as though it were an infernal machine."

"I should hardly think Mrs. Moore would approve of *useless* luxuries," said Aunt Katrina, not with a sniff—Aunt Katrina never sniffed—but with a slight movement of the tip of her very well shaped nose; she followed the movement with a light stroke upon that tip with her embroidered handkerchief.

"Penelope nowadays approves of everything for her Middleton," said Dr. Kirby, laughing again. "I believe she'll deck him out with pink silk curtains round his bed before she gets through."

"Yes—but ivory-handled *brushes*," said Aunt Katrina, confining herself, as usual, to the facts. "And his hair is so thin, too!"

"I must confess I roared—if you will permit the rather free expression. But the brushes came with the other things that nephew of yours sent down; I believe he's trying to corrupt the dominie."

"I am glad, and very thankful to hear that Mr. Moore is going on so well," said Margaret, "there is nothing I care so much about." Carrying her plumed hat in her hand, she left the room.

"He is an excellent man, Mr. Moore—most excellent," observed Aunt Katrina, a little stiffly; "of course we can never forget our obligations to him."

"I should think not, indeed," answered Reginald Kirby, for the first time losing some of his gallantry of tone.

"I am sure we have shown that we do not forget them," Aunt Katrina went on, with dignity. "Margaret has shown it, and Evert; between them they have made Mr. Moore comfortable for life."

"There wouldn't have been much life left in any of you without him," said Kirby, still fierily.

"I beg your pardon, I am not so dependent upon my niece, dear as she is to me, as *that*; I think *such* dependence wrong. You must remember, too, that I have already been through great sorrows—the greatest; my life has *not* been an easy one." The gemmed hand was gently raised here; then dropped with resignation upon the maroon silk lap. "I esteem Mr. Moore highly—haven't I mentioned to you that I do? surely I have. But I *cannot* be deeply interested in him; Mr. Moore is not an interesting man, he is *not* an exciting man. I am afraid that when I care for a friend," said Aunt Katrina, frankly, "when I find a friend *delightful*, I am afraid I am apt, yes, *very* apt, to make comparisons." And she glanced at the Doctor with a gracious smile.

"Pardon my ill temper," murmured the Doctor, completely won again. "After all," he said to himself, with conviction, "she's a deucedly fine woman still."

Three months had elapsed since the burning of the house on the river.

Mr. Moore had remained for four weeks in the neighboring hotel, his wife and Dr. Kirby constantly with him. They had then decided to take him on a litter to Gracias; they crossed the St. John's in safety, and came slowly over the pine barrens.

As they approached the town, Dr. Kirby, who, with Winthrop, was accompanying the litter on horseback, a little in advance, saw a number of people in the road.

"They have come out to meet him," said the Doctor, angrily. "How senseless! how wicked! In his present state the excitement will kill him; I shall ride forward and tell them to go back."

"No, don't," said Winthrop; "I think you're mistaken, I think it will do him good. He has never in the least understood how much they care for him; he has been kept both mentally and physically too low. What he needs now is a richer diet."

"Are you turning into a doctor yourself?" inquired Kirby, with impatience, yet struck, too, by the suggestion. "It is true that I have always said he'd be twice the man he was if he had a glass of port with his dinner."

"This will be the glass of port."

Mr. Moore's litter had curtains, which were down, he had not yet seen the assemblage. His improvised couch was swung carefully across a large wagon, which was drawn by Winthrop's horses on a walk, a man leading them; Penelope followed in another carriage, which Winthrop had also provided.

"I declare—it's all Gracias!" exclaimed the Doctor, as they came near the assembled groups. "Not only our own people, but Our Lady of the Angels' people have come too—there's Father Florencio at the head."

Penelope had now discovered the assemblage, and had bidden her coachman hasten forward. Descending with her weak step, she herself fastened back the curtains of the litter; "Dear," she said, tenderly, "they have come out to meet you—the Gracias people. I know you will be glad."

She kissed him, and rearranged his pillows; then she let Winthrop help her back into her carriage, which fell behind again. Penelope agreed with him, evidently, in thinking that excitement would do the injured man good.

Winthrop, who had dismounted, gave his horse to Tom, and walked himself beside the litter; the Doctor rode on the other side, and thus they went on their way again towards the waiting people.

These people were showing more sense than the Doctor had given them credit for; they had drawn themselves up in two lines, one on each side of the narrow pine barren road, on the right the congregation of St. Philip and St. James, with their senior warden at the end of the line; and, opposite, the flock of Our Lady of the Angels, led by their benign, handsome old priest, Father Florencio. Then, farther on, at a little distance, came the negroes, drawn up also in two lines.

The whites were very still; they did not cheer, they bowed and waved their hands. Mr. Moore looked from one side to the other, turning his head a little, and peering from his half-closed eyes, as his litter passed on between the ranks of friends. It had been agreed that nothing should be said—he was too weak to bear it; but all the people smiled, though many of them felt their tears starting at the same moment, as they saw his helpless form; they smiled determinedly, and winked back the moisture, he should see none but cheerful faces as he passed. At the end of the line the senior warden, in their name, stepped forward and pressed the rector's hand. And then from the other side came Father Florencio, who heartily did the same.

Penelope, looking from the open carriage behind, was crying. But Mr. Moore himself was not excited. He thought it very beautiful that they should all have come out in this way to meet him, it was the sign of a great kindness.

It did not occur to him that it was the sign of a great admiration as well.

When the litter came abreast of the two long lines of blacks, they could not keep back their demonstrations of welcome quite so completely as the whites had done; the Baptist minister of their own race, who was the pastor of most of them, stood, in his Sunday clothes, with his hand up warningly, in order to check their exuberance. One broad gleam of white teeth extended down the entire line, and, "He's come back fum de gold'n gate!" "*Bless* de passon!" were murmured in undertones as the litter passed. And then, behind it, there were noiseless leaps, and hats (most of them battered) in the air; next, they all ran forward over the barren in a body, in order to precede the procession into Gracias.

"Don't shout—do you hear me?—no shouting," said Dr. Kirby, imperatively. He had been obliged to leave his place beside the litter, there was no room for his horse between the close-pressing ranks; now he rode forward in order to keep a control, if possible, over the joyous throng. "If you shout, it will be very bad for him," he went on, threateningly. He had stopped his horse and was addressing them from the saddle; the litter was some distance behind.

"But we gotter do *sumpen*, marse," said one of the men, protestingly.

"Dance, then! But make no noise about it; when he's safely in his own house again, *then* go down to the pier, if you like, and shout as much as you please."

This was done. The negroes preceded the litter through the streets of Gracias, and waited in sympathetic silence until Mr. Moore had been carried into the rectory, and the door was closed behind him; then they adjourned to the pier, and danced and shouted there as if, old Mrs. Kirby declared, with her hand over her little ears—"as if they meant to raise the dead."

"No, ma, no; they mean to raise the living if they can," said her son, when he came in.

He had been more affected than he would confess by that welcome out on the barren. He had not known himself how much attached he was to the mild-voiced clergyman until it had become probable that soon they should hear that voice no more. The danger of death was now averted, he hoped, though the illness might be a long one; in his own mind he registered a vow never to call any one "limp" again;—he had called Mr. Moore that about once a week for years. "There's a kind of limpness that's strength"—thus he lectured himself. "And you, Reginald Kirby, for all your talk, might not, in an emergency, be able even to *approach* it. And turning out your toes, and sticking out your chest won't save you, my boy; not a whit!"

Fond as Aunt Katrina was of the position of patroness, she was not altogether pleased with some steps that were taken, later. "A proper acknowledgment, of course, is all very well," she said. "But you and Margaret, between you, have really given Mr. Moore a comfortable little fortune. And you have put it in his own hands, too—to do what he likes with!"

"Whose hands would *you* have put it into?" Winthrop asked.

"A lawyer's, of course," Aunt Katrina answered.

"I am afraid Margaret and I are not always as judicious as you are, Aunt Kate."

Aunt Kate was not quick (it was one of the explanations of the preservation of her beauty). "No, you're not; but I wish you were," she responded.

Mr. Moore knew nothing of the increase of his income; it was Penelope who had been won over by Winthrop's earnest logic—earnest in regard to the comfort of the poor sufferer lying blinded, voiceless, helpless, in the next room. What Winthrop was urging was simply that money should not be considered in providing for him every possible alleviation and luxury. His illness might be a long one (at that stage—it was while Mr. Moore was still in the river hotel—no one spoke of death, though all knew that it was very near); everything, therefore, should be done to lighten it. If the rectory was gloomy, another house in Gracias should be taken—one with a large garden; two good nurses should be sent for immediately; and, later, there must be a horse, and some sort of a low, easy vehicle, made on purpose to carry a person in a recumbent posture. Many other things would be required, these he mentioned now were but a beginning; Mrs. Moore must see that neither his aunt, Mrs. Harold, nor himself could take a moment's rest until everything was done that could be done, they should all feel extremely unhappy, miserable—if she should refuse them. If she would but stop to think of it, she must realize that.

Penelope agreed to this.

She had cried so much that she was the picture of living despair, she was thinking of nothing but her husband and his pain; but she forced a momentary attention towards Winthrop, who was talking so earnestly to her, trying to make some impression.

He could see that he did not make much.

"Your husband gave his life—it amounted to that—to save Margaret's; she was nothing to him—that is, no relative, not even a near friend, yet he faced for her the most horrible of deaths. If it had not been for him, that would have been *her* death, and think, then, Mrs. Moore, think what *we* should be feeling now." He had meant to say this steadily, but he could not. His voice became choked, he got up quickly and went to the window.

Penelope, who, tired as she was, and with one hand pressed constantly against her weak back, was yet sitting on the edge of a hard wooden chair, ready to jump up and run into the next room at an instant's notice, tried again to detach her mind from her husband long enough to think of what it was this man was saying to her; she liked Margaret, and therefore she succeeded sufficiently well to answer, "It would have been *terrible*." Then her thoughts went back to Middleton again.

"Don't you see, then," said Winthrop, returning, "that, standing as we do almost beside her grave, your husband has become the most precious person in the world to us? How *can* you hesitate?" he said, breaking off, "how can you deny us the pleasure of doing everything possible—so little at best—to help him in his great suffering?"

"Oh yes—his suffering! his suffering!" moaned the wife, the tears dropping down her white cheeks without any distortion of feature. Her eyes looked large; singularly enough, though she was so exhausted, her countenance appeared younger than he had ever seen it; under the all-absorbing influence of her grief its usual expressions had gone and one could trace again the outlines of youth; her girlhood face—almost her little-girl face—had come strangely back, as it does sometimes after death, when grandchildren see, with startled, loving surprise, what "grandma" was when she too was only sixteen.

Winthrop took her thin worn hand and carried it to his lips; her sorrow was very sacred to him. "For you too," he urged—"you who are so tired and ill—let us help you all we can. Do not refuse us, Mrs. Moore; *do* not."

The door into the next room now opened softly, and Dr. Kirby entered, closing it behind him. "No—sit still," he said, as Mrs. Moore started up. "There's nothing to be done for him just now; he's asleep." He called it "sleep," to pacify her. "I came in to say," he went on—"I knew you were here, Mr. Winthrop—that there must *not* be so much noise on this floor; I have no doubt the people of the house are as careful as they can be, in fact, I know they are; but there are others here."

Winthrop turned to Penelope. "*Now* will you consent?" he said.

(She looked at him; she was thinking only of the blessed fact that Middleton was asleep.)

"You hear what Dr. Kirby says?—the house must be kept more quiet. I can clear it immediately of every person in it. The noise is bad for your husband—don't you understand? It will make a difference in his—in his recovery."

"Oh! do anything, anything!" said the wife, wringing her hands.

He pursued his advantage. "You are willing, then, that I should do everything possible—for his sake, you know? You consent."

"Yes, yes," she answered.

"By—all—means," said Dr. Kirby, impressively. "Consent? Of course you consent, Penelope." He had never called her Penelope before in his life. After that he never called her by any other name.

It seemed to Reginald Kirby a natural thing (and a small one too) that these northerners should wish to do everything they could for the dying hero in there; at that time the Doctor thought that the clergyman must die.

Twelve hours later, with the exception of the proprietors and their servants, there was no one save Mr. Moore and his friends in the river hotel. And the house was held empty as long as he remained there. Aunt Katrina never could find out how much those weeks cost her nephew.

But she did find out that her nephew and Margaret together had given the Moores that "comfortable little fortune," though it was not in Mr. Moore's hands, as she supposed; it was in Penelope's.

Penelope herself knew but little about it even now, save the fact (a great one) that where she had once had a dollar to spend in a certain time, she now had ten; they had lived on six hundred a year, they now had six thousand.

Mr. Moore noticed his new luxuries; he knew that Evert Winthrop had sent many of them down from New York, and he felt very grateful; he asked Penelope if she had sufficiently thanked him.

"Why, Middleton dear, he's grateful to *you*," Penelope answered.

She never confessed that it was she herself who had asked for the ivory brushes. Once let loose on that track, her imagination had become wildly lawless; she had not considered the rectory gloomy, as Winthrop had suggested, but there was no doubt but that she would have suspended pink silk curtains round Middleton's bed if the idea had once occurred to her. She had always had a secret admiration for velvet coats—which she associated in some way with King Charles the Martyr—and she now cherished a plan for attiring Middleton in one (when he should be able to be attired), and had even selected the color—a dark wood brown; it would not do for church work, of course; but while he was still an invalid, now—And she lost herself in dreams of satin linings.

On the day after the fire Margaret had left the river.

It was now thought that she had caused the fire herself; she had wakened, feeling somewhat chilled, and had gone across to a store-room in the main building to see if she could get a blanket; having no candle, she had taken a box of matches from her travelling-bag, and had used them to light her way, and probably some spark or burning end had fallen among the stored woollens, and the fire had smouldered there for some time before making its way out.

She was suffering from nervous shock, she knew that she should be of no use as a nurse, at least for the present; Dr. Kirby and Mrs. Moore had reached the hotel, and Winthrop was to remain with them. She could not travel far, but she could cross over to East Angels; she decided to do that.

When she reached the house, Aunt Katrina's voice greeted her: "Oh, Margaret! Margaret! what a horrible fright you *have* given me!"

Celestine, however (there were certain emergencies when Celestine did not scruple to interrupt Aunt Katrina), appeared promptly upon the scene from somewhere, took Margaret up in her arms as though she had been a child, and carried her off to her bedroom.

"Oh, Miss Margaret!" she said, weeping over her one or two big tears as she laid her down on the bed—"oh, Miss Margaret!"

"There's nothing the matter with me, Minerva, except that I am tired," Margaret answered.

And she did look tired; she was so exhausted that she had not laughed over Celestine's idea of taking her up and carrying her, she was glad to be carried.

But having shed her tears, Celestine was now the nurse again. "Don't speak another word!" she said, peremptorily. And then, with careful hands, she undressed Margaret and put her to bed.

At the end of the third day Margaret was able to present herself again in Aunt Katrina's sitting-room.

"I suppose you've got to get it over *some* time," was Celestine's reluctant assent.

"But how in the world, Margaret, did you ever come to go back to that house all alone, *late* at night, and without letting a soul know?" demanded Aunt Katrina, in the course of her cross-examination. "I've *tried* to conceal what I thought of such a freak!"

"It was not late," Margaret answered, "it was early. I changed my mind about sleeping at the hotel, I thought I should rather sleep in my own house, after all; so I went back. Then when I found that Mr. Moore had already gone to bed, early though it was, I decided not to disturb him."

"What a piece of craziness!—and to think, too, that at your age you should have gone wandering about with matches! Well, I am glad that *I* at least have no such tastes; when I say I am going to sleep in a place, I sleep there, and you have no idea what sacrifices I have made sometimes, when travelling, to keep my word—keep it merely to myself; it *is* so much better to do what you say you're going to, and not keep changing your mind. I can never be thankful enough that Lanse was not there; *he* could never have escaped so easily as you did, poor fellow; it really seems almost providential—his having gone off on that journey just at that time. And as to the wandering about with matches, Margaret (for it all comes back to that), it's an excellent rule for people who have those manias never to allow themselves to get out of bed (until the next morning, of course) after once they're in; now do promise me that you will make it yours, at least as long as you are staying here; otherwise I shall be so nervous."

"I wasn't in bed at all," said Margaret.

"A lounge is the same thing; don't quibble," said Aunt Katrina, severely.

Here Betty, hurrying in, fell on Margaret's neck and kissed her, holding her closely in her affectionate arms. "Oh, my dearest child! restored to us from that *dreadful* danger, thank God! To think how near you came—Oh, my dear, dear girl!" She kissed her again, and got out her handkerchief to dry her brimming eyes. "We're going to have prayers in the church, my dear—*thanksgiving*."

"What a pity it is, Betty, that you are so demonstrative! Can't you be glad to see Margaret without boohooing? And when my head is in such a state, too."

"I am very sorry, Kate, I'm sure," Betty answered. She sat down on the sofa beside Margaret; as there was a table in front of her which concealed the movement, she put out her hand furtively and took Margaret's in hers, holding it with tenderness, and giving it every now and then a motherly pressure. In the mean while, she talked as usual to her dear Kate. This was not duplicity on Betty's part; on principle she never opposed Kate now, she was such an invalid, poor thing! In her heart lurked the conviction that if Kate would only "let her figure go," and be just "natural," as she (Betty) was, her health would immediately improve. People's figures altered as they grew older, it was useless to say they didn't; no one could retain a slim waist after forty-five; dear Kate was over sixty,—really it was not *seemly* to be so girted in.

If dear Kate could have suspected these opinions, there is no doubt but that she would have risen from her couch, figure and all, and turned her uncinctured Elizabeth from the room.

On the fourth day Winthrop came over from the river.

Learning from Celestine that his aunt was in a fairly comfortable condition, he had fifteen minutes of serious conversation with her; he told the truth about Lansing Harold's relations with his wife, as well as his relations with another person.

Aunt Katrina was greatly overcome. She cared more for Lanse than for any one; much as she cared for him, she had always admired him even more. She cried—really cried; her handsome face became reddened and disfigured, and she did not think of it. "He was such a *dear* little boy," she said, sobbing. Then she rallied. "If he had had another sort of wife, he would have been different."

"That's what is always said about such men. In any case, there's nothing gained by going back to that now."

"*I* think something is gained; justice is gained—justice for Lanse. And, mark my words, Evert, Margaret *Cruger* has not suffered."

"Whether she has or not, she is going to leave us."

"What?" said Aunt Katrina, quickly, turning towards him her altered countenance. He scarcely knew it, with its reddened eyes and spotted look.

"You thought, I believe, that she was only going to be absent a short time," he went on; "that it was merely that she wished a change. But it was more than that; she has a plan for opening that old house of hers near Cherry Valley, and living there."

"And *me*?" said Aunt Katrina, in angry amazement. "Does she cut herself free from *me* in that way? In *my* state of health?"

"It appears so."

Aunt Katrina remained speechless. Pure dismay was now conquering every other feeling.

"The truth is, Aunt Katrina, you have not been kind enough to Margaret, ever."

"Kind!" ejaculated the lady.

"No. She has done everything for you for years, and you have constantly illtreated her."

"Illtreated! Good heavens!"

"She has therefore decided—and I am not much surprised—that she would rather have a home of her own."

"And you abet her in this?"

"Not at all, I think she had much better stay with you; I am only explaining to you how she feels."

"I don't know that I care to understand Margaret *Cruger's* feelings."

"Exactly; you don't. And therefore she is going."

Aunt Katrina was evidently struggling with her own thoughts. He left her to the contest.

At last, "Poor child!" she said, sighing, as she gently pressed a handkerchief to different parts of her disordered countenance—"poor child!"

Winthrop waited for further developments; he knew they would come.

"It is natural that I should have been cold to her, perhaps, feeling as I did so keenly how unqualified she was to make a congenial home for Lanse. But, as you say, probably she cannot help it, it is her disposition. And now, to think what she must be feeling!—she has, in her way, a strict conscience, and to-day she faces the fact that, by her own utter want of sympathy (which I suppose she really cannot help), she has driven her husband away a *second* time, sent him a *second* time into bad courses! I realize, indeed, that it is the moment when I ought to do everything I can for her, when I should stifle my own feelings, and treat her with the greatest tenderness; don't you agree with me?"

"Fully. But even then I don't know that you can induce her to stay."

"Really—the more I think of it, the more sorry I feel for her, she is deeply to be pitied; I can imagine how crushed *I* should have felt if Peter had deserted me! But if he *had* done so, I should have gone immediately, of course, to stay with some older relative—it is the only proper way. You might represent to Margaret how much better it would look if she should continue, as before, to reside with me."

"Perhaps she won't take so much pains about the 'look' of anything, this time; perhaps she will let people know the real facts; she has always concealed them before."

"They would only be her own condemnation, in any case; everybody would perfectly understand that it was some lack in *her*," answered Aunt Katrina, with decision. "But I think you had better speak to her, and immediately; it *is* so much more desirable, on her own account, that she should remain with me. I don't fancy she cares much for *you*, or she would never have tried to engage you to that odious Garda Thorne; still, you are a relative—- after a fashion, and she ought to listen to you; you might tell her," she added, her voice falling into a pathetic key, "that probably I shall not be left to her *long*."

"My dear aunt, you will outlive us all," said Winthrop, rising. "I will see her, and do what I can," he added, as he left the room.

At first he could not find Margaret, she was not in any of the usual places; he began to fear that she was in her own room, and that he should not find her at all. At last he met Celestine. "Do you know where Mrs. Harold is?" he said.

"Well, Mr. Evert, she's in the garden," Celestine answered, with some reluctance. "I've fixed her up nicely in an easy-chair on a rug, and I've told everybody to keep away, so that she can just rest—that's what she needs. I've let her have *one* book—an easy-looking story that didn't seem exciting. And I'm going out after her in about an hour, to bring her in."

"I won't be any more exciting than the easy-looking story, Minerva; I promise you that."

Celestine watched him go, she was not pleased, but she could not help herself. She shook her head forebodingly, with her lips pursed up; then she went about her business—as she would herself have said.

Margaret was sitting under the rose-tree, in the easy-chair Celestine had mentioned, a rug spread under her feet. She had a parasol beside her, but the tree gave a sufficient shade; over her head Celestine had folded a Spanish veil.

"I thought perhaps we should see you to-day," she said.

"Yes, it hasn't been possible to come before. But of course you have had my letters—I mean about Mr. Moore? I have written twice a day. Is that the book Minerva said was an easy-looking one, not exciting—'Adam Bede?' What do you suppose she calls exciting?"

"The 'Wide, Wide World,' I presume."

He sat down on the bench near her. Carlos stalked out of the bushes, surveyed them, and then, with great dignity, secluded himself again.

"He misses Garda," Margaret said.

"I suppose Garda is still pursuing her triumphant career over there?"

"I don't know what you mean by triumphant. She is very happy."

"That's what I mean; it's extremely triumphant to be so happy, isn't it?"

"I am sure I don't know."

"You mean you have never been either?—Margaret, I have come to speak about your going away. Are you still thinking of going?"

"Yes; as soon as I am a little stronger."

"Aunt Katrina has sent me to plead with you; of course that's the last thing she calls it, but it's pleading all the same. I don't make any plea for her, because I don't think, as far as you are concerned, she deserves the least fragment of one; but I will say that I have told her the whole truth about Lanse at last, and that it has been a great blow to her, I have never seen her so much overcome. She has rallied however, she has taken her line; her line is the tenderest pity for you, *because* you must feel it all to be so entirely your own fault!—you see how much that allows her? But she is so exceedingly anxious—abjectly anxious, to keep you with her, that I think you need fear no unpleasant manifestations of it."

"Aunt Katrina does not really need me. And for myself a change is indispensable."

"But it is so safe for you here—so quiet and protected. It is a species of home, after all. I like to see you, as you are at this moment, sitting in this old garden; it seems to me so much pleasanter for you—with this restful air to breathe—than that bustling, driving New York."

"It may be so. But I need change."

"You cling to that." He paused. "I believe you simply mean freedom."

"Yes, I do mean it. But we are going over the same ground we have already been over; that is useless."

"Everything is changed to me since then," said Winthrop, abruptly. "I have seen you brought back from the very threshold of death, I cannot pretend to be the same."

"I am the same."

"Yes; you didn't see *yourself*—"

"Don't talk about it, please. It is true that, personally, I do not realize it. But when I think of Mr. Moore, I do; and it makes me ill and faint."

"Why shouldn't you begin your freedom—yes; but begin it here?" he went on, returning to his argument. "Aunt Katrina has taken a new line about you. Why shouldn't you take one about her? And about everything? The people here are tiresome, of course; but people are tiresome everywhere, sooner or later, unless one leads a life of just dipping in, never staying long enough in any one place to get much below the surface. You could set up your own horses, your own servants; you could rearrange half the house to please yourself; you could carry it all out, as regards Aunt Katrina, with a high hand; she wouldn't make a murmur, I'm confident! And you could easily take some pleasant trips too from here—to New Orleans and Cuba; there's really a great deal to see. And if you are tired (as I should think you might well be) of always saying where you are going, and where you have been, how long you have stayed or intend to stay, and why, you could lay down a rule that no one should ask you a question. If they should continue to do it, you might throw something at them." His plan seemed to him so good as he unfolded it that it made him jocular.

She returned no answer.

"You don't care at all for what I think, or wish."

"No, I don't."

He looked at her as she sat there with face averted, his expression was that of angry helplessness. "All I want," he went on, trying to curb his irritation, "is to feel that you are safe."

"I shall be safe wherever I am."

"No, you won't, a woman like you cannot be, alone. Of course you will do all that is best and proper, but you are far too beautiful to be knocking about the world by yourself."

"Aren't you confusing me a little with Garda?"

"Your sarcasms have no effect; if I were as innocent in other matters as I am with regard to that effulgent young person, I should be quite perfect. But we won't speak of her; we'll speak of you."

"I am tired of the subject." She looked towards the gate as if in search of Celestine.

"She won't be here for some time yet. Bear with me a little, Margaret, don't be so impatient of the few minutes I have secured with you; what we're deciding now is important—your whole future."

"It is already decided."

He dashed his hand down upon his knee. "There's no use trying to argue with women! A woman never comprehends argument, no matter how strong it may be."

She was silent. Her face had a weary look, but there were in it no indications of yielding.

"You appear to be determined to go," he began again; "if you do go, Aunt Katrina will have the mental exercise of learning to get on without either of us."

She looked up quickly; his eyes were turned away now, straying over the tangled foliage of the crape-myrtles.

"I am sick of everything here," he went on—"East Angels, Gracias, the whole of it. If you are tired of seeing the same few people always day after day, what must I be? There are two spinster cousins of Aunt Katrina's who might come down here for a while, and I dare say they would come if I should ask them; with these ladies to manage the house, with Dr. Reginald and Betty, Celestine and Looth, Aunt Katrina ought to be tolerably comfortable."

Margaret had listened with keen attention. But she did not answer immediately; when she did reply, she spoke quietly. "Yes, I should think you would be glad to go north again, you have been tied down here so long. I am sure we can assume now that there is at least no present danger in Aunt Katrina's case; both of us certainly are not needed for her, and therefore, as you did not speak of going, I thought I could. But now that you have spoken, now that I see you do wish to go, I feel differently, I give *you* the chance. The change I wished for I will create here, I will create it by buying this house from you—that will be a change; I can amuse myself restoring it, if one can say that, when it's not a church."

"You *would* do that?" said Winthrop, eagerly. Then he colored. "I see; it means that you will stay if *I* go!"

"I shall do very well here if I have the place to think about," she went on, "I shall have the land cultivated; perhaps I shall start a new orange grove. Of course I shall lose money; but I can employ the negroes about here, and I should like that; as to the household arrangements, Aunt Katrina would be staying with me, not I with her; that would make everything different."

"Yes; I could not come here as I do now, bag and baggage."

"I should not ask you," she answered, smiling. "I believe in your heart you like no woman to lead a really independent life."

"You're right, I do not. They're not fitted for it."

"Oh—"

"And they're not happy in it."

"It's so good of you to think of our happiness."

"All this is of no consequence, Margaret, it's quite beside the mark. The real issue is this: if I stay, you go; if I go, you will stay."

"I thought you didn't like repetitions; you're always so severe on poor Aunt Betty when she indulges in them."

"You've got the upperhand, and you know it, and are glorying," he said, sullenly.

"Glorying!" said Margaret, with a sudden drop in her voice. "Well, we will say no more about it," she added.

"Excuse me, we will say plenty more. I would do a great deal to keep you here, there's no doubt of that. If I must, I must, I suppose! You may have the place—though I'm fond of it still."

"It must be quite fair?" she said, looking at him hesitatingly.

"You mean that I am not to come back and hang about in the neighborhood? Oh, rest content; I've had enough of the Seminole for a lifetime."

"I presume you will be in a hurry," he went on. "You will expect to have the deeds made out to-morrow."

"Yes, I should rather have it done soon."

"Of course.—How you hate me!" He rose.

She did not speak.

"But I'm not surprised—stubborn fool, ineffable prig as I must have seemed to you all these years! Take the place. And I'll go."

The gate clicked, Celestine was coming towards them.

"But though I acknowledge my own faults, don't imagine I admire such perfection as *you* always exhibit," he went on. "It's too much, you're too faultless; some small trace of womanly humility would be a relief, sometimes." He left the garden. Celestine, coming up, found her patient looking anything but rested. The next moment she put her hand over her eyes, physical weakness had conquered her.

"Just what I expected, men haven't a spark of gumption," said Celestine, indignantly. "He might have seen you weren't fit for talking; anybody could have seen. There, Miss Margaret, there; don't feel so bad, you'll soon be stronger now." And Celestine put one arm round her charge tenderly.

The touch made Margaret's tears flow faster; leaning her head against her faithful New England friend, she cried and cried as if her heart would break.

"You're clean tuckered out, I declare," said Celestine, half crying herself. "Everybody plagues you—I never see the beat! And they all seem to think they've got a right to. Just get real mad, now, Miss Margaret, for once; and *stay* so. My! wouldn't they be surprised?"

This was three months before. Margaret was now the owner of East Angels.

On the evening when she had returned from the landing with her ferns, and had found Dr. Kirby talking with Aunt Katrina, she went to her own room; here she threw off the long, closely fitting over-garment of dark silk, and gave it and the Gainsborough hat to her maid; she had a maid now.

"If you please, Mrs. Harold, there are five letters for you; they are on the dressing-table."

"Very well; you need not wait, Hester, I shall not need you at present."

The woman went out with noiseless step. Margaret turned over the letters, glancing at the superscriptions rather languidly. She did not care much for what the mails brought her at present, excepting Garda's short, rapturous notes with various foreign headings.

The last envelope of the pile—it is always the last letter that strikes the blow—was inscribed in a handwriting that made her heart stop beating. "Mrs. Lansing Harold" was scrawled there, in rather large, rough letters; and within, at the end of the second page—there were only two filled—the same name was signed without the "Mrs."

Lanse had come back to America. He was coming back to Florida. He was on his way at that moment to Fernandina, having selected that place because he had learned that she had "burned down the house on the point," which, he thought she would allow him to say, was inconsiderate. He had made up his mind not to take her by surprise, he would go to Fernandina, and wait there. He was a cripple indeed, this time. And forever. No hope of a cure, as there had been before. It wasn't paralysis, it was something with a long name, which apparently meant that he was to spend the rest of his days in bed, with the occasional variation of an arm-chair. This last journey of his abroad had been a huge mistake from beginning to end (the only one he had ever made—he must say that). But he didn't suppose she would care to hear the particulars; and he should much prefer that she should not hear them, it wasn't a subject for *her*. He had come home this time for good and all, it would never be possible for him to run away again, she might depend upon that. In such afflictions a man, of course, counted upon his wife; but he wished to be perfectly reasonable, and therefore he would live wherever she pleased—with his nurses, his water-pillows, and his back rest—yes, he had come to that! At present it wasn't clear to him what he was going to do to amuse himself. He could use his hands, and he had thought of learning to make *fish-nets*. But perhaps she could think of something better? And then, with a forcible allusion to the difficulties of his present progress southward, and a characteristic summing up of the merits of the hotel where he, with his two attendants, was resting for a day, the short two pages ended abruptly with his name.

His wife had sunk into a chair, she sat staring at it.

CHAPTER XXXII

A week later, Margaret was out to walk on the barren.

She had walked far, though her step had been slow; it seemed to her that her step would always be slow now, her effort must be to keep it steady. She had reached a point where there rose on the green level a little mound-like island of a different growth, its top covered with palmetto-trees. She made her way to the summit; though the height of the little hill was low, the view one obtained there was extensive, like that from a small light-house in a salt-marsh. Where she stood there was a cleared space—the ground had been burned over not long before; on this brown surface the crosiers of new ferns were unrolling themselves, and when tired of the broad barren, her eyes rested on their little fresh stalks, green and woolly, though she no longer stooped to gather them. She did not come home now laden with flowers and vines to plant in the old East Angels garden; the life she had been trying to build up there was suddenly stopped, a completely different one was demanding her. She had been very free, but now she was called back—called back to the slavery, and the dread.

Oh, blessed, twice blessed, are the women who have no very deep feelings of any kind! they are so much happier, and so much better! This was what she was saying to herself over and over again, as, with one arm round a slender tree, so that she could lean her head against it, she stood there alone on the little island, looking over the plain. Not to care very deeply, too deeply, for anything, any one; and with that to be kind and gentle—this was by far the happiest nature for women to have, and of such the good were made. Mothers should pray for this disposition for their daughters. Anything else led to bitter pain.

She thought of her own mother, of whom she had no recollection. "If you had lived, mother, perhaps I should have been saved from this; perhaps I should not be so wretched—" this was her silent cry.

She heard a sound, some one was coming through the high bushes below; a moment more, and the person appeared. It was Evert Winthrop.

"*You?*" she said, breathlessly. "When did you come? How could you know I was here?"

"For once I've been fortunate, I have never been so before where you were concerned. I reached East Angels half an hour ago, Celestine said you were out on the barren somewhere, and Telano happened to know the road you had taken; then I met some negro children who had seen you pass, and, farther on, a boy who knew you had come this way; he brought me here. But I saw you a mile off myself, you are very conspicuous in that light dress on the top of this mound."

"We had no idea you were coming—"

"I couldn't let you know beforehand, because I came myself as quickly as a letter could have come; as soon as I knew you would need help, I started."

"Help?"

"Yes, about Lanse."

"Lanse is not here."

"Oh, I know where he is, he is in Fernandina; established there in the best rooms the hotel affords, with three attendants, and everything comfortable. But this time he did not tell me his plans; he arrived in New York, and then came southward, without letting me know a word of it. I heard of him, though, almost immediately, and I started at once."

Margaret did not reply.

"You will need help," he went on.

"No, I think not."

"Then he has not written to you?—has made no demands? I shall think better of him than I had expected to think, if that is the case; I supposed, from his coming south, that he had intentions of molesting you."

"It would not be molesting."

"*Has* he written to you?"

"Yes."

"What demands, then, does he make—is it money?"

"He wishes me to come back to him, as I did before. But he will live wherever I prefer to live. He is quite willing to leave the choice of the place to me." She spoke slowly, as though she were repeating something she had learned.

"Very good. I suppose you told him that wherever you might prefer to live, there would at least be no place there for Lansing Harold?"

"I haven't told him anything yet. He was willing to wait—he wrote that he would give me a month."

"A month for what?"

"For my answer," she said, drearily.

"It won't take a month. That is what I have come down for—to answer in your place."

She began to look about for the best way to descend.

"I sent the boy who brought me here to East Angels for the phaeton; it will come before long, you won't have to walk back. Now, Margaret, let us have no more useless words; of course you do not dream of doing as Lanse wishes?"

"Yes, I think I shall do it."

"Do you mean to tell me that you wish to go back to that man—after all he has done?"

"I do not wish to. But I must."

"You *shall* not!" he burst out. His face, usually so calm, was surprisingly altered; it was reddened and darkened.

"Nothing you can say will make any difference," she answered, in the same monotonous tone. Even his rage could not alter the helpless melancholy of her voice.

"Do you think he deserves it—deserves anything? You actually put a premium on loose conduct. You reward him for it, while—while other men, who are *trying*, at least, to lead decent lives, are thrust aside."

"He is my husband."

"So good a one!"

"That has nothing to do with it."

"Nothing?"

"No; not with my duty."

"I believe you have lost your wits, you are demented," he said, violently.

"Oh, I wish I *were* demented! Then my troubles would be over."

The despair of these words softened him. She had turned away, he followed her. "Margaret, listen to reason. In some cases it *is* right that a wife should go back to her husband, almost no matter what he has done. But yours is not one of them, it would kill you."

"No more than it did before."

"But it's worse for you now."

"It's exactly the same."

"He left you a *second* time."

"I have only to thank him for that, haven't I? It gave me a respite. Over there on the river, when I learned—when I knew—that he had really gone, I could scarcely hide my joy—I had to hide myself to do it! It was the relief, the delight, of being free."

"The law, you know, would free you forever."

"I shall never take advantage of it."

"Do you think you know better than the law?"

"Yes; the law only touches part of the truth. Its plea would not do for me."

"This is pure excitement. Womanlike, you have wrought yourself up to this new view; but it is without a grain of foundation in either justice or common-sense."

"It isn't a new view, I have always known what I should do. That was the reason I wished to keep the house on the river—so that it could be ready in case he should come back. For I felt that he might come at any time, I was never deceived as to any permanent improvement in his health. I have thought it all over again and again; there isn't a loop-hole of escape for me. Let us say no more."

"I shall say a great deal more."

She put out both hands towards him, with a desperate repelling gesture. "Oh, *leave* me!" she cried.

"I shall not leave you until you have given me an explanation that is reasonable; so far, you have not done it. Time and time again you have put me off, to-day you shall not."

Her own cry had seemed to restore to her her self-control.

"Very well," she said. She folded her arms in her mantle. "What explanations do you wish?" she asked, coldly.

"Why are you going back to Lansing Harold, when you are not in the least forced to go?"

"I am forced; my marriage forces me."

"Not after the ill treatment you have received from him."

"He has never illtreated me personally; in many ways he has never been unkind, many men called good husbands are much more so. He does not drink. If he drank, that would be an excuse for me—an excuse to leave him; but he does not, I have never had a fear of that sort, he has never struck me or threatened me in his life. And I have no children to think of—whether his influence over them would be bad. That too would have been an excuse, a valid one; but it is not mine. He leaves me my personal liberty as he left it to me before. In addition, he is now hopelessly crippled—he has sent me his physician's letter to prove it; his case is there pronounced a life-long one, he will never walk, or be any better than he is now. Are these explanations sufficient? or do you require more?"

"No explanations can ever be sufficient," Winthrop answered. He stood looking at her. "Oh, Margaret, it is such a fearful sacrifice!" He had abandoned for the moment both his anger and his efforts at argument.

"Yes; but that is what life is, isn't it?" she said, her voice trembling a little in spite of herself.

"No, it's not. And it shouldn't be. Why should an utterly selfish man of that kind, who has forfeited every claim upon you a hundred times over—why should he be allowed to dictate to you, to wither your whole existence? Yes, I am beginning again, I know it; but I cannot help it! It is true that I have always talked against separations—preached against them. But that was before my own feelings were brought in, and it makes a wonderful difference? When a woman you care for is made utterly wretched, you take a different view, and you want to seize your old preaching-self, and knock him against the wall! It is *not* right that you should go back to Lanse, it is wicked, as murder is wicked. He does not strike you—that may be; but the life will kill you just as surely as though he should give you every day, with his own hand, a dose of slow poison. You have an excessively sensitive disposition—you pretend you have not, but you have; you would not be able to throw it off—the yoke he would put upon you, you would not be able to rise above it, become indifferent to it; you would never grow callous, he would always have the power of making you unhappy. This would wear upon you; at last it would wear you out; you would die, and *he* would live on! And, besides, remember this—it isn't as though he really depended upon you for personal care; he doesn't need you, as far as that goes, he says so. Give him your money, if you like; give him houses and nurses and servants, every luxury, all you have; but do not, do not give him yourself."

She remained silent. She had steeled herself, so it seemed, against anything he could say.

"You are counting the minutes before the phaeton comes," he went on; "that is your only thought—to get away! Very well, then, you shall have the whole, which otherwise I would have kept from you; I love you, Margaret, I have loved you for a long time. If it is horrible to you that I should say it, and force you, too, to hear, bear this in mind: though I say it, I ask for nothing, I do not put myself forward. I tell you because I want you to understand how near your best interests are to me—how I consider them. I deserve some mercy, I have tried hard to hold myself in check—did I say a word all that night in the swamp? You may imagine whether I am happy, loving you hopelessly as I do! It began long ago; when I thought I disliked you so bitterly, that was the beginning; it was a dislike, or rather a pain, which came from your being (as I then supposed you were) so different from the sweet woman it seemed to me you ought to be—ought to be with that face and voice. I watched you; I was very severe in all I said; but all the time I loved you, it was stronger than I. I feel no shame in telling it; it has made me a better man—not so cold, not so sure of my own perfection. And now, if you will only tell me that you won't go back to Lanse, I will go. And I will stay away, I will not try to see you, I will not even write. And this shall last as long as you say, Margaret—for years; even always, if it must be so. What can I do or say more?"

She had stood still, looking at the ground, while he poured forth these urgent words; she might have been a statue.

"There's an icy stubbornness about you—" he began again. "What is it I ask? One promise, and for your own good too, and then I go out into the world again, bearing my pain as best I can, leaving you behind, and free. I don't believe you know what that pain is, because I don't believe you know, or can understand even, how much I love you. I am almost ashamed to put it into words—I am no longer a boy. I had no idea I could love in that way—an unreasoning, headlong feeling. There's no extravagant thing, Margaret—such as I have always laughed at—that I would not do at this moment; and to feel your cheek against mine—I would die to-morrow."

He had not moved towards her, but she shrank back even from his present distance; white-faced, with frightened eyes, she turned; she looked as if she were going to rush away.

"Don't go,—I will not say another word; I only wished you to know how it was with me, it is better that you should know."

He wished to help her, but she would not allow it, she pushed the close bushes aside with trembling hands, and made her way down alone. They reached the barren; the phaeton was approaching.

"I cannot bear to see you so frightened," he said.

"—I believe you are sorry for me," he went on—his voice was gentle now. "And that is why you are afraid to speak—lest you should show it."

She gave him one quick glance; her eyes were full of tears.

"That is it, you are sorry. I thank you for that; and I shall think from it that you have forgiven me those years when I made your life so much harder even than it was, than it need have been."

The phaeton was drawing near.

"I am going to trust you, Margaret, I believe that I can. You will not speak, you think I ought not to have spoken. But if I go away at once, and do not return, perhaps you will be influenced by what I have said, and by what is really the best course for you;—perhaps you will not go back to Lanse. At any rate I shall be showing you that *I* am in earnest,—that I can, and will keep my promise."

The phaeton drew up before them.

"You must not come with me," she murmured.

"You are to drive, Telano," said Winthrop, as he helped her take her place. He stood there until the light carriage had disappeared.

Then he walked northward to Gracias.

CHAPTER XXXIII

"I said I would not write. And I will not, after I once know that your refusal has been sent. It does not seem to me that I am asking much, it cannot long be kept a secret in any case, and, in my opinion, should not be. Let Aunt Katrina write me what has happened; she won't do *you* any too much justice—you can be sure of that! I left Gracias that same day, as I said I would. I have come back here and gone to work again; a man can always do that."

This letter of Winthrop's was from New York. He had been there two weeks, and there were now but ten days left of the month which Margaret had said her husband had allowed for her answer. He did not speak of this in his letter; but it engrossed all his thoughts.

On the day when he could have had a reply from East Angels, there was no letter from the South. He waited twenty-four hours to allow for delays or accident.

Still nothing.

Margaret did not then intend to reply; it was a case where she would have written immediately (or asked Aunt Katrina to write), if she had intended to reply at all.

"I am not worthy even to be spoken to, it seems; I am the mud under her feet. But it shall not be so easy as she thinks!"

He took the next train bound for Washington, Richmond, and the St. John's River. It was the third time he had made the long journey within the space of four weeks.

He was in such a fever now—fever of irritation and anxiety—that he did not any longer try to keep up his trust in her, to be certain, as he had endeavored to be during the intervening time, that she had been influenced by what he had said, or by her own more deliberate reflections, and that in any case, whether he was to be informed of it or kept in ignorance, she was not going back to Lanse. It now seemed to him possible that, in her strange self-sacrificing sense of duty, she might go. He ground his teeth at the thought.

The leisurely train was crossing the pine lands of North Carolina, making such long waits at grassy little stations to take on wood that those passengers who had a taste for botany had time to explore the surrounding country for flowers. A new thought came to him; it was that he need not have counted so carefully the days of the month, or depended upon that; perhaps she had not waited for the whole time to pass, perhaps she had gone to Fernandina, was already there. Meanwhile—the train crept.

"Oh, can you tell me—will I reach Fayetteville before dark?" said a girl behind him. He knew it was a girl by the voice. She was speaking, apparently, to some one who shared her seat.

This person, an older woman (again judging by the tone), was well informed as to the methods of reaching Fayetteville, the trains, and the hours. This matter settled, they went on talking.

"I have been up in the mountains teaching," the older woman presently remarked.

"Oh," said the girl, sympathetically (falling inflection).

"I have been there a year, and I trust when I came away I left light behind."

"*Oh* yes."

"At present I have no situation, though I have one in view. They are most anxious to have me, but I say to myself, '*Will* I do the most good there? Is it a place where my influence will carry the most weight?' For we should all do the best we can with our talents, it is a duty; I do the best I can with mine."

"Oh *yes*, I reckon so. And you speak so beautifully too. Perhaps you've spoken?—I mean before people?"

"Never in public," answered the other voice, reprovingly; "to my pupils, but never in public. I think a woman should always keep her life secluded, she should be the comfort and the ornament of a purely private home. *We* do not exhibit our charms—which should be sacred to the privacy of the boudoir—in the glare of lecture-rooms; *we* prefer to be, and to *remain*, the low-voiced, retiring mothers of a race of giant sons whom the Muse of History will immortalize in the characters of soldier, statesman, and divine."

"Oh yes," said the girl's voice again, in good-natured, if inattentive, acquiescence.

Winthrop glanced back. The young girl was charmingly pretty, with a sweet indifference in her eyes. The older woman—she was over fifty—was of a martial aspect, broad-shouldered, large-boned, and tall; her upper lip was that of a warrior, her high cheek-bones had an air of resolute determination.

Comfort and ornament of a purely private home, as she had just proclaimed herself, it seemed almost as if her powers would be wasted there; she was a woman to lead an army through a breach without flinching. The giant sons in her case were presumably imaginary, for she gave her name to her companion as they parted: "Miss Louisa Mearns—they *call* me Lulette." Her voice was very soft and sweet.

"Southerner, of course, with those lovely tones," was Winthrop's mental comment as she passed, stepping rather delicately, and, tall as she was, without any stride. "But she's got a thorough soul of Maine, though she doesn't dream of it. There must have been transmigration somewhere among her ancestors." And then from sheer weariness and restlessness he went into another car.

His feeling was that this train would be in North Carolina a week. But it got on. It traversed South Carolina and Georgia, it passed through the cotton country, it crossed beautiful rivers rolling slowly towards the sea, then it made a wide detour round Okefinokee swamp, and at last brought him again to the margin of the broad St John's. It seemed to him that half a lifetime had passed since he left it.

He reached East Angels in the afternoon. Cindy appeared. Yes, Mrs. Rutherford and Mrs. Harold were both at home; they were in Mrs. Rutherford's sitting-room up-stairs. But when she had preceded him and opened the door of that apartment, only Aunt Katrina was there.

"Mercy, Evert! where did you come from?" she exclaimed, in a key rather higher than her usual calm tones. It seemed to him that she looked frightened.

"From New York, of course. You are alone? Where is Margaret?" He spoke abruptly.

"Oh, she's *here*," responded Aunt Katrina, quickly, in a reassuring voice.

But her emphasis told him that it might not be "here" long, it might be some other word. Would that word be "Fernandina?"

At any rate, Margaret was not yet gone.

"What do you mean by 'here?' She's not in the room."

"She doesn't spend every moment with me; I want *some* time for my own reading and—and meditation. She's in the garden, or the drawing-room, I suppose—somewhere about."

"Aunt Katrina, tell me in so many words—is she going back to Lanse?"

"Why—er—why, yes, I believe so." Aunt Katrina's voice fairly faltered.

"You have had a hand in this: you have urged her."

"Well, Evert, she's Lanse's wife, you know."

"Where is she?"

"I have told you already that I don't know."

"Not gone?" he said, with quick-returning suspicion.

"Oh dear no! What are you thinking of?"

"I'm thinking that I cannot trust either of you! When is she going, then?"

"Well, there has been a good deal about that. Back and forth, you know; letters and—"

"*When?*" he repeated, imperatively.

"To-morrow," answered Aunt Katrina, in almost the same tone as his own. "How you do storm, Evert!"

But he had left the room before her words were finished.

Margaret was not in the drawing-room, she was not in the garden. He met Pablo. "Do you know where Mrs. Harold is?" he said.

"She's in der yorrange grove, sah. I ben dar myse'f looken' arter der place a little, as I has ter, en I see her dar." Pablo meant the old grove—his grove; the new grove was on the other side of the house, and was as ugly as a new grove always is. Down to this hour old Pablo had never become satiated with the delight of working in the old grove at his own pleasure and according to southern methods alone; poor little Melissa Whiting's voice had long been stilled, but Pablo was rioting yet.

The old grove was in bloom. It was not so productive now as it had been in Mrs. Thorne's day, but it was more beautiful; Pablo's rioting had not included steady labor of any sort, there had been no pruning, and very little digging; the aisles were green and luxuriant, the ground undisturbed. The perfume of the blossoms filled the air; on some of the trees blossoms and ripe fruit were hanging together.

Winthrop walked on under the bright foliage and bride-like bloom. But there was no sign of Margaret.

"Of course she would not be here," he thought, "or at least she would not stay; it's far too sweet."

At length he saw her light dress. She was not in the grove, as he had thought; she was in a glade beyond it. Here there was an old nondescript pillar, crowned by a clumsy vase. She was leaning against this ornament, with her back to the grove; one arm lay across the top. She wore no gloves, and he could see her pretty hand with its single ring, the band of plain gold. In front of her there was the low curb of an old well, overgrown with jessamine; she appeared to be looking at it.

His footsteps had made no sound on the soft earth, he came upon her before she discovered him.

"I don't think you can be much surprised to see me," he said; "you have waited here to the last hour of your allotted time. You might have gone days ago, and then I should not have seen you at all; but you have waited. It looks quite as if you expected me to come, as if you wished to give me one more final thrust before you joined your excellent husband. Of course I deserve nothing better."

CHAPTER XXXIV

"Yes, I have waited. But it was because I have been trying to—to arrange something," Margaret answered.

She had taken her hand from the old pillar, she stood erect now, with the white shawl she was wearing folded closely round her.

"Something nicely calculated to make me suffer more, I suppose; I haven't been punished enough for speaking as I did."

"It wasn't anything that concerned you."

"That everlasting self-possession of yours, Margaret! Here I come upon you suddenly; you're not a hard-hearted woman at all, and yet, thanks to that, you can receive me without a change of expression, you can see all my trouble and grief, and talk to me about 'arrangements!'"

"You asked me—you accused me—" Her calmness was not as perfect as he had represented it.

"What are the arrangements?" he said, abruptly.

"Do you think we had better discuss them?"

"We will discuss everything that concerns you. But don't be supposing I haven't heard; I have seen Aunt Katrina, and forced it out of her, I know you intend to go back to Lanse—intend to go to-morrow."

She did not reply.

"You don't deny it?"

"No, I don't deny it."

"And the arrangements?"

"I—I had thought of living here."

"Here, at East Angels, you mean? Oh, you wish to bring *him* here? An excellent idea; Aunt Katrina would not be separated longer from her dear boy, and Lanse and his retinue would fit in nicely among all the comforts and luxuries we have between us collected here. Yes; I see."

There was a quiver for an instant in Margaret's throat, though her face did not alter. "My only thought was that perhaps it would be more of a home for me," she answered, looking off over the green open space and the thicket beyond it.

His hardness softened a little. "Of course it would. You surely cannot have had the idea of living at Fernandina?"

"That would be as Lanse says."

"You are determined to go back to him?"

"Yes."

He changed his position so that he could have a better view of her face. "Bring him here, then!" he exclaimed. "Anything is better than to have you wandering about the world, homeless!"

"You would let me come and see you now and then?" he said, beginning again. He spoke in what he himself would have called a reasonable tone. "I could help you in a good many ways; of course, in saying this, you understand that I agree to accept Lanse—as well as I can."

"You must never come."

"Do you mean that?"

"I mean it unalterably."

"It's because I spoke as I did—this is my punishment. But if I promise never to speak in that way again?"

"You must not come."

"Tell me just what it is you intend to do—we'll have it out now. Tell me the whole, you needn't spare."

"After to-day, I wish—I intend—never to see you again—that is, alone. It is hard that you should make me speak it out in this way."

"Oh—make; you are capable of saying whatever you please without being made; whatever will do me the most good and hurt me the most—the two are synonymous in your opinion—that is what you delight in."

She had turned away with bent head.

"You are not as strong as you thought you were; it does hurt you, Margaret, after all, to say such things to me."

There was an old stone seat, with a high back, near the pillar; she sank down upon it.

"What you wish is to have me leave you—tire you and vex you no more. But I cannot go quite yet. I tell you that I will accept Lanse, as well as I can; I promise never again to open my lips as I did that last day; and still you are going to shut your door in my face, and keep it shut; and you assure me it is forever. This is unreasonable—a woman's unreason. Why shouldn't I come occasionally?—what are you afraid of? You will be surrounded by all your safeguards, your husband at the head. But your own will is a safeguard no human power could break; you are unassailable, taken quite by yourself, Mrs. Lansing Harold."

She did not look up.

"And you wouldn't be able, either, to carry it out—any such system of blockade," he went on. "Aunt Katrina would send for me; leaving that aside, Lanse himself would send; Lanse doesn't care a straw what my real opinion of him may be, so long as he can get some talk, some entertainment out of me, and it will be more than ever so now that he is permanently laid up. And if you should tell him of my avowal even, what would he say? 'Of course you know how to take rubbish of that sort'—that is what he would say! And he would laugh delightedly to think of *my* being caught."

Still she did not move.

He walked off a few paces, then came back. "And here, again, Margaret, even if you should be able to influence both Aunt Katrina and Lanse against me, do you think that would prevent my seeing you—I don't mean constantly, of course, but occasionally? Do you suppose I should obey your rules—even your wishes? Not the least in the world! I should always see you, now and then, in some way. I shouldn't make myself a public annoyance; but—I give you warning—I shall never lose sight of you as long as I breathe, as long as I am alive."

She stirred at last, she looked up at him.

"Yes, I see you are frightened; you wish to go—escape, go back to the house and shut yourself up out of my reach, as you usually do. But this time I'm merciless, I feel that it's my last chance; you cannot go (you needn't try to pass me) until you have told me why it is that you wish not to see me again, never again, in spite of the safety, the absolute unapproachableness of your position."

She sat there, her eyes on his hard, insistent face.

"Why do you make me more wretched than I am?" she asked.

"Because I can't help it! There is a reason, then?"

"Yes." She had bent her head down again.

"I thought so. And I am prepared to hear it," he went on.

His voice had altered so as he brought this out that she looked up. "What is it you expect to hear?" she asked in a whisper.

"It's a new idea, I admit—something that has just come to me; but it explains everything—your whole course, conduct, which have been such a mystery to me. You love Lanse, you have always loved him; that is the solution! In spite of the insult of his long neglect of you, his second desertion, you are glad to go back to him; there have been such cases of miserable infatuation among women, yours is one of them. But you do not wish *me* to see the process of your winning him over, or trying to; so *I* am to be sent away."

She got up. "And if I should say yes to this, acknowledge it, that would be the end? You would wish to see me no more?"

"Don't flatter yourself. Nothing of the kind. Recollect, if you please, that I love you; with me, unfortunately, it's for life. You may be weak enough—depraved enough, I might almost call it—to adore Lanse,—do you suppose that makes any difference in my adoring you? Do you think it's a matter of choice with me, my caring for you as I do? That I enjoy being mastered in this way by a feeling I can't overcome?"

"I am going to tell you my life," she said, abruptly.

"I know it already.—How beautiful you look!"

"I ought to look hideous." She walked about for a moment or two, and finally stopped, facing him, behind the old stone seat.

"It will make no difference what you say, I can tell you that now," he said, warningly.

"I think it will make a difference. You are not cruel."

"Yes, I am."

"I never loved Lanse," she began, hurriedly. "In one way it was not my fault; I was too young to appreciate what love meant, I was peculiarly immature in my feelings—I see that now.

"When the blow came, the blow of my discovering—what Lanse has already told you, I was crushed by it,—I had never known anything of actual evil.

"He told me to 'take it as a lady should.' I didn't know what he meant.

"I had no mother to go to. I felt even then that Aunt Katrina wouldn't be kind. In the overthrow of everything, the best I could think of to do was to hold on to one or two ideas that were left—that seemed to me right, and one of these was silence; I determined to tell nobody what had really happened; I would be loyal to my husband, as far as I could be, no matter what my husband was to me.

"So I went back to Aunt Katrina (as Lanse preferred). And I told nothing.

"I have no doubt I appeared cold enough. In the beginning there *was* a good deal of coldness, though there was always suffering underneath; but later it wasn't coldness, it was the constant effort to hide—I had thought my life difficult. But I had yet to learn that there was something more difficult still. I had not loved Lanse—no; but now I was finding out what love meant, for—for I began to love—you."

Winthrop started, the color rushed up and covered his face in a flood; in his eyes shone the transforming light of a happiness which had never been there before. For this man, in spite of his successes, had never attained much positive happiness for himself in life; Lanse, Lucian, many another idler, attained more. Happiness is an inconsistent goddess, by no means has she always a crown for strenuous effort; very often she seems to dwell longest with those who do not think beyond the morrow; there she sits and basks. However, she had come to Winthrop now, and royally, bringing him that which he cared the most for. He thanked her by his glowing face, his ardent eyes.

"It's nothing to be glad about," Margaret had said, quickly, when she saw the change in his face. "I tell you because I cannot endure that you should believe of me what you thought—about Lanse. And also because I am weak—yes, I confess it. You said you intended to see me, follow me; but now that you know how it is with me, you won't do that."

Winthrop's face remained triumphant. "Odd reasoning, Margaret."

"The best reasoning. So long as it was only you, you could do as you pleased. But now that you know that—that others will suffer too—" She paused. "I am sure I have not trusted you in vain?" she said, appealingly.

But he shook his head, the triumph still animated him. "You can trust me in one way; I won't take advantage, that is, not now. But you needn't try to make me think, Margaret, that it's not something to be glad about—to know that you care for me." He laughed a little from his sheer satisfaction; then, in his old way, he put his hands compactly down in the pockets of his coat, and stood there looking at her.

"Is it anything to be glad about—my wretchedness?" she asked, strengthening herself for the contest.

"It makes you wretched? Strange!"

"I am so wretched—I have been wretched so long—that only my firm belief that my Creator knows best has enabled me to live on, has kept me from ending it."

"Why should you be more unhappy than I am? Nothing could make *me* end my life now."

She looked at him in silence.

"If you look at me in that way—" Winthrop began.

She left her place. He stood where he was, watching her, but he was not paying much heed to what she was saying, now. He had the great fact, man-like, he was enjoying it; it was enough for the present—after all these years.

She seemed to see how little impression she had made. She came back to the old stone a second time to complete her story. "I tried so hard—I was so glad when I saw how you disliked me," she began.

"It wasn't dislike."

"I thought it was; and I was miserably glad. What did I take charge of Garda for but because I thought you loved her? That should be my penance, she should be like my own sister, and I would do everything that I possibly could for her, for her sake and yours. She was so very beautiful—"

He interposed here. "Yes, she was beautiful; but beautiful for everybody. Your beauty is dearer, because it is kept, in its fullest sweetness, for the man you love."

But no blush rose in her face, she was too unhappy for that; she was absorbed, too, in trying to reach him, to touch him, so that he would see what must be, as she saw it. "I did all I could for her," she went on, earnestly—"you know I did; I tried to influence her, I tried to love her; and I did love her. I was sure, too, that she cared for you—"

"It isn't everybody, you must remember, that has your opinion of me," interrupted her listener, delightedly.

"But she herself had told me—Garda had told me that she— However, I begin to think that I have never comprehended Garda."

"Don't try."

"I love her all the same. That afternoon when she was on her way to Madam Giron's to see Lucian, and I took her place, it seemed to me that day that an opportunity had been given to me to complete my penance to the full, and crush out my own miserable folly. I could save her in your eyes, and I could lose myself; for, after that, you could have, of course, only contempt for me. I believed that you loved her, I didn't see how you could help it (I don't see very well even now). And I believed, too, that under all her fancies, her real affection was yours; or would come back to you."

"All wrong, Margaret, the whole of it. Overstrained, exaggerated."

"It may be so, I was very unhappy, I had brooded over everything so long. Next, Lanse came back. And that was a godsend."

"Godsend!" said Winthrop, his face darkening.

"Yes. It took me away from you."

"To him."

"You have never understood—I was only the house-keeper—he wished to be made comfortable, that was all. It was a great deal better for me there."

"Was it, indeed; you looked so well and happy all that time!" His joyousness was gone now; anger had come again into his eyes.

"I could not be happy, how could I be? But at least I was safe. Then he left me that second time. And you were there; that was the hardest of all."

"You bore it well! I remember I found it impossible to get a word with you. The truth is, Margaret, I have never known you to falter, you are not faltering in the least even now. I can't quite believe, therefore, that you care for me as you say you do; you certainly don't care as I care for you, perhaps you can't. But the little you do give me is precious; for even that, small as it is, will keep you from going back to Lanse Harold."

"Keep me from going back? What do you suppose I have told you this for? Don't you see that it is exactly this—my feeling for *you*—that sends me, drives me back to him? On what plea, now, could I refuse to go? The pretense of unhappiness, of having been wronged?" She paused. Then rushed on again. "The law—of separation, I mean—is founded upon the idea that a wife is outraged, insulted, by her husband's desertion; but in my case Lanse's entire indifference to me, his estrangement—these have been the most precious possessions I have had! If at any time since almost the first moment I met you he *had* come back and asked for reconciliation, promised to be after that the most faithful of husbands, what would have become of me? what should I have said? But he did not ask—he does not now; I can only be profoundly grateful."

"Yes, compare yourself with a man of that sort—do; it's so just!"

"It is perfectly just. I am a woman, surrounded by all a woman's cowardice and nervousness and fear of being talked about; and he is a man, and not afraid; but at heart—at *heart*—how much better am I than he? You do not know—" She stopped. "I consider it a great part of my offense against my husband that I have never loved him," she added.

"The old story! Go on now and tell me that if you had loved him, he himself would have been better."

"No, that I cannot tell you; even if I had cared for him, I might have had no influence." She spoke with humility.

"Lanse knew perfectly that I did not love him, he knew it when I didn't," she went on. "And I really think—yes, I must say it—that if I had cared for him even slightly, he would have been more guarded, would have concealed more, spared me more; in little things, Lanse is kind. But he knew that I shouldn't suffer, in that way at least. And it was quite true;

my real suffering—the worst suffering—has not come from him at all; it has come from you. At first I had plans—I was too young to give up all hope of something brighter some time. But my plans soon came to an end; when I knew—discovered—that I was beginning to care for you, all my hope turned to keeping in the one straight track that lay before me. I did not think I should fail—"

"I can well believe that!" he interrupted.

"Oh, do not be harsh to me! you do not know—You think my will is strong. But oh! it isn't—it isn't. When Lanse left me that second time, and you were there with me, I knew then that there was nothing for it but to go as far away from you as possible, and to go instantly; anything less, no matter how I should disguise it, would be staying because I wished to stay. And I did try to go; I would not enter that hotel when I saw you on the shore—I went back to the empty house. I dared not stay then. I *will* not now."

"You do well to change the terms," he answered, with unsparing bitterness, "it's nothing but will to-day, whatever it may once have been. I don't believe about your not daring; I don't, in fact, believe—that is, fully—anything you have said."

"Why, then, should I stay here talking longer?" She left the place and entered the orange grove, which she was obliged to pass through on her way to the house.

But he overtook her, he stepped in front and barred the way. "You have been remarkably skilful. I demanded an explanation, I was evidently going to make trouble. So you gave me this one: you said that you had, unfortunately for yourself, begun to love me, that was the explanation of everything; you threw me this to stop me, like a bone to a dog, so that you could get comfortably away. But I have this to tell you: if you had really loved me, you couldn't have argued quite so well! And you couldn't go now, either, so self-complacently, leaving me here in my pain."

"So be it," she said. She looked through the blossoming aisles to the right, to the left, as if in search of some rescuer, some one.

"But what does a woman like you know of love, after all—real love?" he went on, with angry scorn. "As a general thing, the better she is, the less she knows. And I have never denied that you were good, Margaret."

She moved to pass him.

"Not yet. You have reasoned the whole case out too well, there was rather too much reason; a lawyer couldn't have done it better."

"I have had time to think of the reasons. How often each day do you suppose I have gone over everything—over and over? And how many days have there been in these long years?"

"It isn't the time. It's your nature."

"Very well. It's my nature."

"But you needn't suppose that your having that nature will stop me," he said, with a certain violence of tone roused by her agreement with these accusations. "You have confessed to some sort of liking for me, I shall take advantage of it as far as it goes (not far, I fear); I shall make it serve as the foundation of all I shall constantly attempt to do."

Her arms dropped by her sides. "Constantly? I believe there is nothing in the world so cruel as a man when he pretends to care for you." She moved off a step or two. "I do not love you, you say? I adore you. From almost the first day I saw you—yes, even from then. It is the one love of my life, and remember I am not a girl, it's a woman who tells you this—to her misery. And it is everything about you that I love—that makes it harder; not only what you say and how you say it, what you think and do, but what you *are*—oh! what you are in everything. The way you look at me, the tone of your voice, the turn of your head, your eyes, your hands—I love them, I love them all. I suffer every moment, it has been so for years. I am so miserable away from you, so desperate and lonely! And yet when I am with you, that is harder. Whichever way I turn, there is nothing but pain, it is so torturing that I wonder how I can have lived! Yet would I give it up? Never."

The splendor of her eyes, as she poured forth these words, her rapt expression, the slight figure, erect and tense—he could no more have dared to touch her then than he could have touched a shining seraph that had lighted for an instant in his path.

Her eyes suddenly changed. "When I have hurt you," she went on, "it has been *so* hard to do it—so hard!" She was the woman now; a mist had suffused the blue.

He came towards her, he sank down at her feet. "I am not worthy," he murmured, in real self-abasement.

"No, you are not. But—I love you."

He sprang up. "I *will* be worthy. You shall do all you think right, and I—will help you."

"Yes, help me by leaving me."

"For the present—I will go."

"For always."

"Margaret, do not be hard. And now, when I know—"

"You *do* believe me, then?" she interrupted, with winning sweetness.

"Yes, I believe you! It makes me tremble to think what it would be if we were married; they *say* people do not die of joy."

She came out of her trance. Her face changed, apprehension returned—the old fear and pain. She rallied her sinking courage. "We will not talk of things that do not concern us," she said, gently. "All my life—that is, the peace of it—is in your power, Evert, now that you know the truth about me. But I am sure I have not put faith in you in vain."

"Don't you remember saying to me 'Do you wish me to die without ever having been my full self once?' So now I say to you, Margaret, do you wish to die without ever having lived? You have never lived yet with anything like a full completeness. I am not a bad man, I declare it to you, and you are the most unselfish of women; you have a husband who has no claim upon you, either in right or law; Margaret, let us break that false tie. And then!—see, I do not move a step nearer. But I put it before you—I plead—"

"And do you think I have not felt the temptation too?" she murmured, looking at him. "When Lanse left me, over there on the river, don't you remember that I went down on my knees? It was the beating of my heart at the thought of how easily after that I could be freed—freed, I mean, by law—that was what I was trying to pray down. To be free to think of you, though you should never know it, even that would have been like a new life to me."

"Take it now," said Winthrop. He grasped her hand.

But she drew it from him. "Surely you know what I believe, what all this means to me—that for such mistakes as a marriage like mine there is, on this earth at least, no remedy."

"We'll *make* a remedy."

Again she strengthened herself against him. "Do you think that a separation—I will use plain words, a divorce—is right when it is obtained, no matter what the outside pretext, to enable two persons who have loved each other unlawfully to marry?"

"Unlawfully—you make me rage! *Lanse* is the unlawful one."

"That doesn't excuse me."

"Don't put the word excuse anywhere near yourself when you are talking of Lanse; I won't bear it. And nothing is wrong that we cannot possibly help, Margaret; any one would tell you that. If it is something beyond our wills, we are powerless."

"Against my love for you I may be powerless—I am. But not against the indulgence of it."

"You are too strong," he began, "*I* couldn't pretend—" then he saw how she was trembling.

From head to foot a quiver had seized her, the lovely shoulders, the long lithe length of limb which gave her the step he had always admired so much, the little hands, though she had folded them closely as if endeavoring to stop it, even the lips with their sweet curves—the tremor had taken them all from her control; she stood there helpless before him.

"I can't reason, Margaret, and I won't; in this case reason's wrong, and you're wrong. You love me—that I know. And the power for good of such a love as yours—you magnificent woman, not afraid to tell it—that power shall *not* be wasted and lost. Have you I will!" It was more than a touch now; he held her white wrists with a grasp like iron, and drew her towards him. "I hold you so, but it won't be for long. In reality I am at your feet," he said.

She had not struggled, she made no effort to free herself. But her eyes met his, full of an indomitable refusal. "I shall never yield," she murmured.

Thus they stood for a moment, the two wills grappled in a mute contest.

Then he let her hands drop.

"Useless!" she said, triumphing sadly.

"Though you love me."

"Though I love you."

"It's enough to make a man curse goodness, Margaret; remember that."

"No, no."

"Oh, these good people!" He threw his arm out unconsciously with a force that would have laid prostrate any one within its reach. "You are an exception—you are going to suffer; but generally these good people, who are so hard in their judgment of such things,—they have never suffered themselves in the least from any of this pain; they have had all they wish—in the way of love and home, and yet they are always the hardest upon those who, like me, like you, have nothing—who are parched and lonely and starved. They would never do so—oh no! they are too good. All I can say is, let them try it! Margaret"—here he came back to her—"think of the dreariness of it; leaving everything else aside, just think of that. We are excited now; but, when this is over, think of the long days and years without anything to brighten them, anything we really care for. That breaks down the best courage at last, to have nothing one really cares for."

She did not answer.

"I could make you so happy!" he pleaded.

Her face remained unmoved.

"I long for you so!" he went on; "without you, I don't know where to turn or what to do." He said it as simply as a boy.

This overcame her; she left him, and hurried through the grove on her way to the house, he could hear her sob as she went.

Dr. Kirby's figure had appeared at the end of one of the orange aisles; when he saw Margaret hurrying onward, he hastened his steps. Winthrop had now overtaken her, her foot had slipped and he had caught her. Both her hands were over her face, her strength was gone.

The Doctor came panting up. "My dear Mrs. Harold—" he began.

But she seemed to hear nothing.

The Doctor put his hand on her pulse. "Will you go to the house for help to carry her in?" he whispered. "Or shall I?"

"I can carry her myself," said Winthrop. He lifted her. Unconsciousness had come upon her, her head with the closed eyes, her fair cheek, the soft mass of her hair lay against his shoulder.

The Doctor went on with them for some distance; he was not sure that Winthrop's strength would hold out.

But Winthrop's strength appeared to be perfect.

"I will hurry forward then, and warn them," said the Doctor. And he set off at a round pace.

Winthrop walked steadily; at last he reached the end of the white-blooming fragrant aisles, the path entered a thicket that lay beyond.

The fresher unperfumed air brought Margaret to herself. She stirred, then her eyes opened; they rested uncomprehendingly on his face.

Beyond this thicket lay the garden, where they would be in full view; he was human, and he stopped. "You fainted. The perfume of the grove, I suppose," he said, explaining.

Then everything came back to her, he could see remembrance dawn in her eyes, her fear return.

She tried to put her hand up. But it fell lifelessly back.

This sign of weakness struck him to the heart,—what if she should die! Women so slight in frame, and with that fair, pure whiteness like the inside of a sea-shell, were often strangely, inexplicably delicate.

Her eyes had closed again. He held her closely; but now, save for the holding, he would not touch her. For it seemed to him that if he should allow himself to yield to his longing wish and put his lips down upon hers, she might die there, after a moment, in his arms. It would be taking advantage; in her present state of physical weakness her will might not be able to help her as it had helped her before; she was powerless to resist, and she loved him,—oh yes, he knew it fully now, she loved him. But as soon as she should become conscious that she had yielded, then the reaction would come. Between her love and her sense of duty, this proud will of hers had held the balance. It seemed to him that if he should break down by force that balance, her life might go as well.

He went on therefore, he bore her through the garden towards the house. Her face in its stillness had now an expression that frightened him, it was like the lassitude of a person who has struggled to the utmost, and then given up.

The Doctor and Celestine were waiting at the lower door.

Winthrop refused their aid, he carried Margaret up the stairs to her own room, and laid her down upon the bed.

"I will wait below, Doctor. Come and tell me, please, what you make out."

The Doctor had divined a good deal during this last quarter of an hour, in this stricken woman, this abruptly speaking man, he felt the close presence of something he fully believed in, old though he was—overwhelming love; placed as they were, it could bring only unhappiness. He had no confidence whatever in Winthrop, simply because he was a man. In such situations men were selfish (he himself should have been no better); of course at the time they did not call it selfishness, they called it devotion. But in Margaret his confidence was absolute. And it was with a deep, tender pity for her, for all she had still to go through, that he now bent over her.

Winthrop had gone down-stairs; he paced to and fro in the stone-flagged hall below. The door stood open, the deep soft blue of the Florida sky filled the square frame. "If only she doesn't die!" This was the paralyzing dread that held him like a suffocation. He kept thinking how like a dead person she had looked as he laid her down. "If she comes to,—revives, I will go away, and stay away." In his fear, he could consent to anything.

The Doctor came down after a while. They were two men together, so their words were few; they were just enough to answer the purpose. "I think I can assure you that she will come out of it safely," the Doctor said. "She seems unaccountably weak, she will have to keep her bed for a while; but I am almost positive that it is not going to be one of those long illnesses which sometimes follow attacks of this sort."

"But at best it's rather serious, isn't it?" Winthrop asked.

The Doctor looked at him. "Yes," he answered, gravely.

"If you would let me know from time to time? This is my New York address. It will be more satisfactory to hear directly from you. You can tell her I have gone."

"Gone?"

"Yes; back to New York."

"Oh," said Reginald Kirby. Then, "Ah," he added, this time with the accepting falling inflection.

Winthrop was behaving much better than he had thought he would. All the same, it was now the part of every one to speed him on his way. "I will write with great regularity," he said, extending his hand in good-by. "I will write three times a week," he added, with heartiness; he wanted to do something for the man, and this was all he could do.

He returned to his patient. Winthrop went out to order the horses.

He came back while the negroes were making ready. The lower door still stood open, the house was very quiet; he stole up-stairs and listened for a moment near Margaret's room. There was no sound within; he had the man's usual fear—non-comprehension—of a woman's illness. "Why are they so quiet in there?" he thought; "why don't they speak? *What* are they doing to her?"

But there was a very good reason for the stillness; the Doctor had given Margaret a powerful sedative, and he and Celestine were waiting for the full effect.

Winthrop at length left the door; he realized that this was not a good beginning in the carrying out of his promise to himself.

As he passed down the hall on his way to the stairs he happened to have a glimpse into a room whose door stood partly open; here, ranged in order, locked and ready, were Margaret's trunks, prepared for the journey to Fernandina.

Well, if he was to get away at all, he must go at once!

CHAPTER XXXV

Two weeks passed before the Doctor would allow Margaret to begin her night without an opiate, which should numb her constant weariness into some semblance of rest. During this time he himself did not leave East Angels.

At the beginning of the third week the pale woman in the darkened room began to recover some vitality; she spoke to them, she asked to have the curtains drawn aside; she refused their opiates, even the mildest. The Doctor, relieved, went up to Gracias to see his other patients.

That night, about one o'clock, Margaret spoke. "Celestine?"

A tall figure appeared from a dark corner.

"I told you not to sit up to-night; I feel perfectly well."

"There's a lounge here, Miss Margaret. I can lay down nice as can be."

"No, you are not to stay; I do not wish it."

Celestine demurred; but as Margaret held to her point, she yielded finally, and went out. Some minutes after the door had closed, with a slow effort Margaret raised herself. Then she sat resting for a while on the edge of her bed. Her hair, braided by Celestine in two long plaits whose soft ends curled, gave her the look of a school-girl; but the face was very far from that of a school-girl, in the faint light of the night-lamp the large sad eyes and parted lips were those of a woman. She rose to her feet at last, feet fair on the dark carpet, her long white draperies, bordered with lace, clung about her. With a step that still betrayed her weakness, she crossed the room to a desk, unlocked it, and took something out,—a little picture in a slender gilt frame. She stood looking at this for a moment, then she sank down beside the lounge, resting her arm and head upon it, and holding her poor treasure to her heart. She held it closely, the sharp edge of the frame made a deep dent there. She was glad that it hurt her, that it bruised the white flesh and left a pain. At first her eyes remained dry. Then her wretchedness overcame her, and she began to cry; being a woman, she must cry. Her life stretched out before her,—if only she were old! But she might live forty years more—forty years! "And I have sent him away from me. Oh, how can I bear it!"—this was what she was saying to herself again and again.

If the man whose picture she held upon her heart could have heard the words she spoke to him that night—the unspeakable tenderness of her love for him, the strength, the unconscious violence almost, of its sweet overwhelming tide—no bolts, no bars, no promises even, could have kept him from her.

But he could not hear. Only that Unseen Presence who knows all our secrets, our pitiful, aching secrets—only this Counsellor heard Margaret that night. This silent Friend of ours is always merciful, more merciful than man would ever be; for the unhappy wife, now prone on the couch, shaken with sobs; now lying for the moment forgetful of reality, her eyes full of adoring dreams; now starting up with the flush of exaltation, of self-sacrifice—only to fall back again in stubborn despair—for all these changes the Presence had no rebuke; the torturing longing love, the misery, the relapses into sullen rebellion, and then the slow, slow return towards self-control again, all these it beheld with pity the most tender. For it knew that this was a last struggle, it knew that this woman, though torn and crushed, would in the end come out on the side of right—that strange hard bitter right, which, were this world all, would be plain wrong. And Margaret herself knew it also, yes even now miserably knew (and rebelled against it), that she should come out on that hard side; and from that side go forward. It would be blindly, wretchedly; there could be for her no hope of happiness, no hope even of resignation; she scorned pretenses and substitutes, and lies were to her no better because they were pious lies. She could endure, and she must endure; and that would be all. She could see no farther before her now than the next step in her path, small and near and dreary; thus it would always be; no wide outlook but a succession of little steps, all near and all dreary. So it would continue, and with always the same effort. And that would be her life.

She did not come fully to this now, her love still tortured her. And then at last the merciful Presence touched her hot eyes and despairing heart, and with the picture still held close, she sank into a dreamless lethargy.

When Celestine ventured to steal softly in before dawn, she found her charge like a figure of snow on the floor, the lamplight shining across the white throat, the only place where its ray touched her.

The New England woman bent over her noiselessly. Then she lifted her. As she did so the little picture dropped; she had no need to take it up to know whose face was there. "Poor child?"—this was the gaunt old maid's, mute cry. She had the pity of a woman for a woman.

She placed Margaret in bed; then lifting the picture with a delicate modesty which there was no one there to see, she put it hurriedly back in her hand without looking at it, and laid the hand where it had been, across the fair breast. "When she comes to, first thing she'll remember it and worry. And then she'll find it there, and think nobody knows. She'll think she went back to bed herself." Thus she guarded her.

Grim old Celestine believed ardently, like the Doctor, in love. But like the Doctor, too, she believed that marriage was indissoluble; the Carolina High-Churchman and the Vermont Calvinist were agreed in this. Mistakes were plenty, of course; but when once they had been made, there was no remedy in this life; of this she was sure. But how if one happened to be bound upon the rack meanwhile—a woman whom one loved?

The dress-maker, after looking at Margaret again, went off to a dark corner to "offer prayer." But for the first time in her life she found no words ready; what, indeed, should she pray for? That Margaret might die? She was too fond of her for that. That Lanse might be taken? That had a murderous sound, even if you called it "taken." That Margaret's love might cease? But she knew very well that it would not. So all she said was, "O Lord, *help* her!" very fervently. Then she got up, and set about applying restoratives.

A week later, when Margaret had left her room for the first time, Celestine, at work there, restoring for her own satisfaction that speckless order in which her soul delighted, found upon the hearth, mixed with the ashes, some burned bent metal fragments that had once been gilded—the top of a little frame; she knew then that the last sacrifice had been accomplished. A small one, a detail; but to women the details are hardest.

The Doctor had kept Winthrop strictly informed of Mrs. Harold's health. At first the letters were all the same. But after a while he had written that he was glad to say that she was better. For a long time to come, however (he added), any over-pressure would be sure to exhaust her, and then, in case of a second attack, he should not be able to answer for the consequences. Later he wrote that Mrs. Harold's strength would not now be taxed by any more "untoward interruptions;" she had made her intended journey to Fernandina, he was glad to say, and had returned in safety, Mr. Harold having returned with her. Everything was now comfortably arranged at East Angels; Mr. Harold had the west rooms, and the men he had brought with him—he had three at present—seemed to understand their duties fairly well. Mr. Harold was carried every evening into Mrs. Rutherford's sitting-room, which was an agreeable change for all. Mrs. Rutherford herself had improved wonderfully since her nephew's arrival.

Concerning these letters of his to Evert Winthrop the Doctor felt such a deep sense of responsibility that, short as they were, he wrote them and rewrote them, inspecting each phrase from every possible point of view before his old-fashioned quill finally set it down.

This last result of his selection of the fittest, Winthrop received one morning at breakfast. He read it; then started out and went through his day as usual, having occupations and engagements to fill every hour. But days end; always that last ten minutes at night will come, no matter how one may put it off. Winthrop put off his until after midnight; but one o'clock found him caught at last; he was alone before his fire, he could no longer prevent himself from taking out that letter and brooding over it.

He imagined East Angels, he imagined Lanse; he imagined him in Aunt Katrina's pleasant room, with the bright little evening fire sparkling on the hearth, with Aunt Katrina herself beaming and happy, and Margaret near. Yes, Lanse had everything, he had always had everything. He had never worked an hour in his life; he had pleased himself invariably; he had given heed to no one and yielded to no one; and now when he was forced at last by sheer physical disability to return home, all comfort, all devotion awaited him there, bestowed, too, by the very persons he had most neglected and wronged. "Unjust! unjust!"—this was his bitter comment.

If it had not been for the fear that kept him fettered, he would have thrown everything to the winds and started again for Florida that night, he would have swept the woman he loved out of that house, and borne her away somewhere—anywhere—and he should have felt that he was justified in doing it. But Margaret—he had always to reckon with that determination of hers to do right, even in the face of her own despair. And as to what was right he had never been able in the least to confuse her, to change her, as a man can often change the woman who loves him; just the same she saw it now, and had seen it from the beginning, in spite of all his arguments and pleadings, in spite of all her own.

She loved him. But she would not yield. And these two forces, both so strong that they bent her and swayed her like torturers—if the strife should begin again between them, as it must if he should go to her entreating, was there not danger (as the Doctor, indeed, had written) that her slender strength would give way entirely? He had never forgotten the feeling in his arms of her inert form as he laid it down that day. He should never be able to overpower—he felt that he should not—that something, something stronger than herself, which he had seen looking from her eyes that day in the orange grove; this would remain unchanged, unconquered, though he should have carried her away from everybody, to the ends of the earth, and though—she loved him.

He buried his face in his hands. No, first of all she must not die. For there was always the chance that Lanse himself might die; this did not seem to him a murderous thought, as it had seemed to Celestine. It came across him suddenly that Lanse would probably be quite willing to discuss it with him; he would say, "Well, you know, I perfectly appreciate how convenient it would be." Lanse had no fear of death. He called it "a natural change;" none but a fool, he said, could fear the natural.

Winthrop got up at last and went to the window. The brilliantly lighted street lay below him, but he was not thinking of New York. He was thinking of that old gray-white house in the South, the house he had been fond of, but whose door was now closed to him, perhaps forever. For, unexplainably, though he hoped for Lanse's death, he had not the slightest expectation of it in reality; both he and Margaret had the sense of a long life before them. There would be no change, no relief; only the slow flight of the long days and years, and that would be all. He came back to his hearth; the fire had died; he sat down and stared at the ashes.

CHAPTER XXXVI

"How will she appear?" said Mr. Moore. He sat in his arm-chair, his eyes were following the pattern of the red and white matting on the floor.

"'How,' Middleton?" said Penelope, looking up from her knitting reproachfully. "Why, broken-hearted, poor child!"

"Yes, broken-hearted, I fear; broken-hearted," answered Middleton.

Two years had passed since the burning of the house on the point. Mr. Moore was now quite well again, save that he would always be obliged to walk slowly and support himself with a cane. The rectory was more comfortable than it had been in former years, the rector's clerical coat was a better one; but the rector's wife, with that unconsciousness of her own lacks, which, when it is founded (as in this case) upon a husband's unswerving admiration, is not without its charm—the rector's wife was contentedly attired in the green delaine. Penelope indeed had many causes for contentment; it was so delightful to be able to give five-sixths of one's income to the poor.

At the present moment the Moores were listening for the sound of wheels; not the usual rattle, but the muffled grind through sand which came from the roadways of Gracias.

"Hark!" said Penelope, lifting a forefinger. "Yes—there they are!"

Seizing a little head-covering of green wools, the product of her own crochet-needle, she put it hastily on, and giving Middleton his hat and stick, went with him down the path towards the gate. A carriage had stopped, Dr. Kirby was helping some one to descend from the high, old-fashioned vehicle; the young figure in black, the bright hair under the veil, the overwhelming burst of sobs when she saw their familiar faces—yes, this was Garda who had come back to them, come back home, as they fondly called it; she had been widowed for more than a year, Lucian had died in Venice nineteen months before.

They brought her in, tenderly Mrs. Moore took off the crape bonnet; the girl cried bitterly, her head on Penelope's shoulder. There were tears in the eyes of the two men also; it seemed so strange that this bowed black figure should be their Garda, the beautiful, idle, young girl who had had such a genius for happiness that she had been able to extract full measure of it from even an old hammock and a crane.

Lucian had died suddenly of fever. Garda herself, prostrated by her grief, for months afterwards had scarcely raised her head. Dr. Kirby had started immediately, he had been with her through the worst of her illness. But she had not been alone; her devoted friends in Venice were two sisters and a brother, who, singularly enough, were cousins of Rosalie, Lucian's first wife, and of the same name, Bogardus. These staid, stout people had been fascinated with the Spensers from the first.

And when came the overwhelming blow of Lucian's death, the two ladies, Alicia and Gertrude, immediately took charge of the stricken young wife, and did it with a tenderness which even Dr. Kirby pronounced touching, when he himself arrived in Venice—as soon as was possible, but some weeks later. When Garda at last began to improve a little, her lassitude continued; it was evident that she would not be able to travel for some time to come. Meanwhile the poor Doctor's money was running out. Garda did not think of this; at present she thought only of her sorrow, and then, as had always been said of Garda, she never remembered money at all. Of course the Doctor would not confide to these strangers the embarrassments of his position. And no Bogardus, left to himself, would have been able to conceive the idea that a man, in his senses, could have started to come to Venice from the United States with so small a sum in his pocket as the Doctor had been able to provide. But the facts remained the same; Garda could not travel, the Doctor was obliged to say at last that he must go. In this emergency, Trude and Lish-er, as their brother called them, offered to remain with Mrs. Spenser for the present, to bring her by slow stages across Europe to England, and thence to New York, when she should be able to travel; while Dick Bogardus growled, "Much the best plan! much the best plan!" behind them.

The Doctor had never been able in the least to comprehend Dick, he considered him an extraordinary person; Dick was sixty, short in stature, gruff, and worth five millions. Dick, on his side, was sure that the Doctor was a little out of his mind. But Lish-er and Trude would be very kind to Garda, there could be no doubt of that; they showed an almost tyrannical fondness for her even now—the "thwarted maternal instinct" the Doctor in his own mind called it. And so at last it was arranged, and the anxious guardian started on his long journey homeward, with just enough money to carry him to Charleston (where he could borrow of Sally), and barely a cent to spare.

Lish-er and Trude took their time, they had not been so much interested in anything for years; they said to everybody that Garda was like their "own child." This, of course, was a great novelty. But in reality she was more like their doll—a very beautiful and precious one. Garda herself remained listless and passive. But her mere presence was enough for the two old maids; it was a sight to see them purchasing new mourning attire for her in Paris; to such friends as they met they announced that they were "so extremely occupied" that they hardly knew how they should "get through." But it could not last forever, even the buying of clothes in Paris, and at length they were forced to bring their charge over the ocean to New York—where all the other Bogarduses came to look at her, to see for themselves, if possible, what it could be which had roused such abnormal enthusiasm in "Dick and the girls."

"It's amazing how that Garda Thorne always contrives to make everybody serve her turn," was Aunt Katrina's comment, meanwhile, down in Gracias. "Here's a whole New York family—of our best people, too—waiting upon her slavishly, and bringing her across Europe like, like I don't know what;—like Cleopatra down the Nile!"

"I suppose you mean, then, that Dick Bogardus is Antony?" said Lanse, working away at his fish-net. He had learned to make his nets rapidly now, and was extremely proud of his handiwork; he gave away the results of his labors to "fishermen of good moral character;"—it was necessary that they should be moral.

At the moment when Garda was entering the rectory, Margaret, at East Angels, was coming down the stone stairway on her way to the lower door, where the phaeton and Telano were waiting; she was about to drive to Gracias. As she paused a moment on the bottom step to button her gloves, a long shadow darkened the flags at her feet; she looked up; Adolfo Torres was standing at the open portal. After making one of his formal bows he came towards her; a motion of his hand begged her to remain where she was. "I thought you would be going there," he said. "I have therefore brought these—will you take them for me?" Flowers were abundant in Gracias, but the roses he held towards her were extraordinarily beautiful; all crimson or pink, they glowed with color, and filled the hall with a rich cinnamon scent.

"I will take them if you wish, Adolfo," Margaret answered. "But they are—they are very—"

The roses looked indeed as if intended for a joyous occasion; they were sumptuous, superb.

"You mean that they are bright. I know it; I intended them to be so." He still held them towards her.

"Wait a while," she said.

His face changed. "I know you are my friend," he murmured, as if he were saying it to convince himself. His eyes had dropped to his rejected blossoms.

She could see that he was passionately angry, and making one of his firm efforts to hold himself in control. "I will take them if you wish it," she said, gently, and she extended her hand. "I leave it to you. They are wonderfully beautiful, I see that."

"They came from Cuba; I have been watching them growing for nineteen months—for this."

"It is a house of mourning, you know, that I am going to," she said. "It was, as you say, nineteen months ago—a long time; but the remembrance will be very fresh at the rectory this afternoon."

His anger suddenly left him, he raised his eyes from his roses to her face, and smiled. "It's always fresh to me!" he answered. The glow in his dark countenance, as he brought this out, appalled her, it was like a triumph—triumph over death. He walked to the door and tossed the roses into the sunshine outside. "You are right," he said. "I can afford to wait—now!" And, with a quick salutation, he pulled his hat down over his brows and walked away.

Telano drove Margaret up the water-road to Gracias. It was late in the afternoon when she reached the rectory; Dr. Kirby was watching for her, he came down to the gate to meet her.

"She has gone to her room," he said; "we have persuaded her to go and lie down for a while, as she has done nothing but cry since first seeing the Moores.—I am afraid it will be even worse when she sees you," he added, as they went up the path.

Crossing the veranda, he stopped with his hand on the door, looking at his companion for a moment before entering.

There was no one in the world whom the Doctor now admired so much as he admired Margaret Harold; for the past two years he had secretly given her his unswerving help and support. He thought hers, among women, the most courageous and noble nature he had ever known. And the sweetest, also—ah, yes, in its hidden depths, overwhelmingly, enchantingly sweet! The delicacy of her physical constitution, too (and she did not grow stronger), her nearness to breaking down at times—these things had endeared her to the Doctor greatly; for it touched him to see, month after month, her fair youthfulness growing a little less youthful, her sweet face more faint in color, while at the same time, hour by hour, he saw her perform her full task so completely, in all its details as well as its broader outlines. He knew that she constantly suffered, and that it must be so. With his own eyes he saw how she endured. As a physician, if nothing else, he was aware how infrequent is quiet effort, maintained evenly, day after day, in a sex which can upon occasion perform single actions that rise to the height of the superhuman, and are far beyond the endeavors of any man. But here was a woman capable of the steady effort; it was not merely that she had remained with her husband, had allowed him to take possession again of her life and her home; she had made this home as pleasant to him and to Aunt Katrina as so quiet a place could be made to two such persons. She never secluded herself, she was always ready to talk, she brought others to amuse them; she read aloud, she played backgammon and checkers, she tied the ends of the fish nets and kept an account of them. She accepted and acted upon all Lanse's suggestions regarding her dress; she smiled frankly over his succinct stories, which, as has already been mentioned, were invariably good—Aunt Katrina generally managing to comprehend them by about the next day; in addition she directed the complicated household so that no jars made themselves felt; and during all this time, these long two years, no one had heard a syllable from her lips that was sharp in sound; nay, more, that was not sweet.

There are women who are capable of sacrificing themselves, with the noblest unselfishness in great causes, who yet, as regards the small matters of every-day life, are rather uncomfortable to live with; so much so, indeed, that those who are under the same roof with them are driven to reflect now and then upon the merits of the ancient hermitages and caves to which in former ages such characters were accustomed to retire. These being out of fashion, however, the relatives can only wish (with a certain desperation of fancy) that their dear self-sacrificing companions might imbibe from somewhere, anywhere, such a dose of selfishness as should render their own lives more comfortable; and, as a sequence, that of the household, as well.

The Doctor had had these saints as his patients more than once, he knew them perfectly. But here was a woman who had sacrificed her whole life to duty, who felt constantly the dreary ache of deprivation; but who yet did not think in the least, apparently, that these things freed her from the kindly efforts, the patience, the small sweet friendly attempts which made home comfortable.

The Doctor had been witness to all this, as he had been witness also that day in the orange grove, when Evert Winthrop lifted this same woman in his arms, where she lay speechless, tortured by the pain of parting with him.

Her pain was the same now—he knew that; but she had learned to bear it. Unspeakably he honored her.

And now this woman had come to see Garda in her trouble, Garda who was so infinitely dear to him, though in another way. He felt, as he stood there with his hand upon the door-knob, that he must for once—for once—acknowledge the difference between these two natures; he could not be content with himself without it. "I know you will be very good to her," he said—"our poor Garda, our dear little girl; she is suffering greatly, and we must tide her over it as well as we can. Yes, tide her over it; for you and I know, Mrs. Harold, that deep as her sorrow is—undoubtedly is, poor child!—it *will* pass."

He opened the door, and Margaret entered. Then he closed it from the outside, and made his escape. He felt like a traitor; yet he had had to say it—he had had to say it!

But the next moment he was taking himself to task as he walked violently homeward across the plaza. "Don't you want it to pass, you great idiot, that sorrow of hers? How much good can a woman do sitting all her life upon a tomb? she can't even be ornamental there, in my humble opinion. No; it's a thorough waste, a thorough waste!" He entered his old house, still revolving these reflections; he came bursting in upon Ma.

"Ma," he announced, as the little old lady in her neat widow's cap looked up in surprise—he spoke with emphasis, as he was still suffering sharply from having had, as it were, to denounce Garda—"I am convinced, Ma, that it would have been infinitely better for you, infinitely, if you had married again."

"Mercy on us, Reginald!" said astonished little Ma.

Margaret entered Garda's room with a noiseless step, the Moores had thought it better that she should go alone. The blinds had been closed, but a gleam of the sunset entered between the slats, and made a line of gold across the floor; the motionless figure on the lounge had been covered (by Penelope) with that most desolate of all draperies, a plain black shawl. Though Margaret had entered so quietly, Garda seemed to know who it was; she was lying with her face turned away, but she spoke instantly—"Margaret?" And Margaret came and took her in her arms.

"Margaret, I cannot bear it," Garda said, calmly; "I have tried, but it is impossible. And if *you* cannot tell me how to—you the only one I really believe, I shall not try any more. It is decided."

"Time will tell you how, Garda," Margaret answered, putting her hand upon the girl's head as it lay against her breast. "Time, I think, is the only thing that can help us—women, I mean—when we suffer so."

"But it's nineteen months already," Garda went on, in the same desperately calm tone. "And to-day I've suffered just as much as I did in the beginning—exactly as much."

"Yes—the coming home. It will be different now."

"But now's *now*," said Garda, sitting up, and looking at her friend, her face hardened, her lovely lips set in her pain.

"I mean soon, dear."

"I won't believe it unless you swear it to me," Garda went on. She got up and stood looking at Margaret. "If you will swear it to me I will try to believe it, because *you* know me, and *you* speak the truth."

"Very well, then; listen: I am absolutely sure of it," Margaret answered.

"Sure that I shall stop caring so much? stop feeling so dreadfully?"

"Yes, sure."

"But when will it begin?" the girl demanded, shaken with fresh sobs; she leaned down as she spoke, pressing her hands on Margaret's shoulders and looking at her insistently, as if she would draw from her by force a comforting reply.

"To-morrow, perhaps," said Margaret, answering her almost as one answers a suffering child.

"Well—you mustn't leave me."

"I won't leave you to-night at least."

This gave Garda some slight solace, she sat down and rested her head on Margaret's shoulder. "He was buried in Venice—on that island, you know. Margaret, I want to go down to East Angels to-morrow, mamma is there; do you remember dear little mamma?"

But this quiet did not last long. Suddenly she sprang up again, and began walking about the room, clinching her hands.

Margaret went to her.

"I told you I could not bear it," Garda cried, flinging her off. "You said it would stop, and it hasn't stopped at all. It suffocates me, it's a sort of dreadful agony in my throat that you don't know anything about, you—*you*!" And she faced her friend like a creature at bay. "When shall I begin to forget him?—tell me that. When?"

"But you do not wish to forget him, Garda."

"Yes, I do, I wish I might never think of him on earth again," said Garda, fiercely, giving a stamp with her foot as one does in extremity of physical pain. "Why should I suffer so? it's not right. If you don't help me more than you've done (and I relied upon you so), I shall certainly go to him—go to Lucian. *He'll* be glad to see me, he thinks more of me than you do—you who haven't helped me at all! But it will be easy to end it, you will see; I've got something I shall take. I relied upon you so—I relied upon you so!"

Margaret took her hands. "Give me another day, Garda," she said.

"Only one," answered Garda.

CHAPTER XXXVII

One afternoon, six months later, Margaret, under her white umbrella, opened the gate of the rose garden at East Angels. She came through the crape-myrtle avenue, at the end of its long vista, on the bench under the great rose-tree, she saw Garda; the crane, outlined in profile against the camellia bushes, kept watch over his mistress stiffly; another companion, in bearing scarcely less rigid, stood beside her—Adolfo Torres.

His Cuban slips had served their destiny after all, Garda's lap was full of roses. Crimson and pink, they lay on her black dress a mass of color, contrasting with the creamy hue of the paler roses above her head.

There was always the same interest in Margaret; as soon as Garda saw her friend, she left the bench and came to meet her. The roses tumbled to the ground; Adolfo did not glance at his fallen blossoms, but Carlos, stalking forward, pecked at the finest ones.

"Oh, have you got through at last—that everlasting reading aloud and fish-nets?" Garda inquired. "To think that I should have to give way to fish-nets?"

"I was to tell you—Lanse hopes that you will come in before long," Margaret answered.

"Hopes are good. But I shall not come in." And Garda linked her arm in her friend's. "Or rather, if I do, I shall go and sit in your room with you—may I? Good-by, Adolfo; you are not vexed with me for going?" she added. And, leaving Margaret, she went back to him, extending her hand.

He bowed over it. "Whatever pleases you—"

"*You* please me," answered Garda, promptly. "After they have carried off Mr. Harold to bed, those terrible men of his—about ten o'clock generally—then I never have very much to do for an hour. From ten to eleven, that is the time when I am in want of society."

"But you don't expect poor Mr. Torres to go stumbling home through the woods at midnight, just for the sake of giving you that?" Margaret suggested.

"Yes, I do. Mr. Torres never stumbled in his life. And I don't think he is at all poor," Garda answered, smiling.

He had kept her hand, he bowed over it; he did not appear to think he was, himself.

"Yes—from ten to eleven, that is much the best time. Couldn't you come then, and only then?" Garda went on. "Margaret doesn't mind, she's always late."

"Yes, I've a wretched habit of sitting up," that lady acknowledged.

"It is impossible that any habit of Mrs. Harold's should be wretched," announced the Cuban, with gravity. "She may not always explain her reasons. They are sure to be excellent."

"Come, Margaret, we can go after that," said Garda. "If you should tell him that you had a little habit of scalping—small negroes, for instance—he would be sure that your reasons were perfect. And gather up the scalps." Smiling a good-by to Torres, she drew her friend away with her, going down the myrtle avenue. "What are you going to do?" she asked. "May I come and sit with you till dinner?"

"I have accounts to look over; I shouldn't be much of a companion."

"Always something."

"Yes, always something."

"Well, I shall come, all the same."

An hour later she entered Margaret's room, selected a low chair which she liked, and seated herself. This apartment of Margaret's, which was called her dressing-room, though in reality she never dressed there, contained her own small library, her writing-table, the rows of account-books (with which she was at present engaged), and sewing materials—all articles which Garda declared she detested. "It looks like an industrial school," she said; "you only need shoe-brushes."

"Why shoe-brushes?" Mrs. Harold had inquired.

"They always make them—in industrial schools," Garda had responded, imaginatively.

The mistress of the house had not lifted her head when Garda entered, she went on with her accounts. Garda had apparently lost nothing of her old capacity for motionless serenity; leaning back in her chair, she swayed a feather fan slowly to and fro, looking at the top of a palmetto, which she could see through the open window, shooting up against the blue; her beauty was greater than ever, her eyes were sweeter in expression, her girlish figure was now more womanly. After musing in this contented silence for half an hour, she fell asleep.

Some minutes later, Margaret, missing the soft motion of the fan, looked up; she smiled when she saw the sleeping figure. It was a warm day, Garda had changed her thin black dress for a white one; through the lace, of which it was principally composed, her round arms gleamed. She had dropped her fan; her head, with the thick braids of hair wound closely about it, drooped to one side like a flower.

Margaret had smiled to see how easily, as a child does, she had glided into unconsciousness. But the next moment the smile was followed by a heavy sigh. It was a sigh of envy, the page of figures grew dim, then faded from before her eyes, she dropped her head upon her clasped hands in the abandonment of the fresh, the ever-fresh realization of her own dreariness. This realization was never long absent; she might hope that she had forgotten it, or that it had forgotten her; but it always came back.

It happened that at this instant Garda woke; and saw the movement. She came swiftly across to her friend. "Oh, I knew you were unhappy, though you never, never say so! But now I have caught you, I have seen it. And oh, Margaret, you are so changed!—you are the loveliest woman in the world still,—but you have grown so thin; look at your hands." And she held up one of Margaret's hands against the light to show its transparency.

But Margaret drew her hand away. "If I'm thin, I am only following out my privilege as an American woman," she answered, lightly. "Don't you know that we pride ourselves upon remaining slender?"

"Slender—yes; that is what you *were*. Your arms were always slender, and yet round. But now—" She pushed up Margaret's sleeve. "See your poor wrists. Oh, Margaret, I do believe that before long even hollows in your pretty neck will begin to show!"

"How can they, if I always wear high dresses?" said Margaret, smiling.

She rose as she spoke. But if her motive was to escape from further scrutiny, she was not successful; Garda took hold of her and made her sit down on a couch near one of the windows, and standing in front of her to keep her there, she continued her inspection. "Yes, you are thinner. There are little fine lines going down your face. And your face itself has grown narrow. That makes your eyes too large, I don't like your eyes now; they are too big and blue."

"They were always blue, weren't they?"

"*Now* they are the kind of blue that you see in the eyes of golden-haired children that have got to die," pursued Garda, making one of her curiously accurate comparisons.

Suddenly she held Margaret's hands down with her own left hand, and with her right pushed back swiftly the dark hair; it was the hair that lay low over the forehead; for Lanse's taste was still consulted, his wife's dusky locks rippled softly above her blue eyes, having now certainly nothing of the plain appearance to which he had objected.

The forehead thus suddenly exposed betrayed at the temples a wasted look, with the blue veins conspicuous on the white. "I knew it!" said Garda. She sat down beside her friend, and kissed her with angry tenderness. "What is the matter with you?" she demanded, putting her arms round her and giving her a little shake. "You *shall* tell me. What is the matter?"

"A very natural thing; I am growing old, that is all." And Margaret tried to rearrange the disordered hair.

"Leave it as it is, I am determined to see the worst of you this time. You—with all that pretty hair and your pretty dresses—you have managed to conceal it." And again with searching eyes she examined her friend. "You don't care at all!" she announced.

"Oh yes, I do," said Margaret.

"You don't care in the least. But I care; and something shall be done. They have worn you out between them—*two* invalids; I shall speak to Mr. Harold."

Margaret's face altered. "No, Garda, you must not do that."

"But he likes me," said Garda, insistently; "he will say yes to anything I ask—you will see if he doesn't."

And Margaret felt, like a wave, the conviction that he would; more than this, that he would always have said yes if Garda had been the wife instead of herself. Garda would never have been submissive, Garda would never have yielded. But to Garda he would always have said yes.

"I shall certainly speak to him," Garda persisted. "Why shouldn't I not mind what you say, if it is for your good?'

"It would not be for my good."

"But he is kind to you, I know it, because I see it with my own eyes. He thinks you are lovely, he has told me so; he says you are a very rare type. And he himself—he is so agreeable; he says unusual things; he never tires anybody; his very fish-nets are amusing. I like him ever so much; and though he is crippled, he is very handsome—there is such a golden light in his brown eyes."

"He is all that you say," Margaret answered, smiling at this enumeration.

She could talk about her husband readily enough now. As Garda had noticed, he was always kind, his manner had been steadily kind (though not without many a glimpse of inward entertainment gleaming through it) ever since he entered East Angels' doors; he appeared to have taken his wife under his protection, he told Aunt Katrina once for all, and authoritatively (to that lady's amazement), that she must hereafter, in his presence at least, be "less catty" to Margaret. During the one visit which Evert Winthrop had paid to Florida in the same period, Lanse announced to him (in the tone of the old Roman inscription)—"I'm as steady as a church, old lad. I make nets for the poor. I talk to Aunt K. I'm good to the little people about here. I'm a seraph to Margaret."

Garda's present visit at East Angels had begun but two days before. She had been spending some time in New York with Lish-er and Trude. These ladies having written once a week since their first parting with her, to say that they were sure that she must by this time be needing "a drier air," Garda had at length accepted the suggestion; and tried the air. It proved to be that of Ninth Street; and was indeed remarkably dry. This visit to Margaret was her second one; six months before she had made a long stay at East Angels—so long that Aunt Katrina began to fear that she would never go away. The violence of the grief that had accompanied her first return to Gracias had subsided with singular suddenness; she said to Margaret, in an apathetic tone, "I had to kill it, you know, or else kill myself. I came very near killing myself."

"I was much alarmed about you," Margaret answered, hesitating as to whether or not to say more.

Garda divined her thoughts. "Did you think I was out of my mind? I wasn't at all; it was only that I couldn't bear the pain. Let us never speak of that time again—never! never!" She got up, and for a moment stood trembling and quivering. Then, with the same rapidity and completeness, she resumed her calm.

Margaret never did speak of it again. "But how was it that she killed it—how?" was her dreary thought.

During that first visit, Lanse and Mrs. Spenser had become fast friends; every evening she played checkers with him, and she was the only person with whom he did not bluster over the game; she contradicted him; she made sport of his fish-nets; she used his Fielding for her footstool; she put forward the proposition that her own face was prettier than his Mino outlines.

Lanse denied this. "My Mino outlines are not in the least pretty. But then you are not in the least pretty yourself."

"Not pretty!" said Garda, with a protesting cry. "Why, even a little pussy cat can be pretty."

"I have not been able to discover a trace of prettiness in you." He paused. "You are simply superb," he said, looking at her with his deep bold eyes. "What makes you stay on here?" he added in another tone, surveying her curiously.

Garda turned; but Margaret had by chance left the room. "I was going to point to Margaret," she answered; "I stay because I love her—love to be with her."

"Well, you'll have a career," Lanse announced, briefly.

The next day he said to Aunt Katrina, "I should like to have seen that girl before she was married; there's such an extraordinary richness in her beauty that I don't believe she ever had an awkward age; she was probably graceful at sixteen."

"She was designing at sixteen."

"No! For whom could she have been designing down here?"

"Evert."

"And the idiot let her slip through his fingers?"

"Deliver us!" said the lady. "If I've got to hear *you* admire her too!"

Late in the evening of the day when she had threatened to speak to Lanse about his wife's health, Garda came and knocked at Margaret's door. "I wanted to see you," she said, entering.

Adolfo had gone an hour before, and she had been in her own room meanwhile; but she had not taken off her white lace attire, or loosened the braids of her hair. Margaret too was fully dressed.

"What have you been doing?" Garda demanded, suspiciously, as she looked at her. "Not crying?"

"I think I have forgotten how to cry."

"Well, your eyes are dry," Garda admitted. She closed the door, then went to one of the windows and looked out. There had been a heavy rain during the evening, and the air was much cooler; it was very dark. She closed the shutters of all the three windows and fastened them. "It's so gloomy out there! Pine cones? What luck! we'll have a fire."

"Garda—we shall melt!"

"No, the room is too large." She piled the cones on the hearth and set fire to them; in an instant the blaze flared out and lighted up all the dusky corners. "That's better. Only one poor miserable little candle?" And she proceeded to light four others that stood about here and there.

"Are you preparing for a ball?"

"I am preparing for a talk. I'm lonely to-night, Margaret, and I can't bear to feel lonely; how long may I stay? Are you sure you haven't got to go and do something?—say good-night to Mr. Harold, for instance?"

"He has been asleep these two hours. He always has one of his men in the room with him."

"Yes, I know. But why haven't you undressed, then, all this time?" Garda went on, with returning suspicion.

"Why haven't you? But have you no conscience, thinking of poor Adolfo banging into all the trees and falling into all the ditches on his way home?"

"No, Adolfo and I are not troubled about conscience,—Adolfo and I understand each other perfectly. It's in the blood, I suppose; we belong to the same race," said the daughter of the Dueros.

She had been standing watching her fire; now she drew up a chair before it and sat down. "I did not say anything to Mr. Harold about you, after all," she said.

"I thought you wouldn't when I told you I did not wish it."

"I shall do it to-morrow; you are to come north with me the next time I go."

"I shall not leave East Angels."

"I saw Evert in New York," Garda began again, after a short silence. "I wrote a note asking him to come. He came—he came three times. But three times isn't much?" And she glanced towards Margaret.

Margaret had kept her place on the sofa where she was sitting when Garda entered; but she had drawn forward on its casters a tall screen to shield herself from the fire, and this threw her face into shadow. "No, not much," she answered from her dark nook.

"I love to tell you things," Garda resumed, gazing at the blaze. "Well—he wouldn't like me—what would you say to that? I had thought that perhaps he might; but no, he wouldn't."

This time there was no answer from the shadow.

"I used to think—long ago—that it was because he couldn't," Garda went on; "I mean, couldn't care for any one very much; care as I care. But I was mistaken. Completely. He *can* care. But not for me."

She got up and went to the long mirror, in the bright light her face and figure were clearly reflected; here she stood looking at herself for some time in silence, as if touched by a new curiosity. She moved nearer the glass, so that she could see her face; then back to get a view of the image as a whole; she turned half round, with her head over her shoulder, in order to see herself in profile. She adjusted the ribbon round her supple waist, and gave a touch, musingly, to her hair; she lifted her white hands and looked at them; dropping them, she clasped them behind her, and indulged in another general survey. "Such as I am, he cares nothing for me," she said at last, speaking not in surprise, but simply, as one who states a fact.

She looked at herself again. "I don't say he's not a fool!" And she gave a good-humored laugh.

She left the glass and came towards Margaret. "I've got to tell you something," she said. "Do you know, I *tried*. Yes, I *tried*; for I like him so much! You remember I thought everything of him once, when we were first engaged, long ago? I appreciate him better now. And I like him so much!" While she was saying these last words she came and knelt down beside the sofa in her old caressing fashion, her clasped hands on Margaret's knees. But her movement had pushed the screen, and it rolled back, letting the fire-light shine suddenly across Margaret's face.

"Merciful Heaven!" cried Garda, springing to her feet as she saw the expression there; "do *you* care for him?—is that it? The cause of all—the change in you, and in him too? Oh, how blind I have been!—how blind! But I never once suspected it. Don't think of a word I have said, he didn't look at me; I tried, but he wouldn't; he despises me, I know. I like him better than any one in the world, now that Lucian is gone," she went on, with her bare frankness. "But he will never care for me; and a very good reason, too, when it is *you* he cares for!"

Margaret had bowed her head upon her arm, which rested upon the sofa's back. Garda sat down beside her. "How many times have you comforted me!" she said. "If I could only be of the smallest comfort to you, Margaret!"

Margaret did not answer.

"And it has been so all these long years," Garda murmured, after sitting still and thinking of it. "You are better than I am!"

"Better!"

"There isn't an angel in heaven at this moment better than you are," Garda responded, vehemently. "But you mustn't keep on in this way, you know," she added, after a moment.

"I can't talk, Garda."

"That is it, Evert has talked! He has tired you out. I can imagine that when once he is in earnest—Margaret, let me tell you this one thing: you can't live under all this, you'll die."

"It's not so easy to die," answered Lansing Harold's wife.

"You think I don't know about Mr. Harold. But I do. Lucian heard the whole in Rome; I even saw her myself—in a carriage on the Pincio. I know that he left you twice to go to her—twice; what claim has he, then, upon you? But what is the use of my talking, if *Evert* has been able to do nothing!"

Margaret sat up. "Go now, Garda. I would rather be alone."

But Garda would not go. "I could never be like you," she went on. "And this is a case where you had better be more like me. Margaret! Margaret!" and she clung to her, suddenly. "Such a love as his would be!" she whispered—"how *can* you refuse it? I think it's wicked, too, because it's his whole life, *he* isn't Lansing Harold! And you love him so; you needn't deny it; I can feel your heart beating now."

"Go," said Margaret, drawing herself free, and rising. "You only hurt me, Garda. And you cannot change me."

But Garda followed her. "You adore him. And he—And you give all *that* up? Why—it's the dearest thing there is, the dearest thing we have; what are you made of?" She kept up with her, walking by her side.

Margaret was pacing the room aimlessly; she put out her arm as if to keep Garda off.

The girl accepted this, moving to that distance; but still she walked by her side. "And don't you ever think of the life *he's* leading?—the life you're making him lead?" she went on. "He's unhappy—of course he didn't tell *me* why. He's growing hard and bitter, he's ever so much changed; remember that I have just seen him, only a few days ago. It's dreadful to have to say that he has changed for the worse, because I like him so much; but I am afraid he has,—yes, he has. You see he needs some one—I like him so much."

"Marry him yourself, then, and be the some one," answered Margaret, sharply. And by a sudden turn in her quick walk she seemed to be again trying to get rid of her.

"I would, if he would marry me," Garda answered; "yes, even if he should keep on caring for you just the same, for that doesn't hurt him in my eyes. I should be content to come after *you*; and if I could have just a little edge of his love—But he wouldn't look at me, I tell you—though I tried. He is like you, with him it is once. But you are the one I am thinking of most, Margaret. For you are fading away, and it's this stifled love that's killing you; *now* I understand it. Women do die of such feelings, you are one of them. Do you think you'll have any praise when you get to the next world"—here she came closer—"after killing yourself, and breaking down all the courage of a man like Evert, like *Evert*—two whole lives wasted—and all for the sake of an idea?"

Margaret's face had been averted. But now she looked at her. "An idea which *you* cannot comprehend," she said. And she turned away again.

"Yes, I know you think me your inferior," Garda answered; "and I acknowledge that I am your inferior; I am nothing compared with you, I never was. But I don't care what you say to me, I only want you to be happier." She waited an instant, then came up behind Margaret, whose back was towards her, and with a touch that was full of humility, took hold of a little fold of her skirt. "Listen a moment," she said, holding it closely, as if that would make Margaret listen more; "I don't believe Mr. Harold would oppose a suit at all. He couldn't succeed, of course, no matter what he should do, for it's all against him, but I don't believe he would even try; he isn't that sort of a man at least, malicious and petty. If he could be made comfortable here, as he is now? It's very far away—Gracias-á-Dios; that is, people think so, I find; they thought so in New York; so he could stay on here as quietly as he pleased, and it would make no difference to anybody. He could have everything he liked; why, *I* would undertake to stay for a while at first, stay and amuse him, play checkers and all that. It's a pity Mrs. Rutherford dislikes me so," Garda concluded, in a tone of regret.

"Perhaps you would undertake to marry *him*, by way of a change?" said Margaret, leaving her again, with another sharp movement that pulled the dress from the touch of the humble little hand.

"There are some things, Margaret, that even *you* must not say to me," Garda answered, smiling bravely and brightly, though the tears were just behind.

And then Margaret's cruel coldness broke; she came to her, took her hands, and held them across her hot eyes. "Forgive me, Garda, I don't know what I am saying. You don't mean it, but you keep turning the knife in the wound. I shall never do any of the things you talk of, I shall go on staying here. I must bear my life—the life I made for myself, with my eyes open; no one made it for me, I made it for myself, and I must bear it as well as I can. I have said cruel things, but it was because—" She dropped the girl's hands. "I have always thought you so—so beautiful; and if you care for him, as you now tell me you do, what more natural than that he—" But she could not finish, her face contracted with a quiver, and took on suddenly and strangely the tints of age.

"I am not worthy to tie your shoe!" cried Garda, in her soft voice, which even in high excitement could not rise above its sweet tones.

But Margaret had controlled herself again, the spectre face had vanished. "When you tell me that he has changed so much, that he is growing harsh, hard,—that is the worst for me," she said. "I can bear everything about myself, everything here; but I cannot bear that." She paused. "Men are all alike"—she began again. Then she put that aside too—her last bitterness. "Garda," she resumed, "I shall go on living here, as I have said; and it is for always; I am, I intend to be, as far removed from his life as though I were dead. And now—if you will marry him? You are so beautiful he cannot help but love you, you needn't be afraid! You must never come here—I tell you that in the beginning. And he must never come. But"—she moved swiftly forward and took the girl in her arms with a passionate tenderness—"but your little children, Garda, if you should have any, if they could come, it would be good for me; my life would not be so bitter and hard; I should be a better woman than I am now, yes, I am sure I should be better." She put her face down upon Garda's for a moment. Garda could feel how very cold it was.

Then she released her; she began moving about the room, setting the chairs in their places, she extinguished some of the candles; she was quite calm.

Garda stood where she had been left; her face was hidden.

Margaret crossed to one of the windows and threw open the shutters; the cool night air rushed in, laden with the perfume of flowers. Then she came back to Garda. "I will go with you to your room," she said; "it is very, very late." She put her arm round her to lead her away. Garda submitted, though still with her face hidden; they went together down the hall.

There was a light in Garda's room. Margaret kissed her before leaving her. "Good-night," she said.

"I am ashamed," Garda murmured.

"Ashamed?"

"Ashamed of being *glad*."

Margaret went swiftly away, she almost seemed to flee. Garda, standing on her lighted threshold, heard her door close. Then she heard the sound of the bolt within, as it was shot sharply forward.

CHAPTER XXXVIII

"Did you ever hear of anything so absurd?" said Aunt Katrina. "How she will look at sea!—Those prunello gaiters of hers on deck when the wind blows!"

"Jolly old soul," commented Lanse. He was playing solitaire, and had paused reflectively with a card in his hand while he gazed at the spread-out piles before him. "Jolly old soul!—I am glad she is going to see something at last, before she dies."

"What expressions you do use, Lanse! one would think she was ninety. As for seeing, she'll see nothing but Garda Thorne, and have her hands full at that."

"Her eyes, you mean," said Lanse, slipping his card deftly upon a pile which contained already its legal three, and fitting the edges accurately as he did so to those of the card beneath, in order to cheat himself with the greater skill.

Aunt Katrina's comments were based upon some recent tidings. Betty had journeyed down to East Angels that afternoon in the black boat of Uncle Cato to convey to her dearest Kate a wonderful piece of news: Garda had suddenly decided to go abroad for the winter—to Italy, and she had written from New York, where she was staying with Lish-er and Trude, to beg Betty to come north immediately and go with her, "like the dear, kind old aunt" that she was. Betty's mind, driven into confusion by this sudden proposal, was a wild mixture of the sincerest regrets at leaving dear Kate, of the sincerest gratification at this proof of Garda's attachment, and the sincerest (and most dreadful) apprehensions concerning the ocean passage.

Garda's second visit at East Angels—a very short one—had terminated only six weeks before; at that time she had no intention of going to Italy. This, then, was some sudden new idea, and Lanse had amused himself imagining causes for it. He imagined them on such a scale of splendor, however, that Aunt Katrina declared at last that she could listen to no more of them; they were too ridiculously silly.

She brought herself to listen, however, when, four months later, Betty, having survived a recrossing of the ocean, came down to East Angels, with the lion carpet-bag, to tell "everything" to her friend.

Poor Betty had been so homesick in foreign lands that Garda had not had the heart to detain her longer. "And she said that she had hoped I would stay with her a long time, perhaps always," narrated Betty. "And of course I enjoyed being in New York ever so much, of course; and Rome too—Rome was so instructive. But then you know, as I told the dear child, Rome is *not* my home, nor can I make it so at my age, of course."

"It's not age; it's experience," said Kate.

"Very likely you're right, Kate; but then, you know, I've had so little experience; since I came from Georgia with Mr. Carew, ever so many years ago, I've never put my foot outside of Florida until now, and I suppose I've grown like those Swiss exiles we read about, who can't hear that call for cows, you know, that Ranz something, without getting *so* homesick, though to everybody else it's a dreadfully yelling sound,—though I ought to say, too, that as we've next to no cows in Florida, the comparison isn't a *very* good one; but then there were next to no cows in Rome either, for that matter, though it was there that a cow brought up little Castor and Pollux, who built the city—no, no, I'm mistaken, that was Romulus and Remus; Castor and Pollux tamed the horses on the Quirinal; but in either case it shows that the milk must have been good, because they were so strong, you know."

"*Are* we talking of milk, Elizabeth?" asked Kate, in despair.

"Of course not," answered Elizabeth, good-naturedly; "how could you think so? I know you never cared for milk in the least, Kate, and I shouldn't be likely, therefore, to bring it up.—And right there in the Forum I'd see my own flower-garden. And in the Colosseum I'd see our little church here, and even hear the bell."

"Absurd!" said Kate.

"I reckon it was absurd," Betty agreed, though wiping her eyes at the same time. "And at the Vatican, there among the statues, Kate—do you know I was always seeing likenesses to you."

"Oh, well—*that*," responded Kate, as if there might be grounds for associations of that nature. "And Garda Thorne, by this time, I suppose, is living there *quite* alone?" she went on, comfortably.

"Oh no; she has a companion, Madame Clementer."

"Clementi," said Lanse; "I know her—an American, Miss Morris. He ran through all her money."

"Yes, that is the one; the Bogarduses arranged it by letter; they know her very well."

"She's a cousin of theirs, and a very nice woman; about fifty-five. Nothing could be more respectable," Lanse went on, glancing with an amused eye at Aunt Katrina's unwilling face. "You were there some time, Mrs. Carew; I suppose you saw some men?"

"The population seemed to me to consist principally of men," Betty answered, naïvely; "the streets were always crowded with them."

"That's because the Italian women don't knock about. But some of these men came to see you, I suppose?"

"Oh, you mean gentlemen? Yes, a good many came; but for my part, *I* was always gladdest to see Adolfo Torres. *He* wasn't so foreign."

"Is *he* there?" said Lanse, with a delighted laugh; "has he followed her all that distance? Bravo for Adolfo!"

"I don't see where he got the money to go," remarked Aunt Katrina, with one of her well-bred sniffs.

Betty flushed at this. "Mr. Torres has property, Kate," she said, with dignity. Then her usual humble sincerity came back to her. "I don't reckon it's much," she went on. "I've no idea where he stayed, nor anything about it; but I'm sure, whenever he came to see *us*, he always looked like a dignified gentleman."

"Naturally," said Lanse. "Because that is what he is. Well, I give him my vote."

As this conversation was beginning, word was brought to Margaret that Mr. Winthrop was in the drawing-room, and wished to see her. Celestine was the messenger.

"Has he come to stay? You and Looth must put the east room in order, then," said the mistress of the house. "Have you told the others?"

"Yes'm," said Celestine, disappearing.

When Margaret entered the drawing-room, twenty minutes later, Winthrop was there alone. Celestine had told nobody. Minerva Poindexter, meanwhile, sweeping a remote corridor, had had a tussle with her conscience; and gagged it.

"No one here?" said Margaret in surprise. "Where are the others?"

"I didn't come to see the others," Winthrop answered.

Though many months had elapsed since their last meeting, no greeting passed between them beyond this; they did not even shake hands. She had seen upon entering that angry feelings had possession of him, that this time he would not go through any of the forms. This made her only the more anxious to keep to them strictly herself.

"I hope you have come to stay with us a while," she said.

He paid no attention to this. "Shall we go out—to the garden, or somewhere? I wish to see you alone."

"We couldn't well be more alone than this, could we?" she answered, looking about the room.

"But they may interrupt us. If they do, I shall ask you very soon to come out, and you must come." He crossed the room and closed the door. "You got my letter?"

"I was answering it when you came."

"I didn't want a written answer. It came over me, after I had sent mine, that I knew just what you would write in reply—the very words. Not that you have written so often; in two years and a half I think three notes of six lines each would about sum it up. But I know every written phrase of yours just the same; so I have come to get an answer in person—a more sensible and reasonable one."

She did not say, "There will be nothing more reasonable." It was what was in her thoughts; but it seemed wiser not to express her thoughts now.

"How changed you are!" he said; "even in eighteen months so much changed."

"No one here sees such a change." She faced his gaze proudly.

"The same old look! Of course they don't; so long as you keep everything going smoothly and everybody comfortable, they don't want to see any; they never will see one till you're in your coffin."

He was still gazing at her. "Arrange your life as you like," he went on, abruptly, "but at least come away from here. You can do that. And I shall insist upon it."

The fear of him that she had felt from the time of entering was increasing. He had never looked quite as he did at this moment; his voice had never had quite these tones before. The long months that had stretched into years had made no difference, then; everything was to be as hard, perhaps harder than ever!

Her fear caused her to answer with something like appeal. "But I do not wish to go away. I like it much better here than I should like being in New York. It is quiet; I am of some use; I am—I am really contented here."

"Since when have you learned to speak so falsely? You are probably afraid of me! You see, and correctly, that I am not to be put off this time, as I was when I came before—put off with a little preaching, a few compliments and exhortations. You are afraid I shall smash the pretty glass walls you have built up round your sham life here, your charming domestic life, your happy home circle."

"I don't think you have any right to take that tone."

"Yes, I have; the right of our love."

"We must forget that. We are not growing any younger; at least I am not. Men are different, perhaps."

Winthrop laughed. "Very well done, Margaret. But not well enough. You are trying to pretend that you have outlived it; and that I have. But our two faces contradict that; yours is wasted and drawn, and look at me—have I the appearance of a man who is even moderately happy?"

She had not trusted herself to look at him much; she remembered too vividly Garda's description—"changed," "bitter," "hard." But involuntarily now she did look at him. And she saw all that Garda had described; and more.

"What is it you wish me to do?" she asked, hurriedly.

"Come away from here."

"But where?"

"Anywhere you like.—Where I could see you sometimes."

"No—no."

"Very well, then; anywhere you like. And I won't see you."

"It wouldn't do me any good!" These words burst from her almost unconsciously. She dropped into the nearest chair.

He came and seated himself near her in silence.

"You saw Garda before she went abroad?" she said, beginning again.

"Yes."

"She wished to see you, I know."

"How you say that—how timidly! Garda, at least, is not troubled by timidity."

"Perhaps you will go abroad again yourself?"

"Not to see Mrs. Lucian Spenser! Would you like to have me go?" he added.

"Yes."

"I am very much obliged to you. It's a plan, is it?—you wouldn't have spoken of her otherwise. I see; I am growing older, I'm lonely, I'm sad; perhaps I'm wicked. A 'home,' therefore, is the thing I need—you women think so much of a home—and so you've planned this. It's very ingenious. But unfortunately I don't fall in with it. Don't waste any more time talking of Garda," he said, sharply.

Margaret's head was bent.

"It isn't possible that you have thought I *could* care for her, Margaret—such a woman as that. Why, you're trembling" (he rose and pulled down her shielding hand), "you're relieved! You have really dreamed, then, that it might happen!"

"It makes me hate myself," he went on, a mist showing itself in his eyes—"to see your unselfishness; you have thought of this because you believe that it would be better for me, that I should be happier. And if you had succeeded, if it could really have come about, how you would have lived up to it! To the very last hour of your life you wouldn't have swerved."

He looked at her; he seemed to be studying her. Then he grew sarcastic again, perhaps on account of her continued silence. "Garda, on her side, is perfectly capable of having a real affection for me for a while—real while it lasts; she hasn't any especial mission on her hands just now, so that would have done very well. You planned it together, I suppose. You are certainly a wonderful pair! May I ask how far did the plan extend? You would have pampered me up between you (she temporarily); you would have arranged what was 'best' for my life, like two Sunday-school teachers over a case of reform! Once and for all, Margaret, let us put Edgarda Thorne aside; she has nothing whatever to do with the matters that lie between you and me; she is no more to me than an old glove."

He walked about the room impatiently. "Of course I might lie to you," he went on; "I might say that if you persist in your present course—keeping me entirely off, separating your life utterly from mine—I should go to the bad. But it wouldn't be true; I shall not go to the bad, unless becoming hard and disagreeable is that. Later, if you still go on in this way, I shall become callous and selfish probably—self-indulgent. I shall never be vicious or low-lived, I hope; but I am not a woman, I can't live on air—as you will do. Don't see me at fifty-five—I'll give you *that* advice! For *you* will always remain the same; with the exception of growing paler and thinner, you'll be the same till you die; and I really think it would be a greater blow to you than even what we're bearing now to find me like that—selfish, fond of my ease, slow to disturb myself for anybody, mightily taken up with my dinner!—But you don't believe in the least what I am saying to you; I can't bring it before you. I love you—love you at this moment with every fibre of my being." He sat down and folded his arms doggedly. "But I shall not stay sentimental; no man does after a certain age, though women always expect it, as you expect it now."

"What do you intend to do?" he continued, as she did not answer any of this.

"Just what I have been doing."

"You have no mercy, then?" He looked at her with angry gloom.

"If I can bear it, surely you can."

"No, that doesn't follow. Women are better than men; in some things they are stronger. But that's because they are sustained—the ones of your nature at least—by their terrible love of self-sacrifice; I absolutely believe there are women who *like* to be tortured!"

"Yes—sometimes we like it," answered the woman he spoke to, a beautiful, mysterious, exalted expression showing itself for a moment in her eyes.

He sprang from his chair. But the look of his face as he came towards her, frightened her, brought her back to the actual present; moving hurriedly, she put her hand upon the cord of the bell.

"No, not that, that's cruel, that humiliates me—don't, don't. See, it isn't necessary, I shall be perfectly quiet and reasonable now. Here are two chairs; come and sit down. Now listen. I will do all that is proper here—see the people, and make a little visit; then I will go back to New York. After that, in due time, you must tell them that you are tired of Florida, that you need a change; you certainly do need a change, as a plain matter-of-fact; and I see no reason, in any case, for your spending your entire life here. Of course it will be an uphill undertaking to get Aunt Katrina started; she will believe that it would kill her instantly. But it won't kill her; she is stronger than she thinks. As for Lanse, he can make the journey up as well as he made it down; he's certainly no worse. Both of them, if you are firm, will end by doing as you wish, because you are indispensable to their comfort. The thing is that you *must* hold firm. Once established in New York, or near there, I could see you now and then—I mean see you all; Lanse would ask nothing better than to have me about again. I speak in all honor, Margaret—I'm not a vile hypocrite, whatever else I may be. I am growing older; see, I will take your view of that, you are growing older too; why shouldn't we, then, see each other in this way at intervals? where would be the harm? It would brighten our lives a little; and as for the 'home' you wished me to have, its good influences and all that, I could find them there."

"I shall never see you again," Margaret answered, strangely. She had not seated herself in the chair he had placed for her; she stood with her hand resting upon its back.

"What do you mean?"

"All you have said I believe; I believe you would keep to it, carry it out. But with me it would be different—it would be too much pain; I would far rather not see you at all. I love you too much," she added. A burning blush covered her face and throat as she met his eyes. Then it faded suddenly to so deathly a white that his old fear rushed back upon him. He had almost forgotten this fear in the lapse of time; but these terrible waves of color and of pallor, these overwhelming emotions that made her unable to stand—they brought back to him the old conviction, "She has no strength, she will not be able to endure it; she will die!" He took her in his arms and laid her down upon the cushions of a couch, made sick at heart as he did so by the lightness of her weight. Anything but that—that she should go from earth forever; anything but that!

As he bent over her, his heart full of his dread, she looked up; she saw his fear.

"Why—I am not dying," she said, reassuringly, smiling for an instant with almost a mother's sweetness; "it is nothing,—only the faintness that very often seizes me; it has been so all my life, it amounts to nothing. And now will you go? And promise me not to come back?"

"Margaret—that is too much."

"It is the only way; surely I have shown you—told you—in all its shame, my weakness." And again came the burning blush.

He had knelt down beside her. "Weakness!" He bowed his head upon her hand.

"Go," she repeated softly.

"I cannot go!"

She tried to rise, but he prevented her. "Margaret!" he said.

"And must I always be the one?" She did rise, she moved from his grasping hands. "You talk about my dying—*that* would make me die, to have you pursue me, ungenerously, brutally, when I have already such hard pain to bear." With a step that swayed with her exhaustion she went towards the door. "I can only appeal to you, Evert," she said when she had reached it, looking back at him over her shoulder—"I can only appeal to you not to try to see me again. It will be the same with me always, and so I appeal to you for always. I shall never change; and I should never yield; so you can see that it will only make me suffer more."

She turned the latch. "Perhaps, sometime—the years that we give up to duty here—" She went hastily out.

They never met again.

EPILOGUE

It was eight years later at East Angels. Penelope and Middleton had come down for an afternoon visit; Betty was already there, Betty was generally there.

Dr. Kirby had just gone; he had brought to them the surprising tidings that Garda had turned her back upon her many admirers, and was about to bestow her hand upon Adolfo Torres.

The Doctor having gone, "I'll believe it when I see it!" Kate declared.

"But, Kate dear, you can't see all the way to Paris," said Betty.

That same evening, Margaret was sitting beside the lamp in the drawing-room, embroidering something which took her close attention.

Lanse had had his sofa drawn up to the open door of the little high balcony; he was smoking and looking out upon the moonlight.

He, too, spoke of the rumor about Garda. "I wonder why Evert didn't try for her?" he said.

His wife made no reply.

"Never married all this time—yet he was the very fellow for it! Steady, you know; good; a little stupid. It's outrageous the way he treats us—never coming here!"

Lanse was still crippled; but his face remained handsome. Save for his crippled condition, he appeared well and strong.

After a while he turned from the moonlight and sat idly watching his wife's hand move over her work. "Do you know that you've grown old, Madge, before your time?"

"Yes, I know it."

"Well—you're a good woman," said Lanse.